She was driven by desire—and divided by love . . .

Cass whirled around to face Jared. "King loves me and I love him!"

"King loves you as much as he can love, but that's not enough for a woman like you. You need more."

"That's not true. King—"

"It's as true as tomorrow's coming," Jared said ruthlessly. "Do you know what tomorrow is going to bring? I do. And I'll prevent it any way I have to." Jared's hand shot out and captured Cass's face in a caressing vise as he slowly bent down towards her. "Don't destroy my brother. Don't destroy yourself. Let him go. Give your love to a man who can give it back redoubled . . ."

With a broken sound Cass wrenched away from him and stood trembling, her face pale and her eyes wild . . .

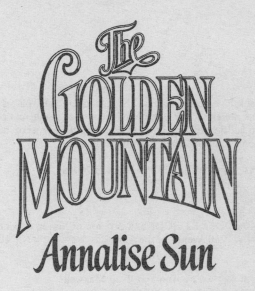

THE GOLDEN MOUNTAIN

Annalise Sun

POCKET BOOKS

New York London Toronto Sydney Tokyo Singapore

An *Original* publication of POCKET BOOKS

POCKET BOOKS, a division of Simon & Schuster Inc.
1230 Avenue of the Americas, New York, NY 10020

ISBN: 0-671-65900-6

First Pocket Books printing December 1990

10 9 8 7 6 5 4 3 2 1

POCKET and colophon are registered trademarks of
Simon & Schuster Inc.

Printed in the U.S.A.

The possessing of gold has been the aim of all races, in all ages, and of all classes of society. The quest of gold has led men to the ends of the earth. . . .

Alfred G. Lock, 1882

BOOK

·›[I]‹·

Prologue

(1889)

"Cassie, bring me a fresh plate! Hurry, girl! We're burning up the last daylight!"

Cassandra Thornton turned and ran back to the wagon whose peeling, faded Gothic letters proclaimed "THADDEUS THORNTON, PHOTOGRAPHIC EXPERIMENTER AND PRACTITIONER." The wagon served as her father's living quarters and portable darkroom all in one. During the summer, when she escaped Mistress Bender's School for Ladies, Cass shared the wagon with Thaddeus. She hoped soon to do so on a full-time basis, at least until she could convince her father that she was capable of creating a real home for him, ending his interminable wandering over the face of the West.

She quickly found the unexposed glass plate in its wooden frame. Scrambling out of the wagon, she ran back to her father as though she were ten years old rather than seventeen. With each step she took she congratulated herself on having donned cut-down men's pants instead of the long skirt required by Mistress Bender. It was the same for the serviceable men's boots Cass wore on her feet; Mistress Bender would have been appalled, but Cass was too practical to wear dainty kid-leather shoes while she helped her father photograph Chinese miners panning for gold in the wilds of California's Sierra Nevada.

Balancing carefully on the slick rocks, Cass worked her way to the point where her father stood knee-deep in the racing water, apparently oblivious to the temperature of the stream. Inevitably, she slipped before she reached him. She caught herself but not before soaking her feet. The water was so cold her toes went numb instantly, for the snowfields that fed the stream were only a few miles away.

"How can you stand it?" Cass asked her father as he took the glass plate.

"Hold this," Thad said, handing over an exposed plate. "Mind the wrapping now. If any—"

"—light gets in, it will spoil the picture," Cass interrupted, finishing the familiar sentence for him. "I know, Papa."

Thad said nothing. His mind was already occupied in composing the picture of small, darkly dressed men bent over in the stream, dwarfed by the magnificent mountains whose rugged peaks glittered with snow behind them. Tenaciously, patiently, impassively, the Chinese washed river gravel in shallow, circular pans, hoping to see the transcendent gleam of gold at the end of their icy labor.

Thad sought a different treasure. He wanted a photograph that would speak profoundly of ordinary men pursuing the barely possible against tremendous odds; men called into wild landscapes by the siren song of gold; and most of all, Chinese men who had come from the far side of the world to the land they called Gum-Shan, the Mountain of Gold, hoping to pan a better future from America's alien soil.

Cass had never fully understood Thad's fascination with the Chinese. When she asked him why he pursued the Celestials, he would look sad and haunted or he would shrug and say that the Chinese had something that he had lost. If she asked what it was, he would say that she wasn't old enough to understand. If she asked why they didn't settle down and build a home, he would simply shake his head and say nothing.

Once, driven by her need for a home, Cass had pushed her father until he finally had answered her: *I'm looking for the right woman to build a home around. When I find her, I'll settle down. You're too young to understand that.*

But Cass wasn't too young any longer. She was old enough to keep a home for her father, and she was determined to do just that. Even his broad-shouldered strength couldn't stand forever against the punishing life he had led. His terrible wracking cough kept them both awake each night. Yet there he stood, up to his knees in ice water, taking photographs of the enigmatic sojourners whose language he didn't speak and whose lives were accessible to him only through the old Globe lens of his camera.

Watching her father with anxious, tawny eyes, Cass catalogued each sign of increasing age. There was more gray than blond in his beard, his face was lined by sun and weather, and the knuckles of his hands were sometimes swollen and painful. Still he pursued the Chinese through all times and circumstances, searching their alien faces for whatever he had lost.

Is it dignity and perseverance you're looking for, Papa? The Chinese have that, but so do other people. Or is it simply the differences between the Celestials and yourself that you love?

And will you ever love your daughter half as much as you love them? Will you let me make a home for you, or will you try to exile me among cold books and colder strangers again, sending for me only during the summers, or when your money runs out and you can't afford to keep me out of your life any longer?

Cass had hated the aching sense of failure that came when her father sent her away from him once more. She had never been able to coax him into settling down in one of the hundreds of towns and villages and settlements they passed through. No matter how pretty or how friendly a place might be, in the end it was always the same—the sound of the wagon's steel-rimmed wheels grinding her hopes into dust and leaving them behind to be blown away by the wind.

It will be different this time, Cass vowed. *This time I'm old enough to make him a home, a quiet place to rest. And he needs that. He's got to see it.*

In the past week he had been talking about Seattle, a city on the edge of the Pacific Ocean, on the rim of what he called "tomorrow's world." The heart of Seattle's downtown area had just been razed by a fire that had burned for two days. Thad hoped that rebuilding the city would provide opportunities for everyone—yellow, white, red, brown, or striped like a barber pole. *There's going to be room for all kinds, Cassie, even the Chinese.*

"Girl, did you hear me? I need another plate. Get cracking. We're burning daylight."

"Do you want me to bring the new lens? It did so well with the sunset light on your last photographs."

"I think it was your hand in the darkroom that turned the trick on those. You've a magic touch, Cassie."

She waded back through the icy water without feeling it, warmed by his words. This time, she wasn't going to be sent away to live alone. She was almost certain of it, and she felt like laughing and crying with pleasure at once.

The wagon's lightproof wooden doors creaked when she opened them wide. Rich, golden light fell across a printing apparatus mounted beside the tiny, lead-lined sink. The van had built-in cabinets for printing paper, developing chemicals, and photo-film plates. Cass didn't need to search for the lens; she was almost as familiar with every piece of equipment in the wagon as her father was. She knew the uses and limitations of each lens, the speed of each camera's shutter, and the pyrotechnical capability of each type of flash powder.

The sight of the flash powder made Cass wonder whether Thad needed it to offset the dying light. She ducked out of the back of the wagon and blinked against the setting sun, squinting until she could see her father standing in the stream whose surface had been turned to burning, molten gold.

As Cass watched, one of the tripod legs slipped. Thad lunged for the camera, righting it, only to slip and fall himself. The chilling, horrifying sound of his skull hitting rock carried clearly through the suddenly quiet afternoon.

Cass ran to the river, trying not to scream, choking on her own fear. By the time she got to the shallows, the miners had dragged her father onto the shore. He lay slackly, his eyes closed. One of the Chinese stood up as she flung herself to her knees beside her father.

"Fall hard hard," the miner said in his pidgin English. "Hit head stone. Worse luck, Missy. Hurt bad bad."

Another miner waded ashore carrying Thad's camera and tripod.

"Save joss box," the miner continued. "He want save. Box much much joss, yes?"

Cass bent over her father and pressed her ear against his chest. She could hear the faint, thready beat of his heart, the sound of his shallow, irregular breaths. He was alive, but only barely.

The next three weeks were the longest and loneliest of Cass's life. She nursed Thad, changed the bandage on his head, bathed him, coaxed water past his lips, kept him warm with her own body. She did everything except breathe for him, but in the end, her efforts were not enough. An hour before dawn one cold mountain morning, Thad Thornton died as he had lived—quietly, gently, inhabiting a past that Cass had never shared, whispering brokenly of lilacs and rainy spring days and a precious beauty that would never come again.

As the sun came up that day, the Chinese miners watched in surprise while the golden-haired girl took a shovel and began to dig on a sandy, gravelly bench above the river. One of the miners objected immediately to his fellows, his voice rising and falling in the shifting minor tones of Cantonese.

"The white woman is burying her father in the middle of the richest gravel. Why does she wish to bring such bad joss upon our heads? She will destroy our luck!"

"Who knows what the white devils think?" answered another miner philosophically. "They are all barbarians.

6

They have no respect for their ancestors. They bury their dead far from home and abandon them."

"At least the white devil's joss box will no longer pick at our souls. Look—" added the third miner in horror. "She is waving at us. She wants us to touch her dead."

"We have to do it and be gone before his spirit takes offense at being abandoned," the first miner said.

Together, the Chinese and Cass lowered Thad Thornton into the grave on the bank of a river that had once held placer gold and now held only piles of tailings, and ghosts.

"Sorry," was the only word the Chinese and Cass shared in common. Each of the miners repeated it many times, bowing so quickly that their black queues swung. Cass nodded as they bowed, thanking each man for his help. Then she turned and went to the wagon, readying it for the trail.

As Cass packed the tiny, clever cupboards and secured the doors, she came across a brass-bound cherrywood box that had once held a Globe lens. Curious, she opened the box. There, nestled on worn red velvet, was an oval frame. Within the frame was a picture of a Chinese woman whose features were delicate, intelligent, and so beautiful that Cass could only stare.

She turned over the frame and removed the photograph, but there was no writing on it, nothing to indicate the woman's name or the reason Thad had kept her picture like a jewel within a velvet shrine. Methodically, Cass searched through the rest of her father's few personal possessions, but found no answer. Nor did she find any other uniquely treasured photographs—not of herself nor even of her long-dead mother. All she found was twenty dollars and the long, heavy gold chain made of nuggets and links that her father had used to secure his watch on the rare occasions when he wore a suit.

In the end, Cass packed the old lens box away inside the small, brass-bound trunk that held all she had of her childhood—the photos she had taken with her to school. For long moments she stood and looked around the wagon, searching for a future. She had only her father's final legacy—an inchoate hope that Seattle was a place that would welcome strangers who wanted to build a better world.

Cass harnessed the old sorrel mule, climbed up to the wagon seat, and started toward whatever future waited on the Pacific Rim.

1

Wrapped in darkness, Kingston Duran knew only the shimmering golden succubus of his dream—gold dust pouring over him, bathing his naked body in soft, unspeakable beauty. He reached for it as he would a woman, but the incandescent vision slipped through his fingers, receding before him, singing to his soul in a thousand tones of gold. Moments later, his eyes opened to a world far less radiant than his dream. Shades of gray predominated, with few hints of the yellow glory that would come when sunlight finally poured through the gaps in Vancouver Island's mountainous spine.

Around King, wind combed restlessly through the twisted firs that grew right down to Alberni Inlet's waterline. Wrapped in a Hudson's Bay blanket, his pillow a heavy wool mackinaw, he envied the wind its long journey over the Pacific Ocean, all those myriad miles untouched by man, wind blowing clean and wild and free.

Sounds from the nearby placer diggings penetrated the wind's howl, telling King that the miners were up and about. He lay quietly, trying to ignore the men's voices, hoping to capture the unfettered sense of being alone in the wilderness. But this wasn't the wilderness, and no amount of pretending would make it so. This was simply a place called China Creek, a stream that had been worked over by tenacious Chinese miners for thirty years. There was about as much chance of making a real strike here as there was of grabbing a handful of sunlight in a hard rock tunnel.

Still, it beats the hell out of being in Seattle, King told himself, trying to still the restlessness of his soul. *Just like this root-rumpled and rocky ground beats the hell out of the feather bunks those two "partners" of mine are crawling out of about now. Wonder which one of them got between that actress's legs first?*

King forgot the question almost as soon as it occurred to him. He had sampled the actress's sexual skills two nights before, somewhere in Victoria. He hadn't been impressed enough to remember her name, much less to share a bunk with her on the steamship trip up the coast.

Impatiently, King stripped away the blanket and stamped into his scarred work boots. The small aches and complaints of his body reminded him that he was thirty-five and hadn't slept outside in months.

City soft, he said disparagingly as he undid his fly and urinated against a huge, thick-barked evergreen. *City bored, too. Damn it all, why does a man have to get old and settle down? Why can't I just be like this old tree, harder and tougher every season?*

There was no answer to that question, except the one that had driven King out of Seattle. He couldn't be a civilized, ruthless empire builder like his little brother, Jared. Nor could King forever roam the wilderness. There had to be something in between. If he was too old to go out and discover gold, the next best thing would be to buy into a producing claim. At least, it had looked that way to King in Seattle. Out here, where the land was only recently tamed, the siren lure of wilderness and undiscovered gold had never been greater.

King put his clothes in order, rolled up his blanket, and pushed through the forest undergrowth until he came to the fire in a clearing on the bank of China Creek. The cook looked up and gestured toward the soot-blackened coffee-pot, where steam curled up invitingly.

"Thanks," King said, reaching for the tin cup that hung from his belt.

The cook grunted.

King expected no more. Nor did he want it. He liked being among men who spent words like gold nuggets. Carefully, King tasted the coffee, and then he stood utterly still. The liquid was raw, vital, hot—the quintessence of every cup of camp coffee he had ever drunk in a lifetime of wandering.

A yearning for the trail burst within King, a need that was so great it was physically painful.

"Morning, Kingston," called a cheerful voice from the creek.

King turned and saw the cleanshaven young Seattle mine promoter who was trying to sell him part of this China Creek placer claim. King's greeting was a grunt that precisely echoed the cook's.

"If you'd slept on the boat, you wouldn't be so surly," the broker said, as he leaped from the rocking dinghy to the sandy shore. He misjudged the distance, sending water splashing up his polished boots and city trousers. "Damn! Well, since you're up, we'll look at the digs. Ed's still in bed with his new lady friend. They won't crawl out for another few hours."

"No hurry," King said dryly. "Chinamen have been picking away at this creek for better than thirty years. If the end of the rainbow were here, they'd have panned the hell out of it by now."

The promoter's young face showed uneasiness, then irritation. "They're nothing but heathens."

King shrugged, finished his coffee in a few great swallows, snapped the dregs into the campfire and hooked the cup back onto his belt. He had been hoping this promoter was smarter than the last one, who had tried to pass off brass shavings and California nuggets as a new placer strike in Washington; but it looked as though this was just one more wild goose chase.

Silently, King rowed himself and the broker upriver until

the stream opened out into a wide, looping series of gravel bars and sinuous overflow channels. The stream itself was clear, pure, cold, as brilliant as liquid diamonds. Water glittered transparently over shallows and gathered in deep pools that were as green as King's eyes. On the far bank, half-submerged logs canted down, damming the narrows to form a series of long, slick pools the color of the sky. Ravens called from one of the fallen trees, jeering the white-headed eagle that was perched on the highest branch of a lightning-killed tree.

Silently, the eagle spread its wings and stepped onto the wind, leaving the ravens behind.

King beached the dinghy on a gravel bar where eleven men were digging industriously. His practiced eye picked out the rudiments of a placer-mining operation—two Sierra rockers, a sluice box with Hungarian riffles and wool-blanket backing, and a short flume to carry water for washing the gravel. Most of the men looked capable of little more than manning shovels or bailing water, but the two men running the rockers were obviously experienced. They moved the handles of the gravel sifters with the smooth, muscular assurance of men who had spent a lifetime sifting gold from pale gravel and black sand.

Those were the men King wanted to talk to; those were the men who had dedicated their lives to the bittersweet pursuit of the golden bitch goddess.

Leaving the broker stranded in the dinghy, King waded across the toe of the bar, knelt, and scooped up a handful of black sand. He rubbed it over his palm and turned so that sunlight could fall over the individual grains spread across his skin. After a moment, he absently rubbed his palm clean on his pants. If there was gold present, it was finer than cake flour.

"Any color?" King asked, walking up to the gray-bearded man who was running the bigger of the two Sierra rockers.

"See for yourself."

As he continued the easy rocking motion with one hand, he ran his finger along the back of the wooden slat on the rocker's chute and held it up for King to inspect. There was a faint gleam of gold on the miner's gnarled finger. King ran his index finger along the same riffle. A few more grains of gold came up.

"Hard work for maybe ten cents a pan," King said.

The miner flashed him a sideways look and nodded tightly.

Suddenly, the man working the second rocker shouted. "Holy Mother of God, look at this!"

King turned and saw a nugget the size of a big marble pinched between the man's wet, gritty fingers.

"Fifty dollars, sure as sunrise," the man said, grinning. "What do you think of that?"

The promoter came trotting over in pants wet to the knees. He grabbed the nugget and turned triumphantly to King.

"What do you think of our pothole now? You still think those Chinamen cleaned it all out?"

King took the nugget and rubbed his thumb over the cool, wet surface. It wasn't pyrite. Nothing else in the world combined the oil-slippery smoothness and the weight of a river-tumbled nugget of pure gold.

"Isn't that something?" asked the broker excitedly. "Feels just like a woman's love-spot."

The corner of King's mouth kicked up in a smile that was almost lost within his mahogany beard. "That's one way of looking at it, I suppose." He turned to the first miner. "Last night somebody told me you worked Olivine Creek. How's this creek compare?"

"Kingston," interrupted the broker, "this man's not an engineer or a geologist. He's not in a position to—"

King cut the promoter off with a single, glittering look. "Any particular reason you don't want me talking to this man?"

"I, er, no."

"Good." King turned back to the gray-bearded miner.

"Kingston, huh?" asked the miner.

"Most folks just call me King."

13

"King Duran. Yeah, I heard of you," the old miner said with a spreading grin. "I gave up on Olivine Creek a few days before you found the glory hole." He shook his head ruefully. "Done spent my whole life coming too late and leaving too soon. Hear you took a couple thousand ounces out of that old crick."

"Close to it," King admitted.

He smiled as he remembered the intense, almost unbearable thrill of reaching beneath clear water and touching pure gold. There was no feeling on earth that could match it. Then his smile slowly faded as he remembered the rest, Jared coming along and turning his discovery into civilization.

"Don't feel too bad about your timing," King said to the other miner. "I have a little brother who makes me look like a piker. Jay found an eastern syndicate to buy out our Olivine claim—pickaxes, gold pans, and ground—for half a million cash. I turned them down flat on my half. Jay sold his. Two weeks later, the strike went as sour as last week's milk."

There was a crack of rueful laughter from the miner. "Yeah, sure do beat all hell how gold comes and goes. Like a female. Ain't no understanding it a'tall."

From high overhead, the eagle's keening call pierced the silence. King tilted his face to the sky and listened as he tossed the nugget into the air. Sunlight caressed the soft, precious metal, making it shine. When the gold landed on his palm, he flipped the nugget to the broker, who caught it reflexively.

"Keep it," the man said, holding out the nugget to King. "Just a little souvenir of our good luck today. You can put it on that famous watch chain of yours. Olivine and Similkameen and China Creek and—"

"I dig my own gold." There was both finality and bittersweet discovery in King's voice; he finally understood that owning a gold mine was no substitute for finding one. "I won't be digging any gold here."

"Why not?" the broker demanded. "What more could

you want, for God's sake? How often does a man find a fifty-dollar nugget in a placer pocket!"

King fixed the broker with a flat, green glance. "About as often as you salt one, I expect."

The broker's mouth opened, but no words came out.

Into the uncomfortable silence came the murmur of clean water, the harsh babble of ravens fighting over a scrap of food, and the eagle's piercing cry. King looked up again, trying to understand why he was sad and angry and empty all at once; it wasn't the first time somebody had tried to con him into buying a salted mine, nor would it be the last. So why did he want to scream back at the eagle?

Shading his eyes, King looked for the bird, whose savage cries still shivered in the air. The eagle was invisible against the blazing golden disk of the sun, but King knew it was up there, high and wild and free.

Fly high for both of us, baldheaded old man. Fly all the way to the sun.

Without looking up again, King turned and walked off the gravel bar, heading back to a city he had come to hate.

2

Wind teased short-lived streaks of white from the cerulean waters of Elliot Bay. Wind shook the slack lines and loosely furled canvas sails of the lumber schooners sitting at their moorings. Wind pulled apart the columns of smoke from the Mosquito Fleet steamers that churned back and forth across the bay. Wind chased discarded newspapers across the green-lumber planking of the wooden wharf. In all, the restless air conspired to ruin the shot Cass had composed on the ground glass of the heavy 18-by-22-inch view camera—a camera that at the moment was balanced on a tripod quivering beneath the repeated gusts of rushing wind.

Although Cass was bent tensely over the camera with the black hood pulled over her head, the wind still tugged free strands of her hair. Tendrils flew and shimmered around her head as though sunlight had condensed into tangible streamers of gold. The long skirt of her sedate navy blue dress billowed and flapped around her knees, revealing something that looked suspiciously like a man's work pants cut off at midcalf. The flying hair and clothes didn't worry Cass; the random motions of *Pacific Winds* as it lay at anchor did. Photographing Duran Shipping Company's ugly lumber schooner was her assignment.

Cass cursed silently, using some of the same words her father had muttered while he stood knee-deep in icy water nearly fifty years before, photographing the Forty-Niners as they gouged both incredible wealth and bitter disappointment from California's fabled earth. Like her language, the wooden camera box with its leather bellows and hand-ground Globe lens had been handed down unchanged from father to daughter.

What had changed was the film itself. The dry-plate film she was using caught light three times faster than the collodion her father had spread on glass plates in his youth. Yet, even that wasn't fast enough for Cass. She wanted this shot to be perfect, to reward the owner of the ship for being independent enough to commission a photograph rather than the usual painting of his ship. On the other hand, an old-fashioned painter had one great advantage over a modern photographer—a painter could imagine full sails, rather than having to wrestle with the complex reality of wind and canvas and sea.

A painter could also gloss over the decidedly unromantic appearance of a battered lumber schooner.

"Damn it!"

Cass erupted from beneath the dark drape and glared at the waterfront, looking for a new angle that would minimize the extraneous motion of the flapping sails and still capture a feeling of trapped, barely contained energy. It was difficult to find drama in a lumber schooner lying at anchor in the deep-water channel just off the wharf, but men who commission portraits of buildings and such want the ordinary surface of their working lives to be imbued with the shimmer of mythic quests.

"Will ye be standing and staring all day, Missy?" roared the schooner's captain through his megaphone. "I dinna know what Mr. Duran is paying you, but the tugboat is costing twenty-five dollars per hour, plus the wages of ten able seamen in the rigging!"

Cass ignored him.

"The tide's running agin us," he bellowed. "We're going to slip that anchor any minute!"

Cass looked at the heavy anchor chain that ran taut into the water ahead of the schooner's bow. The deckhands on the ratlines called back and forth to one another as the ship shivered and jerked at its bonds. Just enough of the men's derisive words and laughter drifted across the water to tell Cass that they were suggesting better uses for a young woman than work as photographer.

Ignoring the sailors as she had learned to ignore all men, Cass bent and gathered up the legs of the heavy wood and brass tripod in her arms. The stand, with its three-foot-long box camera, weighed fifty-three pounds. Years of wrestling with the unwieldy equipment had given her an understanding of leverage and the best uses of what small physical strength God had seen fit to give to women.

"Get your men to work, Captain," Cass called out as she set up the tripod farther down the dock. "You wouldn't want Mr. Duran to hang a photograph of a lazy ship in his office, would you?"

The captain lowered the megaphone and spoke to the boatswain standing beside him. The man whirled and spat orders that set the men in the ratlines into frantic action, swinging like monkeys in a rope-hung cage. Not until Cass ducked back under the camera's black drape did she allow herself to smile. Despite Seattle's handsome boasts of female equality, she knew better than to flaunt her small triumph openly. Victorian men were in no hurry to cede any of their majesty to a mere bloomer girl, even when said "girl" was a woman who wore men's pants underneath her demure skirt.

Through the ground glass Cass studied the inverted image of the *Pacific Winds*. The new angle gave the boat a dashing appearance, emphasizing the flat deck and low scrollwork railing. The wind had even steadied enough that the sails were properly bellied out, like portly shipping magnates and well-fed Empire City tycoons. Working quickly, Cass cocked the shutter and set the exposure time. When she turned to get a fresh plate, she realized that she had left her workbox down the wharf at her original location.

For an instant, Cass had a vision of the box smashed irretrievably beneath the wheels of a passing wagon. A frantic look down the wharf reassured her that the box stood precisely where she had left it. She picked up her skirt and ran down the wharf.

As she grabbed the workbox's leather strap, she saw a man standing only a few feet away, watching her through the big, brine-stained window of a wharf office. The man was tall, powerfully built, and at least thirty years of age. He wore a light brown wool suit, brick red silk tie, a richly brocaded dark gold vest, and an unmistakable aura of command. Cleanshaven but for a dark brown mustache that matched his thick, faintly wavy hair, the man could have been a clerk in the wharfmaster's office, except that his clothes were much too well-made for a subaltern's.

For a moment, Cass froze, compelled by the picture the stranger made as he stood within the cataract of natural light pouring through the windowpanes of the wharf office. The glass glowed with the passage of sunlight, suffusing everything with a mystic gloaming, as though all possibilities, all potentials, everything imaginable had been gathered into the endless, shimmering cataract of golden light. Within that illumination, he stood motionless, watching her with eyes that had the unflinching gray clarity of autumn rain.

She met the man's gaze for a moment longer, then turned away abruptly, unnerved. Without looking back, she fled down the wharf to her camera, feeling as though the stranger had seen through the flesh and blood of the present to the child within her who still yearned, and wondered why wagon wheels had ground her hopes to dust.

3

Jared Duran stood motionless, a massive gold locket dangling forgotten from his fingers as he watched Cass retreat from him. One way or another, Jared had been watching Cass for nearly six weeks. Most often, he had watched her through the work of hired investigators. They brought him the trivial details of her daily life, naming the people who paid to sit for photographic portraits. Without ever having met Cass, he knew that she lived modestly on the second floor of a small house a few blocks up Queen Anne Hill from downtown Seattle. The lower floor of the house served as her studio. Her solitary living arrangement caused some clucking of tongues in the neighborhood, but the detectives had found no patterns of impropriety—no regular afternoon calls by a prominent businessman, no discreet stream of late-night male visitors.

Reading between the lines of the detectives' reports had given Jared an intriguing portrait of a twenty-three-year-old woman who quietly went about living her own life without benefit of masculine protection, support, or company. In the Seattle of 1896, such independence set Cass off from the ordinary run of femininity.

Yet Jared was certain that Cass wasn't a cold woman, indifferent to anything other than glass and chemicals, light and shadows, lives held motionless within a frame. Her best portraits looked beyond the façades of proud businessmen and urban wives to the essential loneliness so often found beneath a polite smile. She found the contrasting threads of resilience and vulnerability, wisdom and madness, creation and destruction that wove through human lives.

As excellent as her commercial portraits were, they were not what compelled Jared. When time permitted, Cass roamed Seattle, shooting photos that had no apparent commercial value. It was these photos that Seattle's Carnegie Library had put on display. Jared had gone and stood for hours, staring at photographs that skimmed instants of time from the ever-changing river of history and transformed them into unchanging images that were beautiful, emotional and—haunted. He had come away from the exhibit feeling as though Cass were trying to freeze the swift currents of time in place before the past slipped forever beyond her reach, leaving her stranded alone in the present.

Jared found Cass's conflicting mixture of emotion and wariness, loneliness and warmth, all too attractive to him. Something in her photographs spoke as directly to his soul as her curving body did to his masculine hungers.

Too bad China Creek didn't hold King. She'll take one look at him, and I won't have a chance in hell of catching her eye.

Not that it mattered. Jared knew he would anger Cass long before she had a chance to understand him, much less to be attracted to him. He was going to take her comfortable little world, turn it upside down, and shake it brutally. Afterward, nothing would ever be the same for her.

Broodingly, Jared looked from Cass working outside in the cold wind to the jewelry he held within his hand. The locket turned slowly, its secrets hanging heavily at the end of a solid gold chain—secrets he was reluctant to reveal. He was stalling and he knew it, a fact that only made him more angry at himself and the circumstances that had trapped him. Stalling was foreign to him, but then, so was his reaction to Cassandra Thornton, the first woman who had interested more than his body in a long, long time.

Yet, he could wait no longer. He would never find a better time than now or a better wedge than Cass with which to split the Chinese community apart from its tong-ridden past. All he could do was hope that the generosity of spirit he sensed within Cass would extend to himself; while she would never thank him for putting the huge gold locket in her hand, perhaps she might be able to forgive him in time.

Perhaps—but Jared doubted it.

Cursing under his breath, he yanked open the office door and walked out into the cold wind off Elliot Bay. Cass hadn't gone far in her retreat from him. She had simply returned to her camera, pulled the black photographer's drape into place, and closed herself off from all but the single slice of reality that lay revealed by her lens.

"Thank you, Captain Soren," Jared called out from behind Cass. "Bring your ship back alongside the wharf now."

"Wait, I'm not finished," Cass said, straightening suddenly and pulling away the muffling black drape.

The captain ignored her.

Cass spun around and found herself staring into the unnerving clarity of the stranger's eyes. Anger flared in her. She wasn't accustomed to having her work interrupted by anyone.

"My God, the last time I got a look like that, I'd cornered a cougar with cubs," Jared said, appreciating the golden blaze of her eyes even as he regretted being its cause. "It's all right, Miss Thornton. I'm Jared Duran, the man who hired you. You'll be paid for a day's work, even if I can't tell the *Pacific Winds* from the wharf pilings." At Cass's look of surprise, his smile widened, and he asked softly, "Did you really think I wanted a picture of that old scow on my office wall?"

Cass looked over her shoulder at the ugly schooner. When she turned back to Jared, his obvious amusement made her angry.

"I'm a photographer, Mr. Duran. I find beauty other people overlook. That's why you hired me."

"Is it?"

Cass said nothing. She disliked being examined as carefully as Jared Duran was examining her at the moment. It made her feel naked.

"I have you at a disadvantage," Jared said matter-of-factly. "It's only temporary, I assure you. If you'll come with me, we can talk more privately."

He stood aside and gestured toward the door of the wharf office. Cass didn't move.

"There's no need to talk privately about a commission to photograph the ugliest scow in Elliott Bay," she said.

"That's not why I sent for you."

One honey-colored eyebrow arched upward. "Really? Tell me, Mr. Jared Duran, why should I want to talk privately with a man who deals in false pretenses?"

"The world is rarely what it seems, Miss Thornton. Or are you too young to have discovered that?"

Cass gave Jared a long, level look. "You call yourself Jared Duran, but I have no proof of that. I have no proof of anything except that you've ruined my chances of getting a decent photograph of an indecently aged lumber schooner. Although," she added, "you certainly act as though you own the waterfront."

"Just a small part of it," Jared said, indicating the glass panel that was inset in the office door. Painted on the panel was "Duran Shipping Company" and in the corner, in discreet letters, "Jared Duran, Proprietor."

Cass weighed the man in front of her for a moment longer before she said distinctly, "I prefer to talk to you out here."

Stifling an impatient curse, Jared reached into his pocket. No matter what the outcome of their conversation, he knew that Cass's first impression of him as a man had left her far more wary than intrigued. He doubted that anything would happen in the next few minutes to soften her opinion. That angered him, but didn't change what he knew must come next. Too much was at stake; the fact that he wanted Cass was irrelevant.

From his vest pocket Jared withdrew a small pouch made of purple velvet. Without a word, he handed it to her.

The cloth had once been thick and lush, but now was worn thin in spots, as though it were old or had traveled great distances rubbing against someone's body. Cass didn't need to untie the drawstring to know that the folds of cloth contained a large, smooth, oval object that was surprisingly heavy for its size. When she turned over the pouch, she sensed as much as heard the rustle of a fine metal chain. She glanced uncertainly at Jared.

"Open it," he urged. His voice was deep and soft, almost seductive.

Cass looked away because she could not bear to meet the intensity of his glance any longer. She eased the drawstring open, held the bottom of the pouch between her fingers, and tipped a heavy gold locket the size of a hen's egg into her hand. Cass had worn her own nugget bracelet long enough to recognize nearly pure gold when it lay cool and gleaming in her hand. Both locket and chain were exquisitely engraved with scrollwork. A single square-cut diamond was mounted in the center of the locket's lid, transforming a handsome keepsake into a valuable piece of jewelry.

Oddly, the locket felt familiar to Cass, as though she had handled its golden weight before.

"Do you recognize it?"

"Only as gold," Cass said slowly.

"I thought perhaps it might be a family heirloom," Jared said.

Cass shook her head in a silent negative that sent strands of hair cascading over her shoulders. The color of her hair and the gold were identical in the sunlight.

"I doubt that the locket is as old as I am," she said. "See how the engraving has barely worn away? Yet the gold itself feels nearly pure, much too soft to hold the marks of man for long."

Jared lifted the locket from Cass's hand. As his fingertips brushed over her palm, she felt his warmth in a startlingly intimate way. She glanced at Jared warily, more surprised by her own reaction than by the impersonal contact of his fingers. He undid the locket's tiny catch with a deftness that was unexpected in a man whose hands were both large and strong. Opening the locket wide, he placed it on her palm.

"Does this help your memory?" he asked quietly.

Cass looked at the photograph inside the locket and felt as though the world had hesitated in its turning for just an instant.

Her own father looked back at her from the locket's oval embrace. In the strong light of the flash that had been used to take the photograph, his eyes were calm and nearly transparent; yet even that hard light hadn't been able to dim their brilliant radiance, a reflection of the urgency that had driven his endless quest for something he could not name.

Did you finally find peace, Papa?

"You know him," Jared said.

"My father. Thad Thornton. He looks so young—"

"That's odd. The picture isn't fifteen years old."

"Yes, I know. I can tell from the suit," Cass said absently. "He almost never wore one. I had forgotten how handsome he was. Even at sixty, his hair was more blond than gray, and he was strong, very strong. His beard is trimmed, too. See? It must have been quite an occasion. He was enjoying it. Look at his smile. I rarely saw him smile like that."

Cass's voice faded as she focused on the tiny, exquisitely beautiful Chinese woman who was seated within the arc of Thad Thornton's arm. Her face was elegant, her expression serene, almost detached, but her fingertips rested on Thad's blunt hand in a gesture that was restrained yet so loving that Cass felt for a moment as though she were intruding.

Even so, she couldn't help looking more closely at the couple. The photographer in her noted that the position of her father's arm around this strange woman's shoulders served not only to shelter her but also to conceal the cable release that he held between his fingers. Thad himself had taken the intimate photo.

"The inscription," Jared urged softly.

Cass glanced at the engraving on the facing side of the locket. There was a horizontal line of script and a vertical line of ideographs.

" 'To my Lilac, from her loving Thad,' " Cass read aloud. The ideographs intrigued Cass, but she could not translate them. As though to learn their meaning by touch, she ran one fingertip delicately over the column.

"'The flower that blooms in adversity knows the greatest beauty of all.'"

Jared's words sank into Cass as though he were speaking directly to her rather than merely translating the ideographs. She looked up into the merciless clarity of his eyes.

"I don't understand," Cass said.

"If you come with me, she will explain everything."

"She?"

"Lilac Rain, the woman in the locket."

Suddenly, Cass remembered her father's dying, incoherent words about lilacs and rain and beauty. Her trembling fingers closed around the locket, snapping it shut, squeezing it until her skin whitened.

She's the one. She's the perfect woman Papa chased all over the West.

"Will you come with me?" Jared asked.

Cass laughed oddly. "Oh, yes, Mr. Duran. I'll come with you. I've been eating Lilac's dust all my life. It's past time that I meet her."

4

The girl was extraordinary.

Her features were delicate, with a suggestion of sensual possibilities so subtle and yet so pervasive that people who had known Tea Rose for all of her fourteen years sometimes stopped and stared at her as though she had just sprung fully formed from their erotic dreams. Even Lilac, who knew better than anyone else the rapier intelligence and unflinching ambition of her daughter, still found herself astonished by Tea Rose's cool perfection.

"If a lotus were ever to bloom beneath winter moonlight, the result would be but a shadow of your beauty," Lilac said quietly.

Tea Rose looked up from the dragon she was embroidering on scarlet brocade. The heavy cloth spilled off the wooden frame onto the angular wooden chair on which she sat and from there onto the rich carpet that softened the floor of the apartment in the heart of Chinatown. The gold thread in the girl's needle gleamed metallically in stark contrast with the darkness of her smooth, straight hair.

"I am your daughter," Tea Rose said. "Of course I'm beautiful."

Lilac's smile was both sad and amused. Once, she had despaired of ever teaching her quick, willful daughter the necessity of showing the world a slave's polite, submissive face. Now, Lilac was having that same face turned on her.

"You may speak freely," Lilac said, switching to quick, lightly accented English. "It is Chow Li's turn at the spyhole. He has no understanding of English." She spoke without looking at the wooden grille on the opposite wall in which the peephole was hidden.

"Are you sure?" Tea Rose asked. Her speech was unaccented and utterly fluent, for she had spoken English, Cantonese, and Mandarin from her first lisping words as a toddler. For better or for worse, her tutors had been men of all classes and stations. As a result, her speech often ranged from scholarly to coarse within the same sentence.

"Am I sure that Chow Li is less than a yard away? Yes. I can smell the opium smoke on his clothes. As for his understanding of English—" Lilac's expression changed subtly, hinting at the ruthlessness beneath her elegant exterior. "Yesterday, I offered to play the turtle game with him."

Tea Rose looked startled in the instant before comprehension came to her. "You spoke in English?"

"Yes. His expression didn't change."

"Then he didn't understand. A man who would play the turtle game with his own hand wouldn't reject the woman he has lusted after for years." Tea Rose laughed musically behind her upraised hand. "The turtle head makes fools of all men."

"Be careful, daughter. You don't understand the turtle's power."

"It has no power over me," Tea Rose said calmly, returning to her embroidery. "Chinese turtle heads or American cocks, it is all the same. 'The tail wags the dog. The bitch wags the dog's tail. Who then is more powerful, bitch or dog?'"

Lilac recognized her own words and felt both pride and fear. She had trained her daughter well. The lust that poked up beneath a man's silk robes would never make Tea Rose's body soften and unfold its scented petals in welcome. She would fight the flowery battle at Tan Feng's command, but her pleasure would come only from the power that men's lust gave her over them. In that coldness lay Tea Rose's greatest strength.

And her greatest weakness.

Because Tea Rose knew nothing of sexual urgency herself, she could only guess at its strength in men. If she guessed correctly, she would please her master enormously. If she guessed incorrectly, she would be badly beaten or strangled on the spot. There was so much for Tea Rose to learn and so terrifyingly little time for her to learn it. Only greater experience would remove Tea Rose's innocent, arrogant certainty that she could control any man solely through his penis.

Impassively, Lilac examined her daughter. Little of the girl's white father showed except in Tea Rose's rare, spontaneous smile and long-limbed elegance. Lilac stood three inches under five feet tall; Tea Rose was two inches over five feet. The girl's black eyes were delicately almond shaped, her nose wasn't prominent, and if her oval face lacked the fullness of a harvest moon, it wasn't a flaw Chinese men seemed to notice. Her skin was light without being repellently so, rather like certain nuggets of river gold, smooth and beguiling in their pale satin luster.

"Is Mr. Duran coming tonight?" Tea Rose asked.

"Which one, Jared or King?"

"Tan Feng would be pleased with either."

"But you, daughter, would be more pleased with King."

Tea Rose's fingers paused, then the slender steel needle resumed drawing the fine metallic thread through silk. "Are you telling me that I must be more careful in showing preference?"

"What is it that draws you to King?" Lilac countered. "His appearance? His laughter? The wildness blazing in his eyes?"

"No," Tea Rose said. "Jared would demand a woman's soul. King would not."

Lilac's black eyes widened fractionally at Tea Rose's shrewd observation. "Jared would give a woman his soul in return," Lilac pointed out softly. "That is a rare thing in a man—or a woman."

"Did my father give you his soul?"

"Yes."

Tea Rose glanced up. "Did you give yours in return?"

"A sing-song girl has no soul."

For long minutes, there was no sound in the room but the subtle shift of heavy silk as Tea Rose worked over the embroidery frame. Except for its spyhole, the small apartment was an oasis of privacy in the crowded squalor of Chinatown, where men rented sleeping space in shifts. But no less a setting would be condoned for Tan Feng's most important prostitute and her daughter, the fourteen-year-old child on whom the tong leader had lavished such extraordinary attention.

"Kingston Duran lives through his body, not his mind," Tea Rose said finally, her voice smooth and cool. She tied off the solid gold thread and severed it with tiny scissors. "King has no use for a woman's soul, and I have no desire to share mine. In that, we are well matched." Tea Rose picked up a needle already threaded with more gold and began to stitch again. "But that is unimportant. I won't be some rich round-eye's China girl. I will be wife to Tan Feng."

Fear squeezed Lilac so viciously that for a moment she couldn't breathe for her fear. Lilac had suspected some such lunatic hope on Tea Rose's part, had even prepared for it, but she had burned much incense in the Hall of Ancestors while she prayed that her daughter's beauty, ambition, and inexperience wouldn't precipitate disaster before the Night of the Good Lady.

"Oh?" Lilac murmured. "When did Tan offer to elevate you to the status of his wife?"

"He will."

"But he hasn't done so, has he?"

"Don't worry, mother." Tea Rose smiled suddenly, enchantingly. "When I am Tan's wife, you won't need to look in your mirror and fear tomorrow. If Tan dared even to talk of selling you, I would bring him to his knees begging for just the scent of my flower."

"Tan may have your miserable flower anytime he bothers to pluck it," Lilac said coldly. "He owns you just as he owns me. Never forget that, daughter. It is Tan's wish that you bring a Duran to his knees with lust. That is why the sing-song girls have so carefully trained you in the ways of teasing and pleasuring the penis. Does a man give his future wife to sing-song girls for educating?"

Tea Rose said nothing.

Beneath her imperious mask, Lilac felt cold claws of fear slide more deeply into her belly. She had lived with fear ever since Tea Rose had discovered that Tan Feng desired her. No matter how carefully trained or how innately clever Tea Rose was in manipulating men, some things could only be understood through direct experience. The connection between male lust, pride, and violence was one of those things. Tea Rose simply didn't comprehend the speed with which lust could turn to killing rage if the man tired of being teased.

Lilac knew that Tan wanted Tea Rose to the point of obsession, yet he feared her power over him. He realized that to give in to his lust would be to hand Tea Rose the razor with which she would slit his throat. As long as Tea Rose didn't know the extent of her power over Tan Feng, he was safe.

And so was Tea Rose.

Lilac understood what her daughter was too innocent and too confident to believe: Rather than be ruled by Tea Rose, Tan would break her; if breaking her were impossible, he would sell her—if he didn't kill her first.

Unconsciously, Lilac reached into the right pocket of her silk jacket. Instead of the worn velvet pouch and reassuring weight of Thad's gift, she found only emptiness. The big locket had always felt so comforting as it filled her hand, the metal warm with her body heat, reminding her of Thad's voice rumbling between her breasts while he caressed her, and his great head like a golden lion's between her tiny hands.

"Mother?"

Lilac's eyes snapped open.

"You cried out," Tea Rose said. "Are you ill?"

Mother watched daughter with opaque black eyes. "You are so young," Lilac said in a soft, despairing voice. "You must learn so much, but most of all you must learn *this:* A man can't be controlled solely by his lust. Because men vie to have you bathe them, you believe you hold the world between your legs. That is not so. Tan has forged your beauty and your body into a weapon for his own use—not into an altar at which he will worship. You have been given special education, training, and freedoms because Tan wants a spy who is well-placed in white society. Sing-song girls are an ancient method of infiltrating enemy clans."

"So are wives," Tea Rose countered instantly.

"Do you really believe that either Duran brother would marry the child of a Chinese prostitute?"

Mother and daughter looked at each other while silence expanded between them, filling the room, crowding them until it was difficult to breathe.

"I will be no man's sing-song girl," Tea Rose said in a soft, final tone.

Again, Lilac reached into her pocket. Again, she found only emptiness and memories. Torn between despair and fierce determination, she watched her daughter's quick, precise use of the needle as she pierced silk and drew pure gold through the wounds. Lilac knew that beneath Tea Rose's youthful exterior lay a merciless clarity of mind that needed only time in which to mature, to grow from a child's erratic insights into an adult's unflinching grasp of the complex nettle of life.

Tea Rose knew much about male lust and little about male pride. Lilac, however, knew of both intimately. What Lilac didn't know was how much time she had left before Tea Rose discovered the depth of Tan's sexual obsession, used it as a weapon against him, and signed her own death warrant in the process.

Fist clenched against emptiness, Lilac prayed that she had bought enough time with her soul and a solid gold locket.

5

"When you told me I'd be safe in your carriage, I had no idea you meant *this*," Cass said wryly. She rapped against the carriage wall with her knuckles, making the iron plate ring like a gong. "This contraption must weigh more than a loaded brewery wagon. No wonder you have eight Belgians in the traces."

"The wagon isn't mine," Jared said. "I just borrowed it for a special trip."

His smile was a flash of white in the dim interior of the armored wagon. The only illumination came through a narrow slit at eye level. When Cass inspected the slit, she discovered that even this opening could be covered with an iron slide.

"It's a gunport," Jared said.

"Good heavens. Why?"

Without a word, he stood up and lifted the heavy wooden lid of the box he was using as a seat. In the faint light, Cass could just make out the dull gleam of a stack of yellow metal bricks nestled in a bed of excelsior.

"That can't be—" her voice died to a hush, "gold."

"Twenty-four-karat and solid clear through," Jared said, lowering the lid and sitting down again. "Refined hundred-ounce ingots. That's just a bit more than six pounds each. Put another way, fifteen hundred dollars apiece. There are ten ingots in each crate."

Cass looked around the interior of the wagon, quickly counting six identical wooden crates.

"You choose an odd way to travel," she said, watching him with eyes just barely darker than gold itself.

"Not really. Gold is the strongest link between the world where we started and the world where we're going." He gestured to the open gunport. "Look out there."

As she moved past him to peer through the gunport, her scent drifted up. His nostrils flared as he inhaled a mixture of rosewater and womanly warmth. It was very difficult not to reach out and trace the long, elegant line of her back with his fingertips. If there had been nothing more at stake than his own future, he would have done it.

Jared's hand balled into a fist. For a moment, he wished that he had his brother's ability to live solely in the present, heedless of past and future alike. King wouldn't have hesitated; he would have reached for Cass and never looked back.

"What do you see?" Jared asked, his voice low.

"Nothing yet. It's too bright."

Cass blinked rapidly, then squinted into the sunlight pouring through the gunport. The street outside was a vast, open-air market. Sidewalk peddlers and street-corner barbers competed for space with the storefront displays of herbalists and gold merchants. Down one alley, sides of fresh pork hung in the open air alongside ropes of sausage, strings of dried fish, and squawking, leg-tied chicken and ducks. Down another alley, a dozen small stands offered early summer produce—vegetables and melons, pungent herbs and oddly shaped mushrooms. In yet another stall, shiny crabs and glistening silver fish lay side by side with clams and oysters and flaccid geoducks in phallic array.

The sidewalks in front of the brick buildings were seething with people. Most of the pedestrians were Chinese, but sprinkled through the throngs were colorfully dressed Japanese, Filipinos, and even a few Koreans with their strange, straight-brimmed black hats and loose white clothes. Ten feet away, a cobbler repaired shoes, and a brawny, bronzed youth executed a series of elaborate calisthenics while whirling a pair of heavy bronze swords above his turbaned head.

"We're in the International District," Cass said, sliding back onto her seat. "Most people just call it Chinatown."

"Did your father talk much about the Chinese?"

"No," Cass said, a touch of bitterness in her voice. "I lived with him only in the summers, Mr. Duran. All we really talked about was photography. Everything else, he kept to himself."

Absently, Cass fingered the heavy chain of the locket she still held. The combination of anger and sadness she felt showed clearly on her face.

"Most of the Chinese in America are from four or five districts in the southern part of China, around Canton," Jared said, watching Cass closely. "They're poor people, farmers who've lost their small parcel of land, dispossessed second sons, and the like. They drifted down the Pearl River to the crown colony at Fragrant Harbor—Hong Kong, it's called—and caught ships sailing east for America."

"They came here to build a better life, just like other immigrants."

"The Chinese are different in one regard from most other immigrants," Jared said. "They have no intention of staying any longer than it takes for them to hack off a piece of the Golden Mountain and take it back home with them. They're sojourners, not immigrants. They're citizens of the Celestial Empire, temporary expatriates from heaven. They make every effort to live here as they lived at home—the same religion, language, clothes, music, culture, everything. More than any other immigrant community, Chinatown is truly a piece of old China transported to America."

Jared leaned toward Cass. In the gloom of the armored

carriage, his eyes were crystalline flashes of light. Cass drew a soft breath, feeling the force of his will reaching out to her.

"You must remember that in the next few minutes," he said distinctly. "You can't judge Chinese as you would Americans. The woman you're about to meet is a rare individual, a brilliant woman who occupies an important position within the context of the Chinese community."

"Go on," Cass said, her voice tight. "Drop the other shoe."

Jared watched Cass, feeling her withdraw from him even though she hadn't moved. Silently, futilely, he cursed what he could not change.

"In addition to being beautiful and intelligent, Lilac is a slave and a prostitute."

Cass swallowed involuntarily. She tried to speak, but found that her voice would not immediately respond. The realization that her father had loved a whore left her speechless.

"I'm sorry," Jared said, "but there's no real way of sugarcoating the facts of Lilac's existence. Chinese women, even wives, are legally chattel. They can be bought, sold, and physically abused, but only within a well-defined social framework. Slave girls are different in that they have no rights whatsoever. Legally, they can be bought, sold, traded, abused, or even killed without attracting particular notice. Lilac has no more freedom of choice than a milk cow. If anyone discovers that you have met her, she could be beaten within an inch of her life. Or killed. That's why I lied to you about photographing the *Pacific Winds;* it gave me a perfectly valid excuse to meet you."

Jared's eyes were so intense that Cass could not bear to look directly into them any longer. She went to the gunport and squinted into the blinding light.

"There are American policemen out there," Cass said.

Though she said no more, Jared understood the implicit question.

"They have about as much effective power in Chinatown as they would in the Four Districts of South China. In

Chinatown, as in China, you can do or be anything you wish, as long as you have the money, strength, and cleverness to make your will stick."

"And you love it," Cass said, her voice almost accusing.

"Yes."

"A Sinophile, like my father."

"No. Your father was fascinated with the exotic and unattainable. I'm fascinated with the pragmatic and sensual. China embodies the essence of both."

The ironclad wheels ground on the cobblestones, reminding Cass of other times, other places, wagons and dust and unhappiness—as her father chased his perfect woman—and forever overlooked the daughter he sent away.

The wagon slowed, turned into a narrow alley between two rows of buildings, passed through a rank of black-clad men wearing black, narrow-brimmed hats, and plunged into the darkness inside a barnlike building. Daylight vanished as big wooden doors swung shut behind the armored wagon.

A sharp knock on the door made Cass's pulse jump.

"Wait," said Jared.

A match flared in the darkness. Gray eyes reflected the light in twin flames watching her.

"Your hair," Jared said. He blew out the match, returning the interior of the wagon to absolute blackness.

Cass's breath came in with an audible rush as she felt Jared's hands gathering up stray locks of her hair, smoothing them with a sensual touch, then deftly twisting them up until each glistening strand was tucked beneath her hat. She thought she felt the lightest brush of his fingers over her cheek, but couldn't be sure.

Another match flared. "Yes. That should do. No blond showing."

Yet, Jared didn't blow out the match. Instead, he watched Cass with an intensity that unnerved her.

"What—?" she asked.

"Cassandra—Cass," he whispered. "I know this won't be easy for you. I'm sorry. I'll help you all I can, all that you let me. Please remember that."

He blew out the match, plunging the interior of the wagon into darkness.

Cass sat very still. She knew that he was attracted to her. Even worse, she realized that she was attracted to him. She didn't want that. Jared was too strong, too self-sufficient, too invulnerable. He wouldn't *need* her. Before she could trust herself to a man, she had to know that she was so necessary to his well-being that he would never leave her behind.

Yet, even knowing that, Cass still found Jared more attractive than any man she had ever met. Far too attractive. Frighteningly so.

"Ready?" Jared asked from the darkness.

Cass swallowed. "I—yes," she whispered, but she knew that she lied.

Jared pulled open the latch on the door and stepped from the wagon. He offered his hand to Cass. She hesitated, then accepted. His hand was surprisingly hard for a businessman; he was even stronger than he looked. He took her weight without giving in the least.

"Watch your footing," Jared warned, steadying her as she stepped down. "It's a dirt floor."

The building was a shadowy inferno, filled with harsh, acrid odors—fire and smoke and red-hot metal. As her eyes adjusted, Cass saw men working all around her. Some were stripped to the waist, displaying muscular, sweat-gleaming bodies. Everywhere she looked, there were flames, furnaces, sparks exploding, and the noise of hammers pounding metal into new shapes.

Nearby, a heavyset Chinese man wearing a leather apron and thick leather gloves took a pair of long-handled tongs and plucked a metal beaker from the depths of a furnace. The beaker glowed yellow-red in the darkness as the man carried it a few feet, then carefully tipped it, pouring the molten contents into a large black mold. A cascade of sparks exploded like fireworks.

Moments later, the smith disappeared in a cloud of steam as he dipped a bucket of water from a trough and poured it over the mold. As the steam cleared, he picked up a heavy hammer and broke open the catches that held the mold together. A perfectly formed skillet slid from the mold. The kitchen utensil was still glowing yellow with heat as the smith seized it with his tongs and dropped it into a washtub full of water. Steam exploded into the air.

Jared took Cass's arm and urged her through the foundry building toward a flight of stairs at the back. They passed another worker carrying several of the newly cast frying pans on a metal tray. At first, Cass thought the pans still glowed from the heat of the fire; then she recognized the muted yellow as their natural color.

"That's gold!"

"Quiet," Jared said urgently.

Dumbfounded, Cass let herself be hustled past a workbench where men carefully painted gold black. When they were finished, the gold pans would be indistinguishable from cast iron.

The room at the head of the long, steep stairs was a cluttered, cramped shop office. There was no one around, although the odor of cigar smoke attested that someone had been there recently.

"Who buys those pans?" Cass asked as Jared closed the door.

"Poor Chinese who come to Fu-shan, work like hell for twenty years, then want to take their gold and go home," Jared said. He walked over to a window and lifted the side of the scarlet curtain just enough to see out. "In China, the only way to keep gold from tax collectors or bandits is to hide it very, very well. Mr. Wan uses gold for all manner of sojourner utensils—tent stakes, swords, stewing pots, even reliquaries."

"Why—"

"Later," Jared said, interrupting Cass. "For now, all you have to understand is that Lilac's full name is Lilac Rain Thornton, and if Tan Feng knows that she has met with her stepdaughter, Lilac will be killed."

6

Against the scarlet lacquered tray, the pot and teacup glowed with the cool radiance of moonlight on white jade. The cup's pale, porcelain fragility expressed an artistic tradition that had raised simplicity and restraint to an art. Cups designed in this manner had made the Ming Dynasty famous in lands far removed from China.

In a single, flowing motion, Lilac knelt and placed the tea tray soundlessly on a teak table. The carved table was like a black dragon crouched in massive silence, waiting for succulent prey to come within reach. Heavy, colorful silk robes whispered as Lilac settled onto her knees to wait with folded hands and bowed head for Tan Feng to notice her presence.

At the moment, Tan was frowning over a scroll that purported to be the manifest of *Fragrant Dreams,* a ship in which the Soong Li Tong had a 49 percent interest.

"Does that eater of excrement think that I have no more brains than his withered turtle head?"

Tan's question was all the more unsettling for the deceptive mildness of his voice. Nearby, Tan's chief accountant moved uneasily, but said nothing because the question had not been directed at him.

"Two thousand dollars in gold doesn't simply vanish like piss into dry sand." Tan glanced up at his accountant. "Did he send full measure of silk and full taels of opium as he promised?"

"Within reason, yes," the accountant answered, bowing quickly and deeply. "No more than the customary percentage was underweight, lord."

Tan grunted and threw the scroll onto a pile of similar papers. "Pay him, but shave the coins to recover our loss. If he complains, tell him to choose his captains and pursers more carefully."

Chin bowed again, gathered up the scrolls, and withdrew.

After several minutes of silence, Tan turned toward Lilac. If she felt his black gaze, she didn't show it. As still as the cup itself, she waited for his pleasure.

Instead of speaking, Tan continued to stare at Lilac. As always, the graceful curve of her neck gratified him, as did the black weight of her elaborately coiled and coiffed hair. If she had been moving in the least, the mirrored ornaments and crimson silk tassels arrayed artfully in her hair would have flashed and shimmered. But she was not moving. Her hands were folded in a position of repose that recalled the purity and serenity of the lotus bud itself.

Tan Feng shifted in the heavy, unpadded armchair, spreading his knees wide and bracing his hands on them. The rubbing of heavy silk and the hollow clicking of the beads on his long mandarin necklace seemed very loud in the silence. Gradually, the irritations of dishonest business partners and the unseemly greed of white merchants faded from Tan's mind. Hands on his widespread knees, he enjoyed the consummate stillness of the woman he had spent twenty years trying to bring to heel.

In his earlier years, he had enjoyed the naked savagery of Lilac's unguarded glance. He had relished their constant, subtle clash of wills, for it had given a rare savor to the moments when he had thrust himself into her body, proving himself her superior. But he had been a younger man then, and his sexual prowess had been legendary. After the successful end of his flowery battle with Lilac, he would go into the women's quarters with a handful of gold; the last sing-song girl to bring him to climax would get the coins. Naturally, the women had shown both stamina and startling ingenuity in their attempts to coax his sated turtle head from its soft shell.

The memories caused a slow, familiar tightening in Tan's crotch. He smiled to himself, pleased that his fiftieth birthday would arrive and find him as hard and blunt as ever. For a moment, he considered ordering Lilac to service him with no more ceremony than if she had been the lowest sing-song girl. The thought of Lilac's narrow, painted lips and clever tongue gave the idea great appeal. The thought of looking into her black eyes and knowing how much she hated him even as she ministered with utmost delicacy to his needs was an added delight.

The thought of having Tea Rose watch and learn caused a lightning stroke of lust so intense that Tan grunted and spread his legs more widely to accommodate his growing erection.

Though there was no doubt that Lilac had heard the low noise, she didn't move. Tan smiled sourly. Ten years ago, he would have had her head between his legs without a second thought. But it wasn't ten years ago. He had a long evening ahead with the two Durans. He couldn't afford to expend his strength on a woman who was too spiritually deformed to accept her place in the universe.

However, he wasn't too tired to bait her. It would serve as a tonic to offset the advancing of age.

"I will take my tea now, woman."

"Yes, lord."

Lilac's voice was as high and pure as the calling of a bird. Tan knew she pitched her voice in that manner for his enjoyment, just as she plucked her eyebrows and forehead, beneath her arms and between her legs in order to make herself more pleasing to him. She used the perfume he preferred, burned the incense he enjoyed, wore his favorite colors, and knew how to bring him intense pleasure with her tiny hands and feet and mouth, as well as in the perfumed recesses of her pleasure pavilion. In no way was she other than a model of feminine obedience.

But Tan knew there was murderous rage seething within Lilac's slender body, a defiance that was as deep as it was invisible. He sensed her hatred in the same visceral way that he sensed who among his men he could trust and who would gut him like a codfish at first opportunity.

Lilac would. He was certain of it.

And Tan also knew he was getting too old to guard his back every second. He should have sold Lilac years before, but she was the only woman he had found who could distract him from the fragile, soul-destroying perfection of her demon daughter. Tea Rose, his personal opiate—if he gave in to her, he would not only be old, but also a fool. And, very quickly, he would be an old dead fool.

The gentle murmur of tea swirling within the delicate white cup filtered into Tan's bleak thoughts. Sensing that she had his attention once more, Lilac lifted the cup in her hands and held it out to Tan in the manner of a supplicant rendering an offering to a god. As always, her movements were elegant, the quintessential expression of a civilization that had spent thousands of years in refining complex social relationships and ceremonies.

If Tan had thought that Lilac performed her duties so perfectly just to please him, he would have been enormously gratified. But he sensed that each artful curve of hand and neck, each tranquil reflection of the contemplative lotus, was a flick of the knife over his skin, a subtle reminder that she would never acknowledge his possession of her. She was an actress playing a part.

See, Tan Feng? See the most perfect woman in the Four Districts. See her and know that she mocks you with every fluting word, every submissive bow, every rippling movement of her body as she serves you. She will never come to you in lust or gratitude or joy. She will never please you simply because it is right and proper for a woman to please her master. She is an evil spirit sent to torment you. She is moonlight on a midnight pond, vanishing from your hands even as you grasp her. Fox Woman.

He should have broken or killed Lilac long ago, but he had believed that he would ultimately master her on her own terms, where mind rather than physical strength was supreme. Letting Lilac choose the battleground had been a mistake that he wouldn't make with Tea Rose. When he could bear denying himself her beauty no longer, he would harvest his deadly little opium flower with consummate care.

And if he felt resentment rather than honeyed submission in her body, he would kill her.

That would be a great waste; fearing that waste was one of the things holding his lust in check. He had spent much money and thought grooming Tea Rose to be a concubine to a powerful round-eye. She would drain business secrets from her lover's brain as surely as she drained liquid pearls from his jade stem. At the very least, she would know in advance if there would be a repeat of the disaster of a decade before, when Seattle's white citizens had turned on the Celestials and had beaten, harassed, burned out, and finally run the Chinese out of the city.

It had taken the Soong Li Tong years to recover from that debacle, which might have been circumvented by forewarning from a single well-placed spy. It would be the height of self-indulgent foolishness to take Tea Rose, to spend the asset of her virginity. Tan had no wise choice but to put off his sexual harvest as long as possible.

Frowning, Tan lifted the teacup to his lips and drank without noticing the exquisitely blended flavors and precise heat of the brew. With equal inattention, he tasted a slice of candied orange. Not for the first time in his life, he wished that he had been born as most men were, with a turtle that slept often and long. Lust was all very well when it could be slaked without difficulty, but when his mind insisted on denying his body's urgent needs, persistent lust became tedious.

"Come, female," Tan said, settling back slightly in his chair.

Narrow-eyed, he watched as Lilac came to her feet with a lithe motion that denied her nearly forty years. She knelt with the same flowing movement. Not by look or word or gesture did Lilac reveal her reaction to Tan's command as she waited between his legs with bowed head and folded hands. Without a word, he opened his robes, revealing the blunt head of his emerging penis.

"I would be soothed," Tan said, "slowly." He savored the warmth of Lilac's breath as it bathed his firming flesh. Just as he saw her tongue, he added, "With your hands. I have other uses for your mouth at the moment."

Lilac's head bowed in elegant, artificial submission. "As you wish, my lord."

There was a rustle of silk as she withdrew a vial of scented oil from a pocket of her robe.

"Are you making progress with Jared Duran?" Tan asked.

"He has agreed to entertain some of his business friends at the House of the Blossom Moon tonight," Lilac said, naming the larger of the two gambling halls that Tan owned. "As you wished, I will entertain the men with music while they eat. Tea Rose will come with me, as you also wished."

"Has Jared Duran mentioned Tea Rose?"

"What could he say, my lord? He has yet to see so much as a photograph of her. You have forbidden her to do more than sit at spyholes while the sing-song girls entertain their clients."

Tan made a low sound, but it was in response to the glide of Lilac's cool, oiled hands rather than to her words.

"Like the moon, that which is beyond reach has more luster," Tan said, his voice thickening.

"Yes, my lord."

The words floated on the warm, scented air rising from his lap. He sighed in a pleasure that was oddly relaxed. Despite Lilac's hatred—or perhaps, because of it—she knew his body better than any woman ever had. The least hesitation in his breathing, the smallest flexing of his thighs, the subtlest shift of his buttocks, and she responded instantly with a new gliding pressure that redoubled his pleasure.

"She will be fifteen soon enough," Tan said. "Then it will be her hands soothing me."

Even Lilac's superb self-control couldn't conceal her surprise. "You do her great honor, my lord."

"Do I?"

"You choose to pluck her flower yourself, thus denying your coffers the wealth her virginity would bring from a rich round-eye."

Slowly, Lilac's nails sank into Tan's vulnerable flesh, stopping just on the dissolving edge of true pain, giving him a peculiar, bittersweet pleasure and cooling his arousal at the same time. Tan groaned at the carefully measured pain that lingered just long enough to accomplish its purpose, then faded, leaving him to enjoy with redoubled intensity being coaxed into fullness once more. Slowly, his whole body tightened within Lilac's skilled grasp, responding like a bow drawn by a master archer's hands.

"I will give Duran that one frail piece of skin that is so valuable," Tan said, closing his eyes but for twin black slits as he watched Lilac's hands and thought of the moment when it would be Tea Rose who knelt between his thighs. The vision brought a vicious thrust of desire that squeezed his breath and loosened his knees. "She will bleed for her round-eye's turtle head, but she will have serviced me in every other way before that moment."

Lilac's hands didn't hesitate despite the fear expanding in her veins. She knew even better than Tan Feng the danger that would come to Tea Rose if she proved reluctant or unsatisfactory in servicing Tan's needs.

"As always, you are wise," Lilac said. "Once Tea Rose has bled, how will her owner know if you henceforth visit her pleasure pavilion?"

The words had a galvanizing effect on Tan, filling him with sexual urgency. Lilac sank her nails deeply into his engorged flesh. He made a hoarse sound and grabbed her wrist, grinding the fine bones beneath his powerful grip. She met his fierce eyes without flinching.

"Forgive me, my lord, but you said you wished it to be slow. With a man of your potency, occasional pain is the only way."

In hot silence, Tan looked at his slave. As always, he could find no hint that she had intended anything except to follow his orders as precisely as humanly possible. And, as always, she had somehow turned submission into war. He should take a stick and beat her until she pleaded for mercy.

Warm drops of oil trickled onto his hot, sensitive flesh. Skilled fingers teased him, cajoled him, coaxed him forth once more. Tan tried to hang onto his anger, but found the emotion being transformed into sudden, hard need. It had always been thus with Lilac. He could only bring himself to beat her when she had sucked the last liquid pearl from him.

Tan's thick, powerful arm shot out. His fingers twisted in Lilac's bound hair as he dragged her head down into his lap.

"Finish it," he said hoarsely.

Lilac bent to her work, relieved that she would soon be free. After a few more moments, she wouldn't have to worry about Tan Feng unexpectedly seeking her out for flowery battle. When she had finished, Tan's turtle head would be content to lie sleeping within its soft shell for a time.

And she would be free to answer Jared's signal when it finally came.

7

"Look down there," Jared said, gesturing toward the world beyond the scarlet curtain.

Cass didn't move. She felt off balance and beleaguered. She had listened without comment while Jared talked about Chinese customs and philosophy, and where Lilac fit within both; Cass had listened, but she hadn't really heard. She was still trying to accept the fact that her father had married a Chinese prostitute.

"You can't see anything from there," Jared said, holding out his hand. "Come closer."

Ignoring his hand, Cass went to the window, stood in front of Jared and felt his breath stirring against the back of her neck. She wanted to turn and scream at him to stop demanding things of her that she wasn't ready to give, but she had learned long ago that giving way to her impulses didn't change anything important. Sometimes—just sometimes—patience and planning did.

Stiffly, Cass stood and looked through the narrow window that opened onto a different world. Three floors below lay the seething heart of Chinatown. The block of buildings that housed the foundry was directly across a narrow alley from a group of structures that looked separate from the outside but were actually connected to one another behind the façades by an interlocking series of passageways and little open courtyards.

"It's a maze," Cass said, interested despite herself as she looked down at the linked gridwork of the square block of buildings. "I'd never have guessed, looking at it from the street."

"Exactly," said Jared. "Most Chinese houses are like that; they present a blank face to the world, but inside, life goes on with all its richness and variety. That particular complex is the Soong Li Tong's temple, the center of Seattle's opium and illegal immigration rackets, and the most active whorehouse in the Pacific Northwest."

"Home of the perfect woman, the one for whom my father forsook all others—including his own daughter," Cass said. "Lovely."

The raw hurt beneath her words caught Jared off guard. He had expected Cass to have difficulty accepting Lilac, but he hadn't expected Cass to be so bitter toward a woman she had never met.

"Prostitution is an accepted profession in China," Jared said calmly. "The Chinese make distinctions among types of prostitutes, according to the women's degree of training and skill. The highest class, the concubines, are educated in mime, music, conversation, culture, chess, and philosophy, as well as in the more obvious sensual arts. Often, concubines become second or third wives to wealthy, powerful men."

"Or to foolish, lonely photographers?"

"Don't judge your father until you've met Lilac."

"I doubt that I'll be in any position to assess her level of 'skill.'"

"I assure you, it is of the highest."

The cool assurance in Jared's voice brought color to Cass's cheeks.

"The next level of the profession is that of courtesan,"

Jared continued tightly. "They entertain more men than a concubine, but often the men pay simply to spend a few hours in the presence of a beautiful, cultured, and gracious woman. If sex occurs between a courtesan and a client, it is usually after what can only be termed a courtship of indeterminate length."

"You're telling me that Chinese men pay these women and get only smiles in return?"

"Yes."

"Amazing."

Jared smiled thinly. "If a guarantee of sex in exchange for money is what a man wants, he goes to the next lower level of the prostitute class—the sing-song girls. These girls have minimal education, but are capable of at least strumming a stringed instrument, singing and entertaining a man before the undressing begins. The lowest class of prostitute is what Americans think of when the profession is mentioned. The Chinese call them saltwater whores. They are the untrained, unwashed, wretched girls who sell themselves to non-Chinese men in ports, lumber camps, gold diggings, and alleys."

Cass grimaced, but said nothing.

"Lilac was once Tan Feng's concubine and is presently one of the most renowned courtesans in America. Sojourners returning to China have made her name known throughout the Four Districts, despite the fact that her unbound feet place her outside the accepted pale of Chinese beauty."

"Her what?"

"In China, it's customary to—" Jared's voice broke off suddenly. "Right on time," he said, looking through the thin opening of the scarlet curtain and then at his watch.

Automatically, Cass reached for the curtain to improve her own view.

"No," Jared said quickly. "Don't touch it. Someone might see it from below."

Cass pressed herself closer to the wall and peered through the curtain. Three stories below, a young man in black pajamas sprinted down the alley from the street and burst into the warren through a side door.

"He's a lookout," Jared said. "Now you'll see what happens when you kick over a tong anthill."

As the watch in Jared's pocket began to chime the hour of ten, the shrill blasts of police whistles pierced the air. Pandemonium broke out within the compound. A squad of men erupted from a shack and scattered to defensive positions like well-drilled soldiers. One dashed off through passageways toward the building at the center of the compound, and two others sprinted toward the other street entrances. They arrived just in time to slam the gates in the faces of two dozen charging Seattle policemen.

The police milled about ineffectually in front of the gates, hammering with their nightsticks and yelling futile orders. Finally five men in suits pushed through the uniforms and went to work on the gates with axes. The sound of metal biting into wood carried clearly through the air.

"Right now," Jared murmured, "women are kicking clients out of bed, gamblers are jumping out back windows, and opium runners are hiding packages all through the walls of the compound."

Below, a thick, powerful giant of a man strode purposefully across an open courtyard at the head of a squad of men. His lime-green robe fluttered with the speed of his passage.

"Tan Feng," said Jared. "That means Lilac should arrive at any moment. Watch the side gate at the right."

Moments later, the small gate swung cautiously ajar, opening just enough for a small, black-haired woman in a flowing silk robe to slide through. She crossed the alley in a ripple of color and vanished into the foundry.

"You can only count on five minutes with her," Jared said. "After that, Lilac may have to run at any moment. It depends on the strength of Tan Feng's gates."

Cass heard the sound of footsteps running lightly up the stairs. Jared went quickly to the door, listened, and opened it. There was a flash of aqua silk, and then the door closed again. Jared bowed to the woman and received a deep bow in return. Then he gently tilted her face and kissed her on one cheek and the other before he turned to Cass.

"Lilac, I'm pleased to introduce you to Cassandra Thornton," Jared said formally. "Cassandra, this is Lilac Rain Thornton, your stepmother. You may call her Lilac, as your father did."

Without another word, Jared stepped from the room and pulled the door shut behind him.

Cass barely noticed. She watched Lilac with wide golden eyes, trying to make the present match with the past. The woman in the locket picture had been warm, radiant, beautiful in a way that brought a shiver of awe. In the flesh, Lilac was a shadow of radiance, pinched by captivity and dimmed by fear. Despite everything, Cass felt an unwilling compassion for the woman who had caused her so much misery as a child.

Lilac bowed and came to stand close to Cass. With fingers that trembled, she reached toward Cass's face.

"Your hair," Lilac murmured. "Will you free it?"

It was the last thing Cass had expected. Without a word, she removed her hat and a few long hairpins and shook out her hair. It fell in a heavy golden veil halfway to her hips, save for the softly curling tendrils that framed her face.

"May I—touch?" Lilac whispered.

Cass nodded, wondering what the other woman was thinking, knowing only that whatever her thoughts, pain trembled in Lilac's voice.

Lilac picked up a handful of the blond strands and ran them between her sensitive fingers, savoring the texture and color, whispering in Cantonese while tears made thin, shining trails down her face. Before the drops could fall onto her clothes, Lilac removed a tiny crystal bottle from her robes, unstoppered it, and caught the tears.

"Lilac—?" Cass said uncertainly, feeling unexpected sadness break over her in a wave, drowning her voice.

"Be happy, daughter," Lilac said in a low, soft tone. "I have touched my golden lion's mane one last time. The final tears have fallen. The bottle is full. I am complete."

49

Cass watched while Lilac stoppered the fragile bottle and placed it within a hidden pocket once more.

"Do you still use your father's camera?" Lilac asked. Her voice was cool and serene, as though the previous moments had never occurred, yet her face had a radiance that it had lacked when she first entered the room. Once again, she was a beautiful girl.

"Yes," Cass said, feeling more off balance than ever.

"Thaddeus would be pleased. He was so happy when he bought it. He said he finally had a camera that could equal my beauty. The first photo he took is the one in the locket."

Unconsciously, Cass's hand went to the handkerchief pocket of her skirt. Her fingertips found and curled around the worn velvet bag and the shape of the heavy locket within. She withdrew her hand and held it out to Lilac.

When she saw the familiar velvet bag resting on Cass's palm, Lilac closed her eyes and turned away in the manner of one refusing to touch that which is not hers.

"Take it," Cass said, trying and failing to conceal the turmoil of her conflicting emotions.

"No." The word was soft, final.

"But it's yours. You're Lilac Rain Thornton, the woman Papa couldn't live without. Take the damned thing," Cass said harshly, looking at the delicate woman who barely came up to Cass's own collarbone. "If Papa had wanted me to have it, he would have given it to me himself."

"A slave owns nothing, not even a last name. I am Lilac Rain. The locket is yours."

Slowly, Lilac turned back toward Cass and opened her eyes. Cass bit back a cry of unwanted empathy at the emptiness she saw yawning darkly beneath Lilac's elegant surface—another child crying about dreams and dust.

"Would your father have wanted you to grow up and sell yourself to any man who had a pinch of gold to catch between his fingers?" Lilac asked calmly.

"No man would want that for his daughter."

"Would you want that for your daughter, if you had one, or your true mother?"

"Of course not," Cass said, her voice tight.

"Ah! I have a daughter, Tea Rose. She is your father's daughter. Do you wish your sister to spend her life as a whore?"

8

Before Cass could even begin to adjust to the shock of discovering that she had a sister, Lilac continued speaking, her voice soft and relentless, like the rain of her namesake.

"Tea Rose is in great danger. I am a slave whom Tan Feng intends to sell. He has tried to keep that knowledge from me, but I know him too well. Tan Feng will ask you to come to the tong hall to photograph me. He knows that I first met your father while being photographed by a previous owner for future sale. Having you photograph me will be Tan Feng's way of taunting me with my own future as a fading courtesan—degradation, opium, death."

"Why?"

"Why does Tan taunt me? Because he has never broken me," Lilac said. Her closed lips curved in a smile that could only be described as cruel. "Selling me will be a great spiritual and sensual loss to Tan. He dreams of fighting the flowery battle with mother and daughter, of having me undress Tea Rose and bring her to his couch, of having me arrange my daughter's body for his sexual ease and pleasure." Lilac paused. "You are quite pale, Miss Thornton. Are you well?"

Cass closed her eyes and drew a deep breath. "I have always prided myself on being a modern kind of woman, one who is able to take the world on its own terms rather than having to be sheltered and cosseted. But the world you are describing to me, where mother and daughter are whores to the same man at the same time—" Cass's eyes opened, and they were bleak. "I can't help asking myself, is this the woman my father wanted above all others? Was it for you he overlooked me? Is a Chinese whore the reason I sometimes still awaken in the night feeling lost and alone?"

"I don't understand."

"I'm sure you don't," Cass retorted. "After all, you're the one Papa wanted. And your daughter. Tea Rose. My—sister. Is she why Papa scorned my offers to make a home for him, because the only home he wanted was with the family he couldn't find?"

"I am sorry if my existence has offended you," Lilac said, bowing deeply. "Tea Rose's life hangs in the balance. Will you listen to me despite the bitterness in your heart?"

Cass laced her fingers together to keep from reaching out to Lilac, whose pain was all too real, a living presence rather than a ghostly echo of the past.

"I'm sorry," Cass said wearily. "I shouldn't blame you for what Papa did or didn't do to me."

"But he is dead, and I am not," Lilac said, straightening. "Nor is your anger. I understand, Miss Thornton. I should have thought beyond my own needs to what yours might be. Yet, there is so little time. May I continue?"

Cass nodded.

Lilac bowed her head for a moment, forcing herself to be calm despite her fear. She desperately wanted to hurry, to let the words spill out, and then to be reassured that Tea Rose would be safe with her half sister; but Lilac had learned long ago that it was far better to know bitter truth than to believe beguiling lies.

"A merchant from Vancouver has already offered eight thousand dollars for me," Lilac said quietly. "Tan Feng wishes more. He will send my portrait up and down the Mountain of Gold, and to the Four Districts as well."

"Eight thousand dollars? But that's a huge amount. With that much money, the merchant could buy the biggest building in Vancouver and have enough left over to buy a fancy carriage and the horses to pull it!"

"Tan Feng believes he can get more. The portraits you will take of me will be the first move in his auction. He is very clever. He knows well the fever that overtakes men when they bid against each other, whether it be in your American poker games or mah-jongg or for the untouched vagina of a beautiful girl."

In the silence, the sound of the hammers from the forge rang out with aching clarity.

"I can't believe I'm hearing this," Cass said finally. "This is America, not China."

"You are wrong," Lilac said in a soft voice. "Look around you. You are the stranger here, not I. This is China. It is you who must learn and I who must teach. Between the teaching and the learning dangles your sister's life. Will you listen?"

"Yes, but I can't promise I'll believe, much less understand. What you are telling me is—impossible."

"Not in China," Lilac said succinctly. "In China, it is as rare for a woman to be free as it is for a white woman to be a slave in America; but my mother was a Samsui, a free woman owned by neither father nor brother, husband nor son nor clan. Samsui believe that women have equal importance with men. Samsui believe in many other things as well—in themselves, in life, in the gods. They even believe in men, but not as demigods before whom women must spend a life of prostration and supplication. Samsui don't believe that women should be bought, sold, or traded without regard to their own wishes. That is why Samsui shun marriage."

Cass said nothing, simply listened and watched.

Lilac almost smiled at the lack of impact her words had on Cass. "You don't understand how unthinkable the Samsui creed is among the Chinese, do you?" asked Lilac.

"As though a milk cow demanded the right to vote?" Cass said, remembering what Jared had told her.

The last thing Cass expected was the ripple of musical laughter that came from Lilac's lips. The fan she pulled from her sleeve to hide her smile gleamed in tones of gold that were like graceful echoes of her laughter.

"Ah," Lilac murmured, slipping her fan back into her

sleeve, "perhaps there is hope, after all. Yes, it is as though a milk cow demanded the right to control her own udder. That is why Samsui spurn marriage. It is our only way of escaping Chinese law, which is a cage imprisoning a woman until despair overtakes her and death is sweet freedom crooning to her. It takes a very strong woman to defy family and culture. My mother was such a woman. All Samsui women were strong. They had to be. They worked for their food as men among men. But they were not, of course, men."

For a moment, Lilac's mask dropped, revealing the bitterness and melancholy beneath.

"The Samsui women I lived among weren't strong enough to stay free," Lilac said. "Slave traders came and took me from my mother because there were no brothers to defend us, no husbands, no fathers, no uncles, nothing but women so desperate to be free that they died rather than be taken. My mother fought as would a man, and died the same way. I fought, too, but wasn't so lucky as she. I survived.

"The men's leader preferred green fruit to ripe. I was nine years old. Again, I was unlucky. I survived rape, not once but many, many times."

Cass made an odd sound and closed her eyes, because she could no longer bear watching Lilac and knowing that she had lived in a kind of hell that Cass could barely imagine. Shame flushed her body—whatever hurt she had suffered from her father's neglect, it had been nothing to what Lilac had endured.

"My God, Lilac," Cass said huskily. "How could anyone survive that?"

"I was a child. I survived capture because death, to me, was unthinkable. My first master saw me writing poetry in the ashes. He realized that I was literate and would be more valuable as a highly trained concubine than as a common whore. Life then became easy for me, much as it has been for Tea Rose. My master made few demands on my body, so I healed with no outward scars. I grew beautiful and very cunning, a combination that caused my master unrest. He sent me to the Golden Mountain, where his cousin was sojourning. I was fifteen."

She paused and judged the state of Cass's mind by the color returning beneath her translucent skin. The beginning of new hope uncurled within Lilac as she saw the other woman's resilience. In some ways, Cass had suffered as rude an awakening as Lilac had suffered on the day she was stolen from her mother. The difference was one of degree rather than kind. Both women had been forced by unpredictable circumstances to confront a reality for which they were ill-prepared.

"Tan Feng saw me in Eureka. He wanted to buy me. My new master refused again and again, for Tan was a man without clan or family, a tong man, a Manchu, and my master was Cantonese. Tan continued to purchase me by the hour or the evening until my master turned his back.

"Then Tan cut my master's throat. His body was used to bait fishermen's hooks, and his power passed to Tan Feng. I became Tan Feng's. I was his when I met your father."

Lilac measured Cass with black eyes that missed nothing. She saw the question even before Cass knew that it existed within her mind.

"What don't you understand?" Lilac asked.

"You were Tan Feng's, yet he allowed my father to—"

"I had no frail maidenhead to protect. What purpose would it have served for Tan to keep me solely for his own use?"

"But he wanted you badly enough to kill for you!"

"He wanted power over me. He had that. While his penis was slack, he had no objection if another man used me. And at one time, he hoped to gain power in white society through your father's hunger for me."

"But my father had no power."

"He was white. Tan Feng is not. In America, that is power."

There was silence before Cass half-asked the question she had promised herself she wouldn't. "You loved my father—"

55

"Love." Lilac sighed. "I bore his child, knowing I should not. I hid from him when I could no longer bear Tan's cruel games."

"What?"

"Tan offered to sell me to your father for twenty thousand dollars. I was more beautiful then."

"Twenty thousand dollars," Cass said faintly. "My God. That's more than my father could have earned in two lifetimes."

"Tan Feng knew that. He enjoyed teasing your father, dangling me as a choice piece of bait and then pulling me away at the last instant. Thad did not understand the game. There was so much that he didn't understand—and so much that he did."

Lilac bowed her head for an instant, then raised it proudly and continued. "I knew your father was planning to steal me, so I refused to look at him, refused to speak to him, spurned him, drove him away with a whore's cruel humor."

"Why?" whispered Cass, appalled.

"Tan would have used your father's love to destroy me. If Tan had thought that I cared for Thad even a little, your father would have been sliced into thin strips and fed to the sea. Tan let other men purchase me because he believed that I hated all men. With Thad, Tan watched me like a snake watching a duckling—but a slave is always a better actress than her master knows."

This time, Lilac's smile was open and cruel and gleaming, sending delicate fingernails of ice down Cass's spine.

"By the time Chinese were driven from Eureka by the whites," Lilac said, "I had driven Thad away. Chinatown was burned to the ground. It was as though Chinese had never lived there." She paused, then added softly. "Nothing remained of the past but ashes. I had been successful. I had killed the beautiful, cruel dream myself, and in my triumph, I wept tears of blood where no man could see."

"You did love him," Cass said.

"I destroyed his soul. Is that love?"

Lilac looked at Cass's golden hair shining in the room's filtered light. With an act of will so great that it left Lilac weak, she refrained from touching her memories once more. But it did no good. In small, unbearably painful ways, Cass was her father incarnate, watching Lilac with clear eyes, speaking to her through lips that held the same curves Lilac had seen in a thousand bittersweet dreams.

"There is little more to the story," Lilac continued in a papery voice. "To escape the riots, Tan Feng took Tea Rose and me to Portland. When there were riots there against the Chinese, we went to Canada. Finally, we left Vancouver and came to Seattle. I never saw your father again."

For a few moments, Cass couldn't speak. At last, she understood what had driven her father to obsessively record the meeting of Chinese and Americans on the Mountain of Gold, America's last frontier, the Pacific Rim, all the same place, yet all very different to each culture; and through the social tumult, her father had bobbed, a tree uprooted by a distant storm, turning and tossing on troubled waters in a vain search for lost love.

Memories rushed over Cass in a seething, battering wave—all the thousands of photos her father had taken over the years in every Chinatown in the West, a frantic odyssey that had ended only at his death. What had seemed to be a lifelong obsession with the exotic had also been her father's relentless search for his woman and his child.

"My father—" Cass's voice broke. She waited a few seconds before she tried to speak again. "He tried to find you. He searched in every Chinatown from Mexico to Canada. He never gave up."

"A white man by himself can do nothing in Chinatown," Lilac said calmly. "We Chinese are too good at keeping our secrets."

"He died calling your name," Cass said, trying to keep the accusation out of her voice.

"Yes," Lilac whispered. "It will be the same for me."

For an instant, Lilac was again the woman in the locket,

touching the hand of her lover, radiant with each shared breath, each memory of warmth. Cass stared, hardly able to believe the transformation. And then she blinked and stared again, for the other Lilac was back, Tan Feng's cruel, merciless slave.

"It was well that Thad never saw me again. Love is a slave's enemy," Lilac said in a voice like incense, both dry and rich with dark, elusive things. "Hatred makes slaves strong. Yet, I want more for Tea Rose than the harsh comforts of hatred. Thad would have wanted that, too. Wouldn't he?"

"Of course he—"

"Then you must steal Tea Rose," Lilac interrupted calmly. "It would have been your father's wish."

Cass felt her heart hesitate, then beat with redoubled speed. "Now? Today?"

"No," said Lilac. "Next week, during the Festival of the Good Lady. That is the one night when the guard on slave girls, concubines, and wives is relaxed. That night, you will become Tea Rose's mother."

"My God," breathed Cass. "You can't just give her away like a kitten! You know nothing about me!"

"Jared says that you are quick, impulsive, wary, generous, and proud. I have seen nothing that contradicts his conclusions. In addition, I have seen that you are resilient and determined. That is good. Guiding Tea Rose in the culture of her father won't be an easy task." Lilac paused before continuing in her soft, unflinching voice. "You must understand, for all her training and precocious wit, Tea Rose refuses to believe that Tan intends for her to service other men. She believes that Tan will make her his wife. That simply is not and never will be true."

Lilac's black glance bored into Cass.

"That is why Tea Rose must not know what is happening until it is too late," Lilac said distinctly. "You must steal her just as Lo Mi—the Old Woman Donaldina Cameron—steals China girls in San Francisco."

"But surely the police would help you?"

"Now that it is illegal for Chinese to come to the Golden Mountain," Lilac continued, "the tongs are becoming more and more powerful. Many of the men who are smuggled in have no other source of protection, no other means through which to live as Men of Han in an alien land. Only the tong can give to them the structure and safety of a family or clan.

"That makes Tan Feng very powerful, even in the white world, because only he can supply the cheap labor that is endlessly in demand. There is no legal way to meet that need now that your government has forbidden Chinese laborers to come to the Golden Mountain. Your laws have made the tongs vital."

Lilac paused to probe Cass with a black glance. She saw only strain and the effort Cass was making to understand.

"Even when America allowed all Chinese to come, your police didn't interfere with the running of Chinatowns," Lilac continued. "We lived by our own ancient customs. We were sojourners with no thought of changing our old ways for a new land."

Cass nodded.

"Now, when Chinese men must be smuggled in, when they live by the hundreds hidden within tong halls, the police are concerned even less by what happens inside Chinatown. They do not want to know, for if they knew, they might be forced to chop down the tree that bears needed fruit—Chinese labor." Lilac looked directly at Cass and said coolly, "That's why you must abandon your foolish hope of going to the police and telling them about Tea Rose's slavery and my own. They do not want to know. They will refuse to listen, but others will hear, and they will whisper, and Tan Feng will be told, and Tea Rose and I will vanish as though we had never been born."

"But—"

"Listen, daughter," Lilac interrupted in a pleasant, comfortless voice. "I am Chinese. I am beyond the reach of your laws. Tea Rose is the bastard daughter of a Chinese whore, also beyond the reach of your laws. For all the good your police can do, Tea Rose and I might as well be in China. Can you accept that?"

"I'm trying to," Cass said finally. "But it seems impossible that there are slaves in America and no one cares!"

"Once," Lilac said, her voice so soft that Cass had to lean forward to hear the words, "I was a brave young optimist such as you. Optimism is not enough, Miss Thornton. Nor is beauty. Only cunning matters, and the strength of will to kill or to die if that is what must be done."

For an instant, Cass saw in Lilac's eyes the soul-deep fury that Tan Feng sensed but could not prove. Beneath Lilac's perfect calm raged a wild animal in whom the memory of freedom could not be quenched. It was the fury of a she-wolf that had been caught in a trap and was gnawing off her own leg in a final, savage bid for freedom.

"When you come to photograph me for Tan Feng," Lilac continued, "give me your decision. Whatever you decide, say nothing in front of Tea Rose."

There was a rapid, urgent knocking on the door. Lilac crossed the room quickly. As she reached for the door, she turned and looked over her shoulder at Cass.

"If you refuse to take Tea Rose," Lilac said softly, "I will cut her throat and then my own."

9

"My name is John Wong," the Chinese man said to Cass. "Mr. Jared Duran sent me for you and your equipment."

"Come in, Mr. Wong," Cass said, stepping aside. "I need to know what's expected of me tonight. Otherwise, I won't know what equipment I'll need to carry out a convincing charade."

"Excuse me, Miss Thornton, but there will be no charade. You will actually take photographs. We will be operating among people to whom conspiracy is a matter of both necessity and preference. They must not suspect you are anything more or less than you seem. Mr. Duran asked me to stress that point with you."

"I have no control over whatever dangers might exist," Cass replied in a clipped voice. "All I can control is myself and my equipment. Unless you wish me to pack up my entire studio and transport it to the Blossom Moon, I'll need more information. What are the conditions there? Light walls, dark walls? Large rooms, small rooms? How much light and of what kind will I have to work with? Who are my subjects to be? Are these to be formal portraits or candid settings? All of these things make a great deal of difference to me as a photographer."

"Of course," said John. "The rooms are illuminated by kerosene lamps, not electric lights," he said. "Chinese houses are darker than your homes in their decorations. Red, the color of happiness and good fortune, is much used. White, the color of death and mourning, isn't favored."

"I see," Cass murmured, mentally adding more flash powder to the list of equipment to be taken. "Go on."

"You are to take individual portraits of Lilac and Tea Rose, and perhaps even of Tan Feng himself, if he wishes." John paused. "That would be quite amusing for a Manchu such as Tan. They're superstitious barbarians at heart, despite their long occupation of the Celestial Empire."

"I take it that you aren't Manchu?" Cass asked dryly.

John bowed. "I'm from the south of China, as are all true Chinese."

"How long have the Manchus, er, 'occupied' China?"

"More than three centuries."

Cass blinked. "That's considerably longer than we've had a nation called America."

"China's civilization is more than four thousand years old. When the men of Carthage were flogging elephants through mountain passes, the Chinese had been enjoying the fruits of a civilization for nearly two thousand years."

"So the Manchus are carpetbaggers and Johnny-come-latelys, is that it?"

John laughed softly and bowed to her. "You are very quick, Miss Thornton, and very correct."

The bow was typically Chinese, yet Cass could see that John was like no other Chinese she had met. He was taller than most, wore his hair in Western style, and wore Western clothes, not the traditional padded silk or cotton jacket and soft cloth shoes of the Chinese. Were it not for his epicanthic fold and flattened profile, he could have walked unremarked among Seattle's Caucasians.

But the difference between John and the other Chinese was deeper than clothes or haircut or lack of accent. Cass realized that he considered himself a citizen of Seattle rather than a sojourner to the Mountain of Gold. Most Chinese males would never have met Cass's gaze directly, or any white person's; with white people, the Chinese were obsequious to a fault. John was polite, but he carried himself with an almost military pride. His face was strong and unlined. Nothing about him gave a hint of his age or his background.

Looking at him, Cass remembered Jared's words about the veil behind which Chinatown hid. In the privacy of their own homes, did all Chinese look and walk and speak like John Wong?

Even Cass's impulsive nature flinched at asking such a bald question of a stranger. Instead, she showed John into her studio while she collected her equipment and packed it into a trunk. By the time she had finished, the trunk was nearly full. Carefully she laid the tripod-mounted camera across the trunk lid.

"I'm ready, Mr. Wong. If you would be so kind as to grab the other handle of this trunk?"

John took both handles and lifted the trunk with an ease that startled Cass. Seeing her expression, John smiled and said, "We did, after all, hammer your steel roads through the tallest mountains in America."

Smiling, Cass bowed in response, giving just enough emphasis to the Chinese gesture that John laughed.

"I see why Jared returned from meeting you looking as though he had been panning for gold—and found it," John said as he loaded the trunk and then handed Cass aboard the four-wheeled carriage.

Taking the reins, John drove the horses at a smart pace. As they turned onto Second Avenue and headed toward Chinatown, twilight was draining into night over the sawtoothed Olympic Mountains that rose behind Bainbridge Island. The evening traffic was light, which gave the pair of well-groomed black horses a chance to display their flashy form. Cass watched the evening sky thoughtfully.

"Mr. Wong," she said, "do you know a Chinese woman called Lilac?"

"Every Chinese knows her. She's one of the most powerful and important people in Chinatown."

"But isn't she a slave?"

"Yes."

"That doesn't make sense."

"In your world, no," John agreed. "In the Chinese culture, it is a fact of life that needs no explanation. Chinese slave girls have no freedom in the sense in which you understand the word, but if they are very beautiful and very, very clever, they can wield power by manipulating their owners."

"Lilac is beautiful. She's quite smart, as well. Yet, I had no feeling that she controlled her owner."

"He didn't kill her when she had another man's child," John said simply. "Nor did he kill the child. I suppose you wish that he had."

"I'm not so mean a person that I would wish my own sister dead, no matter how much discovering her existence shocked me."

"I'm sorry," John said quickly. "I didn't mean to insult you. I'm sure the situation is very—difficult."

Cass nodded and then gave John a rueful smile. "I'm sorry, too. I've been biting off heads ever since I met Lilac. It's not your fault. Please, tell me more about Lilac and Tan

Feng. If I'm going to help my sister, I have to understand her world."

"In many ways, Lilac lives as a queen who is answerable only to her king, Tan Feng. It works well for Tan Feng, too. Owning Lilac brings him respect, admiration, and power among the Chinese. We call it 'face.' Owning Lilac brings Tan Feng much face."

"Because it cost a lot of money to buy her?" Cass asked, remembering the fortune Lilac had mentioned as her sale price.

"That's not the greatest part of it," John said. "In many ways, owning a slave such as Lilac is like cuddling a vixen against your belly—if you aren't strong and careful, you will be eaten alive. Lilac is the wisest and most beautiful vixen ever to stalk a man's soul. She has stalked Tan Feng for twenty years. He is still alive, still powerful, and with every passing day his face increases."

"How did Mr. Duran become involved with Lilac?"

John gave Cass a sideways look. As she heard the echo of her question, she flushed with a combination of embarrassment and irritation.

"Aside from the obvious reason," she added in a clipped tone.

"Among Chinese," John said, "Jared has a reputation for fairness and understanding. When my people have difficulty with the white world, he intervenes." John flicked the reins lightly against the shining black rumps of the horses. They responded with a slightly increased pace. "He has hired many men who would have starved otherwise, either here or in China."

"He is amply repaid for that," Cass pointed out. "Chinese work twice as hard for half the wage of Irishmen."

"Yes," John said softly, "Jared receives full value for his money. So do other men who hire Celestials. But Jared Duran is one of the very few businessmen in Seattle who insists that a foreman who strikes a Chinese be fired. He is the only businessman who has learned our culture. When white labor unions blamed us for taking bread out of Irishmen's mouths, whipping up hatreds throughout the West, Jared supported us. Nearly ten years ago, at risk to his own life and livelihood, he and a few others stood up to the rioters. Every Chinese in the city was expelled, but Jared Duran's actions prevented the kind of bloodbath that happened elsewhere."

John flicked the reins once more. "A few years later, after the heart of Seattle burned, and Celestials were needed to rebuild the city, Jared was ready. He encouraged us with work, with loans, and by means of some genteel arm-twisting among the powerful citizens. His company supplied many workers for Mr. Hill and his Great Northern Railroad. Duran Shipping Company also constructed three of the new buildings on the waterfront after the fire, all with Chinese labor. Jared owns two steamships and several schooners, plus other business interests."

"All that at such a young age? He must have inherited a great deal of wealth."

"He inherited nothing but the ruins of the Civil War," John said. "Jared and his brother, King, were prospectors. Before either of them was twenty, they made a good strike at Olivine Creek in British Columbia. That's where I met them. I've been with Jared ever since. I've watched him turn a handful of gold into a fortune. Despite his Southern upbringing, Jared is very much a Yankee, hardheaded and ambitious, honest, and filled with a vision of the future world he intends to build."

"What about King?"

"He spent his share of the first strike, then went out and found others. He's in Seattle right now, spending the last one."

Cass smiled. "He sounds more adventurous than his older brother."

"Younger brother," John corrected Cass. "Jared is only thirty-two, nearly four years younger than King. Yet, Jared is by far the more reliable of the two. King is—" John shrugged. "King is King. He lives only in the moment, like a fire burning, hot and unthinking."

"You don't like him?" Cass asked, not realizing until too late how personal the question was. "I'm sorry. It's none of my business."

"I admire King," John said, shrugging. "I would like to be that free, but I'm not."

"Because you're Chinese?"

"No," he said, smiling, "because I'm not King. In fact, in one fundamental way, King is more Chinese than I am. King has no desire to change the world. He accepts it for what it is, cruel and beautiful, depraved and holy, dream and nightmare. His greatest desire is to experience all that *is*. Like a follower of the Tao, he is capable of drawing great spiritual insight from something as outwardly trivial as the flight of a moth."

"A poet," Cass said.

John hesitated, then shrugged. "Perhaps."

Though Cass waited, John said nothing else. Cass found herself more intrigued than ever at the idea of meeting Kingston Duran.

Bathed by the gentle glow of street lights, the black carriage rolled from the business district into the mélange of architectural styles that made up Seattle's International District. The buildings were of common brick and stone and wood, but the roof lines and doorways were distinctively angled. Oriental masons and carpenters preferred façades that were less intricate than those in the rest of Seattle. But if the exteriors were plain, the colors were luxuriant. Vivid reds and flashing golds glowed in the lamplight, enriching the night, enhancing the exotic fragrances of sesame oil and garlic, burning joss sticks, and sweet hints of opium smoke.

As John turned off Second onto King Street, he slowed the horses to a walk to avoid running afoul of the teeming foot traffic that spilled off the sidewalks and into the brick-cobbled streets. Porches and balconies that seemed more suited for tropical climates than for the Pacific Northwest appeared. The July evening was cool, but residents sat talking and watching the street.

Everywhere the illumination of street lamps was augmented by round, lacquered lanterns that floated like hot-air balloons beneath the overhanging canopies and verandas. Lamps made of fish skin stretched over a wooden frame and hung with scarlet silk tassels glowed through high windows. The smells of fish and meat and produce and population mingled with the other odors of the streets. The mixture was more pungent than pleasant, as rich and vital as the life hidden behind shuttered windows.

John turned the carriage down a dark, crowded alley. Immediately, Cass sensed a change in her surroundings that had more to do with John's sudden tension than with the alley itself.

"This is called the Street of the Gamblers," John said very quietly, as he let the horses pick their way down the alley. "You aren't entirely welcome here. No stranger is. But don't worry. There's no danger to us right now. For the moment, we're under the protection of a very powerful man."

"Jared Duran."

"No. Tan Feng, the most powerful man in Chinatown." John's smile was more a warning than a comfort as he added softly, "No one has ever made a fool of Tan Feng and survived to tell of it, yet that's what Lilac hopes to do with your help." Black, enigmatic eyes turned toward Cass, reflecting lamplight and nothing more. "Are you sure you know what you are doing, Miss Thornton?"

"The most fascinating part of life is its uncertainty," Cass said dryly.

"Only to an American. Chinese see it differently. One of our oldest curses is *'May you live in interesting times.'* If you step down from this carriage, Miss Thornton, you will step into very interesting times indeed."

Without a word, Cass gathered her skirts and climbed out of the carriage.

10

The Street of the Gamblers was an intensely masculine world. Cass could not see a single female on the street, not one child, just men of all ages and a single costume—loose black pants and dark blue jacket, black silk skullcap, black pigtail descending the spine, black cloth shoes, black eyes watching her.

As Cass stood next to the carriage in her English tailor-made with its burgundy three-quarter jacket and long, simple skirt of dark gold wool, she felt as conspicuous as a naked strumpet at a church social. Cass had deliberately taken some of the fashionable ballooning width from her upper sleeves, had chosen an austere white blouse with a dark, man-styled tie, and had her hair plainly coiffed beneath a modest straight-brimmed hat; but somehow she still felt outrageously feminine and out of place. Even her father's nugget watch chain, which she wore as a triple bracelet, seemed to flash and glitter as though it were the gaudiest of decorations.

Cass pulled her dark wool collar more closely around her neck and told herself not to be ridiculous, that she wasn't the last—or first—woman on earth. Yet everywhere she looked, a single relentless message beat at her in the charged silence: she was different in profound ways that had nothing to do with race or culture. She was *Woman* in a world inhabited by and arranged for *Man*. She was an alien in an alien land, a less-than-human thing with neither importance nor validity.

She was *Not-Man*.

A flash of color materialized in the darkness. The crowd of men parted, and a female appeared. She was very small, dressed in a pale silk tunic and straight-legged, loose pants. She walked with a mincing, tottering, yet oddly graceful motion. Each step advanced her no more than a few inches. As she passed under a flickering street light, the spirals and interlocking curves embroidered on her apricot silk tunic flashed in jewel tones.

The woman passed a few feet in front of Cass, paying her no more attention than if she had been a post. A silent, impassive man dressed in dark silk and carrying a short sword followed the tiny woman. He had more the manner of a bodyguard than that of a man watching a prisoner.

"Is she a slave?" Cass asked in a low voice.

"Yes, but that man is her guardian, not her jailer. She needs no jailer."

"Doesn't she want to escape?"

"Jasmine isn't that foolish," John said. "Where would she go if she ran away? Everyone in Chinatown knows she belongs to Wong Ah Wing, one of Tan Feng's most powerful lieutenants. No one would offer Jasmine shelter for fear of Tan Feng's wrath."

"But once she got beyond Chinatown's boundaries—" Cass began.

"Where would she go?" John asked, interrupting. "Jasmine speaks no English, she knows no one in round-eye society. She would be alone in the world, without even the artificial family of the House of Joy to protect her." John looked down at Cass and added calmly, "Jasmine has an easier life than most Chinese women. She commands a very high price as the second most beautiful courtesan in Seattle."

"Is she? I couldn't see her face."

John shook his head. "Jasmine isn't sought for her face, but for her tiny lily feet. They are feminine perfection. They fit in the palm of a man's hand."

Cass couldn't hide her shock.

"Lily feet are a thing of enormous beauty," John continued, his voice soft. "In China before the Manchus, a woman could not find a proper husband if she had big feet. Between the ages of five and ten, a girl's big toe was bound to her heel until the arch shattered, ensuring that the tiny foot grew no bigger. Despite Manchu edict, it is still the same today among all true Chinese."

"That is—" Cass's voice dwindled in horror as John's calm description of the foot-binding ritual sank into her mind.

"Barbaric?" he offered calmly.

"Even when slaves were kept in America, they weren't maimed. My God—how can the women walk at all?"

"The heel bone is intact and able to bear weight," John said, leaning forward for a final glimpse of Jasmine before the shadows of the alley engulfed her swaying shape. "The difficulty of balance is what gives their walk such incredible elegance."

"It must be—very painful."

"Foot-bound women can't work much nor walk far," John agreed, "but the exquisite lily is worth the cost of maintaining a helpless female." He looked regretfully once more at the shadows that had engulfed Jasmine, then turned his full attention to Cass. "This way, Miss Thornton."

John gestured toward a door glistening with thick red enamel paint and framed in very dark timbers. As though they had been watching from concealment, two men appeared in the doorway. John spoke to them in sharply rising and falling tones that were incomprehensible to Cass as either language or music. One of the men helped John unload the camera and trunk from the carriage, then acted as guide. The other man led the horses off down the alley.

Cass followed John beneath an ornately carved teakwood doorway arch and into the heart of Chinatown. The interior of the plain-faced building was rich and ornate, as intricate as carved boxes nested one within another. The walls of the narrow hallways were hung with embroidered silk tapestries in purples, reds, yellows, and occasional lustrous whites. The designs of the elegant, free-standing dragon statues were echoed in the tapestries and lacquered paintings on the walls. Silent, infused with incense, the passages took odd turns without warning, crossing and recrossing with nothing to distinguish or illuminate them but the golden glow of fish-skin lamps. Somewhere in the background came the exotic notes and unpredictable cadences of alien music—a stringed instrument plucked rather than bowed, a song sung in a voice higher and more nasal than Cass's ear could appreciate.

Finally, their guide pushed open a carved door and ushered Cass and John into a banquet room. A dozen men or more were gathered at one end where a cadre of waiters and servants set steaming dishes on a large table that was already covered with bowls and platters of food. Charcoal burners smoked hotly on the long table, and from their grates rose the scents of food rich and spicy enough to overwhelm the odor of incense.

Cass quickly picked Jared Duran out of the group of men. He was dressed in a well-cut dark blue suit with a lighter blue waistcoat, a white shirt, and a red tie—and he seemed to be instructing a major-domo and two waiters. The Chinese servants listened intently, nodding vigorously to show their concentration and answering in the utterly alien, sliding tones and sudden dissonances of Cantonese. The fact that Jared spoke the language astounded her; as much as her father had been fascinated by the Celestials, he had never learned more than the simplest words—yes and no, thank you and please.

There was a scattering of other white men in the group. Like Jared, they were young and well-dressed. The rest of the crowd was Chinese, all middle-aged or older. They were dressed in sumptuous, colorful silk robes and tunics with horse-hoof sleeves that hung down over the entire hand.

A flash of movement caught Cass's eye as a side door opened and a stranger entered. Immediately, the crowd shifted to face the newcomer. He was tall, Caucasian, and moved with the innate physical ease of a wild animal. His hair and neatly clipped beard were a rich mahogany. His face had been burned dark by sun and wind.

Suddenly he laughed, and Cass remembered John's description: *a fire burning.*

Though Cass had neither met nor seen the man before, she knew that he was Kingston Duran. He seemed to be listening attentively to the Chinese man who came up to greet him, but his eyes were fixed on Cass. Their dark, luminous green color fascinated her. She couldn't look away, despite the fact that she knew she was staring.

King wore a dark suit of forest green plaid wool that had been cut for his powerful, thin-waisted, athletic build. The crisp whiteness of his shirt made his tan appear even darker. A rich black cape was thrown carelessly across his wide shoulders. He carried a low-crowned black hat and an ivory-headed walking stick. His unusually heavy watch chain was hung with big gold nuggets. On another man the chain would have looked gaudy. On King, the gold looked in proper scale.

"Ah, the photographer arrives at last," King said loudly to the men standing close by. "Excuse me, gentlemen. I've been looking forward to this."

King's voice was deep and almost boisterous. For a moment, Cass thought that he must be more than a bit drunk. Yet his posture was as steady as his eyes watching her.

King crossed the room to Cass, aware that every man in the room was watching her. He didn't blame them. The tall American woman with her coiled blond hair, slender hands, and intriguing golden eyes was worth a good, hard look. King usually preferred the rustling silks and lavish laces of bygone fashion, but he had to admit that Cass's fashionably mannish tie, shirt, and jacket somehow accentuated rather than disguised the swell of her hips and breasts.

"I'll take the liberty of introducing myself," King said as his surprisingly slender hand enveloped one of Cass's, "because I'm sure that Jared will somehow forget to do so.

"I'm Kingston Duran, but I would take it as an honor if you would call me King."

His voice was deep, intimate—suggesting that they were

alone rather than in the center of a crowd. Cass's lips quirked in a slow smile.

"But I hardly know you, Mr. Duran."

"I'm very easy to know. Besides, only my little brother is 'Mr. Duran.' If you don't believe me, say 'Mr. Duran' real loud and see who turns around. Just call me King, and no one will be confused."

Smiling, shaking her head, Cass gave in to King's easy charm. If she had thought his approach practiced or artificial, she would have put him off with a single cool glance; but King's charm admitted no artifice. It simply curled up against her like a kitten.

"All right, King," Cass murmured.

"See, that wasn't hard, was it?" he said, bending just a bit closer to her as he smiled. "You know, you're even prettier than Jared said."

Cass gave King a sideways glance. "I doubt that quite heartily, Mr.—er, King. My looks might have interested your brother, but that didn't stop him from throwing me to the wolves. Or she-wolf, in this case."

Dark mahogany eyebrows rose in silent surprise. Then King laughed softly, as though Cass had given him an unexpected present. "Tangled with Lilac, did you? Well, don't feel bad. She and Jay are a good match—both of them have the kind of raw determination that can burn through steel. People like you and me are made of much softer stuff."

King gently squeezed the hand he still held beneath his own. The warm pressure startled Cass, reminding her that she had been standing with her hand engulfed by a stranger's. She started to withdraw her fingers, only to have King's hand tighten.

"Not just yet, Cassie," King murmured. "I must have a reason to stand close to you for just a moment longer. Did you notice the big Chinaman in the red jacket?"

"Yes."

"That's Tan Feng. You saw him this morning."

"Yes."

"Softly, Miss Thornton. Every one of these hard-eyed

little Celestials has assured me he speaks no English, but they're all unprincipled liars, so watch that lovely mouth of yours very carefully."

Color stained Cass's cheeks. "You're a forward sort, aren't you?"

King's smile was as alluring as his laughter. "When my reward is watching roses bloom in your cheeks, yes." He bent a few inches closer to Cass and murmured, "I've spent the last two hours trying to drown their suspicions in rice wine, but they're showing no signs of wear. Unfortunately, I am, so we're going to have to try another ploy."

Then King laughed aloud, as though he had just shared a private joke with Cass. She smiled rather uncertainly, unsure what part of King's manner was performance and what was real. With a feeling of dismay, she realized that she would have preferred to believe that King stood close and held her hand for reasons other than conspiracy.

"Thank you, brother," Jared said coolly as he appeared at Cass's elbow. "I'll take it from here. Come, Miss Thornton. I'll show you where to set up your camera. King, entertain our friends, will you?"

King withdrew as though his next move had been choreographed in advance. Cass turned to speak to Jared, but the pale-ice color of his eyes made her forget the words in her mind.

"You're as tall as King," Cass said, surprised by both the observation and by the fact that she had spoken it aloud.

"An inch taller, actually," Jared said.

"But he—"

Jared's expression suggested that he didn't know whether to curse or laugh. He was accustomed to King's impact on people. Jared had even learned to use it to his own advantage on occasion, although never when a woman was involved.

"Gentlemen," King called out as he turned away from Cass and his brother, "which one of you would care to place a small wager as to whether the toothpicks in that bowl are odd or even in number?"

The Chinese translator conveyed the challenge, and there was a rising babble of acceptance. In the center of silks and incense, King swept the rest of the room toward the long table.

Casually, Jared picked up the equipment trunk and balanced it on his shoulder. With his free hand, he held the tripod-mounted camera. Cass stared for a moment, somehow surprised by Jared's strength, knowing that if King had picked up her equipment, she wouldn't have been surprised at all.

"Quickly, Miss Thornton. We haven't much time. Tan Feng is unpredictable."

"I haven't decided whether stealing Tea—"

"Quiet." Jared looked at Cass for a long moment before he said in a low, urgent voice, "You are here to take photographs, nothing else. You must remember that. Follow Lilac's or my lead in everything, and no one will be hurt."

Thin-lipped and silent, Cass followed Jared to a smaller room that was hung with silk banners upon which ideographs were drawn in black. Two of the walls were formed by tall folding screens of carved teak. The room contained a single dark wooden armchair and a smooth dark wooden table. The furniture had a muscular elegance of design that was essentially masculine. The rug on the floor was rich, vivid, done in alien patterns that were both restrained and vital. The bronze incense burner that was set on the low table was inlaid with designs in silver and gold. A simple glazed pot held narcissus that breathed delicate perfume into the air.

"This room belongs to Tan Feng," Jared said quietly. "It's the only one in the entire tong hall that's not likely to have spyholes and eavesdropping posts."

"How can you think of conspiracies in a room as beautiful as this?" Cass muttered as she knelt beside the trunk Jared had set down.

"With Tan Feng, there's no other choice," Jared said. "In a few minutes, I'm going to bring his lordship in here. I want you to flatter the very hell out of him. Take all the time you need. He's got an ego as big as King's. Use it against him. It may be the only weapon we have."

"I've dealt with difficult subjects before, Mr. Duran," Cass said coolly. "Is he to be my only, er, portrait tonight?"

"While we eat, Lilac and Tea Rose will come to you."

He saw the uncertainty in Cass's eyes and wished he could comfort her. But it was the wrong time and place. All he could do was warn her once more.

"Cassandra—Miss Thornton," Jared said softly, "please remember that the Celestials are very different from us in their approach to relationships between men and women. You simply won't get the respect here that you're accustomed to and deserve. I'm sorry. If there were any other way to accomplish what must be done, I would never have shattered the normal patterns of your life."

"I'm not made of fine porcelain, Mr. Duran. I don't shatter easily."

"I hope you're right."

Motionless, Cass watched Jared leave. She didn't take a deep breath until she was sure that he wouldn't be back. Looking into those uncanny eyes and seeing the pure, raw flamc of Jarcd's will was unsettling in ways that Cass refused to examine.

11

Cass set up her camera, loaded her flash gun with charges of powder and readied film holders. When everything was in place, she looked about the room, selected an exotic but not overly busy backdrop of tapestries and moved the heavy wooden chair in front of it. She paced off the distance between the camera and chair, pulled the camera forward slightly, removed the lens cover, and checked the area of view. As she worked, laughter and the muted cacophony of many voices filtered in from the other room. Occasionally the high, nasal song of the female singer pierced the babble, but it was obvious that the men were more interested in rice wine than entertainment.

Cass checked the distance between camera and chair again, fussed with the focus, cleaned the lens, rechecked the powder in the flash guns, stared through the lens, moved the camera slightly to compensate for the flicker of kerosene light, and began the whole process over again. As always when she worked, the rest of her cares vanished, becoming less to her than the voices from the other room.

When she was finally satisfied that she had achieved the best angle and distance permitted by the circumstances of the room, she put her hands in the small of her back and stretched, arching her spine and letting her head fall back as though she were a dancer. She repeated the motion several times, working out the tension that insisted on drawing her shoulders into knots.

Suddenly, Cass sensed that she was no longer alone in the room. She spun around, then stared with no thought of common manners or the possibility of cross-cultural insult. The Chinese woman who stood motionless in the center of the room was as tall as Cass herself. The woman stood silently, politely waiting to be noticed. Cass started to speak, but no words came.

The woman was the most exquisite creature Cass had ever seen. Her facial structure was extraordinary, with high, slanting cheekbones and a well-defined feminine jaw. Her nose was catlike in its delicacy. Her eyes were also those of a cat, their slant enhanced by the delicate epicanthic fold. Instead of being opaque, her irises had the depth and reflective quality of clear, black water. Her lashes were unusually long and dense for a Chinese woman. Similarly, her black eyebrows had a winged arch that was natural rather than the result of careful plucking and painting. Her mouth was slightly fuller than most, giving a promise of sensuality to the otherwise almost ascetic face.

The intriguing paradox of the stranger's face was framed in a headdress of breathtaking luxury. Ordinary feminine beauty would have been overwhelmed by the sheer opulence of the pearls and occasional brooding rubies that made an open lacework pattern over the high forehead and darkly shining hair. In the manner of all unmarried Chinese women, she wore her hair in a single coil rather than in two. The coil was caught in an intricate jeweled net that covered her right ear. Offsetting and balancing the graceful coil were two ebony sticks nestled securely in her thick hair. From the top of the sticks hung fragile strings of tiny, hammered gold bells.

There was not a line, not a blemish, not a flaw in the pale gold satin of the girl's skin. And Cass, with each passing moment, could see that this was a girl, not a woman.

Then, as though to deliberately confound Cass, the girl lifted her averted eyes and Cass found herself looking into eerie black depths that transcended childhood and womanhood both, primal cat's eyes watching her.

"I am Tea Rose."

Speechless, Cass stared, unable to believe that this extraordinary, calm, feral creature was her own sister.

"You are—beautiful," Cass said almost helplessly.

"You are very kind to find virtue in this worthless person," Tea Rose said, bowing over her folded hands, which were invisible behind the exaggerated length of the tunic's horse-hoof sleeves. Though her English was unaccented, the polite declaration of personal worthlessness was quintessentially Chinese.

The motion of Tea Rose's head set the strings of miniature gold bells to swaying and chiming. Their sweet, tiny cries transfixed Cass. When Tea Rose straightened, the movement sent shimmers of light rippling through the orchid satin of the robe, whose hem stopped just short of brushing the floor.

A vise closed around Cass's heart when she saw no feet extending beyond the embroidered edge of the cloth.

"Can you walk?" Cass asked huskily.

An expression of surprise crossed Tea Rose's face, making her appear much younger and more human than before. "Of course," she said, coming closer to prove her point.

Cass felt nausea rise in her throat with each precious, mincing step that Tea Rose took.

"Is it—very painful?" Cass asked brokenly, swallowing against the nausea that came to her when she remembered John's calm description of how to break a young girl's feet.

"Painful?" Tea Rose asked, puzzled. "No. Why? Does it hurt you to walk?"

"My feet aren't bound."

A graceful movement of Tea Rose's fingers spread wide a lacework ivory fan. From behind the fan came a sound that was suspiciously like a restrained, musical giggle. Saying nothing, Tea Rose used her free hand to pull up the edge of her tunic, revealing an odd pair of shoes—the soles were four inches thick, wooden, and curved upward from the center. The shoes added four inches to her height, but only a small, curving portion of the sole touched the floor. As a result, each movement was delicate, a continual balancing act that imitated the restrictions of the prized lily foot.

The relief that swept through Cass was so great that she barely resisted an impulse to hug Tea Rose.

"Do you know who I am?" asked Cass, her voice careful.

"You are Miss Cassandra Thornton, the white woman whom Tan Feng graciously permitted to enter this house. You are to photograph me and my mother."

Cass hesitated, waiting for more. When Tea Rose remained silent, Cass nodded.

"That's correct. Your English is very good, Tea Rose."

The girl nodded in turn, setting bells to singing softly. "I have had many teachers."

For a hammering instant, Cass's heart squeezed painfully. *What kind of teachers would a beautiful girl find in this Chinese brothel?*

"Is it your wish to photograph me now?" Tea Rose asked demurely.

Once more, Cass tried to drag herself back into the role to which she had been assigned. She felt disoriented. It was becoming a familiar sensation, she realized with dismay.

"Yes, I think that would be best," Cass said faintly,

walking over to the camera and lifting the heavy black cloth. "Sit in that chair, please."

Tea Rose looked at the chair and gasped. "That is Tan Feng's!"

Cass impatiently stepped out from beneath the hood. "I've already done my measurements and positioned my flashes," she explained. "It would take too long to set up again, and there's no other suitable backdrop in the room. Please, sit down."

"But Tan Feng—"

"Won't know," Cass interrupted, ducking back under the hood, feeling more like herself with every instant she looked through the camera's lens, where reality was inverted and once removed. "Sit down."

Tea Rose examined this exotic creature—this fearless woman who had appeared in Tan Feng's very den and appropriated the master's chair with such impunity. All she could see of Cass was the long skirt and boots. The rest was mated with a contraption the like of which Tea Rose had never seen.

As she sat obediently, Tea Rose thought through the ramifications of the situation. If Tan Feng should find out and be angry, she might receive a careful beating from either Kwan or Wing. Their care would be a measure, not of their mercy but of their fear of Tan Feng; Tan would kill the man who put an enduring mark on the most beautiful merchandise in America.

Such a beating would be unpleasant, but Tea Rose decided to risk it. A few strokes from the cane would be a small price to pay for the chance to measure Tan's reaction to this woman who moved with such reckless disregard for Tan's face.

Tea Rose knew her own place in Tan's universe, but she was curious about Cass's. If Tan Feng punished Cass, it would prove he was still all-powerful. If he were forced to kowtow to the woman, then he would lose much face with his men. Tea Rose would have to watch carefully to see whether Kwan or Wing gained Tan's lost face. If it were Kwan who benefited, Tea Rose's future would be secure; he wanted her flower even more than Tan Feng did. If it were Wing who gained face, Tea Rose's future would be more uncertain; Tea Rose knew from time spent at spyholes that Wing obtained his sexual gratification, not from Jasmine's vagina but from her tiny lily feet—feet whose allure Tea Rose could never hope to match. But no matter what happened, Tea Rose had more to gain from sitting in Tan Feng's chair than she had to lose from a careful beating. So she would obey Cass and see what came of it.

The decision took Tea Rose no more than a few seconds to make.

The appearance of Tea Rose's inverted face in the clear lens almost made Cass forget to breathe. Tea Rose was an arresting blend of child and woman. Her face was both complex and simple. Its lines were unchanging, but its impact changed as would a jewel's when turned slowly beneath a light. Light and shadow, smile and sadness, warmth and black winter ice, demure civilization and a primal feline awareness that admitted to no master.

Just as Cass reached for a square of film, the door behind her opened and King Duran's voice swept into the room.

"It's a great piece of luck to have a woman take your picture," King explained as he ushered Tan into the room. "It brings you good fortune with other women, and also insures that—"

Tan Feng's bellow of rage and Tea Rose's high babble of Mandarin apologies filled the air. Tea Rose hurled herself at Tan's feet. Tan's two lieutenants burst into the room, weapons drawn, steel blades gleaming in the flickering lamplight. Cass stood in the middle of the room, staring at the pistol that had materialized in King's hand as he moved to shield her from Tan's bodyguards.

Suddenly, Jared was in the room. His voice was like a whiplash. "Put that gun away, you fool!" he said to King. Then Jared turned to Cass. "What the hell did you do?"

"I don't know! I had just gotten Tea Rose settled in that chair and was getting ready to—"

"Which chair?" Jared interrupted.

"That one," Cass said, pointing.

"Christ!" hissed Jared.

He turned to Tan Feng and spoke rapidly in Mandarin that was serviceable, but little more. "A thousand, thousand apologies, Great One. The white woman is but a barbarian who doesn't understand the customs of true men. She was simply trying to carry out her orders to the best of her lamentably limited abilities. She meant no insult by putting a slave girl in the great Tan Feng's seat of honor."

Jared repeated his Mandarin effusions several times, with minor variations on the theme of feminine stupidity and Tan Feng's greatness. Slowly, the Manchu's face began to lighten as it became clear that it was Jared's pride rather than Tan Feng's that had been diminished. The ignorant woman, after all, was Jared's choice. It had been up to Jared to see that she was properly instructed in civilized behavior. The failure and loss of face were Jared's, not Tan Feng's.

Tan turned and looked at the white woman who wore no platform shoes but was taller than either of his lieutenants, though still many inches shorter than Tan himself. He spoke a few sentences in brusque Mandarin.

"What did he say?" Cass asked Jared.

"He said if you were his, he would beat you until you learned the difference between slaves and men."

Both Cass and King started to react, but an abrupt gesture from Jared cut them off.

"Put the goddamned gun away," Jared said in a low, icy voice. *"Now."*

King met his brother's pale eyes for a moment, shrugged, and slid the pistol back into place beneath his jacket. Jared walked over until he stood directly in front of Cass. She started to speak but he silenced her.

"No. Not now," he said flatly, leaning toward Cass, speaking so that only she could hear. "In this room, you are a thing—more valuable than a barnyard animal or a pet, perhaps, but not quite human."

"I will not be—" Cass said between clenched teeth, but softly.

"Remember why you are here," Jared snapped, leaning even closer and speaking with a bare thread of sound. "If you don't mollify the old bastard, he'll have Tea Rose beaten until she can't walk for a week."

"Are you saying I should kowtow to that—"

"A full kowtow, complete with banging your forehead on the floor, will not be necessary," Jared interrupted smoothly. "He knows what a curtsey is. Do you?"

Cass held her tongue only because Tea Rose still lay prostrate on the floor, bumping her forehead against the rug repeatedly while she sobbed in a high babble of Mandarin. Cass glanced from Tea Rose back to Jared.

"Would he really beat her for my mistake?"

"Yes. But for my mistake, not yours," Jared said. "I should have told you not to use the chair as a prop."

"Why didn't you?"

"Because, Miss Thornton, you have a disastrous effect on my rational mental processes. I forgot!" Jared turned away sharply, bowed—but not deeply—to Tan Feng, and spoke again in Mandarin.

A movement at the doorway caught Jared's eye. Lilac stood there, her eyes wide with fear as she took in the drawn swords of Tan's bodyguards and her daughter stretched out on the floor.

"Lilac," Jared said quickly in English, "please explain to the honorable Tan Feng that Cass meant no insult when she had Tea Rose pose in his chair. My Mandarin isn't up to the task, and Tea Rose is too upset to translate for me."

Lilac looked at her sobbing daughter and spoke in very rapid Cantonese, which Tan Feng understood only in the most rudimentary way, and then only if spoken slowly.

"Enough crocodile tears, daughter! How could you be so stupid as to be caught in Tan Feng's chair?"

"She—the white devil—told me to sit. It was Tan Feng's desire that I be photographed. How could I refuse? I am but a poor slave girl who—"

A torrent of brittle Cantonese from Lilac cut off Tea Rose's words. Lilac went to Tan Feng, knelt, and touched her forehead to the floor while she spoke in the Mandarin dialect she had learned just to please her master. Lilac's effusive praise of Tan Feng's wisdom, restraint, and generosity, coupled with her self-abnegation, had the desired effect on Tan. After a minute or two, he grunted a command to his bodyguards. Their short swords vanished.

Cass felt the tension relax in the room and drew a slow breath. She sensed that something was still expected of her and decided that if Jared Duran could unbend enough to bow to the old goat, she could manage one of the female gestures she had been taught so carefully at Miss Bender's. Cass gathered a bit of skirt in each hand, put one foot behind the other, and bent enough to get the message across.

"Would someone please tell him," Cass said quietly, "that I'm very sorry to have made him angry."

"Lilac is taking care of it right now, but thank you," Jared said.

Tan Feng looked over Lilac's head at Cass.

"Curtsey again," Jared muttered.

"But—"

"Do it."

Cass curtsied.

"You are as arrogant and overbearing as Tan Feng," she muttered as she straightened.

Jared's hands shot out and wrapped around Cass's upper arms with a force just short of pain. He pulled her so close that her face was barely an inch from his own.

"For the love of God, shut up," he said in a voice that was all the more chilling for its softness. "They understand more English than you think. One look from Tan Feng and those guards would cut your throat. Or mine, or King's. Is a scrape to your pride worth that?"

Stiffly, Cass said, "I'm sorry. I didn't understand."

Jared slowly loosened his grip on Cass. He was stung by the anger and unhappiness in her eyes, but he dared not relent. These Chinese understood enough body language to compensate for their lack of English. Any softening of his demeanor toward Cass would be viewed as a fresh insult to Tan Feng. But as he released her, his fingers secretly caressed her. Cass's eyes widened in shock at the sensual touch. She looked into Jared's eyes, saw again for an instant the raw flame of his will, and felt fear shiver through her.

He wanted—too much.

12

"Lilac," Jared said, turning away, "with Tan Feng's permission, will you translate for Miss Thornton?"

A spate of Mandarin was followed by a grunt from Tan. Lilac stood and crossed the room with the curious, swaying, tiny motions of a woman in a perpetual balancing act. She bowed to Cass and asked in a lightly accented voice, "How may I assist you, Miss Thornton?"

For a moment, Cass could only stare at the woman who had been her father's wife. There was nothing warm about the remote perfection of Lilac's makeup and clothing. Even the apricot folds of her elaborate robe had more the frosty sheen of sherbet than the rosy allure of sun-warmed fruit.

Yet, she had wept when she had touched Cass's hair.

"Cassandra," Jared said, sotto voce.

"I'm sorry," she said quickly. "It's just that Lilac is so extraordinary—"

A harsh-voiced question from Tan loosed another spate of Mandarin from Lilac. Instantly, the postures of the three men eased even more.

"She told them that you were struck speechless by Tan's possession," Jared said softly to Cass.

"Possession?"

"Lilac," Jared muttered.

"Oh," Cass said faintly.

Tan nodded minutely, acknowledging Cass for the first time.

"Curtsey."

"Go to hell, Mr. Duran," Cass whispered through her demure smile, but she curtsied anyway. "Now, may we get on with it?"

"Yes."

Cass turned toward Lilac. "If you would please come this way, Mrs. —"

"Call her Lilac, period," Jared interrupted savagely. "Females take the family name of their husbands. Lilac has neither family nor husband. *You must remember that.*"

Cass's lips thinned, but all she said was, "Lilac, I'll need a chair that's, er, suitable for you and Tea Rose to use while sitting for a portrait."

"Of course, Miss Thornton."

Cass waited while the request was relayed. One of Tan's bodyguards left.

"Would Mr. Feng—"

"Mr. Tan," Jared interrupted quickly. "The Chinese use the family name first, because it's most important. The personal name comes last."

Cass cleared her throat and tried again. "Perhaps Mr. Tan would like to look over the camera equipment and assure himself that there is no danger in it."

Lilac was still translating when Tan nodded abruptly, indicating he understood. He approached the camera, looking at it with ill-disguised suspicion. He circled it several times, spoke rapidly to Lilac, and watched while she lifted up the heavy black drapery. He bent over, squinted at the inverted image as seen through the lens, and made a surprised sound.

"My lord wishes to know if all photographs are made upside down," Lilac said.

"Yes," said Cass.

Tan grunted a few words.

"Why is the image upside down?" Lilac asked.

"When light comes through the lens, the glass inverts everything," Cass said.

Tan made a thick sound and looked suspiciously at Cass. Apparently satisfied that she wasn't joking at his expense, Tan turned his attention back to the camera.

"Will it be like that when you take my lord Tan's picture?" Lilac asked.

"Yes," said Cass, "but I will turn the picture right side up and it will look correct."

"This is a very strange instrument," Lilac said, translating in a high, pure voice while Tan spoke. "Many Chinese are reluctant to have their pictures taken. They think you are stealing their souls and locking them up inside your wooden box."

"Is he—er, would you be afraid to have your picture taken?" Cass asked Lilac.

"No. I have no soul to lose," Lilac answered calmly.

Tan broke in once more.

"My lord Tan wants to know what white-devil magic is used by this machine to make the image of a man," Lilac said.

"There's no magic, just Western science. Light and silver salts and chemicals on a plate of glass. There's nothing that he need fear."

"My translation was inadequate," Lilac said instantly. "My lord fears nothing, but he is also very wise. Only a fool rushes into strangeness with the outstretched arms of a woman going to her lover."

"Of course," Cass said, watching as Tan squinted into the camera's inverted world once more. "I'm sure it all seems very strange to him, but photographs are a way of honoring people. Photographs show a person's true strength, so that even the most foolish person can recognize a man's greatness or a woman's beauty just by seeing a good photograph. For example—"

While Lilac translated, Cass went to her equipment trunk

and removed a few pictures. One was a shot of Cass at sixteen, smiling warmly into the lens. It had been taken by her father a few months before he had died. She handed the photograph to Tan Feng, who held it at arm's length and then drew it closer, peering into the image and then comparing it with the woman who stood before him.

"Make you?" Tan asked in harsh English.

"Er, yes, that's me when—"

Jared interrupted. "He wants to know if you took the picture." He bent closer and whispered. "Tell him a professional photographer took it, and change the subject fast. Whatever you do, don't show a picture of your father."

Lilac had acted even more quickly than Cass or Jared. She began a fulsome, misleading translation while Cass quickly selected another photo. It showed an elderly man and woman standing close to one another. The man had a full beard. The woman was dressed in her Sunday best. In the background was a covered wagon.

"These are my father's parents," Cass said. "I look at this picture often. It's all I have to remember them by. That's what photographs are good for. Remembering people and times that will never come again."

"That's the ticket," Jared whispered warmly while Lilac translated.

Again, Tan Feng relaxed before the translation was nearly complete. "White woman small sense got. Pray ancestors. Good good." He grunted and bent over the camera again.

"My lord is pleased that you know the value of revering your ancestors," Lilac said in her high, pure voice. "In China, there is no greater virtue."

"I'm pleased that we have something in common," Cass said as she sketched a small curtsey.

Jared smiled as he watched Cass. She was stubborn, but she was far from stupid. Given enough time, she would have the old tong leader eating from her hand like a tame pony.

Tan Feng grunted a few words.

Instantly, Tea Rose scrambled up from her prone position

onto her knees. She sat on her heels with head bowed and hands hidden in her long sleeves. Cass let out a long breath, relaxing for the first time since the blowup.

"Would Tan Feng like to look at Tea Rose through the lens?" Cass asked.

This time, there was no hesitation. Tan immediately went to stand behind the camera, secure in the knowledge that it was a tool rather than a trick to be played upon the unwary. Lilac told Tea Rose to stand in front of the disputed chair. The lens inverted her image. Tan made an odd sound and stood up to look at Tea Rose. When he saw her looking anxiously at him, he smiled.

"It is all right, my little opium flower," he said, his voice gentle, infusing Mandarin's clear tones with unexpected sensuality. "You are beautiful even when the world is turned upside down, for the spring moon rises in your smile."

Tea Rose's ivory fan flickered open barely in time to conceal the flash of her tiny teeth and tip of her tongue as she smiled at the compliment. The movement of her fan was perfectly calculated, offering Tan a hint of the nakedness of her parted lips while maintaining the proper restraint. Tan's smile widened and his eyelids lowered in response to the seductive hint of tongue he had been permitted to see.

Cass stared at Tan, hardly able to believe the transformation his smile made. Suddenly, he was handsome in a marvelously barbaric way, with the face of a conqueror and the smile of an alien god.

"Will he allow me to photograph him?" Cass whispered to Jared. "When he smiles like that, he is very—powerful."

"If he ever smiles like that at you, run like hell," Jared said dryly.

Cass gave him a sidelong glance, then looked back at Tan Feng, who was bending over the camera once more. This time, he laughed expansively while Tea Rose used her fan with the skill of a courtesan twice her age.

Tan straightened again, backed up several steps, and said in English, "Make."

"Take her picture," Jared said in an undertone.

Cass bridled at the blunt order, but she said nothing. She pulled a film holder out of her box, inserted it into the camera, and bent over to cock the shutter. When she was ready, she picked up the flash gun. A burst of light filled the room, followed by startled cries. The bodyguards' hands flew to the handles of their sheathed swords, and King Duran's hand moved to the butt of his pistol. Lilac immediately called out assurances in Mandarin and Cantonese. After a few moments, the tension subsided again.

Not until Cass was certain that there was no residual trace of a smile on her face did she emerge from behind the concealing folds of the black hood.

"Is something wrong?" she asked innocently.

After one look at Cass's brilliant golden eyes, King threw back his head and laughed. The sound was as clean and untamed as the north wind, a force that expressed itself solely in freedom and movement. Cass stared unselfconsciously at King, fascinated by the sheer wildness of the spirit that lived just beneath the veneer of manners and clothing.

Tan Feng's face went black with rage at the sound of King's laughter, but he said nothing. Quickly, Jared said something in Chinese, then turned on Cass.

"Happy now, Miss Thornton? You almost got a lot of people hurt because of your little stunt. Do you understand yet? *Tan Feng's pride is no joke.*"

"Lay off, little brother," King said, smiling at Cass. "She was just following Tan's orders—and yours."

"Thank you," Cass said, smiling up at King. "It's very kind of you to stand up for a mere female."

"My pleasure. And don't worry about Jay or that big Chinee. No one's going to lay a hand on you as long as I'm around."

Jared clapped his hands in a slow mockery of approval. "Spoken like a true fool, Kingston," Jared said coolly. "Now, if you two children are finished baiting the Asian bear, perhaps we can get through this evening before you both lose your hands."

For a long, taut minute the two brothers stood and eyed each other with a blunt willingness to fight. Then King smiled slowly and rubbed the back of his neck.

"Sorry, Jay. Guess I've been in civilization too long. I feel like a river before breakup, ready to let loose one long howl as I burst the bonds and run free again."

Jared glared, even as he knew deep within himself that he couldn't hold King's behavior against him. King was what he was, and Jared had been wondering how much longer King would last in the city. He had been here nearly six months, which was five weeks longer than his previous record of tolerating civilization. The forays he had made into the outlying country had only made him more irritable. A week ago, King had been complaining about his bad luck at cards. When Jared had offered to lend him money, King had refused, saying that the sooner he lost all his cash, the sooner he would be free to put his face into the north wind and go looking for the only frontier that remained.

"I understand," Jared said softly.

And he did.

Slowly, the tension unwound in both men, leaving behind a heavy feeling in the air, as though incense had been burned. The Chinese men watched closely; it had become obvious to them that, whatever King's superior position in birth order, Jared was the one in control.

"Make now," Tan Feng said.

He strode toward the heavy chair and seated himself with knees spread wide in an attitude of command.

"Quick quick," he commanded.

As she reached for the camera to pull out the plate that was by now overexposed, Cass said to Lilac, "Ask him to sit very still. I wouldn't want his enormous dignity to be blurred. And tell him that there's going to be another flash of light."

While Lilac spoke, Cass removed the used film plate and

inserted a fresh one in the holder. The rubbing of wood frame against the holder sounded loud in the breathless hush that followed Lilac's translation. Cass took three pictures in rapid succession, using flashes of different intensity each time. Jared watched like a diamond-eyed hawk, admiring both Cass's grace and her skill with her equipment. As a man who hired other men, Jared knew how rare it was to find someone who actually knew how to do a job well.

"I have finished," Cass said. "He can move all he likes."

Lilac began to translate, only to be cut off by an imperious gesture from Tan Feng. He spoke quickly in a harsh voice. After only the briefest hesitation, his two bodyguards withdrew. Lilac followed, but her eyes pleaded with Jared every step of the way. Tea Rose stood gracefully and came to stand between Tan's widespread knees. When he spoke to her, his voice lost the deep-throated, gutteral harshness he had used in commanding other people.

"Tell the Duran brothers to go, my beautiful opium dream. The white woman will stay and take more soul-images."

Tea Rose turned around to speak to Jared. A single look told her that Jared had understood the gist of Tan's orders.

"Please, Mr. Duran," Tea Rose said, automatically keeping her voice in the lower register that pleased the Western ear. "It will be just for a few moments."

Jared turned to Cass. "He wants us to leave you alone to take pictures. It's up to you."

The idea of being alone with the proud, volatile Tan Feng made Cass pause.

"I'll be right outside the door," Jared said. "I promise you, Cassandra."

She looked into his clear, steady eyes and for once found the power she saw within him reassuring rather than unnerving. She nodded.

"Out," Jared said to King, jerking his head toward the door.

"Wait just a damn—"

"It's all right," Cass said quickly, putting a new plate into the film holder. "Really."

King looked at her, shrugged, and walked quickly to the door. Jared followed, closing the door behind him.

Cass took a deep breath and felt very much alone.

13

Cass busied herself over unnecessary adjustments to the equipment. When she looked up, Tan had positioned Tea Rose to his satisfaction. She was sitting on his lap, looking up at him with laughing eyes. Her fan was properly raised to shield her mouth, but nothing could muffle the sensual ripple of her laughter as Tan murmured against the jeweled coil of her hair.

Uneasiness twisted within Cass as she pulled the hood over her head. The inverted view of Tan and Tea Rose was no more soothing than the direct view had been. He was running a blunt thumb from the nape of her neck to the division of her buttocks, making her giggle and squirm. He watched the child's motions with heavy-lidded eyes.

But Tea Rose was no longer quite a child, despite her mere fourteen years of age. When light gathered and flowed over her body while she twisted in answer to Tan's thumb, each motion she made emphasized the curves hitherto concealed by her loose clothes. When she squirmed again in response to Tan's probing, his hand slid wholly beneath her buttocks. The looseness of Tea Rose's tunic hid the touch from the camera's view, but nothing hid Tan's smile when his fingers sank luxuriantly into Tea Rose's flesh. He squeezed rhythmically, echoing the deep beating of his heart.

Tea Rose flashed her smile and her fan in precise synchronization. The sudden tightening of Tan's fingers told her that she had been successful; she had displayed the tip of her tongue in an enticement that could never be proven, for the fan had taken away the vision before Tan Feng could be certain that he had seen rather than imagined the glistening allure of her small tongue. She was tempted to try the seductive little trick again, but refrained. Lilac had been quite thorough in her teaching; a courtesan should be like the shimmer of moonlight on a lake, always beckoning, always gone before a man could reach out his hand to grasp her. The sight of her naked tongue had sliced into Tan like a silver razor; to repeat the motion would be to dull its edge.

"Sweeter than opium smoke," Tan said heavily, flexing his hand, searching for the untouched opening of Tea Rose's body, only to be thwarted by the heavy folds of embroidered silk.

"You are kind to notice this worthless child, honorable one," Tea Rose said demurely, looking up at him from behind the safety of her spread fan.

She moved as though to balance herself more securely in his lap, opening her legs a fraction more, hiding her feral smile as she felt the telltale hardening beneath her thigh. As though off balance, she made a soft, startled sound and leaned toward Tan, shifting her weight lightly over his erection, enjoying the narrowing of his eyes and the sudden, revealing tension of his hand between her legs.

"Do you like that, little flower?" Tan whispered, moving against Tea Rose with a slow pressure, drawing her over him again, feeling the sweet-aching heaviness of the turtle head emerging from its shell.

"Like what?" she asked, flicking her fan in teasing concealment of her mouth as she unconsciously increased the weight of her bottom on his hand in such a way that no one could be sure it hadn't been an accident—even Tea Rose herself.

"My tiny, perfect cup of poison," Tan whispered, suspecting that he was being very skillfully teased, but not certain. Her eyes were wide and dark with something that was not quite innocence, yet was far short of the carnal anticipation that swept through him. "Someday, I will play a new game with you," Tan said, enjoying Tea Rose's slow, apparently helpless writhing as he probed her small body. "Someday very soon. Will you enjoy that, black butterfly?"

Cass listened to the alien, incomprehensible murmur of syllables rising and falling without rhyme or reason, and she tried to tell herself that she was letting her imagination run away with her in a way that no decent woman should. Tea Rose was simply an extraordinarily beautiful child who had never been told that, after a certain age, girls didn't sit on men's laps. It wasn't proper. In fact, it was so unseemly as to make Cass uncomfortable.

But what made her most uneasy was the fact that she wasn't certain who was the victim and who the prey.

Nonsense, Cass told herself firmly. *Tea Rose is still a child. Tan Feng has lived a life steeped in corruption. She is no more responsible for his lascivious smile than she is for the circumstances of her birth.*

And then the realization hit her like a blow. *My God, no matter how strange the clothes or how odd the languages she speaks, Tea Rose is my little sister, and she's behaving as though she has no more manners than a puppy.*

"Tea Rose," Cass said crisply, "stop wiggling about like a worm on a hook or you'll spoil the picture. If you can't get comfortable on Mr. Tan's lap, perhaps you should stand next to his chair. Mr. Tan, your dignity will be enhanced if both of your hands are in plain sight."

Though Cass's head was concealed by the drape, her words came through quite clearly. The inverted picture in the glass didn't change. With a bitten-off word of exasperation, Cass checked the focus on her subjects. She moved the camera back a bit to sharpen the definition on Tea Rose before closing and cocking the shutter. Then Cass found her flash gun, held it high to spread the light through the room, and checked her subjects one last time.

"Now, you must hold very still, Tea Rose," Cass said. As she spoke, she pulled out the panel that had protected the plate from exposure. "You must help the one-handed Manchu lord to look dignified."

Tea Rose's body shifted subtly, as though she were seated on a moving surface. Tan Feng's missing hand appeared. He stared at the camera lens in calm arrogance as his palm wrapped over the curve of Tea Rose's right thigh, and his fingers spread wide in a silent proclamation of ownership.

Tea Rose turned her head and looked over her fan at the camera as though it were Tan Feng.

The photographer in Cass responded immediately, tripping the flash gun in synchronization with the shutter, preserving the instant before anything could change; and even as she went through the motions, the woman in Cass felt a chilling moment of fear that Tea Rose was far less innocent than her translucent beauty or her tender years suggested. Yet, in the next second, as the burst of hard white light vanished, doubt returned full force within Cass. Tea Rose was so young, so—flawless.

The girl slipped from Tan's lap with a ripple of graceful laughter, bowing over her folded hands, speaking incomprehensible syllables in high, childish tones, giggling behind her upraised sleeve as though she hadn't had time to prepare her fan before laughter had overtaken her.

"That's all," Cass said to Tea Rose.

"Just one?" Tea Rose asked in disappointment.

"I must save some plates for Lilac and for whatever else Mr. Tan might require," Cass said quickly. Even to herself, she didn't admit that she would break every unexposed plate in her equipment chest rather than see Tea Rose curled up in Tan's lap for another picture. "Perhaps I will be permitted to take more photographs at another time?"

Tea Rose glanced sideways at Tan Feng, who said nothing.

"Perhaps, Miss Thornton," Tea Rose said softly. But even under Tan's subduing glare, she couldn't help but watch with ill-concealed eagerness while Cass removed the exposed plate, wrapped it carefully, and then placed a fresh plate in the holder. "Is it ready now?" Tea Rose asked, her voice low once more, pleasing to the Western ear. "Oh, do let me see it, please, Miss Thornton."

Cass smiled at her impatient little sister. "It will be

several days, I'm afraid. It takes time to develop the image and transfer it to paper. I'll show it to you when I come back."

"If Tan Feng permits," Tea Rose said quickly.

"Of course," Cass said. "I'm sure Mr. Tan will be eager to see the photographs, too."

Tan Feng spoke in low, rapid gutterals, using the throaty, ultramasculine command voice that Cass found so artificial and irritating. The slight lift at the corners of Tan's mouth told her that he had noticed her reaction—and enjoyed it.

"Thank you, Miss Thornton," Tea Rose said quickly. "My lord must return to his guests, and I must be there to translate for him and to taste his food."

"To taste his—?"

But Tea Rose was already withdrawing from the room, her body swaying like a long-stemmed lily in a buffeting wind, her silks whispering secrets that were repeated by the fragile cries of golden bells.

Before the door was fully open, Lilac was in the room, closely followed by Jared. Lilac saw her daughter's nearly invisible smile of triumph and guessed what had happened. Tan Feng's heightened color and constrained walk confirmed Lilac's suspicions.

"Have your image taken, woman," Tan said to Lilac as King entered the room. "Be very still. You must appear as perfect as your daughter. It should be easier for you than it was for her—my hand won't be at your jade gate."

Expressionless, Lilac bowed. Tan Feng watched Tea Rose with a smile that made King uneasy. He looked at Jared.

"What's going on?" King asked.

"I don't know enough Mandarin to catch more than a word or two," Jared said, lying without hesitation. "Guess Tan was just telling her to hold still and follow orders."

King grunted. "Come on. Let's get back before Mulrooney finishes off the good bourbon and leaves the rat piss for us." He turned and smiled at Tan Feng. "When we return to the party, I'll toast your bravery for having your picture taken."

Tea Rose translated so quickly and unobtrusively that after the first few words everyone forgot she was there.

"And my lord Tan Feng will toast your foolishness," she murmured, "and time will see which toast is more farseeing."

King's untamed laughter rang out in the narrow hallway, accompanied by Tan Feng's. Watching them turn and walk side by side down the narrow hall, Cass had the eerie feeling that a gauntlet had been thrown down and taken up, but she could not have said by whom nor for what end.

"You better work fast," Jared said quietly to Cass and Lilac. "Tan could change his mind and require Lilac's presence at any time."

"Only death can be rushed," Lilac said. "Life cannot."

"Jared, we're waiting for you!" King called. "Chop chop!"

Beneath his dark mustache, Jared's mouth flattened into a line of irritation.

"Do what you must," he said, turning on his heel and striding after the disappearing men.

Cass stepped aside from the doorway. Lilac entered the room with the rippling grace of a prima ballerina en pointe. She closed the door behind her back. Instantly, Cass opened her mouth to speak. Lilac moved her head in an emphatic negative that set the mirrors and scarlet silk tassels on her headdress to flashing and swinging. Then she turned and placed her ear against the door.

"I'll set up the equipment," Cass said tightly.

Glancing at Lilac from time to time, Cass dragged Tan's forbidden, heavy chair away from the folding silk screens and replaced it with the frail-looking chair that a bodyguard had brought in and abandoned. When the chair was positioned to her satisfaction, she went through the laborious process of shifting and refocusing her camera and reloading flash guns. Each time she looked, Lilac hadn't moved from her taut position at the door.

Abruptly, she straightened and crossed the room with soundless mincing movements. She came and stood next to the camera, touching its black angles, stroking the tripod's polished wooden legs, pausing over each nick and mar as though remembering the moment when an injury had occurred. Then she went and sat in the frail chair that had replaced Tan Feng's seat of honor.

"Take my portrait, Miss Thornton. Tan Feng requires a beautiful image of the beautiful merchandise he hopes to sell for enough money to end his long sojourn in the Golden Mountain."

Cass bent and adjusted the focus with only a part of her attention.

"You have seen Tea Rose. Do you believe that she is your father's daughter?"

"Yes."

"Are you quite certain?"

"The way she holds her head, the shape of her eyebrows, the line of her smile—it's like looking through a darkened window and seeing him."

Lilac nodded slowly. The motion of her head sent mirrors to shattering light into razor shards of brightness. "He is in your smile, too," she whispered, the words barely loud enough for Cass to understand.

A brilliant explosion of flash powder fixed forever the image of Lilac's mouth poised on the brink of infinite sorrow.

"Such brightness," Lilac said, blinking. "A golden glow is kinder to aged skin."

"You don't need to worry," Cass said, pulling out and wrapping the exposed plate, replacing it with a fresh one. "You can't be much older than I am."

"I will soon be forty."

Cass turned toward Lilac with a look of shocked disbelief. "I don't believe it."

Lilac bowed over her folded hands, accepting the compliment. "It's true, nonetheless."

Her head lifted and she looked at Cass with a serene composure that mocked the very idea of slavery. Fierce light bloomed, stopping that instant of time, fixing it forever on glass. Even before the aftereffect of the light had faded from her retinas, Lilac spoke again.

"Tan Feng sees my time as a courtesan ending. He has bought other women and smuggled them in through Canada. I am training them, passing on my knowledge of ideographs and calligraphy, music, and how to draw the turtle head from its soft shell."

Frowning, Cass worked over her photographic equipment, sensing that there was more to what Lilac was saying than the rippling surface of her words. But the true meaning eluded Cass even as she sensed its presence.

"You have seen Tan Feng. You have seen what he is. Tan is obsessed with the arts of the couch," Lilac observed coolly. "It amuses him to play the turtle game in front of you and to have you know nothing of it. He would never do it in front of other men, however, even white men. Thus, he had everyone leave the room but you and Tea Rose."

"Turtle game?" Cass asked. "What does that mean?"

"Chinese consider the turtle's head and neck to be a symbol of the penis, appearing and disappearing with little warning. To play the turtle game is to—"

"Never mind," Cass interrupted tightly. "I understand. My God in Heaven, that filthy old hatchet man was actually fondling her while—"

Cass's voice died as her skin rippled in revulsion at what she couldn't put into words; Tan had watched Cass while he fondled Tea Rose. At that instant, Cass felt as though all the exotic scents she had been inhaling had clogged her pores, her lungs, her soul. She wanted to put her hands over her ears and shout denials, as the warning Jared had given her after they left the foundry echoed in her mind: *The Chinese are very different from us. Not better, not worse, simply different. If you don't know in your brain and in your belly just how different the Chinese culture is from your own, you won't be able to do your half sister one goddamned bit of good.*

Cass knew it in her belly now, and wanted to vomit, as

though that primal act of refusal would change all that had happened today and all that had yet to happen tomorrow.

The sound of knocking came from the hall outside.

"Have you decided Tea Rose's future?" Lilac asked calmly.

Cass didn't know what to say. Since she had discovered Tea Rose was her sister, Cass had known that somehow she had to remove her from Tan's house of "joy." Even before Cass had known anything of Chinese culture or custom, she had been quite certain of the need to rescue Tea Rose.

But now, Cass had seen her sister for the first time. It was impossible to imagine Tea Rose beyond the exotic confines of silk and incense.

The sound of knocking came again.

Lilac turned her face toward the door and spoke in sliding tones that Cass couldn't understand. The door opened and Tea Rose entered the room with the mincing steps that mimicked a woman's maimed feet. The tiny golden bells in her hair shivered sweetly, whispering music into the incense-laden silence.

As Tea Rose approached, Cass watched and felt that she was poised on a wire stretched from the newly discovered past to the wholly undiscovered future. She felt as though she were about to give birth to a child of her own, a fourteen-year-old changeling who would transform Cass's life more than any tiny infant from her womb might have. Nothing could ever be the same again, and Cass hadn't even had nine months to prepare herself for that new reality. Here was her future, standing before her like an unexpected telegram that might contain either incredible joy or terrible sorrow.

Or both.

"Tan Feng wishes to know when my mother will be finished," Tea Rose said diplomatically.

"Soon," Cass said, listening to her own voice as though it were a stranger's. How could she choose to take or not to take Tea Rose? How could anyone possibly choose wisely under such circumstances? It was impossible.

Yet not choosing was also a choice.

If you don't take Tea Rose, I will cut her throat and then my own.

At Cass's continued silence, Tea Rose bowed and turned to withdraw.

"Tea Rose—" Cass whispered.

The girl heard. She pivoted with the silken elegance of a cat. "Yes, Miss Thornton?"

"I—I want to take a picture of you and your mother."

"Now?"

"Yes. Right now. You're both so beautiful. I'll never forgive myself if I don't get a picture of you together. I'll be very quick. It will be our secret. Tan Feng needn't ever know."

As she spoke, Cass walked toward Tea Rose, until she was close enough to touch fingertips to the girl's flawless cheek. The skin was smooth and taut and almost hot, burning with the banked flame of her vitality. Cass drew in her breath with quick wonder, for she had never experienced another's living warmth in quite the same way. She wondered if it were this vital heat a mother felt when she held a newborn baby to her breast, a sharing of life and flesh that transcended other human bonds.

Tea Rose smiled hesitantly, caught between uncertainty and the cool, gentle caress of Cass's fingertips, a touch not unlike Lilac's in its sweetness.

The girl's smile was like a golden needle piercing Cass's heart; Tea Rose's smile was her father's smile and also Cass's own, past and present reflected and irrevocably joined in a wholly unexpected mirror that hinted at the future.

In that moment, Cass knew that she must take her half sister away from the life that would degrade and destroy her as surely as it had Lilac. No other course was thinkable to Cass. In a way that defied words, she was now joined to Tea Rose.

"Go to your mother," Cass said softly.

Not until Tea Rose's back was turned did Cass look into

Lilac's eyes. Cass nodded once, unmistakably, before she turned away to take a portrait of the past that no longer was, mother and daughter imprisoned together in a cage of birth, culture, and beauty.

14

The Delmonico was the most opulent dining room in Seattle. Cass had never been inside the building, but she in no way felt a stranger because of it. The air was redolent of familiar foods, burning tobacco, and French perfume. The fragments of overheard conversations were in English. The women wore skirts, not pants; their feet were normal, and they walked normally upon them.

"Is this only ten blocks from Chinatown?" Cass asked, trying to shake the feeling of unreality that had been haunting her ever since she had heard John praise the terrible grace of Jasmine's ruined feet.

"Hardly even that much," King answered.

"It seems more like ten thousand miles."

King glanced around with restless green eyes. "Probably why Jay chose the place."

"Jay?"

"Jared. An old nickname. One that he doesn't always like. Not from me, anyway."

"Then why do you use it?"

King smiled, a reckless glint in his eyes. "Makes life interesting. Jay doesn't like that. He likes all his ducks lined up, waiting to be shot. That's why he chose this place—not a Chinaman in sight. Must be the only restaurant in Seattle where Tan Feng's tong men don't even work in the kitchen."

"Frankly, that's a relief to me."

"Is it? And here I had you pegged as an adventurous type."

"I am, but not with other people's lives."

"Don't fret, Cassie. I don't mind adventure."

"I was thinking of Tea Rose's life, not yours," Cass retorted coolly, but she couldn't suppress the warmth in her smile. Nobody had called her Cassie since her father had died. She liked hearing it once more, especially from a man as appealing as Kingston Duran.

King's answering smile was both warm and intimate, making Cass feel as though she were alone with him rather than in the center of a busy restaurant. The realization brought heightened color to her cheeks.

"Do you see Jay?" King asked lazily, knowing that Cass wasn't looking anywhere but at him.

"Er, no."

"Should be around somewhere. He's a regular in the dining room. That's where he makes half his business deals. Me, I'm more comfortable in the bar."

"You're fond of strong drink?"

"No. It's just that all that fancy silver and china out there gives me a rash." King laughed. "Makes me want to throw crystal glasses up in the air and juggle them, just to see what happens. Shall we?"

Before Cass could object, King had placed his fingertips in the small of her back and was gently pushing her toward the far end of the dining room. As he sensed both her hesitation and her surrender to his touch, he felt a lazy kind of heat kindling his blood. He knew he shouldn't be flirting with Cass, shouldn't be brushing against her at every opportunity, shouldn't be watching her, waiting for the flush of warmth that stained her cheeks each time she felt his touch.

He shouldn't be, but he was. He still felt the restless heat of an evening spent with the stimulation of both rice whiskey and adrenaline. Then, too, Cass Thornton's presence next to his hip brought on a different kind of glow. Part of it was her eyes; he had always had a weakness for gold. A lot of it was her body—tall, with a narrow waist and high breasts, and hips full enough to give the heavy skirt a tantalizing sway.

Best of all, every bit of Cass was natural. King felt no

stiffness of corset and whalebone stays against his lightly probing fingertips as he steered her through the crowd. He allowed himself the pleasure of resting his palm fully against her back just above the waist of her dress. Again, there was a sense of hesitation followed by supple surrender. The heat in his blood began to center below his belt, making his pants fit more tightly.

King knew he was rushing Cass, but when she didn't object to his palm subtly caressing her back, he continued the contact. Her warmth radiated into his palm through the smooth burgundy fabric of her jacket. Her fragrance was a compound of cinnamon and faint musk that was as seductive as the heat of her body. King had found himself bending down at any excuse or at none, simply to inhale the scented warmth rising from Cass's nape. In the carriage, it had been all he could do not to pull Cass onto his lap and bury his face in the curve of her neck.

The thought made King smile. He had had to work very quickly to force Jared into the first carriage while taking Cass into the second one. In fact, King had all but lifted Jared by the scruff and tossed him inside the other carriage. The only thing that had prevented an argument was the very real urgency of getting out of Chinatown before Tan Feng was any wiser as to the real purpose of Jared's "business party." Jared hadn't been prepared to jeopardize the success of their mission by arguing over who rode with Cass. King had known his brother would be practical in just that way, and had used it against him.

Through half-open eyes King had watched the woman who swayed easily to the carriage's motions. Her dress and demeanor proclaimed her to be a good woman, not the sort to flirt and fly into a man's bed. But that was exactly where King wanted Cass, even as he told himself that he was a fool—she wasn't his kind of woman, and he wasn't her kind of man. Cass was a woman for tomorrow as well as for tonight. King was a man who had no interest in tomorrows.

Yet, as he watched Cass, he began to sense for the first

time why men turned their backs on the horizon in order to look at just one nearby woman, just one nearby place, just one home.

And if one woman was all a man was to be allowed, Miss Cassandra Thornton wouldn't be a bad choice. She had dealt with Tan Feng very effectively, neither fainting nor dithering nor mewing helplessly when violence had threatened. She had emerged pale but composed from the whole experience, and her golden eyes had glowed with relief when she had seen King walking toward her across the tong hall's dining room. At first, she had taken his arm as though it were a rope pulling her to safety, yet she had made no objection when Jared had insisted that she take photographs of the gathered businessmen. There was strength in Cass. King liked that. Women who clung like living ivy made him restless. Except in bed, of course.

That was the best thing of all about Cass; she didn't object to a man's touch. She hadn't drawn away from the feel of his hand on her backbone, which made him wonder if she would retreat if his hand drifted down to the tempting, concealed curves of her hips.

King curbed the direction of his thoughts, knowing it was as much a hangover from rice wine and whorehouse females as a response to Cass herself. He didn't want to offend her, because women such as Cass were the single feature of civilization that consistently appealed to King. As a prospector, a miner, a gold-seeker, and an explorer, he lived largely alone or in the rough company of other frontiersmen. The vast majority of the time, King liked it that way. Sometimes he hungered for a woman, though. Not just for sex—one way or another, sexual relief was available. But frontier women, what few there were, tended to be as coarse and rough as the men. Even worse, the women were usually as ugly as a hellfire sermon or as ignorant as a boulder, or both. In his footloose lifetime, King had found only a few women he could talk with, and fewer still that he was likely to spend more than an hour with, in bed or otherwise.

Unfortunately, King's fifteen years of prospecting had

also taught him that frontier men were no more interesting than frontier women, by and large. Most of the men had the imagination of a stump and the sensibilities of a hungry wolverine. When King talked to them of his inchoate urge toward the horizon, of the piercing beauty of a raindrop struck by the sun, of the primal scent of evergreen riding the crest of an ice-tipped wind, of the aurora borealis whispering to him about things unseen, unheard, unimagined, all waiting for him, all just beyond the horizon . . . beyond the sunset it lay, something unnamed that had been conceived in midnight, born at dawn, growing into unspeakable perfection just over the curve of the earth, an eternal present where man could walk alone over the pristine face of the earth, a present where everything lay ahead of man and nothing behind, an intoxicating, godlike freedom.

When King talked of those things burning unquenchably in his soul, men looked at him as though he were mad.

Yet, the older King grew, the more insistently those things called to him. Gradually, he had become more comfortable hunting for gold alone rather than with a partner whose only contact with the earth was to squat over it as he emptied his bowels.

Oddly, the only person King had found who understood his hunger for unlimited horizons was the very man who had settled successfully into civilized life—Jared Duran. At times, it amused King that his younger brother had taken root at the Pacific Rim of the continent. And at times, it saddened King, for Jared had been a good companion in the wilderness, a fierce fighter, a dead shot, and a man who understood the beauty of silence as well as the solace of speech. But it had been years since King had been able to lure Jared over the horizon for more than a few weeks at a time.

As King guided Cass out of the dining room, the din of the crowded bar quickly pulled his thoughts from the ineffable to the mundane. Men called out greetings that King answered with a nod or a wave. He had become a regular in the past few months, which in itself was a sign of his increasing restlessness. Alcohol sometimes helped him to touch the ineffable. Most of the time, it simply helped to make the mundane bearable. The longer he stayed in civilization, the more mundane it became, which meant that lately he had often been one of the well-dressed young men sitting at the long cherrywood bar, drinking imported scotch from cut-crystal glasses.

"I see you decided not to find your pleasure in China-town, after all," one of the other regulars said loudly to King as they passed the bar.

The man gave Cass a quick up-and-down inspection, which she returned coolly before looking away without a word. None was needed. Her expression couldn't have made plainer the fact that she saw nothing of interest in the half-drunk young man. Nor was she ruffled by his ill-mannered appraisal; after the exotic dangers of the Blossom Moon, the amiable rakes of the Delmonico weren't worth noticing.

"Miss Thornton, this impolite masher is John Town-send," King explained. "He drinks here every night, drinks a lot, actually, which explains his lack of manners. Mr. Townsend, this is Miss C. A. Thornton, the photographer. She is far too fine a lady to pay attention to a gyppo lumberman like yourself."

After an aloof nod in the man's general direction, Cass allowed herself to be pressured forward by King's hand against her back. In one way or another, he had been touching her since they had left the carriage. She didn't usually allow a man like King such quick liberties. In her position as a single woman, she couldn't afford to. But today had been a difficult one, and there was the interview with the incisive, too-insightful Jared yet to endure tonight. Under the circumstances, the silent, warm, undemanding support of King's touch was welcome.

"That's Townsend Lumber?" Cass asked under her breath when they were beyond the man's hearing. "I've heard he owns half the timber claims in western Washington."

"Says he does, but I think that's just his way of getting

people to take his markers at the poker table," King drawled. He smiled down at Cass. "He owes me a thousand from last week. Every time I run into him he makes some kind of rude remark, hoping I'll forget."

"Forget what?" Jared asked, appearing at Cass's elbow without warning. "That you owe him fifteen hundred?"

"That was Townsend, not Stanhope," King said.

"This way, Miss Thornton," Jared said. "I've reserved a booth at the back."

Before King could object, Jared had deftly disengaged Cass from his brother's touch.

15

Unlike King, Jared was very correct in his manner. He touched only the back of Cass's elbow as he showed her to the booth, seated her, and slid in beside her. King shot Jared a look of amused irritation, but took his seat alone on the opposite side of the booth without protest.

The table was already set with plates of cold chicken, sliced roast beef, and cold spring vegetables. The waiter was fussing with the cork of a bottle of red wine. King looked at the food in dismay.

"Jay, we ate enough for an army at Tan Feng's shindig," King protested.

"Miss Thornton wasn't so lucky. She didn't eat there, and John told me she hadn't eaten before she went."

"How did he know?" Cass asked. "I didn't say anything to him about missing supper."

Jared turned to her. "When I asked if you had eaten, he said there were no food smells in your rooms. Will you permit me to serve you, Miss Thornton?"

Cass felt her stomach stir gratefully at the prospect of food, for she hadn't eaten since morning. With a feeling of relief, she realized that a part of the lightheadedness that had been alarming her was a simple lack of food.

"Thank you," Cass said, meeting Jared's clear glance for the first time since sitting down. "It was very kind of you to think of it."

Broodingly, King watched as the waiter poured bright red wine into three crystal goblets. King stifled a flicker of irritation when Cass continued to look at Jared. King was accustomed to having a woman's undivided attention—or a man's, for that matter. It wasn't conceit on King's part that fed the expectation, it was simply the way people had always reacted to him.

Jared lifted his glass. "To Miss Thornton, not only beautiful, but also brave. Altogether, a very unusual lady."

Cass smiled slightly and shook her head as the two men drank to her. She didn't feel brave or unusual, much less beautiful. She felt tired and famished.

"To partnership in chicanery," toasted King with a grin, lifting his goblet. "Any trio who can fool an old shark like Tan Feng ought to take up confidence games for a living."

Both men touched glasses with Cass, sending a crystalline chime through the booth. Her smile slipped as the sound reminded her of Tea Rose's delicate golden bells and sensual laughter. Quickly, Cass bent her head and breathed in the wine's heady bouquet, banishing the remembered odor of incense. When she sipped, she couldn't conceal a small sound of pleasure. The wine was clean and complex, spreading through her like a sunrise, reviving her. She sipped again to savor the sensation before she set the wineglass aside. It would be foolish to drink too much or too quickly in Jared's presence. He saw too deeply into her, under normal circumstances. As for King—she had enough trouble keeping a proper distance from him, without having wine to addle her intelligence.

Through half-lowered eyelids, Cass watched while Jared dismissed the waiter and served her supper himself. It didn't surprise her that Jared was deft with the serving implements; what surprised her was the instinctive care he used in arranging colors and textures into a pleasing pattern on her plate. She couldn't help thinking that if King had arranged the plate so pleasingly, she wouldn't have been surprised. There was something in Kingston Duran's eyes when he was silent, hints of rainbow shadows and misty distance; he had the eyes of a poet or a visionary or a man who heard voices woven into the wind.

Yet, it was Jared who had thought of her hunger. It was Jared whose actions in placing food on her plate spoke of a sensibility that was frankly artistic. And it had been Jared who had touched her shoulder with a leashed sensuality that had shocked her.

Cass's stomach growled urgently, bringing her mind back to more practical matters. As she ate, Jared watched, taking vicarious pleasure in her appetite. King ignored both of them as he looked over the edge of the booth and slowly spun his empty wineglass in his fingers. Light flashed off the carved crystal surface of the forgotten goblet, sending brilliant rainbow shards scattering through the booth. The goblet looked small and fragile within his grip, for his hand was roughened by mining and scarred by accidents with pick or axe and brawls with knife and knuckles.

When the edge had been taken from Cass's hunger, she realized that Jared was watching her. She looked up, saw his clear approval of her appetite, and smiled. "Thank you again. I never would have expected such thoughtfulness from an empire builder."

"He's a clever devil, my brother is," King said, focusing on Cass with luminous green eyes. "Especially when he wants something."

"King doesn't know how to go after what he wants," Jared explained. "He's accustomed to having it handed to him. Comes of being born with the sun in his smile, I guess. People fall all over themselves to give King whatever he wants."

"Except for you," retorted King softly.

"Except for me," Jared agreed. "I was born with the ability to love my brother for what he is rather than what he seems to be. It's an ability women, in particular, seem to lack." Jared gave Cass a hooded look. "But we're making our guest uncomfortable. Forgive us, Miss Thornton. I have no excuse for my conduct, but you might be so kind as to chalk up King's forwardness to the effects of the rice wine. Then, too, tonight's small charade is the closest to excitement that he's come since he found his last hundred-dollar pan of gold. In its own way, adrenaline is even more addictive than opium, isn't it, King?"

King smiled, poured more wine for himself, and drank. "We fooled Tan Feng, and that's what counts," King said slowly, losing himself in the pure color of the wine as he held the glass up against the candlelight.

"How could you tell?" Cass asked as she delicately cut a piece of chicken, relieved by the change of subject.

"He offered me Lilac as an after-dinner mint." King heard Cass's sharply indrawn breath and winced. "Sorry, Cassie," he said, touching her hand. "I didn't mean to embarrass you." He smiled crookedly. "Jared's right. I've been stuck in civilization so long I'm going sour. I'm not fit company for man or beast, much less a decent woman such as yourself."

"It's all right," Cass said quickly, picking up her wineglass, aware of the faint heat on her cheeks. "Tea Rose—" Cass took a deep breath and tried again. "I'm sure Tea Rose has a rather frank appreciation of the facts of life. I can't mince words if I'm to raise her." She glanced at Jared. "Perhaps you could help me, Mr. Duran. You seem to know more about the life of a Chinese prosti—er, courtesan— such as Lilac than I do."

King's magical laughter rose above the confines of the booth, causing nearby people to turn and smile toward him in automatic benediction.

"I didn't mean that quite the way it sounded," muttered Cass, stabbing a piece of roast beef with unnecessary force.

"What is it about my relationship with Lilac that bothers you—the fact that she is your father's widow?" Jared asked calmly.

"No," retorted Cass. "It's the fact that decent men find it necessary not only to go to a prostitute, but to act as though she were grateful for their attentions. Tell me—do men honestly believe Lilac would tolerate their presence for ten seconds if she weren't forced to do so?"

King's mahogany eyebrows rose in surprise. Jared wasn't surprised; he had learned earlier that Cass had claws.

"Look and learn, brother," Jared said. "God gave decent women tongues like razors. They use them to guard their virtue."

"Virtue never interested me," King said lazily, "so I'm safe. That's why I get along with Tan Feng so well."

Jared's smile was a good deal less endearing than King's laughter had been.

"Don't trust Tan Feng," Jared said. "He may own Lilac's body, but he knows that her spirit is as free as yours."

The words were for King, but Jared had been looking at Cass when he spoke them. He picked up his wineglass and sipped, never taking his eyes from Cass's averted face. He set down the glass with a snap of his wrist, as though he had made a decision.

"I met Lilac years ago in Portland, in a tong hall, under circumstances very like the ones tonight," Jared said. "Tan Feng had something that I wanted—five hundred laborers. Lilac entertained us as she did tonight, singing and serving food, offering the men a glimpse of exotic femininity. Tan and I began bargaining, but failed to strike a deal. He offered me Lilac for the night. To refuse would have been as rude as emptying a chamber pot in the middle of the floor."

Head down, Cass tried to concentrate on her food, wondering why she kept baiting Jared on the subject of his relationship with Lilac.

"Even back then, I had considerable knowledge of Chinese customs, but I didn't know the language worth a damn," Jared continued. "I treated Lilac as the skilled, renowned courtesan she was. Do you remember, Miss Thornton, the differing rules under which courtesans, concubines, and sing-song girls operate?"

A curt nod was Cass's only answer. She refused to look up from the food on her plate.

"Lilac repaid my courtesy many times over. She taught me the intricacies of mah-jongg and Cantonese, which is the dialect the majority of the laborers speak. I also learned a bit of Mandarin, which is the dialect Tan Feng speaks."

Cass wondered if Chinese dialects were all that Lilac had taught Jared during the long hours of night, but she prevented herself from showing any curiosity.

"Tan Feng stalled for three days, and for three nights he sent Lilac to my room. I think he expected me to become so besotted with her skills that I would agree to any price for the laborers."

"That will be the day," King said. "You're all head and damned little—er, heart."

"Don't bet anything important on that," Jared advised without looking away from Cass. "Portland was the beginning of a long and very constructive relationship between Tan Feng and myself. And Lilac, of course."

"Of course," Cass said faintly.

Jared hid his smile behind his glass of wine. He knew he shouldn't bait Cass, but at least it kept her mind off King's damnably charming smile.

"Since then," Jared continued, "I've taken many lessons from Lilac. She is one of the most educated, shrewd, and insightful people I've ever met, man or woman. And one of the strongest. She's also a wicked mah-jongg player."

"Is that why you're helping her? You have difficulty finding, er, mah-jongg partners?"

"I have no trouble finding partners of any kind. I'm helping Lilac because it is the best way of eroding Tan's power over Chinatown. If the Chinese are ever to function fully in our society—which would benefit both cultures—the stranglehold of the tongs must be broken."

"How would stealing Tea Rose diminish Tan's power? She's just a child."

"Tea Rose is his most prized possession," Jared said succinctly. "Losing her to a white woman will cause Tan to lose face. Losing face will diminish Tan's power over his tong men. Without his private army, Tan is just one man.

Without Tan's shrewd generalship, the tong men are rabble. With the power of the tong broken, the Chinese business-men can come forward in safety and assume leadership of their people."

"I see." And she did. Jared was a man with a vision, and it was that vision that burned like an unshielded flame in his eyes. "I wish I were half as certain as you. Turning Tea Rose into an American child is going to be difficult, perhaps even impossible. But I have to try."

"You can't mean that you're really going to do it?" King said, staring at Cass.

"How could I not do it?" she asked simply.

King stared at her for a few moments longer before he smiled and drawled, "Well, Cassie, you could always run away to the north woods with me."

She threw up her hands in a gesture of humorous despair. "You'd have to take me to a place with no mirrors! I couldn't bear seeing my own reflection if I turned my back on Tea Rose." Then, quietly, Cass added, "She's my father's daughter, King. My sister."

For a minute, King simply stared at Cass while he spun the empty wineglass between his fingers with increasing speed until finally the faceted stem became little more than a brilliant blur of color and light.

"Round one to you, Jay," King said finally.

16

Cass glanced at Jared in surprise.

"We had a bet," he said, answering her unspoken question. "King couldn't believe you would take on the raising of a half-Chinese child. I knew you would."

"How?" she asked faintly, guessing the answer even before it came; Jared knew her far too well already—those damned unnerving eyes boring right into her soul.

"The *Pacific Winds* told me," Jared said whimsically, but

his eyes were clear, unflinching. "You photographed that old scow as carefully as though she were the last of the clipper ships. You have integrity, Cassandra. It's that simple."

King looked at the wineglass and sighed noiselessly, wishing that he could disagree with his brother's assessment of Cass. But King was too honest himself not to recognize integrity when he encountered it, so he wished instead that Cass were different, or he were different, or that her golden eyes didn't watch him with an intensity of which even she was unaware.

When King looked up, it was Jared watching him, reading his mind with those uncanny warlock's eyes. King tried to meet his brother's glance, but couldn't. An unspoken warning vibrated between them, a message that King didn't want to hear coming from himself, much less from his brother: *Leave her alone. She's not a toy or an amusement.*

Yet King hadn't met any woman who had half so much appeal for him.

A feeling of confinement throttled King, making his mouth flatten and his fingers clench around the delicate wineglass. He wanted to throw off the night like an ill-fitting coat, to stand up and walk out and not stop walking until nothing was in front of him but the north wind and the dawn giving birth to all possibilities.

Dammit, Cassie, don't lean toward me, don't look at me, don't let that full mouth soften into a smile when you watch my hands. You're not a sing-song girl, and I'm not a marrying man.

Jared's eyes narrowed as he watched the flattening line of King's mouth beneath the trim beard and the tension of his shoulders beneath his tailored suit. Then Jared turned his head and saw Cass studying King's hands with a soft little smile on her mouth, as though she had never seen anything quite so fascinating.

"You're taking a hell of a risk," Jared said flatly.

Cass's head snapped around, and she wondered how Jared had guessed her thoughts about King.

"Tea Rose may be only fourteen, but she's hardly a child,"

Jared continued. "If you have any reservations about taking her, let's talk about them right now. Tomorrow may be too late."

"Of course I have reservations," Cass said, setting aside her fork, no longer hungry. "Tea Rose is very—different. But she is also my father's daughter. I couldn't live with myself if I condemned her to a prostitute's existence." Cass took a deep breath. "God help me, I'm not sure what I'll do with Tea Rose, but I told Lilac I would take her out of Chinatown, and I will."

Jared stared at Cass, then nodded curtly. "All right. We'll bring Tea Rose out for you."

"No," Cass said quickly. "It's not your problem. It's mine. You've done more than enough already, and—"

"We've had more experience with mayhem than you have," Jared said, interrupting. "We'll take care of everything."

"You'll do no such thing," Cass said, pushing her plate away. She leaned forward and looked very hard at Jared. "I appreciate your offer, but I can't accept it. I simply can't impose on you in that way, Mr. Duran. It's my problem, not yours. After Tea Rose went back to Tan Feng, Lilac and I had a few minutes to talk," Cass said, speaking quickly, not wanting her own uncertainty to be sensed by Jared. "Our plan is simple, but it will work."

Jared poured himself more wine and sipped it slowly, saying nothing. King was equally silent. When it came to planning, Jared was the leader; he had the kind of mind that overlooked no detail, no matter how unimportant it might seem. When it came to charging hell with a bucket of water, King was the first man off the mark.

"All right," Jared said finally, his voice neutral. "Would you mind telling me what plan you and Lilac worked out before you came out to photograph the rest of the businessmen?"

Cass hesitated.

"Go ahead, Cassie," King said, yawning. "If he doesn't get it from you, he'll get it from Lilac later tonight."

It was on the tip of Cass's tongue to ask if Jared spent every night in Chinatown, but she refrained. Where Jared spent his nights was no business of hers.

"It's Lilac's plan, not mine," Cass said in a clipped voice. "Next Tuesday night is the Festival of the Good Lady. Apparently that's the one night in seven years when women are allowed to appear on the streets of Chinatown unescorted."

Jared nodded.

"At nine o'clock, I'm to meet Lilac and Tea Rose in the alley where the fishmongers have their stalls," Cass continued. "The alley is close to the edge of the International District. All Tea Rose will have to do is dash across the street and into a cab I'll have waiting there."

Jared frowned. "That sounds as though Lilac has already told Tea Rose about the plan."

"No." Cass frowned. "I'm not sure I understand her reasons, but Lilac was quite insistent. Tea Rose knows nothing."

"Good. That way, if anything goes wrong, Tea Rose won't be blamed. It will all be a complete surprise to her," Jared said. "No matter what the outcome, it will be Lilac who bears the force of Tan Feng's anger."

"No," Cass said firmly. "Lilac will escape with Tea Rose."

"What?" Jared asked, so startled that he forgot to keep his voice low. "Is that what Lilac said?"

Cass looked at Jared in surprise, "No, but it only makes sense. Lilac has as much right to freedom as Tea Rose. It will make things easier for Tea Rose as well. The white world will be strange to her, but she'll have her mother to—"

"No," Jared interrupted. His voice was flat, admitting not even the possibility of contradiction.

"I beg your pardon?" Cass said.

"You heard me. No."

"That's something for Lilac and me to decide, isn't it, Mr. Duran?" Cass said sharply.

"Lilac decided before you ever knew she existed. Lilac

won't come with you, Cassandra. She'll fight you tooth and nail to stay in Chinatown."

"That's absurd! Are you saying that she's so delighted with you and her other male 'guests' that she doesn't want to be free of you?"

"No," Jared retorted. "I'm saying Lilac knows that the daughter's only hope of freedom is if the mother remains captive. Tan Feng won't tolerate losing both of them."

"Tan Feng won't have to 'tolerate' anything. There's a small matter of the law, Mr. Duran. In America, it's against the law to keep slaves. Perhaps some of Seattle's policemen are as corrupt as Lilac believes, but not all of them are. I have a friend on the police force, a big strong Irishman who has been studying scientific investigation, including the use of photographs. He'll be more than happy to accompany me during the Festival of the Good Lady and to intervene if there's trouble from Tan Feng."

"Did you tell Lilac this?" Jared asked, appalled.

"No."

"Does she know you plan to steal her, too?"

"No."

"Thank God," Jared breathed. "That means they're both still alive."

Cass stared at Jared, realizing that his relief was as real as the food remaining on her plate. "Mr. Duran," she began, "what—"

"Jared," he said firmly. "Call me Jared, Cassandra. Partners in crime can't stand on formality. And have no doubt about it. We're partners for the duration of this particular crime."

"But—"

"No," he said, cutting her off. "It's your turn to listen, and to listen as though Tea Rose's and Lilac's lives depended on it. Because they do. Your friend on the police force may or may not be as honest as the day is long. It doesn't matter, because you're going to tell him nothing. You don't want to bet Tea Rose's and Lilac's lives on a cop's honesty or on his ability to keep his mouth shut about the most famous China girl on the West Coast. If even the smallest hint of what we're trying to do gets back to Chinatown, Tea Rose and Lilac are both dead."

"Tan Feng wouldn't—"

"He wouldn't get the chance," Jared said harshly, cutting across Cass's words. "Lilac would kill Tea Rose herself. Didn't Lilac tell you anything at all? Weren't you listening? What the hell were you doing for the five minutes and forty-eight seconds after Tea Rose left you alone and came back to Tan?"

" 'Five minutes and forty-eight seconds,' " repeated King, smiling. "And you looked so calm, too. No one would have guessed that—"

"Stow it," snarled Jared with a flashing sideways look.

King laughed softly, but said no more. Cass looked from one man to the other, not trusting herself to speak. For an instant she had seen the raw flame of Jared's unbridled temper; it was even more unsettling than the icy clarity of his eyes.

"Did Lilac tell you what she would do if you refused to take Tea Rose?" Jared asked, his voice calm, his eyes frighteningly intense.

"Yes, but—" began Cass.

"What did she say?" Jared demanded.

She felt her own temper slipping. Within the fragrant confines of Chinatown, Lilac's words had been believable. In the Delmonico's smoky den, they seemed impossible.

"Lilac said that she would kill Tea Rose," Cass said slowly.

"Do you believe her?"

Cass looked at the flame burning deep within Jared's eyes, and for an instant she was back in Chinatown, where life and death were so very different. Slowly Cass nodded; looking at Jared, she could believe again.

Jared let out a breath of relief. "Well, that's a start. Now, you've got to believe that if anything, and I mean anything, about this gets back to Tan Feng, Lilac will strangle Tea Rose and then kill herself. You are her last hope."

"Then why didn't she come to me sooner?"

"I asked her the same thing."

"And?"

Jared shrugged. "She simply looked at me and didn't answer. Frankly, it doesn't matter, now. Tea Rose will be stolen, and Lilac will remain behind as a small sop to Tan Feng's 'face.' Yes," he said harshly, answering Cass's unasked question. "It's necessary. Otherwise, Tan Feng will have no choice but to send his hatchet men to steal back or to kill both Lilac and Tea Rose, and everything we've accomplished up to that point will be lost."

"That's—" Cass tried to continue, but she felt as though all breath had been wrung from her body.

"Terrible?" offered Jared coldly. "Ghastly? Reprehensible? Yes, all of those and more besides. But not unbelievable, Cassandra. Don't comfort yourself and kill both Lilac and Tea Rose by refusing to believe me."

When Cass would have spoken, he cut her off with a curt gesture and turned away. Only then did she realize that a waiter was approaching.

"More wine, sir?"

"Yes," said King.

"No," said Jared. "Coffee. Black."

Calmly, King said, "I'll have cognac with mine. Cassie, what about you?"

She simply shook her head.

"You must understand Tan Feng's position," Jared continued quietly, after the waiter had withdrawn. "He is a Manchu warlord in a society of anti-Manchu rebels. He rules by force. He has no choice. It's the same way the Manchus have ruled all of China for three hundred years. But Tan is a politician as well as a warrior, in the same way that all powerful men must be politicians."

Cass watched intently and said nothing.

"Tan will tell himself and his men that Tea Rose's loss is a minor thing. Technically, she is still a child," Jared said. "To be blunt, she's still a virgin, rather more in the position of a daughter than a concubine. Daughters have little impact on a man's standing with other men. The addition or loss of a daughter from a man's family isn't a matter of real importance. At least, that's the tack Tan will take; it's the one that will cost him the least face with his men.

"Lilac's loss would be different. She is Tan Feng's most famous possession. If she ran away from him and made it stick, it would be an enormous and probably fatal loss of face for him. He would be the laughingstock of the Chinese. His enemies would assume that he had lost his grip on power. His own men would begin to push hard, testing for further areas of weakness. Very quickly, Tan Feng would find himself fighting for his life."

"All because there is one less sing-song girl in his stable? That doesn't make sense," Cass said. "Tan Feng might be arrogant, but he certainly isn't a fool."

"Exactly," Jared said. "Tan Feng isn't a fool. Lilac is as famous among the Chinese here as Lily Langtry is in the white West. Lilac's fame is also Tan Feng's. The more she is praised, the more Tan Feng's face is enhanced. He can't afford to let Lilac escape. He would be forced to track her down and kill her simply to ensure his own survival. There are too many very tough tong men sniffing the air, waiting for the first sign that Tan Feng is losing his ability to hold them at bay." Jared grimaced and added, "If Lilac fled, you would be in danger, too. You're a woman alone in a world run by men. As such, you are—vulnerable."

"Tan Feng wouldn't dare attack a white woman, Jay, and you know it," King said. "Quit scaring Cassie."

Jared spun toward King so quickly that Cass flinched.

"Save your fairy tales for children," Jared said icily. "You know nothing about Chinatown beyond opium and three sing-song girls in your bed at once. Do you think Tan Feng has access only to tong men? Last week, a decent white woman was beaten half to death by a white thug looking for easy money. If that happened to Cassandra, would anyone outside Chinatown connect it to Tan Feng?"

King's eyes narrowed. For an instant, he looked as dangerous as he had when flash powder exploded and tong men leaped toward Cass.

"If I connected it, there would be some dead Chinks," King said matter-of-factly. "Tan Feng would be the first."

"I don't doubt it." Jared's smile was as cold as his eyes. "I also don't doubt that it would be a lot easier on Cassandra if a little dose of common sense made all the masculine heroics unnecessary."

King smiled, then laughed reluctantly. "You do have a way of taking all the fun out of life, little brother. But I agree. Nobody should lay a hand on Cassie's body—at least, not in anger," he amended, giving Cass a slow, off-center smile.

The waiter's return prevented the sharp retort Jared had on his tongue. He watched impatiently while the waiter set down three coffees and one cognac, picked up dirty dishes, and left.

"If you go to Chinatown with me," Jared said, looking straight at King, "you'll go under my orders or not at all. Your kind of hell-for-leather recklessness could get someone killed."

King picked up the brandy, swirled the liquid in its crystal balloon glass, inhaled, and said nothing.

"Are you in or out?" Jared asked flatly.

For a few more moments, King contemplated the cognac as it twisted candlelight into streamers of gold exactly the color of Cass's eyes. He inhaled again, trying to think of anything but the scented warmth that had curled up from her nape, awakening all of his senses to her presence.

"Are you sure you want me around?" King asked Jared, giving a quick sideways glance at Cass.

"I'm sure I need you," Jared said.

"That's not quite the same thing, is it?"

"No. It's not."

King closed his eyes and sighed almost wearily. "Know something, little brother? Sometimes, I wish to hell it was fifteen years ago, and we were up to our haunches in ice water with our first big gold strike ahead of us."

"Time only runs one way, King."

"Yeah." King's eyes opened, and his smile flashed. "Hell of a thing, time." He drank the cognac with a reckless snap of his wrist. When he set the snifter down, he met his brother's eyes without flinching. "All right, Jay. I'm in, and let the devil take the hindmost."

17

The knock on the front door startled Cass. She jumped, dropping the pillowcase she had just taken from the laundry basket. She snatched the linen from the floor and went to the door. Just as she reached for the carved glass doorknob, she remembered Jared's warning about the vulnerability of a woman living alone.

"Who is it?" she asked.

"It's all right, Cassie. It's just me."

Even before she recognized King's voice, she knew who it was; he was the only person alive who called her Cassie. After a moment's despairing thought for her rumpled appearance, Cass flicked aside the deadbolt and opened the door with a smile of welcome.

"What are you doing out and about so early on a Sunday morning?" she asked.

King's green glance took in Cass's state of easy deshabille. Her bright gold hair struggling free of its confining knot made a lovely foil for her chemical-stained shirt and faded skirt, knotted at one knee to keep the floor-length hem from getting in her way as she went about her housework. King barely noticed the stains or wet spots where she had bent over a washboard to clean her clothes. He had eyes only for the swell of her breasts pushing against the unstarched cotton shirt and the pronounced inward curve of her waist. When he got to shapely bare calves and equally bare feet, he laughed softly.

"Cassie, you're enough to tempt a saint."

"Then I won't have any difficulty, will I? All the saints are in church at the moment." Her welcoming smile faded. "Is everything all right?"

"You mean about Tuesday?"

She nodded.

"Don't worry, sugar. Jared will take care of everything."

"Mr. Duran," began Cass firmly, only to laugh in spite of herself when King looked over his shoulder as though expecting to find his brother there. "All right. Kingston," she conceded, clinging to the more formal version of King's Christian name. "But please, don't call me sugar or—" Her voice faded in exact proportion to the flush climbing her cheeks.

"Don't rush you?" King offered.

Cass looked at him through long amber lashes. He was relaxed and engaging in casual clothes, carrying a bright wool jacket over his arm, his smile like a piece of barely tamed sunlight. "Yes," she said quietly. "I like you, Kingston," she said in a matter-of-fact voice, "but as Jared pointed out, a woman alone is vulnerable. I live alone because the studio I rented came with an apartment overhead, not so that I can, er, entertain male callers whenever the mood strikes."

King's smile faded, leaving only the vivid green of his eyes to animate his face. "I know you're a good woman, if that's what worries you, Cassie." He hesitated, then made an odd, almost helpless gesture with his right hand as he added, "And I know I'm not a 'good' man."

"That's what worries me," Cass admitted. "Oh, I know you're a gentleman. It's just—"

He waited, then prompted softly, "What?"

"You're very attractive," she said simply, "and I'm feeling a little off balance anyway, what with becoming a mother and all."

"A mother!" King said, his eyes going immediately to her waist as though to ascertain how pregnant she might be.

"Yes. Tea Rose will be more my child than my sister."

King tilted back his head and laughed in delight. "Lord, Cassie," he said, "you're good for what's ailing me."

"What's that?"

"Boredom. Too many pinched white faces and brick buildings. That's why you're coming to the races with me."

"I am?" she asked, perplexed by his non sequitur.

King nodded. "I'll bet you're going crazy here, waiting and worrying, knowing there's not a damned thing you can do until Tuesday night."

"Oh, I can wash and iron and clean, and buy a second dresser and bed frame and mattress," Cass said, ticking off each task on her fingers. "Then I can—"

"But you'd rather go to the boat races with me," King interrupted smoothly. As he spoke, he pulled out his watch with its heavy gold-nugget chain, glanced at the time and then at Cass again. "If you hurry, you've got just enough time to comb your hair and put on shoes."

"I think it would be better if I stayed here."

"Would it help to know that Jared will be there, too?"

"Why should that make a difference?"

"I thought you might prefer him to me," King said, his voice dropping as he allowed the Southern cadences of his youth to emerge. "He's much more substantial than I am. I'm just an adventurer and a gold-hunter."

"Do tell," Cass retorted, shooting a look at King's clothes. Though he was casually dressed, the clothes were quite costly. "A woman would be hard put to decide which of you Durans was more outrageous—Jared with his emperor complex or you with that honey-lickin' drawl and wicked laugh."

For an instant, King's eyes widened in astonishment, then laughter overtook him. "Ah, Cassie, I really should leave you for Jared. You'd take the starch out of his collar in nothing flat and make him into a Rebel wildcat again."

"Mr. Duran—Kingston. This may come as an unhappy surprise to you, but I'm not yours to take or to leave for your brother."

King looked into Cass's determined eyes and felt both amusement and curiosity; she was unlike the women he had been accustomed to. In many ways, she reminded him of the Southern women he had known who had shed their silk ball gowns and taken up homespun and rifles for the duration of the Civil War. Yet Cass wasn't hard, wasn't desperate, wasn't visibly fighting for her life. She was simply accustomed to depending upon no one but herself.

"You know, if you were a man, you'd make one hell of a good trail partner," King said.

Cass blinked. "Thank you—I think."

"You're welcome. Now, go get some shoes on or we'll be late." He saw her refusal and spoke before she could. "Jared has some plans to discuss, and there's no better time or place. Steamer races to Tacoma are about as exciting as ferry rides to Tacoma, which is what they are. But Jared said to tell you that he could guarantee you some great photos of the finish because we're going to be aboard the winner of the race."

"The winner? How can you guarantee that?"

"I just acquired a one-tenth interest in the *Alki Point Flyer*. The captain knows if he doesn't win, I'll lose a potful of money and fire him."

"Are you ever serious?" Cass said, struggling not to smile.

King's eyes gleamed with amusement and something more. "Sugar," he drawled, "gold is as serious as I get. If I don't win, the *Flyer*'s captain will be giving orders to a garbage scow."

Cass started to object again to being called "sugar," then gave up. She decided that such familiarity was simply part of King's normal speech patterns; he meant nothing especially personal by the endearment.

Telling herself that she was reassured rather than disappointed by her insight into King, Cass smiled at the mahogany-haired whirlwind with the Southern drawl and the callused hands that had held a crystal goblet with such offhand skill.

"All right," Cass said. "Give me a few minutes to get ready, and we're off to the races."

King reached out and wound a stray lock of her hair around his finger. He smiled slowly, enjoying the rise of color beneath her clear skin. She was a woman drawn in tempting shades of gold, and he was a man who had always loved gold.

Although King knew he shouldn't tease Cass, he also knew he wasn't going to stop. Teasing and touching her was too rewarding a pastime for him to abandon it for the few remaining days he would be held captive in Seattle's over-civilized domain. Little harm could come from the flirtation because he would be gone before she became too tempting for his uncertain self-discipline. Despite his wildness, he had never seduced a good woman, and he had no intention of starting with Cassandra Thornton.

"Don't be long, Cassie," King said in a deep voice, releasing her long strand of hair, letting it slide slowly between his fingers. "I'm a restless kind of man."

18

Match races among the boats of the Mosquito Fleet were Seattle's peculiar addition to the ancient aristocratic sport of yacht racing. The match races were a mixture of nouveau riche self-indulgence and hard-headed practicality; the fastest boat won shipping contracts as well as local fame. The contestants were steam launches, tugs, ferries, and freight haulers. The latter were all-purpose boats that carried passengers and freight around Puget Sound six days a week. On the seventh day, the boats churned at top speed over precisely the same routes for the pure, unrestrained hell of it.

The races were regular summer spectacles that Cass had tried to record in the past. The resulting photographs had been unsatisfactory to her. They had lacked an indefinable something that she had never been able to pinpoint. But it would be different from the bow of the *Alki Point Flyer;* she knew it as soon as she looked through the camera lens.

Cass was in the middle of a logjam made of living ships. All around were rust-bucket working boats and stylish pleasure craft churning the bright waters of Elliott Bay into myriad shades of blue while captains of six of the fastest steam launches on the Pacific Coast maneuvered for position. Whistles screeched, deck bells clanged as urgently as fire alarms, crewmen shouted and cursed each other and the weekend sailors who didn't know a mast from a wharf piling. On the deck of the elegant *Snohomish Pride,* a ten-piece brass band wailed through a ragtime tune for the entertainment of the fashionable ladies and gentlemen aboard, who toasted the band and the racing day with champagne the color of winter sunlight.

"I suppose you own a piece of the *Flyer,* too," Cass said to Jared as she accepted a new film holder from him.

"No," Jared replied, stretching his arms over his head and rolling his shoulders to relax muscles tightened by counting off the hours until the Festival of the Good Lady. "I'm just like you—along for the ride. King can mix business with pleasure but I've never been able to. I'd need a better reason than a hundred-dollar bet to blow a thousand-dollar boiler trying to win a race."

"What about being known as the best?" she asked. "Isn't that worth something?"

"Is it? Do you really give a tinker's damn about what other people think?" Jared asked, rubbing his neck with one hand and loosening his tie with the other.

"I have to care what people think," Cass said. "My reputation is my living."

He watched while she adjusted the legs of the tripod and sighted through the ground glass to compose a picture. She had taken off her broad-brimmed hat, fearing it would be lost in the wind. As a result, her long blond hair was already unraveling into charming disarray. As she emerged from the black hood, she tucked loose strands behind her ears with an automatic gesture that stemmed from necessity rather than vanity; flying hair got in her way as a photographer.

"But if you really cared what people thought, you wouldn't be a photographer living alone," Jared said quietly. "You would be a wife and a mother, and you would live under a man's protection."

Cass shrugged. "Someday, I'll do those things, too."

"When?"

"I don't know. There are too many other things I want to do first, too many pictures I have to take." Cass looked intently past her camera, out to the chaotic pageant of the bay and the invisible ocean beyond. "I'm living on the edge of a continent and at the end of a century. Everything is changing so fast. If I don't grab hold of the present, if I don't catch and fix it in pictures, it's gone for all time."

"Is that bad?" Jared asked, rolling up his shirt-sleeves to reveal forearms surprisingly powerful for a man who wore business suits with such ease.

"Yes."

"Why?"

Unconsciously, Cass caught her lower lip between her teeth, trying to put into words things that were so much a part of her that she rarely thought about them at all.

"When I traveled with Papa all over the West," Cass said slowly, "nothing was fixed. Everything changed from year to year, towns springing up and dying, and the wagon moving and the dust blowing. Only his photographs stayed the same. They became more real to me than the gold camps we visited. The photos would be there next year, unchanged, and the year after that and the year after that. The towns wouldn't be there. All the people, all the hopes, all the dreams—just gone—dust on the wind." Her eyes darkened, narrowed, and her chin lifted in unconscious determination. "It shouldn't be like that. There must be more to life than dust and wind. I can't stop time, but I can save pieces

130

of it so that other people in other times can know what it was like to be alive before the century died."

"History books without words," Jared said softly.

"Yes, exactly! There's so much to catch, so much going on, so much change. I don't believe there's ever been a time or place like this before on earth. You talked of the Chinese and their history stretching back over thousands of years. In America, we have no such deep roots in time. We have only a few frontier stories and a handful of photographs. We need more, much more. Life moves so fast here."

Jared watched Cass intently. As she talked about history and photography and time, her face was transformed. Excitement glowed in her eyes and animated her gestures. In an odd way, she reminded him of King on the scent of a new gold strike—vivid, incandescent, seething with energy.

"Maybe that's why we invented photography and the Chinese didn't," Jared said. "There are wars or famines there, but the same villages remain, the same family names, the same culture. Yesterday and today and tomorrow, time without end."

The words drew Cass toward Jared as though toward a fire in the middle of night. In her life, she had spoken to only a few people about her private beliefs; no one but her father had ever understood. And now Jared.

"It's different on the Golden Mountain," Cass said, gesturing around herself with a sweep of her hand. "Who could have predicted steamboats running sailboats right off the rim of the world? Who could have predicted railroads stitching the two edges of the continent together? A hundred years ago, Seattle was an unpronounceable name. Now it's a city. What will it become a hundred years from now? What will its citizens do and think and be?"

"I imagine they'll be men pretty much like other men— good and bad, greedy and generous, stupid and wise."

"And women," Cass said. "Don't be like the Chinese and forget that without women, their history is finished."

Jared smiled. "I doubt that there will be many women like you. Not in any time or place."

She was startled into silence for a moment, then smiled almost shyly at Jared. Before she could say anything, King's voice intervened, calling for Jared. He ignored the call.

"Kingston wants you," Cass said.

"He probably just needs more money."

"You make it sound as though he were profligate," Cass said, turning back to her equipment.

"He is. He doesn't like money. He gets rid of it as fast as he can dig it out of the ground."

She frowned. "That doesn't make sense."

"He can't bear chains of any kind," Jared said softly, "even those made of solid gold."

Cass knew that Jared was warning her not to become attached to King. It made her angry.

"I don't think Kingston is such a grasshopper as you make him seem," Cass said evenly.

"Grasshopper? Hardly. A horde of locusts, perhaps, or a Blue Norther, or a wildfire."

"What has your brother done to you that you dislike him so much?"

"Dislike?" Jared smiled almost sadly and shook his head. "I don't dislike King. I simply understand him." Jared pinned Cass with an intent look. "I wish I could give that understanding to you, but I can't, can I? And each time I try, I drive you closer to him. Such a beautiful moth to be burned in such a careless flame—" He looked around him at the bay and the churning ships. "Take your photographs while you can, Cassandra. Dip a cupful of instants out of the river Time and freeze them, to brood and smile over forever. We'll talk about Tea Rose later."

Jared didn't wait for Cass's response. He simply withdrew to a nearby spot and leaned on his elbows against the railing, his jacket thrown carelessly over his shoulder. The sun was like Cass, warm, and heedless of where that warmth fell. He let the heat seep into him while the rest of the world buzzed and chattered and swirled around him. Little by little, he filtered out the sounds and motions, fixing his eyes instead on a future only he could see, a time when the gold that had been dug from stubborn, icy streams would be transformed into an empire that would stitch together both sides of the Pacific Ocean as surely as the railroad had joined both sides of a wild continent.

For a while, Cass continued taking photographs, glancing from time to time at Jared as though trying to pierce his silence to the man who lay beneath. He stood motionless, knowing only his own thoughts, indifferent to the shouts and festival atmosphere around him.

Gradually, Cass found herself staring openly at Jared. With his collar open and his sleeves rolled up, he looked somehow both more relaxed and more formidable than he had with cuffs and tie in place. The cords of muscle in his neck were thrown into relief by sunlight and underlined by shadow. His profile was clean-cut, and his dark brown hair stirred in the wind streaming over the bow.

On an impulse, Cass reached down and pulled the small Kodak box camera from her trunk. She moved soundlessly until she was close enough to capture Jared on film. As silent as he, she composed the elements of foreground and background in the viewfinder and snapped the picture. The metallic rustle of the shutter was very faint, as was the sound of Cass winding film.

But Jared heard both. He turned toward her. The new angle made his eyes catch and hold sunlight like finely cut crystal, burning against the darkness of his face. Instantly, Cass took another picture, then advanced the film to take one more.

"Why?" Jared asked.

Cass looked up from the camera, surprised. "I take pictures for a living, remember?"

"I'm not a racing ship."

"No, but you'd make a darn fine prow," she answered.

Jared's laughter was both rueful and relaxed. "Prows see into the future, Cassandra. I'd think a woman with your name would appreciate that."

"The only 'seeing' I do is through the lens." She met his glance squarely. "I also think that it's the only kind of seeing that matters. No one can predict the future, Jared. Towns change. Times change. People change."

"The reality of moth and flame never changes."

"Tell me about yourself and Kingston," Cass said, changing the subject in a firm tone of voice.

"Both of us, or just King?" Jared asked dryly.

"Are you always this—this—"

"Direct?"

"Actually, rude was the word hovering on the tip of my tongue," Cass said, but she did so without heat. The Jared who was watching her now was unthreatening, his intensity only a memory, as though the sun's warmth had ripened and mellowed him. "Which part of the South are you from?"

"Georgia," Jared said, purposely letting the soft, unhurried accents of his youth reclaim his voice. "We Durans are from the ruined section of that state, and frankly, glad to be gone. At least I am. King will have to speak for himself."

"I thought all Southerners were incurable romantics who wanted to fight the Civil War over and over again until they finally won."

Jared smiled sadly. "The only men I ever heard carry on like that were the ones that never smelled burnt powder on a battlefield. Pa got a thumb shot off at Bull Run, but found more honor in the scars he had from farming and breeding buggy horses. The Durans never owned slaves and never planted cotton, so the Old South really wasn't ours to win or lose. We sure as hell lost everything else, though. Carpetbaggers didn't much care what crops a man grew when it came time to steal land."

Pausing, Jared wondered if he should tell Cass about the particular carpetbagger who had learned just how much "free" land could cost. After a moment's reflection, Jared decided to keep the knowledge to himself; it would do Cass little good to know that the two men she was counting on for help had been tried for murder and acquitted only when a mob had gathered and demanded their freedom.

"After Pa and Mama died of the ague, King and I chased

sunsets for a long time. I wanted a place to get rich and build for the future. King wanted gold. The West had both. We never looked back."

"Gold," Cass murmured. Her voice was husky with memories, making the word close to a sigh. "Papa used to call gold the engine of history, driving men hither and yon, dragging civilization after them."

"King hates civilization," Jared said, "but gold is his Holy Grail."

"But you said he threw gold away as fast as he could find it," she protested.

"That's the problem with gold," Jared said dryly. "It's not the Holy Grail. Mortal man can't find the Grail, but he can find gold. Then he has to find something else to search for, some other engine to drive his life. King solves that problem by finding gold and then throwing it away damn near as fast as he digs it out. It's the searching he loves, and the sheer exhilaration of finding something everyone else is looking for. But keeping the stuff?" Jared shook his head. "If he kept his gold, he'd have no reason to look for it, would he? So he doesn't keep it."

"What about you? Do you like looking for gold?"

"I did, once. Then I found it." Jared shrugged. "After that, I became just another pair of strong shoulders to run the Sierra rocker. I shouted as loud as the next man when I saw the gold caught in the riffles, but gold wasn't my succubus. It's different for King. He loves gold the way most men love a woman. He can go on for hours about gold— how you find it, how it looks in the bottom of a panful of black sand, how it feels in your palm."

Jared smiled slowly, remembering King's wild pleasure. "Gold loves King in return," he continued softly. "It calls to him like a woman to her lover, tells him all its secrets, pushes itself into his hands. I've never seen anything like it. I could put King in a group of a hundred men and walk them all over the same piece of countryside. If gold were there, King would be the one to find it. He's uncanny." Jared laughed shortly. "Hell, he's famous: The Man Who Found the El Dorado of the North. That's the name some idiot reporter put on a gravel bar in the middle of Grey's Creek over in Idaho."

"The El Dorado of the North?" Cass asked, excitement lilting in her voice. "That sounds fantastic. I wish I'd been there to photograph it."

"Grey's Creek is a pretty little thing—clear, clean water alive with trout and surrounded by some of the biggest Douglas firs I've ever seen. But by the standards of the West, the El Dorado of the North was a middling strike at best. King and I took out our share of dust and nuggets from the first claim, but half of the gold went to the man who had grubstaked us. The rest of the stream yielded nearly a million that first year to other prospectors, but it played out pretty quickly after that."

"Tell her the rest of the story, Jay," said King's voice. "The part where you came in and made me look like a fool."

Cass turned quickly, smiling into emerald eyes that gleamed back at her as though they shared a private joke.

"You see, Cassie. It's always that way. I seduce the gold from the ground, and Jared makes a fortune. He turned his half of the Grey's Creek take into railroads and ships and all the rest, while I've not got much more to show for it than I did when I walked out of the Bitterroots with scars on my hands and my feet aching from standing in ice water."

"And you've worked very hard to make sure it stays that way. You like hunting gold too well to be tied down by money," Jared said, but there was as much affection as disapproval in his voice.

It was the same for King, who gave Jared a cuff on the shoulder that would have staggered a smaller man. Then King lifted his hat and bowed in acknowledgment of his brother's words. Sunlight glinted like gold dust in King's mahogany hair. "So you keep telling me, little brother."

"But if you had already spent all your gold, how did you get part-ownership in this boat?" Cass protested.

"A busted flush and God's own bluff," King said, laughing again.

"What?"

"Five-card stud at the J & M last night. He'll probably lose the boat tonight at the same table." Jared stretched into the sun again, his head thrown back in pure sensual enjoyment of the warmth. "The only thing that keeps me from envying King's Midas touch in the wilderness is the fact that he uses up all his luck with gold. Cards run cold for him more often than not. As for business—" Jared smiled ruefully and shook his head.

"He's slandering me, Cassie," King said, yawning and stretching as Jared had. "Why, just this morning at breakfast, he told me that he'd probably end up as poor as I am by next week if this crazy railroad deal of his doesn't pan out."

Jared made a lazy swipe at King's chin, missing it and not caring a bit. "I never said I didn't gamble, brother. Just that we do our gambling at different tables, with different packs of cards."

"Yeah, and different packs of wolves, too," King replied. "Frankly, I prefer the frontier wolf that takes you head on and rips your throat out with his teeth. The ones who sneak up behind and stab you in the back with accountant's pencils are too vicious for me."

Jared gave King an amused glance that turned into laughter. Jared knew that he and King were very different people, becoming more different each day, but so far the winds of change had done nothing more than ruffle the surface of the deep reservoir of past experiences and love they shared as brothers.

King felt the same way, whether or not he ever thought about it. At a visceral level, King understood the emotion that bound him to Jared; and King sensed he would never be that close to another human being again. That was one of the reasons he had almost left town when he had seen Cass, wanted her, and discovered that Jared wanted her, too. But King hadn't gone, and it appeared that Cass wasn't going to be held against him.

Smiling, King put an arm around Jared's shoulders in a hard hug. For an instant, the two Durans looked fifteen years younger as they stood on the deck of the *Flyer* and smiled at each other with open camaraderie. The camera shutter snicked and slithered as Cass caught an instant of a past that would never come again.

19

For the first half hour of the race to Tacoma, Cass shot frame after frame of the steamers and spectator fleet. By the time the *Flyer* rounded Duwamish Head and turned for Alki Point, the contestants were so spread out across the surface of the Sound that she could no longer pull them in with her lens. Abandoning the camera, she put her fists in the small of her back, arched and rubbed hard, easing aching muscles.

"Finished?" asked Jared.

"For now." She sighed and looked around.

"King's taking bets on the afterdeck. It's less windy there."

Cass's mouth tightened in irritation; she hadn't known she was looking for King until Jared had pointed it out. Without a word, she turned away and closed up her equipment. When she had finished, Jared escorted her to the afterdeck, where King and the thirty other spectators aboard the *Flyer* had gathered. There, she sat with Jared at a table beneath a green and white awning, drank a glass of cold beer and made desultory conversation while she watched King.

He stood a few feet away, the center of a rowdy group. While their women watched, the men swapped jokes, meaningless insults, and occasional bets. One of the men had drunk more than his share of beer. The jokes he insisted on telling had passed from risqué through bawdy to raw. Cass tried to ignore what she couldn't help overhearing, but she knew that her cheeks were flushed with more than the sun.

Deliberately, she focused on the endless reflections of sky and rugged coastline on the sea's ruffled surface.

"King," Jared called out, his voice cutting easily through the slurred words of the storyteller. "What time is it?"

King turned and looked easily over the heads of his companions. "Did your watch stop?"

"Nope," Jared drawled. "I'm just too lazy to pull it out of my pocket right now."

Laughing, King reached into a pocket and pulled out what looked like a handful of gold. As he separated the watch case from the chain, the words of the tasteless story disappeared beneath the murmurs of delight and astonishment that came from the people who gathered even closer to King.

Nuggets suspended from the watch chain turned and glimmered, taking sunlight and turning it into liquid gold. There were six large nuggets and many smaller ones. The biggest nugget was the size of a plump Georgia peanut, shell and all. The others graded down in size to that of a small marble. The smallest nuggets, the size of flattened split peas, had been soldered between links of the watch chain itself.

"I didn't know gold came in that many colors," said a young woman, watching King with wide blue eyes that reflected the gleam of gold.

"Depends on where the nuggets come from," King said, smiling down at her. "Each placer is different, because no two veins of gold are exactly alike. You see, gold combines with other metals. If there's silver, the gold is light-colored. If there's copper, the nuggets come up a kind of fiery bronze that's as pretty as your hair."

She slanted King a pleased, flirtatious look. Her dense black eyelashes were those of a woman accustomed to stage makeup. "May I?" she asked in a low voice, reaching for the chain.

"I'll hold it while you look," King said, smiling to take the edge off his refusal to let go of the chain. "It's heavier than you'd think. Besides, I'm kind of superstitious about letting it out of my hands. This chain is my luck. I've got a nugget from every placer I ever found that was worth cleaning out."

As King spoke, he gently shook out the chain, holding an end in each hand. The motion set each of the large nuggets to gently swaying.

"This one," King said, pointing to a pink-gold nugget that was the size of a rumpled, fat pea, "came from the Black Hills."

"Did you have to fight Indians?" she asked, wide-eyed.

"No, sugar," King said gravely. "I left that to General Custer. I just panned gold and ran like hell."

With a combination of laughter and bated breath, the people around King urged him to tell more of the story of the watch chain. After a few moments, he laughed and gave in.

While King spoke, gold links and nuggets slipped through his fingers as though he were an earnest Catholic telling his rosary. Names such as Tofino and Bitterroot and Similkameen flowed from his lips, and with them came other names, names rarely spoken in cities, names given by prospectors to tiny creeks on the far side of mountains most people had never heard of. King told of simple hardships and extraordinary results, of men who had walked barefoot through snow and had gone home on crutches with the pockets of their pants torn out by the weight of the gold they had carried.

When King paused and fell silent, someone asked the question that was in the eyes of everyone who had seen the big nugget hanging from the watch chain.

"The big one, King. Where did it come from?"

Without even looking at the chain, King found the heavy nugget with his fingertips and stroked it delicately.

"This old goober?" he asked, as though he weren't certain which nugget hadn't yet had its story told.

There was a chorus of eager agreement. King didn't seem to hear. His emerald eyes were smoky and unfocused as he looked into the past, remembering the season and the day, the hour and the exact instant he had become The Man Who Found the El Dorado of the North.

"It was coming onto summer, and I'd finally talked my

brother into going fishing with me up in British Columbia. Jay didn't believe me about the fishing part, of course. He knew I was broke and thought I was haring after gold again." King laughed richly. "Jay was right. But he grubstaked us anyway, gathered all our supplies, bought pack horses and saddle horses, and gave orders like the general he is."

Cass turned toward Jared, but if he resented King's description, nothing of that emotion showed. Jared was looking at his brother and smiling like a man watching a healthy young animal at play.

"Jay left China John to run his business and took off, swearing that it was the last time he was going to be damfool enough to go 'fishing' in wild country with me. He kept on me about trout every foot of the way, needling me about catching fish with a gold pan and using gravel for bait."

King threw back his head and laughed in delight, sharing with everyone who heard him the pure joy he took in remembering each event that had led to the discovery of gold.

"Well, I dragged Jay about halfway up a little creek that an old prospector by the name of Grey had told me about. It was past high summer by now, and there was hardly enough water in that crick to float a baby trout, which Jay pointed out to me about once every ten minutes. I ignored him and kept on turning over rocks like I was looking for caddis bugs to use as bait. Jay was just telling me that I'd be better off frying up a mess of the caddis for our dinner 'cause there sure as hell weren't no trout around, when I turned over a big rock, and there the nugget was, shining up at me—"

King paused and looked at the piece of gold swinging heavily from the chain. "You know, my mama used to read to me from a book of myths. One of my favorites was about a boy who made wings and flew so close to the sun that the wings burned and he died. I used to dream of that, of touching something so perfect that I burned up and died of it like Icarus.

"When I got older, I discovered that a man didn't have to go to all that trouble just to touch the sun. There are tears of the sun lying cool and smooth and shiny in creeks all over the West. All you have to do is turn over a few rocks and you can hold it all in your hands, the sun and the myth and the dream—"

There were deep sounds of pleasure and near-reverence from the men who watched King's hands and the heavy, tangible sunlight held captive within.

"You mean you find nuggets just laying around?" a young logger asked, looking at his own callused hands as if to ask where he had gone wrong.

There was a moment of silence before the question penetrated King's reverie. When it did, he looked at the young man and smiled an off-center, lazy kind of smile.

"That's right," King said. "I find gold lying around just the same way you go out in the forest and find those big, old Doug firs all neatly felled, peeled, sawed, and stacked up waiting to be sold to city folks by the board foot. No work at all to getting rich."

Everyone laughed, and the logger's laugh was loudest of all.

"I hear that the good strikes have already been made, and there's nothing left but dirt even a Chinaman wouldn't bother with," said the woman whose hair looked like red gold. "What do you think, King?"

"I think there's a lot more gold out there," he said slowly, looking toward the north, "gold lying like the world's most beautiful woman beneath a thousand silky veils of water, just waiting for me to come along and uncover her."

"Then how come you're here and not out hunting more gold?" demanded the man who had drunk too much.

King smiled oddly. "That's a question I've been asking myself about ten times a day lately," he admitted, holding the watch chain up to the sun, letting all the shapes and colors of nuggets catch the light.

The sight of the gold acted like champagne on the people, raising their temperatures, making their eyes shine, sending frissons of anticipation over their bodies.

A man who had been walking alone on the deck stopped and stared, riveted by the sight of the gold dangling from King's fingers. The man's hair and beard had been recently trimmed, his face was weathered, his shirt and suit were obviously new, and his hands looked decades older than the rest of him did. Without apology, he pushed through the group of people until the nuggets were barely inches from his eyes. He studied the nuggets carefully and then began to say names in a voice that sounded like gravel being washed in a gold pan.

"Similkameen," he said. His eyes shifted. "Black Hills. Looks like Idaho gold there." He touched the biggest nugget, testing the edges with his fingertip. "That one weren't far from the mother lode. Could be any one of them cricks up the steep side of British Columbia. Maybe even Grey's Creek. 'Bout the right color."

King nodded, watching the stranger as though one of the gold nuggets had come alive and spoken to him.

The man's scarred fingertip brushed a small, smooth nugget that was the color of moonlight.

"Platinum. Britton Creek?" he asked.

"That's what they call it now. When I was there they called it Eagle Creek." King's mouth curled up at one corner. "Seems like they name every other creek in every other watershed Eagle Creek or Bear Creek or Fish Creek. Makes it pure hell on mapmakers."

The man grinned. "Prospectors spend all their time thinking up ways to spend the gold they never find. Don't have no time left over to think up fancy names for every two-bit ravine they pan."

"Sounds like you've been there," King said, "wherever 'there' is."

"End of the rainbow, like as not," the stranger said. "Never found that rainbow myself, but I've been up the crick and over the mountain chasing it. Name's Dryden," he added, extending his hand to King.

"From the cut of your clothes, it looks like you found a

piece of that rainbow," King said, shifting the watch chain to his left hand and accepting Dryden's with his right. "My name's Kingston Duran, Mr. Dryden. Most folks call me King."

Dryden's eyes narrowed. "You be the man that found Grey's Creek?"

King nodded.

"Pleasure to meet you, King. My name's Nathaniel, but most folks call me Mule."

Recognition lit King's eyes. "You wouldn't be the man whose partner got so sick you packed him out on your back for a hundred miles in the dead of winter?"

Dryden nodded. "Good thing we hadn't had any grub for a month. Durn fool weighed a ton as it was."

King's laughter rose above the heavy beat of the *Flyer*'s engines, but he didn't hear the engine noise any more than he heard the conversations around him. He heard only Dryden, a man who had been where King had been, done what King had done, a man who had held the cool golden tears of the sun in the palm of his hand.

"Where are you prospecting now?" King asked, drawing Dryden aside, ignoring the crowd as easily as he had gathered it around him in the first place.

Dryden's mouth pursed around a silence he was reluctant to break. "North," he finally admitted, as though it cost him a pinch of gold dust to do so.

"All the way to the midnight sun?" King asked, smiling, his voice calm but his eyes burning.

Dryden hesitated, then looked around. Surprise showed on his face as he realized that King had eased both of them away from the crowd of people. He leaned confidentially toward King.

"You know the Stewart River country?" Dryden asked in a hoarse whisper.

"Not firsthand. I saw Ed Schieffelin last month in Portland, though. He talked about the Stewart like he expected the Second Coming of Christ to take place there real soon."

Dryden chuckled. "Wouldn't surprise me. That old hoss was eating bacon and beans and panning the Stewart long 'fore you and me ever heard of gold. But I thought Ed had gone back to Arizona."

King shook his head. "He wants to go north again, but—" King's voice faded. "He's real old, and his eyes have cataracts so bad they look like white quartz. He swears there's God's own strike waiting up north, but he'll die long before it's found."

Dryden shook his head. "Well, we all come to it soon or late. Ed give it a good run and found more than his share of new country. That's more than most men can say when they look God in the eye an' try to lie their way out of hell."

The crack of King's laughter made Cass turn toward him, but he was already walking away, drawing Dryden with him toward the *Flyer*'s bar. King's voice was whirled away on the wind, leaving only snatches of his words for Cass to understand.

"I'll stand the drinks . . . hear about that country . . . gold waiting . . . gold . . ."

Then there was only the wind and the heavy beating of the *Flyer*'s engines. Without realizing it, Cass sat up as though to leave.

"Let him go," Jared said to Cass, watching his brother and Dryden disappear inside. "They'll be reeling in an hour, sure as God made little green apples."

"King didn't strike me as a man who would let liquor get the better of him."

"Whiskey or gold fever, it's all the same," Jared said, yawning and stretching. "He'll be no damn good until it's out of his system."

Silently, Cass watched Jared get up and pump two glasses of beer from a nearby keg that was half-buried in a barrel of chipped ice. He handed one of the cold glasses to her. As he sat down, he moved his chair so close to Cass that his leg brushed hers when he was seated. Startled, she turned toward him. He was watching her intently again.

"There's a problem that you should know about," Jared said quietly, pitching his voice so that no one could overhear.

"Tea Rose?"

"Keep your voice down," he murmured, leaning toward Cass and taking her hand between his. "There are tong men on board. If one of them sees us, I want him to think that I'm courting you."

"Aren't you?" she asked before she could stop herself.

Jared's smile was both an invitation and a warning. "When I court you, *if* I do, you won't have to ask. You'll know. So stop wriggling like a cat with her paw caught in a trap, and look like you're delighted to hold hands with me."

Cass raised her golden eyebrows in a look that was meant to be cool but failed, largely because Jared's fingertips were drawing lazy designs across her palm, sensitizing her skin until she could barely sit still.

"If you want me to sit quietly, you'll have to stop doing that," she muttered.

"What? This?"

Fingertips caressed and goosebumps rippled up Cass's arm.

"Jared Duran, if you don't stop doing—"

Soft laughter cut off Cass's words, but there was no humor in Jared's eyes. She had just opened her mouth to take a strip off him for being so fresh when she saw one of the white-uniformed coolies come out onto the deck. He carried a tray of clean beer glasses, which he placed near the keg. With quick motions he gathered up used glasses, stacked them on another tray, and left.

But before he did, he looked directly over at Cass and Jared.

Only after the door closed behind the man did Cass realize that she was holding onto Jared's hand as though it were a lifeline.

"He was watching us," she hissed.

"Maybe. And maybe he was just checking for dirty glasses."

Cass took a deep breath and tried to slow the beating of her heart. The languid stroking of Jared's fingers over her skin didn't help to calm her.

"Jared, what's going on?" she whispered.

"John was with Jasmine last night. She said that Tan Feng has buyers coming in from Vancouver and San Francisco."

"Buyers?"

"For Lilac."

Cass closed her eyes and bit back useless words of anger. Instead, she simply nodded. "Lilac knows. She told me. But she thought nothing would happen until her portrait was finished and circulated up and down the coast. I've delayed five days on delivery. I'm going to stall until after Tuesday."

"Tan suspects something," Jared said, looking down at the slender, strong hand that he held captive between his own palms. "He hasn't left Lilac unguarded for the last five days. He may insist that she go under guard even during the Festival of the Good Lady."

"Oh, God, no," Cass said in a low voice, feeling her stomach sink. Despite everything Jared had said, she had still clung to the hope that Lilac might be rescued with Tea Rose. "What about—"

"Tea Rose?" Jared asked softly.

Cass nodded.

"She'll probably be with her mother and therefore under guard as well."

"How can we get her out of there?"

"We will. But you won't be with us, Cass. It's too dangerous now. If anybody is hurt, I'm going to be damned sure it's one of Tan Feng's hatchet men, not you."

Cass studied Jared as she would a man who was sitting for a portrait. She saw a man who, like King, wasn't entirely civilized beneath his expensive clothing. But unlike King, Jared had his primitive side on a very short leash.

That only made Jared more dangerous. King would kill in the white heat of rage or battle; Jared would try to think his way out of violence—and if that was impossible, he would kill without passion, without remorse.

"From what Lilac told me," Cass said huskily, "the festival is a bit like our Halloween. The women are allowed to go freely from door to door all over Chinatown, begging for favors."

Jared said nothing.

"That means the streets will be filled with women, not men. Is that correct?"

Slowly, Jared nodded.

"You and King would stand out like pickles in a cracker barrel."

For an instant, Jared's mouth softened into a smile.

"One glimpse of either you or King, and Lilac's or Tea Rose's guards would drag the women back to Tan Feng by their hair," Cass continued. "But me? I'm no threat. I can wander around like the silly, inconsequential white woman Tan Feng thinks I am, recording on film the colorful Celestial celebration. In short, I have a perfect excuse to be there, and you don't."

"Cassandra, I won't—" he began harshly.

"No," she said, cutting him off. "If Tea Rose is guarded, I'm your only hope of getting close to her, and you know it. I'm going to Chinatown, Jared. You can go with me, or I can go alone. Take your choice."

20

The room was still but for the occasional rubbing of silk against silk when Tan Feng shifted position at his desk. In front of him was a sheet of paper listing how much squeeze each of his establishments had paid to Seattle policemen in the past year for the privilege of being left in peace. Tan was quite pleased that he had managed to keep the amount of the payments unchanged while nearly doubling the profits of the brothels, gambling houses, and opium rooms. As a result, Tan not only had managed to pay back his elder brother in China—who had loaned the Soong Li Tong money after Seattle's citizens had burned down Chinatown —but was finally earning a considerable return for his own pocket from his various businesses.

It amused Tan that the Chinese Exclusion Act had helped him to turn an enormous profit on such simple endeavors as smuggling men into Gum-Shan and organizing their work and pleasure from that point on. No matter how much Tan charged for minimal goods, no matter how much he extorted payments from their wages, the men could still do far better for their absent families and for themselves in the Golden Mountain's barbarous, lucrative cities than in the Celestial Empire's orderly, rational lands.

Leaning back in his chair, Tan Feng reflected on the clean perfection of the Celestial Empire and on the brilliant rationality of Confucianism, which told each man his place within the universe and how to fill that place for the maximum benefit of family and society. The practical advice of Confucius had built and sustained the greatest empire on earth. As an instrument of rule, it had no peer; man sustained his family, which in turn sustained society, which sustained the emperor, who sustained the cosmos. For woman, her husband was the incarnation of the Great All. For man, the emperor was the incarnation. From those relationships, all order and purpose flowed.

Yet such fine order could also be—tedious. It allowed no outlet for the animal-within, the natural man, the primitive who lived inside the heart and liver of even the most rational Celestial. To achieve harmony with both the rational and the primitive, Taoism was necessary. While it would be a lamentably inefficient way to rule a country, almost as bad as democracy, Taoism was an admirable philosophy for that part of man's life that overlapped with woman's—the bedchamber.

Tan sighed and reached for the long ivory stem of his opium pipe, which rested next to the shorter, larger-bowled pipe he used for tobacco. His hand hesitated, then withdrew, selecting neither traditional opium nor Gum-Shan's tobacco. Neither drug appealed to Tan on a regular basis. He was a man who permitted himself only one addiction, one obsession—coitus. He would never become one of the hollow-eyed, runny-nosed, stick-limbed addicts who lived like shadows in the darkest corners of the tong's opium rooms.

Far better to exhaust oneself in pursuit of Taoist Harmony, when Yin and Yang, Earth and Heaven, Darkness and Light achieved perfect balance. That balance manifested itself in orgasm, the Ultimate, when man for a brief time attained elemental unity with the universe, ecstasy not only of the flesh but of the soul as well. By its very nature, each successful act of coitus added to the sum total of harmony in the universe.

Understandably, a matter of such gravity as the continued health and perpetuation of the universe commanded careful study. While white devil ministers and priests bent their minds and backs to the study of the number of angels resident on the average pinhead, committed Taoists made a careful study of the methods and physical aids most conducive to attaining orgasm, which was man's sole, certain means of attaining oneness with the Great All.

Tan Feng wasn't alone in his study of the Ultimate. Many Chinese had made a lifelong study of the spiritual and cosmic importance of orgasm. Two thousand years before Lao-Zhu put forth his view of natural man and harmony, calling it Tao or the Way, the Yellow Emperor had put the importance of studying man's sexuality much more succinctly: To understand the head, one must first know the tail.

And to understand at all, Tan believed that one must go to the most venerable source. For the Chinese, the Yellow Emperor's *N'ei Ching Su Wen*—the oldest known discourse on human sexuality—was just such a source. In the intervening four thousand years since the Yellow Emperor, the book had been copied and illustrated many, many times, but never with more finesse and enthusiasm than by Taoist monks and nuns.

The Emperor's Nine Glorious Postures had proliferated and become rather extraordinary in the course of time, but Tan considered that development more of a challenge than a deterrent to further study. If one of the positions recommended for achieving the Ultimate seemed frankly improbable at first encounter, Tan simply called for the services of his most flexible sing-song girl and whatever ancillary attendants and sex aids were required to correctly position her. To Tan, no matter how one approached the fabled one square inch of female anatomy, the mystic connection was well worth whatever awkwardness might occur along the way.

A familiar tightness spread up from Tan's crotch as he mentally considered the Celestial Empire's four thousand years of ingenuity and experimentation focused on increasing the harmony of the universe through orgasm. The flowery battle between Yin and Yang, Woman and Man, fought in darkness and in light, on a couch or in a swing, by stealth or by frontal assault—so many ways of thrusting jade stem between jade gates, thrusting again and again with variations of depth and direction until the instant of clouds and rain came, and man was transfixed within the Great All.

Someday, Tan would teach Tea Rose each variation, each scented battle, and he would feel her cloudburst, and she would feel his.

Tan took a breath and expelled it harshly through his nose, trying to restore discipline to his body. Even as he tried, he knew his efforts wouldn't be wholly successful. An old Chinese proverb explained his predicament perfectly: A wife will never be as alluring as a concubine; a concubine cannot compete with an illicit lover; and an illicit lover can never be as exciting as an inaccessible woman.

Tea Rose was Tan's inaccessible woman. So, in many ways, was Lilac. For all the thousands of times he had fought the flowery battle with Lilac, Tan could count on a single hand the number of times he knew with great certainty that he had brought her to orgasm. Lilac was never more inaccessible than when Tan was buried so deeply that the ivory pleasure ring he wore at the base of his jade stem was inside her gates.

Long ago, Tan had decided that it would not be that way with Tea Rose. Her hidden springs would well forth at his mere touch, and she would experience the Ultimate repeatedly, until she begged him to end her pleasure-pain. Only then would he permit himself to know the clouds and rain within her. He would withdraw quickly afterward, his jade stem still hard and proud, the clear victor in the flowery battle.

Tan grunted in approval of his plan. Then with a swift, controlled motion, he positioned a piece of rice paper in front of him on the desk, tested the ink in its flat stone saucer, and took up a brush. Each black stroke was boldly begun and elegantly completed. For an educated man such as Tan, writing was more than a means of communicating with his elder brother in China, it was an act of reverence that celebrated China's long history of culture and civilization. No error of thought, style, or execution would be permitted in the letter. A botched communication would insult his elder brother Tan Wu and be a great loss of face for Tan Feng himself.

After completing the obligatory effusive praise of his elder brother and modest denial of his own self-worth, Tan enumerated the extent and success of his thriving businesses. He asked that two hundred more men be smuggled to Vancouver, Canada, and from there to Seattle. In addition, he asked that fourteen more girls between the ages of eleven and sixteen be purchased and sent to him. They needn't be educated or even particularly pretty; he would be using them as saltwater whores rather than as sing-song girls for his Chinese clientele. The elder Tan Wu not only would save money by buying the least desirable of the girl children who were for sale, but would not need to add to their training, as the white devils didn't care about flute or mandolin, song or poetry, finesse or elegance. They cared only to root like pigs.

Tan paused in his writing as he wondered how best to word his next statement. His elder brother had proven very reluctant to divest the family of a possession as illustrious as Lilac Rain. Tan Feng had no intention of sending Lilac home as elder brother Wu had suggested. Tan had no doubt that Lilac would have his elder brother castrated and drained of his life force within months. Yet, to suggest that the eldest male in the Tan family couldn't cope with a mere slave girl would be a mortal insult—and would raise the unwelcome question as to how well the younger Tan was coping with his stubborn slave.

Forgive your awkward, foolish younger brother, but I have just discovered that which would have become apparent long ago to a man of your experience and wisdom. The renowned Lilac Rain is actually a Fox Woman let loose among mortal men. A very young Fox Woman, to be sure; no doubt she has only a handful of the many thousand years required before she can go to the Celestial Gates and summon the Dragon-Lover to sate her.

Even so, it would be very lacking in piety and respect for this worthless younger brother to inflict such an evil spirit on your honorable elder self. Therefore, I must respectfully and with great earnestness decline your kind offer of tutelage for the female. Nor can I keep her any longer in my house. There is the very great chance that her true nature would be revealed to one of her clients, causing much loss of face for the family of Tan.

Thus, I have sold the fledgling Fox Woman to a white devil in Vancouver for half her weight in gold. Let the vixen drain his Vital Essence while giving none of her own in return. Let him die trying to touch the Ultimate within the Fox Woman's insatiable pleasure pavilion. Or perhaps she will achieve Unity with unwashed timber beasts and illiterate prospectors who think that the only use for a woman's mouth is to bathe their crusted turtle heads.

Tan lifted the brush and made a sound of satisfaction. He

could think of no better vengeance for the woman who had refused to accept her position within the universe.

After eyeing the letter critically once more, Tan tested the ink stone and worked swiftly to conclude his letter as a scholar should, from a single mixture of ink.

With the gold from the sale of that miserable Fox Woman, I come closer to the fragrant moment when my miserable and unworthy self will be allowed once more to breathe the perfect air of the Celestial Empire. I grow weary of Gum-Shan's barbarities, its toneless language, and its fish-belly faces.

I ask that my most honorable elder brother choose my successor from among his own worthy sons or from among my own unworthy progeny, for I will soon be turning my tear-gladdened face toward the Celestial Empire once more. The most beautiful flower ever to grow in the Celestial Garden nears the age of her blooming. Many men will vie with one another to purchase the right to first pierce the perfection of her flower heart. The sale of her precious hymen will give me enough wealth to come home and live as an honorable man should, in reverence and unity with his family.

Tan was working over the last ideograph when there was a dazzling burst of sound from beneath his chair. He leaped to his feet, and in doing so, dragged the brush across the face of the letter, leaving a black gash.

Even before Tan was standing, he had catalogued both the noise and its probable source—firecrackers and Tea Rose. Spreading his legs wide and putting his fists on his hips, he thundered, "Who dares to disturb my silence?"

Tea Rose heard and laughed softly behind her fan. On any other day, she would have been throwing herself at Tan's feet and begging for mercy, but today was the one day in seven years that a woman could wreak small havoc in the domain of man without fear of punishment. Tea Rose had enjoyed it thoroughly, running from room to room at unexpected intervals, lighting the firecrackers' neatly plaited fuses with a burning incense stick.

The door in front of Tea Rose jerked open to reveal a furious Tan Feng looking balefully at her through a veil of blue-white firecracker smoke. The ferocity of his glare set her heart to hammering in sudden fear.

"You ruined more than my silence, you miserable imp! You caused me to mar a letter to my elder brother."

It might be the one day in seven years when a female could tweak the beard of her master, but there was a limit to such insolence, and Tea Rose was afraid that she had transgressed it. She had learned the slave's lesson well; she could not confront strength, she could only subvert it. With a scented rush of fabric, she sank to her knees.

"Oh, noble lord, please forgive this worthless slave girl who was foolish enough to believe that honorable tradition excused thoughtless female acts this one day in seven years."

Tan stared down at Tea Rose's submissively bowed head and didn't know whether to laugh or to curse. While she purported to apologize to him, she reminded him of her traditional female rights on the Festival of the Good Lady. It was the day of the turning worm.

Even so, it would be wise for him to curb that sharp little tongue before some man took offense and cut it off for her, leaving her to choke to death on mouthfuls of her own blood.

"Look at me, worthless one," Tan snarled.

Slowly, Tea Rose looked up. Unshed tears magnified her clear black eyes. Her painted lower lip trembled as though she were a frightened maiden being introduced to the flowery battle for the first time.

Knowing he was being manipulated and not particularly caring, Tan let his appearance of anger slip away.

"Precious one," he said, cupping Tea Rose's face in his hands and catching the unshed tears on the balls of his thumbs. "Take care lest even your great beauty be not enough to offset a man's righteous anger."

"Yes, lord," Tea Rose whispered through trembling lips. "You are very kind to this worthless one."

He grunted. "Now tell me what new things Jasmine and Lotus Moon have taught you."

"You are the kindest of all masters, lord."

Tea Rose grasped one of Tan's ankles and pressed her lips against the soft cloth of his black-and-white shoe. For an instant, the fingers of her right hand slipped inside the shoe to press against his flesh. The hiss of Tan's swiftly indrawn breath was her reward.

"Did Lotus Moon teach you that?" he asked, as Tea Rose straightened into a kneeling position once more.

Beautiful confusion showed on Tea Rose's face. "Teach me what, honored lord?"

Tan stared into her clear eyes and felt both excitement and a cautionary chill. The animal-within scented a mate, but the rational, Confucian part of Tan's mind sensed something more sinister, a Fox Girl watching him with eyes darker than a moonless night.

"To excite a man by touching his foot," Tan explained.

A small smile crossed Tea Rose's lips, to be quickly followed by the screen of her fan as she laughed.

"Oh, no, lord," Tea Rose said. "In matters of the feet, it is Jasmine of the golden lilies who teaches. Lotus Moon's skill lies in touching the sacred pouch and the jade stem. Such skills are difficult to learn, however, with nothing more than a carved ivory implement to practice upon."

Tan rumbled but said nothing. He knew what Tea Rose was angling toward. Most sing-song girls of fourteen had not only witnessed but also participated in coitus in all its varied forms. Tea Rose had not, except for stolen glances through peepholes.

"May I ask a question, lord?" Tea Rose murmured.

Tan nodded.

"There is a position known as 'horse pawing the air'—"

He made an encouraging sound.

"Even with the pillow books, I fear I would be impossibly awkward if a man asked that of me. You are a man of extraordinary expertise in the arts of the bedchamber. Would you find it within the great well of your generosity to explain to your worthless slave how that position is managed by Lord Yang and Lady Yin?"

It wasn't the first time Tea Rose had asked Tan to elucidate when pillow books fell short of their teaching goals, but her requests had been more and more frequent of late. And he had been more and more tempted to comply in the most direct manner possible. Especially now, when her young mouth was barely a hand's-breadth away from his crotch. All that had kept him in check was the suspicion that guile rather than innocence prompted her sweet requests.

"Are you impatient to know the fire within the pleasure pavilion?" Tan asked mildly.

"Forgive my forwardness, great lord," Tea Rose said, her voice fluting as softly as a sleepy bird. "I am but a worthless female. In the presence of such masculine splendor as yourself, my foolish tongue betrays my secret thoughts."

"Which of the young men did you have in mind as your Lord Yang?"

"None, lord! I would rather have a blow from you than a thousand days of caresses from any other man."

The earnest face and sweet voice were both balm and stimulant. Tan looked down at Tea Rose and smiled, knowing that she wanted to try out her increasing store of sensual skills on him.

"Part my clothes, precious one," he said, his voice unusually deep.

Tea Rose's eyes widened in an instant of surprise, but she obeyed without hesitation. The hands that reached for the opening of his clothes trembled slightly. Even before she pushed aside the edges of his tunic, she knew that he was aroused. His heat burned through the loose silk of his pants as his erection nudged free of confinement. She stared in awe at him, watching as the fabled pearl of intense desire formed on the turtle head's tiny mouth.

"I will oversee your teaching from now on," Tan said slowly, savoring the play of emotions across Tea Rose's usually composed face as she saw his jade stem thrusting toward her. "I will be Lord Yang to your innocent Lady

Yin—but not tonight. Tonight, you will bring your mother to me. Together, we will show you how to execute the horse pawing the air, and many other positions as well. You will help us, and you will learn."

"Yes, my lord," Tea Rose said, her voice neutral, her body quivering in a combination of anticipation and fear.

Before she could rise, Tan caught Tea Rose's face between his hands. He felt her subtle trembling and smiled.

"But first," he whispered, "you will play upon my warm jade flute some of the songs you have practiced on cold ivory. Long have I waited for your sweet tunes. Play well, precious one, and you will receive the gift of liquid pearls."

Guided as much by instinct as by training, Tea Rose touched the tip of her tongue to his hot flesh and tasted for the first time the essence of a man.

21

From where Cass had set up her camera at the south end of the Street of the Fishmongers, it seemed as though the whole International District were alive with colored lanterns and laughing women. Cass tried to capture the rushing moment by framing figures against well-lighted backdrops, but the heady sense of play coursing through the women defeated the fastest film Cass had. In groups of two or three, women moved freely along the sidewalks and in the streets, boldly greeting one another and singing as though they were at play within the concealment of their master's walls.

"They're like exotic birds freed from a cage," Cass said as three colorfully dressed, gaily laughing women walked by.

John said nothing. He was too busy watching the shadows for danger.

One of the women Cass watched was a plump, moon-faced girl whose single long black braid had been interwoven with strands of silk until it reached almost to the ground.

She waved toward the camera in an act of boldness that made her companions burst out laughing in nervous pleasure.

"The Festival of the Good Lady comes only once in seven years," John said finally, looking at the women and hoping for a glimpse of Jasmine's mincing steps.

"In Chinatown, perhaps," Cass said in a clipped voice. "In America, things are different."

John glanced from Cass to her photography van, which was stationed across and a hundred feet down the street. The horses had grudgingly become accustomed to the flash and rattle of firecrackers; the animals no longer threatened to pull free of their ties. Jared and King had positioned themselves within the closed wagon so that they could see Cass clearly. Both men were determined not to let her out of their sight.

"I think if I put more flash powder in the gun I might be able to catch the next group of women as they cross the street," Cass said. "Would you hand the gun to me, please?"

Despite Cass's initial irritation at having a bodyguard, as the night wore on, she gradually realized that Jared had been right to insist on having a man at her side. Beneath the festive air, there was a dark current of unruliness in the crowds of men and boys who stood around on street corners and at the mouths of Chinatown alleys, watching the passing parade of women. The spectacle was so unusual, so rare, that the men were more ill at ease than the women.

The banter between the sexes seemed good-natured enough, but Cass didn't trust her reading of the situation. After having seen Tea Rose fling herself at Tan Feng's feet in terror and beg wildly for forgiveness, Cass had realized that she had no way to judge accurately the flash points of the Chinese culture.

"It's the teenage girls who feel the greatest joy," John told her. "Tonight, they return to the freedom of childhood. All Chinese children—boys and girls—can move freely on the street, but once a girl reaches a marriageable age, she must retire to her home. She's never again allowed out without a father, brother, husband, or bodyguard."

"How do the women stand for it?" Cass muttered.

"A Chinese woman might well ask how you can bear to be so unwanted as to be allowed to wander the streets like a homeless dog."

Cass felt a flash of anger, but told herself it sprang from nerves. That, she knew, was only part of the truth; it also made her furious that an educated man such as John Wong could calmly equate a woman's freedom with that of a homeless dog. She doubted that he viewed the quality of his own freedom in such a jaundiced manner.

"Tell me, John," she said, looking him in the eye, "do Chinese men see themselves as homeless dogs?"

John smiled. "Yin is not Yang. Women measure the amount they are cherished by the thickness of the walls separating them from the outer world. What is true in China is even more necessary here in Gum-Shan, where there are so few Chinese women and so many men."

"I can't tell you how grateful I am to have been born into a culture where a man simply says 'I love you,' instead of breaking both my feet to ensure that I stick around long enough to be suitably cherished by him."

John's laughter drew some glances from across the street, where two young women stood poised on the edge of the sidewalk. For an instant, Cass's heart felt squeezed between her ribs. Then one of the women turned, revealing a face whose features were far too coarse to be Tea Rose's. Cass was chagrined to find she felt not only disappointment but relief.

Only then did Cass admit to herself that she was uncertain of how Tea Rose would react to being stolen. Cass couldn't imagine a person who wouldn't be grateful to be freed of the life that awaited Tea Rose; but then, Cass still couldn't imagine a culture that systematically maimed its women in the name of cherishing them. She knew there must be other disturbing cultural differences she had yet to encounter, as well as things she took for granted about American culture that would horrify Tea Rose.

Tea Rose is going to get a chance to test all those fancy theories about 'hybrid vigor,' Cass told herself bracingly. *And I'm afraid it will be a test for good old American vigor as well.*

But all she said aloud was, "More flash powder, please."

22

A hundred feet away, inside the darkened van, Jared Duran watched the crowded sidewalks intently. Like Cass, his eye was caught by the dark-haired girl who resembled Tea Rose. He touched King's sleeve, then shook his head.

"I thought so, too," King agreed, "but I didn't see Lilac."

"Don't count on seeing Lilac. If there are bodyguards, she'll divert them to give Cass a chance to grab Tea Rose."

King pulled out his gun and checked the bright brass primers and cartridges by the light coming through a crack in the van's wooden side. The visual check was unnecessary. He could tell by the weight of the weapon that it was fully loaded. His fingertips and ears assured him the hammer and cylinder were moving smoothly.

"Lilac will have all hell to pay if Tan figures out what happened," King said absently. "Probably even if he doesn't."

"There's no help for it. If she doesn't lead Tea Rose over to the camera, there's no way Cassandra can grab her. Besides, it was Tan's idea to ring in Thad Thornton's daughter for the photos. At least," Jared smiled thinly, "he thinks it was his idea. Hell, maybe it even was. He's a tricky, cruel bastard. But none of that matters now. Cassandra's here. We're here. It's up to Lilac to accomplish the rest."

King grunted. Nothing mattered now but the darkness and the men lying hidden within the wagon's closed box. King shifted his big body just enough so that the crack of light fell on the gun in his hands. Once again, he checked each chamber individually through the hinged side-gate at the back of the cylinder. Jared watched the ritual with understanding amusement. Nobody liked waiting, but King liked it far less than most.

"Why are you still carrying that blunderbuss?" Jared whispered.

"Colonel Colt may be old-fashioned but he's real reliable. Made a whole lot of wild towns real damn tame."

Jared pulled a heavy, blue-steel revolver from his waistband. "Want to see what the future has to offer?"

"What the hell is this?" King muttered, taking the weapon from his brother and holding it in the streak of light.

"Webley-Fosbery, self-cocking, top-break revolver," Jared said. "Fires twice as fast as your single-action relic and reloads three times faster."

"Webley-Fosbery, huh?" King said. "British, I suppose?"

"Right."

"You got a limey gunsmith for those awkward little moments when the damn thing jams?" King gibed. He handed the pistol back to his brother and put the Colt back into the blade of light.

The stuttering racket of nearby firecrackers splintered the silence. When the last echo had gone, King spoke softly.

"I'm leaving, Jay. Soon as we get Tea Rose locked up safe, I'm going north. It will be a long time before civilization comes to the country Mule Dryden described."

"Are you going alone?"

"Mule will partner me if I go. But that's not what you meant, is it?"

"No."

"Cassie?"

"Yes."

"I've never met a more appealing woman," King said frankly.

"Neither have I."

"Yeah, I figured as much. Don't suppose you'd be of a

mind to share her? It worked for us once. Remember that red-headed gal from—"

"No. I want Cass as a wife, not a toy."

"Shit," King hissed under his breath. He squinted into the darkness but couldn't make out his brother's expression. "She's leaning toward me, Jay."

"Don't they all—at first?"

King sighed and swore again.

"You'd be no damned good for her," Jared pointed out.

"I know." There was silence, then King added, "But you know something else, brother? She could be real damn good for *me*. You see, there's a part of me that looks at Cassie and sees a home and children and fires burning in the night, welcoming me home."

"Do you hear what you're saying?" Jared asked in a low voice. *"Welcoming you home.* Where have you been, and how long were you gone, and how long would it be before you left her alone again?"

There was a long silence before King said, "All or nothing at all, huh?"

"Life is always that way, King. You've just never admitted it. Now it's here, staring you in the face: You can't build a home and run free in the wilderness at the same time. You have to choose."

"Other men do both."

"Not with a woman like Cassandra. She's not a sometime thing. She's a woman to share your life with. All of it, King. Or none of it."

In the darkness, the small sounds of King testing his revolver once more sounded oddly distant. At last came the distinct click of the cylinder being put into place again.

"I'll go north," King said.

Jared didn't try to conceal the relief he felt. "Do you need a stake?" he asked instantly.

"Nope. I'm going to sell my railroad shares."

"If that's not enough, I'll make up the difference."

King laughed softly. "Glad to get rid of me, aren't you?"

"This time, yes."

King's big hand settled onto his brother's shoulder and squeezed affectionately. "You know the hell of it, Jay?"

Jared waited.

"This time," King said quietly, "I'm afraid I'm leaving something behind that's almost as good as whatever is ahead."

It wasn't a comforting thought for either brother. Saying nothing more, they waited together for Lilac to appear, letting the silence between them expand until it was part of the night.

23

"Speak English," Lilac instructed.

As Tea Rose followed her mother into her room, the girl tried to control the conflicting emotions racing through her. With an effort, Tea Rose schooled her face into the pleasant neutrality of expression that Lilac had taught her. As soon as the door was closed behind them, Tea Rose began talking English in a high, excited voice.

"Tan Feng is even more potent than the fabled Yang-Ti," she said quickly, thinking of the long-ago Celestial Emperor who had built pleasure houses every half-mile along the royal roads he traveled. "I brought Tan to orgasm twice before you came to the room," she said proudly.

Lilac looked at the flush on her daughter's face. Tea Rose's eyes were like wet black crystal, and her lips had a sensual shine. Lilac wondered whether a sense of accomplishment or simple sexual excitement was responsible for the heightened coloring.

"Did you enjoy that, daughter?" Lilac asked calmly, concealing her fear with the ease of a lifetime of practice.

"Enjoy? I have been trained for Tan Feng's enjoyment, not he for mine." Tea Rose laughed openly, using neither sleeve nor fan for concealment, for she was alone with her mother. "Ah, mother, it was very sweet to wag the tail that wagged the dog! I had but to put my hand on his penis and his vital essence flowed. It was so easy, so very easy to make him groan and twitch and pulse. If that is enjoyment, then *yes,* I enjoyed."

Despite her worry, Lilac couldn't help an amused smile. Tea Rose had been so attentive to Tan, so sweetly eager to assist in coitus, that Lilac had feared her daughter desired Tan as a young woman desires a potent male. But the sheen of excitement on Tea Rose's young face came from successfully exercising her female power, not from some newly awakened—and dangerous—sexuality.

Lust was what Lilac feared most of all, what she had trained her daughter to resist from earliest childhood. Lilac didn't want Tea Rose to become as addicted to clouds and rain as Tan Feng himself. Lilac herself had known no such addictive pleasure, until Thad. Before he came into her life, she had been a highly skilled courtesan, feeling nothing, concentrating upon her task as though the man were truly a flute and she a master musician. But Thad had taught her that she had a soul; with him, she had first felt the Ultimate burning through a lifetime of hatred to sear her newly discovered soul.

"Mother? Can we go into the streets now?" Tea Rose asked eagerly.

"First, we will bathe, and then I will dress you as though you were four again," Lilac said, touching Tea Rose's smooth cheek. "I will hug you and tickle you and comb your hair into a beautiful maiden's coil. Then I will take your hand and lead you into the Good Lady's Night, where women are free."

Tea Rose smiled uncertainly, wondering why her mother's smile and words pierced her heart like needles of ice that vanished before the source of pain could be found.

"Mother—?"

Lilac turned away and began undressing before her tears could be seen.

24

"Jay."

"I see them," Jared answered softly. "Down the alley by the third fish stall. Both wearing dark clothes."

"Which one has the flashy gold fan?"

"Lilac."

"How do you know?" King asked.

"I gave it to her."

King started to say something, then saw two other figures following the women at a distance of thirty feet. "Damn it! Tan put two guards on them."

Jared said nothing until he identified both men. "The short, thick one is Zhu. The big bastard in the bowler hat is Kwan. He's a hatchet man from way back, used to come into the camps to collect debts for Tan. Last time I bumped into him, he was carrying a pistol."

"So much for getting away quietly," King said, easing toward the van's door. "You have any druthers?"

"I want Kwan." What Jared didn't say was that Kwan also had the job of beating Lilac when she displeased Tan Feng. "I know how he moves. If either one of them gets close to you, watch out for his feet. They'll kick your head off before you can see it coming."

When King reached for the door, Jared stopped him.

"The women are too far away," Jared said. "Let them get closer. Every step now could save a bullet later."

King didn't argue.

"See any more guards?" King asked.

"No, but don't count out the men who are milling around. If they see two white devils attacking two tong men, they might get excited enough to do something stupid."

Across the street, the crowds were so heavy that Cass and John couldn't see that Lilac and Tea Rose were approaching. While maintaining the illusion of a working photographer

—minus the flash powder, which Cass had decided would call too much attention to them—Cass was studying the full, smiling faces of the passing women. Suddenly, John hissed softly under his breath. She followed his line of sight down the alley and caught a glimpse of Lilac's drawn face before she was screened once more by the random motions of people passing by.

Cass turned and looked at the closed van. Jared and King had gotten out and were standing in the van's shadow, visible only to someone who expected to see them. Their attention was focused down the alley, which was narrow but not completely walled in by buildings. A piece of the night sky showed through, where the ruins of a brick building gave wordless testimony to the fire that had leveled Chinatown years before.

One of two young Chinese men who had been loitering in a doorway lit a string of unusually large firecrackers and threw it into the street at the mouth of the alley. The loud reports sent women running in all directions, clutching the hems of their silk gowns and shrieking with mock fear.

Lilac had anticipated the panic for she had paid the two youths a handful of brass Chinatown coins, explaining that she wanted her daughter's Festival of the Good Lady to be as exciting as possible. At the instant the firecracker barrage began, Lilac grabbed Tea Rose's arm and darted into the overlapping shadows that engulfed the ruined building. She shielded the girl's glittering headdress with her dark cloak and watched the fleeing women through slitted eyes.

"Mother, it was only firecra—"

The sharp pressure of Lilac's fingers silenced Tea Rose in midword.

Still laughing at the antics of the squealing, fleeing women, the two bodyguards turned back to their charges.

The alley was empty.

Kwan grunted a harsh command. Zhu joined him in a dash down the alley and into the street, head swiveling as he looked for Tan Feng's women.

Instants later, Lilac saw Kwan returning to the alley on

the run. Without warning, she yanked Tea Rose farther into the shadows and covered her completely with folds of her dark cloak.

"Do not move or speak."

Lilac's words were a bare thread of sound, but Tea Rose heard them. Lilac was bent over her daughter, concealing both of them beneath the flowing cloak, and her lips brushed Tea Rose's cheek. One of Lilac's small hands lay across Tea Rose's mouth. The other held a knife against her daughter's throat.

Motionless but for the hammering of her heart, silent but for the inner scream only she and the Great All could hear, Lilac waited to see whether Tea Rose would live free in an alien society or die by her own mother's hand in a nameless Chinatown alley.

25

Kwan paused at the side alley and peered into the darkness. Zhu came pelting back from the street, shouting that the women had disappeared. The men were so close that Lilac could hear them confer in sharp, frightened tones.

"The miserable females must be near," Zhu argued. "We looked away from them for only a moment. They can't have—"

"Stop barking like a dog," Kwan snarled, cutting off the other man's words. "Run to the House of the Folded Lotus. Tell Wang-Sing to bring soldiers from the tong. Promise a reward for anyone who finds the wretched creatures. Run! Tan will castrate us if we lose his females!"

Without another word, Zhu turned and sprinted toward the teahouse. At the head of the alley, Kwan looked down the street to the right and saw nothing more than he had seen the last time, which was a round-eye woman stealing images of foolish Chinese women who quacked like ducks while they pretended to be men for this one night in seven years. There was nothing of interest when Kwan looked to the left, where more Celestials milled and seethed through the heart of the Chinese district. He looked long and carefully at the figures, but saw none who resembled his charges.

After a final glance, Kwan moved farther into the alley until he blocked the intersection of byways and narrow paths between buildings where he had first lost sight of Tea Rose and Lilac. He waited in the shadows, his body poised, his head turning slowly. As he searched the darkness for movement, his nostrils flared as though he scented the prey he couldn't see.

Although Kwan no longer completely barred the way to the street where Tea Rose's freedom waited, Lilac knew that it wasn't yet time to move. She had no means of forcing Tea Rose to run to freedom and no time to explain to her terrified, motionless daughter why running away from Kwan was necessary. Barely breathing, watching through eyes that were slitted to avoid reflecting random lamplight, Lilac waited, her hand steady as she held the knife against Tea Rose's throat.

Suddenly, two large men appeared at the mouth of the alley, silhouetted against the brighter illumination of the street beyond. Lilac recognized Jared's familiar outline and felt a wild surge of hope that she wouldn't have to take her beloved daughter's life.

Tea Rose felt the trembling of her mother's hand across her mouth as the knife dropped away from her throat. That was the only warning she had before Lilac yanked her to her feet and began racing down the alley toward the main street.

King saw the shapes hurtling toward him out of the darkness and the swift movement of the hatchet man deeper in the alley. There was no mistaking the steel gleam of the pistol that sprang into Kwan's hand as he turned toward the sound of the fleeing women.

With the savage grace of a wild animal, King struck, driving Jared to his knees, forcing him out of the line of fire. *"Down!"* King shouted at the same instant. *"Get down!"*

Lilac sent Tea Rose sprawling onto the grimy cobblestones of the alley just before Kwan's pistol spat a brilliant tongue of fire. Even as Jared rolled aside, he registered the sound ripping through the night; like King, Kwan was using a .45 caliber pistol. The incandescent muzzle flash and harsh, rolling thunder of King's .45 answered as he slipped the hammer repeatedly with his thumb, firing with incredible speed. Kwan dove over a ruined brick wall and rolled to his feet like a cat while bullets whined and ricocheted. King flicked open the side-gate and began reloading with quick, steady hands.

"To the street!" Lilac commanded Tea Rose in a low, harsh voice, speaking English so that Kwan wouldn't understand. "Crawl on your belly like a snake!"

Behind them, Kwan's pistol began firing again.

"Goddammit King, get down!" shouted Jared as he sighted down his own pistol barrel from his prone firing position.

Still standing, King continued reloading without a pause, methodically shoving out one spent shell at a time and replacing it with a fresh bullet.

Jared's .38 had a higher voice than either .45, but it was just as terrifying. Tea Rose didn't need her mother's urging to leave behind the bullet-shattered night of the alley. Heedless of the dirt and stinking garbage, she kept her face down and began clawing and slithering through the alley toward the golden glow of the street ahead. Whimpering too softly to be heard, Tea Rose hugged the cobblestones and the base of the building as she passed opposite the point where Jared was. Kwan continued firing until an empty chamber rolled around. He began reloading as quickly and methodically as King had.

Jared broke open his pistol and sent all six spent cartridges scattering across the alley's cobblestones in a ringing shower of brass. Instants later, six fresh shells were in place.

"Go," he said softly, knowing that King would be waiting for just such a signal.

King darted into the cover of a fish stall while Jared fired two evenly spaced shots to keep Kwan pinned down and unable to fire. From his new position, King snapped a shot down the alley, keeping Kwan down and allowing Jared to move forward. The brothers' motions were well-coordinated, quick, and required no communication after the first word. When Kwan returned fire suddenly, both Durans fired back. Kwan withdrew once more, going deeper into the alley's darkness.

"He's moving," King whispered. "Cover me."

The eerie ballet of Duran advance and Kwan retreat resumed, punctuated by pistol shots. Tea Rose snaked away from the battle a few inches at a time, her eyes fixed on the golden safety of the street that lay fifty feet ahead of her.

26

Less than two minutes after the first shot was fired, Cass had already scooped up and thrown all her equipment into the back of the van where Jared and King had hidden earlier. The black horses Jared had insisted on using that night were snorting and stamping nervously in the traces despite John's hand on the bridle of the lead horse.

"Go find Tea Rose. I'll bring the wagon," Cass told John as she scrambled into the driver's seat.

John hesitated, for Jared had been very explicit in his orders that Cass be protected at all times.

More shots shattered the night.

Without a word, John turned and ran toward the mouth of the alley. Cass had divided the responsibilities with unarguable pragmatism—if necessary, John could pick up Tea Rose and run through the night with her. Cass could not.

At the last instant, John slid to a halt behind the protection of one of the buildings at the mouth of the alley. He looked around the corner just as a muzzle flash illuminated the night. The figures of Jared, King, and the brief glitter of a woman's headdress lying on the dirty cobblestones were imprinted on John's retinas. Even as he realized that the headdress was Tea Rose slowly eeling toward him, he knew that he could do nothing more than wait for her to come within reach. If he called out to her, bullets would answer, endangering both their lives while accomplishing nothing that patience couldn't do better.

The sound of a buggy whip's whistle and snap came through the darkness behind John. He heard the rhythmic beat of the blacks' hooves and the jangle of harness as Cass drove the team into a slewing turn near the alley. When the horses came to a wild-eyed halt, the back of the wagon was just visible from the alley, and the horses were positioned for a dash out of the International District. One of the blacks half-reared as John materialized out of the shadows in back of the team.

"No!" he said, grabbing Cass's arm when she would have rushed past him to the alley. "Don't go near the mouth of the alley. It's dangerous."

"Where are Tea Rose and Lilac?" Cass demanded.

"Crawling toward the street. One of the hatchet men controls the open places of the alley. Jared and King are closing in on him to give Tea Rose time to reach the street in safety. You can do nothing but wait."

Suddenly, both Cass and John heard shouts from up the street, toward the Soong Li Tong quarters. A single glimpse told Cass that the gunfire had attracted a squad of Tan's men.

"Which way is the man in the alley facing?" Cass asked urgently.

"What?"

"The hatchet man. Is he facing toward this street or toward the back of the alley?"

"The street."

"Do you have a gun?"

"Yes."

"Hold the horses right here. Shoot up the street if you have to, but *hang onto the horses at all times.*"

John started to question Cass, but she had already jerked

free of his hand and vanished into the back of the van. No sooner had he leaped to the bridle of the lead horse than Cass emerged from the van with a large tin of magnesium flash powder in one hand and the flash gun in the other.

"Twenty seconds," John warned, watching the rapid advance of Tan's men. "No more!"

Cass lifted her skirt and sprinted to the edge of the wooden sidewalk that ended at the alley's mouth. Throwing herself flat on the walkway, she poured a trail of powder in the dirt from the street to as far as she could reach into the alley with her arm. Then she tipped the tin on its side so that powder spilled over the end of the impromptu fuse she had just made. Her hands were shaking so hard that she was afraid for a moment she wouldn't be able to work the striker on the gun's powder tray.

Suddenly, a spark sizzled into the powder.

"Close your eyes!" Cass shouted, hoping the Durans could hear. She threw herself away from the alley, tucked herself into a ball against the building and covered her own eyes.

The short trail of powder became an incandescent snake twisting across the dirt toward the upended can. Flame met the several pounds of powder inside the stout container. For an instant the explosion was trapped inside the can; then there was a thunderclap from escaping gasses as the can burst in a ball of blazing light. The horses screamed in fear, a sound as shocking as the shattering violence of the explosion itself; but it was the light Cass was counting on, the blinding brilliance that all her subjects complained of when they looked directly at the flash tray.

The tong men were ten feet away when the magnesium can exploded. There were screams of surprise and fear followed by absolute confusion as the temporarily blinded men groped about, trapped in a choking cloud of smoke.

The astonishing flash of light had come from behind the Durans, as had Cass's warning cry. Jared had reacted instantly, understanding as soon as he heard her voice what Cass was going to do. Intent on reloading his pistol, King had been slower. As he jacked out the last shell, the alley around him suddenly had stood out in stark relief, a world of blinding white and razor shadows, and then only shadows, the blackness of hell itself engulfing him in the moments before his vision returned.

Kwan wasn't so fortunate. He had been staring at the spectral, twisting line of light when it had exploded into a dragon that ate the world, burning itself onto the back of his eyeballs.

"Zhu!" Kwan screamed, calling to the man he had sent away for reinforcements. "Where are you?"

There was no answer but a girl's high shriek. The sound ended abruptly.

Kwan shouted again. The muffled grunts and curses of the blinded, retreating tong men came back to him, telling him that he was alone. He began spraying the alley with bullets as though that would somehow slay the dragon that had taken his sight.

Jared aimed carefully, but before he could pull the trigger, Kwan spun around and flung himself into the darkness.

"Let him go," King said hoarsely. "Grab Tea Rose, and let's get the hell out of here."

The sound of King's voice brought Jared instantly to his brother's side.

"Where are you hit?" Jared demanded.

"Leg. High."

"Can you walk?"

"You ever known a time when I couldn't?"

Cass saw the two men staggering toward her and felt her heart turn over in fear. She left the horses and ran to John, who was struggling at the door of the van, trying to subdue the terrified Tea Rose and get her into the wagon at the same time.

"Put her in back and sit on her!" Cass said, shoving both of them through the door into the van. "Jared! King! Over here!"

As Jared and King neared the wagon, Jared could see the sweat on his brother's pallid face. Blood glistened wetly from his thigh to the top of his boot. He was breathing hard and fast through clenched teeth, trying to stay conscious by blowing the pain away.

Then Jared saw men coming from all sides, from behind, men slipping from shadow to shadow, directed by Kwan's voice as he regained his sight.

King made a hoarse sound and collapsed. Jared bent, took his brother's full weight across his shoulders and then straightened, carrying him.

"You'll have to drive," Jared said in a strained voice, his strength taxed by his brother's weight.

Jared caught only a glimpse of Cass's pale, set features before she spun away from him and raced forward to untie the horses. Jared boosted King into the van and scrambled in after him to sit facing out the open door, King's pistol in one hand and his own in the other. He barely had time to brace himself before the buggy whip whistled and snapped like a small caliber gun, launching the horses into a frantic gallop from a standing start.

From the shadows of a refuse heap, Lilac listened to the last, frightened scream of her daughter borne back through the silence.

When nothing more reached Lilac's straining ears but the normal sounds of night, she stood and ran toward the regrouping tong men, her voice rising and falling in chilling laments, her fingers clawing her hair in an agony of emotion over her stolen daughter. Men gathered around her, firing questions in Cantonese. They were answered by the universal language of a mother's grief for a lost child.

27

Lilac lay at Tan's feet, babbling hysterically in Mandarin about the fiery demon that had come and stolen her daughter. Tan had heard the story many, many times already, and the result was always the same.

Tea Rose was gone.

"Silence, miserable female!" Tan snarled.

After a moment, Lilac subsided into wild sobs, allowing the other men to speak without having to shout over her wailing laments.

"So, the photographer stole Tea Rose," Tan said.

Kwan and Zhu bowed deeply to Tan Feng.

"It must be, lord," Kwan said, his voice hoarse from strain. Each time he looked at Tan's black eyes, Kwan felt the cold winds of eternity blowing across the back of his neck. "She had her three-legged demon device set up in the street near the alley, yet when we looked for her, she was gone. Only she could have loosed the burning demon that—"

"The only demon in that alley was Lilac Rain," Tan said harshly. He dug his fingers into Lilac's disheveled hair and yanked her to her feet with cruel strength. *"Fox Woman.* You have ridden my soul too long, sucking my vital essence in flowery battle and giving none of yours in return."

The face of a grieving woman looked back at Tan—but beneath the tears, triumph glittered. He sensed it, just as he had always sensed the essential Lilac hovering beyond his reach, forever eluding him.

"I am Lilac, your slave," she sobbed, "and I am a mother whose only child has been stolen by the Old One! Why do you punish me when I did nothing wrong?"

Tan made a harsh sound of disgust when Lilac used the nickname of Donaldina Cameron, the Christian woman who had made a wide reputation for herself by stealing young Chinese prostitutes from their masters.

"This is Seattle, not San Francisco," Tan snarled, wrenching Lilac's head slowly, twisting her neck, forcing her body to follow clumsily. "There is no Old One here. There is just a Fox Woman scheming against her master."

Kwan and Zhu watched dispassionately, each hoping that Tan's rage would be vented on the woman rather than on themselves.

"How did you know Miss Thornton was his daughter?" Tan asked savagely, each syllable clipped and harsh. "You hadn't seen him for many, many years. He never knew you were in Seattle. You had never even seen her as a child. How did you know she was Tea Rose's half sister?"

Kwan and Zhu looked at each other uneasily, wondering what Tan was talking about.

Even if Lilac had wanted to answer Tan, she couldn't have because his hand in her hair had twisted her neck until air was blocked in her throat.

"I should kill you, Fox Woman," Tan whispered, his face only inches from Lilac's. "But I'm not finished with you just yet."

He released his grip on Lilac abruptly, throwing her to the floor where she lay gasping for breath. When he looked from her to Kwan and Zhu, they flinched.

"There are four traditional deaths for those who have displeased their lord," Tan said without emotion. "I will not use the death of Ten Thousand Cuts. Nor will I separate head from body so that it will be impossible for you to join with your ancestors. Nor will I tie hang you from crossed timbers and strangle you from below. As I am not the Emperor, I have no silken cord to give you with instructions that you accomplish your own miserable deaths."

Tan stepped over Lilac and walked across the room to his men. He looked from one to the other, his face impassive. "You continue to live only because she is Fox Woman, a demon no man can be expected to control."

Both men relaxed slightly. Tan saw, and smiled.

"Wing!" Tan barked.

Wong Ah Wing stepped around the carved folding screen that had divided him from the rest of the room.

"Thirty strokes each with a very thin and limber cane," Tan said. "If they cry out even once, cut off their useless balls."

Wing bowed. "And the female, lord?"

"Strip her, take her to the gambling rooms, and see that she drinks urine from each man there. Afterward, bind her hands and feet to my bed so that she can't move."

Wing bowed again.

"Watch her very carefully," Tan said. "If she escapes or manages to kill herself before I am finished with her, you will spend the rest of your miserable life as a eunuch, pissing through a straw."

28

King Duran lay trapped in the middle of a blossoming red explosion that expanded and receded in time with his heartbeat. It was an erratic rhythm, nothing to depend on, nothing to hang onto, and he needed something to hang onto very badly. He tried to call out to Jared, but when his mouth opened, blood poured out, dyeing the world red until pain came, a white agony that ate his soul until he writhed and prayed for death.

Across an immense distance came a gentle voice, a woman's husky plea, his own name repeated over and over, calling him back from darkness. Soft hands caressed his face, his arms, his naked chest, his loins—a fountain of gold dust flowing coolly over his body. He let it bathe him, washing agony away. Then he reached for the golden streamers, only to have them elude his grasp, allowing pain to rush back in, a white screaming that ended only when gold dust poured over him once more. Sighing a name, he pulled the gold around him and let himself slide into a darkness that held no threat, for he was wrapped in caressing gold.

Sitting next to the bunk, Cass looked at her hair tangled in King's big hands and felt tears scald down her cheeks.

"What did he say?" Jared asked.

" 'Cassie—gold—' " she murmured.

Gently, she tried to ease King's fingers from her hair. When he made a sound of pain, she smoothed her hand over his forehead, caressing and soothing him until he became calm once more. A handful of her hair still remained within his grasp; to remove it seemed to cause him distress. She sat up carefully, held close to him by a silken leash of her own long hair.

From the corner of the room came splashing sounds as the doctor finished washing off his surgical instruments. Jared turned and looked broodingly at the man in whose hands King's life had been balanced. The hands were steady now, a considerable improvement over what they had been when Jared had dragged the doctor from a drunken poker game.

"Ice water has its uses," Jared observed.

The doctor looked up from packing away his instruments in a worn leather bag. He smiled frostily. "You're lucky my heart didn't stop."

"You're lucky *his* didn't," Jared countered, gesturing toward the ship's bunk where King lay so white and still.

"Strongest man I ever operated on," the doctor said, fastening his surgical bag with quick motions. "The wound is clean, the artery stopped bleeding, and the bone wasn't broken. I'd say God is on your brother's side. If he follows the instructions I left with the young lady, he should mend just fine. If he gets an infection—" The doctor shrugged. "God's will be done."

"What about Tea Rose?"

"The little China girl? She'll sleep the rest of the night on what I gave her. I left some more with your man in case she gets hysterical again."

"Thank you."

"I'll be by in the morning," the doctor said. "If you need me before then, my surgery is at this address."

Jared took the card. "Doctor?"

"Yes?"

"I'm relying on your discretion."

"I don't doubt it, son." The doctor smiled. "Half the citizens in Seattle do. I've never disappointed one of them. But I've no nurse you can trust. They jabber like crows before a storm."

"We'll manage."

Jared saw the doctor to the *Flyer*'s gangplank and then stood for a few moments in the damp night, gathering himself for what was yet to come.

It could have been worse, he told himself silently. *And it could have been a hell of a lot better, too. King could have been less a hero or less a fool. If only everything had gone just a little more smoothly.*

But it hadn't happened that way. King had been both hero and fool, saving Jared and making a target of himself.

The word of the battle was already spreading on the streets of Chinatown. Tan was not feeling merciful. He believed Cass and Lilac had acted in concert to spirit Tea Rose away from him. Cass was beyond his reach. Lilac was not.

Jared raged internally at the thought of the revenge Tan had taken, Lilac defiled by every man in the tong.

A few feet away, Elliott Bay's cold black water licked against the steamer's hull. From the wharf came the sudden glow of a match, then the scent of a cigarette being lighted. Two sentries talked softly in the night. Somewhere forward, a line stretched and groaned as the tide drew the steamer tight against its moorings. The prolonged, inhuman cry of stressed rope was preferable to the sounds King had made while he lay barely conscious beneath the surgeon's knife.

Jared turned and went back inside. He stopped opposite King's cabin to greet the sentry who sat outside the cabin where Tea Rose dreamed opium dreams. Jared hesitated, then opened the door, knowing he wouldn't feel at ease until he had assured himself that the prize that had been won at such cost was still safe.

A single lamp burned on the wall, casting soft light on the polished brass and walnut paneling. The cabin seemed far too silent to hold any life. The slight figure of Tea Rose didn't stir even when Jared bent over her bunk to feel her reassuring breaths measured against his cheek. Only when he was certain that she was alive and well did he turn away, going to King's cabin.

Entering, Jared closed the door soundlessly behind him. Cass was sitting on a chair she had pulled up against the bunk. As he watched, she bent over and brushed her lips against King's pale forehead, then lay her head next to his on the bunk. For an instant, Jared closed his eyes against the sight.

Don't do it, Cass. Don't fall in love with a man who can never love you in return. God, if only once, just once, a woman could look past King's smile to the lone wolf beneath.

A hundred other "if onlys" raced through Jared's mind. If only King had had the sense to take cover himself. If only Kwan had missed entirely or shot Jared instead. If only Lilac hadn't been so carefully guarded. If only Tea Rose could have been trusted with the truth. If only Tan had agreed to sell Tea Rose or Lilac or both. If only Thad Thornton had never fallen in love with the wrong woman.

If only his daughter weren't falling in love with the wrong man.

Unaware of Jared standing behind her in the large cabin, Cass half lay with her face close to King's. Her long, unbound hair was still caught within his fingers. She made no effort to free herself. It pleased her to be needed, to know that the feel of her hair soothed King even when he was half-delirious with pain and shock. Slowly, Cass brushed her mouth over King's cheek once more, savoring the difference between his skin and the crumpled softness of his beard. He smelled of sweat and gunpowder, antiseptic and something less definable—wild as a falcon, elusive as lightning, elementally male.

And the touch of his beard against her skin was more intriguing than the feel of ermine.

Jared saw the sensual flutter of Cass's long eyelashes as she savored the textures of his brother. Biting back a curse, Jared peeled off his dark jacket and threw it into a corner. His dark blue shirt was stained with King's blood as were his pants and boots. King's blood everywhere, a red tide of life that had barely been stemmed in time. The blood was dried now, black and stiff, grating on Jared's skin. With quick, savage motions he ripped the cloth free of his body, sending buttons dancing and rolling across the cabin floor.

The sounds had told Cass she wasn't alone. She sat up and gently freed her hair from King's grasp. Then she turned and saw Jared's naked, shockingly powerful back and glanced away quickly, shaken and not knowing why. Jared's strength shouldn't surprise her; she had seen him pick up King as though he were a sack of flour. As for a bare torso, she had been the one to take off King's bloody clothes while Jared "enlisted" the doctor. There was no reason for her to be disturbed by the sight of Jared's bare, powerful back, yet she was. She looked away.

Jared pulled open the door of an armoire and shook out one of King's shirts. He pulled it on, not bothering to fasten the buttons, and then went to the small, built-in bar on the far side of the cabin.

"Brandy?" he asked quietly.

"Yes, please," Cass said without turning around.

Moments later, Jared's arm reached over her shoulder. A cut crystal tumbler with two fingers of brandy in it appeared beneath her nose.

"Shall I hold it for you?" he asked.

"I can manage, thanks."

His hand brushed over hers as she took the glass. His skin felt cool and dry and—calm. She wondered if he ever lost that tight control of self, or if it went all the way to his soul.

Cass took a sip of brandy, shuddered, and took another sip. Some of the clammy residue of fear that had coiled queasily in her stomach began to ease.

"If you hear men outside the door, don't worry. They're Pinkertons."

"Guards? Why? Is there still danger?"

"Who knows? If there is, they'll take care of it. That's why I hired them."

"What's going on?" Cass demanded, turning to face Jared.

Jared hesitated, then shrugged. "You were recognized

tonight. Tan is offering a reward for information about you and Tea Rose. Somebody is watching your studio right now."

"There are hatchet men watching my apartment?"

Jared shook his head and looked from the amber in his glass to the golden flow of Cass's hair. "That's just the problem. They aren't hatchet men. They're Seattle cops."

"Policemen? Working for Tan?"

"Tan compromised the Chinatown Squad a long time ago," Jared said wearily. "They've been overlooking his gambling and girls and opium dens so long that they've gotten used to the money. They've got a vested interest in helping him stay on top, and he's using that."

He sipped brandy. "I underestimated Tan's political strength. Now, there isn't a place in town that's safe. As soon as King can be moved, the three of you are going into hiding. I need some time to make his reputation stink so badly that no white politician can defend him."

Cass stared into the fragrant brandy, dimly realizing that her hand was shaking so that the liquid trembled in rings of agitation.

"I thought once we stole Tea Rose it would be all over," Cass said in a low voice.

"I'm sorry. It's just beginning."

"What do I do now? How can I fight Tan Feng and the police and Tea Rose all at once?"

So lightly that Cass couldn't feel it, Jared stroked the glistening blond hair that fell over her shoulder.

"You won't have to fight alone," he said very softly. "I'll be with you every step of the way."

King let out a long, groaning breath. Instantly, Cass bent over him and stroked him as though he were more precious than life itself. Blindly, his hands searched for and found her hair once more.

Jared stood and watched in frustration while the brother he loved fought against the wound he had taken so that Jared wouldn't be hurt. All that seemed to reach King in his thick, pain-ridden half-sleep was the feel of Cass's hands and her hair locked within his grasp as though it were the wealth of the world.

Forgetting that Jared was in the room, Cass bent and kissed King with aching gentleness, wishing that she could do more for him than merely sit and watch his pain.

"Any sign of fever?" Jared asked.

Cass straightened abruptly, embarrassed by the tense edge in Jared's voice.

"No," she said in a low voice. "No change."

"Don't worry, Cassie," Jared said, his voice tired and rough with irony as he used King's nickname for her. "I'm not going to see you kiss King and then rush out and tell the world. But I am going to tell you that King had a ticket north in his pocket when he was shot. He was going gold hunting again."

Cass's look of hurt surprise gave Jared cold comfort.

"He didn't tell you?" Jared asked, finishing his brandy in a single swallow.

"Why should he?"

Jared's smile was like his voice, sad and angry and tired. "Your protests would be more convincing if his fingers weren't so firmly tangled in your hair."

"He could hardly be held accountable for that in his condition, could he?"

"No," Jared said. "In fact, sweet Cassandra, I'm certain he doesn't even know you're here. He's not an intentionally cruel man. He meant to let you go."

"What are you talking about?"

Without answering, Jared moved until he stood at the head of the bunk and looked down at King with clear eyes that saw too much. King's breathing was still too shallow, too quick. His face was far too pale. Even the mahogany fire of his hair was dulled. Jared stroked the back of his fingers down his brother's cheek in a gentle caress. The flesh was firm and vibrant, telling of the life that burned strongly beneath the pallor.

Cass looked from Jared's fingers to his eyes and felt tears clenched in her throat. No man who was so cold, so controlled, could possibly be as sad as Jared looked right now.

"What—what did the doctor say?" she demanded fiercely. "Isn't King going to be all right?"

Jared looked at Cass with eyes as clear and remote as a mountain spring.

"King will be fine," Jared said after a long silence. "It's you I'm worried about, Cass."

"That doesn't make sense."

"It will," he said softly. "It will."

29

Tan Feng nodded curtly. Wing struck Lilac once more across her naked breasts with his open hand. The stinging report of bare skin on bare skin rang like a pistol shot in the room. The blow staggered Lilac, sending her slamming against the wall. She bit back a groan that would reward Wing's efforts. The marks of previous blows on her breasts stood out in great red welts.

"Good God, is all of this really necessary?" a man asked in English, his voice showing his distaste.

Tan looked at the white man with hooded eyes.

"You want woman signee paper, chop chop?" Tan demanded harshly.

Robert Salyor grimaced. He had a lawyer's respect for documents and signatures. He also regarded himself as tolerant, when it came to other cultures. If Lilac had been white, he might have tried to reason with Tan Feng, but she was Chinese and a whore in the bargain.

Even so—

Reluctantly, Salyor nodded. "It was her daughter who was kidnapped. She has to sign the complaint. Too bad she's so well known. It would be easier to use one of your other prostitutes. A willing one."

The smile Tan gave Salyor wasn't meant to comfort. "She

all time al'lays bad bad sing-song gril. Bad *bad,*" Tan added with emphasis. He was irritated by his inability to communicate in English, but he didn't trust Lilac to translate for him.

And Tea Rose was gone.

Lilac stared at Tan with eyes that were savage with pain and anger and something more, something as elemental and ungovernable as night. She levered herself away from the wall despite the fact that her hands were bound behind her back. Head erect and spine straight, she waited.

Tan measured Lilac's strength and felt frustration eating at his control. No matter what punishments he devised to humiliate Lilac, she faced him with the pride of an empress. She knew no shame, acknowledged no master, bowed to no man's rules within her wretched soul. The more cruel he was to her, the stronger she became, using his own strength to defeat him.

"Fox Woman," Tan snarled in Mandarin. "You will lick dog parts and fuck pigs if you do not sign the paper."

Lilac's black glance went from Tan's face to his crotch. "There will be no difference," she said, "except, perhaps, in size. Even a small dog would be bigger than your insignificant tool."

Tan's skin took on a dark flush of rage as he walked closer to Lilac. She watched him with hatred and a curious, chilling triumph lighting the depths of her eyes. Yet, when Tan stood close enough to strike her, he didn't raise his hand.

"I know you, Fox Woman," he said, his voice vibrant with the same elemental darkness that glowed in Lilac's eyes. "You hope to make me lose control and kill you. That will never be. Nor will I permit you to kill yourself. I will keep you bound and alive until I die. I will use you to piss in until you choke. I will cut away your beauty inch by inch, and then I will stitch you up and start all over again. I will teach you fear."

Tan struck like a leopard unleashed, catching Lilac flush in the face with the back of his clenched fist, once, twice, three times, blows so fast they were a blur. Lilac's head snapped back and banged against the wall. Caught off guard, she couldn't control a cry of pain. Tan had hurt her before, but not like this, as though she were an object with no value. In the past, he had always been careful to preserve her beauty.

Tan looked at Lilac's dilated pupils and nodded in satisfaction.

"You are listening to me now, Fox Woman," he said, playing idly with Lilac's nipples. "That is good. Even demons feel pain, don't they?"

If Lilac had wanted to answer, the agony shooting through her when Tan twisted her nipples would have made speech impossible. Unmoving, she watched him out of wide black eyes. Very lightly, Tan's fingers touched the bruises forming on Lilac's face where he had struck her. Three drops of blood welled, one scarlet drop from each blow, glistening testimony to Tan's precise application of pain. Cupping her face between gentle hands, he bent until he could kiss the marks he had placed upon her once perfect flesh.

"Ah, my beautiful lover," Tan murmured, stroking her sadly, caressing her with a tenderness that was as real as his cruelty had been. "My own scented lotus, my lithe warrior of white jade limbs. No female will ever equal your beauty in the flowery battle, not even your own daughter. I will never sell you, sweet demon. I will keep you bound always to me, and your spirit will follow mine at death. How will you spend the time between now and eternity, my savage Lady Yin?" Tan asked, looking deeply into Lilac's black eyes. "Begin again with me as though it were the first time, the first night, and you were a maid trembling in her scarlet bridal bodice. Joy or pain, ecstasy or agony, love or hatred, orgasm or torment. I can give you all of them or none of them or one or two or three." He lowered his mouth to her lips and whispered, "What do you choose, my bittersweet Lilac Rain?"

Waves of heat and ice alternated dizzyingly in Lilac's body as she was swept by a fear such as she had never known. Tan the warrior, the conqueror, the arrogant lord; that Tan she knew and had fought successfully for many, many years. Tan the lover, the supplicant, the persuader, the poet; this Tan she had rarely glimpsed and never overcome.

And she was afraid.

Lilac opened her mouth, and her pink, glistening tongue arched toward Tan's lips, met his in a deep kiss, slid between his teeth until she was deeply in his mouth. She stroked him with aching gentleness, tasting him—and then her jaws snapped shut, and her teeth sliced through her own tongue, severing flesh and thick blood vessels in a single slashing instant.

The salty, smoky taste of Lilac's blood filled Tan's senses. With a gutteral cry, he caught Lilac as she swayed. Already her breasts were covered by a scarlet bodice of blood, travesty of bridal joy, and her life rushed from her with every beat of her heart.

From a great distance, Lilac heard Salyor's shouts and Wing's harsh answers as they raged at one another, sound without meaning, one English, one Cantonese. Sounds faded in and out, then merged into a single low roaring. Pain was a living, fiery animal in her mouth, consuming her, choking her.

Is this what the phoenix feels when it burns—?

The question was never spoken because Lilac had no tongue; but oblivion held the answer. Soft darkness swept down, surrounding her utterly. At the last instant, a distant, widening circle of brilliance beckoned to her. Like a phoenix rising from ashes, Lilac flew toward the light.

As the last of Lilac's life finally drained between Tan's fingers, the fury and grief he felt immobilized him. He made no sign, no sound, because he knew in his soul that no screams could ease his pain, no curses could relieve his rage, nothing could change what had been done.

Motionless, silently raging, Tan understand too late that he had loved Lilac as much as he had hated her—and he wondered if her hatred had been mixed with love in just the same agonizing way.

30

In the hours before dawn, Tea Rose lay awake, ignoring the strange, clammy pillow beneath her cheek. The dampness came not from tears, but from the draught of laudanum she had half-swallowed and held in her mouth until she could let the bitter liquid drip unnoticed from her lips onto the pillow. The opium that was still within her system gave a surreal quality to her thoughts, but nothing was as unbelievable as the tactile memory of a knife at her throat, held by her mother's own hand.

Why? What have I done, mother? Why do you hate what you once loved? Is it simply that Tan comes at my touch and not yours, that I am young and you are not?

Tea Rose had held the big locket clenched in her hand for so long that she couldn't tell where her skin ended and the gold began. The diamond was as deeply set into her flesh as it was into the precious metal itself. But it was the picture that was engraved indelibly on Tea Rose's mind, her mother's radiance, and the white man's gentle strength.

This is your father, Tea Rose, and also mine. You are my sister. Sleep, now. You're safe with me. Tan Feng can't ever touch you again.

Cass's words echoed and re-echoed in Tea Rose's mind, fading and increasing, fragile and booming, words that meant everything and nothing, words changing her life beyond belief.

Ah, mother, what have you done to me?

BOOK

⋅⋅◄[II]►⋅⋅

31

Jared rested for a moment on the long sweep-oars of the racing scull and listened to the water lap at the thin veneer of wood that lay between him and the cold Pacific. Beyond the eastern horizon the summer day had just begun, breathing the first golden veil of sunlight over land and sea alike. He loved this time of day, the silence and the openness, the feeling that he was soaring while the future condensed around him. Out on the water, he could think without interruption. Out here, the future was as close as dawn.

As Jared sat on the gently rocking surface of the sea, he visualized the sharp line between night and day rushing over the curve of the earth, binding all the distant lands and peoples together in a single radiant tide of light. Although he rarely spoke about it, he believed that the Pacific Ocean and the fiery ring of land that surrounded it formed a gateway to an extraordinary future, one in which Europe would play only a secondary part. It would be the relationships between Pacific Asia and the Pacific Rim of the New World that would make up the watersheds of mankind's future history. Paris, Rome, London, even New York—all would become what Cairo and Constantinople and Jerusalem already were, cities whose time of glory lay in the past, not the future, for they were oriented toward the Atlantic or Mediterranean, not the Pacific.

In the future, the names that rang through history would be Canton, Shanghai, Hong Kong, Tokyo. Their Western counterparts would be Sydney, Los Angeles, San Francisco, Seattle, and Vancouver. Today, most of those Western cities on the edge of the Pacific were more a promise than a reality, particularly in Australia, a country so new that its adolescent insularity hadn't yet had time to ripen into a cosmopolitan view of the world. Insularity wasn't simply a Western problem, unfortunately. The Celestials clung to their past as tenaciously as limpets, insisting that China was the center of the universe and all other nations and peoples were inferior.

But as trade increased and the peoples of the Pacific Rim mixed and made bargains and married, a new culture would slowly emerge, freeing dreams from the stranglehold of the past, giving mankind a limitless future. Jared intended that his offspring be a part of that future, riding the waves of Pacific change, helping East and West not only to meet but to anneal into a potent new culture.

That future was to Jared what gold was to King—a Holy Grail whose pursuit was uniquely worthy of his mind and mettle.

Gold-seeking had never been enough for Jared, as it was for King. When they had cleaned out a series of small placer pockets in nameless creeks on the western watershed of the Rocky Mountains, King had spent his gold as he found it, for it was the search that fed his soul, not the gold itself. Jared had spent no more gold than he needed to live. The rest had gone into a soft leather bag whose sides slowly had swelled and rounded like a pregnant woman's belly.

When the time of birth came, Jared had looked at a map and chosen a port city on the western edge of the continent, because he knew that throughout history, access to saltwater trade had separated the powerful cities from those landlocked into a dreamy contemplation of a distant past when the world had been flat and trade had moved overland rather than overseas. The city Jared chose was Seattle. It had a proven port, was surrounded by natural resources with which to build the future, and was new enough to have a first-come, first-served attitude toward power and trade.

In Seattle, Jared invested part of his gold, banked the rest, and shipped out on a lumber schooner carrying planks from Henry Yesler's Washington sawmills to Canton on the Pearl River in southern China. Over the next eighteen months, Jared made landfall in every major port on the Pacific, from the foreign settlement on the Sumida River in Tokyo, to Victoria Bay on Hong Kong's Fragrant Harbor, to Moreton Bay in Queensland. He fought and drank and bargained, and prospected for information over more than a third of the world. He learned rudimentary Cantonese from a shipwrecked Chinese sailor and decided that the sultry, salty tropics were not the place for him to build an empire.

When Jared returned to Seattle, he found King waiting impatiently, filled with rumors of gold. Jared took most of his money and bought a four-masted schooner named *Marlborough.* The rest of his money he used to stake himself and King to the pursuit of gold.

That became the pattern of the next decade for Jared. When he wasn't gold-hunting with King, he sailed the Pacific in the owner's cabin of half a dozen ships, buying and selling and trading, and most of all learning. He learned to decipher Chinese ideographs, and he read voraciously. He stayed in Hong Kong until he could not only understand but also speak Cantonese. He sailed the classic trade routes, and visited the backwaters as well, until the horizons of the Pacific Rim countries were as familiar to him as the shores of Elliott Bay.

Each time Jared came back to Seattle, he stayed longer. Each time he went gold-hunting with King, Jared was away for less time. He was ready to put down deep roots, to find a woman who could share his dream, to have children with her who would inherit that dream.

With that thought, the image of Cassandra Thornton condensed in Jared's mind. Everything he had seen in the ten days since they had stolen Tea Rose had reinforced his belief that in Cass he had found a woman to equal his dream. The initial attraction he had felt for her had grown stronger and stronger, doubling and redoubling with each meeting, his mind and body shouting to him that he had finally found a woman he could love, a woman who was beautiful but not vain, courageous but not foolhardy, intelligent but not dry, passionate but not undisciplined, sensual but not promiscuous.

Unfortunately, she was also young enough to fall in love with King Duran.

And she had.

Narrow-eyed, Jared looked over the pointed stern of the rowing scull, where the sun was rising above the blunt, forested form of Duwamish Head. As the light intensified, he could see the brown patchwork outlines of clear-cut logging operations interrupting the green velvet landscape. The patchwork grew greater every year, silently proclaiming the city's vitality, a tumbled confusion of homes and industries, greed and hope.

Seattle was as unruly and unpredictable as a bar brawl. In that much, building an empire based in the city was rather like placer mining. But no matter how often Jared had tried to explain that to King, his brother had simply shaken his head and said that it wasn't the same at all. King said Jared was simply chasing money. Chasing gold was different. Gold was the ineffable made tangible, proof of glory, incorruptible. Perfect.

Tears of the sun.

They were the only tears that moved King, the only reality that gripped his soul. Out of all the emotional colors of mankind, all the possibilities of life and feeling, he saw only one—the search for gold. When he was in the city, King's hunger for it drove him to gambling, liquor, and sweet-scented, good-looking women.

Like Cass.

Jared bent over the oars, gathered himself into a tight, tucked position and then drove hard with legs and arms in a smooth release of power. He paced himself at a steady sixty strokes a minute back across the water toward the Alki Point Rowing Club, enjoying the feel of his own strength, the deep steady breaths, and the sweat that told him his body was working hard and well.

In the past, when Jared and King had wanted the same woman, they had flipped a coin or shared her, no hard feelings and no regrets. Jared was so accustomed to women being drawn to his brother's wild flame that he had stopped resenting it about the same time that he had started to shave. Resenting King made as much sense as resenting a mountain for being taller than a man. Jared wasn't a mountain; he was a river, deep and swift and silent, flowing always toward the future.

And in the end, Jared knew that rivers wore mountains down into plains and then rolled on to the boundless sea.

Cass couldn't see past King to Jared. The sight of Jared didn't bring a flush to her face and a startled look to her eyes, as though she were surprised to find herself in love. It was King who received those swift glances, those soft half-smiles, the caress of her gentle fingers. Cass had chosen her man, and that man was not Jared.

But King's soul already had a mate—the quest for gold.

Jared's stroke went up to seventy a minute. He drove himself hard, wishing that there were another way to do what must be done, knowing that there wasn't. King lacked the ability or the desire to sustain love for any length of time. He was simply too involved with his own soul to share it with a woman. He might woo her, bed her, perhaps even foolishly wed her, but he would never be able to sit still long enough to learn how to love her.

If only I hadn't asked King to stay and help with Tea Rose's rescue.

One more "if only" to add to the long list.

But Jared had asked because he had known that there was no man on earth he would rather have at his side in a fight than King Duran; and King had agreed to stay because there was no man on earth he would rather stand by than Jared Duran; and all the regrets and "if onlys" in the world wouldn't change one damned thing. The past was out of reach, and the present was out of control.

32

Roger Harwell was already seated at a clubhouse table that overlooked the open water of the Sound. The attorney saluted Jared with his coffee cup and looked toward the bright rowing shells stacked on the wharf.

"What makes a gentleman of leisure such as yourself work so hard?" Harwell asked.

Hair still slick from his shower, Jared smiled and took a chair. "Gets my heart started."

"Coffee works faster and doesn't make you nearly as sweaty. You want some or have you started drinking the Chinese brew?"

Jared glanced at the lawyer. "I don't pay you a monthly retainer to keep track of my personal tastes."

Harwell looked uncomfortable. "Hell, Jared, I don't care if you drink green tea and eat dried fish and go to Chinatown for, um, entertainment. But if half of what I hear is true, I'd better start reading criminal case law if I want to do you any good."

Without a word, Jared picked a cinnamon roll from the basket in the center of the table. When the roll was buttered to his satisfaction, he returned his attention to Harwell.

"I thought I had asked you to find out about a civil case filed against Cassandra Thornton," Jared said.

"So you did, and so I did. But the deeper I looked into the case, the more I wondered whether you needed me or a member of the bar who is experienced in criminal defense. The civil case against Miss Thornton involves the alleged kidnapping of a Chinese woman by the name of Tea Rose."

"Kidnapping?" Jared took a bite, chewed, and swallowed. "Is that what the police are calling it?"

"No. That term was introduced by the young woman's husband. Some Chinaman named Wong Ah Wing. He's even got a Chinaman's marriage license proving they're man and wife."

"Her husband, is it? That will come as something of a shock to the young lady, since she's only fourteen years old."

"Then you *do* know something about this mess," Harwell said.

Jared shrugged. "Obviously, Tan Feng thinks I do. His lawyer has been trying to serve a subpoena on me for a week now."

"Who's Tan Feng?"

"Wing's boss."

"Oh." Harwell shrugged. "Well, subpoenas aren't a problem. That's a fishing expedition. I can get it quashed. I'm more concerned about the rest of it. The pleadings make it sound as though the girl were ripped from the bosom of her family by great force and violence. There's even some mention of two unidentified white men who mounted an armed invasion that resulted in the injury of several decent and honorable citizens of Chinatown."

Jared shook his head in amusement. "Invasion? God in heaven but you lawyers do dress a thing up, don't you? You make a street-corner shoving match sound like Armageddon."

"You pay me three hundred Yankee dollars a month to do exactly that," Harwell retorted. "Wing is paying Robert Salyor a lot more to do the same thing in his behalf."

Jared knew that it was Tan Feng, not Wing, who was paying Salyor, but there was no reason to make an issue of it.

"Salyor—Salyor," Jared mused aloud. "I've heard that name recently. Isn't he the man who just won the big divorce case down in Portland?"

"The same. He's good, Jay. He ties local judges in knots until he gets what his client wants."

"Which is what, precisely, in this case?" Jared asked.

"I talked to Salyor yesterday afternoon, off the record, just to see what this Wing wants. He'll be more than happy to let you off the hook if you'll just tell him where Tea Rose and Miss Thornton have gone."

"Presuming, of course, that I know where they are," Jared said.

"He's convinced you do. I don't know what his reasons are or whether they're valid. That's your business. Frankly, I'd rather not know. But I must advise you that Salyor is going to squeeze you as hard as the law allows until he gets what his client wants."

"He wants Tea Rose," Jared said flatly.

Harwell tried and failed to conceal his irritation. "Is all this fuss about a Chinese tart? Hell, man, send the little baggage back to her own kind. A scandal like this could ruin your future in Seattle. Citizens here don't hold with immoral—"

"When I want a sermon, I hire a preacher," Jared interrupted coolly.

"I doubt that you spend much money on preachers," Harwell muttered.

Jared helped himself to some scrambled eggs from a covered dish on the table, signaled to the waiter that he needed coffee, and waited while it was poured.

"What should I expect from Salyor?" Jared asked after the waiter had moved away.

"He'll come at you like a steam-powered buzz saw, but that's what he gets paid for. He's only as tough as his client."

"Wing is just a stalking horse. It's Tan Feng we have to worry about. He's tough enough for two men."

Harwell sighed. "That's unfortunate. Wing's legal position is better than yours."

"Why?"

"He's trying to recover a stolen wife. You're trying to hang onto an illicit toy."

"Tea Rose is fourteen. A bit young for me, don't you think?"

"What I think doesn't matter. In the law's view, fourteen is too young for a whore."

"But not for a wife?"

"We try not to interfere in other people's customs."

"Particularly when the fifty-year-old judge happens to have a wife who just turned sixteen," Jared said sardonically. "Let me tell you something, counselor. Tan Feng is a whoremaster. Wing is one of his lieutenants. Tea Rose is neither Wing's wife nor my mistress. Tea Rose is a virgin who is approaching the day of her greatest value—the day her maidenhead is sold to the highest bidder in a travesty of the wedding ceremony as we know it."

"What?"

"You heard me. If that shocks your delicate Christian sensibilities, you won't be much help to me."

Harwell drummed his fingers on the table as he frowned at Jared's lean, hard face.

"Are you sure she's a virgin?" Harwell demanded bluntly.

"Yes."

"Then what in hell is Salyor trying to prove? He's no fool. He knows that the courts have been tolerant of Chinese customs—forced marriages and the like—but no judge in America is going to turn a child over to some opium-stained whoremaster. I don't care if Salyor's got a marriage license signed by the highest muckety-muck of the biggest joss house in town. It just isn't going to happen." Harwell hesitated, then added reluctantly, "Of course, the law won't view Miss Thornton's guardianship very favorably, either. She is a young woman living alone, with no means of support except photography and no formal church affiliation or record of attendance. If it goes to court, Salyor will make Miss Thornton look like little more than a prostitute herself. Wait," Harwell said quickly at Jared's hard look. "I'm sure Miss Thornton has impeccable morals. I'm equally sure that Salyor will drag her name through the mud. In the end, no matter how spotless her private life may have been, her reputation will be ruined."

Jared clamped down on his anger, knowing that Harwell

was only telling the truth. That was one of the reasons Jared didn't want the matter to go to court. Cass's name would never recover from the scandal—particularly when King's reputation with women was thrown into the unsavory stew.

"Did Salyor say anything about Tea Rose's parents?" Jared asked finally, forcing himself to put into words the question that he feared silence had already answered.

Despite his casual tone of voice, Harwell knew Jared well enough to sense what the answer meant to him. The lawyer tilted his round face to the right and studied his client.

"No," Harwell said, after a long look. "Not a word. Why?"

Jared didn't answer. He stared out the window at the blue morning light for a long time. Harwell watched what seemed to be a stiff battle for control. When Jared spoke again, his voice was soft, and his words were careful.

"I'm not a lawyer, but it seems to me that a mother's claim to a child would take precedence over a purported husband's, particularly when the so-called bride is fourteen."

"Yes, I would think so. Particularly if the girl's virginity could be proven."

"If necessary, it can be. Are you sure Salyor never mentioned Lilac Rain?"

"No. Who is she?"

A dead woman, Jared thought. *You'll pay for her death, Tan Feng. You'll pay if I have to burn down all of Chinatown and drive you like a stinking rat from the ruins.*

"Tea Rose's mother," Jared said, his voice still soft.

"Then why in God's name isn't Salyor using her? Even if she's a prostitute, she's better than——"

"Lilac is dead, probably buried in some cellar or cut up for fish bait, but certainly dead. Tan Feng killed her, or had her killed."

Harwell measured the controlled anger in the man across the table from him, and chose his next words with great precision.

"Can you prove that?"

Jared shook his head. "No Chinese will speak out against Tan. It would be suicide."

"Then we may have a stalemate as to the best guardian for Tea Rose, unless you want to testify. I wouldn't recommend that, by the way, considering the criminal charges that might eventually arise in this case. It could be made to look very bad for you," Harwell said bluntly.

"What? A lawyer admitting that facts don't speak for themselves in the eyes of the law?" Jared asked coolly.

"The first thing you learn in law school is that facts aren't facts until somebody testifies to them," Harwell answered. "Like it or not, that's the system."

"It's the system in the courtroom, counselor, but not in the real world."

"Do you have something in mind I should know about?"

"No. I don't think you should know about it at all. There is one thing that might help you, however. Tea Rose is Miss Thornton's half sister."

Harwell shrugged. "She's still a China girl, and Wong is still her husband."

"Yes, I thought the law would see it that way." Saying nothing more, Jared pushed back his chair and left the room.

Outside the club, John was waiting with the carriage. Jared tossed his case in the back and swung up beside John on the front seat.

"Well?" Jared asked.

"They've changed detectives again," replied John, picking up the reins. "The others pulled back this morning, but then these men appeared. They're over in the trees. They've been looking for a lost golf ball for the past twenty-five minutes."

Jared turned and pretended to fumble with his briefcase on the carriage's back seat. In the process, he stole a glimpse of the men who were following him.

The two men were dressed casually. They could have been businessmen on their morning walk or golfers out for an early-morning match. Behind them, Jared caught a flickering glimpse of brown, which he assumed marked the position of horses tethered behind the screen of trees.

John started the carriage horse and turned onto the road toward town. After a moment, Jared looked back and saw the detectives toss aside their cigars and move swiftly toward the trees. By the time the carriage had gone a quarter-mile, the two men had galloped off the golf course and melted into the early-morning traffic, maintaining a constant interval between themselves and the Duran carriage.

"They're pretty polished," Jared said, taking a final quick look.

"Tan and Salyor must be spending a fortune, which means they still don't know where Cass and Tea Rose are," John said.

"For these small things we're grateful," Jared muttered. Then, "Take me to the *Seattle Post-Intelligencer* building."

Jared said nothing more until he climbed down in front of the newspaper offices.

"Keep tracking that railroad stock," Jared said, "but don't buy any yet. And John?"

"Yes?"

"Find out how Lilac died."

33

Along the shoreline, the icy azure of Puget Sound dissolved into a fragile foam that resembled peach blossoms whirled into curling windrows. Above the reach of wind and wave, the Lincoln green of midsummer lawns rolled in manicured perfection to the feet of houses even whiter than the foam.

The beauty of the day and of Bainbridge Island was lost on Tea Rose. She took as much pleasure in the lattice garden house overflowing with blooming fuchsias as a prisoner would in the bars of his prison. And like a prisoner, her gaze was fixed on freedom, the ragged skyline of Seattle eighteen miles across the water, jutting above the surrounding forest.

Somewhere in that angular line of buildings was her home. Somewhere out there in the distance, Jasmine sat with her tiny lily feet in a pan of scented water while she bathed and trimmed and finally wrapped once again in silk bindings her most precious assets. Somewhere out there, Lotus Moon sat patiently, her hands around her ankles and her feet lifted higher than her head, stretching her joints and muscles again and again in order to maintain the flexibility so prized by Tan Feng in a sing-song girl. Somewhere out there, Lilac and Tan were locked in endless flowery battle, his jade stem buried deeply within her supple body. Somewhere out there—

And Tea Rose was here, exiled to this freedom that was a more confining prison than any room within the Soong Li Tong's warren of buildings.

"Tea Rose, where are you?"

Tea Rose heard Cass's call and ignored it. She couldn't bear the thought of going back into the drab house, its interior colors those of death, its furniture too soft and of an awkward height. The smells of the house were strange and unappealing, the outer walls of its rooms so filled with uncovered glass that it was like living on a spotlighted stage. Only in King's room was Tea Rose more at ease, for there the heavy drapes were drawn, and the wall coverings and bedspread were made of a rich crimson brocade. Whenever possible, she sat in King's room, listening to his restless tossing and ragged breathing, thinking of all the ways in which her world had changed, devising plans for returning to the world she knew.

Once Tea Rose stole back into Chinatown, Lilac would accept her daughter again. Tea Rose was certain of it. She would be a very obedient daughter, saying nothing to distress her mother, never again teasing Tan Feng with firecrackers and an impudent laugh. Tea Rose would be home again, and all would be well. She would eat sticky rice and sweet pork and fried noodles and vegetables with color and texture; and food would come to the table properly cut, so that people didn't have to wield dull little knives and clumsy forks, hacking food down to a civilized size.

And never, not once again in her life, would Tea Rose have to stare at the rotten milk called "cheese" and try not to vomit what small amount of food she had already managed to sneak past her sensitive nose.

"Tea Rose! Come help me with King!"

Once Tea Rose knew that it was King rather than lunch that had caused the summons, she responded quickly. As she rose, her legs tangled in the awkward, limp skirt that Cass had cut off and hemmed for her. Tea Rose hated the skirt; it had the color and sensual appeal of dog droppings.

"Someday I will rip this off and leave it for the pigs to piss on!" Tea Rose whispered savagely, yanking folds of skirt from between her legs so that she could move quickly.

The wool cloth of her skirt rubbed harshly against thighs accustomed only to cloud-soft silk. The cotton blouse chafed her neck and her breasts. But the shoes were the worst—brown and stiff, rubbing raw spots on her tender feet.

When Tea Rose hurried in the front door and past the furniture in its white dust covers, she caught a glimpse of herself in the hallway mirror. She frowned fiercely and hurried on, hating the pale image that had glared back at her, a ghost face surrounded by a funeral room draped in white.

Gone were the bee-stung scarlet lips and pearl face powder and peach-blush cheeks. Gone was the flashing, glittering, chiming fascination of her headdress. Instead, she was nothing but a wretched child in pigtails and ugly clothes more suited to a scullery maid than to the pampered female she had been in Tan Feng's house.

"Where were you?" Cass demanded, then said quickly, "Never mind. King's fever is up again. You'll have to help me wash him down. Get the water."

Without a word, Tea Rose went to the bathroom and drew

a pan of cool water from the white enamel and brass faucet. Of all the strangeness she had endured since being kidnapped, the bathroom was the greatest. The house was the summer home of a wealthy businessman, a friend of Jared's. It contained the most modern of conveniences. There had been nothing in Chinatown like the icy porcelain toilet and bathtub, the wash basin and S-shaped drain. Tea Rose delighted in the ease with which she could bathe. It was some small, soothing compensation for the luxuries she had lost.

Carefully carrying the shallow basin of water, Tea Rose walked into King's room. Cass had already stripped away the bedcovers and was unbuttoning King's black pajama top. The pajama bottoms looked quite odd—the left leg was intact, but the right leg had been cut away a few inches below the crotch to allow access to King's wound.

"I'm sorry," Cass said, turning to give Tea Rose a weary smile as she put the basin on the bedside table. "I know this isn't a proper thing for a young girl to do, but I've had so little sleep in the past ten days that I'm clumsy, and I don't have the strength to turn him over any more, and I never know when Jared is coming and—I'm sorry, I know this is embarrassing to you, but—there's really no choice."

Tea Rose looked curiously at Cass. "Embarrassing? Why?"

"We can hardly bathe King with his clothes on, can we?"

Tea Rose waited, but there was no further explanation. When Cass fumbled in her attempts to get the pajama top off King's lean yet heavy body, Tea Rose stepped forward. In this, at least, she was accomplished. The difference between a man's body in Chinatown and a man's body on Bainbridge Island was insignificant.

"Let me," Tea Rose said.

To Cass's surprise, the girl stripped off the pajama top with a minimum of fuss. In fact, she moved so fast that King's pajama pants were halfway down around his hips before Cass realized her intention.

"Stop!"

Puzzled, Tea Rose looked up. "It's all right, sister. I will be careful of his wound."

"No, that's not it," Cass said quickly. "We don't have to bathe all of King right now. I can finish when you leave."

"I don't understand. His legs are heavier to move than his arms, and you said you were tired—"

King muttered sounds that could have been words. Cass remembered the feel of his burning heat through the pajama top. The infection in his leg was finally abating, but the fever itself came and went without warning.

"You're just a child," Cass said. "I can't ask you to deal with a fully naked man. I'll manage that part without you. I became accustomed to it when I nursed my father before he died."

At first, Tea Rose thought that Cass was teasing her. Then the girl realized that Cass meant every word—she believed that a nude male body would embarrass Tea Rose. With an automatic motion, Tea Rose covered her laughter with her hand. At first, Cass thought the girl was embarrassed.

"I'm sorry," began Cass, only to have Tea Rose cut across her words.

"Ah, sister, don't worry about shocking me. I know all about a man's cock and balls and ass."

Cass closed her eyes and drew in a sharp breath. Tea Rose's combination of youthful innocence and gutter English still had the ability to shock Cass. She had made it clear that she wouldn't tolerate casual coarseness in Tea Rose's speech.

"Tea Rose," Cass said tightly, "this isn't a whorehouse. If you expect to do well in polite society, you'll have to watch your language much more carefully."

The girl's mouth flattened with the impatience that surged up in her every time she ran up against her half sister's baffling customs.

"Yes, yes," Tea Rose muttered, sweeping the pajamas down King's body. "Penis and testicles and buttocks," she said, touching the parts casually as she named them. "Is that better, sister? Does the fact that it takes three times as long for me to describe reality somehow make it less shocking to you?"

Without waiting for an answer, Tea Rose dipped the cloth in water, wrung it out, added soap, and began washing King's face. When she glanced up again, Cass was staring at her.

"You look like a fish thrown into the bottom of a boat, sister," Tea Rose murmured. "What do you think I did when I wasn't learning to read and write in two languages, or playing the mandolin so that I could sing sad songs of unfulfilled desire? I learned what a man's body is and what a woman's is, why Yin and Yang are what they are, lock and key, and how to make the key strong and hard. I have bathed more men than you have kissed."

Cass closed her eyes. She was tired, so tired—never in her life had she been so long with so little sleep. She felt like a wire stretched taut and then stretched even more, until it vibrated with tension.

I can't deal with this sweet-faced, foul-mouthed child. I can't cope with her, and with King's fever, and with waiting for Tan's men to find us, and with King so ill that he thrashes and turns and moans. Oh, God, let him heal! Let him heal so I won't spend my life wondering if I killed the man I love trying to redeem a half sister from a hell she weeps to return to.

Opening her eyes, Cass looked at the girl whose beauty was so angelic once it had been washed free of a strumpet's paint and dressed in decent skirt and blouse. As Tea Rose bathed King with gentle, impersonal hands, she looked closer to ten than to fourteen, until she twisted to the basin again and the fabric of her blouse drew firmly across high, perfect breasts.

Tea Rose's physical maturity had come as a shock to Cass. Somehow, she had expected Tea Rose to be as shapeless as the tunic and pants she had worn. Cass had expected a laughing child and had gotten something quite different. She had never thought of herself as prudish, but she was a world away from Tea Rose's matter-of-fact acceptance of sex.

Without a word, Cass took a clean basin, drew fresh water in the bathroom and returned to help Tea Rose bathe King. Somewhere between his ribs and his knees, a combination of exhaustion and pragmatism overcame Cass; she simply didn't have the energy to be bothered by King's nakedness. It was as though she were bathing King alone, except that the task was easier, four hands working to wash and rinse and roll King onto his side, so that he could be washed and rinsed once more. While they bathed him, they soaked the dressing on his wound, loosening the crusted bandages. When the last layer was ready to come off, Cass hesitated.

"You do fine with nakedness, but how are you with gore?" Cass asked bluntly.

"Abortion is a skill every sing-song girl learns."

"I — see." Cass expelled a hard breath, appalled by Tea Rose's words and unable to conceal it. "Well, this shouldn't give you any problem, then. Bring a fresh basin of water. No, not that basin. The clean one on the dresser."

As gently as possible, Cass peeled away the last of the dressing. King moaned softly, but his eyes didn't open. Despite his nakedness and the cooling bath, his skin was hot and dry to the touch. The wound was puffy, raised, welted—a raw hole gouged out of living flesh. Despite the wound's ugliness, there were no red lines radiating out from it into healthy flesh. Each time the dressing was changed, there was less pus than before. Even in the dim light, the blood that flowed in the wake of the removed dressing was a fresh, brilliant scarlet.

"Don't worry, sister," Tea Rose said, seeing Cass's concern. "The flesh isn't rotten. Bend over the wound and take a deep breath. There is no sweetness of decay. He's a strong man, as strong as Tan Feng, perhaps."

"I've never known a stronger man than King," Cass said, cleaning the wound carefully.

"Then you have never known his brother."

Shrugging, avoiding the thought of Jared, Cass said only, "King is different."

"Yes, he is," Tea Rose said. Unnoticed, her hand stroked

the beguiling softness of King's beard, enjoying its unexpected texture. "But don't give your soul to him, sister. He doesn't want it."

Cass paused in the act of applying medicine. "You've been raised to believe men want only sex," she said carefully, trying to match Tea Rose's bluntness, "because sex is all that sing-song girls are trained to provide. There is much more between a man and a woman than sex."

Saying nothing, Tea Rose looked up from King's body into the golden glance of her half sister. Tea Rose's eyes were pieces of elemental midnight polished into clarity. Cass looked into their black depths as long as she could bear it, then looked away, feeling chilled and baffled. She was almost a decade older than Tea Rose, yet the girl's utter self-confidence was more than a match for Cass's own.

At times, Cass had the distinct feeling that, having discovered her discomfort with the prostitute's trade, Tea Rose subtly and continually baited Cass on that very subject. Never once had Cass found any hint of maliciousness in Tea Rose's expression or voice, yet sometimes Cass sensed its presence quite clearly.

When King's leg had been bandaged once more, Cass and Tea Rose worked together to change the sheets, which were wet from his sweating and from the bath itself. First, they rolled King onto his side and made one half of the bed, then they rolled him back to the middle and made the other half. Tea Rose faithfully followed Cass's instructions with the baffling bedcovers. In a third of the time it usually took, both King and his bed were fresh. Although he hadn't awakened, the activity had excited his wound, raised him to half-consciousness and left him fretful, despite the laudanum the doctor had recommended as a painkiller.

Cass put her fists on the small of her back and stretched, easing the aching muscles. "Thank you, Tea Rose. You can go back to whatever you were doing. I'll call you when it's lunch-time.

"May I sit with you, sister? I'll be very quiet. You won't even know I'm here."

"Of course," Cass said, giving Tea Rose a tired smile. "We haven't had much time to get acquainted, have we?"

"Opium makes talk difficult."

Cass wondered if she were being baited once more, but there was only pleasantness on Tea Rose's face, nothing to suggest that she resented having been kept drowsy and submissive on laudanum for the first five days of her stay on Bainbridge Island.

"It was either that or tie you to your bed," Cass said crisply. "King needed all my time. I couldn't be chasing you up and down the island."

Tea Rose smiled slightly. "But you're very fast."

"Comes of having whole feet and decent shoes."

For a moment, the half sisters looked sideways at one another and then they both burst out laughing, remembering the wild chase through formal gardens that had ended with Cass bringing Tea Rose down in a flying tackle amid scarlet geraniums. It had been Tea Rose's first—and, so far, final—bid for freedom.

Impulsively, Cass held out her hand. "Come and sit next to me, Tea Rose. I'll tell you about my childhood, and you can tell me about yours, and we'll both try very hard not to be shocked."

After a moment's hesitation, Tea Rose took her half sister's hand.

Cass smiled encouragingly. "It will work. Honestly. But we both have to try."

Oddly, Tea Rose's pleasant smile didn't reassure Cass.

34

King rolled over fitfully, fighting the black cloud that engulfed his mind. The pain in his leg dragged him up into the half-consciousness that had become familiar since he had been shot. He opened eyelids made heavy by opium and struggled to focus. A golden nimbus glowed in front of him, an incandescent color that was brighter and softer than the finest gold dust he had ever poured from one palm to the other in pure sensual fascination.

"Gold," he whispered hoarsely, reaching for it.

His fingers trembled, then strengthened, allowing him to grasp the elusive treasure. Senses heightened by opium found the texture of the gold odd, different from what he had anticipated. But then, gold was always less than he expected, always ultimately disappointing, and yet—and yet—the search remained urgent, compelling, the very core of life itself. He had to have gold, and once he attained it, he had to let it slide through his fingers so that he could seek it all over again.

But not now. Now he was too weak. Now he needed—something—

The level of opium in King's body made logical thinking impossible and sensual responses inevitable. He succumbed to sensual need, struggling to bring the gold to his face, to taste and touch and bathe himself in its unexpected, miraculous presence.

"King," Cass murmured. "It's all right, darling. Go back to sleep."

His restless thrashing had awakened Cass from the makeshift pallet that lay on the floor next to his bed. It was four in the morning, the darkest hour of night, when lamps and human spirits burned at their lowest ebb. As she bent closer and stroked King's forehead and cheeks soothingly, her unbound hair swung out to meet his reaching hand. Lamplight transformed her hair into myriad threads of molten gold.

"Don't—leave me," King said, tangling his hand in the golden mass, pleading with it this time to be all that he had hungered for and never found. "Just once—just this once—keep your promise."

"Shhhh," murmured Cass, stroking King slowly. "I'm here, King. I'll stay with you. Go to sleep."

"Stay—"

"Yes. I promise."

King let out a ragged breath that was almost a groan. He struggled against the opium claiming his system, as he strained to see his dream finally made tangible, the ineffable reaching out to him as he had always reached out to it, cool tears of the sun glittering and beckoning to him beneath a river as transparent and as deep as life itself.

Slowly, the gold condensed into focus—golden eyes watching him, eyes set within a nimbus of shifting, gleaming gold. After an enormous effort, King managed to lift his head from the pillow.

"Cassie?"

"Yes. Lie down, King."

His head swayed as he tried to focus beyond her. "Who else is here?"

"No one."

His breath came out in a low groan of disappointment. "But I thought I saw—"

Cass waited, but King collapsed and appeared to fall asleep again, his fingers tangled within her hair. When she tried to pull free, his fingers tightened their grasp, holding onto the radiance he could see only in his dreams. Cass looked longingly at her pallet, then gave up and stretched out beside King on the big bed, carefully avoiding his injured leg. In two hours, it would be time to give him more laudanum. She had no doubt his restlessness would wake her long before then.

It wasn't King's thrashing about that awoke Cass; it was being pulled into his arms sometime after dawn.

"King? What—"

"Shhhhh," he said, watching her with eyes so widely dilated that only a thin rim of green was visible. "This is a dream. Don't wake me."

Cass's protest was lost in King's mouth as he kissed her. The touch of his tongue against hers made her stiffen. Her muffled sounds made no impression on him, and despite his injury, he was more than strong enough to hold her in place.

With an effort, she turned her head aside, only to feel his mouth tease her cheek, her chin, her neck. Then his hand was beneath her breasts, between them, caressing first one and then the other with hungry urgency.

"King, no," Cass said, trying without success to push him away.

"Cassie—yes," he said, seeking her mouth again, stilling her protests, holding her without hurting her.

After a time, the touch of tongue against tongue intrigued Cass. Curious, she touched him in return, tasting the odd flavor of laudanum and the faint underlying saltiness of King himself. Suddenly, his tongue thrust fully into her mouth, filling her, and then retreating only to return again in a rhythmic seeking.

The depth and intimacy and hungry duration of the kiss went beyond anything she had ever experienced. She began to feel strangely dizzy, disoriented, as though she rather than he had been the one drinking opium-laced syrup. The realization that King's hands were caressing her breasts only enhanced her sense of disorientation. When his mouth finally lifted, she could hardly breathe.

"Stop," Cass said in a low voice that was almost a moan.

"Why?" King asked thickly, picking at the buttons of her nightgown, feeling her tremble.

"You're sick."

"The bullet went through my leg, not my balls. If you don't believe me, all you have to do is put that soft little hand of yours between my legs and check."

"King!"

"Go ahead, sugar. It will feel a lot better without the washcloth getting in the way."

"You—but—didn't the opium—I thought—"

King's slow smile was more dangerous than the hand that had worried three tiny buttons free of their holes and was working on a fourth. "Opium, huh?" he said. "Well, you can forget giving me any more of that crap. I'll take honest pain to those crazy dreams. Except for this dream. This one I like."

"The doctor said—stop that," she gasped, realizing that she was being unbuttoned.

"Then we agree. No more opium unless I fix the dose."

"No, I meant stop unbuttoning me."

"I will, eventually. How many of these damned things are there, anyway?"

King pulled himself half upright to pursue his task, then stopped. Pain twisted visibly across his face, cutting through the opium-induced sensuality.

"Lie down," Cass urged, putting her arms around him in order to ease him back down onto the bed. She felt him press his face between her breasts. His low groan of pain vibrated through both their bodies. "Darling, please lie down," she whispered. "Please. I can't bear knowing that you hurt."

Eyes closed, King slowly acquiesced to being lowered onto the bed. The intense, stabbing agony removed the last opium veil from his mind, bringing reality into focus with razor clarity. He opened his eyes and saw that Cass was real rather than a tantalizing dream.

"Oh, God, Cassie, I'm sorry," he said, eyes narrowed against even the dim illumination of the room. Breath hissed between his clenched teeth as he fought to control the combination of fierce pain and even more fierce desire that warred within his body. "I thought it was a dream, and then it was real and I've wanted you since the first time I saw you, and your breasts are so beautiful beneath that damned gown that it's driving me crazy."

Cass looked down at herself and realized that the sheer lawn of her nightgown did little to conceal her body. Automatically she crossed her arms over her chest, but nothing could hide the scarlet flush that consumed her from her breasts to the roots of her golden hair. She closed her eyes against the waves of embarrassment flooding through her.

"Don't," King said, his voice gentle. "You're a beautiful woman, Cassie. There's nothing to be ashamed of in that."

"No decent woman would—"

"Fuck decency," King said angrily, shocking Cass into silence. "Do you want to know what real decency is? It's you risking your butt to rescue a little China girl and then staying up night after night washing down a stranger's body, stroking his hair, talking to him, giving him water, changing his bandages, emptying his bedpan, sleeping on the floor next to him. To me, Cassie. To me. It was you all the time, wasn't it?"

"Tea Rose has helped me," Cass said faintly.

"Tea Rose is a sing-song girl. A man's naked body means no more to her than an unsaddled horse means to you."

Cass closed her eyes again and fought against the disorientation sweeping through her. Her life had been turned on its head and then yanked inside out since she had stood on a wharf and taken a picture of an old lumber scow two weeks ago. She could scarcely accept that it had been only fourteen days. Things she had never before questioned about herself and her beliefs and her family were suddenly like a thousand snares set out around her, tripping her no matter which way she turned.

Is this what Tea Rose feels like—uprooted, adrift, nothing to depend on but herself, a self that she doesn't know nearly as well as she thought she did?

"Cassie?" King said gently. "I'm sorry about the language, about touching—I didn't mean to insult you."

Slowly, Cass opened her eyes and looked at the man she barely knew, the man whose body was more familiar to her than any but her own had ever been. With a distant sense of shock, she realized that she had liked his deep kiss, the feel of his hands on her breasts, the intimacy of being so close to another human being. She hadn't felt insulted by King. She had felt—wanted. It was a heady experience to be the focus of those green eyes.

"Cassie? Say something, sugar. Don't be mad at me. I woke up opium-fuzzy and you were lying there against me, all warm and soft and golden."

"It's all right," Cass said.

"Is it?" King asked, searching her eyes.

"Yes," she whispered, smiling down at him.

"Cassie," he said, the word a sigh. "Come here for just a moment. Don't worry. It's all right. I won't hurt you."

"It's you I'm worried about, not me."

"Is it?" King gave Cass a slow, lazy smile that made her heart turn over. "Then don't move, sugar girl. Stay just where you are for a minute. Promise me?"

Bemused, Cass nodded.

King's hands came up and resumed their task of unbuttoning the tiny fastenings on Cass's bodice. Her hands flew up like startled birds, getting in his way.

"You're moving," he said, then smiled teasingly at her. "You wouldn't break your promise to a sick man, would you? Just thirty seconds more. There's nothing to blush about, Cassie. No one needs to know anything about this. Just you and me and the night—"

While King talked, his fingers worked. Before Cass knew what had happened, her bodice was undone, and King's warm palms had smoothed the cloth away and tucked it beneath her breasts, baring them while still leaving her shoulders and arms covered. As he looked at her, he made a sound that was mingled pleasure and pain, for the sight of her full breasts framed in white lace was both exquisite and unbearably arousing.

"Cassie," he whispered, but no more words came from his full lips. Silently, he held out his arms.

She hesitated.

"Despite what I said earlier, I'm too weak to do anything but cuddle," he admitted softly. With delicate care, he ran the back of his fingers down the warm slope of one breast. "Would you mind that? My head resting on your breasts? A man who sleeps like that won't have nightmares."

Cass didn't know that she was going to agree until she felt herself stretching out next to King. His beard caressed one of her breasts in the same instant that his tongue found the nipple of the other.

"King!"

"What's wrong, sugar girl?" he said, nuzzling gently, stroking each sensitive aureola with beard and lips and tongue. "Babies do this all the time."

"You're not a baby," Cass said, but the effect of her protest was spoiled by the huskiness of her voice.

"I feel as weak as one." King's tongue swirled around her nipple, drawing it out until she felt both hard and velvety in his mouth. "God, Cassie, I wish I were well," he murmured, groaning, nuzzling against her, enjoying her helpless response.

"Go to sleep," she said, hoping he couldn't hear the catch in her voice or feel the strange shivers that took her without warning. Streamers of pleasure coursed through her body as his tongue caressed her, making her want to arch her back. Of their own volition, her fingers worked into King's hair, encouraging the pressure of his mouth against her breast.

Cass didn't know whether she was relieved or disappointed when King followed her soft command and fell asleep. Even after the last odd ripples in the pit of her stomach stilled, she lay awake for a long time, feeling the warmth of King's breath between her breasts, wondering at how her life had changed so quickly, how she had come to lie with a man in such trembling intimacy—and knowing that she didn't really care how it had happened.

In a world gone awry, she desperately needed the comfort of King's living warmth, the reassurance of his arms around her, the piercing sweetness of his caresses telling her she wasn't alone anymore.

35

With no expression on her face, Tea Rose stood looking at the useless, oversized wooden hammers and the equally useless wooden balls, each painted a color of the rainbow.

She had learned the intricacies of fan-tan, mah-jongg, and chess in order to play them with her mother or Tan Feng. Croquet was different. Tea Rose couldn't imagine one single use on earth for the ridiculous, frustrating game.

"Gently, Tea Rose. You must stroke the ball, not bang it as though it were a baseball," Cass said.

"Stroke the ball," Tea Rose repeated neutrally. Then, "What is a baseball?"

"A ball used in another game."

"Americans are very fond of games and balls," Tea Rose said, her voice as bland as her expression.

Looking away quickly, Cass pretended to have misplaced the next wicket as an excuse to hide the faint color rising to her cheeks. She knew that she was foolish to react to an innocent use of the word "balls" merely because of what King had said three nights before about the location of his wound. Yet, she couldn't think of that night without a quickening of her heart and body.

The memory of that night was quickly followed by the memory of the night after, when King had refused to sleep until Cass stretched out beside him on the bed. She had insisted on wearing a robe and a nightgown and keeping both fastened, only to awake in the darkness before dawn with King's face pressed between her bare breasts. Sleepily, she had started to do up her gown, only to have King capture her hands. His mouth lazily caressing her breasts had felt far too good to argue over in her sensual, barely awake state. When he had sighed and fallen asleep once more, she had left her clothes undone, enjoying the feel of his beard and breath against her naked skin.

As though sleeping cuddled next to Cass were the medicine he had been lacking, King's wound was healing quickly. His fever had broken. Since the first night she had let him sleep with his head on her breasts, he had measured out his own doses of laudanum, declaring that he would rather hurt than have no more brains than a kitten.

After Cass had seen that King grew stronger with each

hour, she hadn't argued any more. His resiliency and strength amazed her. He had taken over care of his own most intimate needs, although he insisted that he couldn't wash his legs effectively, so Cass had continued doing that when she changed his dressing. And he watched her the whole time, his eyes a lazy, smoky green that made her hands tremble. She looked forward to changing his dressing now, to bathing his long, powerful legs, and to the moment late at night when she would stretch out on the bed next to him and go to sleep in his arms.

Cass was startled from her thoughts by Tea Rose.

"I'm sorry," Cass said. "Did you say something to me?"

"Yes, sister. I think I should teach you more Chinese words."

"All right."

Tea Rose held up her mallet. "In Chinese, this is *yu-ching*. The ball is—" She hesitated, and then her smile bloomed anew as she made her choice among sexual euphemisms— she had finally found a use for the ridiculous game of croquet. "The ball is *chieh-shan-chu.*"

Cass repeated the words several times, trying to reproduce the precise intonations required for the Chinese language. When she had those words under control, Tea Rose pointed to the wicket.

"That is *ch'iung-men.*"

Again, Cass practiced until she had the intonations correct.

"The game itself is called *fang-shih.*"

Cass repeated the new word, then said, "I didn't know you played croquet in Chinatown."

"We don't," Tea Rose answered promptly.

"Then why do you have a name for the game?"

Tea Rose took a long time lining up wicket and ball and mallet before she said, "We don't have to do a thing to know that it exists." She bent gracefully, swung back the mallet, and hit the ball smartly, sending it zipping through the metal arch. "And that is *yun-yu,*" she finished triumphantly, despite the laughter that kept her mouth hidden behind her hand.

For the next twenty minutes, Cass played croquet using only the Chinese words Tea Rose had taught her. The girl ended up laughing so often that it was difficult for her to play at all. Cass didn't get irritated that her pronunciation of the strange words apparently was so bad as to be laughable. She was too pleased to see Tea Rose happy to mind being the source of that amusement. By the time the game was nearing its conclusion, Cass was laughing as much as Tea Rose.

Just as Cass was lining up her final shot, a flash of white out on the blue waters of the Sound caught her eye. A blunt-bowed launch was steaming around the point, heading toward the boathouse in the protected cove that bordered the mansion's grounds. Cass recognized the boat immediately as the one Jared used when he came to check on them. But it had been only two days since his last visit, and the launch wasn't coming toward them from the usual direction.

She peered at the man at the wheel, but the sunlight's glare had turned the windscreen he stood behind opaque. Her heart beat in sudden fear that it wasn't Jared at all, but one of the men who had been looking for her.

John appeared on the foredeck and waved. Cass let out a sigh of relief.

"Look!" Tea Rose called, her voice high with excitement. "It's China John. He promised to bring me hoisin sauce and garlic and vegetables that aren't canned or withered, and hundred-year-eggs."

Eyes sparkling with anticipation, Tea Rose clapped her hands together, unable to contain her excitement at the thought of all the edible wonders coming ashore. Cass smiled and held out her hand to her half sister.

"Come on," she said. "Let's go down and meet them."

As always, there was an instant of hesitation before Tea Rose took Cass's hand. Cass no longer worried about it, for Jared had assured her that it was simply the Chinese way not to touch or to demonstrate affection in public—which meant that Cass was doubly pleased when Tea Rose smiled almost shyly and took her hand.

"Okay. Now lift your skirt in the other hand—not that high," Cass added hastily, laughing. "Ready? Let's go!"

Together, they ran down the sloping green lawn. Their laughter reached the shore before they did, echoing in the boathouse, making both men grin as they hopped out and went about securing the boat. But when Cass and Tea Rose hurtled through the boathouse door, Jared's smile faded. He wasn't looking forward to what he must tell Tea Rose.

"Is something wrong?" Cass asked, her smile vanishing after a single look at Jared's face.

John glanced quickly at Jared, wondering what he was going to say.

"Guess I'm just cranky after five hours of playing cat-and-mouse with Tan's hirelings," Jared said casually.

"His hatchet men followed you?" Cass asked, shocked.

"No, I'm used to losing them. But Tan hired some more white detectives. They're harder to lose. In fact, they're too damned good. They figured out I was using the boat to get to wherever the two of you were hiding. Today, they were waiting off Alki Point for me to go by, trying to look like fishermen. Took me most of the morning to get rid of them." Jared finished tying off the bowline before he turned back to Cass. "So stay inside during the day, and keep Tea Rose with you. They have binoculars."

"Are the men dangerous?" Cass asked bluntly.

"They won't try to kidnap you, if that's what you mean. They just want to serve some papers on you."

"Papers?"

"Tan Feng has hired a lawyer as well as private detectives."

"But I thought you said Tan Feng would avoid the law."

"I said he'd avoid complaining to the police," Jared corrected. "Lawyers aren't cops. Wong Ah Wing has filed suit in civil court. He wants his wife back."

"Wife?" Cass demanded, her voice rising. "Tea Rose?"

"Yes." Jared looked at Tea Rose. Shock, and the beginning of fury, showed on her face. "I see that you're as surprised as I was by the news of your marriage."

For a moment, Tea Rose didn't speak. When she did, her voice was low and very carefully controlled. "The man who is my husband. Are you sure he isn't Tan Feng?"

"Positive. I read the original document, not merely the translation. Your husband is Wong Ah Wing."

Tea Rose's face became tight with a rage that burst out in a torrent of sharp Mandarin. "I am no wife to that outhouse rat, that liquid stool of a diseased dog, that eater of shit, that fucker of pigs and—"

"Enough, female!" Jared said in Cantonese that was as cold and precise as her Mandarin had been. His voice was deep, gutteral, harsh—the command voice of a Chinese male.

Shock showed on Tea Rose's face for an instant, but her reflexes were deeply ingrained. Automatically, she put her hands together and bowed over them, speaking in Cantonese, Jared's language of choice. "A thousand pardons, master. This lowly slave forgot herself in the presence of—"

"Tea Rose," Jared interrupted more mildly, switching back to English. "Just shut up for a minute, will you? Most sing-song girls would be delighted to be first wife to a man of Wing's status. Or do you still believe that Tan Feng is so far into his dotage that his mind has clouded, and he will take you for his own concubine? Or did you aspire to be his second or third wife? Or, perhaps, his first, since his Celestial wife died in China two years ago?"

Tea Rose raised her head proudly, telling Jared that Lilac had been right; her beautiful, intelligent but inexperienced daughter had believed Tan Feng wanted her as wife, not as a toy for his idle hours.

"Use your very agile brain, Tea Rose," Jared said, his tone matter-of-fact. "If Tan Feng had ever planned to have you as his wife, or even as his concubine, it would be his name on that paper, not Wing's."

There was nothing Tea Rose could say to deny that truth,

so she remained silent, watching Jared with black, unflinching eyes. He returned her look for a long moment before he glanced back over at Cass.

"Wing filed papers two days ago in civil court, claiming that Tea Rose is his legal wife and that you've stolen her," Jared said. "If pressed in a criminal court, the charge would be kidnapping."

"But I'm her sister," Cass said. "And she's only fourteen. No court in the world would give her back to—"

"You're wrong," Jared interrupted, his voice flat. "The courts in Seattle have adopted a live-and-let-live attitude toward Chinese customs. Wing has a piece of paper his lawyer claims is a valid Chinese record of a Chinese marriage of a Chinese male to a Chinese female. The paper is even decorated by what purports to be Lilac's signature, all witnessed and countersigned by a couple of Tan's soldiers. The judge, no matter what his private opinion might be, will have a tough time ignoring that piece of paper."

"You can't mean that a judge might order me to give Tea Rose back to Tan Feng?"

"Wing, not Tan."

"It's the same thing and you know it!"

"Not on paper, and paper is all that matters in a court of law."

"Are you saying that I'm supposed to hand Tea Rose over to a—a lecher and a whoremaster?"

Jared smiled his comfortless smile. "No, Cass. I'm saying that we may have to fight them in the courts to see that our side is heard. I already have one of the best civil lawyers in the state taking a quiet look at the suit. In the meantime, we want to make very sure Tan doesn't find you or Tea Rose. You haven't seen any unusual activity here on the island, have you? Any strangers going from house to house, asking questions?"

Cass shook her head. "We haven't seen anyone but you and John."

Jared looked relieved. "Good. That means they're still

trying to figure out if you're on Bainbridge or some other island, or if my boat rides are just red herrings, and you're both really still in the city. In any case, this will be the last visit I make for a while."

Unhappily, Cass looked from Tea Rose to Jared.

"I think—"

Cass's voice caught at the thought of being left alone to deal with Tea Rose and King. Although Jared hadn't been present most of the time, when he had been in the house, it had been an enormous relief to her. The same strength of mind and body that had unnerved her under normal circumstances was very welcome in this crisis. Even so, she knew that there was too much risk in his coming back. In fact, he should stay as far away from them as possible.

"I think that's probably best," Cass said quietly to Jared. "You've got a reputation to protect. What would your bankers and other backers think if they found out you were harboring a fugitive from justice and the runaway child of a Chinese prostitute?"

"I don't give a damn what my various partners and 'peers' think," Jared said. "In any case, by the time they find out, the story will be more along the lines of 'a noble young man coming to the defense of an American child who has been sold into virtual slavery at the behest of a gambler, whoremaster, and opium runner.'"

Jared's slow, off-center smile reminded Cass very much of King. She found it impossible not to smile in return.

"I have enough friends in the newspaper business," Jared continued, "that I could permanently poison Tan Feng's well if I pushed hard enough. I've already sent him that message via an intermediary. The *Post-Intelligencer* has a team of reporters talking to American Chinese at this moment, asking questions about the man who's known as the 'Emperor of Chinatown.'"

"Is that what the Chinese call Tan?"

"No, but they will after today. That's what I called him the whole time I was being interviewed by the *Post's* top crime reporter. I did the same speech for their designated do-gooder, the one who writes columns lamenting the low state of human morality in general and Seattle's citizens in particular. The labels I put on Tan Feng will stick like tar and feathers."

Cass smiled unwillingly. "You're a confidence man at heart, aren't you?"

"I'm whatever gets the job done. Speaking of con men, how's my brother?"

The faint color that came to Cass's cheeks at the mention of King made anger flicker in Jared's blood; that delicate blush told him that the golden moth had finally succumbed to the siren call of the flame.

No emotion showed on Jared's face while he digested the unwelcome discovery. He had known Cass's attraction to King would inevitably increase while she nursed him. Jared had accepted it because there had been no choice but to accept what could not be changed. He or John had been out to the island as often as possible, but the brunt of the nursing had unfortunately fallen to Cass. There were no itinerant nurses who could be trusted with the secret of Tea Rose and "The Chinatown Gunman" whose identity had been hinted at but never printed in the newspapers. Then there was the matter of the reward Tan Feng had lately offered for the whereabouts of an injured man of King's description and a girl called Tea Rose—

"King is much better," Cass said. "His fever hasn't come back. He rarely takes the pain medicine. The wound is healing cleanly. In fact," she added with a worried frown, "I caught him trying to get out of bed at noon."

Jared shrugged. "That's King. He hates confinement."

"But he should be in bed for at least two more weeks."

"I know. Now, try to convince him. Hell," Jared said in sudden frustration. "I was going to move him back to Seattle as soon as he was better, but now—" Jared swore beneath his breath. "I can't risk it. The reward Tan Feng is offering is just too big."

"That's all right. I don't mind taking care of King." Cass looked earnestly at Jared. "Truly, I don't."

"Oh, I believe you, Cass. I just don't like it." Jared's thin smile made Cass flush. "John and Tea Rose are going to cook for us," he said in a clipped voice. "Call me when the food is ready."

"Where will you be?"

"Having a little chat with King."

36

When King saw his brother coming up the front lawn to the house, he groaned and pushed away from the bedroom window. Using a straight-backed chair as a clumsy crutch, he slowly pulled himself back into bed.

By the time the bedroom door opened, King was lying back against the pillows, pale and breathless from his forbidden excursion. Jared glanced at the chair, the rumpled throw rug beneath the window, and finally at his brother's drawn face.

"I thought that was you in the window," Jared said. "You don't have the sense that God gave a goose, do you?"

King smiled a bit ruefully. "I hate being laid up like a side of beef."

Jared grunted, spun the straight-backed chair around and straddled it, facing King. Without a word, Jared folded his arms across the backrest and eyed his brother with a steady, unwinking gaze.

"Jesus, Jay, a look like that makes a man feel like he's being sized up for a coffin," King grumbled.

"You keep prancing around on that leg, and that's just what I'll be doing."

King breathed out a huge sigh and a string of words heard more often around campfires than in silk-hung bedrooms. Jared waited until the epithets hissed into silence. He was good at waiting, which was one of the reasons King had always ended up turning to his younger brother for money when luck ran low.

"All right, spit it out," King said finally, watching Jared with narrowed green eyes.

"Tan Feng has a big reward out for you."

"So?"

"Dead or alive."

"Shit."

"Yeah. Shit. You can't walk across the room without breaking a cold sweat, so sending you up north is out of the question, isn't it?"

King looked uncomfortable but said nothing.

"Isn't it?" Jared repeated softly.

"Let it go, Jay."

"No. Not this time. This time, it's all the way to the bone."

For a moment, King closed his eyes and wished very hard that he were either stronger or weaker, or that his brother were a different kind of man. But wishing didn't change anything. When King's eyes opened, Jared still was staring at him with the bleak, appraising eyes of a man who neither sought nor gave quarter once the battle had begun.

"I wouldn't leave even if I could," King said slowly, searching Jared's clear, comfortless eyes, silently asking for more understanding. Or less. "Is that what you're driving at?"

Jared nodded.

"I've done a lot of thinking," King continued, choosing his words carefully. "I'm not as young as I was. I don't heal as fast. Maybe it's time for me to think of settling down, staying in one place, living like other men."

"Other men have jobs. Day after day after day. Same city, same building, same people, same work."

King let out another explosive breath. "If it's that bad, why the hell do you do it!"

"I didn't say it was bad, King. You did."

228

Jared said nothing more, simply waited with the kind of predatory patience that King had never been able to match.

The wound in King's leg ached fiercely, protesting his recent exercise. The reminder of his weakness enraged King. He kicked free of the blankets with savage impatience. Pain lanced through him. He welcomed it. This pain was clean, obvious, understandable, remediable. It wasn't like a shimmering gold dream crooning to him until he woke with a restless mind, and a rigid cock, and the knowledge of Cass's softness so near, tormenting him endlessly, pain without cure—save once.

"To stay, I'll need income," King said, and his voice seethed with all that he hadn't said and wouldn't say. "I'm no good with money, and I know it, so I'm turning all my stocks and cash over to you. I'm not asking for an empire like you're building, just a steady living that—"

"I can't take that kind of responsibility for you," Jared interrupted, his voice emotionless.

"Funny, neither can I." King sighed and made a half-angry, half-helpless gesture with his hand. "Then will you sell some of my railroad stock and rent me a place to stay?"

"You can stay with me."

"No. Not this time. It wouldn't work."

For a moment, Jared became utterly still, knowing without hearing the precise words that King intended to become Cass's lover.

"I thought you were going to use those railroad shares to stake you and Mule Dryden for a run up north," Jared said.

His voice was calm, but King knew his brother too well. He had seen that look on Jared's face the night he crouched in a shadowed Chinatown alley, coolly feeding shells into a pistol in the middle of a gunfight.

King smiled crookedly. "You'll stake me when the time comes."

"No."

King's eyes widened with surprise. He shrugged. "Then someone else will."

Jared came to his feet in a single catlike motion. He made no sound as he walked the few steps to his brother's bed.

"If you seduce her," Jared said distinctly, "I'll treat you like a stranger. If you get her pregnant, you better run and run hard, because I'll be on your tail. Don't let me catch you, King. I swear to God, *Don't let me catch you.*"

For a long moment, King met his brother's savage glance. Then King made a fierce, anguished noise, as though he were being pulled on a rack.

"What if I marry her?" King demanded. "What then!"

Jared's eyes glittered like ice. "Are you going to marry her?"

"How the hell do I know what will happen?" King asked roughly. "Christ, Jay, I could have died! I don't know about tomorrow, and I don't care. Tomorrow is your specialty, not mine. Mine is living *now.*"

"What about Cass? Where does she fit into your tomorrows?"

King opened his mouth to answer, but no words came. He had already said all that he could, all that mattered, all that was true.

He didn't know.

It was the same for Jared. He had already said all that mattered, all that was true, and King hadn't been deflected from his pursuit of sweet disaster.

Jared stood and left the room without saying another word.

37

Cass stood in the kitchen listening to Tea Rose and John converse in harsh, staccato Cantonese while they worked. Between them lay exotic cooking implements and even more exotic vegetables in colorful array. When Jared came into the kitchen, Cass looked toward him and smiled in unconscious relief. Before she could tell him how nice it would be to hear English again, he began talking to Tea Rose in Cantonese.

"Is there anything I can do?" Cass asked almost desperately, gesturing toward the food laid out ready for cooking.

Tea Rose was chattering so earnestly to Jared that neither of them heard. It was John who looked up from the sizzling, fragrant oil in the wok and shook his head.

"Thank you, but it's easier to do it ourselves than to explain what has to be done."

"Oh. Of course," Cass said.

Feeling an absurd impulse to cry, she turned away and walked quickly out of the kitchen to the workroom she had set up, but the familiar sight of camera and tripod, flash gun and powder, wooden plate frames and other photographic equipment didn't soothe her as she had hoped they would. She still felt cast adrift, floating helplessly, a stranger alone in a once-familiar world.

And tonight I'll fall asleep in King's arms again and wake up in the darkness with my breasts bare and his tongue licking my nipples until I tremble, and nothing will seem real—everything a dream, no past, no future, just me and King and the darkness.

That was the most unreal thing of all, yet she knew she needed King's comfort too much to deny herself his arms. She would do nothing to prevent the moment she awakened feeling cherished and warm, heat coursing through her veins, and the velvet rasp of his tongue making her bite back soft moans. Each night, she gave King more of her body, never meaning to, not knowing how to stop, because in the darkness there was nothing but the sweet racing of her blood and his love words whispering against her skin.

Last night, his hands had stroked her all over, rubbing her with soft insistence from heels to neck again and again, sliding her gown and robe up until she had felt the shocking touch of his hand between her naked thighs, his warm palm sliding higher. She had struggled in earnest then, hurting him without meaning to, and their fragmented apologies to one another had tangled in the darkness. She had rearranged her clothes and finally fallen asleep in his arms once more—and had wakened in the morning with his hand between her legs, his fingers curled in the golden hair that grew lushly at the apex of her thighs.

After the first, shocked instant of discovery, she had lain rigidly, too embarrassed to move. Slowly, very slowly, she had realized that she liked the feel of King's hand lodged so innocently against her, touching her in a way no one ever had. She had lain watching him with an odd, shimmering feeling in the pit of her stomach, wishing that he would wake up, and at the same time frightened that he would awake. She shouldn't be in bed with him, not like this. She shouldn't be; yet she needed this very intimacy, this sweet cherishing of herself, too much to turn away—no matter what the cost.

Now, looking at her camera without really seeing it, Cass wondered what this night would bring. She knew that soon, very soon, she must stop lying down next to King to sleep. He was healing so rapidly. In a night or two or three, he wouldn't need the comfort of another human being beside him to hold the residue of opium dreams and painful nightmares at bay.

But she needed that comfort. She needed him in a world gone suddenly strange, full of alien words and unexpected responsibilities. And Jared's eyes watching her, always watching her, seeing more than she wanted anyone to see.

"Cassandra?"

She made a startled sound when she realized that Jared was real, standing in front of her.

Watching her.

"Is it d-dinner time already?" she stammered, trying to still the frantic beating of her heart.

"Yes. Are you all right?"

"Of course." She smiled brightly, emptily. She yearned for the darkness before dawn when she would lie in King's arms, no longer confronting the world alone. "What are we having?"

"Most of the food will be strange to you, I'm afraid."

"What isn't, lately?" she asked, her tone caught between the bitterness of tumultuous days and the secret balm of the hours before sunrise.

"I'm sorry. I thought it would comfort Tea Rose to have familiar food. Especially now."

"Has something else gone wrong?"

"Her mother is dead."

Stunned, Cass could only stare.

"I'll tell Tea Rose," Jared continued, "but first I want her to laugh and be young for the last time."

Jared turned away. Cass followed him to the dining room, protests wedged futilely in her throat, her emotions numbed by the feeling of sheer unreality that was undermining her sense of self—adrift until she could be anchored by King's arms.

The meal only increased Cass's sense of being out of place, out of time. The colors were strange, the combinations of flavors were exotic, the chopsticks impossible to control. Conversation flowed around her in meaningless syllables that rose and fell harshly on her ears.

No wonder Tea Rose turned and ran the first chance she had, Cass told herself as she stared at yet another unfamiliar pile of diced food. *If I turned and ran, would someone come after me and tackle me among the geraniums?*

She looked up, saw Jared's clear, unnerving eyes watching her, and didn't look up again until Tea Rose's Cantonese became a flood of bitter English.

"Freedom! Don't talk to me about the joys of freedom, Mr. Duran. I wear wretched clothes that cut into my skin, I eat food whose stench makes me want to vomit, I hear only English monotones everywhere I turn, and my half sister stares at me in horror if I talk about what I know best. I am a prisoner in a house draped with the color of death! If this is freedom—"

"No," Jared interrupted, setting aside his ivory chopsticks. "I'll tell you what freedom is, Tea Rose. Freedom is a woman who fights her entire lifetime against crushing odds and still retains her heart and mind intact. Freedom is a woman who doesn't believe she has a soul, but who fights fiercely for that soul anyway, hoping that maybe, just maybe, in the darkness of death, she will see the face of the one man who loved her without reservation. Freedom is a woman who will bite through her own tongue and choke to death in the arms of her mortal enemy so that her spoiled daughter won't have to lift her heels to her ears for every man who has a hard cock and a handful of brass coins."

Tea Rose's black eyes widened and her lips parted in a soundless cry of denial, but there was no denying the bleak truth in Jared's eyes. A tide of silence rushed higher and higher within her, washing over her, strangling her, drowning her; and within that void, the memory of her mother's words whispered: *First, we will bathe, and then I will dress you as though you were four again. I will hug you and tickle you and comb your hair into a beautiful maiden's coil. Then I will take your hand and lead you into the Good Lady's night, where women are free.*

Tea Rose's anguished scream of understanding made the hair at the nape of Cass's neck quiver. Even as she rushed forward to comfort Tea Rose, Jared was already there, catching the girl's hands before her nails could shred skin from her flawless cheeks in an action that was both ritual and primal reality. He gathered her rigid body against his own, taking into his own flesh the heedless violence of her fists and nails, shielding her from her own wild grief.

After the first raging minutes passed, Tea Rose collapsed into racking sobs interspersed with words that moved Cass to tears, even though she didn't understand them. Jared carried Tea Rose into the darkness of the white-shrouded living room where he sat in a rocking chair, holding her close, murmuring words and stroking her gleaming black hair with his hand while the chair glided back and forth, back and forth.

Minute upon minute passed, first a handful and then ten, fifteen, twenty, thirty, and still Tea Rose's body shook with terrible sobs. Her voice had splintered into raw, ragged sounds of grief that were older than civilization or language, older than everything but the tears welling up and spilling from her eyes.

Finally, Cass came and stood in front of the rocking chair. If Jared knew she was there, he didn't acknowledge it. He remained with his head bowed over Tea Rose as though to shield her from the golden reflection of the light coming from the dining room. Silently, Cass held out the bottle of laudanum where Jared couldn't fail to see it. Without interrupting the motions of the rocker or his hand stroking Tea Rose's hair, Jared shook his head, refusing the opiate.

"Are you sure?" Cass whispered.

Slowly, Jared's head came up. As he looked at her, Cass finally realized that Tea Rose wasn't the only one who wept for the loss of Lilac Rain.

38

Cass closed Tea Rose's door softly and stood for a long moment in the darkened hallway. No sound came from within the bedroom, no hint of movement or restlessness. Either Tea Rose truly slept, or she was able to discipline her body into a perfect semblance of sleep. Cass didn't know which. Nor did she need to know. Tea Rose would never run away from her half sister's world again.

In the week since Tea Rose had learned of her mother's death, she had changed. She was far older now. Her silences were those of an adult, as were her words. She spoke carefully or not at all, as though she were finding her way through a hall of mirrors studded with pitfalls and steel traps. There were no more outbursts against the food or clothing, rituals or language; there were only Tea Rose's feral eyes and probing questions about American customs until Cass was exhausted with the answering.

There was no peace for either of them, except at night.

"Cassie?"

King's soft voice made her hand tremble, sending light from the candle shivering over the walls. Each night Cass faced the hungry warmth of King's arms, and each night she knew that it must be the last—and each night she prayed that it would never end, leaving her alone once more.

"Cassie? Where are you?"

She walked quickly to King's room.

"Why are you awake? Do you need laudanum?" she asked, standing in the bedroom doorway.

King looked at the golden hair tumbling around Cass's shoulders.

"No, Cassie. What I need is you."

"King—"

His name was said almost helplessly, but she walked into the room with no further protest. If she didn't lie next to him, he woke and thrashed restlessly. For the past five nights, she had been awakened in her own room by the sound of him limping heavily around, wild as a caged wolf. She had wanted to go to him, but hadn't.

Now she could stay away no longer.

"Come here, sugar girl," King said, smiling and holding out his hand to her. "Lie down beside me. Men and women bundle all the time. It's a fine old American custom."

"But you said it hurts you—?"

An off-center smile flashed within the sleek masculine beard. "I can survive that kind of hurting. I can't survive without touching you. Come here, sugar girl. Let me pet you until I fall asleep."

His fingers caught in the warmth of hers. He felt the fine trembling in her body as he pulled her closer. His leg ached, but at a distance. He had used enough opium at places such as the Blossom Moon to know that a small amount worked as an aphrodisiac, while anything greater diminished sexuality to little more than a vague wish. It had taken him nearly two weeks of experimenting with the laudanum, but he had finally discovered just how much would take the edge off the wound's pain without bringing about a sexless opium stupor.

"But I don't want to hurt you," Cass whispered.

"It's a sweet kind of ache," King said, tugging her down onto the bed. "Don't you feel it, too, just a little?"

The trembling of the candle in her hand was all the answer King needed. He took the brass candleholder and set it on the bedside table as he pulled Cass closer.

"I've missed you. Don't go away from me tonight," he whispered, brushing his lips over hers. "Lie with me. Let me hold you. Let me touch you."

The feel of the mattress giving slightly beneath Cass's weight as she lay down sent fingers of tantalizing heat through King's groin. He barely stifled a groan. He knew he was playing with dynamite. He could sense the lit fuse sizzling shorter and shorter, but he didn't know where it would end. That was much of the tantalizing excitement. It was almost like searching a river for gold, knowing in his gut that it was within reach, but not knowing when he would first touch its shining surface.

King pulled the blankets up over Cass, shutting out the damp chill of the room. He kissed her lips until they softened and stopped trembling. Without thought, without caution, without hesitation, he slid his tongue into her mouth and then out again, penetrating and retreating in slow rhythms that made her moan.

"Ah, Cassie, you taste like gold, you feel like gold, I want to—I—want—"

With a throaty groan, King eased the blankets over both of them, covering their heads, bringing blessed darkness to his opium-sensitized eyes. Cass turned onto her side as his fingers worked quickly over the ties of her robe and the maddening tiny buttons of her nightgown. Finally, he could push all cloth aside and bury his face in the feminine beauty of her breasts. He breathed in deeply, filling himself with the scent of her. Even before he turned and licked the tip of one full breast, he felt her shiver, felt the heat of her reaching out to envelop him, felt the nipple drawing up into an exquisite velvet hardness.

Hungrily, he pulled her erect nipple into his mouth, sucking on her rhythmically as his hands kneaded her waist, her hips, her thighs. He ached to lie between her legs and feast without restraint on her breasts, on her belly, on the secret folds of skin she had let him touch only once, briefly—just enough to drive him nearly wild with her humid softness.

Without warning, King's right hand shifted, sliding up between Cass's thighs until he penetrated the dense nest of hair and caressed the sultry flesh beneath.

"King—"

"You're so soft," he said, holding Cass close with one powerful arm and probing her softness slowly despite her stiffly held legs.

"King, no," Cass said quickly.

"Don't be shy," King murmured, nuzzling her breast, tickling it with his teeth and tongue. "Sugar girl, sweetheart, so soft, like a handful of gold dust heated by the sun. Ah, don't tighten up so. Let me touch you. Or is it the wrong time of month to play?"

"I don't know what—" The words unraveled in a helpless moan as his fingers found their goal.

"When did you last bleed?" King asked against her skin. He smiled, feeling the heat flushing her breasts, knowing that if it weren't too dark, he could have seen the tidal rush of blood brightening her clear skin. "It's all right, Cassie. Every woman bleeds, and every man asks about it at times like this."

He felt her take a deep breath and he waited, sucking on first one nipple and then the other, feeling her response in the slow relaxing of her tense thighs.

"This morning," she whispered finally. "I stopped bleeding this morning."

"So that's why you stayed away from me these last nights. I thought you were angry or—"

King's voice died as he felt Cass's secret flesh grow moist at his caresses; he could take Cass tonight, could end the violent tightness in his balls. He tried and failed to control the fierce hunger that sent blood rushing to his groin, transforming him. A groan threaded though his clenched teeth as his fingers moved more urgently between her legs.

"Cass? Are you angry with me, sugar girl?"

The feel of her hands on his face, his neck, his shoulders, was like fire. He wanted to pull her hands down his body and teach her to stroke and rub him until he came, finally ending his sweet torment. But he didn't have to settle for the limited satisfaction of her hands. Not tonight. Tonight, he could push deeply into her, sheathing himself in her heat until he could take no more and he burst.

"I'm not angry," Cass said, her voice trembling as she smoothed his beard, cupped her palm against the hard tendons of his neck, slid her hands beneath the loose pajama collar. "I'm just—"

"Afraid?" King's mouth found her breasts again. He teased her with teeth and tongue and the soft warmth of his mustache.

"I don't know," Cass said honestly. "Oh, King, I don't know! Everything is changed, everything is different, everything is upside down and inside out. I don't know what's right and wrong or good and bad or—"

Her words ended in a ragged sigh as his mouth shaped one of her breasts with increasing demand. He heard her sigh, felt her body soften to him, and pulled her closer to his hips. Pain splintered through the muffling haze of opium and desire. She felt him flinch and tried to pull away, but he was much too strong.

"King," Cass whispered, stroking him soothingly, "that's enough. Your leg—I can't bear hurting you."

"Then let me keep touching you," he said hoarsely. He rolled fully onto his back. "Come here."

"But your wound—"

"Let me worry about my leg," King said, his voice rough.

"I'm not as weak as you think." Then he heard his own impatience and said, "Oh, dammit, I'm sorry, Cassie. I didn't mean to snap at you. Come here," he urged, his voice gentler as he pulled her closer. "Put your leg across my stomach, and sit on me like I'm a tame old pony."

Before Cass could object, King simply pulled her right leg over his body and lifted her into place. She didn't struggle for fear of hurting his wounded leg. When he released her, the feel of his muscular, silk-clad abdomen resting between her naked thighs made her forget to breathe, much less to struggle.

"Sit down, sugar girl," he whispered, running his hands up and down her taut, bare thighs. "It's safe. I won't buck you off. I promise. It's all right. This way, I can touch you without hurting my leg. That's it, sweetheart, relax. Now, bend over just a bit more—"

As King spoke, he ran his hands hotly over Cass's body, pulling up her nightgown and robe until no folds of cloth were caught between their bodies. She bent over slowly beneath his pressing hands, bringing her breasts within reach of his mouth. He caressed their tips with hands and tongue, caresses that had become familiar in the past weeks, caresses that both reassured and pleasured her.

When Cass was pliant once more, her breathing quick, her breasts hot and slick from his mouth, King eased his right hand between her legs. She stiffened, lifting slightly away from his intimate touch. His seeking, stroking fingers followed her, taking full advantage of the access she had inadvertently given him when she raised herself onto her knees. One of his fingers found the opening she had instinctively been trying to conceal. He slid deeply into her undefended body.

"King—"

"Hush, sugar girl," he murmured, probing and retreating, first one finger and then two, feeling the exciting, clinging heat of her body. "It's all right," he said against her mouth, kissing her as she knelt above him with her legs opened and her breasts brushing his lips. "So soft. I've never touched a woman like you, sugar sweet and soft as gold dust. And warm. Lord, you're warm," he whispered, sliding his fingers again and again between the tender folds of skin she no longer tried futilely to protect. "Sugar girl—oh, God, it's so sweet, it's like dying. That doesn't hurt you, does it?"

"N-no, but—"

His tongue slid into her mouth, cutting off her words, filling her with rhythmic advances and retreats that matched those of his long fingers. After a few moments, he couldn't bear teasing himself any more. It seemed as though he had wanted her for a lifetime, had been hard for all eternity, his erection beating against the silk confinement of his pajamas. He reached down and freed himself, trying to ease the fierce ache by rubbing his blunt tip slowly against the soft, yielding folds of her body. It wasn't enough. He was in agony, on fire, wild for more than the sultry butterfly kiss of her barely parted lips. Before she could fully realize that it was no longer his fingers probing between her legs, he gave a hoarse cry and thrust into her at the same instant that his hands gripped her thighs, forcing her down until he was buried in her.

"Cassie—" King gasped, "Sweet—hot—gold."

She was so tight, yet she yielded, surrounding him, accepting him like a second, much hotter skin. He had felt nothing to equal it in his life. He retreated just for the violent pleasure of thrusting into her again and yet again, calling her name, feeling his climax coming in a wild rush of golden light, burning up, groaning between his clenched teeth, jerking with the repeated convulsions of his release.

King's ragged, harsh groans frightened Cass more than his hands clenched fiercely on her thighs or the burning pain of his hardened penis lodged deeply within her body. The pain was minor; the fear for his health was not.

"King?" she asked urgently.

There was no answer but a tearing groan and a final convulsion of his powerful body.

"Oh, God," Cass cried. Her hands flew to his face. "King—*King*. What's wrong? Are you bleeding again? King, answer me!"

The blinding aftermath of climax ebbed from King, allowing him to hear more than the roaring of his own blood. Slowly, his eyes opened and focused on Cass. She made an incoherent sound and burst into tears. Gradually, her fragmented words began to make sense to King. He tried to stifle his smile, and then his soft laughter, but it was impossible. He felt too drowsy and far too fine to do anything but let the warm aftermath of sex wash through him.

"Sugar girl, there's nothing to worry about," King said finally, lifting Cass's chin to give her a lazy kiss. "I'm fine as frog's hair." He laughed softly. "You're the best medicine a gunshot wound ever had."

"But you groaned like you were dying."

"Innocent little sugar girl," he whispered. "That's the way sex is for a man." He yawned and shifted Cass until he could nuzzle against her nipples. He wanted to suckle her, to hold onto the sensual moment, but he was too spent to keep the world from spinning away in a haze of satiation and opium and the throbbing of his wound marking off each heartbeat as he slid toward sleep. "No tears—next time," he said drowsily, looking at Cass and forming each word with an enormous effort.

"What?"

"You—sugar girl," King said, his voice fading and his eyes closing as sleep reached up to claim him. "Next time—you won't be—a virgin."

In the guttering light of the candle, Cass watched sleep claim King between one breath and the next. His eyes closed fully, his face relaxed, his hands slid away from her legs, and the full pressure of him within her body ebbed. She took a broken breath, realized she was crying, and tried to stop. She couldn't.

Slowly, Cass moved off King, only to see scarlet blood bloom in the candlelight. Reflexively, she looked at his wound. The bandages were the purest white. Then she saw a glaze of red on the half-aroused male flesh that had so recently been in her body. She looked at her thighs and realized that it was her own blood, not King's.

Disoriented, shaken, unable to stop crying, Cass went to the bathroom, drew a basin of water, and rinsed away the blood of the virgin she no longer was.

39

Tea Rose watched through clear black eyes as Cass put her fists in the small of her back and stretched for the second time in as many minutes.

"Why do you continue to work if you're tired?" Tea Rose asked, glancing from the camera to the wan blond woman who was even now looking around the shrouded living room, sizing up yet another photograph in which she would try to make shadows speak as clearly as light.

"Because I love what I'm doing," Cass said absently. "I love taking a blank plate of film and using it to make people see how much beauty and mystery lie around them. I love making people look and remember before it's too late, and everything is gone but hazy memories."

"Black and white, like an ideograph."

Cass looked toward Tea Rose and smiled almost sadly. "Don't forget the gray. Lots and lots of shades of gray. The older I get, the more shades of gray."

"That stands to reason, sister. The Chinese see death as white, Americans see it as black; that leaves only gray to describe life."

"And colors," Cass said. "Someday, man will learn to capture colors with his plates of film."

"Like crimson, the color of good fortune?"

"To Americans, red is the color of danger," Cass said. "Danger and blood."

"But danger and blood aren't the same thing," Tea Rose

objected mildly, turning away from the composition Cass had created of a sheet-draped chair and a man's forgotten pipe. "Blood can be both good fortune and bad danger. There is the monthly blood of a woman's fertility, which is good. There is blood from a man's injury, which is bad. There is the blood a woman bleeds for her first man, which is neither necessarily good nor bad, simply a fact. Blood can be many things."

Cass's slight flush didn't escape Tea Rose's eye. Dispassionately, the girl decided that her conclusion was correct—the blood she had found on King's sheets a few days before hadn't come from his wound. A slight frown creased Tea Rose's forehead, for she knew that Jared wanted Cass. Tea Rose also knew that, without Jared, Cass wouldn't have the knowledge or the skill to protect herself from Tan Feng's certain vengeance, which meant that Tea Rose was more vulnerable now than she had been before King had driven his cock into Cass, a wedge to separate the two Duran brothers.

But perhaps it wasn't what it seemed. Perhaps Jared was like the Arab sultans she had heard of, men who so abhorred a virgin's blood that they kept special studs to break maidenheads, so that their masters' way would be eased. Tea Rose had heard of no Americans who acted in that manner, but no custom was too bizarre for people who routinely ate rotten, rigid milk, and the more it stank, the more they praised it.

Perhaps the fact that Cass was one brother's woman would tie all of them together more closely, thus increasing Tea Rose's own security. In China, it wasn't unheard of for brothers to share a favored concubine. Unfortunately, it was even more common for brothers to be jealous of one another's presence. Each wanted to believe that the woman they shared desired his jade stem more than his brother's. Each brother wanted to know that only he was truly welcome to make the fire within the pleasure pavilion.

To Tea Rose, each brother was a fool, for no woman who had a real choice would accept a man's penis poking into her body. But no woman did have a real choice, whether she were first wife or second concubine or saltwater whore. The only choice a woman had was in how many men pushed between her jade gates, and under what circumstances.

Tea Rose didn't know what the circumstances were with Cass and Kingston Duran. She would find out, however, and then she would know how best to ensure her own safety.

"Will Jared come today?" Tea Rose asked casually, shifting her grip on the flash gun she held.

"I don't know. It's dangerous."

Tea Rose made a sound that could have meant nothing or everything. As though an afterthought, she said, "I think I might like Jared."

Cass looked at her, surprised. "Of course. Why shouldn't you like him?"

"Why should I like any man?" Then, before Cass could answer, Tea Rose remembered the night when she had learned that her mother was dead. Jared had held her, wept with her, comforted her, and asked nothing of her in return. "It was very pleasant to be held by a man who didn't want to put his cock—excuse me, his *honorable penis*—between my legs."

Cass was considerably more accustomed to Tea Rose's vocabulary than she had been a few weeks before. Even so, she shot Tea Rose a warning look in the instant before surprise turned into amusement, and amusement into laughter. Within moments, Cass was laughing so hard that she couldn't speak.

Tea Rose, whose words were never casual, much less inadvertent, was delighted. She covered her mouth and laughed, too, feeling more at home than she had ever expected to feel in this strange white house. She had many memories of Jasmine, Lotus Moon, and the other sing-song girls making jokes about the men who came and went from their bodies with little more fanfare than digestive gas.

"Oh, I shouldn't laugh," Cass said, struggling to control herself, "but 'his *honorable* p-p—'"

It was no use. Cass was laughing too hard to speak.

"Of course you should laugh, sister," Tea Rose said, giggling. "What else are men good for but women's private laughter?"

"Not all men are like that, just—just—" Cass began gamely, only to break into helpless laughter again.

If the sounds Cass made were closer to hysteria than she wanted to admit, she no longer had the energy to care. The combination of a week of King's lovemaking, followed by restless, broken sleep each night, plus her constant unhappy anticipation of Jared's reaction when he discovered that she and King were lovers, had left Cass too worn out physically and emotionally to be sensible.

"Not all men want only a woman's, er, I mean—" Cass began, only to have Tea Rose interrupt.

"Ch'iung-men," Tea Rose said, laughing behind her upraised hand.

The word sounded very familiar to Cass. As she repeated it, she remembered playing croquet with Tea Rose before Jared had forbidden them to leave the house.

"Ch'iung-men?" asked Cass, pronouncing the word correctly.

"Very good, sister," Tea Rose said, clapping her hands in delight.

"But I thought that meant wicket," Cass protested.

Tea Rose bent her head modestly and laughed into her delicate hands.

"Tea Rose," Cass said, trying and utterly failing to be stern. "You didn't—?"

Nodding, laughing, Tea Rose admitted her deception. *"Ch'iung-men* means 'coral gate,' the entrance to the *chin-kou."*

"Coral gate," Cass repeated, smiling and shaking her head at the joke that had been played on her. "What does *chin-kou* literally mean?"

" 'Golden gully.' "

"My God," Cass said, then raised her own hands to hide her dropped jaw. Suddenly, she was laughing again. "I don't believe it! The golden gully!" She sank to the floor and laughed until she couldn't breathe. "Tell me," she demanded between gasps of breath. "The croquet mallet. *Yu-ching.* Is it—is it—"

Tea Rose nodded, smiling widely behind her hands. "The jade stem, sister. Or, as you say, the penis."

"Go on," Cass urged. "What is *chieh-shan-chu?*"

"The pearl on the jade step."

"Just one?"

"Are American women built so differently?" Tea Rose asked, startled. "In Chinese men, the jade stem strokes the woman's single pearl."

"Women?" Cass said, confused. "I thought we were talking about men."

"Not unless white men have a—" Tea Rose frowned, trying to remember the English word. "Ah, yes. Clitoris. *Jui-t'ai,* the 'jewel terrace' of a woman's pleasure," she explained. "And the game itself, *fang-shih,* translates as 'delight on the couch,' not croquet. So now you know, sister, why I laughed so much when you learned the Chinese words for 'croquet.'"

When Cass remembered herself earnestly repeating the proper—or improper—word each time she picked up the croquet mallet and stroked the ball, sending it through the wicket to strike the wooden peg beyond, she began laughing all over again, laughing until tears gathered in her eyes and ran down her cheeks. After a moment, Tea Rose sank down on the floor next to her, her hands on her stomach, laughing without thought of modesty, as though she were alone with her mother once more.

"What in hell is going on?" demanded a deep voice from the door.

Instantly, Tea Rose covered her mouth, hiding her pink tongue and small white teeth. Cass turned her head so quickly that hairpins flew and blond strands tumbled down, completing her dishevelment.

"King! You're supposed to be in bed. What are you doing up?" Cass asked as she scrambled to her feet. The white sheet covering a chair wrapped around her ankle, tripping her. She caught herself on the tripod before she fell, kicked free of the cloth, and looked anxiously at King. "Is something wrong?"

"I got damn tired of looking out the window and wondering where you were. Then I heard you two laughing fit to split something, and decided to see what was so damned funny."

Cass looked at King with her heart in her eyes. He was leaning against the doorjamb to ease the weight from his injured leg. The ivory-headed cane that he had formerly used only for show he was now using of necessity. In his mutilated black pajamas, with his rumpled mahogany hair and his burning green eyes, he looked improbably handsome.

"You're supposed to be asleep or at least resting," Cass said anxiously, hurrying through the room of shrouded furniture to stand close to King. "Let me help you back to your room."

"No," King said curtly. "Cabin fever is what's wrong with me. I'm sick and tired of that damned room."

He jerked away from her hand on his arm, only to lose his balance. He caught himself, but at the cost of using his injured leg. For a moment, he went very pale and leaned heavily on the cane. When he raised his head again, Cass was standing with her hands pressed to her mouth. Tears glittered in her eyes, and her face was as pale as his.

"Ah, Cassie, don't look like that," King said almost roughly. "I'm not worth your smiles, much less your tears." He put his hand under her chin and kissed the salty drops away. "It's just pain, sugar girl. It passes. Besides, I'd rather hurt a lot than be caged a second longer. So instead of standing there crying, why don't you come for a hobble with me around the garden?"

King's lazy, off-center smile made Cass want to laugh and cry, kiss him, and then hammer on him until he showed more sense about taking care of himself.

"We can't," she said finally.

Anger hardened the handsome lines of King's face. "I'm

real tired of being treated like an invalid. I'm a man, not a doll to be fussed over and then put on a shelf when you get bored and go off to play with your other toys."

The accusation was unfair. King knew it as soon as the words went past his lips; Cass had spent every waking minute with him, leaving him only when he slept, or when his irritability at being caged drove her away.

"I'm sorry," King said harshly. "And I'm also god-damned tired of being sorry." He smacked his palm hard against the doorjamb in a burst of frustration. "If I don't get out of this house, I'll go crazy!"

"Tan Feng has hired detectives to search for us," Cass said, keeping her voice even with an effort. "They think we're on Bainbridge Island. Every day, they cruise the shoreline in a boat and watch the houses. Sometimes, they ride over the roads on horseback. They don't have any schedule, so we can't predict when they'll appear. That's why Jared hasn't come for a week."

She moved even closer to King and smiled up at him uncertainly. "And that's why we can't go for a hobble in the garden."

That was also why the doors were barred, the drapes were drawn, and a loaded pistol was placed within her reach at all times. But Cass said nothing about those things, for she knew what King's reaction would be; he would demand that the responsibility for protecting them be his. That simply wasn't possible while he was injured and in pain, forced to take careful rations of laudanum before he unbuttoned her nightgown and caressed her breasts and his hands slid down to her waist and beyond.

"You look far too handsome to be standing around in torn pajamas," Cass said huskily, smiling and standing on tiptoe to kiss King's bearded cheek. "Come on. Let's get you back to bed."

King looked into Cass's golden eyes. "Sugar girl," he murmured, his voice going no farther than her ears, "if I thought that was an invitation to a lover rather than an order to an invalid, I'd race you to the mattress. But you're always so damned worried about my leg that you spend your time fretting instead of feeling. I'm not near as fragile as you think, and I'm damned tired of being treated that way."

Cass closed her eyes, trying to conceal her hurt at King's words. "I can't bear seeing your pain and knowing it's my fault that you were injured," she said finally, opening her eyes. "If I were the one lying in bed, and you were the one who had caused my injury, wouldn't—"

"Stop it, Cassie. Jared asked me to go, not you."

"But—"

"No," King said harshly. "You listen to me for a change. A few weeks ago, I thought you were one hell of a lovely woman, but I didn't go down that dark alley for you or even for Jared. I went because I never feel so alive as when I could be killed at any second. I went because it's as close to wild as this goddamned city gets, and I was sick to death of card games and bourbon and easy women. I was spoiling for a fight and I got it, and my only complaint is that I didn't kill the Chinaman who shot me."

King's hand came up beneath Cass's chin, holding her in place, forcing her to meet his smoldering green eyes. "I'm a simple man, Cassie. I like simple, uncluttered things—fire when I'm cold, food when I'm hungry, drink when I'm thirsty, room to roam when I'm restless, and," he added, brushing his lips over hers, "my own Lady Gold to pleasure me."

Cass smiled despite her residual tears and whispered King's name, but he was still talking and didn't hear her.

"Freedom is what I need, sugar girl, not a bedroom cage. That's all I ask. A simple thing for a simple man."

King's final words carried to Tea Rose, who waited as she had been trained to wait, motionless, soundless, demanding no more of the human beings around her than would an elegant piece of furniture. But she wasn't a chair or a table; she was a girl with an unusually keen mind and the training to put it to use. Tea Rose knew King's insistence on seeing freedom as a simple thing would have the effect of making her own freedom even more precarious. Whether Cass acknowledged it or not, Tea Rose believed that Jared had been driven away when Cass chose King. That left only one man to guard and defend where once two had stood. Now, that lone man was yearning to be elsewhere.

Tea Rose had no doubt that King in time would leave; and when he did, Tea Rose would be what her mother had once been, a woman without power in a world run by men for their own comfort. As King was a man, his careless behavior wasn't unexpected. However, it had to be dealt with. Somehow, Tea Rose had to do what hundreds of generations of Chinese women had always done: She had to use man's self-absorption to reinforce her own chances of survival. Tea Rose didn't know how she could accomplish that in King's case. She only knew that it must be done.

Freedom is not a simple thing, Kingston Duran. Your brother understands that, but you do not. My white sister understands, but you do not. I understand, but you do not. My mother understood best of all, and she is dead. Perhaps you will have to die before you understand. Perhaps not. It doesn't matter.

All that matters is that I don't die simply because you haven't learned that freedom isn't a simple thing.

Impassively, Tea Rose watched Cass urge and cajole King back to his sickbed. When Cass returned to the shrouded living room, Tea Rose still hadn't moved. Cass didn't notice the girl until she spoke.

"Shall I distract him?"

"Oh!" Cass put her hand over her suddenly hammering heart. "Tea Rose, you startled me. I was so worried about King that I'd forgotten you were waiting for me."

"Shall I play poker with him for a time so that you may take photographs of white and black and gray?"

"He's still so weak," Cass said distractedly.

Tea Rose's small bow of acknowledgment was essentially Chinese. "Don't worry about him, sister. He is strong."

"He almost died."

"But he lives, and he is stronger every day." Tea Rose hesitated, knowing that Cass wouldn't like what was going to be said next; yet there was no choice. "Let me entertain him for a time with that odd instrument you call 'guitar' and with cards and with—"

"No. He needs rest." Cass heard her own abrupt refusal and sighed. "I'm sorry."

"The more you fuss over him, the more restless he becomes. Let me divert him for—"

"That's not necessary," Cass said coldly.

"Is my avoiding King another of your rules?" Tea Rose asked in a slave's emotionless voice. "You have so many of them, like an herbalist his potions. And like potions, there are few rules that can be swallowed without effort."

Cass looked at the bland-faced, soft-voiced girl in front of her and wanted to scream with frustration. Cass didn't know how to deal with Tea Rose when she erected that implacable wall of polite neutrality between them.

"Rules and potions are alike in one other way, too," Cass said finally. "You don't have to like them, but you have to swallow them just the same."

"Some rules, like some potions, make people more miserable rather than less."

"You make yourself miserable," Cass retorted, "not rules or potions or any other damned thing. Can't you accept that you're no longer a royal Chinese strumpet, coddled by some corrupt old hatchet man who can see no farther than your face and your body?"

"Is it my beauty that bothers you, sister? There is no need for jealousy. King prefers gold to black jade."

"What bothers me has nothing to do with men in general or King Duran in particular."

Tea Rose's lips curved in a smile far too old for her face. "That's impossible. Everything women do revolves around me."

"Perhaps in China, but not here," Cass snapped.

"Men are the same everywhere."

"You're wrong. You think that it's enough just to catch a man's roving eye. That's only the beginning, Tea Rose. You have to be able to hold a man, too. With your heart and your mind and your soul. That's what love is. That's why men and women spend their lives together. But you know nothing about that," Cass said scathingly. "All you've been trained to handle is cock and balls and ass."

"That same training attracted and held your father. From what you have told me, he died wanting my mother, not yours."

"He died loving your mother, which is far more important than simply wanting her," Cass said, reining in her uncertain temper. "Lilac didn't use her sex to hold our father. He could have found a thousand whores—Chinese, Indian, or white—to service his male needs. Your mother used something else to hold him, something quite different. She gave herself to him, not just her body but her *self.*"

"Self," Tea Rose said slowly, as though she were tasting the word and found it odd. "Self is another English word for soul, isn't it? My mother told me that a sing-song girl has no soul."

"Yet your mother died so that you would be free of Tan Feng. She gave you to me because she wanted me to teach you that life is made more complicated by your extreme beauty, not less, and that love is much more than two bodies rubbing together in the dark. If she thought your beauty and your sex were enough to sustain you through life with your soul intact, she'd have left you with Tan Feng."

"Most men want no more than two bodies rubbing," Tea Rose said, her voice calm and yet vibrant with all that had to be said. "Have you thought about that? Have you given more than your body to King? Has he asked for more from you? Will he die calling your name? I don't think so, sister. He is one of those men whose soul belongs to the Great All, not to a mere woman. That's why he can never stay in one place. His soul is always calling to him from another place."

Cass opened her mouth, but was too stunned to speak. It didn't matter, for Tea Rose was still speaking—softly, relentlessly.

"Perhaps my mother hoped to give a final gift to your father, who believed she had a soul. Perhaps she sent me to educate my father's white daughter in the ways of Yin and Yang, man and woman, light and dark. Have you thought of that, sister?"

40

Heavy silver tapped hollowly on well-made china plates. The drone of conversation filled the dining room of the Pioneer Club, but the tables were spaced discreetly so that the diners could speak without worrying about being overheard by curious neighbors.

"Sure you wouldn't like a glass?" Robert Salyor smiled and gestured with the wine bottle as he finished filling his own glass again. "It's a truly exceptional French claret. As for *in vino veritas,* our little chat is entirely in confidence. You don't have to worry about making any damaging disclosures to me."

"I have no damaging disclosures to make to you or anyone else," Jared replied coolly, looking at the permanent flush alcohol had left on Salyor's sagging cheeks. "Get to the point, Mr. Salyor. I don't have the time to fence over a leisurely lunch."

"Ah, the impatience of youth."

Jared waited, saying nothing. When Salyor made much out of tasting the wine as though it were his first sip rather than his third glass, Jared put his napkin on the table and moved as though to stand up.

"Mr. Wong Ah Wing is interested in a truce," Salyor said quickly. "He's willing to forget the whole misunderstanding."

For a moment, Jared studied the attorney. He smiled thinly. At one time, Salyor would have made a good poker player, but no longer. Poker required a clear head and a steady hand. Salyor no longer had either.

"I don't give a damn what Wing is willing to forget or remember," Jared said. "Tell me about Tan Feng."

"Wong Ah Wing is my client, not Tan Feng."

Jared pushed back his chair.

"Oh, all right," Salyor said hastily. "Wing or Tan Feng, what's the difference?"

"If you don't know, I'm wasting my time watching you pretend to taste wine while you're still hung over from a quart of cheap bourbon."

The flush on Salyor's cheeks heightened. "When I say 'my client,' you may be assured that Tan Feng is in agreement with whatever settlement I propose."

Jared settled back into his chair and waited.

"Mr. Wong is willing to grant his wife her freedom if that's what she wants," Salyor continued. "In turn, he merely wants to be reassured that she really wants to leave him."

"She does. She has."

Salyor ignored him. "My client is willing to withdraw his lawsuit—"

"The suit is doomed," Jared interjected.

"—and to publicly state that Tea Rose is free to live where she wishes. No matter what her decision, he will personally guarantee her safety." Salyor sipped wine, looked at Jared and added, "I've been told that you understand Chinatown well enough to know how valuable such a guarantee of safety might be."

Jared said only, "What does Tan Feng get in return?"

Salyor sipped at his wine again before he spoke, making Jared wait. "He wants only that which is already his. First, the diamond-studded gold locket that the girl stole from her mother. I understand that the locket was really Tan Feng's property in any case, and—"

"Cut the bullshit," Jared interrupted. "You aren't in front of a jury."

Salyor drank more wine, poured more, and said, "My client also wants his good name back. He wants all the hand-wringing, moralizing newspaper articles to stop."

Jared's look of surprise was quite convincing. "Then he should drop the lawsuit. He's the one stirring around in the muck, not me."

"He hasn't connived with reporters to ruin your name, however. He said to tell you that he found your tactic both reprehensible and instructive. It seems that the lurid stories about corruption behind the Great Wall of Chinatown have forced the police to pay more attention to certain business interests that are really of no concern to Seattle's white citizens."

Again, Salyor had told Jared nothing new. John had already told him that Tan Feng had been forced to permit several raids of his opium dens as a show of the police department's efficiency. Tan could afford such raids now and again in order to satisfy the most importunate white moralists, but any more than an occasional, carefully planned raid would cut deeply into his profits.

"You know how it is with the law," Jared said. "It's always butting into other people's business." He paused, thinking rapidly. "All right. I'll call off the yellow press, if he'll call off his bounty and his detectives." Jared moved to stand once more. "Good day, Mr. Salyor."

"There's one more thing," Salyor said, looking at his wine rather than at Jared.

"What?"

"Just a formality. My client wants to hear the girl's choice from her own lips. He wants to be sure that she's doing precisely as she wishes, rather than what she has been coerced into doing by Christian zealots."

Every instinct Jared owned warned that he was being lured toward a trap. For a minute, he neither spoke nor moved, simply studied the lawyer.

"Your newspaper scandal made a great deal of the so-called slavery in Chinatown," Salyor said, allowing sarcasm to enter his voice for the first time. "Women being held in bondage against their will—wives and concubines and prostitutes alike. It really was very cleverly done, if a trifle salacious. But that's what the moralists like, isn't it? Sex and slavery and sin." Salyor lifted his glass as though to toast his own words. "I'm not a suffragist, but those stories made me want to march in behalf of the benighted females of the Celestial race."

Jared said nothing.

Salyor smiled ingenuously. "You and I are men of the world, Mr. Duran. We know that things aren't as simple as they seem in the newspaper. What some carefully misguided reporters call 'slavery,' most Chinese regard as the natural order of things. As far as that goes, Mr. Wong assures me that he values his wife so much that he must be sure that this Thornton woman hasn't been too hasty in her attempts to imitate the redoubtable Donaldina Cameron. A prostitute might have wanted to be saved, but a wife?" Salyor shrugged. "His seeing the girl is a reasonable request. After all, witnesses did see her fight against her captors the night she was kidnapped. I'm told her screams were quite heart-rending."

"How many witnesses?"

"How many would you like? One, five, fifteen? The whole population of Chinatown? That can be arranged, Mr. Duran, I assure you."

"What kind of wife is still a virgin after nearly a year of supposed marriage?" Jared countered.

Salyor paused. "A virgin? Remarkable, if true."

"It's true. Count on it."

There was a frown, then a shrug. "There's no need for either of us to go to the trouble of producing proof," Salyor said finally. "You say the girl is a virgin, and she's happy to live in a society where being a Chinese is just slightly preferable to being a rabid dog. Naturally, her husband finds it difficult to reassure himself that her choice is freely made. Let her tell her husband in person. Let him reassure himself of her welfare. It will all be done on neutral ground, of course."

The sounds of the dining room seemed muted and far away as Jared considered the lawyer's words.

"Tea Rose is a fourteen-year-old child who is presently in

the custody of her half sister," Jared said. "No court in this state is likely to change that."

"Really? A single woman of questionable morals such as Miss Thornton?"

"You have witnesses to her questionable morality, I presume?" Jared asked softly.

The savage glitter of Jared's eyes made Salyor hesitate, but in the end the lawyer went ahead.

"It only takes one witness to ruin a woman's reputation, but more can be arranged, if necessary. Do you really want this to go to court, Mr. Duran? If Tea Rose truly made a free choice, why do you hold back? It's only just and moral that you—"

"You'll have to pardon me," Jared interrupted. "I find a lecture on any kind of morality sounds odd from the lips of a drunken word-merchant whose fee comes out of the earnings of prostitutes."

Salyor's hand tightened on the wine bottle he had just used to refill his glass.

"Don't call me a pimp, Duran. I know all about your affair with the Chinese whore that whelped this girl. Now, it looks like you're after the daughter, too."

Jared caught Salyor's wrist with his powerful fingers and squeezed until the lawyer's face became as pale as salt.

"You have badly misjudged me, Miss Thornton, Lilac, and her daughter," Jared said softly. "I'll accept your apology this time. If it happens again—but it won't, will it?"

Jared's fingers tightened until sweat shone on the lawyer's face, and a greenish tinge of nausea replaced the alcoholic flush on his cheeks.

"Sorry—" Salyor gasped.

Jared's grip eased. He picked up a napkin, wiped his fingers very thoroughly, dropped the linen on Salyor's plate, and stood up to leave.

"Tell Tan Feng I'll think about his offer."

41

"God," complained King with only half a smile, "you do know how to brighten up a man's day, don't you?"

"Things aren't that bad," Jared said, stacking up the certificates and putting them back into an expanding folder. "The bank's outstanding loans are still sound. The bank itself will survive. It will just be a year or so before you see any return on your original investment."

"Then I'll have to sell my shares."

"You can if you want to, but people are panicked right now. The going rate for Bank of the Great Northwest shares is just a few cents on the dollar."

"Hell, Jay, that won't keep me for a week, much less buy me a place to live in the city."

"If you wait six months, you'll probably be able to recover seventy-five cents on the dollar," Jay said. "In a year, it will be 100 percent. In two years, 140 percent."

"Two years? In two years I could be dead! What about you? Did you get cleaned out, too?"

Jared shrugged. "My losses will be more than offset by the fact that Mr. Hill is finally ready to run a shunt up to the Canadian border, where he'll tie into the Canadian Pacific railway system. The harvest of Canada's interior wheat lands will be shipped out on James J. Hill's grain cars." Jared smiled. "But first, he has to buy the right-of-way from me."

The sound King made conveyed a combination of boredom and irritation. He levered himself to his feet and walked around the bedroom, ignoring the stiffness and complaints of his wound. He had been out of action for much too long. Having Jay appear and talk about bad investments and small financial panics did nothing to soothe King's savage impatience with his physical restrictions. For the first time in his life, he needed money for its own sake, yet he was no more interested in fiscal manipulations now than he had been when he was a babe sucking milk from his mother's breast.

"You're so damned good at making money," King said, turning to confront Jared. "Can't you take care of this mess for me the way you always have?"

"No."

The refusal was no less final for its softness.

"You really meant it, didn't you?" King said, understanding finally. "You're treating me like someone you just met. Like a stranger."

"I always mean what I say. You know that."

King watched Jared stand up with the muscular ease of a man in the prime of his physical strength. Uneasily, King realized anew how ruthless Jared could be.

And then King remembered the second thing that Jared had promised: *If you get her pregnant, you better head north.*

There could be no doubt now that he had meant each word.

Jared reached into the breast pocket of his finely tailored jacket and pulled out a small, neatly tied parcel. He threw it to King, who caught it reflexively.

"French letters," Jared said. "Use them."

Red tinged the skin above King's beard for a few seconds as he balanced the package of condoms on his palm.

"Jay—" King said, then his voice died and his eyelids closed, because he couldn't bear to see a stranger looking at him through the cold gray eyes of the brother he loved. King's big hands moved restlessly, almost helplessly. "I—Christ, Jay, you're the last person on earth I ever wanted to hurt. But Cassie is—different. She's gold dust, all soft and sleek and shining in my hands. I had to have her."

There was no answer. King opened his eyes and saw that Jared had walked from the bedroom as though King were a stranger whose painful explanations meant less than the cries of Pike Street fishmongers.

"Dammit, Jay," King called hoarsely. "She wanted me. She wanted *me!*"

If Jared heard, his steps didn't hesitate as he went to the kitchen. Tea Rose was teaching Cass how to prepare fresh vegetables in the Chinese manner, using thin slices and odd angles.

"John sends his regrets," Jared said to Tea Rose.

The girl smiled over her shoulder. As always when he hadn't seen her for a while, Jared was struck by her beauty.

"More welcome than regrets are the hundred-year eggs he sent with you," Tea Rose said, her voice musical. Even at times of excitement, she no longer forgot to pitch her voice for American ears. "I didn't know how much I'd missed them until I bit into one."

Cass shook her head in disbelief. "How you can turn up your nose at good clean cheese and then happily eat gray pickled eggs and god-awful-looking chicken feet is beyond me."

"I ate the cheese," countered Tea Rose.

"One bite only. And I ate the wretched chicken foot."

"One bite only."

The two women looked at each other and laughed.

Jared noted with approval that Tea Rose no longer tried to hide her amusement behind the narrow sleeve of her blouse. That was just one of the many signs of her growing ease with her half sister and American customs. He was relieved that Tea Rose was accepting her new home, for the old one lay forever beyond her reach.

Did she realize that, or would youthful, wishful thinking make her vulnerable to whatever trap Tan Feng had prepared?

"There's something I have to discuss with you," Jared said to Tea Rose. "Would you allow me to show you the view from the lattice house?"

Cass's hands froze over the vegetables, then resumed slicing carefully. "I thought we were forbidden to go outside."

"Tan Feng has called off his dogs for the moment."

Jared's voice was an uncanny echo of the controlled, neutral tone that Cass had first encountered among the

Chinese. His expressions, each of his movements when he was around her, were controlled. He was distant without ever giving cause for her to reproach him.

"The lattice house sounds heavenly," Cass said, setting aside her paring knife. "I've been cooped up so long that—"

"Forgive me," Jared interrupted, "but it would be better if Tea Rose and I spoke alone. Later, Tea Rose will tell you whatever is necessary for you to know."

The clear ice of Jared's eyes was even more unnerving to Cass today than it had been the first day they met. She hadn't known then how his eyes could warm with laughter and affection. She hadn't known that he was capable of gentleness. She hadn't possessed the least idea of the thoughtfulness he could display. But she knew those things now, which made their absence all the more painful. Conspiracy, danger, and shared concern for King had forged a bond between her and Jared. She hadn't suspected the depth and strength of the bond until today, when he had cut it without a word or warning.

As Cass had anticipated, a single glance at her had told Jared that she had become King's lover. Yet Jared had shown none of the contempt that she had feared. There had been—nothing. Since the moment a few hours before, when he had walked into the house and seen the flush mounting her cheeks as she met his eyes, from that instant Jared had been a scrupulously polite stranger.

Unhappily, Cass realized she had looked forward to Jared's visit a great deal. He brought a nameless kind of strength that was so unlike King's volatile, charismatic presence. Without knowing it, Cass had come to count on Jared's friendship and support. She cared for him much more than she had realized. Now his friendship was lost.

But not his support. Cass was certain that Jared wouldn't turn his back on Tea Rose.

"Of course," Cass said, her voice husky with hurt and regrets. "I'm sorry, Jay. I didn't mean to intrude."

Jared nodded, silent.

Cass went back to preparing unfamiliar vegetables. They

felt strange in her hands, all the wrong size, the wrong weight, the wrong texture, color, smell, everything wrong.

"May I suggest that you change your soft Chinese shoes for the hard American variety?" Jared said to Tea Rose. "The ground is still wet from last night's rain."

When the sound of Tea Rose's whispering footfalls disappeared down the hall, Jared spoke calmly to Cass's back.

"King will be irritable tonight. Don't let him take it out on you—it will only make him feel more guilty, which will make him more irritable, which will make him more guilty and more irritable, until finally he turns on you like the cornered animal he is."

"You make it sound as though I'm the one who has cornered him."

"You are," Jared said in a matter-of-fact tone. "You're a good woman, and King is a decent man underneath all the wildness. Now that you've seduced him—"

"I never se—" she said, whirling around.

"Bullshit," Jared said savagely. "You wanted King the instant you saw him. You would have gotten over it in time, but luck wasn't on his side. So King spent the last few weeks half-pickled on opium, hurting, and as weak as a day-old kitten. You were there by his bed the whole time, bathing and petting and comforting him—"

"He was hurt," Cass interrupted, her voice raw. "He needed me."

"He needed a nurse, and you floated in and out of his mind like a golden opium dream. You should have had enough wit to get beyond his reach, but you didn't, and King has never comprehended the simple truth that tomorrow comes as surely as death. So he took what you offered, and tomorrow came and he's cornered. He bedded you in an opium haze. The opium is fading, leaving him to confront the prospect of wedding you, settling down, finding work, supporting a family."

"You make that sound like a death sentence," Cass said angrily.

"For King, that's just what it is."

"No! King loves me, and I love him."

"You're infatuated with him. All women are at first. As for King, he loves you as much as he can love anything tangible, but that's not enough for a woman like you. You need more."

"That's not true. King—"

"It's as true as tomorrow coming," Jared said ruthlessly, overriding Cass's words. "Do you know what tomorrow is going to bring? I do. I'll have to watch the brother I love and the woman I could have loved destroy each other. But I'm not going to let that happen. I'll prevent it any way I have to, any way I can." Jared's hands shot out and captured Cass's face in a caressing vise as he slowly bent down to her. "Don't destroy my brother, Cassandra. Don't destroy yourself. Let King go. Give your love to a man who can give it back to you redoubled."

With a broken sound, Cass wrenched away from Jared and stood with her arms wrapped around herself, trembling, her face pale, and her eyes wild.

In the doorway, Tea Rose waited and watched with consummate stillness.

42

Jared settled Tea Rose into the lawn swing and sat down next to her.

"You would have made a fine queen and an even finer spy," Jared murmured, smiling thinly. "But then, you were trained to be both. May I smoke?"

Surprise flickered for an instant in Tea Rose's eyes. "Is that a question that requires no answer?"

"A rhetorical question," Jared said, watching her absorb the word with a slight nod of comprehension. "In China, it would be."

"In China, a man would never ask. He would simply do as he pleased without all this fuss."

"In America, men ask women's permission in certain things as a sign of respect."

Tea Rose bowed to Jared in the manner of a student to a respected teacher, but he sensed that she was unimpressed by American men's respect for women of any race.

"I dislike the smell of opium," Tea Rose said, "but I would never bar a man his pleasures."

"It's only tobacco, I assure you. I dislike more than the smell of opium," Jared said dryly.

He lit a small black cigar, enjoying the gentle bite of smoke in his mouth. For several moments, he sat and smoked quietly, looking out over the water toward the mainland. The air had been still most of the day, leaving Seattle veiled in the smoke of cookstoves and sawdust-burning steam plants. A four-masted cutter with fully rigged sails beat its way north out of Elliott Bay. The last light of the day dyed the sails a deep saffron.

Without looking away from the sweep of land and sea and sky, Jared asked softly. "What do you want to do with your life?"

"Do?"

"Yes."

"Do—" Tea Rose said, repeating the word many times, as though she had just encountered it in a new context and was trying to fix it forever within her quick mind. "I'm not certain I understand what you mean."

"In America, you may do anything you want with your life. You may take photographs as your half sister does, or you may go to school and become a scholar and teacher, or you may get on a horse and explore mountains and deserts. You may choose to *do* anything."

Tea Rose was quiet for a time, thinking about the implications of Jared's words.

"In China you don't 'do,'" she said finally. "You simply are. You are a peasant or a merchant or a soldier or a songbird. Once you are something, there is no difficulty deciding what to do."

Jared smiled. "You have your mother's incisive mind."

"Not my father's?"

"Your father was a man like King. His thoughts didn't have the clarity or urgency of his emotions."

Tea Rose rocked the chair swing slowly, staring out over the darkening water and thinking about all the possibilities of life open before her. Jared sat and smoked his fragrant cigar and wondered what was going on in Tea Rose's mind, in Cass's mind, in Tan Feng's; and if it would be possible to bring King to his senses before he irrevocably ruined the lives around him.

"I don't know what I want to do," Tea Rose said after a long silence. "I do know what I *don't* want to do."

"Which is?"

"I won't be any man's sing-song girl," she said softly.

Ghostly fingers touched Jared's spine at Tea Rose's quiet statement. She had inherited not only Lilac's intelligence, but also her unflinching resolve.

"I hope that's a choice you'll never have to make," Jared said. "Your 'husband' sent his lawyer to see me."

The swing hesitated in its backward motion for an instant, then resumed its rhythmic swaying. Other than that, Tea Rose showed no outward reaction to Jared's words. She simply sat without moving but for the small motions of her legs pushing the swing.

"Wing has agreed to allow you to choose between your Chinese family and your white family. But you'll have to choose in his presence. And, of course, Tan Feng's. If you agree to meet with them, I'll set up a time and a place."

"I have no Chinese family. My mother is dead. My only family is my white sister, and she won't be family for long."

Surprised, Jared turned and looked at Tea Rose. The black clarity of her eyes made an extraordinary contrast to the pale, translucent gold of her skin. He wondered if any man could ever grow accustomed to her exotic beauty.

"Just because Cassandra is foolish in her choice of men," Jared said, "doesn't mean that she will abandon you."

"If she marries, it will be as though she had never been her father's child," Tea Rose said. "She will be part of the Duran family, not the Thornton family, and I will be a female with no family at all."

"In China, what you say is true. It's not true in America. Cassandra will take the family name of the man she marries, but she will never turn her back on her father's other child."

"This is true?"

"It's as true as you are beautiful," Jared said matter-of-factly.

The smooth curve of Tea Rose's eyebrows arched upward. "You call me beautiful, yet you don't desire me. Why? I wouldn't refuse your touch as my half sister did."

"I like you, Tea Rose. That's more lasting than lust."

"But far less powerful. It doesn't bind you to my wishes. Lust would."

"You have been trained to use your sex as a weapon against men."

"Are you saying that I frighten you?" Tea Rose asked, amused.

Jared smiled slightly. "If I desired you, you'd scare the hell out of me, Tea Rose. But I don't want you sexually, so I can simply appreciate your beauty and at the same time pity the poor son of a bitch who both wants *and* gets you."

Tea Rose laughed softly, revealing a flash of small white teeth. "'May your fondest wish come true,'" she murmured.

Jared smiled slightly as he heard the ancient Chinese malediction. "You might pass on that sobering bit of wisdom to your half sister."

"I tried."

"And?"

"My elder sister dresses me as a child, often speaks to me as a child, and thinks of me as a child. Why should she believe that I have more wisdom than she does on the subject of men?" Tea Rose looked sideways at Jared, giving him the full benefit of her midnight lashes and gleaming, mischievous smile. "I'm glad you don't desire me, Jared Duran."

He shook his head. "You're lying, little minx. But go

ahead and flirt. It will keep you in practice and amuse both
of us."

"There are other things I could practice that would amuse
both of us more. I have some small skill in playing the flute."

The euphemism wasn't lost on Jared, but he knew what
was driving Tea Rose—survival, not desire.

With a flick of his wrist, he sent his cigar sailing out of the
lattice house onto the wet ground. He held out his hands to
Tea Rose palms upward, as though to show that he was
unarmed.

"Put your hands in mine," he said softly.

Uncertainly, she did as he asked. His much larger, far
more powerful fingers curled gently around her vulnerable
ones.

"Look at me."

Tea Rose lifted her head and looked at Jared with eyes
that were too dark to reveal the shadows within.

"Because you and Lilac lived in a world where your only
safety lay in your ability to arouse and satisfy a man's lust,
you came to believe that unless a man wants you, you're
powerless against him."

Jared paused and searched Tea Rose's eyes, wondering
how he could make her understand, wondering if such
understanding were even possible for her. She had come
from a world where sex was both the medium of exchange
and the only power women held over men.

"With some men, manipulating their lust is the quickest
way of making them do what you wish. But not all men are
like that, Tea Rose. Sex is necessary for a man, but by itself
it's not a sufficient reason for a man to protect and care for
one woman. Tan Feng, whose sexuality is legendary, was
vulnerable to your mother not only because of her couch
skills and beauty, but also because of her mind and un-
quenchable will. Sex alone would never have held Tan."

"Perhaps. Yet that doesn't tell me why you don't desire
me."

"I want a mate, a companion, a wife, a mother for my

children, a passionate woman whose mind will fascinate me long after my body is sated."

"And a China girl can be none of those things to you?"

"You could be all of those things except one."

Tea Rose waited, searching the crystalline eyes of the man whose protection meant the difference between freedom and a prison whose only escape was suicide.

"You don't desire me, Tea Rose. You don't watch me with longing in your eyes. Your color doesn't heighten when I stand near you and," Jared gently stroked the pulse in her wrists, "your heart doesn't beat faster when I touch you. You want to know me better, but only so that you can manipulate me better. You're pursuing me now only because King, who might have been vulnerable to your beauty, is already in thrall to something else."

"You are describing my doom," Tea Rose said with aching calm. "Together, King and Cass will drive you away. King—" Tea Rose's voice faded. "Whether in a day or a month or a year, King will leave to seek the Great All, and then I will be taken by Tan Feng once more, because no man will remain to protect me." She watched Jared with outward composure, but her eyes were those of a wild animal. "Don't you understand? Tan Feng is like time itself, wise and patient and cruel. If I can see the shape of the future, so can he. He will wait, and then he will take me."

"You'll be under my protection as long as I live, Tea Rose. I'll make sure Tan Feng understands that."

"Words," she whispered. "Just words, gone with a breath."

"What would convince you?"

"If you wanted me, I would be convinced," Tea Rose said, "but you don't. If you would marry me, give me the protection of your name—?" She looked searchingly at Jared. "But you won't, because my pulse won't quicken for any man, even one as powerfully malc as you. Tell me, how can I believe you will help me when I possess no power to reward or to punish you, and Tan Feng does?"

"What do you mean?"

"You have much business in Chinatown. Without Tan Feng, you would have no laborers."

There was no accusation in Tea Rose's voice, simply the belief that Tan had a way to punish or reward Jared.

"Without me, Tan Feng would have no work for his laborers," Jared pointed out. "In business, we're stalemated." It was that stalemate he was working to break right now, but he had spoken of that plan to no one, not even to Lilac. A Chinatown without tongs would have been too much for even Lilac's wisdom to imagine.

Tea Rose closed her eyes and shook her head slowly. "I don't understand you, Jared Duran. You don't want me, yet you say you will help me. Why?"

"I promised a woman called Lilac Rain."

It was not a lie, but still Tea Rose was not satisfied. "Why?"

"Because I believe the future of this country lies in the joining of our two cultures, and that joining must begin somewhere, somehow, no matter the inconvenience or cost. I believe in that the way my brother believes in gold. In a very real sense, you are that blending of cultures. *You* are what I believe in, Tea Rose. I won't abandon you. I can't. It would be the same as abandoning my dreams."

In the deepening twilight, crickets began rasping softly into the silence. From the edge of the woods came the low, haunting call of an owl. Not until the last tremors of the cry faded did Tea Rose withdraw her hands from Jared's.

"I will see Tan Feng," she said. "His offer, at least, I will understand."

43

Neither the hot bath nor the skilled contortions of Lotus Moon had managed to release the emotions seething beneath Tan's impassive surface. Though his jade stem finally hung flaccidly over the sacred pouch, his mind was still turgid with rage at the circumstances that had taken from him two of his most prized possessions.

Fox Woman, gnawing on my soul.

Tan knew he would die with the memory of Lilac's blood as fresh as the instant it first had gushed from her mouth over his hands. He would die wanting her, cursing her, writhing with the certainty that she had eluded him in the very instant he thought he had achieved his greatest victory over her.

For a few seconds, Lilac had softened toward him. He had sensed it in her body, seen it in her eyes, tasted it on her tongue—and then there had been only the taste and sight and smell of blood, blood taking Lilac from him and leaving only the spectral sounds of demon laughter echoing within his mind. The final flowery battle had not been fought; now, it never would be. There was no victory, no defeat, no surcease to the raging sexual heat of his body.

Except Tea Rose. Only she might dim the savage brightness of Lilac's memory. Tan remembered the widening of Tea Rose's clear black eyes when he had pulled aside his clothes to reveal the fullness of his jade stem. When she had touched him so delicately, she had combined a virgin's trembling discovery with a courtesan's consummate skill. The combination had brought him to climax quickly, repeatedly, and each time his essence spurted, she had looked up at him with awe in her eyes and a smile on her glistening lips.

Fox Girl, even more dangerous than her mother. Fox Girl, drinking my essence, becoming stronger as I become weaker. Is that why you died, Lilac Rain? Did you know that I could quench my obsession for you in your daughter and my obsession for your daughter in you, thus defeating both of you? But one alone, just one obsession—.

Fox Woman, you have destroyed me.

Even as the words echoed in Tan's mind, he refused to acknowledge their truth. Lilac had been only a woman whose legendary beauty had been fading, a courtesan on the downward slide to becoming a saltwater whore. He should have sold her sooner, when she had been worth her weight in gold.

But he hadn't sold her, because Tea Rose's black eyes and slender little hands had begun to consume his imagination. He had hoped to keep Lilac until Tea Rose was safely installed as a white man's mistress. Then he would have both an extraordinary price for her maidenhead and the opportunity to take her in flowery battle without diminishing her value.

Tan had thought through his actions so carefully. If taking Tea Rose repeatedly wasn't enough, if he found himself in danger of becoming obsessed with Tea Rose, he had planned to buy back Lilac at a fraction of what he had been paid for her. After all, she would be merely a sing-song girl or saltwater whore by then, her face and body coarsened by the hundreds of men she would have been forced to service each week. Her mind, however, would not have been dulled; and it was Lilac's mind that gave the flowery battle with her such unique excitement, unique savor, unique danger. Tan could have broken her body with a single blow of his fist. It had not been the same for her mind. Even when each of his motions excited the pearl on her jade step, she had watched him wisely, measuring his increasing arousal until she sensed that he was on the brink of clouds and rain; and then she had used her body with terrifying skill, sucking the essence from him before her own essence flowed.

But a few times, just a few, he had managed to burst her cloud before she burst his. Then he had known the exquisite, matchless violence of her body convulsing in helpless pleasure around his jade stem.

Tan made a low sound as he felt his crotch tighten.

Fox Woman, take your savage spirit elsewhere. You have tormented me enough for one lifetime. Or have you found that even the Dragon Lover himself can't sate you? Have you come back to suck me dry as well?

No answer came to Tan from the haunted shadows of his

mind. He grunted, and stared at his desk, finally seeing the drying ink in its stone saucer, the patient abacus on whose smooth beads he would add up the week's gains or losses. He looked at the half-written letter to his eldest brother; the ideographs were elegantly formed, but they didn't say what must be said.

Reluctantly, Tan picked up his pen, drew the tip through the ink that remained, and wrote quickly.

This is a demon-ridden society. White devils came and stole the beautiful merchandise whose sale would have brought enough gold to allow my return to Celestial shores. The Fox Woman was so vexed at the loss of her daughter that she gnawed through her own tongue and bled to death. Thus, I have no gold from Lilac's sale as I had planned. The cursed police have twice raided me in recent days, causing further losses.

Yet, even the worst flood brings new soil. The miserable white go-between I purchased came to me an hour ago. The wretched thief who stole Tea Rose has no interest in her coral pleasure pavilion. He has agreed to bring the girl to me in front of witnesses.

And there, in front of witnesses, she will agree to come back to me.

44

Tea Rose rode in the stern of the rowboat like a Chinese princess. The young English sailor who manned the oars had watched her, every stroke of the way from the boathouse to the *Alki Point Flyer,* which was waiting in the deeper water off Bainbridge Island.

"I been Hawaii many many time," the sailor said finally, speaking in a sing-song pidgin, "but never see Chinee girl wear real dress. You speekee English, luv?"

Tea Rose had been ignoring the sailor's stares. Now, she

turned toward him and gave him a look that took in everything from his rakishly tilted hat to the worn-out soles of his shoes.

"I'm American," Tea Rose said in her soft, unaccented voice. "I 'speekee' English better than you do."

"Half white, eh? Which half is prettier?"

The sailor's leer left no doubt that the question had a double meaning. With a smile like a knife being unsheathed, Tea Rose told the sailor that he had the prick of a cooked mushroom and the face of a shithouse rat. As she spoke in Cantonese, the sailor understood only that her eyes made him a bit uneasy.

"Speak English, luv. I don't understand Chink."

"And I didn't understand your question. Perhaps I can get King to explain it to me."

"King? What's he, a laundry man?"

"Mr. Kingston Duran is part owner of the steamship that employs you. Perhaps you would like to repeat your questions to him?" Tea Rose suggested softly.

They made the rest of the trip in silence. Tea Rose occupied her time in making sure that the package she carried didn't get soiled by water from the bottom of the rowboat. The parcel contained a dress made of eggshell white silk that had come from the finest mill in Hong Kong. The dress had been created for Tea Rose by a French seamstress who was much valued by Seattle society women. Jared had brought the seamstress, cloth, and a sewing machine to the island. A day later, he had taken the seamstress and the sewing machine back to Seattle.

The closer the rowboat glided to the mosquito fleet steamer, the more impressed Tea Rose became. The ship's brass fittings, mahogany, and glass were all polished to a high sheen. The entire craft glowed in the morning sunlight. She had never seen such a beautiful ship, and it had come especially to carry her back to Seattle.

Tea Rose's lips shifted into a tiny smile. The ship was grander than anything Tan Feng had. She enjoyed having it at her beck and call, but the courtesan in her knew that

Jared had ordered the preparations for Tan's bemusement, not her own. Jared understood the ancient game of increasing face in front of one's enemies.

"Hand her up, boys," Jared said from the railing. "Do it properly, or I'll have your hides."

Two young sailors helped Tea Rose aboard as carefully as though she were made of thin crystal. Even so, they couldn't help staring at her from the corner of their eyes, fascinated by her beauty.

"Cassandra settled King in the salon. She's waiting for you in King's stateroom." Jared took Tea Rose's parcel from one of the sailors before he turned back to her. "I'll show you the way."

Thanking him demurely, Tea Rose tucked her hand through Jared's arm and permitted him to escort her to a cabin. Jared smiled down at her, enjoying the nearly hidden light of mischief in her eyes. Tea Rose was a consummate actress, and at the moment she was playing the part of a proper young American girl.

At the third stateroom, Jared stopped and knocked on the gleaming mahogany door. Around them, the ship shivered into life as her boilers were stoked and steam rose to drive heavy pistons.

"Cassandra?" Jared called. "Tea Rose is here."

"Thank goodness," Cass said, throwing open the door. "Hurry, Tea Rose. We don't have much time before we reach Seattle, and I suspect your hair won't take easily to curling."

Cass pulled Tea Rose into the cabin, shut the door in Jared's face, and went to work on transforming her half sister into a living symbol of sweet American virginity.

By the time the *Flyer* docked, all that remained of Tea Rose's Chinese heritage was her faintly tilted eyes. From her white kid leather shoes and gloves to the cut of her formal day dress, Tea Rose was occidental rather than oriental. Her thick, straight hair had been subjected to a curling iron until it formed shining, loose curls that cascaded down her back to her hips. Part of the shining mass of hair had been combed back from her face and held by a big silk bow of the same eggshell color as her dress. The muted white of the dress brought out the pale, nearly translucent quality of her skin. The simple, innocent style of both hair and dress were heightened by the single piece of jewelry Tea Rose wore— the large locket with her parents' picture inside.

Just as the *Flyer's* deep-throated whistle announced the ship's arrival in Seattle, Cass stepped back and measured the results of her handiwork. She looked, and then she stared, motionless, unable even to speak. The transformation was extraordinary. Tea Rose was innocence incarnate.

"What's wrong, sister? Is that wretched ribbon crooked again?"

Cass shook her head almost helplessly and said, "I think Eve must have looked like you. No wonder Adam couldn't say no."

Tea Rose's smile was all the more beautiful for being sad. She went to the wardrobe, opened its door, and looked into the mirror. The silk ribbon was a miserable substitute for gems and chiming golden bells. Naked skin was less appealing than the sensuous, rich drama of rice powder and crimson lip rouge. The silk of the dress was luxuriant, but Tea Rose had chosen its color to remind every Chinese who looked at her that her mother had died only weeks before. As for the kid gloves and shoes—

"Why do Westerners insist on wrapping themselves in the skins of dead animals?" Tea Rose asked, wrinkling her nose in distaste.

"Probably for the same reason that the Chinese insist on wrapping themselves in the skins of dead worms," Cass retorted.

Tea Rose blinked, then laughed. "Do I really seem as odd to you sometimes as you seem to me?"

"Not so much now, but in the beginning, yes, I'm afraid so."

There was a knock at the door and Jared's voice calling to Tea Rose.

"Come in," Tea Rose said, turning toward the door.

When Jared opened the door, Tea Rose watched him intently. She saw his eyes widen in surprise and admiration, heard his appreciative laughter at her skillful transformation, and knew that he still didn't desire her. Slowly, she curtsied, holding his eyes with her own.

"Will I do, my lord Jared?"

"I'm your friend, not your lord."

Tea Rose straightened and walked gracefully over to Jared, stopping only when she was bare inches away from his body. "Will I do, my friend Jared?" she asked in a low, husky voice.

"You'll do very nicely, and you damned well know it, minx. You're exquisite," he said simply, "but then, you always are."

Cass watched Tea Rose flirt with Jared and felt an odd anger rise within her. There was a combination of innocence and sensual assurance in the girl's manner that made Cass wonder what Jared and Tea Rose had done in the lattice house while they "talked." Had Jared seduced Tea Rose after Cass had refused him so abruptly?

The thought made outrage seethe in Cass. Jared might have been free to come and go from Lilac's bed, but Tea Rose was a different matter entirely.

"I don't see why any of this is necessary," Cass said, not bothering to conceal her anger. "No American judge would give a child to Tan Feng's hatchet man. Why didn't you file to have Tea Rose awarded to my custody as I asked you to do?"

Jared looked up from Tea Rose's flawless face into Cass's furious golden eyes. "Does this mean that you're speaking to me again, Cassandra?"

Silence stretched between them until Cass knew that he wouldn't say another word until she answered him.

"Does this mean you're apologizing for your behavior?" Cass asked coldly.

"What behavior?"

"You know precisely what I mean."

"I'm afraid I don't. Explain it to me."

Again there was silence.

Tea Rose watched the clash of wills and felt fear grow in her heart. No good could come of a fight between the two people who were most important to her welfare.

"What do you want from Jared, sister?" Tea Rose asked, breaking the taut silence.

Startled, Cass turned away from Jared. The expression on her face told Tea Rose that Cass had forgotten there was anyone else in the room.

"An apology," Cass said tightly.

"Why should a man apologize for wanting you?" Tea Rose asked, her voice calm, curious. "Isn't that why you wash your hair until it's fragrant and brush it every night until it has the fire of melted gold? Isn't that why you wear clothes that are cut to cling to your breasts and waist and hips?"

"Tea Rose." Jared said no more. He didn't have to.

She turned and looked at him out of magnificent, wide black eyes. "Forgive me, friend Jared," she said, her lips parted and trembling with distress. "I forgot that truth is only for Chinese half sisters."

"Sharpen your bittersweet wiles on someone else," Jared said, stopping the trembling of Tea Rose's glistening lower lip with his index finger. "You forget, I knew the master who taught you."

"How could you!" Cass said, her voice shaken by fury at the implications of Jared's finger caressing Tea Rose's mouth. "She's just a child, Jared. How could you seduce her as though she were a woman who—"

Tea Rose's laughter cut across Cass's angry words.

"Seduce me? Ah, sister, if only he would, I would burn incense in every joss hall in Seattle." Then all humor vanished from Tea Rose's face as she turned to confront the woman whose blood was half her own. "Why are you so angry? You share the couch with one brother. Why shouldn't I enjoy the touch of the other?"

"You are a child, Tea Rose. What I do with King is none of your business. In any case, there's more to it than—"

"—two bodies bumping in the dark," Tea Rose interjected coolly, her voice an eerie echo of Lilac's precise intonations. "I agree. There's protection from other men. I have none, yet you rage at Jared when he looks my way. If you're so jealous of Jared's smiles, why did you insult him when he offered to give you much more than two bodies bumping?"

"He never—"

"You know nothing of yourself and men," Tea Rose interrupted coldly. "You've put us all in danger with your foolish infatuation, yet you rage at Jared because he hasn't taken your advice. I've lived outside of Chinatown barely a month, but I know why Jared hasn't gone to court to have my life assigned to you."

"Why?" Cass demanded.

"It's very simple, sister. The white world considers sex a sin that can be redeemed only by marriage. Is there a judge alive who would give me to an immoral woman rather than return me to my lawful husband?"

Cass went white as a wave of sickness swept over her at the thought of having her relationship with King discussed in court, all sweet intimacy destroyed, all privacy, all that made it more than two bodies rubbing in the dark.

"That's enough, Tea Rose," Jared said quietly.

"Why can't I speak?" Tea Rose asked passionately. "Why should I listen to my sister's lectures on men and women, right and wrong, when her blindness puts my own life at risk?"

Tears welled in Cass's eyes, making them huge. Helplessly, she looked from Tea Rose to Jared.

"I'm sorry," Cass whispered. "I didn't think—"

"I know, sister. You didn't think."

Anger and unwilling compassion warred within Jared as he saw Cass's distress. Tea Rose's assessment of the situation was correct, but unnecessarily cruel. Cass was white to her lips. With a silent curse, Jared caught Cass in his arms, supporting her. She stiffened for a moment and then sagged against him, crying silently. He held her, stroked her hair, felt each curve of her body as though it were being branded onto his own; and he cursed the manipulative girl who was watching them with triumph burning in her black eyes.

"Don't blame yourself, Cass," Jared said roughly. "Even if you'd never met King, Tan Feng's lawyer would have found men to testify against your virtue. The judge might have believed us in the end, but—" Jared's voice softened. "It's all right," he murmured, holding her, rocking her slowly against his chest. For a long, agonizing moment, he allowed himself to brush his cheek over Cass's bright, fragrant hair; then he put her away from his body. "Tan Feng is waiting for us. Go wash your face, and see that King doesn't break his fool neck going down the gangplank."

When the stateroom door closed behind Cass, Jared turned to look at Tea Rose. She returned his glance calmly, her eyes as clear as black crystal.

"You will treat your elder sister with respect, or you will find yourself living alone."

Instantly, Tea Rose's small hands came together. She bowed deeply over them. "Yes, lord," she said, the familiar Cantonese words coming quickly to her tongue.

This time Jared didn't correct her.

45

Hungry for the clean air of Elliott Bay, Jared left the cabin and went on deck. Once there, he leaned on the railing near the gangplank and watched the life of the port city swirl along the docks. As cargo was shifted from warehouse to hold, the hoarse cries and careless curses of sailors and stevedores mingled with the crack of teamsters' whips and the hollow boom of hooves on wooden planks. He let the sounds wash over him, replacing the bitter words that had come before.

A man's laughter soared above the waterfront noises. The sound was so inviting, so filled with life, that Jared knew it could have come from only one man. He turned and leaned his elbows on the railing as he watched his brother approach the gangplank.

In deference to the importance of the occasion, King had allowed Cass to trim his beard until it lay like a sleek pelt along the line of his jaw; but nothing could subdue the fire that burned within the mahogany depths of his hair. The subdued color of his suit heightened the sense of untamed strength coiled just beneath, impatient to be free. Only King's hobbled walk and ebony cane seemed at home in civilization.

As he laughed, King's free hand slid caressingly down the back of Cass's dark dress. Her face was turned up to him, and her eyes reflected his burning life. Jared watched the two of them and tried to forget what Cass had felt like in his arms a few moments before.

King smiled down at the woman who watched him, and his whole stance changed, becoming gentler. For an instant, he looked at Cass as though he would absorb her into himself, and then he laughed again.

At that moment, Jared wondered if he had been wrong, if Cass were indeed the one woman on earth who could hold King without destroying him. And then Jared wondered how he would endure a lifetime of listening to their laughter, of seeing the woman he wanted more than any other worship King with her eyes, her smile, her body.

Suddenly, King's cane slipped on the uneven gangplank. He caught himself on his wounded leg and then stood very still for a few moments, racked by pain.

"King," Cass said, her voice breaking over his name. She slid her arm around his waist. "Now will you let me help you?"

With a lithe twist of his body, King pulled free. "I told you, I'm through being treated like a doddering Civil War amputee. It's past time I stood on my own two feet."

Cass started to object, only to stop at the look on King's face.

"Don't frown so, sugar girl," he said, smiling down at her. "I've doctored myself back from worse injuries with whiskey and coal tar. It's time I got out and started making some money at the tables again. Sure as hell, the cards can't be any colder than my investments have been. If word gets out that I'm laid up, everyone I owe money to will gather like crows and pick me clean as a skull."

Cass opened her mouth to argue, but realized it was futile. She released King and watched anxiously while he walked down the gangplank with the uneven grace of an injured cat. From the corner of her eye, she spotted Jared leaning against the railing, watching his brother. She hesitated, then walked over to Jared.

"Can you do something with King?" Cass asked. "You know as well as I do that he's in no shape to pick up where he left off. He's risking permanent injury."

"King has always done what he wanted without asking my permission. That's not likely to change."

Cass closed her eyes for an instant before she looked up at Jared with too many shadows in her golden eyes.

"Are King's money problems so serious that he has to push himself right now?"

"You're asking the wrong man."

"But he told me you handled all of his finances."

"I used to. I don't any more."

Cass didn't need to ask why. She clasped her hands together, as though to keep from reaching toward Jared in a silent plea. Without looking away from her bent head, Jared drew a slender cigar and a match from the gold case he carried in his breast pocket.

"None of this would have happened if it weren't for me," Cass said with desperate calm. "King was injured helping me rescue Tea Rose. Then he and I—we—" She closed her eyes and shook her head. "Then you and King argued, and now Tea Rose is frightened, and I've really made a mess of things for everyone."

"The day that little opium poppy is scared is the day I'll walk on water from here to Bainbridge Island," Jared said. He snapped a sulfur match into flame with his thumbnail and puffed quickly, drawing the small cigar into life. "And before you get a bellyache from eating too much crow, you might remember King's part in all this, and mine, and Tan Feng's."

"And my father and Lilac?" Cass added, attempting a smile and failing. "Let's not forget them."

"I'll never forget Lilac Rain," Jared said softly. "Tan will burn in hell regretting what he did to her, and I'll be the man who sends him there."

Cass looked at Jared's glittering eyes and felt as though the deck had dropped away beneath her feet. Without a word, she turned and hurried after King, whose eyes reflected the immediacy of life rather than the certainty of death.

46

Tan Feng and his double column of men were a short black sword slicing through the crowded street of Seattle's International District. Throngs of people parted before Tan and fell back toward the wooden sidewalks like dark waves falling away from the carved prow of a ship. Faces impassive, bodies erect, colorful tong banners snapping overhead, the thirteen men strode down the center of the street.

Tan had prepared himself carefully for this meeting. His naturally high forehead had been emphasized by a barber's razor. In addition, the barber had skillfully worked delicate black silk threads into Tan's queue, lengthening it until the end nearly touched the ground. On his head, Tan wore a crimson silk skullcap trimmed at the bottom in sable and decorated on top with a large crystal nob. A long black tassel fell gracefully from the center of the nob. As with the hip-length necklace he wore, the hat was a sign of his rank.

Dressed in a vivid emerald silk tunic and black pants, Tan was a potent green flame burning against a sea of drab citizenry. He walked staring straight ahead, as though the rest of humanity resided just beneath his gaze.

Closest behind Tan in the double column of men were Kwan and Wing. The two bodyguards wore black, from their silk skullcaps to the ends of the formally oiled queues that hung to their calves. The additional length of their queues had been achieved by adding black silk rags shredded into thin strips, a process that was less time-consuming and costly than the fine silk threads Tan's barber had used. Both Kwan and Wing walked with hands stuffed inside their black jackets. Each bodyguard wore the heavy, short sword that custom decreed and, in addition, his palm rested on the butt of a loaded revolver.

Behind Kwan and Wing walked ten more men, important tong soldiers all—collectors of the informal protection tax, enforcers of order, opium runners, managers of tong gambling halls. Each man was feared and respected within the shadowed reaches of the International District. Each man was a living reminder of the pervasiveness of Tan's power. He and his tong exerted their influence at every level of nonwhite society, from the wealthy merchants' silk-hung residences to the stinking toilets of the lowest opium dens and whorehouses.

If the District's citizens had become dubious about the extent of Tan's power in the aftermath of the loss of Lilac and Tea Rose and the raids on his opium dens, the doubting citizens had only to look and see the white men who had preceded Tan into the Christian mission building, bringing with them the precious merchandise that had been stolen from Tan.

The Methodist Church Mission on the edge of Chinatown had been agreed upon as neutral ground on which to meet and hear Tea Rose's decision. The idea of meeting in the church amused Tan Feng. The place might be revered by Christians as a place of much joss, but Tan wasn't intimidated by the god of the white devils, a god whose son had died in middle age without siring so much as a half-witted son to mark his passage. Of what use to a true Chinese was a god so weak that his jade stem couldn't provide sons to respect and honor and continue the family line?

Tan's entourage turned a corner and marched up the street that led out of Chinatown. On the sidewalk, two policemen in blue woolen uniforms watched impassively. One officer chewed on a dark piece of Peking duck he had just plucked from a rack above the cutting block of the fowl-seller's small stall. The other policeman stood idly, his hands clasped behind his back. On any other day, the two men might have challenged the right of Tan's tong to parade armed through the streets, but not on this day. This day, each policeman had a twenty-dollar gold piece to brighten his pocket.

The twelve men behind Tan came to a coordinated halt at the bottom of the steps leading up to the church doors. Tan spoke rapidly over his shoulder, harsh commands that sent his soldiers dashing to positions up and down the street. Kwan, Wing, and one more bodyguard remained at Tan's elbow. Not by so much as a glance did any of the tong men acknowledge the stares of the common citizens of Chinatown. Kwan and the black-dressed bodyguard marched up the steps, opened the doors wide, and waited stiffly for Tan to pass. Three steps behind Tan came Wing, the putative focus of the meeting.

Inside the church, it was dark and cool, redolent of incense and spicy candle wax. A handful of altar candles provided the only illumination. When Tan's eyes adjusted, he recognized Jared Duran standing at the end of the long center aisle between the pews. Beside him, dressed in bleak white, a female stood with her back to the street door. Her hair was an undisciplined black waterfall tumbling down her back nearly to her knees. When she heard his footsteps, she turned around.

Tan Feng drew a deep, almost involuntary breath as he recognized Tea Rose.

There was nothing left of the sweet, mischievous Chinese child in this female with black eyes and pale lips and wild hair. More American than Chinese, utterly unadorned, wearing a mourning dress that followed the curves of her body with an indecency that would have embarrassed a saltwater whore, all that was recognizable of Tea Rose from the past was the violent impact of her beauty.

That hadn't changed. Nothing would change that, even death. Fox Woman had been reborn in the flesh of her daughter.

Tan took a few steps forward before he could prevent himself. The impassive, powerful lines of his face flowed into a scowl that brought uneasy murmurs from the people sitting in the front pews. The sounds filtered through Tan's fierce emotions, reminding him that he wasn't alone. Slowly, his eyes focused on the pews. At least a dozen people looked back at him; five were Chinese. He scanned the faces, recognizing merchants and businessmen and the smith who forged frying pans and utensils from placer gold that returning sojourners smuggled back into China. The men in the pews were prominent members of the Chinese community, men of much face.

They were also Christians. In China, their religion wouldn't have mattered. For thousands of years, the Celestial Empire had absorbed the storms of every new religion carried by traders or conquerors over the face of the earth. Buddhists, Muslims, Christians, Shintoists, Jews, all called to their disparate gods from joss houses built on Chinese soil; and the great mass of the Chinese people went on unchanged, worshipping their ancestors, having sons, being worshipped by those sons in turn.

It was different in America. Here, Chinese Christians had turned their backs on much of what made China unique. More white than Chinese, they burned joss sticks in tong halls only as a form of social insurance. It was their impotent Christian god whom they feared, not Tan Feng.

"Welcome, Mr. Tan Feng. We are pleased to have you with us," Jared said clearly. He gestured toward the pew where Cass sat with King and four Pinkertons whose faces were as expressionless as those of the Chinese soldiers.

Jared spoke in English, a discourtesy that instantly registered on Tan. Jared knew Cantonese and even some Mandarin, but he intended to force the tong leader to muddle through in broken English or to rely on an interpreter. It was a subtle way of underlining the death of Lilac and the defection of Tea Rose. Nor could Tan simply speak Mandarin, for then he would be forced to rely on Tea Rose to translate his words for the American businessmen who had come to sit in judgment on this dispute between two communities.

Tan turned to Kwan and spoke in clipped Mandarin. "Bring Spring Moon."

Kwan bowed and went to the last pew at the rear of the church. There, waiting in the motionless silence perfected by countless generations of Chinese women, sat Spring Moon. Years before, she had cost Tan the price of three sing-song girls, but he had paid it without complaint. It wasn't Spring Moon's beauty that made her valuable, for she had little of that; bilingualism was her lure. She was the English-speaking daughter of Chinese Christians who had been reduced to penury by a long-ago spring flood. Formerly, she had been the Madame Pao of Tan's Portland brothel, where her language skills had been very useful to Tan's business ambitions within the white community. After Lilac's death, Spring Moon had become the Madame Pao of his Seattle brothel, as well as his personal translator.

Without appearing to, Tea Rose watched the woman coming up the aisle. Spring Moon was neither young nor old, beautiful nor ugly. She was tiny, and for that reason she had inherited Lilac's luxurious clothing. Today, Tan had chosen for her to wear a sumptuous peach silk tunic and pants embroidered with brilliant designs. Her hair was elaborately coiffed and held in place by a headdress made of pearls and pink jade. Tiny mirrors flashed with each movement she made, and jade pendants clicked musically on the headdress fringe. Her hands were concealed beneath the pendulous horse-hoof sleeves, and her feet were hidden within folds of silk from the loose pants. She moved with the tiny, precious, swaying motions of a footbound woman.

"She wears my mother's clothes," Tea Rose said so softly that Jared barely heard.

Jared said nothing.

Spring Moon had reached into her sleeve and pulled out the gold-filigree fan Jared had once given to Lilac. He showed no outward sign of the anger in his gut, for Tan would seize upon that anger and turn it against Jared in front of the assembly.

Spring Moon stopped a few paces from Tan and bowed deeply before she turned to Wing and bowed less deeply. Jared couldn't hear the spate of mixed Mandarin and Cantonese that passed among the Chinese. He had to wait for the high, sing-song translations of Spring Moon. She turned and bowed to Jared, but the bow was a poor, shallow thing. Even before Spring Moon straightened, Tea Rose spoke softly.

"Pretend not to understand her English. I'll speak for you."

Jared nodded. Then he caught the brief flick of Tan's wrist beneath his long sleeve. Instantly, Kwan and the other bodyguard slipped between pews until they commanded the side aisles. Other tong soldiers moved in silently from the street, reinforcing Tan's position.

It won't help you, you son of a bitch, Jared thought with satisfaction. He had noted the look of shock and sexual hunger that had passed over Tan's face when he first saw Tea Rose dressed as a proper American miss. In that instant, Tan had realized that he had been outmaneuvered by Jared, and it was too late to undo the damage. *Bring in the rest of your army. Bring in all of Chinatown. It won't matter. Your cock is your only weakness, and I'm going to drag you all over the landscape with it.*

Jared made a small gesture with his left hand that brought King and the Pinkertons to their feet. King, his limp barely noticeable, came to stand near Jared. The four Pinkertons quietly took up positions blocking the side aisles. All four wore suits whose coats were unbuttoned to facilitate drawing a pistol. Silently, the tong men and the Pinkertons eyed one another with cool professional interest.

"Most Honorable Tan Feng sorry-sorry come joss house

with soldier," Spring Moon said in an artificially high voice. "Must protect honorable self when thief steal even wife."

Jared turned to Tea Rose. "I can't make heads or tails of what she's saying. Would you please translate for me, Miss Thornton?"

Tea Rose nodded her head gravely, then turned and curtsied to the citizens gathered like a petit jury in the front rows. In flawless English, she relayed Tan Feng's insult.

A low word from Tan galvanized Wing. He strode forward, stopping only when Jared moved to cut him off. Wing glared at Jared, then looked beyond him to Tea Rose.

"Precious wife, you are safe now. The Most Honorable Tan Feng will protect you from these white devils who stole you. Come. We will go home and drink tea and smile, knowing you are safe once more."

Wing spoke in Cantonese, his native dialect. It was also the dialect of the Chinese businessmen who were sitting quietly, listening with great interest.

Alone in her pew, Cass looked from Spring Moon to Tea Rose, for the contrast between them was both instructive and stunning. Spring Moon hobbled on maimed feet several steps behind her master; Tea Rose stood on whole feet next to Jared, a man who was friend rather than master.

Tea Rose, Cass pleaded silently, *look at Spring Moon and see what you would become. Don't let your anger at my mistakes send you back into slavery.*

The answer to Cass's prayer came quickly.

"I have no memory of being your wife," Tea Rose said in English, looking at Wing.

The expression on her face was one of innocent distress. Its impact was heightened by her soft voice and earnestly clasped hands. Her eyes, however, were those of a predator looking for warm flesh.

The high sing-song of Spring Moon's translation pierced the silence.

"Wife, why do you shame me thus?" Wing asked angrily. "Have I not given you my name and my house and my protection? What demon possesses you? Where is the sweet

Tea Rose whose soft voice and shy smiles gave beauty to my home?"

"I'm sorry that you are distressed," Tea Rose said, looking at him earnestly. "I'm afraid I have no memory of anything but my honorable mother, who recently passed away."

The murmurs of the citizens rose. Jared heard enough to know that the American component was impressed by Tea Rose's virginal innocence. The Chinese citizens were struck by her manners, more American than Celestial, yet still respectful for all of that.

Rather grimly, Jared smiled; it had been Tea Rose's idea to wear white. Obviously, she had also decided that she would plead a simple lack of memory rather than confront the issue by denying that she was Wing's wife.

It had been a shrewd decision, if the speculative murmurs were anything to go by. The white men looked at Tea Rose and saw a ravishing, rather bewildered child. The Chinese looked at Tea Rose and saw a female that must have been possessed by demons, for only such a possession could explain her defection and subsequent loss of memory. Men on both sides supported Tea Rose; yet she had not declared for either side. Wing was effectively stalemated.

Tan Feng had apparently reached the same conclusion. He turned and spoke to the men sitting in the pews. His Cantonese was serviceable, but little more. The fact that he spoke it rather than his customary Mandarin was a form of flattery to the Cantonese who watched him with unblinking attention.

"I think the poor female is not the only one here possessed by demons. What other reason than malicious demons could there be for wise and honorable men such as yourselves to listen to a husband and wife bicker over things that matter only to them? Or do man and wife come to Christian joss houses to argue over the cost of chickens and rice, and how to build the fire in the pleasure pavilion?" Tan smiled sadly. "This things are private matters, family matters. What has the Celestial Empire come to when neighbors interfere in a man's family? Go home, honorable neighbors, before there is much loss of face all around."

"These men are here because I asked them to be here," Jared said in Cantonese. "Their presence is an honor to your face, not an affront. These men will take Tea Rose's decision and spread it up and down this coast of the Pacific Ocean. You won't have to go to the effort and expense of publishing the fact of Tea Rose's safety from harassment in broadsides nailed to every building in every Chinatown in America. The men gathered here will take care of that for you, freeing your energy for endeavors more worthy of a man of your standing."

Tea Rose translated for the white businessmen while Tan listened impassively.

"Your kindness is noticed and understood," Tan said, nodding very slightly. "I will, of course, repay you in some small measure."

The Chinese shifted, knowing well the threat that lay beneath Tan's polite words. As though their movements had attracted Tan's attention, he turned again toward the pew of honorable men, bowed slightly, and began speaking in Cantonese. After a moment, Spring Moon began translating into English in a voice so soft that it didn't disturb the flow of Tan's words.

"Have you heard of the newspaper stories that call a Celestial female's honorable position within the hierarchy of man and gods slavery?"

Murmurs of unhappy agreement rose from the men, who had been distressed by the articles' portrayal of Chinese men as barbarians who enslaved women and ate dogs.

"Americans call their females 'free.' We call their females pitiable," Tan Feng continued, "for they have been forced out of the protection of the home to work in factories for wages a coolie would scorn.

"Americans call our females slaves. We know that our females are cherished and protected, especially in Gum-Shan, where Chinese females are so lamentably rare." Tan Feng paused thoughtfully before he continued. "A wise man would say that the Celestials and the Americans cherish their females differently. Our females wear pants and theirs wear skirts; our females bind their breasts flat to diminish the contrast between chest and waist, their females wear instruments of torment made of whalebone to heighten the contrast between breasts and waist. But whether in China or Gum-Shan, females have breasts and wear clothes according to the custom of their country."

Tan waited until Spring Moon's high voice became silent. "Tell me, wise men," he said in a ringing voice, "have we so little face that we must bow our heads and listen while white devils tell us how to dress our females?"

There was a long, uncomfortable silence. Finally, the goldsmith stood, bowed to Tan Feng, and said, "Most Honorable One, we are merely the grass on which the elephants play. Our desire is not that one elephant or the other win; all we want is to avoid being trampled."

"Grass," Tan said. He grunted in disdain before he turned and went closer to Tea Rose. "And you, precious one?" he asked, smiling at her as he hadn't done since he had opened his robes, giving her the gift of his virility. "Do you choose to live as a female alone in a devil land? Do you cut yourself off from your honorable husband and family?"

The church became utterly silent.

Cass looked at Tan Feng's handsome, compelling face and bowed her head over her hands, praying that Tea Rose would see beyond Tan's looks to the reality of the slave master beneath.

Not until the silence in the church had become unbearable did Tea Rose lift her head and meet Tan Feng's glance. Tears glittered in her beautiful eyes and left silver trails down her flawless face. When she finally spoke, her voice was husky with uncertainty and regret.

"Forgive me, most Honorable Tan Feng, but my mother is only recently dead, and I have no memory of a husband at all. My only family is my sister, Miss Cassandra Thornton, daughter of my father. Surely a man of your great wisdom understands that a child belongs with the family of her own blood?"

Check and mate, Jared exulted silently. *Wiggle off that hook, Tan Feng.*

"You have no memory of a husband," Tan Feng repeated carefully, his voice both deep and tender. "What of me, little flower? Do you remember me?"

"If *you* had called yourself my husband," Tea Rose murmured, "I'm certain that I would never have forgotten it."

Understanding burned in Tan Feng's eyes. He smiled at Tea Rose with a cruelty that made Cass's skin ripple in fear. He moved closer to Tea Rose until only she could hear his words. For a moment, he stood and looked down at her with hooded eyes.

"Beautiful black butterfly," he said caressingly, "enjoy your wings while you can, for someday I will rip them off and feed them to you."

Tan turned and walked back down the center aisle of the church toward the front doors. As he passed between the silent rows of pews, silk rubbed over silk with a sound not unlike that of a snake sliding across warm sand. Before he reached the outer doors, they were flung open by his men. For a moment, Tan was a towering shadow framed by a rectangle of dazzling blue-white light.

And then he was gone.

47

With a combination of unease and disgust, King Duran watched the milling activity behind the stock exchange's wooden rail. He hadn't been in the place since he had been shot three months ago. To his jaundiced eye, nothing much had changed. Traders still darted and gabbled like geese in a grain field. Well-scrubbed young men in wilted white shirts and crooked bow ties still scribbled the names and prices of stock issues on the chalkboards against the back wall. About the only thing different was that the names of some of the companies had changed; King didn't recognize a dozen of the issues being bought and sold. It didn't bother him, because he was even less interested in the stock exchange than he had been three months ago.

A young page made his way back through the seething crowd of traders, followed by a stockbroker named George Simon.

"Hello, stranger," Simon called out, grinning and advancing with a hand poised to shake King's in welcome. Simon was a man with pale skin and a darkly waxed mustache. He wore his hair parted exactly in the middle of his head and slicked down with brilliantine, an affectation left over from the days when he had been a barber rather than a broker.

"Morning, George," King drawled. "How's business?"

"Great, just great," the broker said enthusiastically. "People are beginning to buy again. First time in three years that I feel really optimistic about the future. Other folks feel the same way. The room has really come alive. Can't you feel it, like bubbles in champagne?"

The corners of King's mouth curled into a small smile. "Can't say as I do, but I'm glad to hear it. Why don't you go on out there and rustle me up a buyer for this?"

As King spoke, he reached into the breast pocket of his suitcoat and produced a thick sheaf of stock certificates. The printing was in a baroque style emphasized by heavy use of gold foil and colored inks. Simon's cheery smile tilted a little when he saw the name on the certificates.

"Uh, West Seattle Electric Railway," Simon said.

"Right. That's the traction company you and Jared dumped on me last year, remember?"

Simon started to say something, hesitated, cleared his throat, and asked brightly, "You sure you want to get rid of those shares right now? What about your stock in—"

"I've sold off everything else," King said. His green eyes

narrowed, and his nostrils flared as though he scented something unpleasant. "You don't look real happy anymore, George. What's the matter? You tired of doing business with me?"

"No, nothing like that," Simon said, laughing briefly. "It's just that this might not be the best time to unload your West Seattle shares."

"That doesn't make sense. You just said the market was rising like bubbles in champagne."

"Not for traction companies," Simon corrected. "People are still a little wary of them. Streetcar ventures won't realize their full potential until development picks up again and people start building houses out there in West Seattle."

"When is that likely to be?"

"Oh, a year or so, maybe three."

Deliberately, King looked around the room, trying to rein in his growing temper. He was damned tired of being told to wait a year or two or three to get his money out of his investments.

"I don't have that much time," King said flatly, focusing on the broker again. "I need to sell now."

Simon drew a deep breath. "I guess I didn't make myself clear, Kingston. There isn't any market for West Seattle traction company shares at the moment. Hell, I can't give those shares away, much less cash them in for you."

King tilted his head to the left and studied the broker as though he were a new and unappetizing form of life. "Try that again," King invited.

"The exchange has stopped trading those issues because nobody will buy them."

"Just like that? I pay ten thousand dollars in honest gold, turn my back, and when I turn around again, all I have is a handful of paper tarted up like a whore's face? What the hell kind of business are you running here?"

King's voice carried very well despite the exchange's normal noisy turbulence. Nearby brokers turned and looked at King, but he didn't shift his glance away from Simon's unhappy face. Slowly, King leaned forward, towering above the broker like an avalanche poised on the brink of breaking loose.

Simon took a step backward and said, "If you paid more attention to your business, you'd know that a San Francisco holding company bought up most of the available shares in West Seattle Electric Railway about two months ago."

"So?"

Simon shrugged. "So the holding company closed the line down."

"What? Buy a streetcar line and close it down? That doesn't make sense!"

"The line wasn't generating much revenue," Simon pointed out.

"Then why buy it in the first place? Who the hell owns this holding company, anyway?"

"Nobody knows. There's some talk that it might be a James J. Hill stalking horse, a corporation he created secretly just to pick up the West Seattle right-of-way. You see," Simon added, when it became clear that King didn't comprehend the intricate interplay of forces that made or broke stock issues, "Hill's Great Northern Railway is still trying to find a downtown depot site in Seattle. This buy-up might have something to do with that depot."

"Then what's the problem? I'll be glad to sell Mr. Hill my shares at a fair price."

"You're too late," Simon said patiently. "Two months ago, the San Francisco outfit began buying up every share it could get its hands on until they got one share over 50 percent. It took less than a week. Then they stopped buying and shut down the line. There hasn't been a share of West Seattle Electric Railway move across the board for nearly two months."

King stood motionless, his anger stalemated by the fact that he didn't understand the manipulations that had led to his shares becoming worthless. All he understood was that ten thousand dollars in gold had vanished as though he had never scooped it from beneath icy veils of water.

"Two months," King repeated softly, thinking of all that had happened in those weeks while he healed and hid from Tan Feng, golden opium dreams and Cass enveloping him in gentle flame. And the past month, in which he had tried and repeatedly failed to find a bearable niche for himself within Seattle's civilized boundaries. The only thing that had kept him from going crazy was Cass's undemanding, generous gift of herself. She accepted him without reservation, asking nothing, living only in the moment—as though she knew that to ask about the future would be to cage him, driving him away.

She deserved better than he gave her, and he knew it, and it galled him all the way to his wild soul.

"I'm sorry, Kingston," the broker said, looking uneasily at King's bleak face. "I tried to get hold of you so you could get in on the action, but you'd disappeared. Nobody knew where you were, so after a day or two I quit looking. I had other clients to cash out."

"Did you try Jared?"

"Couldn't find him, either," Simon said. "Like I said, the whole buy-up lasted only two, maybe three days. I tried to take care of you, but—" He shrugged helplessly.

"So now what?" King asked, fanning the stock certificates in his hand as though they were colorful, oversize poker cards. "What should I do with these?"

"Hold onto them, by all means," Simon said, his voice rich with encouragement. "Things change fast, Kingston. Someday there may be a market for your West Seattle shares again."

"But in the meantime, I can't get two cents on the dollar, is that it?"

"You could use them as markers in poker games with your brother. He lost twice what you did." Simon's smile became a grimace when he realized that, at the moment, King's sense of humor was as bankrupt as the traction company. "I'm sorry," Simon said, but even as he spoke, a triumphant shout from a corner of the room drew his attention.

"Why should you be sorry?" King drawled, his eyes nearly

opaque with fury. "You collected your commission, didn't you? Isn't that what a commission agent does—take a notch out on the way up and on the way down, too? Sort of like the house share of table stakes. No matter who gets cleaned, the house makes money, right?"

"There's rather more science in the stock market than in stud poker," Simon said, turning back to King. "There's nothing personal in what happened, Kingston, so taking it personally won't help. It's just the nature of things. The invisible hand of the free market gives to some and takes away from others."

King's right hand flashed out without warning. His fingers gripped the stockbroker's neck just above the bow tie.

"Someday," King said, "that 'invisible hand' is going to wrap itself around your neck and squeeze until you choke on all that fancy science."

Simon tried to back away, only to find himself trapped between King and the wooden railing that separated the trading floor from the lobby.

"Now just a minute, you can't—" began Simon, only to be interrupted.

"I can't do what?" King retorted, squeezing lightly. "You know something? You're what I hate about cities. They're full of scavengers. They run in packs like dogs."

King's voice cut through the racket, bringing a spreading pool of silence in its wake.

"Here," King said, flinging the share certificates in Simon's face. "If they're worth something, you hold them. If not, use them to wipe your ass."

48

Three hours later, King was still seething as he stood with one polished boot on the brass rail and one elbow on the marble bar of the Humboldt Grill. He had been drinking steadily but not hard since he left the stock exchange. The bartender, a bearded man with the build of a blacksmith, pointed at King's nearly empty beer glass and raised his eyebrows. King looked at the glass for a moment, studying it as though it were a crystal ball, and then shrugged.

"Sure, why the hell not?" King asked carelessly. "It's only another nickel, unless the price went up while I was in the gents'."

"Nope, still just one buffalo to a glass," the bartender said as he pumped another glass of lager. He set the dripping drink on the marble with a solid smack of glass meeting stone. "Beer's the last thing to go up. It's God's way of making hard times tolerable."

"In hard times, are we?" King asked. "Thought I was the only one hurting."

"Hell no," said the bartender, swiping his rag across the marble. "I'm so flat broke right now I could slide under that spittoon by your feet and it wouldn't even gurgle."

The bartender laughed deep in his barrel chest as he wiped his way down the bar to draw another beer and chase dust on the pyramid of shot glasses on the back bar, leaving King alone once more. King didn't object. He had had all the company he could stand for a time. A long time.

That was why he had come to Humboldt's bar. It was a good place to drink alone. Its clientele ran to hard-drinking loggers, boom boat operators, and other men of the lumber industry. King didn't know any of them, so he didn't have to worry about being drawn into their conversations. And if the place got rowdy at night, that was fine, too. A good brawl would get King's blood running and clear the cobwebs out of his mind. He needed to think about the future, to plan, to organize; and all of those things were alien to him.

Without really seeing it, King stared at the golden glow of the beer in front of him. He had been where he was now before, but it had never seemed quite so constricting. He had squandered a decent fortune in the past seven months —good times and bad investments and worse luck at cards. He wasn't sure which of the three had cost him the most money, nor did he care. He had settled his bills and debts this morning and had found himself to be a far poorer man for it.

A few hundred dollars remained out of more than twenty thousand.

One corner of King's mouth turned up in an ambivalent smile that was invisible beneath his mustache and beard. It had been a long and glorious slide down to penury, every bit as entertaining as it had been the other three or four times he had gone the same route. Boom and bust out, boom and bust out—the ageless sine curve of life for prospectors like himself who chased placer gold, found it, spent it, and chased it again.

Boom and bust—but no more boom.

The gold trail was closed to him, and the stock exchange was priced out of his reach. He needed cash, but his only real skill was useless in the city, where money came from printing presses and dollars were doled out by the week. No boom was possible here. Nothing but a lifetime of not-quite-busted.

Other men have jobs. Day after day after day. Same city, same building, same people, same work.

If it's that bad, why the hell do you do it!

I didn't say it was bad, King. You did.

The memory of his talk with Jared made the beer turn to acid in King's stomach. It wasn't the idea of physical labor that dismayed him; he had the strength and stamina to outwork four men, and had done so many times in the past. But what good did physical strength do him in the city? Here, King's skill with a pan and water would get him a job washing dishes in a hotel, and his skill with a pick and shovel would qualify him to muck out livery stables. He couldn't see spending a lifetime doing either one.

That left his skill with a pistol. Wearing a badge and shoveling drunks out of the gutter had about the same appeal as shoveling horseshit. About the same pay, too. Of course, he could always find employment on the other side of the badge. Bank robbers probably made a decent enough living, and sure as hell they didn't die of boredom in the process.

A corner of King's mouth kicked up again. He drank a cool swallow of his beer and lowered the glass again. The glow of the golden liquid caught and held his eye. The money that remained from his fortune would be enough for a very bare-bones stake for the country Dryden had told him about. Prospecting was what King should do, what he would have done, except that doing it didn't solve the rest of the problem—Cassandra Thornton.

When King heard himself calling Cass a problem, he groaned softly. She deserved better than that, much better, and that was a problem, too.

Cassie, what the hell am I going to do?

No answer came, nothing but the fool's gold of the beer. King knew that marrying Cass wouldn't stop up his ears against the siren call of the ineffable. In fact, marrying her would be even more unfair than seducing her had been. He was the worst candidate in the world for matrimony, yet Cass wasn't made to be a man's mistress; she was made to be a man's partner.

"Cassie—" King whispered softly to the golden swirl of beer in the glass. "I don't want to hurt you, sugar girl. I don't want—"

A whoop of laughter made King look up from his beer. Five feet down the bar were two lanky youngsters in their early twenties. Both wore loggers' tin pants and heavy, double-aught calk boots whose sharp spiked soles chewed up the green lumber floor of the bar. Their conversation and their cocky attitude identified them as toppers, the high flyers of the woods. Their job was to tie themselves to a tree a hundred and fifty feet up the trunk and then lop off the top of the tree with a double-bladed axe honed so fine that loggers made a show of shaving with it.

Without rancor, King listened to the men's wild laughter. He knew that they were bucking a stacked deck in a way that he never would; the odds were that one of the two young men would be dead within three years and the other would lose his nerve and take up ground leads or bucking crosscut saws in the jackpit. The odds were even better that the dead man would leave a widow, who would marry another logging man.

Women rarely married prospectors more than once. It wasn't that prospectors died young. It was just that they were home only one month out of twelve or sixteen. The difference between being married to a prospector and being a widow was quite simple; widows could remarry.

Just beyond the toppers stood a dour, middle-aged drinker—whose clothes proclaimed him to be a lumber-schooner captain—hoisting one last shot of bourbon and a glass of H. Weinhard's Lager before heading out Puget Sound to Australia with an overload of green lumber stacked man-high on the deck. With luck, the captain would be gone three months. Then he'd be back for a few weeks to see his wife and his children, if he had any. Either way, his voyage would be shorter than any of the last five prospecting trips King had made.

And when the captain grew tired of roving, he could always transfer his skills to an easy berth on a coastal freighter or a mosquito fleet steamer, a job that would allow him to sleep in his own bed, with his own wife, every night. King wasn't so lucky. There was no handy, nearby, part-time way to be a prospector. His work required ten thousand square miles of unexplored land and the unfettered time to pan every promising inch of its streams.

Just beyond the schooner captain stood a solitary figure wearing the stained buckskins of a professional hunter. His clothes were dark with sweat and blood, and stiff with soil. Even to loggers who were accustomed to sweating hard and bathing rarely, the hunter stank. He was halfway through a bottle of bar whiskey, drinking from a shot glass with the numbing regularity of a metronome, and then tamping each charge down with a swallow of beer from a thick mug. Once he had hunted buffalo, but that way of life was irretrievably gone. Now, he supplied some of the fancy restaurants in town with fresh game. Elk, bear, deer by the dozen, wild geese and ducks in season—he killed and dressed them all like a roving wilderness slaughterhouse, forgetting or ignoring the frontier's first rule: Kill what you eat and eat what you kill.

Poor bastard, King thought, taking another swallow of beer. *He made the same mistake I did. He thought the frontier would last forever. We were both wrong. The frontier died before we did.*

But not up north. There's a lot of land up there. Maybe even enough for my lifetime.

Yet King couldn't go and find out.

"That one go flat, did it?"

"What?" King asked, focusing on the bartender.

"Your beer. Did it go flat?"

King smiled oddly. "Doesn't everything?"

Before the bartender could answer, King dug a cartwheel out of his pocket and flipped the coin onto the marble bar. The silver dollar rang musically as it spun around and around until it lost momentum and fell still.

"Keep the change," King said.

"Last of the big spenders, huh?"

King didn't hear. He was already gone, striding through the Humboldt's back door as though he had fifty miles of wilderness to cover and only half a day's sunlight ahead. He turned up the alley toward First Avenue, going past the seamy crib houses and bars of the Tenderloin. Nothing was open for business yet, but one of the prostitutes was out in the back yard of a dusty Victorian house, handing a bulging bag of laundry to a small man wearing dark clothes and a queue. Her shrill orders and his sing-song reassurances rang through the alley.

At First Avenue, King turned west, heading back into the respectable reaches of the city. The afternoon sun was hot. It felt good, beating through the dark cloth of his trousers, warming the muscles of his injured thigh. Other than giving him a mild ache when he roamed the city all day, his leg had healed. The wound was little more than a tender pink knot of scar tissue on his muscular thigh—that, and memories of pain and sensual opium dreams.

And Cass, of course—the woman he loved as much as he would ever love anything he could touch.

Walking quickly, not wanting to think because there was nothing new to think about, King had just reached the Olympic block with its rough-quarried granite facades when someone called his name. He stopped in front of one of the stores and turned around. A short, slightly built man wearing workman's clothes and a straight-brimmed felt hat was smiling and holding out his hand to King.

"Mule Dryden!" King said, smiling widely and smacking his own palm into the other man's grip. "What the hell have you been up to? Damn, it seems like years since I've seen you! Let me buy you a beer."

Dryden's face creased into a wide smile. "It's only been three months, but I know what you mean. The city does that to a man. Comes of having too many clocks around."

"What have you been doing?"

"Rustling a grubstake. Took much longer than I thought it would."

"You're going north?" King asked.

The yearning in King's voice told Dryden more than words could have. It was the way Dryden felt himself. He jerked his thumb at the storefront.

"I wasn't sightseeing," he said happily.

King turned and noticed the store for the first time: Cooper and Levy. Behind the tall display windows were stacks of supplies and equipment, everything from flour to dynamite and a thousand things in between. Cooper and Levy supplied mining camps and logging operations all along the West Coast. A man could buy everything he needed from the store except guts, strength, and good luck. When it came to prospecting, King had been born with more than his share of all three.

"When are you going?" King asked, his voice rough.

"Tomorrow."

"Where you headed?"

Dryden hesitated. King laughed and slapped him on the shoulder.

"Afraid I'll get a jump on you?" King asked, understanding without resentment Dryden's silence. "Hell, man, even if you told me of another Sutter's Mill strike and drew me a map to boot, I'd be weeks behind you by the time I got a stake together."

Dryden tipped the flat-brimmed hat back on his head and smiled self-consciously. "Sorry, King. Old habit. I'm leaving for Alaska."

"This late in the season? I thought you were a cautious man."

"Like I said, it took longer to gather a stake than I'd expected."

"Still, I'm surprised you don't wait until spring. There's some brutal weather between you and sunshine in that country."

Dryden shrugged.

King's eyes narrowed to lines of shining green. Adrenaline swept through his veins, clearing out the mellowing effects of beer. "Someone made a strike."

It wasn't a question. King knew that nothing else would have convinced a shrewd old hand such as Dryden to take on an Alaskan winter.

"Sure as hell wish I hadn't been shot," King muttered. "If we'd partnered three months ago, we'd be up there right now, ass deep in placer gold."

"Maybe, maybe not. She's a right tricky piece of country up there."

"Can you tell me where?"

"Aw, hell, sure I can. Come on," Dryden said, jerking his thumb at the store again. "It's no secret, if the truth be told. A lot of men already know. I'll show you close as I can on the map in here."

Cooper and Levy's interior was papered with a dozen maps of the northwest, including one that was spread out on the glass top of a display case. The map sketched out in rudimentary detail the vast wild country from the Gulf of

Alaska to the Arctic Ocean. Curling through the center of it like a thick blue vein was a line marked "Yukon." Dryden stabbed his finger at a point about halfway up the river from the Beaufort Sea.

"Circle City," he said confidently. "Danged place is so new they don't even have it on this map yet, but it's there, all right. More than a thousand people already, and growing like spring wheat."

"Then it's too late," King said, looking hungrily at the map. "The good ground will all be staked. Nothing will be left but Chinaman's pickings."

"Come late spring, yes," Dryden said slowly. "There'll be hell's own stampede up there when they start bringing out gold. But so far, only talk's come out."

"What kind of talk?"

Slowly, Dryden drew a circle on the map with a scarred fingertip. "Some say they'll take a million dollars in gold out of here come summer."

"A million?" King whistled. "That's some cleanup."

King looked at the map's scale and began quickly marking off distances with his thumbnail. There were only hints as to the topography, or the number and size of rivers, streams, and creeks.

"You're not the kind of man to go against a northern winter just for some fancy talk," King said, looking up sharply.

"I saw some gold," Dryden admitted. His voice softened and he smiled. "She's coarse and clean, mostly dust with a few old beat-up nuggets that come a good ways downstream from the mother lode."

"How much a pan? Five cents? Fifty? Five dollars?"

"Don't know. I heard a man say something about fifty-dollar pans, but it was probably just whiskey talking."

King's hungry glance fixed on the invisible magic circle inside which mapmakers had had little more than speculation to record. There had been rumors of gold in the Yukon for as long as King had been prospecting, but there had been little proof. The country was too wild, too remote, too cold for all but the most hardy—or foolhardy—of prospectors. Even when the rivers weren't frozen, the ground remained locked in ice a few feet beneath the surface. The winters were so cruel that almost nothing moved over the land but man. A few birds, fewer rabbits, no deer, no elk, no bear, nothing a man could get his teeth into. During the long winter, there was little for man to eat except the supplies he had packed in himself.

"How many men are prospecting up there now?" King asked slowly, watching the map with burning green eyes.

"'Bout two hundred, last I heard."

"You going overland?"

Dryden shook his head. "That's a fool's route, from what I heard. I'm going upriver." He tapped the map with a fingertip that had been flattened and deformed by frostbite years before. "The last steamer leaves St. Michael, right here, about the first of September," he said, pointing to a spot on the Alaskan Coast just north of where the Yukon emptied into the Pacific. "With any luck, I'll be able to catch her. I'll winter in Circle City and be set to pound stakes on a likely claim come the thaw next spring."

King looked at the rest of the map, tracing the line of the river farther inland. It was a long, long way from anywhere, which only added to its appeal. That was where what he sought would always be, beyond the reach of man.

"If there's dust here," King said, indicating Circle City, "what about upstream? Say about here?" He stabbed the spot marking the confluence of the Yukon and another smaller river.

"Some folks think so," Dryden conceded. "But a man's got to eat. There's nothing to live on out there 'cept bark and a rabbit or two if you're pig-lucky. That's the Klondike area I was telling you about a few months ago. But it's in Canada, and it's a lot easier to get into heaven than it is to get into that Yukon country. I want to get rich as much as any other man, but I don't plan to kill myself doing it."

"The Klondike—" King's fingertips stroked the surface of the map as though he could actually touch all that might be there. "It would be worth the risk. Hell, I came closer to dying in Seattle than I ever did hunting gold."

"There's gold in Circle City," Dryden said, tapping the spot with his mutilated fingertip. "They've proved that. Nobody's proved there's gold in the Klondike country, and lots of men have died trying."

King's untamed smile flashed like the sun coming out from behind clouds. "But Mule, you know as well as I do that if two hundred men have already found gold, there's damn little left for number two hundred and one."

Reluctantly, Dryden nodded. "Maybe so, King. Maybe so. But I can't risk my life for a handful of maybes. Too old, I guess, or too smart. Besides, that country would be pure living hell on a white woman."

"So?"

"So, I'm married," Dryden said, smiling at King's look of surprise. "Two months ago, I found me a widow with grown kids. Now I eat good food and sleep right warm at night, and I don't have to buy drinks for the house to get someone to listen to me talk. It was her idea that we go north. Said she was itchy as I was to see new country. She's home packing right now."

King smiled oddly. "I wish you luck, Mule, and your woman, too."

"Oh, we'll do fine. If I don't turn up a likely claim in Circle City, a friend of mine has a spot for me as foreman on a sluice-box crew. I'll get a percent and a half of the cleanup and not have to risk another round of frostbite and pneumonia for it."

King knew that a miner's wages and a cut of another man's take wasn't much different from a city job; Dryden wouldn't starve, but he had no chance of touching the sun, either.

As though reading King's thoughts, Dryden smiled a little sadly. "I know," he said, "but a man's got to grow up soon or late. You and me were born in the wrong time, King. The great strikes have all been made, and all the best placers are already panned out. So a man has to work another man's claim for wages, or work in the city for wages." Dryden shrugged. "I'd rather be in Circle City than Seattle. Up north, I stand a chance of staking my own claim on the side, maybe even finding a small placer pocket or two. Down here, all I stand a chance of finding is a gold watch when my eyes are too old to read time."

"If your wife will go to Circle City with you, why not go on to the Klondike?"

"You ever been there?"

"No."

"If hell was ice instead of fire—" Dryden shrugged. "Millie's too good a woman to chew up in a useless hunt for gold, and that's all there is to it."

"A bird in the hand is worth two in the bush?"

Dryden smiled. "That's just what I told her."

King wondered if Dryden would be as happy with his bird in hand a year from now, or even a month, but he didn't ask. It was a choice each man had to make and live with for himself.

A bird in hand—and another just over the horizon, calling to him in every scintillating color of the rainbow, even those colors he had never seen, nor even imagined. Especially those.

Unimaginable.

49

Slowly King Duran's image condensed beneath the clear developing liquid. Cass swirled the exposed plate with a practiced wrist, washing the glass as thoroughly as a prospector washed a pan of promising sand. With each passing second, the chemicals laid down an image in light-sensitive silver salts on the plate. First, the dark slashes of King's eyebrows and hair and beard appeared. Then the outlines of his face were sketched in.

As King's eyes condensed from the chaos of the developing fluid, the hair on Cass's nape stirred. In the hard light of the flash powder, the emerald color of King's eyes had become splinters of pure translucent silver. They were the eyes of a dreamer, a poet, a visionary, a mystic. They were eyes that looked through life to—what? What did King see that other men did not?

He belongs to the Great All.

"No," Cass said aloud, swirling the plate mechanically. "Tea Rose is wrong. King loves me."

Yet, the more clearly the image of her lover condensed from chaos, the more Cass feared it. Unwittingly, she had captured her most secret fears about King on glass plate, preserving them forever.

Another picture, sugar girl? I think Tan Feng was right. I think you're trying to steal my soul.

No, I'm just trying to reveal it.

King and Cass had laughed together at her words before he had pulled her into his lap and not let her go until she was disheveled and breathless, and photography was the farthest thing from her mind. She loved being close to him, holding him, knowing that the green blaze of his eyes was focused only on her. She loved his warmth, his kisses, and she had come to enjoy having him within her body as well. When she was with him, she thought of nothing beyond the moment she was living in.

At this moment, however, King wasn't around to muddle Cass's insights with his lovemaking. There was nothing but herself, and the plate between her hands, King's image condensing into timeless reality, a fragment of a man's restless soul captured forever.

Looking at the image now, Cass realized that she had been avoiding her intuitive understanding of King. When she was with King, she concentrated on the line of his lips or the sensuous brush of his mustache on her skin, or on teasing him into the laughter that made her feel as though she, too, had touched the sun.

King hadn't been laughing for this picture. He had laughed less and less in the past weeks. Cass told herself that he was concerned about finances, although King had brushed off the idea when she mentioned it. He had told her brusquely that money was the least of his problems—money couldn't cure boredom. Then he had seen her unhappiness and pulled her into his arms, apologizing for upsetting her, telling her that everything would work out in time.

But how much time do we have? Cass silently asked the image condensing on the plate. *You live in a hotel so shabby you won't let me go there to visit you. You have no job, you won't take money from me, you won't ask Jared for work or financial advice or—*

Cass's hands trembled as she moved the plate within the developing solution, fixing King's image forever. In his wing collar and cravat, chalk-striped coat and trousers, he looked very handsome. He also looked not quite real. The thick pelt of his hair and beard were at odds with the constraints of boiled collar and intricate cravat.

She should have listened to him.

Another portrait in suit and tie, Cassie? If it's the truth of my soul you're after, you'd better photograph me in a flannel shirt and rough pants, with a miner's pan in my hands.

Cass, who routinely tried to coax her clients into less formal sittings, had ignored King's suggestion. She had pulled the black photographer hood over her head and had begun taking photographs of King as though pursued by devils. Without knowing why, she had instinctively shied from the idea of photographing King in clothes that matched the calluses and scars on his hands. Now she understood. She hadn't wanted to confront his reality, the elemental energy in his soul that would give him no peace, the same elemental energy that had drawn her inevitably to him in the first place.

King wasn't a businessman in an expensive suit. He was a prospector who would buy a Hudson's Bay blanket and a pack, and then live out of them for the next year, somewhere out there beyond the pale of civilization.

Why couldn't you have been more like Jared? Just a little, darling, just enough to hold still, to—build a life. Love, love, I can't go over the horizon with you. Can't you see? If I abandon Tea Rose, I won't be able to live with myself.

Not that you've asked me to go. Or to stay. Or anything. Don't you have any plans at all, King? Aren't I part of them?

Why couldn't you and your brother have been born in one skin, one man? Your fire and his endurance, raw energy and icy intellect combined.

There was no answer but the truth that Cass was too honest to ignore any longer. King's unfettered soul was the core of his attraction for her: he had been places few other people had; he had seen things, felt things, discovered things; and she had wanted to see, feel, and discover those things through him before all those experiences vanished, unremarked and unrecorded, into the expanding void of the past, everything turning to dust and being blown away.

She was afraid that her love was a prison for King, rather than an undiscovered country opening in front of him, beckoning him to explore its dangers and rewards. Could anything she offered fill the hunger in him?

For she had no doubt that a hunger was there. She had heard the siren call of the horizon in his words, had seen it in his eyes, had sensed it in his brooding silences.

Part of Cass wanted to go with King, to hear the siren's honeyed call rising on the light of dawn, to touch the sun. She knew that part of King wanted the comforts of a home and a woman's love. Part of him, part of her—but would that be enough to build a whole life on?

She wondered if King understood her fears, or if he even thought beyond the coming night, when he would walk soundlessly into her room, undo her nightgown and whisper love words against her bare flesh as he parted her legs, seeking the warmth within. Like the energy burning in King's eyes, he existed without question or demand, asking nothing of the present or future.

But Cass did. She hadn't the melancholy visions of her namesake prophetess, but she knew that the future was forever becoming the present. Whether man noticed or ignored it, time existed, and tomorrow came, willy-nilly. She had learned to plan for tomorrow, but King had not. Now, all she could do was to pray that King's lack of money wouldn't drive him back into the wilderness before their love had had time to grow into the depth of emotion that lasted a lifetime.

Don't go, my love. Please. Stay with me until Tea Rose is grown. Then I'll go wherever you want.

50

The private dining room was far too dim for James Jerome Hill. Even the short, gray days of Seattle in November were brighter than the interior of the restaurant.

"Grauer, let's have some light in here, some *electric* light," Hill grumbled, his voice reverberating from deep in his barrel chest.

One of the well-polished attendants in the empire builder's retinue came to attention and hurried away to find a waiter.

"I don't understand why people keep on using candles," Hill complained. "Electric light is much superior."

"Some people prefer the past," Jared Duran said. "Their memories are illuminated by candles, not electricity."

"I've little time and less use for nostalgia," Hill replied.

Part of Hill's testiness came from the fact that he was blind in one eye. That blindness was the focus of newspaper cartoonists all over the West; they relished depicting the president of the Great Northern Railway as a buccaneer with a black patch over one eye and his good eye burning as fiercely as one of the glaring single headlights on Hill's highballing express engines.

Other than his monocular vision, Hill's physique was too unremarkable for the requirements of caricature. He was short and sturdy, with a bland Scottish face and a white spade beard. His dress was as conservative as his public lifestyle. The only thing unusual about him was that he understood the connection between railroads and social growth better than any man alive. As a result, the Great Northern was the most powerful business force in the Northwest.

It had taken Jared a great deal of planning, hard work, and skillful stock manipulations to get to the point of eating dinner at Hill's table. Now, Jared was on the edge of finding out if his plans were going to pay off with more than the ambiguous pleasure of Hill's company in a dimly lighted, overly expensive restaurant.

A pair of waiters appeared with electric lamps, which were quickly plugged into wall sockets and placed on the supper table. Hill picked up the lamp that had been set in the middle of the table and moved it to one side, allowing him to see his tablemate more clearly.

"Better. I like to see a man's eyes when he talks to me."

However, Hill wasn't yet ready to talk. He seized his knife and fork and attacked the slab of rare roast beef on his plate. He cut the eye of the loin into proper bites, dabbed them with horseradish, and ate them one at a time, quickly and efficiently. Then he gave a sign, and one of the waiters swept the plate away and placed a glass of red wine before him. Hill sipped, patted his white mustache with the heavy linen napkin, and was ready to talk business.

Jared signaled the waiter that he, too, was finished with his plate, although he had eaten only a bite or two. He sipped the wine without tasting it, set the glass aside, and waited for Hill to open the game. Silence spread between the two men for more than a minute while Hill stared at Jared and Jared returned the gaze. Finally, Hill broke eye contact and laughed.

"You are a cool one, aren't you, Duran?" he said.

"I have nothing to be hot about at the moment."

Hill snorted. "I don't need your railroad, young man. I've built the Great Northern all the way across this country without any help, and that includes those thieves in Washington, D.C."

Jared smiled. Hill's railroad was the first transcontinental system that had been built without land grants or government subsidies, and Hill was rightfully proud of that fact.

"If I can do that," Hill concluded, "I can surely run a line north to British Columbia without your help."

"You could," Jared agreed, "but it would be foolish. You didn't build a transcontinental railway by being a foolish man."

"Two pieces of steel thirty miles long—that's all you've got to offer me. I could choose another route, or I could parallel your right-of-way yard for yard. My crews could put down thirty miles of track in two weeks. If I did, your little railway wouldn't be worth a handful of spit. You'd be lucky to sell out for five cents on the dollar."

Jared nodded. "I've supplied crews of Chinese who could put down three miles of track a day. You could go around me as you've gone around a hundred other short lines. But as for another route—" Jared shook his head. "I don't think so, Mr. Hill. You've played communities one against the other all the way across the country by keeping your route plans a secret. If one community didn't offer you enough, you chose the other. Divide and conquer is one of the oldest strategies in the world, and one of the best. Unfortunately, you've come up against something you can't divide and conquer."

"You?" Hill said. "Don't overrate your own—"

"Not me," Jared interrupted. "The Pacific Ocean. You can't play the alternate route game because you've already committed yourself to projects at both ends of my line. Now you've got to connect the mills in Everett to the timber on Whidbey Island. You can do that with my line, or you can build its twin from scratch."

Hill sipped red wine for a moment, then finished his glass in a single gulp. Instantly, a man stepped forward and poured more wine. With outward calm, Jared watched and waited to see whether his gamble had paid off.

"Do you always play your cards face up?" Hill asked finally, real curiosity in his voice.

"No."

Hill grunted. "You've got three hundred thousand tied up in that line, and you've held it for two years. I'll give you four hundred thousand. That amounts to 12.5 percent appreciation per year. That's a more than ample reward."

"Your arithmetic is correct. Your estimate of me is not." Jared smiled slightly. "A duplicate line would cost you no less than one million, two hundred thousand dollars. I'll settle for one million, which leaves you bragging rights on two hundred thousand."

"Your line is outdated," Hill pointed out. "It needs a great deal of work. Four hundred thousand dollars' worth of work, according to my appraisers."

"It could be brought up to the Great Northern's standards for less than two," Jared replied. "I'll split the cost with you. Nine hundred thousand."

Hill peered across the table with his one good eye, then held out his right hand. "Nine hundred thousand in Great Northern stock. Done."

"Cash," Jared countered immediately. "Stock can be watered too easily."

"I wouldn't bother watering stock for that amount, but— done. Nine hundred thousand dollars in cash."

Jared shook hands across the table, and tried not to show the intense elation sweeping through him.

"Now that that's done," Hill said, settling back with wineglass in hand, "satisfy an old man's curiosity."

"About what?"

"Business, son. That's all that's worth a man's attention."

Smiling, Jared wished that Tea Rose could have been with him at the dinner. She, too, had an endless curiosity for business matters. She also had a gift for them. Her ability to manipulate, and understand how men used power, had at first shocked then intrigued Jared. Many of his visits to Cass's photographic studio had ended up in intense, three-sided conversations about Seattle's future. Cass had a fascinating visceral understanding of the range of human emotions, an understanding that Tea Rose lacked; Cass wouldn't have agreed with James J. Hill that business was all that was worth a man's attention.

Neither did Jared agree, but he hardly planned to point that out to the man from whom he had just wrung a very handsome profit.

"Go on," Jared said, sipping his own wine, noticing it for the first time.

"Why on earth did you buy up all that useless traction company stock?" Hill asked.

Jared's eyes snapped open. "I beg your pardon?"

"Don't worry, son. I won't tell anyone. There's no profit in it for me that I could find. You covered your tracks real well," Hill added with a smile. "Cost me a lot to unravel your trail, but it was worth it."

"How so?" Jared asked.

"It told me how close to the vest you can play, which told me that you had me sewn up tighter than a tart's corset before you agreed to have dinner with me tonight. When you play your cards face up, it's because you've got an unbeatable hand and you're smart enough to know it. So why did you want West Seattle Electric Railway?"

"Almost everyone in town thinks the Great Northern is in the market for downtown right-of-way and a depot site. West Seattle controls both, or so most people think."

"Do you?"

"Why else would anyone buy the company?" Jared asked neutrally.

Turning his head slightly to bring his good eye fully to bear, Hill studied the younger man in the cold white glare of the electric bulb.

"We'll take your railway, but not your traction company," Hill said. "I intend to build a tunnel beneath the downtown area someday and run my lines right through to the waterfront. So I'm not interested in your West Seattle property. Sorry, but you guessed wrong."

"Which just proves that no one is as shrewd as you," Jared said, lifting his glass to James J. Hill in a silent toast.

Hill watched while the toast was drunk, knowing that

Jared hadn't told him the full truth, and knowing also that Jared had said all that he would say on the subject.

Jared sipped wine again, but it was the taste of victory rather than alcohol that sang in his blood.

51

"Would Mr. Tan Feng care for a glass of red wine?" Salyor asked.

Smiling cordially, the lawyer stood at the sideboard, a bottle of wine poised over the mouth of a crystal glass. He was surprised to see a look of distaste spread across Tan's face just before the Manchu sucked air loudly through his teeth, making a deliberately rude noise. Abruptly, Tan turned away and studied an oil painting on the office wall, pretending he had not understood the question.

"Lord Tan Feng no drink wine," Kwan announced carefully.

"Perhaps some coffee?"

"No come here drink."

Salyor poured himself a glass of the claret and carried it back to his desk. He was weary of the arrogant Chinese, but not of the monthly retainer Tan paid into Salyor's bank account. Even so, Tan's belief that he was the superior in the lawyer-client relationship was very tiresome to Salyor.

The lawyer's oil painting of European flowers and fruits didn't interest Tan Feng. Neither did the other still life, of husked corn and squash and three dead ring-necked pheasants. The pheasants had originated in China, but if they had been used in a Chinese painting, they would have been depicted alive, in black and white, with only the most subtle use of color to suggest the living reality.

Tan grunted and looked at the floor. It was covered with a hand-knotted silk carpet designed in a dragon pattern. He pointed at it and spoke in Mandarin to Kwan.

"Lord Tan Feng ask where come carpet," Kwan translated.

"I bought it in San Francisco," Salyor said with a trace of pride. "An excellent rug. It cost me almost four hundred dollars."

Tan Feng spoke again to Kwan.

"My lord own many like rug. Cost in China one ounce gold. Twenty dollar." Kwan hesitated while Tan spoke again. "You want more like rug? Forty dollar."

The drinker's flush on Salyor's face deepened. "One's all I need," he said, turning to Tan. "What do you want today, or did you come here to discuss cheap rugs?"

Tan spoke in quick, harsh sounds.

"When Tea Rose return?" Kwan asked.

Salyor shook his head firmly. "I've explained that many, many times. So long as Jared Duran is protecting her, we don't have much chance of prying her out of her half sister's hands."

There was another round of rapid Chinese, followed by Kwan's translation.

"Lord Tan Feng give much money, much much," Kwan said, pulling a pouch of gold dust from his tunic and dropping it onto the desk. "Each month three hundred fifty dollar. Each month Tea Rose no come. Why this?"

Salyor settled into the leather chair behind his desk, ignoring the poke of gold. "The sum of which you speak is a professional retainer for work I have done and am continuing to do on Tan Feng's behalf in my capacity as an officer of the court. I have filed suit, I have—"

Tan spoke quickly again, interrupting.

"No understand 'officer of the court,'" Kwan said. "Lord Tan Feng say in China if man pay official, man get something back."

Salyor looked puzzled for a moment before he laughed. "So the old son of a bitch thinks he bribed the court through me, does he? He thinks a few ounces of gold guaranteed that I'd get his little China doll back for him."

The sound of a second leather poke thumping onto the polished walnut of Salyor's desk startled him. As the bag landed, it tipped over and spilled a stream of gold dust onto the wood. Salyor glanced down at the dust with wide eyes. Experience told him that there was at least eight ounces of gold in the bag.

"What's this for?"

"Message boy," Kwan said.

Salyor looked up and saw Tan Feng's contemptuous black eyes staring at him.

"I'm not a—" Salyor began, only to be cut off by Kwan.

"Listen message you deliver. Listen good."

52

Cass and Tea Rose labored in the sweet light of late afternoon, trying to position the tripod on the uneven footing of the steep hillside. The Denny Hotel towered above them like an ancient fortress, complete with balustrades and flat arches. Cass loved the baroque splendor of the downtown landmark, which had been started in 1891, only to stand empty and half-completed since the Crash of 1893. She had been trying to catch the changing patterns made by the shadows of the past and the incomplete arches of the future across the face of the building as it stood vacant, waiting for its own time to finally come.

With a last squint through the lens, Cass started to lift her hand in a signal for Tea Rose to expose the plate. Before Cass could do much more than form the intention, Tea Rose had whisked off the cap. The girl's quickness was a constant revelation to Cass. Tea Rose had learned to read people's habits and actions so accurately that it was uncanny.

A slave's skill, Cass thought uneasily. *But she's not a slave anymore.*

Tea Rose replaced the cap as meticulously as Cass herself would have. Tea Rose had a patience that was truly extraordinary; never once had she shown irritation or boredom when Cass had become lost in her photography for hours on end, barely noticing the beautiful girl who handed her new plates and wrapped up the exposed ones. In fact, Tea Rose never complained about anything at all anymore, even the presence of cheese in Cass's cooler.

Nor did Tea Rose ask for anything. Her small room was kept painfully clean, as were her clothes. Over Cass's protests, Jared had insisted on supplying Tea Rose with a complete wardrobe of Western clothes. Her house clothes were colorful and made of soft fabrics. Her outside clothes were made to blend into the life of the city streets without a stir, including the hats that all but concealed her beauty.

No matter what happened, Tea Rose made no complaints, no requests, said nothing to tell Cass what went on behind those clear black eyes. Tea Rose worked hard and willingly, learned with astonishing speed, and saved her enthusiasm for the huge, dark books on economics, industry, and history that Jared brought to her. Those books, Tea Rose read with complete concentration, asking questions of Cass from time to time, and quizzing Jared unmercifully during his frequent visits.

At first, Cass had been uncomfortable in Jared's presence. In time, she had relaxed, largely because Jared rarely looked at her and never spoke to her about anything other than Tea Rose. If King wasn't there, Jared usually stayed for dinner, and the three of them would talk until late at night. If King was there, Jared would stay only long enough to drop off whatever books or small gifts he had brought for Tea Rose. Cass often found herself wanting to ask Jared to stay, for she enjoyed his wit and cosmopolitan view of men and societies; but she never requested that he remain once King arrived. She knew Jared would refuse politely—and very finally.

Cass emerged from beneath the black drape, put her fists in the small of her back, and stretched. As she did, she noticed a man standing just outside the entrance of a nearby saloon. He was watching Tea Rose.

"Sister?" Tea Rose asked, seeing Cass's sudden stillness.

"The man over there," Cass said.

"He has watched us for the past five minutes."

Cass hesitated. It wasn't unusual for the two of them to be stared at, for photography hadn't been practiced outdoors in Seattle long enough to have become commonplace. Nor did Cass have reason to be nervous of any attack; she and Tea Rose were hardly alone, for the streets were alive with people.

Even so, Cass found the man's surveillance disturbing.

"He's coming this way," Tea Rose said.

In silence, the two women waited while the stranger walked up to them. As he drew nearer, Cass saw that the man was dressed in a well-cut dark business suit and an equally dark hat pulled down over his eyes. His pale skin was flushed with red across his nose and cheekbones. He moved oddly, as though he were just a bit uncertain of his footing, a gait that Cass attributed to the nearby saloon.

When he came close, Cass stepped between the stranger and Tea Rose.

"Good afternoon, Miss Thornton," said the man.

"I don't know you," Cass said. "Excuse me, but the light is fading, and I have more photo—"

"We haven't been introduced," he interrupted, "but we have friends in common."

"I doubt that."

"Tea Rose, it's nice to see you looking so well," the man said, ignoring Cass.

"Who are you?" Cass demanded.

"Robert Salyor, attorney, at your service," he said, lifting his hat and bowing slightly.

"What do you want?"

"Nothing for myself. In fact, I've come to give you some information."

"We want nothing from you. Please leave us alone."

Salyor's eyes narrowed. "A woman who's no better than she has to be can't afford such grand airs, dearie."

Ignoring the flush that stained her cheeks at the man's

allusion to her relationship with King, Cass turned to Tea Rose. "Help me pack up. We're leaving."

"The information concerns your connection with Jared and Kingston Duran," Salyor said, watching Tea Rose.

"You pack the plates," Cass said to her half sister. "I'll take care of the camera."

Tea Rose looked from Cass to the lawyer, then spoke in a voice too low to carry beyond Cass. "Sister, information is worth more than gold. If what he says is true, we're the stronger for knowing it. If what he says is lies, then we know what our enemies wish us to believe. In America, ignorance may be bliss, but in China, knowledge is."

Cass hesitated, then nodded slightly, because she had come to respect Tea Rose's acumen in sizing up people and situations. "All right, but be prepared to grab up your skirts and run like the very devil if I give the word." Without waiting for an answer, Cass turned and faced Salyor once more. "Come no closer. We can hear you quite well from where you are."

With an irritated look, Salyor complied. "Are you familiar with the West Seattle traction company that went bankrupt a few months ago?"

"No," Cass said.

"Yes," said Tea Rose at the same instant.

Salyor smiled. "The long and the short of it is that all the investors lost their shirts. The stock issue isn't worth the paper it's printed on. Kingston Duran held a lot of stock. So did Jared Duran."

"Men quite frequently lose money on the stock exchange," Tea Rose said calmly. "That's the nature of gambling."

"King Duran lost more than he could afford to."

"That, too, is the nature of gambling."

The girl's calm voice made Salyor uneasy and angry at the same time.

"There was no gambling in that sense on this deal," he retorted. "A San Francisco holding company began buying

West Seattle's stock earlier this summer. On the surface, it looked like the usual run of business—traction companies are bought and sold every day. But underneath the surface, it was something unique. First, the holding company bought up majority control of West Seattle's stock, then the company turned around and effectively cut its own throat by disbanding before any of the stock could be resold. It was as though the West Seattle Electric Railway company had never existed."

Cass looked puzzled, but Tea Rose nodded, understanding everything except why Salyor was telling them about a defunct company in which both Durans had invested and lost money.

"No one could figure out who was behind this San Francisco holding company and why it had acted so irrationally. The company's principals were shielded by a series of corporations that existed only to hold each other's paper. There were no outside transactions at all."

Salyor paused and drew a deep breath as he organized the rest of his presentation in his own mind. He had the distinct feeling that Tan Feng would be dangerously irate if the message was garbled.

"Intensive investigation revealed that the owner and sole proprietor of the San Francisco holding company is none other than Jared Duran."

Tea Rose's eyelids narrowed fractionally as understanding came, but it was too late to stop the man from talking, too late to drag Cass beyond hearing, too late to prevent Tea Rose's security from being shaken down to its terrifyingly fragile foundations.

In this case, the Americans had been quite correct: ignorance had been bliss.

"That's ridiculous," Cass snapped. "Jared's an excellent businessman. He wouldn't buy out a company only to destroy it and his investment at the same time."

"If business were all he had in mind, no," Salyor said. "I believe the explanation is—how shall I say it?—more personal. I believe Jared Duran set out to ruin his brother. And I believe he succeeded very well."

For a long moment, the only sound in Cass's world was that of her heart beating within her chest. She stared at Salyor, her face as pale as the white cotton blouse she wore, wondering if he was lying, and at the same time sensing that the truth wouldn't be that simple.

Damn you, Jared, Cass seethed silently. *What gave you the right to ruin King for the sake of some petty revenge?*

There was no answer, nothing but rage churning inside her mind, making it difficult for her to think, even to breathe.

Tea Rose watched Cass with something close to pity in her eyes. She put her hand on her sister's arm in an unusual show of affection, before turning her black glance back to Salyor.

"Did Tan Feng give you any other information to convey to us?" Tea Rose asked.

Shocked, Cass looked at Tea Rose. "What makes you think it was Tan Feng?"

"Is there any more to the message?" Tea Rose asked, ignoring Cass for the moment.

"Your husband will take you back, but you must come with me right now. Tomorrow will be too late."

"No!" Cass said in a raw voice. "Never!" She spun around, took two quick steps, and bent over her equipment trunk. When she straightened, she was holding an old army pistol. With a quickness that spoke of familiarity, she cocked the hammer. "You work for a slaver and a whoremaster," Cass said to Salyor, her voice filled with loathing. "Don't ever come close to Tea Rose or myself again."

Salyor took one look at Cass's blazing golden eyes and decided that it was time to have another drink in the saloon halfway down the block.

The two women watched in silence until he disappeared behind the saloon's door. Carefully, Cass uncocked the pistol and replaced it in her equipment chest.

"How did you know he was from Tan Feng?" Cass asked, when she turned back toward Tea Rose.

"True or false, the information didn't come from friends," Tea Rose said. "Tan Feng is the only enemy we have who would benefit from a falling-out between the Duran brothers. Tan can't defeat Jared's power in the white community, but he can make sure that we are cut off from Jared's protection. Then only King will stand between us and Tan Feng. King is a warrior, not a general. He can fight magnificently, but he has no chance of outwitting a man such as Tan."

Tea Rose's matter-of-fact summary startled Cass. "I rather suspect you're a general yourself," she said. "Is that what you think about while I compose pictures?"

"Someone must think about the future after Jared has gone," Tea Rose said.

"Is Jared leaving?"

Tea Rose gave Cass a narrow look. "Will he have a choice, sister? He ruined his brother, your lover. Even if you are willing to forgive that, King won't. He is a man in golden chains, and the dragon of rage prowls his soul on razor claws. When he finds out what happened, he will attack."

"No," Cass said. "We can't let Tan's lies—"

"Lies?" interrupted Tea Rose. She smiled. "What makes you think Jared didn't ruin King?"

"Jared is ruthless, but he loves his brother more than he is angry with him over me. Jared loves King as deeply as I do."

"You're wrong, sister. Jared loves King more deeply than you. No, for once you must listen to me. Jared loved my mother as well, yet he helped you to steal me, knowing all the time that my mother would be defiled by Tan Feng as a result. Jared loved her, yet he left her to die alone in Chinatown."

Tea Rose watched her words sink into Cass like blows, making even her lips turn pale.

"Tan Feng will see that his message reaches King," Tea Rose said. "You can't prevent it. All you can do is plan how to limit the damage."

"I don't believe Jared did it. He's not that petty!"

Tea Rose said no more, because there was no point to it; Cass had resisted knowing the truth of both men from the start. If Tea Rose were to survive Tan Feng's latest gambit, she would have to act quickly.

Your husband will have you back—

Tea Rose's lips parted in a feral smile. She had no husband.

Yet.

53

Tea Rose drew curious looks as she hurried through the crowds along Yesler Way. It was rare to see a girl alone on the downtown streets, much less a beautiful half-Chinese girl dressed in Western clothes. After stopping people twice to ask for directions, Tea Rose found the lumberman's bar.

She had never been in a saloon, but after a quick look through the double swinging doors, she recognized it as part of the male world from which females were excluded except as harlots. The décor consisted of scuffed wood, paintings of coyly draped nudes, stuffed moose heads, and more varieties of bottled whiskey than Tea Rose had known existed before that moment. Her hope of finding King inside the bar strengthened. She knew that he would relish this atmosphere. King enjoyed women, but he was at home only with men. In civilization, he sought out the blunt strength and largely good-natured shouldering of other men.

The day shifts at the Elliott Bay mills and lumberyards were just over. The bar was crowded. Tea Rose pushed through the doors and stood for a moment, looking from face to face in the crowd. Gradually, the din of conversation faded as man after man stopped in midsentence to stare at the exotic flower that had appeared without warning among them. Though nothing of what Tea Rose felt showed on her face, she knew a distinct stirring of satisfaction as she measured her effect on the men. Beauty was her only weapon in the flowery battle all women were fated to fight.

A man's laughter rose above the bar's residual conversations. The sound shimmered like sunlight in the smoky air. Tea Rose turned immediately toward the laughter, knowing that it could only have come from Kingston Duran.

He was seated at a round table toward the back of the bar, playing cards with four other men. As though he sensed Tea Rose's approach, he looked up from his cards.

"Hello, little sister," King said as Tea Rose approached. "Is something wrong?"

"I need to talk with you."

"About what?"

"Gold."

King's green eyes narrowed as he focused his whole attention on Tea Rose. There was a muscular ease to his posture, yet currents of vitality coursed through him, a vivid life that was concentrated in the luminous green eyes measured her. At that instant, Tea Rose appreciated for the first time the masculine power that had transfixed Cass.

My poor sister. She might as well have tried to teach lightning to come to her call as to marry this man.

Without looking back to his cards or at the men around the table, King threw in his hand. "Deal me out, boys. A gentleman never keeps a lady waiting."

King had guided Tea Rose out of the bar and into the street. The November wind blew around them, sending cold air up beneath Tea Rose's skirt. A pair of padded pants would have been more sensible in Seattle's chilly climate, but Tea Rose didn't wear Celestial clothing anymore, not even in the privacy of her own bedroom.

"In here," King said, pushing Tea Rose gently into the lobby of a small, run-down hotel.

Without conversation, they climbed two flights of creaky, scarred wooden stairs. The smell of the place matched the floors and walls—dirty, ill-used, and unappealing. King took a key from his pocket, opened a door whose number had long since been torn away, and ushered Tea Rose inside the room where he had lived since he had left Bainbridge Island.

"Sit down," he said, removing a backpack and pile of maps from the seat of a small, straight-backed chair. A few sweeps of his hands restored order to the unmade bed. He sat on it, turned to Tea Rose, and said, "All right, let's have it."

Tea Rose didn't hesitate. She had thought through her plan very carefully and had decided just how far she could push King without alienating him.

"Do you still want to hunt gold in Canada?" she asked.

King froze. "Who told you about that?"

"The house we live in is small. Your voice isn't."

"If you heard, you know why I can't go," King said curtly.

"Money? Or my sister?"

His eyes narrowed. "Both."

"No," Tea Rose countered softly. "Only one. Money."

"That's not true."

"Isn't it?" she said, cutting across King's words. "If you wanted to marry my sister, you would have by now. At the very least, you would have asked her to be your wife."

King tried to keep silent, but it was impossible. He was a man in a trap. The fact that the trap was of his own making didn't make the steel jaws biting into his soul any less brutal.

"I've thought about it," he said savagely. "Goddamn it, I've thought about it until I'm going crazy!"

Tea Rose waited. She knew the battle going on within King; now, she wanted to hear him state it aloud, admit his unhappiness—and then she would offer him all that he wanted. Freedom.

With a bitter curse, King closed his eyes and put his head into his hands. "I love Cassie as much as I can love any woman," he said huskily. "That's why it's tearing me apart. Every time I think about leaving, I remember how she smiles when she sees me walking toward her, how she watches me when she thinks I won't notice, how she feels and smells and tastes when she gives herself to me." He made a low sound that was a curse and a plea and Cass's name all in one. "I never should have touched her, I wouldn't ever have touched her, but I thought—I thought she would be the one to stop up my ears so I'd never hear the bitch goddess calling my name again."

Silent, alert, motionless, Tea Rose watched and weighed the man who sat in front of her with bowed head. King had been drinking, but not enough to make him either maudlin or foolish. Saying nothing, she unbuttoned the top of her blouse, reached inside, and brought out the heavy gold locket. The long chain slipped easily over her head. Suspended from her outstretched hand, the locket turned on the end of its chain. With each turn the large diamond flashed and gleamed, and light ran over the gold as though it were breathing, moving, alive.

"King," Tea Rose said softly. "Look."

Slowly, his head came up. His eyes widened and then narrowed into intense green slits. When he held out his hand, the big locket came to him still warm from Tea Rose's body. He opened the catch, expecting from the size of the case to find a watch inside. Instead, he found a picture— Lilac and a white man he had never seen.

"My parents," Tea Rose said.

King said nothing, simply looked at the two people until Tea Rose's elegant fingers took the locket from him again. Closing it, she turned the locket face up on his palm. The diamond quivered with light.

"Beautiful," King said.

"Valuable," Tea Rose corrected. "Take it. You can sell it for enough to stake you to the Klondike."

Surprise flickered in King's eyes. "What?"

"I want to be rich," Tea Rose said, choosing her words carefully. "The bitch goddess loves you. She'll come gleaming to your hands while other men look in vain for the smallest flake of gold dust. I want half of what you find."

King's bittersweet smile was as gentle as his fingertips

smoothing over the locket's dense gold. "It's not that easy, Tea Rose. I could come up empty."

"Perhaps I'll bring you luck."

"The rivers can't be used until spring, and by then every man with two hands and a hole in his head will be crawling all over Circle City. I'll need more than luck to find gold then. I'll need a goddamned miracle."

"A flower is a miracle," Tea Rose said. "Its petals open despite wind or storm or cold, and from that blossoming comes the seeds of new life." She paused and then said simply, "A tea rose is a flower."

King looked at Tea Rose's exquisite, almost inhuman beauty as though for the first time. Black, faintly tilted eyes watched him in return, the unwavering stare of a supremely confident person.

"Is there no other way to the Klondike but the river?" she asked after a few moments.

"Overland. I don't know if it's ever been done."

"Perhaps a man such as yourself has never tried."

King smiled. "Maybe not." He looked at the locket for a minute, then two, three. Finally he spoke. "If I strike gold, I'll give you half, but—" He shrugged and stopped speaking.

"What?"

"It won't do you any good, China girl," King said bluntly. "You might have turned fifteen, but you're still too young to own anything on your own."

"But I'm not too young to marry. As your wife, I'll have the protection of your society's laws rather than being at their mercy."

King froze. Before he could gather his wits enough to speak, he felt slim, warm fingers sealing his lips.

"Listen," Tea Rose said, her voice low and musical, coaxing, knowing that the next few moments would determine the course of her life. She would rather he marry her instantly, but knew that he would refuse. Eight months from now, however, or a year, hundreds of tomorrows—and

331

King understood only today. "Listen to me, King. If you don't find gold, you owe me nothing. If you do find gold, I won't take your freedom from you. I don't want it. I want your name, the protection of being your wife. In return, I'll give you children if you want them, a home when you want it, a place of refuge without arguments or tears, a place that asks nothing of you, even your presence.

"When you tire of your bitch goddess and come to the city once more, I'll cook your favorite meals, hang upon your words, bathe you slowly, caress you if you desire, pleasure you until you think you're dying. When you tire of your wife, you may have other women, as many as you like, as often as you like, and if they don't please you, I'll find women who do.

"When the bitch goddess sings sweetly to you again, I'll mend your clothes, pack them, prepare food for your trip, and send you away without sad words and wailing. Marrying me won't be a jail; it will be a kind of freedom such as you've never known before."

King looked into the clear black eyes that were so close to his and felt as though he were being undressed slowly, nothing hidden, nothing held back, until he was naked; but still the baring kept on, layers of doubts and dreams and hopes peeling away until finally only his impure soul remained; and even then Tea Rose didn't flinch from him. She knew him better than he knew himself, and she accepted him without reservation, asking nothing of him but his name.

"Think about it," Tea Rose said softly, sliding her hands up King's hard thighs. "Other people are drawn to you, they come to you bearing their innocence in both hands, as though it were a fine gift. They don't know that their innocence is a burden that crushes you. Don't fear me, King," she said, caressing him intimately, feeling his reflexive hardening at her touch. "I have no innocence."

"Tea Rose—my God."

King's breath rushed out hotly as he grabbed her small

hands. With a gentle smile, Tea Rose slid from her chair, knelt between King's knees and kissed the hands restraining her. Her tongue slid between his fingers, caressing the inner skin just enough to make King realize how sensitive his hands could be. His grip loosened as he responded to the sensual assault.

"You don't have to answer me in words," Tea Rose said, biting him with exquisite care. "If you keep the locket, I'll know you've agreed."

Then Tea Rose slipped from King's grasp and left the room as silently as a shadow.

He stared at the closing door and felt as though he were waking from an opium dream. The weight of gold was unbearably heavy in his palm, unbearably perfect. For a long, long time, he stared at the locket, until its golden glow blurred and ran in scalding streams down his face.

Cassie—

King's hand clenched with crushing force, yet the gold remained unhurt, untouched, untouchable, perfection made tangible, its siren call whispering to his soul.

54

"She's called the *Haitian Republic*," the broker said. "A beauty, isn't she?"

The man watched with avuncular pride while the steamship forged past the office window that looked out on the choppy waters of Elliott Bay.

Jared's expression was less enthusiastic as he studied the ship. The white hull was streaked with rust, and the woodwork needed varnish badly, but she rode lightly in the water and steam poured from her twin stacks in roiling streams, which meant that the crew trusted the boilers.

"*Haitian Republic*," Jared said thoughtfully. "Isn't that supposed to be the voodoo ship?"

The agent's grizzled eyebrows shot up in surprise that Jared knew what was supposed to have been a tightly held secret. "Didn't think you were a superstitious man, Duran."

"I'm not."

The agent gestured with an open hand toward the steamer, which now was making a wide turn in preparation for returning to the wharf to present the port side of the ship for inspection.

"Personally, Duran, I think that voodoo is a bunch of hooey. Does that look like anything except a well-constructed work boat with a decade of service left in her?"

"The *Haitian Republic* has been on the market for four months because sailors are superstitious," Jared said, leaning back in his office chair, watching the broker with ice-pale eyes. "The ship's reputation is bad enough to reduce its market value by—oh, 50 percent."

The broker looked unhappy, but offered no counter arguments.

"I'll pay you fifty thousand in cash, tomorrow, provided that you get a priest to exorcise her, have her repainted stem to stern, and rechristen her."

With a sigh, the broker accepted the inevitable. "Sold," he said. "What name do you have in mind?"

"Haitian Republic is a name for an Atlantic steamer. Call her the *Portland*. One more steamer with that name won't hurt."

"You're a real sentimentalist, aren't you, Duran?" the broker said, shaking his head. "She'll be ready next Thursday. Drop by the office. We'll have a little ceremony, signing her over."

"Skip the ceremony," Jared replied brusquely, returning his attention to the papers piled on his desk. "I want her to put to sea as soon as possible. I've just picked up a contract to resupply some warehouses in St. Michael."

"St. Michael, Alaska? That's clear to hell and gone up on the Bering Sea."

"I'm aware of that," Jared said, looking up. Whatever else

he had been going to say was forgotten when he saw Cass standing in the doorway. Her face was pale, and there was a fine trembling of her hands as she clutched her purse. "Thank you, Mr. Carstairs," Jared said without looking away from Cass. "I'll expect to hear from you by next Thursday."

The broker took one look at Cass, tipped his hat, and said, "Excuse me, ma'am." He eased out of the office, pulling the door closed behind him.

"What's wrong, Cassandra?"

"You," she said, her voice raw. "You're what's wrong. You drove him away!"

An odd stillness came over Jared's body. "King?"

"Who else?"

"Are you pregnant?"

The question was so unexpected that Cass couldn't believe that she had heard correctly. "What?"

"Are you pregnant?" Jared repeated, his voice cool and his eyes unreadable.

"No."

Jared let out a slow breath and closed his eyes for a moment as relief loosened the deadly tension that had claimed his body. When he opened his eyes, Cass was watching him with cold anger.

"Does King know that?" Jared asked.

"Who the hell do you think you are, asking such—"

"Does King know that you're not pregnant?" Jared demanded, cutting across Cass's words.

"Yes, damn you."

"Good. I told King if he got you pregnant, he'd better start running and running hard because I'd be right on his tail," Jared explained. "You're not pregnant, so you can't blame me if King took off."

"Somehow, I never expected you to lie," Cass said in a thin voice. "Not to me."

"I'm not lying. I've told you the exact truth."

"But not all of it.

"What have I left out?"

Cass looked at Jared's winter-colored eyes and felt fury snaking through her veins. The world came and swirled around Jared and went on, leaving him untouched. He was the opposite of King, who reacted to the world with laughter or anger or desire, anything but the icy composure of Jared Duran.

"Always in control," she said furiously. "Always a cut above the turmoil of people who laugh and hurt and *love*. Everything you do is planned and calculated down to the last red cent."

"You don't know me at all," Jared said. "But then, you never wanted to know me, did you? Even before you saw King. You've never forgiven me for turning your neat little world upside down."

"Is that why you drove King away, just to get even with me for not wanting you?"

"I didn't drive—"

"The hell you didn't," Cass accused, too angry to hold onto her temper a moment longer. She reached into her purse, grabbed a bulky paper envelope and hurled it at Jared. He caught it reflexively. "You won! You won, and King and I lost and—" Her voice broke. "But you don't care about that, do you?" she asked raggedly. "All you care about is winning."

Cass spun around and jerked the office door open, but Jared was already on his feet and moving fast. His hand shot over her shoulder as he slammed the door shut again.

"Just a damn minute," he said roughly. "If I'm going to be tried, found guilty, and then flayed alive, I'm going to know what the hell my crime was."

Cass tugged once, futilely, on the door handle before she turned to confront Jared with eyes that blazed hotly against the pallor of her skin. For long seconds he measured her, then nodded and withdrew his hand. When she made no move to flee again, he opened the manila envelope she had hurled at him.

A heavy gold chain studded with nuggets slid out of the envelope into Jared's hand. He made a sound of disbelief as he recognized gold from Grey's Creek and Eagle Creek, Black Hills and Tofino, Bitterroot and Similkameen; and he heard the ghostly echo of his brother's voice saying *I'm kind of superstitious about letting it out of my hands. This chain is my luck.*

The metal felt too heavy, too cold, as though its special beauty had vanished with King.

A business card slipped out of the envelope. On the front was "Kingston Duran, Esq." On the back was a brief message: *Goodbye, Cassie. I'm sorry.*

Jared looked at the gold in his hands. Sadness clenched in his throat for the brother he understood too well and for the woman who hadn't understood King enough.

"He gave you all he could, more than he ever gave any other woman," Jared said finally. "Try not to hate him."

"Hate him?" Cass asked, in rising tones of disbelief. "Rest assured that I reserve that fine, black emotion for you, Jared Duran."

"Why?" Jared asked, fixing her with narrowed eyes. "Because I told you this would happen? I thought better of you than that, Cassandra."

"You bastard," Cass whispered furiously. "You never gave King a chance to find out if he could make a home with me. When King and I became lovers, you set out to ruin him. You systematically bought out or undercut every venture he had invested in. Suddenly, he had no money, nowhere to turn, nothing to do but to go back to the wilderness. You ruined him!"

For a long time, the office was silent, save for the ticking of the clock.

"'Ruin,'" Jared said finally. "You're raging at me because I 'ruined' King. That depends on how you define ruin, doesn't it? By any realistic definition, I didn't ruin King. I helped him."

"By making him a pauper?" Cass retorted.

"No. By doing the one thing you wouldn't do," Jared said grimly, pinning Cass in the merciless clarity of his gaze. "I did what I could to set King free. It's the only way he can be happy. I love him, Cass, and I know him better than you ever let yourself know him."

Pain welled up in Cass. She wavered as though she had been struck.

"Am I so lacking as a woman that I can't make King happy?" she asked, agony and anger tearing her voice apart. "Or did you do this to get even with me for choosing him over you? You won. King's gone. But that's all the success you'll have. If I were a man, I'd cut out your heart and feed it to the crows."

"Is the truth so hard for you to take?" Jared asked savagely. "King was going to leave you sooner or later. The only question was when, not if. Would you rather he left a year from now, or two, or three? Talk about ruining a man! What do you think it would have done to him to desert his wife and children—or his lover and her bastards? It would have destroyed him, *but he would have done it just the same*. He can't survive in captivity. It's that simple. Face it, Cass. He was the wrong man for you. He knew it, even if you didn't."

"Wrong for me?" she repeated bitterly. "Compared to whom? Yourself? You're a machine, not a man. You have a cash register for a heart, and an account book to record your fondest memories. What woman wouldn't choose a man like King, no matter what his faults, over an ice monster like you?"

Jared's eyes darkened, and his lips flattened with the pain that he could no longer conceal. "Cass," he whispered, reaching toward her, "I'm not what you think I am. Please—"

She struck his hand away. "Don't touch me. Ever!"

Silence stretched between them like black lightning, silence broken only by the sound of Cass's quick, ragged breaths. Deliberately, Jared turned his back on her. The sound of the door handle moving seemed as loud as a shout.

"Before you leave," Jared said distinctly, "answer this: Was it Tan Feng who told you about King's finances?"

Cass made a startled sound. "You're as devious as Tea Rose."

"Meaning?"

"She guessed right away that Tan Feng was behind that wretched lawyer."

"Robert Salyor?"

"Yes."

Calmly, Jared marked Salyor out for a future of bad luck. "Despite your hatred, I will continue to be a frequent visitor at your house."

"The hell—"

"That's enough, Cassandra," Jared said, his voice like a whip.

Cass flinched, despite her anger.

"I promised Lilac that I would protect Tea Rose," Jared continued. "I keep my promises. It's just as well King has gone. He would have taken out all his frustration on me, and one of us would have been hurt or killed, and it would have been a hell of a mess." He stopped, struck by a thought. "Tea Rose. She knew."

"Yes. She was with me when Salyor told us."

"I see. Undoubtedly Tea Rose assumed you would tell King about the traction company stock. And you would have, wouldn't you?"

Unconsciously, Cass backed up a step, only to come up against the door. The Jared who was watching her was a different man from the one she had known before.

"Would you have told King?" Jared repeated, his voice as hard and colorless as his eyes.

"I wouldn't have meant to, but how could I have kept the truth from him forever? I can't lie to someone I love."

Jared watched Cass in silence, then he opened her purse and dropped in the card and gold chain.

"Take it," he said. "The chain is yours, even though you no more appreciate its meaning than King appreciated your innocence."

By the end of November, King had worked passage north for himself on a steamer that hauled cut lumber and general cargo for small coastal settlements along the Inside Passage. As a result of his work, King was physically fit again, the last residue of his injury reduced to a bare murmur of complaint beneath the thickly layered muscles of his thigh. When the steamer anchored offshore at Skagway in early December, King handed his pack over the side and dropped with feline ease onto the flat-bottomed lighter. He grabbed a pole and helped the crew guide the craft ashore on the tidal flats in front of the remote village.

Alaska's southern coast was almost as moderate in climate as Seattle. In the winter, gray clouds rolled in off the north Pacific and wrapped the lowland in a dripping embrace for hour after hour, day after day. While rain was the rule at the lower elevations, snow was the rule in the mountains. Weather's rules, however, were often broken. Thus far, the winter had been mild. At the moment, it wasn't even raining, although there were quantities of white to slate gray clouds roiling about. Thin, highly slanted sunlight poked through the clouds to illuminate Skagway's unimpressive collection of shacks and the occasional more ambitious building. Beyond Skagway rose mountains that were swathed in green forest and gray rock and very little snow or ice.

King slung his pack over one shoulder and headed for the general store. A few minutes with the storekeeper confirmed King's hopes; Chilkoot Pass wasn't yet locked into winter.

"'Course, that's just my eyeball opinion," the storekeeper added, laying out the last of the supplies King had requested. "You want it from the horse's mouth, you look for Harlan Wintermoon. He come in last night from t'other side."

"Where's he staying?"

"Wherever he fell," the storekeeper said, shrugging. "Damn fool 'breed can't hold his liquor. That's why he come out. Ran out of booze." The storekeeper looked over the modest pile of supplies. "Traveling kinda light, ain't you?"

"I always do."

"Ain't no place to get grub between here and Circle, 'cept Dawson, and those old boys in Dawson ain't gonna want to sell much, what with it being winter and all."

"Dawson? Where's that?" King asked, reaching into his pocket for the worn map of the interior he had bought in Seattle.

"Ain't on no map," the storekeeper said, "but she's there just the same. Hear tell they hit poor man's gold up there in three different rivers."

King felt the familiar rush of adrenaline hitting his blood. Rich man's gold was still in its hard quartz matrix; mining that kind of gold cost money, lots of it. Tons of rock had to be blasted and pickaxed and processed before ounces of gold could be collected. Poor man's gold was river gold, loose gold, placer gold that erosion had already mined from a hard rock matrix and washed downstream until bits and flakes collected in pockets that a man could clean out with no more equipment than a pan, a shovel, and his two hands.

"Harlan Wintermoon, huh?" King said, refolding his map. "I'll look him up."

"Even if he's sober, won't do you no good. You ain't bought enough supplies to get you to Dawson, and a man can't live off that land in winter. Ain't nothing to live off of 'cept ice and evergreen bark. An' that's assumin' you ain't froze to death already in a blue norther. Mister, that's one hell of a lot of assumin'. She's rough country out there. Real rough."

"No argument there," King agreed, assembling his supplies.

With swift skill, he put the sugar, bacon, flour, salt, and coffee into his pack along with a batch of deer jerky he had bought in the last settlement. He was going to be traveling light and fast, and praying that the mild weather held.

But King knew that even the mildest winter in the interior was frigid. A man burned fierce amounts of energy just staying alive, much less traveling at the pace King was going to have to maintain. But he had learned a cold-country survival trick from one of his partners, a man who had once lived with the Eskimos; for keeping alive in icy weather, no food beat pure fat.

"Anyone around here keep a milk cow?"

"Try Ma Swenson up to the north end of town."

"Thanks," King said, hefting his pack and heading out the door.

"Mister," the storekeeper called after him, "you're a damn fool if you try for Dawson before spring!"

King waved in acknowledgment, but kept on going. He soon discovered that Mrs. Swenson did indeed have two milk cows. Only one was producing at the time, but King sweet-talked Mrs. Swenson out of twelve pounds of butter.

"Look at this weather," she said with disgust, gesturing at the dripping trees and patches of blue sky as she wrapped the butter in waxed paper. "Andy promised me real winters in Alaska, but the snow never lasts on the ground. Our ice skates are getting rusty."

"Ice skates?" King said. Suddenly, he threw back his head and laughed in delight. "Ice skates, by God!"

Ten minutes later, King was the owner of a pair of solid Swedish steel skates. He strapped them onto his pack along with a pair of snowshoes.

"You know a man called Harlan Wintermoon?" King asked, hefting the weight of his pack, testing its balance.

"Everybody knows him. He does odd jobs until he can buy whiskey, then he drinks until it's gone. Good hunter, though; I'll say that for him. He eats fresh meat when the rest of us are pining for it."

"Have you seen him lately?"

"Try the Indian settlement at the head of the inlet. He usually sleeps it off there, if he gets that far."

"Thank you, ma'am."

"My pleasure. We don't see many strangers around here. It's nice to hear a new voice."

King smiled. "If there's gold in the Klondike, you'll be hearing a lot more of them."

Mrs. Swenson shook her head. "The river route out of St. Michael is much easier. Only a fool or an Indian goes cross-country."

"Or a gold-hungry man."

Mrs. Swenson was still shaking her head when King strode out of sight wearing the heavy pack, his pace that of a strong man accustomed to walking long distances.

Skagway was ragged and small, but Dyea was little more than scattered huts. King found Harlan Wintermoon in a lean-to that should have collapsed several winters before. There was no furniture, no windows, nothing but a smokehole in the ceiling and a bedroll thrown onto the dirt near campfire ashes. Harlan lay on the blankets, groaning about a hangover as big as a mountain. When King offered the hair of the dog from a silver hip flask, Harlan took it without hesitation. A few minutes later, he was sniffing appreciatively at the bacon and biscuits King was making over a new campfire.

"What'd you say your name was?"

"King Duran."

"Well, thanks, King Duran. I was feeling real poorly."

King smiled, handed over a plate of food and watched Harlan fall upon it like a starving wolverine. King didn't know when the barrel-chested, thickly muscled man had last eaten, but obviously it had been too long.

Gently but relentlessly, King began asking questions. Harlan answered between—and often during—great mouthfuls of food. Within minutes, King knew that he was on the right trail. The network of prospectors, miners, guides, and traders who were the vanguard of civilization had all been pushing into Alaska's interior and northwest Canada for years, hunting the gold that everyone knew must be there, somewhere. But it was a huge, wild country, as unforgiving as it was beautiful. It had taken men a long time to find the kind of gold that was worth going back to civilization and bragging about.

"Lotta white men in Circle," Harlan said, belching and mopping up bacon grease with a hunk of biscuit. "That's upstream of Fort Yukon."

"Not far enough. Any place with an opera hall is too damn civilized for me."

Harlan chuckled.

"What about the new place called Dawson?" King asked.

"Dawson's no place yet. Crazy men there. Winter coming, and they dig in the river instead of hunting meat."

"Gold?"

"Hell yes, there's gold. There's always been gold there."

"You found any?"

Harlan gave King a look from bleak black eyes. "You ever know an Indian that found gold and lived to get rich from it?" Then Harlan shrugged. "Makes no nevermind. If I had gold, I'd drink all the time and never hunt. I like hunting almost as much as I like drinking." He leaned back onto his elbow and scratched his thick neck lazily. "Tell you, though, there's gonna be some happy white men there come summer. Place called Rabbit Creek has a new name—Bonanza Creek."

"Rabbit Creek?" King asked, pulling out his map.

Harlan sat up and pointed to the creek with a greasy finger. Like many frontiersmen, he couldn't read many words, but he read maps very well.

"Lot of stakes going in along this creek," Harlan said. "Last August, a white man name of George Carmack found a nugget you could choke on. I heard of men getting thirty-dollar pans just by wading out to a gravel bar."

King whistled softly. "I've worked claims where I'd have settled for thirty cents a pan."

"I heard of hundred-dollar pans and cleanups worth twelve times that," Harlan said matter-of-factly, "but you can't eat gold. Come spring, they'll trade it all for a haunch of venison. Got any more of that whiskey?"

King uncapped the silver flask again.

"What's the ground like?" King asked, watching Harlan drink.

"Bastard's froze solid in winter." Harlan belched and sighed contentedly. "Not much better in summer. That don't bother Joe Ladue, though. He staked out his town, called it Dawson, and started in building a sawmill. Damn fool. How the hell you going to pan for gold when the water's all froze up? And they call Indians crazy—"

"The men will dig in the winter, stockpile the pay dirt, and wash gravel in the summer," King said.

"Yeah, but when do they hunt?"

"They'll buy meat from hunters like you—and they'll damn near pay its weight in gold."

"Crazy," Harlan said, shaking his head. "Work their butts to bone all winter digging out a pound of gold and then paying it in spring for meat a man could've shot for his own self in an hour. Don't make no sense." He belched softly.

King shrugged. "I'll bet men are pouring in from all over right now," he said, looking beyond Harlan, looking through the gaps in the lean-to walls to the place where the mountains rose, a granite barrier separating him from the golden interior.

"White men are crazy, but they ain't *that* crazy. From what I hear, everyone's staying put in Circle 'til spring. When the breakup comes, they'll go upriver and drive in stakes."

"Must be a lot of claims already."

Harlan shrugged. "Man told me there were thirty claims registered at Fortymile. That's not a drop in the bucket."

"In other words, a man could still stake a pretty claim if he could just get to the creek."

There was silence, then Harlan belched softly. "Good biscuits," he said. "Bacon was fresh, too, and the whiskey wasn't rotgut. You did me a favor, showing up when you did, so I'll do you one back. Don't be fooled by rain here. On the far side of Chilkoot Pass, it's fifty below. Only way to survive is to hole up like a wolverine or a bear."

"Hole up or keep moving, one or the other," King said.

"A man'd be a fool to do it that way. Take a boat to St. Michael and hole up. Come spring, you can do a thousand miles of river sitting on your butt."

"I'm not going to St. Michael. I'm going to do what you did—take the Chilkoot Pass."

"I was booze hungry and dead lucky. If a storm'd caught me, I'd be froze board stiff right now. I ain't going back until spring, no matter how good the pass looks."

"What's it like between the pass and the lakes?"

"Pretty," Harlan said simply. "Kill you quicker than it will kiss you, though. I took to the river from Dawson all the way up past Lake Bennett. Good way to travel, long as you don't go through a thin spot and freeze 'fore you drown. Them river currents eat away at ice, no matter how cold it is."

"Much snow?"

Harlan shook his head. "Too cold to snow. Have to warm up forty, fifty degrees at least 'fore it snows." He fixed King with an opaque black stare. "Winter-over with me here. Come the melt, I'll take you to Dawson. You cook, I hunt, we'll both be fat."

King considered the offer, then shook his head regretfully. "Come spring, it'll be too late to stake a claim. The good ones will be long gone. You don't know what it's like on the outside. Times are hard in the cities and have been since the crash in ninety-three. When word of Klondike gold hits Seattle, all hell's going to break loose. Every man who ever carried a pick and a pan will be on the trail north." King held out his hand and shook Harlan's ham-sized hand firmly. "But thanks anyway. If I need a partner, I'll pass the word back to here."

"Here's where I'll be," Harlan said. He stretched, then settled back onto the rough wool blankets and closed his eyes. "There be snow in the pass, and it's man-deep in the creases. Don't let that smooth river ice fool you. One mistake, and you're dead as a brass monkey's balls."

56

Tan Feng watched while Precious Pearl served him tea. The girl had Lilac's elegant neck, but lacked her elemental grace of movement. When Pearl looked up at him, it was with fear rather than with banked fires of rebellion in her eyes. Her eagerness to please him not only was boring—but made her clumsy on the couch. It had been different with Lilac Rain, who had known how to bring him to the brink of climax and then hold him there long past the point where pleasure became pain and pain became ecstasy.

Even as Tan told himself that he couldn't expect Lilac's level of skill from a girl barely fifteen, he remembered Tea Rose and the Night of the Good Lady, when both mother and daughter had been with him on the couch. For those hours, he had been more potent than even the fabled Yellow Emperor. Just the touch of Tea Rose's fingertips, the pointed tip of her tongue, the small palm between his legs—

Tan Feng shifted in his chair. Instantly, Pearl looked up, spilling tea in her haste. Her eyes were wide, frightened, and her clothes retained the smell of the opium rooms. Tan looked right through her, dismissing her as less important than the buzzing of outhouse flies. He had hoped that Pearl's youth and prettiness would ease his gnawing need for the dead Fox Woman and her missing daughter. Unfortunately, Pearl's easy fright was tedious. She could bring him to clouds and rain twice in rapid succession, but so could any female. After laborious effort, Pearl might call forth his vital essence a third time, but never a fourth. It had been much different with Tea Rose and Lilac Rain.

From the hall beyond Tan Feng's office came the sound of footsteps. Tan knew from years of analyzing sounds behind his back that it was Kwan who waited beyond the closed door.

"Enter," Tan Feng growled.

Pearl jumped, spilling even more tea.

"You are as clumsy as a duck with a twisted foot," Tan snarled, his face drawn with disgust. "Take yourself out of my sight. If you spill my tea again, I will sell you as a saltwater whore. *Get out.*"

Whimpering with fear, Pearl kowtowed rapidly, grabbed the tea tray and vanished. Kwan watched her go with a hungry expression on his face. Tan knew that his lieutenant wanted Pearl. If she persisted in her clumsiness, Kwan could have her—but he would have to go down to the docks and stand in line to claim his soiled prize.

"Well?" Tan grunted.

"King Duran got off the lumber boat at Skagway."

"Where is he now?"

"That is not known. The detective refused to follow King past an Indian settlement called Dyea. The man believes King went inland, following rumors of a big gold strike somewhere in the Vast Unexplored."

"Gold," Tan said, relaxing into his chair once more. His eyelids lowered as he examined Kwan. "Where? How much?"

"There is a camp called Dawson, on the Klondike River, which feeds into the Yukon River, which empties into the Bering Sea," Kwan said, repeating the English names as though they had been carefully memorized, which they had. Kwan had been a very careful man since he had lost Tan Feng's prized female. Each time Kwan might have been inclined to carelessness, the tender scars on his buttocks and calves reminded him of the most thorough punishment he had ever received. "There is much gold, if the rumors can be believed. Word of it is whispered in Vancouver, where your sing-song girls have been paid in gold unlike any we have seen before."

"Show me."

Kwan stepped up to the desk, pulled a soft leather poke from his tunic and poured gold into Tan Feng's broad palm. Tan stirred the flakes and dust with a fingertip, but it was the nugget that caught his attention. Its color was subtly unlike any nuggets Tan had collected, and its shape indicated that the gold had spent a long time being tumbled and smoothed by water.

If there was more gold such as this, there would be many, many men chasing it. Young men. Foolish men. Hungry men. Men who would pay extraordinary amounts of gold for the ease to be found within that one square inch of female anatomy.

"Collect these rumors. Bring them to me."

Kwan bowed. "Yes, lord."

"What of the other Duran?"

"He is frequently with the two females. Whatever unhappiness his brother's disappearance caused was not enough to separate Jared Duran from the Thornton female."

Tan grunted. He had gotten rid of one Duran, but the more dangerous one still remained. Tan had hoped that it would be otherwise, that Jared would have been driven away. So long as he remained Tea Rose's protector, the white community would not tolerate Tan's stealing her back. Nor would the tong tolerate further disruption of their business if Tan incurred the white community's wrath. Much as it galled Tan, he knew he was stalemated.

Even worse, his pursuit and loss of Tea Rose had cost him much money and much face. Rumors of his difficulties had reached his elder brother in China. With every tong ship that arrived, Tan expected to be ordered back to China or to be demoted to running a lesser tong operation in Vancouver.

Then there was Kwan, whose lust for Pearl was rapidly surpassing his loyalty to Tan. That had to be dealt with, but not just yet. First, Tan must find out who within the tong had allied himself with Kwan.

"Continue having Tea Rose watched," Tan said. "Sooner or later, there will be a chance to reclaim her."

"Yes, lord," Kwan said, bowing deeply.

Long after Kwan left the room, Tan Feng sat alone and poured the particles of gold from hand to hand, thinking of riches and hungry men and the first hot touch of Tea Rose's tongue. If there was gold in Canada, he would go there, recoup his fortune and his face, and return triumphantly to China.

But first he would steal Tea Rose.

57

The initial five miles of the Chilkoot trail had been level. Then the rough wagon road had disappeared, and the path climbed up to a narrow, rock-strewn canyon that was choked with spruce and hemlock. For two miles, King scrambled along the edge of a furious milk-white stream, the heavy pack balanced carefully on his back. He saw no one, heard no one, smelled no woodsmoke. The temperature went from chilly to cold. By the time he reached the high flats at a place called Sheep Camp, he was in the bottom of the clouds. He could not go on, for the short hours of day had passed, leaving only cloud-mist that moonlight could not penetrate. He camped in a stunted grove, the last such trees he would see until he went up through the pass and descended once more to timberline.

The next morning, the clouds cleared long enough to give King a daunting view of the steep, barren incline that pitched up to the tiny notch called Chilkoot Pass. The trail went up a fifteen-degree slope from Sheep Camp before twisting and doubling and scrambling across a jumbled talus slope. From there, the going became much harder. The last mile was a slope so steep it was like climbing stairs. Under normal winter conditions, the climb would have been all but impossible. King's luck and the weather held. He was over and through the pass in six hours, despite the hundred-pound pack on his back.

Beyond the shadow of the coastal mountains, winter had the land deeply within its grasp. The temperature fell with every mile farther inland, but unlike the coastal air, the inland air was so dry it made skin split and bleed. King ignored the discomfort as he worked his way downward through the man-deep snow Harlan Wintermoon had described.

Within a day, King had reached the shores of Lake Bennett, which was a gleaming expanse of windswept black ice. He traded New World snowshoes for Old World ice skates and set off onto the lake, falling repeatedly until he mastered the skates; and then he raced over the ice like a man born to steel runners, not slowing until he came to the frozen river that was the lake's outlet and one of the headwaters of the Yukon River. He watched his route carefully on the river, where flowing water could tunnel under the clear black ice, leaving it dangerously thin.

Using every bit of the short northern days and all but a few hours of the clear, moonlit nights, King pushed on into the interior through air so cold and dry it seemed to squeak at his touch. He skated when he could, hiked or snowshoed when it was necessary, and ate on the move, stopping only when forced to by fatigue or occasional bouts of bad weather. If he was on the move, he ate jerky and butter. When he built a fire, he cooked biscuits and bacon and drank coffee that tasted as though made by angels in heaven. He fell asleep instantly, waking at the first hint of color in the sky. Minutes later, he would be up and moving along the river system that was gradually fattening into the Yukon itself.

Christmas flew past with no more notice than another lemonade-colored dawn, and an empty sky, and the frigid world beneath King's feet. In places, the river ice was so clear that he could see more than a fathom's thickness of captive swirls and bubbles frozen in place, and below that the liquid river itself, a great black glass snake, twisting and testing the strength of its transparent prison. In the days that followed, he skated and ate and snowshoed, and ate and walked and skated and slept, and even in his dreams, he was moving, moving, moving across the black-and-white night, the blue-and-white day, the hours of lemon dawn and brass twilight—nothing alive but himself in all the land.

The new year came to King in the middle of a long, transparent stretch of river ice that would have been nearly invisible beneath his feet but for the reflection of moonlight from the icy, wind-polished surface. By his best reckoning, he was no more than a few days of fast travel from Dawson. He had been on the go for almost eighteen hours when he coasted to a stop in a fine spray of ice chips gouged out by his steel runners. Breathing easily, warm despite the intense cold surrounding him, he searched beneath layers of wool clothing until he found his watch. Moonlight flowed over his shoulders, bathing him in pale light, making the watch's face gleam.

It was a few minutes before midnight. King toasted the coming year with water from a canteen kept warm by his body heat, stretched and adjusted the thick straps on his pack. Suddenly, a golden glow suffused the northern horizon, as though dawn had chosen to come at a new time and from a new direction in order to celebrate the new year. Golden currents flowed across the sky, first just a few, and then more and more until they merged, becoming spectral rivers whispering to one another as showers of gold dust bridged unimaginable midnight distances, golden light seething gently, bathing the black face of night.

Transfixed in the midst of gold, King let the aurora bathe him as well, washing away the past, beginning everything anew—the year, the night, the land, himself, all new, all untouched, nothing behind but black ice, nothing ahead but the golden nimbus of the ineffable. Elation built in him, sweeping through his body in wild currents of joy. He threw back his head and laughed, as though man had never been cast out of Eden into a world of disappointment and despair, where man and his soul were always divided, always seeking and never finding each other.

Laughter poured out of King into the limitless night, sounds as rich and pristine and wild as the aurora itself.

When King's watch began to chime the midnight hour, he bent forward like a racer and counted off the last seconds. As the final chime struck, steel runners dug into the ice, driven by the powerful muscles of King's legs. Instants later, he was racing down the river toward the aurora singing to him, skating hard and fast, steel flashing, his laughter an invisible banner trailing behind. He was a great black bird flying beneath the seething golden sky, skimming over the back of a prehistoric, ice-sheathed snake. He was the first and only and last thing alive in a world that stretched to infinity in all directions, but loneliness was impossible because extraordinary currents of life poured through him, life hot and sweet and limitless. He was the black river and the transparent ice, the wild horizon and the empty land, the pristine night and the seething golden aurora.

And he was free.

58

The last punishing sounds of firecrackers sputtered into the silence, leaving behind echoes and coils of smoke and the afterimage of fire blazing behind Cass's eyelids. She didn't mind the bitter smoke, for it explained the tears searing her eyes at the hour of the new year.

"Happy New Year!" Tea Rose called, clapping her hands and jumping back, as yet another string of firecrackers danced into life at the touch of a match. "Of course, if we were in Chinatown, we wouldn't be celebrating yet, but—" She shrugged. "We're here, and there are no colorful dragons to snake through the streets, frightening and delighting little children. At least, the firecrackers will frighten away evil spirits."

"Happy New Year," Jared said to Tea Rose, smiling at her excitement. "The Chinese have firecrackers and dragons. In America, it's the custom to exchange a hug and a kiss in honor of the new year."

Tea Rose went into Jared's arms, hugged him, and stood

on tiptoe to receive his kiss. As always, she searched his eyes and his body for any sign of lust when he touched her; as always, she found only amused affection and no sexual desire.

"In China, a man pays off all debts and ends all grudges so that the dragon of anger can't wound the coming year," Tea Rose said, searching the icy transparency of Jared's gray eyes before she turned and said to Cass, "It's a custom I would like to keep in my new life, like ancestor tablets and stir-fried vegetables and firecrackers. Is that all right, sister?"

"Of course," Cass said absently, hearing only the request, not really understanding what Tea Rose was asking.

But then, there was much that Cass hadn't understood lately, most of all the loneliness, the ashes of loss that remained after the fierce fire of her rage had burned out. She had gone through celebrating Thanksgiving and Christmas in an emotional daze, teaching new customs to Tea Rose, learning new customs in return, smiling little, laughing less. During all of it, Jared had come and gone, stitching through their lives like a steel needle, binding up the fabric that had been rent by King's departure.

Cass couldn't have coped without Jared. She knew it, resented it, and she was helpless to do anything to ease her resentment. She looked out the window and saw the shadow of Tan Feng's hireling, and she knew that only Jared kept the tong lord at bay. She looked into the past that sometimes haunted Tea Rose's black eyes and knew that only Jared's strength kept her half sister from becoming a cruel tyrant.

Worst of all, Cass looked at the line of Jared's profile, saw the long-legged power of his walk, caught the feline grace of his body when he turned at a sudden sound—and saw King all over again, a knife slicing into her, wounding her until she had to bite her lip against crying out.

Did I mean so little to you, King? Do you ever think of me, miss me, want to hold me? Did you love me at all, or was I just a sweet, soft, foolish thing to amuse you until you were well again?

Even as the thoughts echoed in her mind, Cass heard Jared's words again.

He loved you as much as he loved anything tangible.

The words had been meant to comfort, but they were a scourge against her naked soul. If she accepted Jared's words, she would have to let go of King forever, even in the silences of her own mind; for she would know, finally, that King could not love her as she needed to be loved. She could be touched. She lived and breathed and wept. She was tangible, real, earthly.

Imperfect.

And King's soul yearned after something that was none of those things—something untouchable, perfect. But if Jared was wrong in his understanding of King, there was still hope, still a chance that King could love something enough to live with it.

But if Jared was right—

"Sister? Have you heard anything I've said?"

Cass blinked, releasing two transparent tears. "I've been thinking."

"About forgiveness?" Tea Rose asked, watching her sister closely.

Cass blinked again, but no more tears fell. "After a fashion," she said in a husky voice.

"Have you forgiven Jared?" Tea Rose asked, ignoring the stillness of the man next to her.

"Have you forgiven Tan Feng for marrying you off to one of his men?" Cass asked.

"Touché," Jared murmured, looking at Tea Rose. "Your sister has rediscovered her claws. I think the match between you will be a bit more even, now."

"You're being unfair to Jared," Tea Rose said, ignoring him, concentrating on Cass. "Jared didn't make King what he is. If you have to rage at something, rage at God."

"God didn't buy King's stock and then ruin it."

"What difference does that make?" Tea Rose asked in a voice of cool reason. "If the stock had been gold, King would have spent it by now. Do you really believe that an extra two months or four or six would have made King love you enough to live like a captive bird in your hand?"

"I didn't want him to live in chains. Why does everyone think I wanted King's freedom? I didn't! I just wanted—" Cass's voice broke.

"What did you want?" Jared asked in a gentle, coaxing tone.

"I wanted to share his freedom," she said raggedly. "I wanted to feel the hot currents of life I sensed in him. "I wanted them to flow through me, too."

Jared's eyes closed for an instant, concealing the pain he was helpless to hold entirely at bay. When he was able to speak, his voice was too husky, almost hoarse. "Did they?" he asked.

"What?"

"Did you feel those hot currents of life?"

"No," she whispered, "there wasn't enough time for that kind of sharing. We didn't have enough time!"

"For you, sister," Tea Rose said. "For King, there was more than enough time. That's why he left."

"Tea Rose," Jared said, his voice harsh.

The girl's expression shifted, becoming pleasant, neutral, removed. "I am sorry, Lord Jared," she said in high-pitched Cantonese as she bowed over her folded hands. "I have forgotten how offensive simple truths are to my sister."

"King's truth is not simple," Jared said curtly in the same language.

"Your elder brother is gone. He does not write to soothe the pain of his absence. He sends nothing to my sister, not even the fact that he is alive and well. These are simple things, my lord."

"Here is another simple thing, sharp-tongued female. The more you criticize King to Cass, the more she blames me for his loss. Is that the end you desire?"

Eyes of black ice searched Jared's face for the space of several breaths. "I had hoped for the opposite response, that she would see the truth, that she would look away from the man she cannot have and see you, the man who would demand her soul but would give his own in return."

Jared's breath came in sharply, but he didn't deny the truth of Tea Rose's insight into what he had once wanted from Cass, and no longer believed he would ever have.

"What you wish will not happen," he said. "I have taken her old life from her by giving you to her care. I have taken her first love from her by understanding him better than she did. I do not believe she will forgive me for those things, just to make your own life more secure. She will not forgive me tonight. She will not forgive me in a lifetime of new year's nights."

"Then she is a fool."

"She is capable of sharing her soul in love. To you, that is a foolish thing; but don't mistake your sister for a fool, for then you will misjudge her. That could be very dangerous for you, as dangerous as your misjudgment of Tan Feng was."

Tea Rose made a soft sound of comprehension and bowed deeply. "You have instructed me, mentor. Please accept my humble gratitude, and forgive my foolish attempts to teach the sun how to bring light and warmth to the day."

This time, there wasn't the least whiff of sarcasm in Tea Rose's manner. It was the same when she turned toward Cass, who had listened to the rapid, incomprehensible exchange of Cantonese with a feeling close to despair.

"I'm sorry, sister. My foolish words caused pain. That wasn't my desire," Tea Rose said softly. "I'm not worthy of your care."

Cass looked into the clear midnight radiance of her sister's eyes and felt tears burning once more. Wordlessly, Cass held out her arms. Tea Rose came to her sister without hesitation, clinging to Cass, the only person on the face of the earth who shared her blood. Cass closed her eyes and hugged Tea Rose in return, needing the warmth of another human being in the darkest minutes of the new year.

Jared watched the embrace with a hunger he would never

acknowledge. He knew Cass wouldn't ever be a tenth so generous with him. He had taken too much from her and hadn't been permitted to give her anything in return.

Soundlessly, Jared walked from the room and let himself out into the new year's night.

59

The light was thin and watery as King slid down a snow-covered bank onto the rumpled ice of a small creek. He had come more than twenty miles already, but that wasn't why he had turned up a feeder creek to seek shelter. The temperature had risen steadily throughout the day. Now it was in the twenties. The wind felt raw, damp, and it reeked of the snow held within the black belly of the oncoming storm. He hunched against the wind and turned upstream, hoping to find a natural shelter in an overhang on the lee side of the creek bank.

The odor of snow became mixed with an unpleasant musky smell. King stopped and sniffed the wind as carefully as a wild animal, but the smell swirled away on the wind. He waited, emptied his lungs through his nostrils, and tried again. The only odor was that of the snow that had just started to dance on the wind; nowhere was there any trace of the wolverine's distinctive odor.

King took another breath, every instinct alert. There was no animal more savage or dangerous than a wolverine. Even a hungry grizzly would walk away from a fresh kill rather than contest the meal with a sixty-pound wolverine. A pack of wolves retreated rather than risk injury fighting a wolverine. In the cold, even the smallest wound could prove fatal to predators that survived through speed and endurance.

King was no different. Alone in the frigid wilderness, his health was his life.

After a final deep inhalation, King went on up the creek. A few moments later, he spotted a game trail beside the stream. Nothing had passed that way recently but the wind. Any tracks that might have been left had been filled in by loose snow. He knelt and brushed snow away with careful hands, seeking tracks that might have hardened beneath the dusting of new snow.

Suddenly, the musky scent returned. It was stronger, much too strong. With adrenaline hammering in his veins, King surged to his feet and spun around in time to see a dark, low blur the size and shape of a small bear erupt over the far bank. The animal moved raggedly yet very quickly, bushy tail erect.

Wolverine.

Even as the animal's identity registered in King's brain, he tried to shuck his pack and get his pistol out. The pack's strap caught inside his right elbow, and the weight dragged his gloved hand away from the pistol. Silently, wildly, he tried to twist free.

The wolverine slammed into King's legs, toppling him. Jaws wide, snapping, snarling, the wolverine lunged for King's throat. Reflexively, he jerked his arm up as he wrenched aside, shielding his jugular. Powerful jaws clamped on the upper half of his left arm. All that saved him from having the arm torn off was the fact that the thick leather pack straps had somehow become tangled. The straps acted as a tough, flexible armor over part of his flesh.

King's fist came down high on the animal's muzzle, pounding on the unprotected eyes. The wolverine hung on to King's arm, bunched its shoulders and haunches, and jerked repeatedly, as though King were a carcass from which the animal was trying to tear a meal. Snarling as savagely as the wolverine itself, King switched tactics and tried to gouge out the animal's eyes. The thickness of his gloves defeated him, protecting the wolverine from counterattack.

Hot, bright, rich blood welled up from around the wolverine's clenched teeth. King saw the spreading scarlet and knew that he had never been closer to death. Adrenaline shut out any pain, slowed down time, made his own snarls sound distant, unreal. A massive, muscular twist freed his right arm from the pack. He ripped at his right glove with his teeth, yanking it off, and clawed for the pistol once more. This time, it came to his hand with icy ease. He cocked the weapon as he drew it, slammed the muzzle down against one of the wolverine's eyes, and pulled the trigger.

As suddenly as it had begun, the battle was over.

Snarling in a combination of victory and rage, King levered apart the dead wolverine's jaws with the pistol barrel, freeing his arm. Then he slumped back into the snow, dragging breath into his lungs in great gasps, while the wolverine's limp form draped alongside him like a spent lover.

After a few minutes, King forced himself to sit up, then to kneel, then to stand. He had had enough experience with injury to know that the effects of adrenaline would quickly wear off, leaving weakness and pain behind. He had to get moving, to find shelter and fuel, build a fire, melt water, wash his wounds, bind them, eat and drink to restore lost blood; and he must do it all quickly, before shock took his strength, killing him more slowly and cruelly than the wolverine would have.

King stood over the dead predator, cradling his injured arm, and shaking with adrenaline. He spat, trying to clear the brassy taste of fear from his mouth.

"Guess you never had to fight another wolverine, did you?"

They were the first words King had spoken in weeks. They made him smile, then laugh, as he had at the coming of the new year. The wild currents of life coursing through him had never felt hotter, brighter, more vivid.

Nearly perfect—Icarus close to the sun, but not dying. Not yet.

Only on the next day, when King lay sick and weak from fever inside the dead wolverine's den, did he remember what he had left behind—Cass's sweet breath and sun-bright hair, the taste of golden scotch, waking on a cool morning in bed with Cass's breasts beneath his cheek, a slice of fruitcake laced with rum, the glow of candles on a Christmas tree, candles that were her eyes when she turned to him and smiled—

All behind him. All of it.

King groaned and thrashed, but the dreams remained with him, haunting him. If he could have gotten to his feet, he would have packed and dashed off onto the trail again.

But he would have headed north, not south, leaving loneliness behind, for he was certain that this time he would finally touch the sun.

60

For a long time, King lay within the wolverine den's foul-smelling shelter while the storm outside raged over a land newly white. The eerie wailing of the wind became a part of King's dreams, Cass coming to care for him once more, Cass weeping tears of gold from eyes that were blind river nuggets; and when she opened her mouth to call his name, a stream of gold dust gushed forth instead of living breath.

Only the wind heard King cry out at the dreams that were racking his body as surely as fever and pain. After a time, the dreams came less and less often, slowly releasing King's mind, even as the fever released his body. His thoughts turned again to the needs of survival.

The smell of the wolverine's lair no longer bothered him. Inside the den, he was kept surprisingly warm, in part by the fur of the very animal that had nearly killed him. The wolverine's lush pelt was spread beneath King, keeping the ground's bitter cold from seeping into his body while he slept.

When King had skinned the animal, the reason for the ambush had become clear—the wolverine's left hind leg had a deep wound in it that looked no more than a week old. Partially crippled, slowly starving to death, the animal had been doomed until the wind had brought the scent of warm, large, living prey. A man's flesh would have kept the wolverine alive long enough to heal. Now, the wolverine's carcass lay rigid at the back of the den.

At first, King hadn't been hungry enough to eat the strong, unpalatable meat. In the end, he became as desperate as the wolverine itself had been, forced by a recent injury to attack an unaccustomed source of food. But the wolverine had lost, and its flesh sustained a man's life, rather than the other way around.

King lost track of how long he lived in the rank den— sleeping, dreaming, rousing himself only to feed the small fire and to eat. When he finally emerged from the lair, he was as much wolverine as man.

The first few days of travel were like an extension of King's dreams and nightmares, a time of howling wind and weakness, and finally the slow, steady strengthening of his indomitable body. He existed as the animals did, knowing only the white land and the empty sky and the wind's savage conversations. He merged seamlessly with the elements, asking nothing of himself or the land but bare survival.

Then, without warning, the wind shifted, bringing with it the scent of smoke. King's nostrils flared, drinking in the unexpected odor. He had smelled no fires other than his own since he had left Dyea. For a time he stood transfixed, wondering if he would remember how to speak, how to act, how to be a man among other men. Then he shook off those thoughts as though they were snowflakes gathered on his shoulders, and he skated on. When he rounded a deep bend, he saw a huddle of log cabins and gray-white canvas tents at the other side of the river. As he skated closer, he could see tiny figures moving around the cabins. Before he reached the riverbank, three sled dogs came dancing across the frozen river toward him, towing a sled carrying a bearded man in a bearskin coat. Straggling across the ice after him came a handful of men with the pinched look of hunger on their faces.

When the dog sled drew close, the bearded driver got off the runners in front of King.

"Don't know where the hell you come from," the man said, thrusting out a mittened hand, "but if you brought food with you, I'll trade you ounce for ounce in gold."

For an instant, there was silence. Then King threw back his head and laughed, forgetting his fever, his encounter with death, his injury, his hunger. All those things were in the past and he was alive in the present.

And the present was paved in solid gold.

61

Dawson was everything that King Duran had ever dreamed, and more. More than a ton of gold had been dug out in the six months since the discovery claim had been staked. The silky, heavy metal was everywhere—in glass jars on counter tops, in hide pokes that dangled from every man's belt, and in the sawdust that covered the green lumber floors of the most important building in town, Joe Ladue's saloon.

Dawson was also a nightmare unfolding, an eerie tribute to gold's power. In August, the town hadn't existed. By the middle of January, the population was four hundred men and a handful of women who had to be seen to be believed. There were four plank buildings, dozens of log cabins, and scores of tents whose luckless inhabitants endured temperatures that rarely crawled above zero in sunlight and often dropped to fifty below during the eighteen-hour nights. Food was in short supply. So was everything else.

Except gold.

The people of Dawson didn't complain about the hardships, for gold was all they cared about. Most of the population was made up of experienced prospectors who had been searching for color in and around Circle on August 16, when word had come downriver about George Carmack's big strike up Klondike way. On August 17, Circle had been all but deserted.

Before the leaves turned, most of the possible five-hundred-foot claims along Bonanza and Eldorado creeks had already been staked. So had all the other likely prospects along the braided skein of streams that drained the wilderness surrounding a bald-topped mountain called the Dome, twenty miles distant from Dawson. There were two dozen streams in the land between the Indian River and the North Fork of the Klondike.

Gold had been found in six of them.

Each new strike fueled Dawson's euphoria, pushing it closer and closer to true dementia. Men forgot to eat, to sleep, to build fires, to go through all the mundane motions that added up to survival. Tents bloomed like stained mushrooms amid the scraps of raw wood left behind by miners who had been patient enough to throw up tiny log cabins in between prospecting for gold.

They found fine dust and smooth nuggets and blunt flakes. They found three-hundred-dollar pans and million-dollar claims—and no end in sight. One creek after another turned up golden until men wondered where the gold began and if it would ever end, and still pans came up smiling gold, and hungry men squatted in ice water until their muscles locked and their empty bellies shriveled.

And there was no end to gold.

The rivers froze, yet even that didn't stop the gold-crazy miners. They simply built fires to melt the frozen ground, dug shafts no wider than their shoulders, built more fires, dug deeper and deeper, stockpiled the pay-streak dirt on their claims, and kept on building fires and digging—waiting for the day when water would melt and gold could be washed from gravel once again. They sank the narrow shafts into the ground until they reached bedrock, or until they struck river gravels left over from an earlier time, when the various streams had run in different courses.

No one knew why or how or when these rivers had changed their courses. Men only knew that such changes had taken place, and that within the cold embrace of those abandoned river gravels, gold would be found.

Prospectors who hadn't yet staked a claim fanned out frantically from Dawson, seeking the white gravel that characterized paying ground. They panned up and down existing creek and stream valleys, looking for the golden smile. When it was too dark or too stormy to prospect, they speculated in existing claims—trading and partnering, dividing and bartering, thinking and speaking and dreaming only gold; and in each man was the heady certainty that he was on the cusp of personal history, smack in the middle of the golden bull's-eye—a modern Midas who had only to reach out to turn dirt into gold.

A few mushers had come upriver by dog sled from Alaska, but King was the first man to come in from the south, along the overland route. He became an instant celebrity, not only for his battle with the wolverine but for the fact that he had been so recently in the outside world. The gold seekers were hungry for food, but they were starved for news. The Canadians wanted to know about Queen Victoria's health, and the Americans wanted to know who had won the 1896 presidential elections.

Despite the scarcity of food, in the first few weeks, King found himself a welcome guest in tents or in cabins at mealtime. The meals themselves were predictable, for miners of the Klondike lived mostly on beans and bacon. Many had begun to show the first signs of winter scurvy, for they had been living without fresh food even in the midst of summer's bounty.

King talked to everyone, listened to everyone, and with each new fact he learned, his inner laughter burned more brightly. The golden bitch goddess followed no obvious pattern in the Klondike. Discovery claims were scattered randomly over the various watersheds that drained the wooded slopes of the Dome. No single river had a corner on the mother lode, wherever that might lie. Even more curious, no single creek or watershed had gold up and down its whole length. Eldorado and Bonanza were where the white gravels of the old river courses were most often found; claims along those two creeks had veins of pay dirt that were studded with hundred-dollar nuggets.

But the white gravel itself was as elusive as lightning, appearing and then disappearing without warning. One shaft in the middle of a claim might yield pay dirt so rich that the nuggets could be seen from twenty feet away, while another shaft dug right beside the first might prove as barren of gold as a granite gravestone. Charting the probable lie of the white gravel was done by guess and by God.

King listened not only to the men, but also to the land and to the golden succubus who whispered in his dreams. He walked the different watersheds repeatedly, by sunlight and moonlight, getting a feel for the variations in the land along the creeks. As he walked, he hunted ptarmigan and hare, trading mouthfuls of fresh meat for staples, such as flour and beans and salt; for in a town where everyone had gold, gold could buy nothing but whiskey.

King dug in various places, collecting enough gold in one way or another to fatten a poke, but he found nothing that matched the savage laughter burning in his soul. Never had he felt the bitch goddess's presence so clearly, consuming his soul in anticipation of ecstasy; yet never had the bitch goddess been so elusive to the man who loved her above all else.

Three times in the first few months that King was in Dawson, the town emptied over rumors of yet another strike on one of the Dome's rumpled watersheds. The first time it happened, King followed a rumor that whispered of an Indian finding forty thousand dollars in the tangled roots of a recently fallen tree. There was no truth to the story, but it enlivened table conversation for a few days. That was something that Dawson very much needed—leavening.

The can-do, rough-and-tumble community spirit that prevailed in most mining districts was in short supply in Dawson. Part of the poor spirit was the result of dwindling stocks of food; part, simple cabin fever, as men who had been partners too long in too small a space began to object to matters so trivial that outsiders never understood what all the fighting was about. Part of the ill humor came from the fact that gambling and whiskey in Ladue's saloon were the best entertainments available, so men drowned their boredom in a clear amber river that seemed as endless as the time spent in windowless cabins waiting for a storm to pass.

But most of Dawson's meanspiritedness could be attributed to the growing desperation among two groups of men. The first group was composed of men who had staked the solitary claim permitted under Canadian law and had found nothing; the second group was made up of men who had found nothing worth staking.

King was among the latter, yet he was far from desperate. Each night, he slept with the seductive whisper of gold in his dreams. Each day, he awoke and wondered if this was the day the bitch goddess would come to him, pouring herself into his hands.

Gradually, the other prospectors realized that the man they called Wolverine Duran was among those who had yet to stake a claim. When questioned about it, he smiled and shrugged and said something about Lady Luck; then he asked about their own claims, where the white gravel was and where it wasn't, about what kind of ground they were bringing up from their shafts. The men answered King's questions without reserve, for he was one of them—a prospector who had struck gold before and would strike it again any day now.

Dawson began taking bets on just which day Wolverine Duran would find a piece of dirt worth staking.

King confused everyone by spending the month of April moving chains and holding markers for William Ogilvie, a Canadian government surveyor who was virtually the sole representative of law and order in the entire district. Ogilvie's job was to sort out the tangle of claims that had resulted from the stampede the previous summer. Claims were designated by number, using the site of the original discovery as a landmark and measuring up- or downstream from there.

In the beginning, the system was self-administered. Some miners proved to be more precise in their measurements than others. By spring, the resulting chaos had become institutionalized by custom and less civil means, such as fists and pistols; only a sober, incorruptible, meticulous man like Ogilvie could have made sense of the overlapping claims, and then made his interpretation of claim boundaries acceptable to the miners.

For more than a month, King and Ogilvie paced up and down Eldorado and Bonanza creeks, measuring and restaking claims. Barred by law and conscience from staking claim himself, the Canadian surveyor couldn't be accused of trying to line his own pockets by shaving a rich claim and then staking out the newly unclaimed land for his own. Thus, if Ogilvie said Forty Above Discovery on Bonanza encroached improperly on Forty-one, or that there was an unstaked partial claim between Sixty-two and Sixty-three Below Discovery on Eldorado, the prospectors adjusted their stakes and kept their grumbling to themselves. If there had been any whiff of bribery or favoritism, Ogilvie's job would have been impossible. The fact that the stone-fisted, whiskey-sodden miners accepted Ogilvie's word as law was a tribute to the man's unflinching rectitude.

In the month he worked for Ogilvie, King earned minute wages but learned the boundaries of the district intimately. He came away from the job with an understanding of the pay dirt around Dawson that no other man could equal, much less surpass.

And still King staked no claim.

62

King could feel the changes in the air even before they began to show on the ground. Sunlight came sooner, stayed longer, and slanted less. Throughout April, there had been periods of thaw nearly every day. On some of the scrub-covered slopes above the mining claims, bare earth was showing through the snowpack. Spring was coming, and with it the breakup of river ice. Soon hordes of men would battle their way upriver and overland, lured by the certainty of gold. King had to stake his claim, and he had to do it quickly.

But where?

The question had plagued King since he had first learned how scattered the original discovery claims were. He had hoped that questioning the other prospectors would clarify the pattern, but it hadn't. He had hoped that walking the land with Ogilvie would bring understanding, but it hadn't.

While King had wrestled with the elusive geography, the population of Dawson had slowly increased. Prospectors and woodsmen from downstream had begun to make their way up the highway of ice that was the Yukon. A few rugged men had even come in from the south, following the route that King had blazed from the Alaskan Panhandle. Gradually, by ones and twos and threes, men filtered in to Dawson from all points of the compass, men who had been prospecting the Northwest Territories for years, men who had been in transit to Circle before they'd heard rumors of a Klondike thick with poor man's gold.

Some of the newcomers took up abandoned claims or staked in fresh territory downstream of producing claims, while others bought into proven claims or took jobs on promising claims while they looked for their own piece of gravel. The rest of the men found their place in Dawson at the commercial sluice boxes, or by becoming merchants or land speculators, restaurant owners or gamblers, sneak thieves or laundrymen who filled their pokes with gold panned from water that had been used to wash miners' mud-caked britches.

Still, King waited to file the perfect claim.

Finally, one of the newly arrived gamblers approached King with an offer to split the betting pool fifty-fifty if King would just pick a piece of dirt and stake it on a certain day. King laughed and went back to watching prospectors from outlying claims lose a hundred dollars a hand, just for the company of the others at the table. King drank rounds of whiskey purchased with hundred-dollar nuggets pried from the frozen turf, and watched Dawson grow until there were more than three thousand people clotted together in the raw countryside.

And at night, King poured over maps he had made, notes he had taken, snippets of fact he had heard. He correlated everything, recorded it on a map, and stared at the result until his eyes refused to focus, searching for the pattern that had to be beneath the outward chaos of the discovery claims. The bitch goddess might seem capricious, but she was bound by the rules of gravity and bedrock and possibility. A pattern for the Klondike goldfield existed. All that remained was for King to discover it and stake it out.

Again and again, he went over the basic facts. Gold first occurred in a mother lode, a network of gold-enriched quartz veins that radiated through hard stone like an exploded sun. Rich man's gold. If a prospector wanted that kind of gold, he had to go after it with a rock drill, pickaxe, and dynamite. Originally, all gold had been locked up in stone.

But nothing natural was unchanging. Time and water slowly eroded even the hardest stone, freeing the gold within. Because the gold was heavy, even the smallest flakes sank and were tumbled along with other stony debris, continuing to sink, until they became lodged in the riverbed itself. There, gold of all shapes and sizes collected and continued to sink slowly, slowly, through the loosely packed gravel, displacing other riverbed debris, until finally bedrock was reached and the gold could sink no farther. There, the gold remained year after year, millennium after millennium, while more gold filtered down from the mother lode, and was bounced and tumbled and sorted and rounded, and finally deposited on the gravel bed to begin a slow sinking to bedrock.

Finally, a flood would cut a new channel, or a landslide would divert the river, or the water would eat away old bends and create new ones in a slowly writhing progression that only the mountains lived long enough to see or appreciate. Eventually, the old, gold-laden gravel beds were left high and dry, and the gold-bearing stream cut a new, lower course over the land, deposited new gravel beds, and hurried on to meet the distant sea. The pattern was repeated again and again until the mother lode was exhausted and no more gold-bearing gravels were laid down by that stream.

That was why gold was never found on a watershed above the mother lode. That was why a prospector panned upstream from a placer strike to determine both its extent and its probable richest point. The bigger and rougher the nuggets, the closer to the mother lode. The smoother the nuggets and the greater proportion of dust to nuggets, the farther from the mother lode. Like water, placer gold relentlessly sought the lowest possible level to which it could sink. That was why placer miners didn't stop digging until they came to bedrock, for that was where the richest gravels were.

The Klondike strikes followed many of those rules, but they seemed to defy or ignore others. Most troubling was the fact that the gold from each strike appeared equally rounded and contained about the same proportion of nuggets to dust as the other claims, which suggested that the mother lode was roughly equidistant from all the strikes. The Dome was the only place that was uphill of all of the placer strikes; therefore, the Dome had to hold within its bulk the secret of the Klondike's mother lode.

Yet, not one of the Dome's higher streams had shown color.
King stared broodingly at the map showing the Dome's higher elevations, which were utterly naked of stakes. When the breakup of the ice came, he was certain that men would swarm over the Dome in search of the gold that experience and common sense insisted had to be there; but King's gut instinct told him that they would not find gold. The distance from the Dome's forty-five-hundred-foot peak to the big strikes simply didn't impress him as great enough to account for the smoothness of the nuggets and the fact that the proportion of dust to nuggets was so high.

Frowning, King retraced the richest strikes once more. Bonanza Creek meandered down the east face of the Dome to the low, scrub-covered foothills. There, the creek joined Eldorado just above Carmack's original discovery. Together, the two streams flowed down into the Klondike a few miles above where it emptied into the Yukon. Almost without exception, the prospectors had concentrated their attention on those two streams or on the Dome itself, for they were as certain that gold washed downhill as they were that the sun rose in the east.

King was also certain about the natures of gravity and gold—but once he had seen seashells embedded in the jagged rock of a mountain peak. He found it easier to believe that the landscape itself slowly changed shape than that sea animals climbed mountains and mindlessly bored their own graves out of solid stone.

If sea bottom could become mountaintop and then be worn away utterly by rivers and carried to the sea once more, it was fair to assume that watersheds could change, too. New river systems would form to drain new mountain ranges, washing out new mother lodes, rounding off the gold, depositing it in riverbeds that themselves changed constantly, slowly, relentlessly, carrying away the mountains one grain at a time until the land changed again, and the old river system vanished even as the mountains had.

But the river's placer gold would remain behind, incorruptible, unchanging, caught within gravels so old that nothing remained of the landscape through which the river had originally flowed. There would be no rhyme or reason to such placer deposits, because they would follow the logic of a watershed long since flattened, a watershed that today was being cut through by new streams that flowed over new courses in response to new elevations and new mountains.

King traced and retraced the present course of riches with his fingertip, then sat motionless, staring at the map with half-focused eyes. Abruptly, he stood and left the cabin with long strides. Outside, sunlight filled the land to overflowing. Water dripped from eaves and ran in crystal rivulets to low points on the ground. Slowly, the outer skin of the land was thawing, water pooling and flowing downhill, water washing away the icy grip of winter, one tiny drop at a time.

The liquid sparkle and murmur of meltwater didn't penetrate King's concentration. Half walking, half running, he clambered up a thawing trail that led to a bench above Bonanza Creek. From there, he scaled the hillside, aiming toward a small notch. Many men had been there before him throughout the winter, but they had been hunting firewood, not gold. He followed the loose network of trails that had been worn into the snowpack by prospectors who had scavenged winter wood on the slopes upstream from Carmack's original discovery claim. King climbed upward without pause, driven by his need to see the land itself rather than a smudged map. From the top, there would be a grand view of Bonanza Creek's paying claims.

Despite the pouring sunlight and patches of bare dirt that had begun to show through the melting snowpack, the air itself was cold. As King gained the crest of the hill that separated the Bonanza watershed from Eldorado, his attention was caught by a flicker of movement in the middle of a bare patch of ground. He stopped and saw the first hoary marmot of the season sunning itself at the entrance to its burrow on the south-facing slope. When the little animal saw King, it gave a shrill warning whistle and dove underground in a blur of grayish yellow.

King smiled at the high whistle, which underlined the fact that this was true spring, not a false time of warmth between icy bouts of winter. He felt bad about running the marmot back into the frozen ground; it had been a long winter for man and beast alike.

"Don't worry, fellow. I won't be here long. I just came to look at the—"

King's voice died. In a few swift strides, he was at the marmot's burrow. In front of it was a mound of dirt that had been pushed out to make the underground passageway. Mixed in with thin soil and slowly decaying bits of wood, pieces of pale, water-rounded gravel shone against the dark earth. Hardly able to believe his eyes, King knelt and grabbed a fistful of the cold, stony soil, then tore it apart with fingers that were shaking from the onslaught of adrenaline.

The gravel at the mouth of the burrow looked just like the coarse white conglomerate that had yielded Carmack's first nugget, just like the pale pay dirt that appeared and disappeared from riverside claims without rhyme or reason. But the paying claims were at the bottom of the hill and the marmot's burrow was at the top. What was river gravel doing at the top of the hill?

If seashells can grow on mountaintops, why can't a hill once have been a river bottom?

Sweet, wild laughter seethed within King, but he held it in check. A quick look around assured him that he was alone. No one else moved on the hillside in search of firewood. No one else was within view down below. He turned back and studied the burrow. It was shallow, for this was permafrost country, with ice a year-round resident a few feet below the surface of the land. He could hear vague scrabbling sounds from beneath, as though the hoary marmot were enlarging its home at the top of the notch. Breath half-held as though he were fearful of waking from a dream, King looked once more at the gravel ringing the entrance to the burrow.

Nothing had changed. The white gravel still looked the same as that found down below on either side of the hill in pay-dirt claims staked along two separate river courses. King scattered the top layer of gravel with his hand, sorting through it automatically, trying to make his mind believe what his senses were shouting at him: *he had struck pay dirt.* He thrust his fingers into the gravel and threw it into the air, scattering it wildly. Dirt and rounded white pebbles and sunlight fell around him, sunlight that was pale and cool; and then a gleam of fire that was both pure and perfect, sunlight condensed into solid gold.

King let the rest of the pebbles fall to the ground, keeping only the satin heaviness of a nugget bigger than his thumbnail. Slowly, his fingers closed over the water-rounded gold until it was wrapped in his strong hand, hidden in darkness once more; but it was a darkness warmed by the heat of King's body. Sitting on his heels, shaken by tremors of excitement, he looked out over the land while his heart tried to beat free of his chest. He could hardly believe that he had found placer gold in river gravels high above present-day creeks. But gold was there just the same, gold in white gravel, pay dirt so rich that a big nugget had come instantly into his hands as though summoned.

Dazed, wondering, King looked around the hillside bench. Much of the scrub timber had been cut down during the past winter. Here and there, in spots where meltwater had washed away the thin soil that was no longer protected by living trees, pieces of white gravel showed through like scattered bones. From where King sat, it looked as though the little notch in the hilltop was paved with riverbed gravel. The longer he looked, the more he became convinced that he was sitting in the middle of the bed of a long-vanished river, and that ancient river was the source of placer gold, not the modern streams called Bonanza and Eldorado.

Closing his eyes, King visualized the map he had made and studied for so many hours. The notch where he sat was on a line that tied together the richest areas of Bonanza Creek and the best claims on Eldorado. The nose of the upthrust hill he was sitting on separated the two watersheds, but was made of exactly the same stony ingredients. It was as though a wedge of cake had been cut and shifted upward from the body of the cake itself. The position was different, but the raised piece of cake was just the same as the lower pieces on either side—and the pieces on either side of King's cake were called Bonanza and Eldorado. The ground beneath his feet was every bit as rich as the richest claims that had yet been staked in the Klondike.

He was sitting on top of a mountain of gold.

Laughter as pure and beautiful as gold itself poured out of King, a sound of exaltation and joy that no one heard but

King himself. It was enough. It had always been enough. That, like the satin perfection of gold, would never change.

With the last echoes of laughter ringing around him, the man known as Wolverine Duran finally staked his claim.

63

"What the hell you do a damfool thing like that for? You're, by God, a thousand yards from the nearest pay dirt and all the hell up a barren mountain to boot. None of them little feeder creeks have shown enough color to fill a man's tooth, yet you go and waste your one claim way up on the bench! What the hell got into you?"

Poke Martin wasn't the first man to ask that question of King, but he was the first one to do so to King's face.

King smiled into the amber whiskey that lay all but untouched within his glass and said, "I took a notion."

The heavyset young miner made a sound of pure disgust. "You lived with that damn wolverine carcass too long. You're plumb crazy."

"Probably," King agreed. "How's your own claim doing?"

"Ain't worth a fart in a windstorm. Me and three others is working for Black Joe. He's too crippled up to move. Winter near killed him."

"I'll pay you a hundred and fifty a week to work for me, and 5 percent of the first month's cleanup if you stay past four weeks. If you leave before then, you get only wages."

Poke stared, blinked, and stared again. "The hell you say."

King smiled into his whiskey again, sipped lightly, and set the glass back down on Ladue's bar. "Take it or leave it."

"It's done took," Poke said, reaching out and shaking King's hand heartily.

"Good." King turned to face Poke fully. "You start now. I've got lumber to haul up to the bench. The sooner we get a rocker and sluice built, the sooner we know how rich we'll be."

Poke looked puzzled. "You need a rocker already? When did you have time to dig your trail shaft?"

"I didn't."

"Then how in hell do you know there's any color to wash out?"

"I asked a marmot."

Poke's eyes widened. "That's plumb crazy."

"So is gold, my friend. So is gold."

Shaking his head, muttering about chechakos—greenhorns—who had no more sense than a chicken, Poke followed King out of the saloon. The hot-stove prospectors around Dawson had spent a lot of time making up tales about how crazy Wolverine Duran was, but none of those tales topped the bare fact of an experienced river prospector like Duran claiming to have found placer gold on a hilltop bench. Any fool knew that was something only a chechako would do.

The idea of placer gold on the bench high above the river was so preposterous that nobody even bothered to scramble up the slippery, muddy trail to the site of King's claim. The bench became known as Chechako Hill, and the sages of the Klondike shook their heads every time they looked up to the highlands where two tiny figures labored tirelessly in darkness and light.

But despite their orthodoxies, the prospectors were a forgiving lot. When Wolverine Duran brought down his first hundred ounces of gold—gold that was absolutely indistinguishable from the riches of Eldorado and Bonanza—the miners who had laughed loudest were the first to claw their way up the muddy hillside to stake their claims with shaking hands and pounding heart.

By the time the ice went out of the Yukon, the highlands above Bonanza were covered with stakes, and men worked round the clock in a frenzy, stripping white gravel from the mountain of gold.

64

A ringing bell awoke Cass from a deep sleep. Confused, she sat up in bed, trying to identify the source of the sound. It wasn't the doorbell, which meant that it had to be the telephone. She rolled out of bed, muttering at the thing called Progress. She had had the phone for three months, but she hadn't gotten used to the fact that people who would never show up at her doorstep at odd hours of the day or night felt no such compunction when it came to intruding on her life via the telephone.

"I'll get it," Tea Rose called.

Cass abandoned her futile search for her slippers and sat on the edge of the bed, waiting. A moment later, Tea Rose came to the door and turned on the bedroom light. Even mussed from sleep, the girl's beauty was startling. Cass wondered if she would ever get used to it.

Of course I will. I've gotten used to everything else. Even the fact that King didn't love me—and Jared didn't hate me.

"It's Henry Marshall," Tea Rose said.

Cass sensed the excitement glittering just beneath Tea Rose's calm surface. In the twelve months they had lived together, Cass had learned to catch glimpses of the Tea Rose who lived behind the emotionless façade. Gradually, Cass had realized that Tea Rose had an intensity of mind and purpose that rivaled Jared's.

As always lately, Cass's mind caught and held on Jared. She had finally accepted that his assessment of King had been correct: King might indeed have loved her, but not enough to live with her. As for her own love—she had begun to wonder about that, too. She wondered if she hadn't been off balance, lonely, infatuated with King's dark radiance and the knowledge that he had needed her very badly while he healed.

But that wasn't enough to build a life on. King had healed, and he had left—and lately, she had begun to remember odd things about the few brief months she had known King. Things such as how much she had looked forward to talking with Jared, how often she had wished he would stay instead of leaving every time King had appeared, and how it had been Jared's quiet strength that had kept her own fear at bay, even when King had been present. Jared had always been there.

And she had always turned away from him, seeing only King.

"Sister? Are you awake?"

"Did Henry say what he wanted?" Cass asked as she felt around with her bare toes until she encountered a slipper pushed under the bed.

"No, but he was very excited."

"How could you tell?" Cass asked, for the editor of the *Post-Intelligencer* rarely showed any emotion but impatience.

Tea Rose shrugged. "How do you instantly know what will make a good photograph and what won't?"

"Talent, experience, and hard work," Cass said dryly.

Tea Rose smiled and bowed slightly over her clasped hands. "Exactly, sister. To me, people are as clear as photographs are to you."

Cass didn't argue. She had come to respect Tea Rose's incisive, precocious understanding of human nature. Unfortunately, the girl's pragmatism still left Cass feeling from time to time as though she had been dropped from a great height into ice water.

"He won't know that you have only one shoe on," Tea Rose pointed out, when Cass persisted in her search for the missing slipper.

With a sigh, Cass kicked off the slipper she had found and walked barefoot to the phone box on the wall by the front door.

"Good morning, Mr. Marshall," she said. "Or is this a late 'Good evening'?"

"I don't care and you won't either once you hear the news. I've got a great job for you!"

Cass hesitated. She had done some business with Marshall since the *Post-Intelligencer* had acquired the capacity to print photographs, but she had mixed feelings about journalistic photography. The images Marshall wanted seemed long on drama and short on everything else.

"Mr. Marshall," Cass said, yawning, "I'm not going to race through the city before dawn to take a gruesome picture of a mother wailing over the charred body of her child."

"I know, I know," Marshall said, his words soothing, but his voice impatient. "You're an artist, not a hack. That's why I want you."

"How have you stayed a bachelor?" Cass demanded, half exasperated, half flattered. "You sure know how to catch a girl's attention."

"That's how I've remained a bachelor," Marshall shot back.

Cass laughed. Marshall was a shrewd editor. She liked him, even if she didn't entirely like his profession.

"I'm giving you first shot at this," he continued. "You interested?"

"I'm awake, so I must be interested," Cass said. "But I can't commit to a pig in a journalistic poke."

"How does a shipload of gold sound to you?"

"A shipload of gold?" Cass repeated. "That sounds like an overstatement."

Tea Rose felt her heart hammer. She started to reach for the phone in the instant before she brought herself back under control. She stood with breath held, vibrating with urgency, saying nothing, thinking of a gold locket and King Duran, who had said nothing to her.

And who had left without returning her locket.

"The ship is the *Portland.* It belongs to the Duran Shipping Company. It's a beat-up old scow that's been on the Alaska run. It's coming down the Sound right now, loaded to the gunwales with a million dollars' worth of coarse gold from that new strike up in Canada. You heard about the San Francisco end of the story, didn't you? It was the lead in yesterday's late edition."

Cass had seen the wire service reports from San Francisco in the *Post-Intelligencer*. An Alaska steamer named the *Excelsior* had arrived from the north two days before, carrying a dozen gold miners who were supposed to have struck it rich in the Klondike. The miners had caused a small riot in San Francisco when they came staggering down the gangplank, headed for the U. S. Mint, laden with suitcases, wooden crates, and leather bags full of raw gold.

The story had been electrifying. Even Tea Rose, who normally accepted everything without comment, had been visibly excited. Newspapers all over the country, tied together by the newly formed telegraph wire services, had sent the story coast to coast as though it were the Second Coming of Christ rather than a handful of lucky prospectors carrying gold to the mint. The miners had been quoted at length as they talked about the Big Cleanup, God's Own Strike, nuggets lying thick on the ground, gold dust choking the crevices, a mountain of poor man's gold waiting to be hauled to the mint.

Cass had dismissed most of the quotes as whiskey talk, tall tales, and a shrewd editor's idea of what would sell papers. Even so, she had read the story carefully, as she had read every piece of news from the Northwest Territories for the past seven months. At one time, she would have yearned to go to photograph the first, wild rush of the discovery, but no longer. Her affair with King had taught her the difference between dreams and day-to-day reality. Men like the prospectors—like King—were beautiful shooting stars burning against the mundane backdrop of real life. For better or worse, they set other people to dreaming, to yearning, to hurting themselves by falling headlong on the ground, as they tried to catch a falling star.

It was another kind of man entirely who had the vision, determination, and strength to build the enduring monuments of mankind. Men such as Jared Duran. They were the men who left their mark upon time, who built cities and nations, railroads and steamship lines and banks, who led people in war or peace, who had families, who built empires and made decisions and lived with them; and other people lived with them, as well.

For better or for worse.

Without realizing it, Cass sighed. "I read the story, Mr. Marshall. Frankly, I didn't believe half of it. Did anyone bother to add it up? A million dollars in gold would literally weigh a ton."

The telephone line hummed for a moment before Marshall said slowly, "A ton of gold. My God—makes a man restless just to think about it. It would be a great headline!"

"If it were true."

"Oh, my reporters have seen the gold. The *Portland* left Alaska a few days behind the *Excelsior*. Jared Duran called me when the *Portland* was sighted off Victoria. He offered his fastest launch to my reporters. They've been and come back already, though the *Portland* is still a couple of hours out."

There was a hard knocking on the front door.

Cass jumped, startled. "Wait a minute, Mr. Marshall. Someone is pounding on the front door."

"I'll take care of it," Tea Rose said, feeling she would explode if she didn't have an excuse to move. She went to the door, opened it a crack, and looked through. "Yes?"

"My gawd, he said he was promised to a looker, but you beat hell out of anything I ever seen! Oh, 'scuse me, Miss. My name's Mule Dryden. I come from King Duran, only everybody calls him Wolverine nowadays. Miss Cassie around?"

Tea Rose looked over her shoulder. Cass stood rooted to the floor, able only to nod her head. Tea Rose reached past Cass, opened the door, and stood back.

"They've got the gold, no question about it," Marshall continued, his voice a distant buzzing in Cass's ear. "It's going to be the biggest thing to hit Seattle since the fire. I'm putting out an extra edition right now, and I want full photo coverage when the boat gets in. Will you do it?"

Helplessly, Cass pictured the arriving steamer in her mind's eye. Somewhere on the rail, she saw a face that was familiar. Too familiar. She wasn't sure she was ready to confront her bittersweet memories in the flesh, to see again the man she had failed to hold with her offer of herself and a home.

Funny, I never realized how much King reminded me of Papa—loving him, nursing him—losing him.

"Ma'am," Dryden said, looking at the woman who leaned against the wall as though all the strength had run from her body. "Are you all right?"

"Yes," Cass whispered.

"I have a message from King."

"Wait," Cass said, cutting Mule off with a tight gesture. "Mr. Marshall, I'll do your photographs. You can develop them in your lab, or I'll do them myself."

"If Billy doesn't find you, bring me the prints two hours after the *Portland* docks."

"Fine."

Without another word, Cass hung up and turned to Mule Dryden. "Tell me," she said tightly.

Mule dug into his pocket and brought out a small poke. Gently, almost reverently, he loosened the tie and carefully shook a single large water-smoothed nugget into his palm.

Tea Rose bit her tongue until tears came to her eyes, but she made no sound.

"This here nugget is the first from the biggest strike King ever made, and maybe the biggest strike ever made by any man," Mule said. "Only time will tell." He took Cass's trembling hand and tipped the nugget into her palm. "He said it belongs with the others he gave you." Mule turned to Tea Rose. "And he said to tell you he's never welshed on a deal, but he's not coming out until the cleanup is done."

Tea Rose nodded tightly, hanging onto her self-control with a lifetime of harsh discipline.

"I'll be going now, ma'am," Mule said, turning back to Cass. "I got other messages to deliver. Good day to you."

She tried to speak, to ask more questions, but Mule had

already turned and headed out into the night, shutting the door behind him. Cass looked back at Tea Rose just in time to see her sister crumpling in a faint. Cass just managed to catch the girl and drag her the few feet to the sofa. Kneeling next to her, she chafed Tea Rose's hands together and slapped her cheeks lightly.

"Tea Rose?" Cass asked. "Tea Rose!"

The girl's black eyes opened. At first, she seemed dazed, then suddenly she laughed. The musical, triumphant sounds were so unexpected that Cass wondered if she should slap Tea Rose's cheeks harder to bring her out of hysteria.

"What's wrong with you?" Cass demanded.

Radiant black eyes focused on Cass. Tea Rose started to speak, and laughter bubbled out with her words.

"Nothing is wrong with me, sister. Everything is right. I'm rich, and I'll never have to kowtow to anyone again. Ever! I'm free of Tan Feng and of all your silly rules!"

The sweet laughter gave Cass chills. It wasn't simply that she didn't know what had set Tea Rose off; it was that the girl apparently had seen her time living with Cass as a kind of prison.

"I don't understand," Cass whispered.

Tea Rose smiled with heartbreaking beauty. "I know. There's so much that you don't understand. Sometimes, I envied you that sweet innocence, but not now. Now, it doesn't matter any longer. Nothing matters except the gold that will be mine." Tea Rose took a deep, shaking breath. "I wish Mother were alive. I could buy her ten times over and myself as well. But if she were alive, I would still be a slave, rather than a rich China girl." Tea Rose closed her eyes. When she opened them again, they were enlarged by unshed tears. "Remember that camera you admired last week? I'll buy it for you. I'll buy ten like it and hang red ribbons from all of them. I'll buy you a studio in the busiest part of town, a new wagon, new horse, new lenses, everything!" She clapped her hands together and laughed softly. "I'm rich!"

"What are you talking about?"

"I staked King in his hunt for gold. I'm his partner!"

"What?" Cass whispered, staring at Tea Rose.

Smiling, shimmering with barely contained exultation, Tea Rose nodded.

"How? When?"

"After we talked with Tan Feng's messenger, I went to see King," Tea Rose said. "I gave him the locket so that he could be free to hunt gold."

Cass closed her eyes, unable to believe what she was hearing. "You went to King? You urged him to leave? Why, Tea Rose? What had I done that you would hate me so?"

For a moment, Tea Rose looked confused. "You're not making sense, sister. I don't hate you. In any case, what does that have to do with my staking King to—oh, I see. You think that I did it only to hurt you." Tea Rose shook her head. "I'm not that foolish. If it weren't for you, Jared would still protect me, but only with great difficulty; and if I were cruel to you, Jared would punish me severely. So why would I do something that would make you hate me? That would benefit only Tan Feng. Do you understand now?"

Cass shook her head, more at a loss to understand than she had been before.

Patiently, Tea Rose explained what had been instantly obvious to her nine months before. "I need you for my own safety. In order for you yourself to be safe, you must be under a man's protection. You are so cruelly transparent, sister. You would have told King what Jared had done, and then King would have gone into a rage. No matter what happened after that, only Tan Feng would have benefited. So I gave King the means to escape the woman he couldn't bring himself to marry. He left, which is to his benefit and mine, whether or not he ever discovered gold. Jared remained and protected us very well, which is to our benefit. Jared didn't have to defend himself against the violent rage of the brother he loves, which was to Jared's benefit. Tan Feng was thwarted once again. Everyone benefited but our enemy."

"Where was the benefit to me?" Cass asked, her voice far too soft, too strained.

"Do you know what happens to people who try to chain lightning, sister? They go crazy or die. The longer King stayed, the greater the chance that you and Jared would been destroyed by your attempts to hold King. Then I would have been defenseless and Tan Feng would win."

"Tan Feng. Tan Feng. You say his name like a god's, invoking him whenever it suits you—and it suited you to separate King and me before we ever had a chance! You manipulate other people's lives for your own comfort and call it beneficial. You are cruel and call it kind!"

Tea Rose sighed and gave up trying to explain, tired of a subject she had gone through so many times in her own mind. "In any case, it's done and can't be called back."

Cass opened her mouth, but no words came out. She looked at the gold nugget in her hand and wondered how much of what Tea Rose had said was true and how much was simply self-serving.

And Cass wondered the same of her own words, her own thoughts, her own fears and hopes.

What does it matter? Cass asked herself brutally. *King didn't love me enough to stay. Everyone knew it but me. What good does it do to scream at Jared and Tea Rose for my own blindness?*

Cass's fists clenched until the nugget ate into her soft skin. She stood swiftly.

"Even if everything you say is the exact truth," Cass said carefully, looking down at Tea Rose's deceptively delicate face and trying not to scream, "you have acted with great selfishness. Your first thought has always been for your own comfort, your own safety, never for anyone else's. How can you be that way?"

"How can I not? Everyone is that way."

"You can't believe that. Lilac died so you could be free."

"My mother died because Tan Feng was going to sell her as a saltwater whore," Tea Rose said patiently, once again explaining to Cass things that were obvious to her half sister. "Mother took me from Tan Feng to punish him because he wanted me more than he wanted her."

Cass could only stare at Tea Rose's calm, beautiful face. "What are you saying?" Cass whispered, horrified.

"The very truths that my mother trained me so carefully to observe. If Tan Feng had offered me marriage, I would have gone back to him, because he is powerful and I could have controlled that power. But he married me to a man whose lust is only aroused by perfect lily feet. I would have no power over such a man, so I stayed with you and sought to learn another culture, another kind of power. I found it. In the end, I benefited from my mother's death and from Tan Feng's anger and from my own wit. That doesn't make her a saint or him a devil." Tea Rose sat up, feeling in control of herself again. "As for myself, I have tried to teach you to be less trusting, but it has been futile. You see only what you want to see. It's much more comfortable for you to trust in goodness than to confront evil. I understand your choice, but it's not mine."

Tea Rose looked at Cass's pale, lovely face and sighed.

"Ah, sister," Tea Rose said, standing up and hugging Cass with surprising strength. "I'm sorry that the news of gold loosened my tongue. I shouldn't have said anything. There's no benefit to anyone from my hurting you. Come. Let's photograph the ship of gold for Mr. Marshall."

Cass struggled between an impulse to shout at Tea Rose and the urge to hug her sister in return. In the end, the impulse toward love won out, as it always had in Cass. She put her arms around Tea Rose and hugged her fiercely.

"Tea Rose, you don't have to fight so hard against the world, not any more, not here, not with me. In my world, you can love and be loved and be stronger for it, not weaker."

Tea Rose smiled sadly, hugged her sister with equal strength, and said no more about men and women and the curious disaster known as love.

65

Cass drove the reluctant horse through the chilly pre-dawn to the Duran Shipping Company wharf. With an odd sense of déjà vu, she realized that she had been in this exact place when it had all begun a year before—the gold locket and Lilac and Tea Rose, Jared and King. Without warning, the past condensed around her once more, Jared's unnerving eyes looking past her businesslike façade and seeing the intensely vulnerable woman beneath; Jared asking her to accept a half sister she had never known existed; Jared standing by her when everyone else had vanished; Jared, always Jared, and herself always turning away from him, yearning after a shooting star.

Why? she asked herself for the first time.

Jared saw too much of me, she answered quickly.

What do you have to hide and withhold?

Jared didn't need me. King did.

For a time, yes. But he is gone and Jared remains. And Jared—needs. Not as a weakened man needs, temporarily, but as a strong man needs. Forever.

Cass closed her eyes and swayed, feeling on the brink of a frightening discovery about herself and the brother of the man she had thought she loved. It was Jared whose image came to her in the dark hours before sleep, not King's. It was Jared whose rare smiles made her laugh with delight. Jared's walk and strength and quickness no longer recalled King to her. Jared had become light, and King had become shadow.

"Cassandra?"

For a moment, Cass thought it was Jared calling to her, and her heart beat wildly. Then she realized it was Tea Rose.

"Where do you want to set up?" Tea Rose asked again.

It took several minutes for Cass to put the Duran brothers out of her mind so she could concentrate on the job ahead. She looked at the eastern sky. Dawn was just coming on. By the time the ship docked, the sun would be over the horizon, but not by much. She would need her fastest film and clearest lens. That meant the Kodak, not the cumbersome glass plate camera.

"Farther up the wharf," Cass said.

It quickly became apparent that the wagon wouldn't make it out anywhere near the end of the crowded wharf. Despite the early hour, word of the ship had spread through the city.

"Damn," Cass muttered, looking out over the crowd. "I'm too far away for the Kodak, and things will happen too fast for the big camera."

"I'll stay with the wagon," Tea Rose offered. "You go on to the end of the wharf."

Cass hesitated.

"Quickly," Tea Rose said. "The ship will tie up soon, and you'll miss the best shots."

For an instant more, Cass hesitated, but the sight of people streaming toward the waterfront decided her. She stuffed extra rolls of film into her skirt pocket, leaped from the wagon, and began weaving through the people who were crowding forward onto the wharf. The murmur of the crowd was like a distant wind fretting the trees, words half-heard, elusive, fading and then coming again, borne on the wind; and all the words were variations on a single theme.

Gold.

Cass tried not to hear, tried not to feel the contagion of gold fever, but it was impossible. The necklace of gold nuggets that had once been King's watch chain weighed heavily around her neck, physical proof of the words whispered on the wind. Once, she had been tempted to hurl King's chain and all that it stood for into Elliott Bay. Instead, she had joined King's with that of her father, whom she also had failed, and she now wore the heavy result around her neck.

When Cass neared the Duran offices at the end of the wharf, a boy in short pants and a cap with a turned-up brim stood on a box, chanting a newsboy's sales pitch. She checked the light level, composed the picture, and took it while the boy chanted on, oblivious to everything but hands holding out silver coins to buy his story of gold.

"Extra! Extra! Read all about it! Ship of gold comes to Seattle! Get your paper right here!"

The block-letter headlines were even more shrill than the boy's chant.

GOLD! GOLD! GOLD! GOLD!
Sixty-Eight Rich Men on
The Steamer *Portland*
STACKS OF YELLOW METAL!

While an old man sorted slowly through a leather change purse for the exact amount in pennies, the boy twitched and pranced, anxious to get on to other customers.

"Business good?" Cass asked, as she worked over the camera, composing a shot that would catch the boy's impatience and the unshakable calm of the old man, who had seen too much of life to get excited about anything.

"Yeah, but nothing's as good as gold. I'm going to sell these papers, and then I'm off to the Klondike to make my fortune. I'm gonna be rich!"

"Do you know where the Klondike is?" Cass asked, shifting angles.

"North of here somewheres," muttered the boy. He grabbed the money from the old man's hand, shoved a paper toward him, and then was off and running through the crowd once more, selling papers in a high, frenzied voice. "Extra! Extra! Extra! Mountain of gold found in Klondike! Extra! Extra! Read—"

The boy's cries were lost in the triumphant scream of the *Portland's* whistle as it approached the wharf. The sound sliced through everything, an inhuman cry that was both exhilarating and savage.

But it was nothing compared to the answering roar of the gold-hungry crowd.

66

Thousands of roaring voices shook the windows and made the timbers of the Duran Shipping Company wharf vibrate. Inside the wharf office, Jared looked up from the papers piled on his desk and smiled humorlessly. He hoped that those cheers would be only the beginning of gold madness. Already rumors of gold had been landing like sparks in a pile of sawdust, setting off leaping fires of excitement.

The men who had come stumbling off the *Excelsior* in San Francisco were rumpled specimens of the common man's dream—working men with no prospects one day and wealthy as Midas the next. Already, the Klondike miners had become celebrities. According to the wire service stories Jared had read, the crowds in San Francisco had treated the prospectors like returning war heroes. A few of the miners had responded by strewing nuggets from hotel windows to the throngs below.

The crowds in Seattle, a city made by and for working men, would be no less wild in their response to the presence of poor man's gold. There was going to be dancing in the city streets before the day was done and probably minor riots as well. If things went as Jared hoped, before the week was out, thousands of men would be on steamships headed north. Others would flock to Seattle's docks from every town big enough to have a newspaper. Of those thousands and hundreds of thousands, only a few would ever see gold in their own hands.

But you couldn't tell men that, when gold frenzy struck, for each man was certain that he would be the one blessed by the golden goddess.

With clear, calm eyes, Jared read the Extra edition that had been dropped on his desk before the ink was dry. For once, the banner headlines were an understatement. Next to the newspaper on the desk were copies of the *Portland*'s manifest, which had been delivered to Jared's office by a launch that had easily outpaced the slower steamship. The prospectors' boxes, satchels, and bags contained not one ton of gold as the newspaper said, but more than two. Two tons of gold lying heavily in the ship's hold, lifeless metal gleaming, calling to men's souls with a sweet singing that couldn't be denied.

Jared had experienced the contagion of gold and gold rushes at first hand. He understood the immense lure of instant, easy wealth. He had felt the call of unclaimed gold in his blood and had answered with wild exhilaration. But for him, the call had become weaker each time he heard it, rather than stronger. He had looked at the handful of lucky miners, seen a hundred or a thousand luckless men for every one that came up golden, and then Jared had looked beyond the lucky and the unlucky alike, focusing on the instant towns built upon rumors of gold.

Panning for gold was an uncertain process at best. Selling supplies to miners was not. For every man made fabulously wealthy by a gold strike, five men made fortunes transporting and supplying the unlucky miners with food or equipment or excitement. Jared had no desire to own saloons or whorehouses or even respectable emporiums. He was a man who believed in the transportation of goods and men by rail or sea. Every miner and every supplier of miners had to use transport of some kind. Jared wanted to supply that transportation. For the Klondike, that meant steamers capable of taking on the Inside Passage while filled to the gunwales with men and supplies on the northward run, and heavy with gold on the southward run.

Jared sat back and stared out the window, but it wasn't the rowdy crowd that held his attention, it was the future. If the Klondike was a quarter as rich as he suspected, the Northwest—indeed the entire circle of the Pacific Rim countries—would be transformed by Klondike gold in ways that went far beyond the accumulation of individual wealth.

Gold was the lifeblood of the world's economy, and gold had been in short supply compared to the demand for capital with which to finance the industrialization of the Western world. The effects of the ongoing economic depression had been magnified by the relative scarcity of gold. A major new strike could be the engine driving Seattle into the twentieth century, allowing the city to take her place alongside great present-day ports such as London and New York.

The Klondike gold fields were thousands of miles from anywhere. Seattle was the closest American city of any size, which meant that the Klondike's wealth would funnel back into the national economy through Seattle. And with any luck at all, a good deal of that wealth would be carried aboard Duran ships.

The *Portland*'s whistle and the crowd screamed at each other again, bringing Jared's thoughts back to the present. He sighed and rubbed his eyes wearily. He had spent most of the past two days awake, adjusting his professional plans to take advantage of the Klondike strike. There had been his personal future to consider as well. The fast launch that brought him a count of the wealth in the *Portland*'s hold had also retrieved a copy of the *Portland*'s passenger manifest. Jared had been even more interested in the sixty-eight men aboard than he was in the gold. Once he had ascertained that King was not among the passengers, Jared had studied the list for other names he recognized, hoping to find a trustworthy source of firsthand information.

Only one name stood out: M.E. Haynes was a well-known figure in the Far Northwest, a staff sergeant of the Royal Canadian Mounted Police and one of the few policemen of any kind west of Winnipeg. Jared intended to buttonhole the officer as soon as the boat docked. Although Jared had more information about the Klondike strike than most men, he wanted very much to confirm the extent of the gold deposits. If the major part of the cleanup had been removed already, the rush would quickly peter out. If there was more gold, much more, it would become the kind of event on which empires were founded.

But Jared had to have more information before he could decide whether to continue his commitment to the Klondike strike or to sell the steamboats he had mortgaged his domain to buy, cut his losses, and retrench to await another opportunity. Other than the fact of gold on the two ships, Jared had found only a few concrete sources from which to estimate the extent of the strike. The best source was a Canadian pamphlet called *Information Respecting the Yukon District,* which had been published the previous spring. The information had come from a government surveyor's report filed by a man called Ogilvie. The report had made clear that the Yukon strike easily surpassed that of the Circle City discovery of the previous year.

Jared had managed to glean a few other indications of the Klondike's potential from brief, unconfirmed, and fragmentary reports that had appeared in a number of papers around the United States. A Chicago paper had even reprinted a dispatch from one of its own reporters, a man who had himself staked on Eldorado. A few men had made it out of the area before winter set in; at least three of them had wintered in Seattle before returning to the northern gold fields. Jared had spent a good deal of time with each of the men, assaying the possibilities of the Yukon in his own way.

As a result, Jared knew more about the region than did many of the men who had wintered there and who were now fighting the swarming clouds of mosquitoes and blackflies as they washed pan after pan of pay-streak gravel in the tributaries of the Yukon. Each time new word had leaked out of Klondike gold, Jared had expected the stampede to begin. Each time he had been wrong. He had a fortune tied up in three new steamers that were awaiting orders to head north. Today, there weren't enough passengers and freight contracts to justify owning the ships. But tomorrow—ah, tomorrow.

That was why Jared had made the Duran Company's fast launch available to the reporters of the city's largest newspaper. Jared didn't have a stake in Eldorado or Bonanza, but with one of the largest steamer fleets in the Northwest, he had a definite stake in the Yukon itself, and he intended to maximize the value of his investment. If the rush materialized, he would look like a prescient entrepreneur. If the rush fizzled, he would look like a fool, and he would be nearly broke, as well.

If two tons of raw gold didn't set fire to men's imaginations, nothing would.

The *Portland* was now a hundred yards off the end of the wharf. The stumpy little boat's prow was scarred from fighting through the last remnants of the Alaskan sea ice and its superstructure was streaked with rust and coated with brine salts. The rails were thick with passengers. As the ship drew slowly closer, they came into focus. The men looked like refugees from a disaster. Their faces were covered with unkempt whiskers and their clothing was torn, patched, and all but worn out. Their skin had been burned dark by the summer's endless sun.

Jared wondered what the men were thinking as they saw the people thronging the wharf. The population of the entire Yukon district probably numbered less than the crowd that seethed on the wharf, roaring with a single voice.

Welcome back, gentlemen, Jared thought, smiling an odd, off-centered smile. *I don't know whether civilization is ready for you, and I'm damn sure you aren't ready for it, but welcome back, anyway. I've waited a long, long time for this particular ship to come in.*

Settling his hat onto his head, Jared stepped out onto the wharf as the captain slid the stubby little steamer into its berth with calm efficiency, oblivious to the growing roar of the crowd.

"Show us the gold!"

One man's deep-throated bellow rose above the random shouts of the throng. Other voices took up the cry, then more voices and still more, until the ragged chant shook the wharf.

"Show us the gold! Show us the gold! Show us the gold!"

The prospectors at the rail whistled and waved. One of the

men bent down and slowly lifted the leather valise that had rested between his feet. Sun-darkened face split by a fierce grin, the miner struggled to hoist his precious burden high.

"How much?" yelled the deep-voiced man who had set off the first chant.

The miner's shouted response was buried beneath the new chant: of "How much? How much? How much?"

Jared smiled as the crowd's excitement hit him like a current of electricity, making the hair rise on the backs of his arms. Up to that moment, the Klondike rush had been like an avalanche poised on the lip of a precipice, more potential than reality.

But now, that avalanche had cut loose and started downhill, gathering momentum with every second.

While the short gangplank was being lowered from the *Portland,* Jared pushed through the crowd toward the edge of the wharf. The crowd surged and pressed forward in mindless urgency. Suddenly, Jared spotted a camera held above the seething crowd. The lens was aimed in the general direction of the *Portland* as the camera was triggered, the film advanced, and then the release triggered once more. The slender arms and graceful hands holding the camera could belong to only one woman. Brusquely, Jared shouldered his way through the crowd until he was next to her.

"Hello, Cass. Hell of a way to take pictures, without even looking."

"Not everyone is as tall as you are," she said in exasperation. "I can't see!"

"Want to be taller?" Jared invited.

The white flash of his smile was the only warning Cass got. His hands locked just beneath her rib cage, and she was boosted high over the heads of the crowd. All thought of objecting fled when she saw the pictures her new vantage point would make possible. She worked quickly, finishing off the roll.

"I have to change film," she called down.

Jared lowered Cass to the wharf again, letting her brush

slowly over the length of his body. Even when her feet touched the planks, he didn't release her. She twisted around in his hands to tell him that she could stand on her own two feet, only to realize that his braced body was all that was keeping the throng from pushing both of them into the bay.

A ship's officer came down the gangplank, blowing shrilly on a whistle, trying to clear a way through the crowd for the passengers. On either side of him, two burly seamen accomplished much more by simply shoving against the front rank of people in the crowd. As soon as the officer recognized Jared, the two seamen went to work clearing a space for him. Cass found herself positioned perfectly at the base of the gangplank as the first of the prospectors came down it.

Her first shot was of a grinning, roughly dressed man with a tangled beard. He was staggering ashore carrying a hundred and sixty pounds of gold in a wooden crate on his shoulder. The next picture was of a pair of miners walking uncertainly down the gangplank with a blanket suspended between them. Both of them were pale and gaunt, as though they were suffering from consumption. Halfway down the gangplank the men paused, coughing and panting from the exertion of carrying the blanket suspended on a pole.

The two heavily burdened miners finally reached the dock just as the blanket tore, spilling leather poke bags onto the wooden planks. One of the pokes fell open, disgorging a pile of gold dust the color of freshly shelled corn. The sight of the precious metal electrified the crowd. Men were shocked into silence for an instant. Then the crowd gave a hoarse roar and surged forward, nearly overwhelming the ship's crewmen who had gathered to keep the gangplank clear.

The two prospectors laughed. One of them bent over, scooped up a palmful of the coarse yellow dust and flung it over the nearby spectators like a priest scattering holy water. Men tried desperately to catch the wealth that pelted their faces like golden sleet.

"That's right," the prospector yelled. "It's gold! Now,

which one of you boys wants to earn twenty dollars by fetching a wagon and helping us haul this to the mint? I'm not going to work another day in my whole damned life!"

Twenty dollars was two weeks' wages. A dozen teamsters shoved forward, offering their rigs. The spontaneous action was too quick for Cass's film, but she kept shooting anyway, shifting position, trying to freeze the moment forever. Other prospectors came down the gangplank lugging their own piece of the golden mountain, their weathered faces split by grins.

"Your lumber scow has become a ship of gold," Cass said as she thrust the camera into the lightproof bag she wore tied around her waist. She changed the film by touch alone, working quickly, automatically.

"Or a ship of fools. Either way, it's not the first time for the *Portland*," Jared said, looking at Cass. His glance took in her sun-bright hair and unusual golden eyes, the full curves of her lips, and the shine of excitement coloring her cheeks. "She was a smuggling ship once. She carried hundreds of Chinese in from Canada." Jared looked around. "Where's Tea Rose?"

"I couldn't get the van close enough, so she stayed with it."

Jared hesitated, then was distracted by a long strand of Cass's hair as it lifted on the wind and brushed softly over his mouth.

"Sorry," she said, moving her head in a futile attempt to control her hair without removing her hands from the lightproof bag. Even as she worked, she decided that she would expose this last roll of film and then go back to the van. There she would set up her glass plate camera for an overview of the ship and the crowd and the new sun slanting over the bay.

Her hair lifted again, blowing across Jared's lips. Again, Cass apologized.

"I don't mind," Jared said slowly, tucking the flying hair behind Cass's ear with the same deliberation he had let her slide down his body. "I like your hair."

Her fingers fumbled with the film. The intensity in Jared's eyes as he watched her sent frissons of awareness through her, for she finally understood that he was not a man who would come and go from her life like a wild wind, leaving her alone and lonely.

The crowd surged against Jared. He flexed but didn't give way to the mindless urgency of the people who wanted to get just one inch closer to gold.

"I suppose you'll send the rest of your fleet to Alaska?" Cass said almost huskily, threading film by feel alone as she watched Jared's clear eyes.

"My ships will leave by dawn tomorrow," Jared said.

"And you? Will you be going?"

"No. I've had my gold rush. This one belongs to King."

Cass went very still at Jared's casual allusion to his brother. King had been the one topic that was never introduced into their wide-ranging discussions.

With a feeling of anger and helplessness, Jared watched the animation drain from Cass's face. It had been nine months since King had abandoned her, yet even the mention of his name made her flinch.

The wind tugged at Cass's collar. Beneath the cotton, Jared saw the gold chain. King's chain, King's nuggets, King's past, King around her neck like a slave collar. Angrily, Jared looked at the evidence that Cass was no closer to getting over King than she had been the day he left.

Without another word, Jared looked past Cass to the ship tied at the end of his wharf and tried to forget how very good she had felt in his hands, how her hair had caressed his lips, how she smelled like sunshine, and how her eyes were more beautiful than any gold ever found by man. Almost distantly, he wondered if he were going to be forever the third corner of the triangle of doomed lovers.

The thought both enraged and saddened Jared. He had never pursued lost causes in his entire life. Cassandra Thornton would be no exception. He would not be like her—wasting his life looking over his shoulder at the past, stumbling over and ignoring the possibilities that lay at his feet in the present. He had hoped she would get over King. He had been wrong. It was time to do what he would have done if Cass had been a business investment—cut his losses and get on with his life.

Jared focused on a flash of scarlet along the *Portland*'s rail. A tall, burly man in the bright red uniform coat of a North West Mounted police officer stood looking out at the crowd. Jared turned to the nearest crewman.

"See that Miss Thornton isn't shoved into the bay."

He went up the *Portland*'s gangplank without looking at Cass again.

67

Gold fever spread from the prospectors to the front ranks of the crowd, and from there, on up to the shore with the speed of chain lightning. The rough clothes of the newly wealthy prospectors only made the luster of the gold they carried more overwhelming. There was nothing about the miners to suggest that they were unusually intelligent or strong or quick. There was no more reason for Lady Luck to smile on them than on any of the men pushing and shoving on the wharf to get within touching distance of gold.

If they can do it, so can I.

It was in the mind of every man who saw the flash of precious metal. The words became a whispered vow that hummed like distant thunder long after the lightning had passed.

Tea Rose could hear it, feel it, almost taste it, from her vantage point atop the van. People hurried past her without a glance upward, caught up in the swelling thunder of mass delirium, having eyes only for the ship and the gold. She, too, had eyes for nothing else; but unlike the crowd, the victory she was tasting wasn't vicarious. The gold was hers. Half of what King had found, plus a marriage that would ultimately free both of them from unhappy choices. Never again would she fear the day when she would confront slavery or death—and would choose one or the other. Never again would she have to wear clothes and eat food she hated rather than offend the only person who stood between her and Tan Feng. Never again would she have to school every thought, every emotion, even the very beating of her heart, so as to give no clue to what kind of person lived within the deepest reaches of her mind.

Trembling with a feeling of wildness she had never before known, Tea Rose threw back her head and exulted in a silence that she was too well trained to break, even now.

I'm free of all of you! Do you hear me? I'm finally free!

An arm snaked around Tea Rose's ankles and jerked, yanking her feet out from under her. Waving her arms in a futile attempt to regain her balance, Tea Rose toppled off the van into the arms of Wong Ah Wing. She opened her mouth to scream, but all that came out was a whimper, as an ether-soaked gag was shoved into place. With a soundless cry of raw rage, Tea Rose sank beneath a breaking wave of midnight. Moving quickly, Wing dumped Tea Rose in the back of the closed van, untied the horse, and whipped the animal into a trot.

Few people gave any notice to the wagon moving away from the *Portland*'s berth, for their eyes were blinded by gold.

68

Cass fought free of the worst of the crowd until she stood where she had left the van. At first, she couldn't believe that it was gone. Assuming that Tea Rose had moved the wagon beyond the reach of the throng, Cass stood on tiptoe and looked over the heads of the people who formed the ragged edge of the crowd. Still, she saw no sign of the van.

"Miss Thornton! Miss Thornton!"

Cass turned and saw Billy Marrow, a stringy teenager who

made his living doing errands for the *Post-Intelligencer* staff. At the moment, he was running toward her, panting with the unaccustomed exercise.

"Mr. Marshall said for me to get whatever you have. He's getting requests from San Francisco and Chicago and even New York. The whole world is going crazy."

Quickly, expertly, Cass checked the fastening on the lightproof sack before she handed it over to the boy.

"Be careful, Billy. If anything happens to the film, Mr. Marshall will skin both of us alive."

"Amen," Billy said fervently. "I'm just glad I found you. When I saw your wagon going off, I—"

"What?" Cass interrupted. "Who was driving?"

"Don't know, ma'am. I only saw the back end."

"How long ago?"

"Oh, just a few minutes. I was clear over there, and it took me a while to—"

"Which way was the wagon headed?" Cass demanded, fighting to keep fear from her voice.

Billy gestured vaguely over his shoulder in the direction of the city. When he saw that she was going to ask more questions, he turned away with a mumbled apology.

"'Scuse me, ma'am, I gotta go. Mr. Marshall was real careful to tell me just how quick he wanted these pictures."

"Billy, wait!"

The boy waved, but didn't turn around or slow his pace. Within moments, he had vanished into the swelling ranks of people coming toward the wharf. Cass gathered her skirt in one hand, climbed up on a wharf piling and balanced precariously. The vantage point showed her only streets filling with more and more people, men and women hurrying toward the wharf, as word of gold swept through the city like lightning through darkness.

Cass leaped off the piling, held up her skirt in one hand and her camera in the other, and began running back up the wharf. By the time she had battled her way to the ship's gangplank, she was disheveled, panting, and half-wild with fear for Tea Rose.

"Jared!"

The anguish in Cass's cry spun Jared around like a blow. He ran down the gangplank toward her, shoving men aside, never looking to see where they fell. Without thought, Cass threw herself toward Jared, knowing that he would keep her from falling. Hard hands caught her by her upper arms, supporting her, as she sagged in relief at having reached him.

"She's gone," Cass panted. "Tea Rose is—gone. The van—gone. Ten minutes—maybe more."

Jared didn't waste time asking questions. He knew that Cass had given him all the important information she had. At his signal, two burly crewmen broke ranks and pushed their way forward. Forming a triangle with Cass in the middle, the men shoved through the crowd until they were standing where Cass had left the wagon. Jared issued crisp orders. The two men ran off in opposite directions, looking for more Duran Company employees to put out the alarm for the missing photographic van and its beautiful passenger. Jared thrust a key into Cass's hand.

"Wait in my office for word."

She shook her head.

"We won't be able to get a buggy through the streets," Jared explained impatiently. "We'll have to do it on foot. You're too—"

"I'm as strong as you are," Cass cut in.

"As stubborn, surely," he muttered, but wasted no time arguing with her. "Hold my hand tightly. If we get separated, it's you I'll be looking for, not Tea Rose."

Strong fingers laced between Cass's, joining her to Jared. There was a leashed power and vitality to his touch that was almost shocking. She had no time to resist or adjust. Swiftly, Jared set off for the city proper, towing her behind.

The celebration had spread from the waterfront to the entire downtown area. The sidewalks and streets were so crowded with people that streetcars had quit moving. Bicyclists and horsemen dashed through the streets, only to be brought up short by an immovable wall of flesh. Pistol shots and firecrackers split the air as though it were the Fourth of July.

Nowhere did Jared or Cass see her van mired in the crowd.

After thirty minutes, Jared pulled Cass into the shelter of a recessed doorway. Nearby, the owners of a store that specialized in mining supplies and dry goods had hired a three-piece brass band to attract attention. The noise was hardly necessary; the store was already jammed with men snapping up Northwest maps, food, tools, and weapons. Despite the crush inside, a salesman stood on a soapbox at the store entrance, shouting over the band's noise.

"Hurry, hurry, hurry! Get your mining supplies before they're gone! Shovels and picks, maps and compasses, dried beans and coffee, sugar and jeans. Everything a man needs to dig his fortune out of the Klondike. Hurry, hurry, hurry! While you dither, your neighbor's getting his and yours, too. Hurry, hurry, hurry!"

Men staggered out of the store laden with hundreds of pounds of supplies, men who had no better idea of where they were going than when they had first heard the name Klondike, just after dawn. The men were beyond rationality, drunk on the idea of poor man's gold.

"This is futile," Jared said, lifting his voice over the crowd's noise. "Whoever was driving the wagon obviously got out before the streets were this jammed. I'll take you to your home. Wait there for word."

"But—"

"If Tea Rose escapes," Jared said, talking over Cass's objections, "she'll try to get word to you there."

Escapes. If Tea Rose escapes.

"Tan Feng," Cass said, hopelessly.

Jared read the name from Cass's lips more than he heard her speak it. He nodded. There were other possible reasons for Tea Rose's absence, but none of them was very likely.

Tan Feng was a near certainty.

"I'll find her," Jared said, gripping Cass's hand. "Do you hear me, Cass? I'll find her."

BOOK
❧[III]❧

69

Somewhere, on the other side of the intricately carved shutters, it was raining. Tea Rose watched the trail of a single drop that had penetrated the shutters to reach the windowpane. The raindrop touched and slid down the glass like a single tear. Distantly, she wondered what it would be like to have the freedom to cry. The thought passed quickly from her mind, for her self-discipline had become as reflexive as breathing itself; she would attempt to see nothing, hear nothing, feel nothing, and most of all, she would remember nothing, not even how long it had been since she had once more become Tan Feng's possession.

Seven months, eight—Tea Rose had no way of knowing. She knew only that she had awakened from an opium stupor that could have lasted hours or days or weeks. Since then, she had existed in a self-imposed state of suspended animation, a prisoner with a life sentence, her jail a small room so cleverly hidden near the eaves of a three-story house that it didn't exist in the eyes of the rest of the world.

That was as it should be, for the rest of the world didn't exist within the room.

The only way Tea Rose knew that she lived within the walls of a tong brothel was that she could hear the voices of women calling to each other in Cantonese beyond her hidden room. Their conversations left no doubt as to their occupation. At first, Tea Rose hadn't been able to tell whether the house was located in Gum-Shan or China itself. She doubted the latter, but she did have opium-hazed memories of a timeless interval enclosed within an even smaller room that rocked, and was permeated by the smell of the sea.

After she had awakened within her prison room, the opium haze had cleared. She had quickly learned the trick of narrowing and half focusing her eyes when she stared through the shutters. With the new perspective, she had decided that the red-and-white flag she could barely make out beyond the shutters must belong to Canada. The city itself was probably Victoria or Vancouver. Either way, it didn't matter.

Both cities were beyond the reach of Jared Duran's influence.

Following that discovery, Tea Rose had devoted all of her mind to escaping on her own, rather than to hoping for rescue. She had been permitted out of her room less than a handful of times, but that was enough to tell her that the building was a maze of false walls and narrow, blind corridors that led in circles. The door to her prison cell was concealed behind a carefully constructed tin relief sculpture. A thoughtful Chinese might have seen through the decoration to the door that was concealed behind it, but an outsider would never have noticed.

Any aid from within the house was unlikely. Tea Rose was permitted to speak to no one but Wing or Tan Feng. Nor did she have anything with which to bribe the jailers in the room beyond. Once she had accepted the improbability of her own escape until circumstances were altered, Tea Rose—changed. She found in hatred the only kind of freedom left to slaves.

Lilac Rain was reborn within her daughter's beautiful body.

Quietly, calmly, using every bit of her insight into human

nature, Tea Rose set about to break Tan Feng. Between meetings with him, she played the lute, pursued the exercises necessary to maintain maximum flexibility on the couch, and continued embroidering the same scarlet tunic she had worked upon when Lilac was alive, the tunic that would one day be Tea Rose's "marriage" dress.

She didn't permit herself to dwell upon the fifteenth birthday she had celebrated in relative freedom as a white woman's half sister. Barely a year of such freedom as white men permitted their women had been Tea Rose's. Her sixteenth birthday had passed within tong walls, where the outer world didn't exist. Nothing existed but the lute and chess games and pillow books and Tan Feng's inexhaustible jade stem.

And hatred. Hatred existed, a burning core of black ice. Hatred expressed as Lilac had expressed it, in perfect discipline. Like her mother before her, Tea Rose eluded Tan Feng most completely in the very act of servicing him most skillfully. Her weapon was the valuable maidenhead Tan hadn't yet pierced. Her victory would come the day she goaded him into taking her as a man took a woman, not a boy; because she knew Tan wanted her that way—woman, not boy. He was obsessed with her jade gates and the pearl at the step and the pleasure pavilion beyond. It was to those parts of her body that he addressed his skills, trying to burst the cloud that he knew was within Tea Rose, just beyond his reach. He had never succeeded. When he could bear no more of her sensual baiting, he thrust into her lesser pleasure pavilion and rode her buttocks in a frenzy of release.

Wind rattled the shutters fiercely, announcing a new squall line coming in from the northwest. Rain squeezed between the tiny spaces in the shutters until the imprisoned window shed slow streams of moisture. The sight soothed Tea Rose in an odd way, as though the glass wept the very tears she herself could not. She touched the small window with her fingertips, reassuring herself that nothing had changed.

It hadn't. The thin, cold glass would shatter at a touch, yielding a thousand razor invitations to take her own life.

Lilac's example was never far from Tea Rose's mind; she knew that she always had the means of suicide, even without the glass window. Tea Rose hoped to find another way. Her reluctance came not from fear of death, but from a determination not to be defeated before she had some measure of revenge upon Tan Feng. At the very least, she wanted to goad Tan into breaking her maidenhead, thus depriving himself of much of her value. Even better would be to have the pleasure of killing him in an unguarded moment upon the couch.

And if she were to misjudge the moment and goad Tan Feng into killing her instead, that also would be a victory. Her death would deprive Tan Feng of the one thing he wanted in life even more than he wanted her pleasure pavilion to convulse in climax around his jade stem—he wanted enough gold to go to China and become a man of importance within his family and his province, and perhaps even within the Celestial Empire itself. Her sale would be the key to acquiring much of that wealth. All that remained to be seen was whether Tan Feng would take her, sell her, or kill her first; or if she would manage to achieve his death at any time in between.

Motionless, utterly silent, Tea Rose watched the window weep and thought of the single sharpened chopstick she had concealed between the layers of her bed pallet.

70

The storm that gave Tea Rose vicarious tears wasn't even noticed by Tan Feng. He was working over account books that had just begun to show profits once again after the disastrous twenty months following Lilac's death. Jared Duran, the man who had been the mainstay of Tan's labor market, had systematically poisoned the well from which both men had drunk so profitably. Laborers from the Soong Li Tong were now shunned by many Seattle businessmen. When Tan had made inquiries as to the reason, it had been made clear to him that the situation wouldn't change so long as he remained head of the tong.

The loss of revenue had seriously undermined Tan's position within the tong, as had continuing raids by policemen who refused to stay bribed. He had barely managed to hang onto power long enough for his elder brother's middle son to arrive from China. It had been a bitter disappointment for Tan not to be permitted the pleasure of putting his own son in the position of tong leader, but the decision had not been his to make. His nephew's succession had been swift and brutal; Tan had slit Kwan's throat, Wing had strangled Spring Moon, and their bodies had been displayed for the edification of the ambitious among the tong. Any plans to displace the new tong leader had died with Kwan and his paramour, who somehow had found enough courage to aid Kwan's plots against Tan.

Sighing, Tan pushed aside the abacus and entered the final numbers in the account books. He reached for his opium pipe, then withdrew his hand. Too much opium dulled his mind. Too little simply aroused his lust, making him easier prey for Tea Rose's supple, enthralling body. She had proven to be a delicious, cunning warrior in the flowery battle. He had managed to keep his obsession for her in check only by keeping her hymen intact.

Someday, he was afraid she would goad him into taking her in that final, fundamental way. He knew she wanted that, just as he knew Tea Rose withheld her own climax for the same reason Lilac had—to punish him, to declare herself the victor in the flowery battle, absorbing his essence and giving none of her own in return.

As always, the thought of Tea Rose made Tan's turtle head stir and stretch beyond the margin of its soft shell. When the blunt, sensitive tip prodded against his silk clothes, he smiled in anticipation of going to Tea Rose's tiny, hidden room and locking the door behind him. He would let the first battle be won by her hot, clever mouth. The second time, he would bind left ankle to left wrist and right to right, rendering her excitingly helpless, and then he would coax forth the rosy pearl, teasing and seducing until either he or she could bear no more.

Each time they had remained locked within the tiny room, he had lured Tea Rose closer to the brink of the Ultimate; and each time, he had been the one to be pushed over.

Tan Feng smiled. There was no way he would rather spend a rainy afternoon than locked in scented battle with Tea Rose. She was in every way a supremely worthy adversary, and perhaps today's battle would be the magic one in which Tea Rose would learn the exquisite defeat of clouds and rain. And if she didn't pour out her essence the first time or the second, there was always the third time or the fourth, when he would be more in control of himself and his hungry jade stem.

"Lord Tan?"

Tan's head snapped up, in the same instant that a gleaming knife appeared in his hand.

"Walk less softly, Wing, or I might mistake you for one like Kwan," Tan said, returning the knife to its concealed forearm sheath.

Wing bowed. "Forgive me, lord."

"What do you want?"

"Word has just come that the Thornton female and Jared Duran have a piece of paper that means we must permit her to search for Tea Rose in the tong buildings. The police can do nothing for us this time except warn us. Soon the female will be here."

"She is an abscess on my crotch," Tan muttered. "She has been to every Chinatown from here to San Francisco. May her children rot within her womb."

"Permit me to kill her, lord."

"Not until you can kill Jared Duran as well," Tan said

dryly, "and that will be a long time indeed. In Canada, we are both equally strong—or weak." Tan shrugged. "A stalemate is not a victory, but neither is it a defeat."

"But the female neither mends his clothes, nor cooks his food, nor warms his bed, nor bears his children. She is not related to him by clan or marriage," Wing said calmly. "No man would miss such an insignificant thing if I killed her."

Tan grunted, but didn't bother to explain to Wing that the woman a man doesn't have will always be more fascinating than the one he does have. Wing, who had a rather lazy turtle head, did not appreciate how a man could become obsessed by one specific woman, much less a woman with big feet. Wing would fuck a dog if that dog had lily feet. That was one of the reasons Tan trusted Wing; unlike Kwan, Wing didn't desire Tea Rose.

"No killing," Tan said shortly, "unless Tea Rose's room is discovered. Then, we will kill who we must, hide the bodies, and go to another place." He made a dismissive gesture. "In any event, we are leaving soon for the Klondike." He smiled and added, "There is no more lucrative place to sell women than in a town full of newly rich peasants."

Tan stood up abruptly and strode across the room. "I will be with Tea Rose to see that she makes no sound. Stay close to the Thornton female. If the room is discovered, lance my abscess with your sword. I grow weary of not being able to sit in comfort for more than a few days at a time."

In Tan's bedroom, Wing lifted away the large tin sculpture that decorated the far wall. Tan unlocked the hidden door and walked inside, closing and locking the door behind him. He stood motionless until he heard the sound of the sculpture being returned to its place, concealing the presence of the tiny room from anyone outside.

Tea Rose was kneeling on her pallet in the correct position of a female waiting to serve her master. The pose was not only graceful, it was also necessary; there was only space in the room for a narrow pallet and an embroidery frame, from which hung lush folds of scarlet silk. Ignoring Tea Rose, Tan went to the embroidery frame. Needles and strands of the finest pure gold thread waited close at hand. Inside the wooden frame, pulled taut by its tiny prison, a golden phoenix opened its wings above the surrounding flames.

"The embroidery is almost complete," Tan said.

"Yes, lord."

Tan stroked the silk with appreciative fingertips. "You have done well, precious one."

"You are very kind to this worthless female. The honor you give to my insignificant self is much too great."

The high, perfectly pitched music of Tea Rose's voice made frissons run over Tan's skin, as though a trickle of ice water had slid without warning down his naked spine.

"You have much of your mother in you."

Tea Rose bowed deeply over her invisible hands. "Thank you, most generous lord. My mother was a skilled practitioner of the flowery arts. If I can but touch the least part of her shadow, I shall be greatly honored."

Tan listened to the nuances of tone and word while his fingertips stroked the golden embroidery that had been created with such patience and skill. He wondered what Tea Rose thought about while she worked alone in the tiny room. Did she hate him for her mother's death? Did she look forward to his visits as a break in her isolation? Whom did she talk to in the silence of her mind? Was she learning to want him? Did blood thicken her jade gates at the thought of his hands undressing her and his fingers gently penetrating, testing the resilience of that fragile, vastly valuable skin that protected the inner pavilion?

"Look at me, my tender opium flower."

Slowly, Tea Rose's head came up. Wide, faintly tilted black eyes focused on Tan Feng. For an eerie instant, he thought he saw a demonic flicker of fire; then he realized it was only the reflection of a crimson bridal dress in Tea Rose's pupils. Even so, another frisson of unease went over him, sharpening his senses to the glittering edge he relished. It was almost like looking into the eyes of Lilac Rain once again.

"How is your mother?" he asked suddenly.

"Dead, lord."

"Do the dead speak?"

"I do not know, lord. I am not a mystic. I am but a sing-song girl trained to play upon flutes of living jade."

"Do you hate me for your mother's death?"

"All things die, honorable Tan. Why should I hate the generosity of the great man who feeds and shelters my worthless body?"

"Do you miss your half sister?"

"I do not remember a half sister, lord."

"If I caned your breasts, would you remember?"

Without looking away from Tan's eyes, Tea Rose unfastened her tunic top and let it slide from her shoulders. Beneath the tunic, she wore a simple wrapped blouse, which came undone with a few motions, leaving only the silk bodice that held her breasts close to her chest. She unfastened the bodice and let it fall away.

Tan stared into Tea Rose's clear, unblinking eyes and felt his own excitement rising. It was as though the past two decades had never been, and a young Lilac knelt before him once more, her words and body gracefully, consummately submissive and her fury a black flame burning invisibly. He couldn't see or hear or taste or feel that flame, but he sensed its feral presence as surely as he counted his own accelerating heartbeats.

And he smiled.

"I will burn much incense in praise of the Great All," Tan said in a low voice as he walked to Tea Rose. He didn't stop until he was so close to her that his clothes brushed her face. Slowly, he opened the folds of cloth, savoring the special ache in his groin that told him he would be inexhaustible today, his body endlessly responding to the sleek violence hidden within Tea Rose's thousand veils of discipline. "Surely, no other man has known two such women."

Tea Rose slid her tongue out, then slowly closed her jaws, letting her small teeth sink into the soft pink organ of sensation, making it quiver in glistening invitation.

The battle had begun.

* * *

By the time a heavy black carriage pulled up in front of the house next door and disgorged four dark-coated men, plus Cass and Jared, Tan Feng had lost two skirmishes to Tea Rose's skilled mouth and small hands. Naked, sweating, still shuddering in the aftermath of touching the Ultimate, Tan stripped away the last of Tea Rose's clothes and admired her as she half reclined on the heaped pillows.

"Surely, my lord is not tired?" Tea Rose asked softly.

Watching Tan's eyes, Tea Rose's hands slid from her breasts to her thighs to her knees and then farther, until her slender fingers embraced ankles whose delicacy was equaled only by that of her wrists. Slowly, sinuously, she lifted her legs until her heels brushed her still flawless coiffure.

Tan made a low sound that was half sigh, half curse, all pleasure, as blood returned in a rush to his crotch.

Tea Rose slid her hands down her bare legs until she was lying normally once more. Then, slowly, she raised her legs again, watching Tan's eyes. She had learned that of all the positions her flexible body could attain, this was the one that excited Tan almost beyond bearing, for it seemed to render her helpless, and at the same time it fully revealed to him the object of his obsession.

The position was exciting for Tea Rose, as well, for she knew that one day she would goad Tan into breaking her hymen by taunting him with the one square inch of her that he wanted but refused to damage by taking. She might look utterly helpless, but she was never more dangerous to him than when she offered the pink, forbidden depths of her pleasure pavilion. She knew it as well as he did, and the knowledge made her heart beat heavily in anticipation.

Would this be the day of her revenge?

"Ah, the honorable turtle stirs," Tea Rose said. "He is thirsty, great lord. Let him drink from me."

"But you have no water for him," Tan said, circling the forbidden territory with his fingertips.

"Where there are clouds, there is surely rain."

Tan looked at Tea Rose and smiled, despite—and because of—the taunting sexual challenge of her body. He knew what she was after, and why. He also knew that the battle excited her, even as it excited him. The closer each came to the edge of the precipice, the more intense the excitement became for both of them. Tan had one advantage in this kind of flowery battle that was also a disadvantage. Because he knew the unspeakable ecstasy of the Ultimate, he was doubly lured to its edge; and he knew from past experience just where that edge of oblivion was. Because Tea Rose had never touched the Ultimate, she did not know how far she could safely go. The act of taunting him made her jade gates glisten with excitement, as much as the agile tongue that was curled out to him in invitation right now.

"My precious poison," Tan said hoarsely.

Knowing he should not, unable to resist, he circled her jade gates repeatedly with his fingertip, then slowly pushed inside. The frail barrier waited as always, half a finger deep. Some maidenheads could be carefully stretched to allow access without breaking, and some were so narrow as to present almost no barrier at all to a modest jade stem; but Tea Rose's veil was both wide and fragile, and Tan's jade stem was not modest. There was no way to cheat a future buyer. Sighing, Tan Feng slowly retreated from the precipice.

"You could have *Pao* knit me a new maidenhead."

At first, Tan thought that he had spoken aloud. When he realized that Tea Rose had followed his thoughts so exactly, unease streaked through his body.

"Pao is not fit to gut fish, much less to perform an operation of such delicacy on your pleasure pavilion. Her last patient died of infection."

"The girl was sickly. I am strong." Tea Rose flexed the muscles of her buttocks and saw the visible leap of Tan's response. "If I have no water for your turtle, honorable lord, it is because your liquid pearls have never filled my humble pavilion," she said coaxingly. "Is it not true that even the most well-used pump must be primed? If that is true, then what of one that has never been used? Would it not need even more fluid to make it work properly? I would overflow for you, my potent lord, if you would but show me the way."

Tan laughed at the whimsical, musical earnestness of Tea Rose's voice. Humor was a new addition to the flowery battle, one which pleased him enormously, for it told him that she was becoming very confident of her skills. He wanted that, for Lilac had been most vulnerable when her confidence had been highest.

Slowly, Tan Feng shifted until he was kneeling at Tea Rose's jade gates. Carefully he looked only at her eyes, not quite trusting himself to see the essence of his *yang* so close to the essence of her *yin*.

"Sweetest of poisons, do you want me so badly, then?" Tan whispered, watching Tea Rose's eyes, caressing her languidly with his hands. He saw the leap of excitement in her when he allowed his jade stem to probe very lightly at her gates.

"Oh, yes," Tea Rose said, her breath catching, unable to contain her anticipation of the victory that was suddenly so very close.

"But you are not a pump," Tan said, smiling, despite the cost of controlling himself. He measured the excitement in Tea Rose and decided that it was finally time to introduce a new weapon into their flowery battle, the weapon that he had withheld in the hope of just such a moment of vulnerability on her part. "You are a pearl, and that most precious of jewels should be polished only by the softest of cloths."

As Tan spoke, he shifted position until his tongue found the pearl Tea Rose's excitement had revealed.

For a moment, Tea Rose was too surprised by the reversal in their normal roles to be disappointed at the postponement of her victory. The sensuous moisture that she had stubbornly refused to supply was suddenly flowing from his tongue over her jade gates, increasing her sensitivity enormously. Her first impulse was to huddle around herself protectively until she understood the new responses of her body, but she knew that she must do nothing of the kind. If Tan realized that he had disconcerted her, she would be giving him a potent weapon in their battle.

"My lord," Tea Rose said urgently, "I cannot pleasure you when we lie this way. If you would but let me turn and—"

Abruptly, she stopped speaking, unable to believe what she thought she had just heard.

The sound came again, Cass's voice calling her half sister's name—*and it came from just outside the room.*

71

"Tea Rose! Tea Rose, where are you?"

Before Tea Rose could cry out in answer, Tan's hard, broad palm clamped over her mouth. Swiftly, he shifted position, pinning her in place with his right arm, her hands and heels above her shoulders, rendering her utterly helpless.

"If this room is discovered, your half sister will die." Tan said very softly.

Tea Rose wondered how Cass had found her, and if her sister had been so foolish as to come alone. Between the silence and the sound of rain came the murmur of other voices, speaking English, men's voices. Still, Tea Rose made no attempt to cry out, for the voices could have belonged to the tong's customers.

"Tea Rose! Answer me! What have they done to you?"

The anguished cry came from no more than a few feet away, but Tea Rose made no motion, no sound.

"Empty room," Wing said loudly. "See see? Come, female. Come quick quick. Waste time much much."

"If so much as your stinking breath touches her, I will cut off your shriveled balls and feed them to you."

The whiplash of Jared's Cantonese electrified Tea Rose.

Jared would not be fool enough to walk unguarded into Tan Feng's den. Jared would have men with him, men whom he could trust. Most important—if Cass were hurt, Jared would kill Tan Feng no matter who tried to intervene.

Watching Tan's eyes, Tea Rose deliberately sank her teeth into his hand until blood flowed. His face flattened into a grimace of pain, but he didn't remove his hand. Instead, he sharply increased the pressure against her mouth, wedging her jaw open with the side of his hand, preventing her from biting any more deeply into his flesh. He stopped just short of breaking her jaw. The pressure he exerted made it impossible for Tea Rose to utter any more than a low sound that just as well could have come from the creaking, storm-battered house.

Tea Rose felt the pain only dimly, for her body was flooded with adrenaline called by the silent, savage battle. Writhing, twisting, she fought to free her mouth from its living gag and her legs from Tan's imprisoning arm. Tan watched, and smiled grimly, despite the pain from Tea Rose's teeth. He moved his hips in slow counterpoint to her writhing, holding her down, and at the same time rubbing his turtle head over her straining flesh as the familiar, always new fire claimed him. It was deeply arousing to watch Tea Rose's discipline come apart beneath the maddening knowledge that rescue was so close at hand, and simultaneously, so far from her grasp.

"Lie quite still, sweet poison, or it will be the skin of your belly that drinks my liquid pearls rather than your thirsty pavilion."

The words meant nothing to Tea Rose. She continued to writhe futilely, while rain drummed down, muffling the sounds from the next room. Then she heard the voices retreat, withdrawing into the hall, fading, dying, drowning in the same rain that made Tan's words a soft, flicking goad, like the feel of his blood slowly dripping from his hand to pool in the hollow of her neck.

Finally, Tea Rose's struggles succeeded in freeing one hand. Blindly, she groped among the pillows and bedcovers until her fingers found the chopstick she had so patiently sharpened. With a soundless snarl, she rammed the point into Tan's side.

He grunted as much in surprise as in pain, for his ribs had taken the brunt of Tea Rose's attack, breaking off the point of the chopstick. Even as she raised it for another strike, Tan shifted. The stiffened fingers of his right hand punched into her diaphragm, driving out her breath, making it impossible for her to groan, much less to scream for help. He wrenched his hand from her mouth, struck her wrist a numbing blow, and threw aside the broken, bloodied chopstick that had fallen from her useless fingers.

No sooner did Tea Rose's lungs begin working again than Tan calmly, deliberately closed her mouth and nose with his hands, keeping her just on the edge of consciousness and life. She forgot to fight, to defend herself, to hold onto discipline; she forgot everything in the primal, excruciating need to breathe. She didn't hear the grinding of steel carriage wheel rims against wet cobblestones as Jared and Cass left. She didn't feel Tan's hands releasing her. She didn't see Tan's slitted black eyes watching her, measuring her, waiting for the moment when the realization of her own survival would act as an aphrodisiac, ripping away more veils of her self-control.

Suddenly, Tea Rose felt the agonizingly beautiful rush of air back into her lungs. After a few moments, the scarlet and black cleared from her vision, revealing Tan kneeling between her thighs.

"Lift your ankles once more, black butterfly."

Too dazed to fight, Tea Rose obeyed with the ingrained reflexes of a lifetime of submission.

Instead of delivering the pain Tea Rose had expected and earned, Tan's fingers brought pleasure as they skillfully polished her jade gates. Slowly, she realized that he wasn't going to have her caned or beaten for attacking him. Hardly able to believe that she had escaped painful retaliation or death, Tea Rose stared up into Tan's black eyes.

"Do not look so frightened," Tan said gently. "Did your mother not teach you that, in the heat of flowery battle, blood sometimes flows?"

Before Tea Rose could gather her wits to answer, she felt Tan's fingers dipping into her vulnerable body and then retreating, spreading a sensual moisture over her hot skin, rubbing slowly, tenderly polishing the pearl of her pleasure.

"I was wrong to withhold *yang* from *yin*," Tan said after a time of silence and touching that had made the pearl sit high on its soft cushions. "It's time that you know the pressure of me within your beautiful gates."

At first, Tea Rose didn't understand—and then she realized that it was Tan's jade stem at her gates, not merely his hands. It was his smooth, blunt turtle head parting her, not his fingers. The knowledge swept through her in a wave of excitement unlike anything she had known since she had stood on top of the photography van and exulted in her freedom.

Somehow, some way, she had snatched an important victory from utter defeat.

Tan saw Tea Rose's excitement and firmly bridled his own sexual response. Very slowly, he penetrated her, stopping just short of the precious maidenhead.

"I can go no farther without rain," Tan said coaxingly. "Just a small amount, my sweet poison. There is no rush to the Ultimate."

Tea Rose looked down and saw Tan's blunt turtle head slowly coming to her, retreating, returning, stopping short of the instant when she would be victorious. Excitement spread up through her, making her breath shorten with impatience and the radiating pleasure that came with anticipation of her victory.

"Tan," she said, the word more groan than name.

He made a low sound of satisfaction as he felt Tea Rose rain softly on him.

"Yes, little opium flower, like that," Tan murmured, penetrating and retreating, holding himself in check until sweat stood on his dark skin. "If you want me, you will have to rain just a little more, yes, precious one, yes, a little more, a little—"

The excitement that Tea Rose had felt returned redoubled as Tan deftly plucked the pearl at the jade step, sending heat racing through her blood until she shuddered with impatience for the victory that she sensed was so close to her grasp. This time, it wouldn't elude her. This time, victory would be hers.

And then it was hers, exploding through her in waves of pleasure.

Tan felt the hot bursting of Tea Rose's cloud wash over him. For a handful of seconds, he fought grimly to hold himself in check, for there was nothing he had ever wanted more than to penetrate the frail hymen and feel her convulsing around him. But he could always have the victory of complete penetration. He could have this particular victory only once, her essence washing over him repeatedly, and his own essence withheld.

When Tea Rose slowly grew still, Tan withdrew and then took her as he always had, thrusting into her lesser pavilion. Even then, he didn't release his self-control. He waited until her eyes opened and focused on him in the disbelieving aftermath of having been one with the Ultimate for the first time in her life.

"My most precious poison," Tan said, sliding his finger past her jade gates, stroking her hymen. "Most precious, indeed."

Tan smiled as he saw the realization dawning in Tea Rose: she had lost, not won. His hips moved slowly as he found her still-shimmering pearl, plucked it as he had before, and watched knowledge of defeat and renewed climax take Tea Rose simultaneously, repeatedly, relentlessly; and he was, as he had always been, inexhaustible.

72

Usually, Cass loved Seattle's winters, when moisture was drawn in shades of silver and gray and black across sea and sky and land, everything merging into one. But now, she had come to associate winter with despair. First her father, then King, then Tea Rose—separate losses defined by the same turning of the season from autumn sunlight to winter rain, her emotions going from denial and hope to acceptance and defeat. King and Tea Rose were gone, and nothing Cass could do would change that fact.

She looked from the portraits of Tea Rose to those of her father and King. She had caught those moments, fixed them within silver frames—and lost the people themselves, the past repeating itself endlessly, the wagon leaving another town behind, steel wheel rims grinding up the past to dust, which the wind blew away—everything gone, farther away each day, each hour, each heartbeat.

Unconsciously, Cass touched the heavy necklace she never removed, counting the nuggets with her fingertip, feeling the smooth, water-polished gold without really being aware of it any more than she was aware of the slow rain of tears down her cheeks.

Why didn't you tell me what you were looking for, Papa? I loved you. I would have tried to understand. At least, I would have known why you kept turning away from me—

Her fingertips moved on to the heavier strand of chain, where large nuggets lay heavily against her skin.

Have you finally touched the sun, King? Is it as beautiful as you dreamed? I hope so. I hope that something finally equaled the fire in your eyes and in your soul. God knows that I didn't.

Her fingertips came to the Klondike nugget and paused, as she remembered the man called Mule Dryden and his message of riches for Tea Rose.

I'm sorry I didn't understand sooner, Tea Rose. I couldn't believe that everyone didn't want the same things I did, a home and love and—

Love.

Better that I had wanted gold. It, at least, is tangible, real, possible. But you already knew that, didn't you, Tea Rose? My God, what a price you paid for my ignorance. I'm sorry, sister, for all the good that does you or me.

There were too many things she had understood too late—her father, King, Tea Rose. And Jared. Jared, most of all.

Jared, who had given Cass so much in the past eighteen months and never asked for anything in return. When she had floundered in her attempts to understand Tea Rose, Jared had been there to help out. When Cass's earnings hadn't covered the extra income needed for Tea Rose, Jared had set up a trust in Tea Rose's name and paid Cass from the trust, despite her protests. When Tea Rose was stolen, Jared had helped Cass to pursue Tan Feng as relentlessly as the Furies themselves. When she succumbed to discouragement and self-doubt, Jared had taken her to dinner or to a concert or to a gallery; and always he had talked to her about her art and his dreams for a future when the countries of the Pacific Rim were bound by a web of business and marriage, a limitless future calling to man with a voice more beautiful than gold.

Cass had listened and had finally understood that the hot currents of life and love that she had yearned for all her life ran more deeply through Jared than through any man she had ever known. She hadn't meant to discover that, any more than she had meant to fall in love with him. But she had. Each day, each meeting, each conversation—each was a stitch taken with a golden thread, binding her to him slowly, almost secretly, until she awoke one morning and finally knew the difference between infatuation and love.

Too late.

She wanted to be Jared's lover, his woman, his wife, to have the privilege of sharing his home and his future, of bearing his children, of cooking his meals and caring for him in a thousand small ways.

Too late. Just as she had learned too late about her father, King, Tea Rose.

Lost in the past, Cass didn't hear the soft knocking at her front door or Jared's voice calling to her. She didn't hear his footsteps approach the sitting room of her studio and then stop in the doorway.

Silently, Jared looked at the woman washed in golden lamplight. Tears glittered amid her long eyelashes and shone on her cheeks, tears as golden as the nuggets her fingertips were running over ceaselessly, as though she were telling a private rosary. Jared looked from the necklace to the framed portraits arrayed across a bookcase. Though there were portraits of Thad and Tea Rose and even of Jared himself, Jared saw only the image of King's untamed eyes staring at the world; and Cass staring back through the imprisoning glass, crying.

The sadness and rage Jared had hoped to purge himself of long before swept through his blood, and along with them, the desire he felt for the woman who wept golden tears over the irretrievable past.

"He wouldn't have wanted your tears."

Jared's voice was low, resonant with suppressed emotion. Slowly, Cass turned toward him, surprised, not by his presence but by the fact that he had brought up the one subject that both of them had tacitly avoided for eighteen months: King's brief affair with Cass.

"I know," she said. "He wanted very little from me. Just my body."

"That's not true."

"I think it is. Of all that I offered to King, my body is the only thing he took."

"Did you offer those things to King, or to the man you thought King was?"

Cass closed her eyes for a moment, then smiled with such sadness that Jared had to clench his jaws against a sound of protest. He didn't want to care about her, but he did. Was it the same for her with King? Did she fight a losing battle against loving him?

"You, Tea Rose, Lilac—" Cass whispered. "You see people so clearly that it's—frightening. Yes, I offered those things to the man I thought King was. But did you know that part of King *was* that man? Part of him wanted a home and a hearth and a woman's love. Part of him, part of me—not enough for a whole life for either one of us. I should have seen that, but I didn't. I was blinded by what I thought was possible."

"Anything is possible."

"Yes," Cass said, sighing. "But some things aren't very likely, are they? For instance, it's possible that we'll find Tea Rose, but it's not very likely, is it? Not quickly. Not before Tan Feng ruins her."

"'Ruins' her?"

"Please don't bait me, Jared," Cass whispered. "You know I'm not quick or clever or intentionally cruel. To say *fornicate* takes too long and *fuck* is too coarse."

"Is that what King did? Did he ruin you?"

"Most people would say yes."

"What do you say?"

"King gave me all that he could."

"And you still love him."

Slowly, Cass shook her head. The motion made light run in golden streams over her hair and the nugget necklace and the tears on her skin.

"Don't lie to me or to yourself, Cass. You still love King."

"No. I simply don't hate him. Is that wrong? Should I hate him because we were wrong for each other?"

Jared said nothing as he watched the delicate fingertips stroking and counting gold nuggets. It was impossible for him to believe Cass's denials of her love for King when she clung so tightly to the one part of King that he had been able to leave with her.

"For a time, I think I did hate him," Cass continued. She sighed. "Just as I hated you and Tea Rose for being right about King. I discounted what you said about King being the wrong man for me because I knew you wanted me. As for Tea Rose, I couldn't believe that a girl so much younger than I knew more about life and men than I did. Finally, I realized that you both had been right, and then I hated myself for being so stupid as to see only the part of King I wanted to see."

"You were innocent, not stupid," Jared corrected softly.

"Now who's lying to whom?" Cass countered dryly.

Jared's smile was so brief and yet so beautiful that Cass stopped fingering the necklace and extended her hand to him as though in greeting.

"You should smile more often, Jay."

His face became expressionless, polite, as remote as the echoes of wagon wheels rolling by in the night.

"I'm sorry," Cass said, lowering her hand to her lap. "I've no right to criticize your smiles or lack of them." Closing her eyes against the tears she couldn't control, she leaned back into the overstuffed chair. "I know you haven't forgiven me for misjudging King and for setting off the chain of events that condemned Tea Rose to slavery again. Nor is there any reason you should forgive me. I was wrong, but other people have paid for my mistakes, Tea Rose most of all."

"Don't blame yourself for—"

"Why not?" Cass interrupted, her voice flat. "You blame me. You've hated me since the day Tea Rose was stolen."

"You're not making sense. I don't hate you, nor is it your fault that Tan Feng was shrewd enough to pick the one day when there was such chaos in the city that he could steal a woman in full daylight and never be noticed."

"If Tea Rose had been given to me by the court, do you think Tan Feng would have stolen her? And if he had, do you think the American and Canadian governments would have been so indifferent to the outrage? No, of course not," Cass said, talking before Jared could. "So why didn't we go to court? Because we knew we would lose. And why would we lose? Because—"

"Cass," Jared interrupted.

"—because I was immoral, loose, fallen—a woman no better than she had to be, a hussy, a—"

Jared's hard hand covered Cass's mouth. *"Stop it."*

For a few instants, there was only silence and the scalding flow of tears over Jared's hand, and then he could bear the heat of her skin no longer. He lifted his hand away, as though he had been burned.

"I don't hate you," he said in a clipped voice.

Her eyes opened. Their golden depths were magnified by tears.

"Such a polite lie," Cass said, her smile eclipsed by despair. "Thank you for trying, I guess, but it's not necessary to hide the truth from me. I already know what you think of me. Since the day Tea Rose was stolen eight months ago, you've barely been able to tolerate touching me. You would have nothing to do with me if it weren't for your promise to find Tea Rose. Well, you needn't worry about that any more. I absolve you of your promise. You're free, Jared.

"Once, just once, I'm going to do something right. I've worked double hours in the past eight months and saved every bit of money I could for this. I'll find Tea Rose. We were so close to her a few days ago in Vancouver. I know it. I'll find her if it's the last thing I ever do on this sad earth."

Jared was too shocked to comprehend fully what Cass was saying. He was still caught by her ruined smile and the fact that she was so sensitive to the nuances of his emotions that she could precisely pinpoint the day when he had decided to distance himself from her as much as possible.

"Cass, it's not what you think."

"Please don't," she said, trying to smile again, failing again. "You forget, I've seen you with people you care about, with Tea Rose and King and Lilac. You touched them, Jay. You don't touch me."

"I tried to," Jared said. "Twice. And twice you turned away from me. I'm not like you, Cass. I won't destroy myself over someone who can't be loved."

"'Can't be loved'?" Cass repeated, her voice rising and then breaking. "Why? Because I was King's lover? Did you turn your back on Lilac because she was Tan's or my father's or God knows how many other men's lover before she was yours?"

"I didn't love Lilac, not in the way you mean, not in the way you loved King, or in the way your father loved Lilac, or in the way I would have loved you."

"'Would have'—'can't be loved.'" Cass made an odd sound and clenched her hands until her nails dug into her soft palms. "Why was my infatuation with King such a heinous sin that you can never forgive me? Was my virginity so important to you?"

Jared hesitated, then told the blunt truth. "In all but one way, I didn't give a damn about your virginity. A woman takes her first man in ignorance. She takes her last man in full knowledge of herself as a woman."

"If you believe that, then why do you hate me so?"

"You had given yourself to no other man. The fact that you gave yourself to King was a measure of your feeling for him. That was the single important fact of your virginity." Jared saw Cass's pale skin and golden tears and downturned mouth, and he had to fight not to take her into his arms. "Please believe me, Cassandra, *I don't hate you.*"

"Please believe me, Jared, *I don't believe you.*" Cass's laughter was more painful than her tears had been. "Never mind, never mind, never mind. It's all gone, all in the past. Dust." She took a deep, shaking breath and stood up. "So what brings you here tonight? Do you have more news about Tea Rose?"

"No. John told me he had seen you three times since we came back from Vancouver, and each time you looked more pale. Are you ill?"

"Yes. No." Cass set her fists in the small of her back and stretched. "We were so close to her, Jay. So close I felt as though I could touch her. And then—nothing. I've thought about that a lot. That and other things."

"King," Jared said, his voice soft, unflinching.

"I think about King much less than you believe. We were together for barely eight weeks. He's been gone nearly ten times that." Cass looked broodingly at Tea Rose's photograph. "Often I think about my sister, whom I knew for much longer than King, and understood even less well. I think about Lilac Rain and my father, and steel wagon wheels grinding everything to dust. I think about you, Jay. You saw so much that I wasn't ready to see.

"And sometimes, when it has rained for forty days and forty nights, I sit in this chair and pretend that you don't hate me, that you will walk through the door and take me into your arms, and we will comfort each other as though I were Tea Rose and Lilac had just died."

"Cass," Jared began, but he could say no more without losing his self-control.

"But I'm not Tea Rose, and Lilac died eighteen months ago, and Tea Rose is Tan's slave anyway, and I've paved my personal road to hell with the very best of intentions," Cass continued, her voice as soft and colorless as her lips. She turned away from Jared and looked at the forgotten hearth fire. "It's cold in here," she said absently, rubbing her hands over her arms. "Lately, it always seems to be cold."

73

Cass didn't know that Jared had come to stand behind her until she felt his hands moving gently over her arms, bringing warmth to her chilled skin. When she turned toward him, he lifted her into his arms, walked the few steps to the overstuffed chair and sat down. In silence he held her, stroking her back soothingly, feeling the scalding glide of her tears against his neck and the fine trembling of her body against his. Slowly, he rocked Cass.

"If you're crying for King or Lilac or Tea Rose," Jared said after a time, "then go ahead; your tears aren't wasted. But if you're crying because you think I hate you—" Jared bent until his lips were so close to Cass's skin that he could sense her heat. "If you're crying for me, please don't. I don't hate you, Cass. I could never hate you, even if I tried." Then he whispered, "And God forgive me, I have tried."

Once, twice, three times Jared sipped the tears from Cass's eyelashes. At the first touch of Jared's lips against her eyelids, Cass went very still. He froze, expecting her to turn away from him once more. Instead, she turned toward him, lifting her face as though to the sun.

"Jay," Cass whispered. Her hands crept up the front of his soft wool suitcoat and, trembling, rested on his cheeks. She brushed her lips over his chin, the line of his jaw, one corner of his mouth, kissing him blindly, trying to tell him how much it meant that he truly didn't hate her. "I don't deserve your forgiveness, your friendship, but I need—this."

Eyes closed, feeling nothing but the butterfly brush of her lips, Jared told himself that Cass meant no more by the caresses than her simple statement of truth: she needed his friendship and comfort. So he pulled the pins from her hair and stroked its unbound softness with a slow, invariable rhythm, holding her gently, trying to ignore the heavy rush of his blood that nearness to Cass had brought ever since he first had seen her eighteen months before.

For long minutes, Cass was soothed by the slow stroking of Jared's hands and the masculine textures of cleanshaven cheeks and silky mustache. She drew a deep, contented breath and sighed as she leaned against him, enjoying his warmth, his resilience, his strength. When his weight shifted subtly, she pressed closer in response, holding onto him as though she were afraid he was going to get up and leave. But he didn't. He simply held her in return.

"Better now?" Jared said, his voice husky.

She nodded. The motion rubbed the scented softness of her hair against his cheek, caressing him. His body tightened in helpless response.

"Cass," Jared said finally, almost roughly, "I think it's time for me to go."

"Why?"

There was silence, then Jared said, "Because all you want from me is friendship. I want more than that from you. I always have."

Cass straightened until she could see Jared's face clearly.

He made no attempt to hide the silver blaze of his eyes, the passion he had been so careful to conceal from her since King had left. Cass lifted trembling hands to Jared's face as she said his name over and over again, kissing him between each word, trying to tell him that it was all right, that she wanted more from him, too; but all she was able to say was his name.

"Cass?" Jared whispered.

"Yes," she said simply.

"What does that mean?"

"Whatever you want from me, whatever I have to give is yours."

Cass felt the passionate shudder Jared couldn't control, heard the thread of a groan he couldn't suppress, and tears flowed down her cheeks once more as she realized how much of himself he had hidden from her.

"Are you sure?" he asked in a raw voice.

"Let me show you how sure I am," she said, lifting her face, seeking his mouth with her own.

"Wait," Jared said, pinning her in place with his strong hands. "I have to be certain you understand. I've wanted you too much for too long. I don't trust myself to share a few kisses and then get up and leave. Once I kiss you, I won't be able to stop short of taking you."

The idea that she could affect Jared's steel self-control to that degree stunned Cass. His self-containment was one of the things that had both fascinated and frightened her about Jared since their first meeting; and it was the thing that had made King seem so much—safer.

"I understand," she whispered.

"God, I hope so," Jared said, his voice almost rough as his hands came up to frame her face, "because it's too late, and you're too close. I want you until I'm shaking with it."

Despite Jared's hunger, he lowered his mouth to hers by

slow fractions, as though to give Cass time to change her mind. With a small sigh, she stretched up to meet him. The brush of his mouth over hers was incredibly sweet. The tip of his tongue tracing her lips, tasting her smile, tasting her, made her breath come out in a husky moan that was Jared's name. Golden tendrils of sensation and desire licked out from the pit of her stomach, making her shiver. He felt her trembling and could wait no longer. With a quick, almost fierce motion, he opened her mouth beneath his.

Jared tasted of coffee and brandy and something much more elemental, a flavor as unique as his signature. His taste swept over Cass's senses, consuming her, completing her— then he withdrew and she whimpered softly, wanting more of him.

"Again," Cass breathed, opening her eyes slowly. "Please, Jay. You taste like sunlight, all clean and golden and hot."

"Cass—my God," Jared said, feeling his self-control sliding away with every breath, every accelerating heartbeat, every glance at her parted lips and glistening tongue. "Do you know what you're doing to me?"

"Is it what you're doing to me?"

He smiled, making her catch her breath and wonder why she had ever thought him cold.

"What am I doing to you?" he asked softly.

Cass started to speak, looked into the diamond brilliance of Jared's eyes, and forgot everything else. She eased her fingers into his thick, dark hair and pulled his head down to hers.

"Let me taste you," she said. "Let me—"

Cass felt as much as heard her name whispered against her lips, then Jared's tongue was in her mouth, caressing her, tasting her, stroking her in slow, deep rhythms. She kneaded his scalp with slow, catlike pressures of her fingertips, holding him close and then closer still, tasting him, trembling with pleasure as the kiss lengthened and deepened into a sensuous melding that was unlike anything she had ever experienced. When one of his hands moved from her hair to her neck, and from there to her shoulder, her breasts tightened in a rush that made her ache. She wanted him to stroke her, undress her, and kiss the taut flesh that hungered for his mouth.

Not knowing what she did, Cass twisted slowly in Jared's lap, trying to get closer to him as his fingers traveled from her neck to her waist, leaving buttons undone, revealing the full rise of her breasts beneath her thin camisole. When his hand slid under the cloth and took the weight of one breast, she couldn't mask her soft sound of surprise. He went very still.

"Cass?" Jared said hoarsely. "Didn't you understand what I meant?"

"Yes," she said, twisting slowly, increasing the pressure of his hand on her breast. "I just didn't understand how good it would feel." She gasped and shivered as his thumb rubbed over her stiffening nipple.

"Do you like that?" Jared asked, watching her face, seeing sensual response replace surprise.

Her answer was another soft whimper of discovery as he caught the velvet hardness of her nipple and rolled it slowly between his fingers, tugging at her, hearing her breath break into fragments of pleasure. Her uninhibited response went to his head and his groin at the same time, making him dizzy. He clenched against the claws of need that were sinking into him more deeply with each sweet sound Cass made.

With quick, urgent motions Jared unbuttoned Cass's dress. The thin ribbons of her camisole slid softly through Jared's fingers until that cloth, too, parted. Her breasts were full, taut, quivering with her broken breathing, and their tips were hard with desire.

Through half-opened eyes, Cass watched Jared's face as he looked at her. She saw the leap of blood in the vein at his left temple, the smoky intensity of his narrowed eyes, and the tiny flaring of his nostrils as he took in a quick breath. Suspended in sensual anticipation, she waited for the burning caress of his mouth. When it didn't come, she felt a disappointment so great it shocked her. Before she could ask why he held back, he spoke.

"You're even more beautiful than I had dreamed."

Jared's deep, husky voice was like a caress. Cass's breath came in sharply, then out again in a soft rush of sound, as she watched him bend down to her. Slowly, he turned his face from side to side, stroking her sensitive nipples with his mustache, tasting her with tiny flicks of his tongue until her back arched in an instinctive movement that was both invitation and demand. Jared laughed softly and took the tip of one breast into his mouth, shaping the taut, velvet flesh to his tongue, tugging on her with a suction that was both tender and fierce.

The golden tendrils in the pit of Cass's stomach burst in a shower of sensation that tore a small sound of surprise from her lips. This time, her startled cry made Jared smile with the knowledge that he was giving her a kind of pleasure new to her. When her fingers threaded through his hair and held his head to her breast in sensuous demand, he responded by redoubling the gentle assault of his mouth, caressing her nipples until she twisted slowly in his lap, her skin flushed and her breathing broken.

Jared stroked Cass's waist and the curving invitation of her hips and thighs, unfastening and pushing away cloth with each caress until there was nothing beneath his palm but smooth skin and a burnished gold triangle of hair. Cass responded to the gentle pressure of his palm between her legs by parting them, opening herself to his touch with an unthinking abandon that would have shocked her if she had been aware of it; but she was aware of nothing except the satin rasp of his tongue over her nipples and the golden bursts of pleasure shimmering through her body at each rhythmic tug of his mouth.

Restlessly, hungrily, Jared's hand stroked Cass's stomach, her legs, the smooth warmth of her inner thighs—and each motion of his hand separated her legs a bit more, until finally, there was no barrier to touching the hot, secret center of her body. Still he held back, fighting to control his own hunger, wanting to give Cass every kind of pleasure a man could give to a woman. With delicate care, his fingertips repeatedly circled the hot folds of flesh between her legs, barely touching her, inciting her to a new threshold of sensitivity.

It was like being brushed by fire. Cass moaned and drew up one knee in a sensual reflex that was as old as man and woman and passion. Jared could no more resist her wordless invitation than he could stop his own heart from beating rapidly. His finger slid between soft folds of skin, penetrating her in a slow, deep caress that unraveled her. He felt the incredible softness that caressed him in return, felt the liquid heat of her response, and knew she welcomed him within her body.

When Cass felt the hot overflowing of her response, her eyes opened in shock. She tried to apologize, but she didn't know what to say. Her whole body tightened as she fought against the liquid waves of pleasure that sought release with each sweet sliding motion of his hand.

"Jay, stop, I—" The word became a moan as Cass bit her lower lip in an attempt to control the shimmering, glittering heat that pulsed between her legs.

Reluctantly, Jared lifted his head, releasing the rosy nipple he had shaped into a rigid velvet peak. But he didn't release the satin heat of Cass, for he had dreamed too long of being within the sultry intimacy of her body.

"What's wrong, love?" Jared asked huskily.

The ball of his thumb stroked across the tight bud that passion had lured from its hiding place within her softness. At the first touch of his thumb, she gasped. Heat washed through her, spilling over, bathing his hand. She tried to speak, but all that came out was a ragged moan as she convulsed gently around him, heat welling up in liquid pulses of pleasure until she cried out once more.

When Jared realized that Cass was trying to apologize, he bent and kissed the words away from her lips.

"I've dreamed of this a thousand times," he said, kissing

Cass between words, tasting her even as he redoubled the sliding, gliding pressure of his fingers within her, wanting to touch all of her, to know all of her, to feel the sensuous pulses of her response when he immersed himself in her. "But I never dreamed that you would come to me so hotly, so perfectly. I love your heat, your cries, your passion bathing me. Don't fight against yourself, love. Let go and come to me."

Cass tried to breathe, to speak, to move, but she could do nothing except close her eyes as his sensual penetration continued, dissolving her bones. Jared's name on her lips became a litany of wondering pleasure as he dipped into her body repeatedly, deeply, caressing her most sensitive skin with her own silky heat, rubbing the swelling bud of her pleasure until it burst into a thousand brilliant shards. She cried out as ecstasy splintered through her, wave after wave ravishing her, giving her completely to Jared.

Smiling, despite the harsh urgency of his own need, Jared watched Cass's climax radiate through her body, flushing her creamy skin with a passionate heat. Cass's long eyelashes quivered, then opened, surprised to discover that the room was filled with lamplight rather than the glittering darkness of sensuality. She looked down the length of her naked, flushed body, framed in the unfastened folds of her own clothing. Jared's lean male hand was nestled intimately between her open thighs. With a sense of shock, she realized that he was still within her. A flood of embarrassment stained her smooth skin. She looked into the silver blaze of his eyes and knew that he had watched her, had watched his hand caressing her, had watched her abandon herself to him in the golden lamplight with no thought of modesty or restraint.

"You're very beautiful, Cass. Don't be embarrassed," Jared murmured, smiling down at her as she lay in delicious deshabille across his lap. "No, not yet," he said, gently preventing her from closing her legs or covering herself. "I like looking at you. And I think you like me to, don't you?"

Even as Cass blushed, a delicious shiver of ecstasy lanced

up through her, then another and another, echoing the slow rubbing of his thumb, motions she saw as well as felt. From the corner of her eye, she caught Jared's slow smile and knew that he was feeling her response as clearly as she did, for he was in the center of her gathering sensual storm.

"I'm glad you like it," Jared whispered, bending down to Cass. "Next time, it will be my mouth instead of my hand, and you'll like that, too."

The shocked sound Cass made was lost in the deep, slow kiss Jared gave her. By the time he freed her mouth, any protest she might have had was forgotten in the golden tendrils of pleasure shimmering through her once more.

"Hold on to me, love," Jared said.

Cass made a startled sound as he shifted beneath her suddenly. She laughed softly as he stood up, still holding her in his arms. She had forgotten how strong he was beneath his civilized clothes. The thought of peeling off those layers of cloth and sinking her fingers into his resilient, muscular warmth excited her.

"What an odd little sound," Jared said, smiling down at Cass as he carried her toward her bedroom. "Am I tickling you?"

Cass shook her head. She stretched until she could kiss the hard line of Jared's jaw. "I was just thinking of how good you'll feel without your clothes." She heard her own words and blushed, then forgot any embarrassment when she felt the shudder of response that went through Jared's powerful body. "You don't mind?" she asked, her voice low, hesitant. "I don't seem to be able to control myself with you, Jay. You make me—shameless."

The husky confession sent an exquisite, agonizing heat through Jared's groin. He closed his eyes and hung onto his self-control with every bit of discipline he had.

"I'm glad," he said finally, "even though hearing you say that makes me want you so badly that it's killing me."

Despite Jared's urgency, he was gentle with Cass when he reached the bedroom. He lowered her to her feet, freed her from the tangle of unfastened clothing that hadn't yet been cast aside, and then stripped off his own clothing with impatient movements. When he had finished, he straightened and found Cass staring at him. He stood motionless, watching her as she measured his power and potency.

"May I touch you?" she whispered.

"Yes. Of course." Jared shuddered with a need that denied the calmness of his voice. "Oh, God," he said hoarsely, "touch me, Cass. I've waited so long—"

Her fingertips traced the line of tendon and muscle in his shoulders, his arms, his chest. She kneaded his hot flesh with clear pleasure, savoring the male textures of hair and muscle, nuzzling through the thickness of his chest hair with her tongue, tasting him, kissing him, caressing him until he couldn't control the primitive sounds of pleasure that she drew from him with her mouth. When her hands rubbed slowly down his chest to his abdomen, his breath came in and wedged. She hesitated, looking up at him in a wordless question.

"Whatever you want, as much or as little," Jared said, his voice rough. "Just touch me. Feel what you do to me, what you've always done to me from the day I first saw you."

Jared's breath came out in a low groan as Cass's fingers explored the length of his erection. She made a sound of mingled pleasure and surprise when she stroked the blunt tip.

"So smooth, like satin," she murmured. "Hot." She made another soft sound of discovery. "I can count your heartbeats." Half closing her eyes, smiling languidly, she circled him as though she were warming herself at his fire. "Do you like this, too?"

The slow, sensuous, sliding pressure of her hands was rapidly stripping away Jared's control. He braced his body against the climax he felt growing within, a wild pressure demanding release. He had hoped Cass would want to touch him, but he hadn't expected it; not like this, with such sultry curiosity and open pleasure.

"I like it—too much," Jared said through his teeth.

"Too much?" Cass looked up, puzzled.

"I want to be inside you when I come. Does that shock you, Cass?"

Her eyes widened into pools of gold as surprise and sensual curiosity fought within her. A few moments later, curiosity won. "And I want to watch you," she said in a husky voice. "Does that shock you, Jay?"

"Cass," he groaned. "My God—"

She felt the gentle leap of his flesh between her hands, saw his features flatten and darken as though he were in agony; but it wasn't pain she had brought to him with her words and her touch. She knew she had given him ecstasy, and she smiled with the knowing.

She was still smiling when Jared lifted her onto the bed and followed her down onto the soft mattress. He put his hands beneath her knees, flexing her legs, opening them, and then he sheathed himself inside her with a single fierce motion. She was hot, willing, slick, yet so tight that he was shocked. She whimpered at each of his movements. The sounds were soft, but he heard them, and remembered that she wasn't accustomed to having a man inside her.

"I'm sorry," Jared said in a low voice, holding himself completely still. "Are you all right?"

Slowly, Cass opened her eyes.

"Love, love," he said, kissing her gently, "I'm so sorry. I didn't mean to hurt you."

"Hurt me?" She shivered and moved her hips languidly, loving the feel of their bodies so deeply joined. "Jay, if you give me any more pleasure, I'll die of it."

Cass's words transformed him, renewing him between one heartbeat and the next. He laughed softly and rocked in slow, powerful counterpoint to her own movements, and he drank the soft whimpers of ecstasy from her mouth.

"Cass," he whispered, biting her lips, calling her name, rocking against her, feeling her shimmering heat overflow. "We'll die together, locked together, moving. Come with me, love. Come with me."

Cass tried to answer, but she couldn't speak, she couldn't breathe, she could do nothing, for she was transfixed by the elemental fire radiating up from their joined bodies. Jared felt her ecstatic shivering in the instant before his own control was burned away. With a hoarse sound, he sank into her, holding her fiercely while they burned as the phoenix had burned, ecstatic death and fiery rebirth in one.

74

King had long since decided that hell was cold, not hot, and was furnished with frozen river cobblestones rather than crimson flames. In the Klondike, fire was friend, not enemy; and there was never enough of fire's precious light and warmth to go around. Up on the mountains, and along the slopes and the sinuous curves of Bonanza and Eldorado, the world was white and still, and sunlight came for only a handful of hours each day. Most of the time, there was only the light of lanterns, stars, and the changing moon reflected from the billion flakes of ice.

The surface of the land was pure and silver-white, as unsullied as heaven and as frigid as hell. The true paradise was subterranean, at the bottom of mine shafts whose flame-pinkened mouths breathed plumes of smoke into the dark sky. Deep in the mine shafts it was warm, for fires burned there ceaselessly, melting soil and gravel until they had thawed enough to give way before pickaxe and shovel.

The windlass that straddled the China Girl's original mining shaft squealed as King turned the crank, drawing up two tandem buckets of half-melted pay dirt. Grunting with effort, he lifted the heavy wood buckets and walked quickly to the sluice box, which would be useless until the melt came. He dumped the pay dirt onto one of the many huge piles that had been built up around the sluice. Gravel rattled and soil slopped down the side of the pile, freezing solid before King had walked back to the shaft's glowing pink mouth. He went to the woodpile, gathered up fuel, and loaded it into the buckets. His breath turned to fine ice crystals that sank and merged with the ground fog as he hurried back to the windlass.

"Coming down!" King hollered into the shaft.

"Yo!" Poke called back.

King lowered the buckets and then slid down the rope himself, ignoring the makeshift ladder he had nailed to the inside of the narrow shaft.

"How's the fire in the east drift going?" King asked as he tucked sticks of wood under his arms.

"'Bout like a fire in a icebox," Poke said, shooting a stream of tobacco juice between his teeth. "By the time the danged wood thaws, there's enough smoke in the tunnel to choke a regiment of Injuns."

King smiled. "But all over the tunnel walls you can see the gleam of gold reflecting the flames."

Poke's soot-blackened face split into a grin that displayed few teeth, each of them heavily stained. Winter scurvy had been hard on Poke. "That you can, Wolverine. Right pretty sight, all that gold just waitin' to be dug out. How much you reckon you have by now?"

With a shrug, King turned aside. "Won't know until the melt comes and we can sluice out the gold."

"Bet by the end of summer you got two, maybe three hundred pounds of gold."

Laughing, King shook his head. "You've been eating too much smoke," he said, whacking Poke on the shoulder. "Any coffee left, or did you drink it all?"

"Coffee, beans, and bacon in there," Poke said, jerking his chin toward one of the tunnel mouths that opened up from the main shaft. "Course, you got to crawl on your belly in frozen muck to get to 'em."

"Poke, I've spent so much time on my belly in this damned hole, I'm beginning to think I'm a fire-breathing snake."

King crouched over and duckwalked partway down the tunnel until the ceiling lowered, forcing him onto his hands and knees. The last few feet, he was on his stomach, levering himself forward with his elbows and the sides of his feet.

The beans, bacon, and coffee were at the end of the drift, where fire smoked and flared fitfully, surrounded by frozen earth.

Despite the barely breathable air, the warmth made the ragged tunnel a haven. For a moment, King just lay quietly and listened to water drip from overhead and turn to steam with a hiss at the first touch of flames. When he reached for the coffee and food, he discovered that the dying fire had kept everything thawed but not actually warm. He grabbed the plate, snaked out backward until he could sit up, and ate quickly. Even though it was at least fifty degrees warmer down in the tunnel than it was above, his coffee was dead cold by the time he finished it.

"She 'bout burned out?" called Poke.

"Close."

"Well, let's get to her. Can't dance, and it's too damn cold to plow."

King traded tin plate and cup for a pickaxe and went back into the tunnel. Working with the economical motions of a man who had done the job countless times, King raked out the fire and stacked the charred, smoldering remains at one side of the tunnel. He was careful to waste as little wood as possible, for it had become almost as precious as gold. All the easily gathered fuel had long since been burned, and chopping wood took time and energy that men would rather use looking for gold.

Grunting, swearing at the occasional ember that burned through his clothes, King gouged out the ceiling above the former fire. Soggy earth and pale gravel rained down on the hot tunnel floor, sizzled, and cooled. King scraped the pay dirt past his body to where Poke could load the buckets. It was grueling, grinding labor, the kind that had been done throughout history by slaves whose only other choice had been certain death.

But King was a free man who chose to slave for gold, and Poke was a free man who slaved for good wages and the chance to work alongside the man who had become a legend among prospectors: Wolverine Duran, the man who had killed a wolverine with his bare hands and found gold in its hollowed-out den. The fact that King had shot the wolverine and had found gold in a hoary marmot's burrow made no difference to the men who told and retold the story of Wolverine Duran, the man who lay down with the bitch goddess and got up dripping gold.

Working quickly, despite the awkward conditions and the cold that seeped into the marrow of his bones, King enlarged the tunnel and sent the scrapings back to Poke.

"How's she look?" Poke called anxiously.

"The drift's moving left."

"But it's still there?"

"It's still there, Poke, white and shining as the teeth you lost."

The other man's laughter came up the tunnel, followed by the popping sound of his mittened hands clapped together in glee.

"Then there's more gold waitin', sure as God made little green apples."

Poke's glee drew a smile from King, but no more. The first summer had been a heady rush of gouging out pay dirt and sluicing it, cleaning the riffles of gold so that more pay dirt could be gouged out and sluiced, so that there would be more gold smiling back up at him through veils of water. Despite the grinding physical labor, each day had been its own reward. The cache of leather pokes beneath his cabin floor had swelled silently, replete with dust and nuggets the size and smoothness of tears; and still the layer of pale gravel had gone on and on, a stone river permeated by the tears of the sun. King had never encountered a placer deposit like it—capricious, inexhaustible, infused with riches.

When the melt came, King had already decided that he would hire other men to gouge out the pay dirt below, while he sluiced out the riches above. There would be plenty of men looking for work after the melt, hordes of gold-hungry men who had arrived too late to stake out a piece of the golden mountain. They would work for wages, and King would work like one of the damned, awake night and day guarding the sluice, breaking up arguments among bickering, disappointed men, overseeing the gathering of firewood and the stoking of the fires so that the frozen ground could be worked, making arrangements for the shipment of gold to Seattle, and a hundred other things in the bargain—

King bit back a curse. The finding of gold was one thing; the mining of it was another thing entirely, and the less appealing of the two by far. Whenever he had struck it rich before, he had gotten word out to Jared, who had come in and organized either the mining or the sale of King's claim, whichever made more sense.

But those days were gone. King had seduced and abandoned the golden woman his brother had wanted to marry; now, King's partner was a little China girl who would be his wife come this time next year.

When you tire of your bitch goddess and come to the city once more, I'll cook your favorite meals, hang upon your words, bathe you slowly, caress you if you desire, pleasure you until you think you're dying.

King had thought of Tea Rose's words more and more often in the bleak winter weeks when gold lay frozen within pay-dirt piles, waiting for the melt. He had spent more than a year in the Klondike, more than a year without a civilized woman's silky voice and satin skin, more than a year in the rough company of other men or work-hardened whores, more than a year laboring in the bitch goddess's rocky, frozen bed. He could feel gold's hold on him loosening with each passing day.

Maybe this time, I'll be free. Maybe this time, the bitch goddess will sing to me no more.

Even as the thought came to King, so did the answer— Tea Rose's words whispering to him as seductively as gold itself.

When the bitch goddess sings sweetly to you again, I'll mend your clothes, pack them, prepare food for your trip, and send you away without sad words and wailing.

When, not if. King would go in quest of the ineffable once more, for he hadn't found it here, where gold was all around him, yet still not touching him, not in the way he needed to be touched—to know something so perfect that it consumed him utterly.

Marriage to me won't be a jail, it will be a kind of freedom such as you've never known before.

King hoped Tea Rose was right. But even if she were wrong, at least she wouldn't be hurt by his leaving. He wouldn't lie alone and haunted in the sliding, uneasy instants before sleep, wondering if somewhere a golden woman wept for him, tears falling, sliding between the cracks of the earth, tears turning to gold that called to him in a thousand beautiful voices; and the golden woman left behind, crying. Tears sliding into the earth, turning to gold, whispering to him, crying, turning and returning, cycle without end.

75

Jared awoke slowly in the hour after dawn with Cass's warm weight pressed against his side. He turned and saw the bright mass of her hair falling over her cheek and his shoulder. The golden strands were turned molten by the light streaming through the partly opened curtains of her bedroom. Gently, he smoothed the hair back from her face. She made a soft sound and snuggled closer to him, nuzzling his hand, seeking his touch even in her sleep.

The realization made both tenderness and desire flare within Jared. Two months of being Cass's lover hadn't diminished his passion for her. If anything, he wanted her more now, not less.

And he feared that wanting more each day, not less. He hadn't meant to become her lover. He hadn't meant to be anything at all to her so long as she wore King's brand like a slave collar around her slender neck. But when she had wept because she thought Jared hated her, his ruthless instinct for self-defense and survival had been dissolved by Cass's tears. He had held her, kissed her—and now he lived in dread of the day King would return to claim the woman who wore the symbol of his greatest accomplishments around her neck.

Will it be this spring? Will King come downriver with the broken ice, a fortune in his hands and the sun in his smile? Or will undiscovered gold keep him up there for one more summer, one more winter, one more spring, a year in which Cass might come to love me more than she loves King?

Cass stirred, murmuring, then rolled over and fitted her back spoon-fashion along Jared's torso. The back of her thighs rubbed over the top of his, and her hips nestled against the male flesh that she took so much pleasure in arousing and then holding within the teasing restrictions of her mouth or the satin depths of her body.

There was no doubt in Jared's mind that, whatever the state of Cass's heart, her body was his in an elemental way. Their mutual sensuality was a constant revelation to him. He had known nothing like it with any other woman, even the highly accomplished Lilac Rain. And Cass's reaction had told him that she had known nothing like it either, even with King.

Yet still she wore King's necklace, locking herself within a prison of gold, locking Jared outside.

Broodingly, Jared stared at the links of gold shining up between parted strands of her hair. Cass wore no other jewelry, not even a ring. Just the necklace that he had once wanted to snatch off her, but had not, for it served to remind him how much of a fool he was to lie next to her, wanting her, loving her—and knowing that it was just a matter of time before he lost her to King once more.

Cass, Jared asked silently as he ran the ball of his thumb lightly down her naked spine, *why can't you love me enough to leave the past behind?*

There was no answer but her sleepy murmur of pleasure as his hand glided down to her buttocks, tracing the line of darkness dividing the full feminine curves. Gently, he eased her legs apart and caressed the incredible softness within her. He sensed her changing as he touched her, felt her body becoming even softer, more sultry, and he wondered what her dreams were like.

Is it King you dream of when your body is hot and slick, or is it me?

At the thought that Cass might be dreaming of King, Jared withdrew his touch. Cass rolled restlessly onto her back, murmuring a sound that could have been Jared's name.

The sleepy, satin allure of her was too great for Jared to resist. He slid his leg between hers, found her humid softness once more, and shuddered with need when she melted at his touch. Even though she was far more asleep than awake, the sweet, familiar pressure of his body between her thighs made her open her legs to receive him. His mouth shaped first one nipple, and then the other, into a sensuous peak while her hips moved beneath him in dreamy offering. When he felt her melting once more, he penetrated her with slow intensity, growing inside her until they were melded into a single body, and she came apart around him in a rush of heat, calling his name. The sound of his name fragmenting on her lips rent Jared like raw lightning, convulsing him.

"Love," he said huskily, and then he could say no more, for her climax had become his, unraveling him in a series of savage, exquisite pulses that left him spent within her.

"What a wonderful way to wake up," Cass said dreamily, nuzzling Jared's ear and stroking the sleek muscles of his back. "You should spend the night more often, and to hell with the gossips who have nothing better to do than peer out at the world through dusty curtains."

Jared laughed softly. The motion stirred him within her.

"Mmmm, that's nice, too," Cass said, moving her hips.

Jared groaned at the wonderful sensations she caused in his still erect flesh. He whispered her name and began to move in slow counterpoint to her motions, enjoying the gliding intimacy of being joined to her.

"It's a miracle I haven't gone broke in the last two months," he said, bending down to bite her lips softly. "I'm only at the office half the time I used to be."

"The miracle is called a telephone," Cass murmured, biting his tongue gently. "It lets you be in two places at once."

"Speak of the devil—"

"Hmmm?" Cass murmured.

"That ringing sound from downstairs."

"The telephone?"

"The telephone," he agreed.

Reluctantly, Jared rolled aside, freeing Cass to answer the importunate intruder. She looked around for her robe, but found only the dress shirt she had hurriedly stripped from Jared the night before. She shoved her arms through the sleeves and ran barefoot downstairs, shirttails flapping. Jared followed a few moments later, wrestling with slacks that hadn't been cut to accommodate a fully aroused man.

A single look at Cass's smiling, excited face told Jared that his worst fears had come true: King was coming back to Cass.

A combination of grief and rage swept through Jared that was almost blinding. He spun around and walked away, not trusting himself to overhear Cass's joy. He went to the kitchen and made coffee with barely restrained violence. By the time Cass hung up, the water was whistling shrilly through the kettle's metal spout.

"Jay!" Cass called, her voice high with excitement.

"In here."

"They found Tea Rose!"

"What?"

"Tea Rose! A group of twenty Chinese men and women went through Chilkoot. The Pinkertons are certain that Tan Feng was among them and if Tan was there, so was Tea Rose. Oh, Jay, we've found her at last!"

Palms flat, Jared leaned against the countertop and tried to gather his thoughts, but all he could think of was how grateful he was that it hadn't been King's voice that had made Cass glow with excitement. Jared took in an aching breath and expelled it harshly, frightened by how deeply rooted within him Cass had become. He hadn't meant for it to be this way.

"Slow down, love," Jared said, pulling Cass into his arms and rocking her against his body. "Start all over. The Pinkertons traced a group of twenty Chinese, and Tan Feng was among them. Where did they go?"

"The Chilkoot."

"What?"

"The pass. The Royal Canadian Mounted Police logged them through last week, which means they're somewhere in the interior by now."

Jared shook his head in disbelief. "A group of twenty?" he asked quietly. "Tan must be in more trouble than I thought. He's staking everything on one roll of the dice."

"What do you mean?" Cass asked with alarm.

"The Canadians have a detachment of Mounties at the top of the Chilkoot to enforce one rule: Every man who crosses Chilkoot into the wilderness has to carry with him enough equipment and supplies for a year—two thousand pounds."

Cass thought for a moment. "A ton of food per person? How are people carrying that kind of load?"

"A hundred pounds at a time," he said dryly. "The usual practice is to lug your ton over to the shores of one of the lakes—Lindeman or Bennett—and start building boats or rafts to float everything downstream to Dawson. But wives get a break. They only have to carry an extra hundred pounds of food, so long as they're traveling with their husbands."

"Most gold seekers are men. One ton of equipment and supplies per man. That's madness."

"Or simply a shrewd effort to keep Americans out of Canadian gold fields. Whichever is the truth, Tan is mounting a major expedition. Even if half of his people are so-called wives, he's still hauling better than ten tons of supplies with him."

"But why?"

"Because I drove him out of Seattle and was close to forcing his own tong into driving him out of Vancouver. He's desperate. He's gambling everything on one last turn of the cards."

"What's he planning to do?"

Jared grimaced, thinking of all the reports he had been reading, information gathered by the Pinkertons and funneled back to him. "There are between twenty-five and fifty thousand men in tent cities on Lindeman and Bennett," Jared said finally. "They have nothing to do but drink and wait for the thaw. Tan Feng will offer them—diversion."

The color drained from Cass's face. "Tea Rose," she whispered.

Jared gathered Cass into his arms. "Not yet. Not on the trail. Tan hasn't changed. He's still fixated on Tea Rose's virginity. He won't spend that until he can get the highest price for it. That will be in Dawson, where men have more gold than they have ways to spend it."

Cass fought against the despair rising up within her when she thought of what her own ignorance had cost Tea Rose. There had to be something Cass could do, some way to redeem past mistakes.

"Wait," she said, her voice vibrating with hope. "Tan Feng is trapped until the melt. All we have to do is go to Lindeman or Bennett and—"

"Don't even think of it," Jared said harshly, cutting across her words. "Do you have any idea what conditions are like on that trail?"

"I was raised on gold rushes and in gold camps, remember?"

"Not gold camps like this one, you weren't. I've got six ships in and out of Skagway and Dyea all the time. It's hell on earth in the interior. They've stripped the slopes around Lindeman and Bennett of trees for firewood and boats, they're five hundred miles from Dawson, and there aren't a handful of Mounties to keep the lid on in the whole damned territory. There's hunger, disease, and brutality of the worst sort. It's no place for any woman, much less a decent one like you."

Cass smiled slightly. She looked at herself, barely covered by her lover's shirt, her body still slick from their mutual passion. "Decent?"

Jared's breath came in with a sharp sound as he saw the shadow of pain on Cass's face. He knew it hurt her to be his mistress rather than his wife; and he also knew that he would never ask her to marry him while she wore King's necklace. Yet, each time Cass hurt herself stumbling over the nature of their relationship, Jared couldn't help sharing her hurt.

"Damn it, Cass, you know that's not what I meant."

"I know," she said quickly. "Besides, the state of my *decency* is my own concern, not anyone else's."

"Not even the man who's your lover?"

"Not anyone," she said, her voice raw. "You've given me so much, Jay. Please don't think I was hinting for more."

Blindly, Cass reached down to wrap the shirt more completely over her nakedness. Jared had shared himself with her as no other person ever had; not King, not her father, not anyone. For that, she loved Jared as she had never loved anyone, not her father, not even King Duran. Jared had given her life itself and had never demanded one thing of her in return.

"The important thing is that Tea Rose is in one place and can't be spirited away until the melt, which is at least four weeks away," Cass said, her voice as level as her glance. "That will be plenty of time for us to take a steamer to Skagway and take the trail from there to Dyea and over the pass. It's only thirty miles from the Chilkoot to Lake Bennett."

"I see I'm not the only one who's been keeping track of the Klondike," Jared said. "Or has King been writing to you, too?"

"No. King would have no reason to write to me," Cass said, her voice low. "Is he—well?"

Jared grimaced at the husky hesitation in Cass's voice. "He's ass-deep in gold. What more would King ask of life?"

"Health. Most of the stampeders are ill, some of them desperately so."

Jared grunted. "No case of miner's two-step is going to bring down Wolverine Duran, if that's what you're worried about."

"Wolverine?"

"King," Jared explained. "Somewhere between Chilkoot and Dawson, King was ambushed by a starving wolverine. It was touch and go, but he survived, killed the wolverine, ate it, and added a whole new dimension to his legend."

"I didn't know."

"Really? I'm surprised he didn't send you a wolverine fang for that damned necklace."

"It's not just King's necklace," Cass said, touching the gold defensively. "My father's nuggets are part of it as well, and the clasp once belonged to my mother. It's the only part of her trousseau that wasn't sold to buy supplies for Papa's photography."

"How touching. King lives only in the present, and you wear the past around your neck like an albatross. You two are a real pair to draw to."

Cass flinched at the coldness in Jared's voice, the whiplike sarcasm she hadn't had used on her since the day he had accused her of seducing King.

"The necklace has nothing to do with finding Tea Rose," Cass said, trying to conceal her anger and hurt.

"It has everything to do with finding Tea Rose," Jared shot back, "because she's nothing more than the excuse you've been looking for to go running off to Dawson after King."

For a moment, Cass was too shocked to answer. "That's not true!" she said finally, her voice rising.

"The hell it isn't. No woman goes slogging over the Chilkoot on the half-assed hope of finding a highly trained whore who is probably leading Tan around by his cock and has no intention of letting go until she wrings out the last ounce of her vengeance."

Cass went pale. "I thought you cared for Tea Rose."

"I love Tea Rose," Jared said flatly, "but that doesn't mean I'm blind to what she is. She has been thoroughly trained to have only one emotion—self-interest. She has demonstrated her training to you time and again, but you refuse to see it. She's like King, only King came by his self-absorption at birth, rather than by training. And you refuse to see that, too. You think everyone has your capacity to love and be loved. They don't, Cass. They simply can't love the way you do. Don't destroy them and yourself by assuming that they can."

Cass tried to speak. Jared gave her no chance.

"I love King and Tea Rose," Jared continued in a low voice, "and I know how badly they can be hurt by your innocence. Long after they betray you by the simple fact of being themselves, your generosity and ability to love will haunt them, undermining their self-esteem, telling them that there is something missing in their souls, *something they can do nothing about without destroying everything they are.*

"Can't you understand that, Cass? There is no greater cruelty possible than to show a person a glimpse of something incredibly beautiful—something that person will never be able to have for himself. If you love King, truly love him, you'll let him go."

Slowly, Cass shook her head, ignoring the tears that scalded her eyes. "It's not King," she whispered raggedly. "It's Tea Rose. And you're right, Jay. My innocence destroyed her. If I hadn't been King's lover, she would have been legally under my care, and none of this would have happened."

"That's not what I meant!"

"But it's true," Cass said in a strained voice. "I failed Tea Rose horribly. I would be less than human if I didn't do everything possible to get her back. And if she doesn't want to come back with me, if she truly prefers to live with Tan Feng, then I'll give her my blessing and never interfere again. But I have to hear her say it, Jay. I have to know it's her own choice rather than my own stupidity that condemned my half sister to life as Tan Feng's whore!" Cass took a swift, shaking breath. "I'm going to Skagway."

"Not on one of my ships, you aren't," Jared said coolly. "I won't lift a finger to send you back to King."

"It's Tea Rose I'm going after, not King!"

In taut silence, Jared weighed Cass. He wanted to believe her. That was why he couldn't. He wanted it too much to trust himself. All he had was a lifetime of experience that had driven home a single message again and again: King was a fire, and women were moths drawn inevitably to his flame.

"I think you're fooling yourself again," Jared said in a clipped voice. "You're going after King. But I'm not going to help you. If you go, you go alone."

Cass closed her eyes and swayed as though she had been struck: Jared had never asked anything of her; now he was asking her for the one thing she couldn't give without destroying herself.

Like her asking King to stay. Like her asking Tea Rose to be gentle. Asking them to destroy themselves.

"And when I come back?" Cass whispered. "Will you—?"

Cass's voice died. She swallowed, but she wasn't able to finish her question.

It didn't matter. Jared knew what she was asking.

"Don't come back to me, Cass. Unlike you, I learn from my mistakes."

76

The Chilkoot was a punishing trail, even in summer. In winter it was ill-defined and mud-choked at the lower levels and perpendicular, ice-clad, and avalanche-prone over the last four or five miles. Pack animals could make the climb about halfway to the pass, but only at great cost; above Skagway, there was a deep ravine filled with the frozen, emaciated bodies of horses that had died along the trail. Two-footed packers took over for the final, steep pitch, fueled by gold fever and grim determination.

But even the most resolute human beings had to bow to nature. It had stormed every day of the two weeks Cass had been trying to get through the Chilkoot Pass. Nor was she the only one waiting impatiently on the lower slopes. Frustrated stampeders had disembarked from ships and piled up between tidewater and Sheep Camp like flood debris behind a dam. Some men had managed to get over, despite the wet spring storm. Most had not. They waited with growing restlessness for the storm to end and their dreams to begin.

Finally, the late-April sun won out. A hot golden light, a warm wind, the promise of rebirth and growth—all poured through the clear sky. During the hours of light, water trickled and ran everywhere, making the snow sparkle with the savage light of the rejuvenated sun. During the hours of darkness, everything froze again, making a slick glassy surface where men had walked before and would walk again with the coming of dawn.

A few women would walk as well, Cass among them. Most of the women on the trail were camp followers of one sort or another—actresses or dancehall girls, or plain unabashed prostitutes. Usually, they traveled under the protection of a pimp. The rest of the women were wives, who were likewise protected by a man. Cass was an anomaly, neither wife nor whore, and as such she was the focus of the men around her. At first, it had been flattering; soon, it became frightening. She protected herself by ignoring the speculative glances and turning aside the coarse invitations with a cool refusal. When that didn't work, she had a twin-barreled .41-caliber derringer always within reach.

Dressed as a man, a pack on her back and her face covered with soot to protect against the blinding brilliance of sun reflected from icy snow, Cass stood with other stampeders in the darkness before pre-dawn, waiting to become part of the thin, living line of black that stretched up the coldly gleaming pass. Nearly a mile long, the single file line of men clawed toward the summit, moving in slow lockstep, each man carrying a pack nearly as big as he was, each man no faster than the man ahead.

No one moved quickly. Men struggled upward, bent over nearly double, trying to hold position on the slippery ice steps, straining to find a balance between the urgency of gold hunger and the elemental reality of gravity.

"Ready?"

Cass turned toward Harlan Wintermoon's voice. Since he had adopted her, she hadn't had to rely on the derringer for protection. She had trusted Harlan immediately, despite his harsh face, alcohol breath, and overwhelming physique. Perhaps it had been because he was King's friend, and he had come to her after he had heard that "a Duran woman" was trying to get over the pass. Or perhaps she had trusted Harlan because of simple desperation; without him, getting through the Chilkoot would have taken fifty separate climbs up the Golden Stairway with a forty-pound pack on her back each time. Harlan, with his massive strength and soul-deep determination to get back to wild country, could make the trip three times in a day, carrying two hundred pounds each time. Cass was as determined as any man, but her body was not equal to the task. Even carrying a pack that weighed barely thirty-five pounds, she could climb to the summit only once a day.

"I'm ready, but you must be exhausted after yesterday," she said.

A grin split the ragged stubble on Harlan's face. "Been packin' freight fer strangers all winter. Now I'm doin' it fer my own wife. I kinda like that."

Cass heart stopped, then picked up at a faster pace. She and Harlan weren't married in the eyes of the law, much less the Lord, but they had a piece of paper signed by a drunken, defrocked priest that stated they were man and wife. It was a marriage of convenience that would end at Lake Bennett, or at Dawson, if Tea Rose had gone on. Harlan hadn't the money to buy his own ton of supplies, and Cass hadn't the money to pay someone to haul her supplies up the Chilkoot. They had pooled her supplies and Harlan's massive strength, and had taken on the pass along with thousands of other stampeders.

This would be Cass's third and final trip up the Golden Stairway; she had insisted on carrying her own *wife* allotment of one hundred pounds of food. Harlan had taken the rest, repeatedly trudging up the grueling slope with a huge pack on his back—drunk. Having made up his mind to go back to the wild country, he was savagely impatient to get past the white man's absurd restrictions.

"Don't you worry," Harlan said, finishing off the last of his pint bottle and pitching it into a urine-stained snowbank. "Friend of King Duran's is a friend of Harlan Wintermoon. Won't touch one shining hair on your pretty head."

"I know," Cass said, meaning it. "I just don't know how to thank you."

"Don't want it. Got a mean itch for the Yukon that even booze can't cure. So step lively, Miz Cassandra Thornton Wintermoon. Gonna be a strong sun today. Sooner we get over, better I'll feel. Storm left too much wet snow on them glaciers by half."

Shouldering her pack, Cass took her place on the trail that would end in hundreds of icy steps hacked out of a thirty-degree slope. She was glad to leave behind Sheep Camp's makeshift *hotel* and trampled, garbage-strewn snow, but she wasn't glad to get back into the hellish, grunting, straining, mind-numbing line of men. She knew from experience that progress up the last, steep pitch was both difficult and excruciatingly slow.

What awaited her on the summit was only marginally less numbing. While the pass itself wasn't much to look at— stony pinnacles rising five hundred feet on either side of a rock-strewn notch—what man had done to the Chilkoot surpassed belief. Nearly every square foot of the pass's four acres was covered with piles of supplies.

Everywhere a man walked, he walked on or among caches of food and equipment dumped by packers, marked with flags and then left unguarded. The piles grew by fifty or a hundred pounds or two hundred pounds with each trip up, until the stampeder's quota of one ton was met. Hundreds of tons of flour and beans, sugar and salt and bacon, lay in cloth sacks half-buried by snow. Sleds as well as stacks of shovels and lumber stood exposed to the elements.

And that was just the beginning. There had been seventy feet of snow the past winter. Two more layers of supplies lay completely buried, waiting for the thaw.

The Golden Stairway's twelve hundred icy steps led directly to chaos. The relatively flat land at the summit camp permitted dog sleds to be used in place of human packers. The air reverberated with the howling and snarling of huskies and the curses of mushers trying to keep order in the traces. The result was seething havoc, the supply depot of a ragtag army on the march, with each man his own quartermaster, drill sergeant, and pack mule.

After two hours of climbing, Cass and Harlan had made barely more than a hundred yards, moving in lockstep with the rest of the damned. The sun had fulfilled Harlan's promise—a hot yellow-white light burning holes through two feet of new snow. Cass tied on the crude, effective snow goggles that Harlan had made for her by putting slits in bark. The glasses cut by 90 percent the amount of light that reached her eyes, saving her from the snow blindness that had plagued so many men.

As Cass struggled upward, sweat mixed with soot on her cheeks, slowly washing away the protective coating, revealing her skin to the burning rays of the sun. She didn't notice her exposure, any more than she truly noticed the broad pack straps digging into her shoulders. She had learned that she climbed better if she simply blocked out everything except the step ahead, then the next, and the next, until the goal was reached or Harlan pulled her out of the line to rest.

The new snow was heavy, wet, clinging to Cass's boots and pant legs, weighing her down. Head down, breathing out great plumes of silver moisture, she labored to join the one hundred thousand other people who had poured into the Yukon since she had taken pictures of Jared Duran's first shipload of gold. But she wouldn't think about that, for then she would think about Jared, and her steps would falter, and her vision would blur with tears.

Don't come back to me, Cass. Unlike you, I learn from my mistakes.

She caught herself with her hands before she fell flat. Harlan pulled her to her feet, looked at her with dark-eyed concern, but said nothing when she faced the summit without a word, put her head down, and continued her climb.

The line in front of Cass moved forward one step, then two more, then a half dozen in a rushed, eccentric rhythm. The hand-carved stairway was little more than a foot wide, icy, slanting at odd angles, treacherous. None of the people who walked within touching distance of one another spoke except to curse the person who slowed progress by so much as a heartbeat. Shuffling, coughing, groaning, the living line crept toward the Mounties' post at the top.

There, under the unblinking eye of a Maxim gun, each person's supplies would be weighed until the magic number was reached, and the stampeder was allowed to slip through the door to his dreams—or nightmares. Foolish, magnificent, greedy, touching, desperate, sublime, quintessentially human, the living line inched toward golden immortality.

Cass was halfway up the twelve hundred steps when the sun lifted above the rim of the Chilkoot Pass's natural bowl. The man in front of her slowed, then bumped to a halt. Cass looked back over her shoulder at the line that stretched down to the packers' station the stampeders called the Scales. The gray canvas tents stood out against the new snow like dirty rags. Off to the east, the cable lift dragged sled-loads of freight up the pass at the kind of rates only a man already rich could afford. Beyond the cable was a broad, fanlike slope dotted with tiny figures. It was the return route for packers, many of whom hiked along the razorback ridge from the summit for a half mile and then slid back down to the Scales on snow shovels or on sleds made from the hides of dead pack animals. For the less adventurous or sure of foot, there were return trails worn so deeply into the snowpack that they had become narrow, ice blue passageways with gritty floors and with eerie shadows sliding along head-high walls. At some points, the packers' return trails overlapped the Golden Stairway, but the stampeders never got lost; the way to gold was up, and up, and up some more.

Squinting even through the protective goggles, Cass peered all the way down the mountainside to the boomtown of Dyca. The trail up from tidewater was cleanly defined in the new snow, a solid black line of men and animals ferrying supplies up the canyon, past Sheep Camp, and into the valley called the Scales that lay below Chilkoot's summit.

A muffled sound on the slope at Cass's left caught her attention. She turned in time to see a snow cornice drop off a rock and flop heavily onto the snow-covered thirty-degree slope. The slippery, wet lump of snow rolled a dozen yards, picking up more mass, then began to lose momentum. The tiny avalanche came to a stop without triggering a larger slide.

Cass turned to ask Harlan a question, but his curt gesture cut her off. He was listening intently while he peered at the slopes on either side of the bowl. There were no obvious cracks or gaps in the snow cover, but snow often melted unevenly beneath the frozen crust, invisibly separating the snowpack from the ice fields and glaciers beneath.

"No good. Too slow," Harlan said, measuring the distance they had yet to climb. "Snow too soft. Sun too hot. Bad damn feeling. We're goin' back."

"But we're halfway there," Cass protested.

Harlan didn't waste time arguing. He grabbed Cass's arm, jerked her off the Golden Stairway and set off across the snowpack to a return trail. A few others had the same idea.

Men broke away from the main line and scattered across the steep slope, looking for a route down. The gaps in the line were quickly closed by men who saw only the remaining steps and heard only the siren call of gold.

"Hold on."

With no more warning than that, Harlan lowered Cass into one of the packers' downhill trails, which was trampled only waist deep into the snowpack at that point.

"Go first," Harlan said, dropping into the trail beside her. "Go fast."

A single look at Harlan's grim face answered all of Cass's questions. Heart beating heavily, she turned and began walking as fast as she could on the slippery, bumpy surface. Behind her, another muffled thump came rumbling down from the pass as more snow slid free of its moorings.

With a few ruthless motions, Harlan stripped off Cass's pack and threw it aside. Even as he worked over the straps of his pack, he pushed her ahead.

"Faster," he said, grunting as he heaved off his pack.

Cass doubled her speed, moving much more easily without the awkward pack. Even so, she slipped and skidded every few steps. Most of the time she regained her balance without help. The rest of the time Harlan's fingers gripped her like steel bands until she found her feet once more.

Beyond the confines of the downhill trail, the line of men climbing the Golden Stairway suddenly rippled and blurred as packers and stampeders alike decided that they would wait for a safer time to claw their way through the Chilkoot. Harlan and Cass were still a hundred yards from the bottom of the slope when they heard the pounding sounds of boots behind them. Here, the trail was a virtual tunnel, with room for only one person to walk at a time. Cass increased her speed until she was all but skating over the treacherous trail, but the hurried pounding of boots kept on getting louder, closer.

"Get a move on, dammit!" shouted a voice. The cry was joined by other voices. "Get the hell out of my way! Move! Move! The whole fucking mountain's coming down!"

462

There was a thud and a hoarse grunt, and Harlan snarling at the men to get hold of themselves or they wouldn't have to wait for the mountain to kill them—he would do it right now. The panicked shouts turned into surly mutters. Cass was all but running now, moving as fast as she could without falling, knowing that she was holding up the people behind. She tried to stop to let everyone by, but Harlan simply locked his hand into the back of her jacket and half-carried, half-pushed her ahead of him.

"No," he grunted. "Too many of 'em. Stomp you flat as a flea."

Cass ran.

By the time the trail broke out onto the flats, where the panicky men could pass around Cass, she was breathing hard and raggedly. A thousand men milled around the staging area called Stone House. Rumors were shouted on the air like battle cries. Someone yelled that a wall of wet snow had broken loose and would sweep down the slope any second, killing everyone at Stone House. Another voice tried to calm the crowd, arguing that the danger had already passed.

Harlan ignored the arguments and soothing advice alike. He kept a fistful of Cass's jacket in one hand as he trotted purposefully across the Stone House flats toward the slope that led to Sheep Camp, which lay below, beyond the reach of avalanche.

The mountain muttered again, drowning out men's shouts, giving voice to a long, rumbling complaint that made the ground tremble.

The main trail to Sheep Camp was already choked with fleeing stampeders who yelled and fought and hardly moved faster than a walk. Harlan took one look, shifted his grip so that his hand was under Cass's arm, and set off at a hard, steady trot for a ravine that eventually would open onto Sheep Camp's safety. Others had the same idea. Soon the ravine was alive with panting, cursing, slipping, sliding men.

Cass and Harlan had gone about four hundred yards when the mountain lost its grip on its rotting white mantle.

Harlan heard the deep, almost subliminal sigh of the newly born avalanche, felt the shivering vibrations in the air, and flattened out in a dead run.

"There!" he grunted, pointing toward a rock cornice fifty yards away.

Cass was breathing in great, ripping gasps by now. Her feet seemed to touch the ground only every third or fourth step, as she was propelled forward by Harlan's massive strength. From the corner of her eye, she saw a huge patch of snowpack slithering toward them, gaining speed with every second, moving faster and faster, and then faster still, easily overtaking the tiny, frantic figures that fled before the breaking wave of solid snow. She knew that she couldn't outrun the avalanche, but Harlan might if he weren't anchored by her.

"Let—go!" Cass gasped, trying to free her arm.

Harlan tightened his grip and lengthened his stride. Cass knew instantly that struggling further might cost them both their lives. She concentrated on running as fast as she could. The snow was deeper in the ravine, for no trail had been broken by lines of packers on their way back down the mountain. The drifts Harlan and Cass ran through first were ankle-deep, then knee-deep, then deeper. On all sides of them were screams of panic and hoarse, panted prayers.

Then there was only the deep cry of the avalanche. Harlan cursed in rage and frustration as he forged ahead in great grunting leaps, dragging Cass through ever-deeper drifts of snow. They were still five yards from the shelter of the rock when the leading edge of the avalanche licked around their ankles in an icy caress. Abruptly, Harlan yanked Cass off her feet and hurled her toward the rock cornice.

Before she could fall, a twenty-foot wall of snow swept her up with a long, consuming roar. Instinctively, she tried to swim in the icy white torrent. It was impossible. She slammed up against the rock cornice, was pushed around its side by the force of the racing snow, and finally tumbled into the uncertain shelter behind the stone.

* * *

When Cass regained consciousness, she didn't know whether she was still dreaming or truly awake. Voices called at a distance, voices cursing viciously and praying fervently by turns. The light was diffuse, pearly, sourceless, and the air itself was almost solid.

She was cold, and there was no warmth anywhere.

She was bound, encased in ice, helpless, motionless, and her voice was both one of the fragmented chorus and separate from it, for she called out not to heaven or hell, but to the man she would die loving.

There was no answer.

She called out again and again, while recent sweat became a thin layer of ice on her skin, cold seeping through her flesh, her bones. For a time, she stopped calling and listened, hoping to hear the only voice that mattered to her—Jared's voice—calling her name, telling her that he had forgiven her for loving him too late.

All that came back to Cass through the snow were the voices of the damned, dying men encased in a frigid white hell.

One by one, the voices blurred and then fell silent. She cried out again and again—Jared's name, shaped by lips as pale as snow—and then her lips were snow, motionless, and the cold went all the way to her soul.

77

A thousand men labored over the shifting, treacherous white surface of the mountain. Some were digging parallel trenches or poking through the loose snow with long poles, searching for bodies. Other men dug frantically where voices had been heard shouting up from beneath the snow. In many cases, digging out the still-living victims was impossible; snow flowed like white mud, filling in shafts long before rescuers could reach the victim buried far below. People trapped beneath the avalanche called out to one another, talking to keep up their spirits. One by one, the voices faded as the heat of life was absorbed by the deep, frozen shroud.

"Yer name Duran?"

Haggard, grim, his eyes blazing like shattered ice against his face, Jared turned toward the rough-voiced stranger.

"I'm Jared Duran."

"Heard yer lookin' fer a woman?"

"Yes."

"Blonde?"

"Yes."

"Think we found her."

"Alive?"

The man hesitated, measured the savage light in Jared's eyes, and hedged. "See fer yourself."

Jared handed his shovel to another man, vaulted out of the trench he had been digging in the snow and followed the ragged stranger to Sheep Camp, where the dead were being laid out and the laborious process of identification had begun. Only thirteen bodies had been found so far, but everyone knew that there would be many more. There had been too many men on the mountain when the avalanche had come down.

"There she be."

Jared took one look at the pale, bloody face and felt the world give way beneath his feet.

Don't come back to me, Cass. Unlike you, I learn from my mistakes.

"Haven't found her husband yet. They're diggin' nearby."

"What?" Jared asked, hardly hearing, for his own last words to Cass were echoing cruelly in his mind, drowning out everything but the knowledge of irretrievable loss.

"Harlan Wintermoon, the 'breed. She shacked up with him to get through the pass. Good packer, that Harlan. One of the best."

Hearing the words without understanding them, Jared sank down on his knees beside Cass and searched for signs of life. He found no pulse, no warmth, no stirring of breath. He kissed her very gently, breathing warm air into her partially opened lips. It was like kissing snow.

Without thinking, feeling nothing but a violent, silently screamed denial that this could happen, Jared pulled out his linen handkerchief and very gently began wiping away the blood that had dripped down from beneath her hair to congeal on her cheeks in ghastly imitation of life's color. When her face was clean, he gathered her unresisting body against his chest and held her, rocking her as he had once rocked Tea Rose, shaken by grief and rage and bleak despair.

This time he wept alone, hearing nothing but the tolling of the past.

Don't come back to me, Cass. Unlike you, I learn from my mistakes.

But what could he learn from sending her off to die alone? If he had swallowed his pride and gone with her, instead of following her like a thief because he couldn't force himself to let go of her, if he had been with her, none of this would have happened. He could have sent their supplies over Chilkoot Pass on the freight cable in a single day. The two of them would have been at Lake Bennett by now, searching for Tea Rose among the tent cities and sawpits of the men who waited for the melt.

And if it were King for whom Cass truly searched, then so be it. Better that she love another man, and live, than lie so cold and still in Jared's arms.

"Son, you better get that cut taken care of 'fore you bleed to death."

The words didn't penetrate Jared's grief, but the gruff sympathy of the hand gripping his shoulder did.

"What?" he asked hoarsely.

"You're bleeding like a stuck pig. Here, let me see how bad it is."

Fingers searched over his face and scalp with brisk efficiency and found nothing.

"Where'd you cut yourself?" the man asked.

"I didn't," Jared said dully, looking down at Cass's still face. "It's her blood." And then realization came, ripping away the blinding veils of grief. *"She's bleeding. She's alive."*

The man bent and unfastened Cass's jacket with blunt fingers. He thrust his hand between the buttons of her shirt, ripping one off.

"What the hell—" began Jared.

"Quiet!" interrupted the man fiercely. He frowned and closed his eyes in the manner of someone concentrating intensely. "Be damned," he said finally. "Still pumping, but not by much." He lifted his head and yelled, "Blankets over here! We've got a live one!"

Jared stared at the man's gray-streaked, ragged beard and weather-burned face. "You're a doctor?"

"Used to be. Then I killed a man." He came to his feet as blankets were thrust into his arms. "All right, son, let's wrap her up and find out how good you are at breathing for two."

78

The first time Cass awoke, she thought she was dreaming. She was being rocked very gently, and the man she loved was calling her name, breathing warmth into her, holding her. Sensing that agony would come with full wakefulness, she made no effort to pierce the golden veils of comfort offered by the dream. Smiling softly, she tried to touch his lips, but could do no more than whisper his name.

"She say something?" asked Peters, sitting upright in the steamer cabin's chair.

"My name," Jared said, brushing Cass's fingertips with his lips before tucking her hand beneath the covers once more.

"She recognized you? Thank the Lord. Sometimes, when they sleep for days, they don't remember anything when they wake up. If they wake up."

Jared smiled crookedly at the man who had shared the vigil by Cass's bedside. "I'd rather thank a renegade doctor called Peters. Anytime you want anything—money, a job, anything—you come to me."

Peters scratched his ragged beard. "I'll take a bath and a bottle of whiskey and call it even."

"John," Jared called.

The outer door of the ship's stateroom opened instantly. "Yes?"

"Give the good doctor anything he wants, and then make sure he doesn't fall overboard and drown."

"What about you?" Peters asked, grinning.

"I've got more than I deserve already."

Jared didn't look up from Cass's pale face when the other men left. For long, silent hours he had listened to her steady breathing, soothed her when she whimpered and cried out in fear, and absorbed the miracle of her life—her skin warm and soft, her heart beating, her breath warm.

Her eyes opened and focused on him.

"Jay? Is it really you?"

The husky question sent relief shivering through Jared. "Hello, Cass. How do you feel?"

"Terrible," she whispered.

"Better to feel terrible than to feel nothing at all. You were damned lucky." Jared stood up and retrieved a teapot from a small stove. "The doctor said you might like some tea."

"Please."

Jared poured some, helped Cass to sit upright, and tipped the china cup against her lips. The liquid was warm and rich with honey. It soothed the rawness in her throat that had come from screaming Jared's name to the uncaring snow.

"Thank you," Cass said, turning and brushing her lips across his hand. "I owe you so much, more than I can ever repay, and it seems that I'm always arguing with you instead of thanking you for the very things I used to blame you for." She heard her own words and smiled weakly. "I'm not making sense, am I?"

"You've been through hell," Jared said. Beneath his mustache, his mouth was grim. "Do you remember what happened?"

"Snow. There was snow everywhere, and it buried me." Cass's breath came in sharply. "Harlan! We've got to find him, Jay. He saved my life."

Gently, Jared pushed Cass back down into the bedcovers. "You're too weak to get up. Lie still."

"But he could be hurt! I can't just lie here and—"

"He was found almost a week ago," Jared interrupted.

"A week? Are you sure?"

"A big man, part Indian from the look of him? Strong as a bear?"

She relaxed and lay back again, struggling no longer. "That's Harlan. He's even stronger than you. He tried to throw me above the wall of snow."

"He almost made it. That's why you're alive. You were close enough to the surface that people could dig down to you before you froze to death."

Golden eyes searched Jared's. "He's all right, isn't he?" she asked anxiously.

Jared hesitated. "He didn't make it, Cass. I'm sorry."

Cass closed her eyes against the hot welling of her tears. "He could have saved himself if it weren't for me," she whispered. "Oh, Jay, he could have saved himself."

"No man worthy of the name would save himself at the cost of someone weaker," Jared said. "Harlan Wintermoon was a man. I would like to have known your husband."

"Husband—"

Cass shook her head and laughed brokenly, but could say no more. A black tide of exhaustion and weakness welled up to claim her. Because it was neither cold nor white, she gave herself to sleep willingly.

When she awoke, Jared was no longer there. It was China John who fed her soup and hot tea and fussed over her until she slept—and woke and slept again. By the fourth day, she was feeling much stronger.

"Where are we?" Cass asked, when John came in answer to the little bell she had been given to ring.

"Aboard the *Pacific Star*."

Cass made an exasperated sound. Getting information out of John was like prying nails from green wood.

"I'd guessed we were aboard a ship," she said dryly, gesturing to the gimbaled lamps, the tiny stove, and the flat-bottomed decanters set into niches on the small sideboard. "But we're anchored, aren't we?"

"Yes."

"Where?"

John hesitated.

"Fine. I'll get out of bed and look for myself."

"We're anchored off Skagway," John said hastily. "Dr. Peters doesn't want you out of bed for another week."

"Dr. Peters may not get his wish." Cass sat upright, waited for dizziness, and was pleased when none came. "I'm feeling much better. Where's Jared?"

"Duran Company launched twelve steamers in the past month. He's overseeing their run to St. Michael."

"Then why was he in the Chilkoot?"

"I don't know."

"Where, precisely, is Jared now?"

"I don't know."

"Is he on this ship?" Cass asked impatiently.

"Yes."

"Please tell him I want to talk with him."

"He's very busy."

"I understand. I'll save him some precious time. I'll go wherever he is."

"Perhaps I could answer your questions."

"Only Jared can answer my questions."

"You are a very stubborn woman."

"Thank you."

John looked at Cass coolly. "You and your blind stubbornness have put Jared through living hell. If he'd wanted to talk to you, he wouldn't have sent me to play nursemaid."

"What, precisely, were your instructions?"

"To see that you have everything you need."

"Fine. I *need* to talk to Jared. Alone."

John stood up, turned, and left without another word. A few minutes later, Jared opened the door to the cabin.

"You must be feeling better," he said, closing the door behind him. "John said you wanted to talk to me."

"I wanted to thank you for—"

"That's not necessary," Jared interrupted flatly.

Cass stared at Jared for a long, silent moment. "You're still angry with me, aren't you?"

"No," he said softly, certainly. "I had no right to be angry with you in the first place."

"You had no *need,*" corrected Cass. "It's you I love, Jay. You, not King."

Jared's smile was gentle and yet so distant that Cass had to bite back her words of protest.

"It's all right, Cass. You don't have to sell yourself again to get to King. All you have to do is tell me when you want to leave for Dawson."

"Sell myself?"

"Your husband. Harlan Wintermoon."

Cass shook her head numbly, not even feeling the tears that ran down her face. "All Harlan wanted was enough supplies to get past the Mounties. I had the supplies, but I didn't have the strength. That was the beginning and the end of our *marriage.*"

Jared's expression didn't change.

"Don't you believe me?" she asked.

"About Harlan? Yes. About King—" Slowly, Jared shook his head. "You were willing to die to get to King. I discovered that I would rather have you alive under any circumstances—even as King's lover—than to hold your corpse in my arms. I'll give orders that we leave immediately for St. Michael."

"It's Tea Rose I must see," Cass whispered with aching calm. "Not King."

"Of course," Jared murmured, not believing a word of it. "Tea Rose." He pulled out a soft handkerchief and crossed the room to Cass's bed. He blotted her tears as though she were a child. "The ice on the rivers could break at any time. The lakes will be slower to open. As you're too weak to go over the Chilkoot, the fastest way for you to get to Dawson is by steamer after the ice goes out."

"Dawson?"

"By the time we get there, Tea Rose will be in Dawson." And so would King. Both Cass and Jared knew it. Neither one said it aloud.

"Are you sure?" Cass asked finally, knowing only that she must get to Tea Rose.

That hadn't changed. Nothing had changed—except that Cass had died and been reborn and Jared wasn't angry with her any more. Nor was he passionate in any way. He didn't watch her with undisguised hunger burning in his eyes. He didn't walk across the room to be close to her, didn't touch her for the sheer pleasure of the silent communication, didn't bend over and breathe in her scent as though she were a bouquet of spring flowers. He was kind and gentle and patient—and as distant as the moon.

"There are rumors that Tan Feng plans to auction off his ten women one at a time in Dawson," Jared said calmly. "Tea Rose will be the last. He expects her first night to bring more than her weight in gold."

"That's—barbaric. Can't something be done?"

Jared's smile was as cold as the snow that had once encased Cass. "How many women did you see in the Chilkoot?" he asked softly.

"Ten, perhaps." She smiled wanly. "It was hard to tell, dressed the way we were."

"How many policemen?"

"Outside of the post at the top, none, and only two or three up there, I think."

"What was Sheep Camp like?"

"What do you mean?"

"Gambling? Drinking? Fights?"

Cass nodded.

"How many men were going over the pass?" Jared continued, his voice soft, his eyes intent, relentless.

"Thousands."

"There will be more than thirty thousand people in Dawson when we get there. All but a handful will be men. If there is one Mountie in Dawson for every two thousand miners, I'll be surprised. If any of the men going over the pass now finds ground worth staking, I'll be shocked. Those men will have spent their last penny and their health on a wild goose chase, because all the good ground was claimed before the *Portland* ever tied up at the Duran wharf."

Jared paused and tried to soften the truth, but there was no way to make it more palatable. "When the men figure out that all their debt and hardship was for nothing, they're going to be angry, resentful, and spoiling for a fight. Do you think the Royal Canadian Mounted Police will risk starting a riot by preventing a pimp from raffling off his sing-song girls? Hell, Cass, even if Tea Rose were as white as you, they wouldn't interfere. The whores are working harder than the Mounties to take the fighting edge off the miners."

Unable to take the intensity of Cass's haunted eyes any longer, Jared turned away. Since the moment he had met her, he had been the source of unsettling, often unhappy facts for Cass. It was no wonder she preferred King, who could solve all problems with a Colt .45 or a ticket north.

"I'm sorry," Jared said finally, still looking away from Cass. "I didn't mean to put it quite so brutally. Chalk it up to one more in a long list of failures of my personal charm."

Cass was too surprised by Jared's apology to say anything. The idea of Jared failing at anything seemed impossible to her. He radiated a hard, white-hot certainty of his own power that had frightened her at first, then reassured her, and finally, had consumed her body and soul in a way that King's easier radiance never could have. She had thought that King needed her, needed her love, needed someone to share his life; but he had not. She had thought that Jared needed no one—had she been wrong about that, too?

She studied Jared as though she had never looked at him before that instant. What she saw made her heart turn over with compassion. Exhaustion had drawn his face into hard planes, and made his eyes look like splinters of ice against their dark circles. His mouth was a thin line, as though it took so much effort for him to keep going that he had none to spare for smiles or laughter. His thick, dark hair was rumpled from his fingers running through it in a silent anguish he would never permit himself to speak aloud.

And he was turning away from her.

Slowly, Cass became aware that, even with his back all but turned to her, Jared was aware of her scrutiny. Once, that realization would have unnerved her; now, she simply accepted it as part of the man she loved.

"Will I ever be able to surprise you?" Cass asked, smiling a sad, off-center smile.

Jared turned and looked at her, not bothering to conceal his reaction. "You always surprise me, Cass. Every time I look at you, you're more beautiful to me. Your generosity humbles me. It's like sunlight or rain, given to rich and poor, wise and foolish alike, with no thought of the cost to yourself."

"Or them?" she asked.

Jared remembered his bitter words to Cass about the cost of her generosity to Tea Rose and King. "I was jealous of King, and I was speaking for myself, not him. As I said, your generosity humbles me, but I'm learning from it."

"Generous or foolish, or somewhere in between, I owe you so much," Cass said in a trembling voice, taking Jared's hand in her own. "Hold me."

Jared's eyes closed for an instant as his features were drawn into harsh lines by the pain tearing through him. Slowly, almost helplessly, he lifted Cass's warm hand to his lips and kissed it with a tenderness that brought fresh tears to her eyes.

"You don't owe me anything," Jared said against her skin. "I didn't save you for my personal benefit. I saved you for the same reason I saved King and tried to save Tea Rose— the world would be a much poorer place without you. You don't have to give yourself to me again, Cass. You're free, all debts paid, and no regrets that matter."

Jared kissed the palm of her hand a final time, breathed in her scent, and released her. Her fingers twined through his and tugged until his hand was tucked against her cheek. Very gently, he disengaged himself from her warmth.

"Please don't," Jared said softly. "I've had all I can take of loving my brother's woman." Before Cass could speak, Jared's hand sealed her lips. "No, Cass. Listen to me. Even if you believe you're going to Dawson for Tea Rose, you'll inevitably see King there. He'll be stronger than ever, harder, wilder, more fascinating; and he'll be weary from another round with the bitch goddess who controls his soul. He'll see you, and he'll remember all the heedless beauty you gave to him once before, and he'll wonder if maybe, just maybe, he was right and you're the one woman on earth who can hold him. He'll want you, need you, come to you—"

"And if you were my woman, I would kill him.

"So you can't be my woman, Cass. You can only be what you have always been—King's woman, not mine."

"I love you."

"Yes," Jared said softly. "I know. Just as I know you love King more. Women always have, always will. It just took me a long time to admit it. Much too long. I held a corpse in my arms, and she looked just like you."

"Jared—" Cass cried, but it was no use.

The door closed silently, and he was gone.

79

A tent city lay like a beached flotilla, stretching from the frozen shores of Lake Lindeman through a boulder-choked canyon, and on to Lake Bennett's equally frozen length. The slender, serpentine, mountainous margins of both lakes hosted thirty thousand stampeders sheltered beneath everything from one-man pup tents to huge circus tents flapping and belling in the wind. The air rang with the sounds of hammers and whipsaws and the savage curses of men whose partnerships were being torn apart by the physical misery of dragging two-man saws through green wood, transforming logs into planks for crude rafts, boats, and masts. Malamute teams rushed snarling through the ankle-deep slush that formed on the surface of the lake's slowly rotting lid of ice. The teams narrowly avoided being run down by drunken stampeders who had discovered that a mast, a canvas sail, a log, and a gale-force wind could combine into a hair-raising ride across the mushy surface of the ice.

No matter what their size or shape, most of the tents were clustered around Lake Bennett, for it was there that the ice would first break apart and be washed downstream, bringing the promise of spring to the Yukon's headwaters. It was at Lake Bennett that the air seethed with anticipation, as the sound of distant, breaking river ice came like gunfire on the wind. Rumor had it that great black cracks were showing in the river ice. On the lake itself, the ice had thinned in some places until the water's green surface shone eerily through.

More than seven thousand boats of all conceivable sizes, shapes, and degrees of reliability waited in ragged rows along the shore, piled to the gunwales with thirty million pounds of supplies. The dreams the boats carried weighed nothing, but without them, the flotilla would never have been conceived, built, loaded, and manned under primitive, impossible conditions.

It was the strength of those dreams that baffled Tea Rose, each stampeder's certainty that if only one man of all the gathered thousands was to be blessed by the bitch goddess, he would be that lucky man. Tea Rose didn't know whether the men were all fools or simply mad, if they were victims of false hope or minions of Mammon; she only knew that she was among them, but not one of them, just as she was among the Chinese prostitutes, but not one of them. She wasn't earning her passage on her knees or on her back, servicing five or ten or thirty men a day, an endless procession of wagging cocks poking into her.

Tea Rose serviced only one man in an inexhaustible pas de deux of advance and retreat, goad and submit, temptation and satiation, physical virgin and practiced whore. Neither Tan Feng nor she was winner or loser in the naked battle; and both of them waited, watched, prayed for the correct moment to strike and emerge victorious.

"What are you thinking, sweet opium?"

Without looking up from her embroidery frame, Tea Rose took another golden stitch and said, "I am a sing-song girl, lord. Of what would such as I think?"

"Of jade stems and pleasure pavilions and the Ultimate."

"My ass grows tired of those things," Tea Rose said beneath her breath in English.

"What?"

"My lord?" she asked, reverting to Mandarin and looking up as though surprised by his inquiry.

"I thought you said something."

"Nothing worthy of your attention, lord. I was merely despairing of my clumsy fingers. I must get the fire finished before we set sail. The ice will go out soon, and the river will be too uncertain for me to stitch upon."

Tan shrugged. "There will be much time in Dawson for you to work."

"I think not, lord," she said. She tied off a golden thread and severed it with a single, neat motion of her teeth. "We will have two weeks, perhaps three, possibly four; and then the steamboats will come in from St. Michael, and there will be many whores in Dawson. You will get your best price for me before then."

Tan froze. "Who said I was going to sell you?"

"No one, lord."

Tan's blunt, powerful fingers dug into Tea Rose's hair. A casual movement of his wrist levered her head back on her neck until her throat was a taut arc, and she had no choice but to look at him.

"Who?" he demanded.

Tea Rose opened her mouth and curled out her tongue as Lilac once had, sensual invitation and warning in one.

"Fox Woman told me," Tea Rose said, smiling thinly. "She comes to me often, telling me the secrets of your mind and body. You believe you will sell my maidenhead, and then you will keep me for yourself until you win the flowery battle, or you wish to impress a businessman. Then you will send me to his room—and then I will wear a bridal gown of blood that puts me forever beyond your reach."

Her tongue curled out again, taunting him.

Tan could neither control nor completely conceal the cool frisson that went over his nerves as he looked down into Tea Rose's calm, fathomless black eyes. Never had she more resembled Lilac Rain than at this moment, when she taunted him with the glistening pink softness of her mouth, and at the same time, reminded him that she could escape as her mother had done.

Abruptly, Tan Feng bent and caught Tea Rose's tongue between his teeth, holding it in a vise that delivered a measured amount of pain. When reflexive tears filled Tea Rose's eyes, he continued the punishment for a long count of three before he released her.

"Watch your tongue, female," he said softly, "or I will bite it off for you."

"This miserable female is not worried, lord," Tea Rose said, sliding her hand deftly between his legs, flicking her fingertips over his slack penis. "A man whose turtle head is too soft to pierce my frail virginity must also have teeth too soft to sever my tongue."

No other person alive could have insulted Tan in such a manner and have avoided brutal punishment for it. All that kept Tan from beating Tea Rose was the animal certainty that once he lost his control with her, he would kill her. Even worse, she knew his weakness. He was sure of it.

That was why she taunted him.

"Fox Woman," Tan said hoarsely, feeling himself grow until he overflowed Tea Rose's clever, treacherous fingers. "One day you shall come eagerly at my command. One day you—"

Ragged shouts drowned out the rest of Tan's words. Tea Rose's fingers stilled. He tightened his grip on her hair, stretching her head back even farther, until the meaning of the shouts registered.

Bennett Lake's lid of ice was breaking up.

Tan Feng threw Tea Rose aside and rushed out of the tent to bellow orders at his men.

The lake shore was absolute chaos, with boats being launched in a thumping, bumping wave of humanity that crowded the small margin of unfrozen water stretching between the muddy land and the crumbling ice. The ice gave way first at the downstream end, tugged apart by the currents of water as the lake overflowed into the headwaters of the Yukon. Great chunks of ice swirled and dipped and bobbed in an improbable ballet, partnered by an even more improbable array of green-lumber craft piloted by men whose only experience with a ship had been a steamer ride up the Inside Passage.

By the second day of breakup, every mile of Lake Bennett's length was alive with boats. The wind came up with the sun, whipping the water into icy froth, driving the ragged armada before it like an invisible hand sweeping leaves from a green marble surface. At twilight, the wind died, stranding the boats in silence. Somewhere, a man began to sing about salvation and an angel's golden chariot swinging down to receive his soul. Other voices joined in, then more and more voices until the ancient hymn rose above the mountains to the stars beyond, filling the world with the multifaceted voice of humanity singing to its own soul.

Hearing it, Tea Rose wept for the first time since her mother had died.

80

"Lord God above. I'm seein' it, but I ain't believin' it."

Poke's words drew King from the brass railing of the Elite Bar to the doorway. The bar looked out on Front Street in what had become downtown Dawson City. Crystal shot glass in hand, King stood beside Poke, sipped decent whiskey, and watched a chechako who hadn't yet gotten his land legs after two weeks on a heaving raft. The man missed a step on the boardwalk and staggered headlong into the knee-deep muck of Dawson's main street.

"Where'd they all come from?" Poke asked.

"Everywhere men use gold for money," King said dryly. "They've come to see the elephant, but they've come too late. All that's left is the part right below the tail."

Shaking his head, Poke watched the crowds.

No longer locked out by winter ice, the Klondike stampede was now running free, riding the crest of spring floods, rampaging through Dawson. In less than a week, the city had gone from a population of five thousand to fifteen thousand, and still men poured in, with no sign of letup. The huge tent cities upstream at Dyea, Lindeman, Bennett, and Teslin, and downstream at Circle and Fortymile, had become overnight ghost towns as they disgorged their contents onto swiftly flowing rivers. Rafts, rowboats, and flat-bottomed upper Yukon steamboats had deposited thousands of men and a few women on the half-frozen muskeg bar just south of the mouth of the Klondike.

Sober estimates from checkpoints upstream predicted that Dawson's population would double again in the next few weeks. A hundred thousand people had set out for the

Klondike goldfields. Scores of thousands had dropped out en route and hundreds more had died, but at least forty thousand were still on the trail.

And they were all coming to Dawson, every man jack of them.

King had been waiting for the stampede to hit the Klondike for the past fifteen months, waiting and knowing that when it came it would be time for him to leave. The Klondike pay dirt had all been staked; there wasn't an inch of the richest creeks or the white-gravel highlands that had not been claimed. For now, the stampeders were high on simply surviving and arriving in Dawson's fabled streets. In a few weeks, the chechakos' exhilaration would become malaise, as they realized that all the poor man's gold was already owned.

Then, Dawson would turn violent. By the end of summer, the discontented, surly, and disheartened would have left, having reclaimed or stolen the boats that were now stacked three deep, abandoned on the river's edge.

For every prospector who departed, at least one merchant would stay to take gold from the pockets of die-hard chechakos and seasoned sourdoughs alike. Already, the flats between the original Dawson settlement and the mouth of the Yukon had become a single, sprawling tent city, complete with haphazard commercial and residential zones, burgeoning industrial sections, and one or two whorehouses; and every person in that seething mix had just one goal in mind.

Gold.

But if gold was hard to find, it was ever harder to hang on to. If a man earned a month's Outside wages in a week of working over a sluice, buying food and shelter for that week cost at least four times what it would Outside. Boom prices matched the boom town that had seen more than four thousand pounds of gold pass through its streets the previous year.

"Lord God," Poke repeated.

King knocked back the whiskey in his glass with a single,

quick motion. "Don't blame the Lord God for this," King muttered. "Blame the bankers and merchants and empire builders. Next thing you know, there'll be churches and schools and soda fountains, and men will be fined for spitting on the sidewalk and for not wearing starched collars."

"Aw, don't be so sour. You'd give your left ball for a real nice woman right now, and you know it."

King's lips twitched as he tried not to laugh, but it was impossible. "You're right, Poke. But that's the trouble—I want the civilized woman *and* both my balls."

Poke laughed, too, pleased that he had managed to penetrate his boss's growing irritability. "That's the ticket, Wolverine. Grab it all and let the Devil suck hind tit. What say you and me go on a toot and celebrate? That last cleanup was real fine. Musta been five pounds of pure gold in them riffles."

King looked at the young man who was already gaptoothed and stooped over from the Klondike's punishing demands. Poke wore six months' of beard, and his hair hadn't been cut—or washed—for the same amount of time. He wore patched wool Mackinaw pants and a faded, buttonless undershirt held together at the collar by a safety pin. His hat was the color of mud, and the consistency as well.

Poke looked like a beggar, but little leather bags full of gold swung from the rope that held up his pants.

Dressed in a pair of worn corduroy pants, a woolen turtleneck so worn that it wouldn't stand a washing, and a battered Borsalino felt hat, King looked similarly disreputable by the standards of the Outside. King didn't care. Fancy clothes would come in with the first river steamboats; if he felt like it, he would buy clothes whose cost equaled their weight in gold.

King returned to the bar and ordered a bottle of whiskey. It was smooth, bright scotch, an astounding change from the sharp, cloudy rotgut that had been the rule in Dawson before the ice went out.

"Better order two, Wolverine," the bartender suggested.

"I bought a case of this stuff from a stampeder yesterday, and I'm down to three bottles already."

"Put my name on one of them," King said. "I haven't had anything so smooth since I was a tycoon back in Seattle."

"You'd better be a tycoon now," the bartender said. "It's going to cost you an ounce of gold for an ounce of whiskey. That would put the bottles at somewheres over two hundred dollars each."

King pulled a leather poke from his belt and dropped it on the rough-sawn planks that served as a bar. "Take what you need for two bottles, and buy a round for the house. I hit a streak of pay dirt the other day that went five hundred dollars to the pan, and I haven't had a chance to spend any of it yet."

The bartender hefted the poke, grunted, and turned to the small balance scale at the back of the bar. "Two bottles, a round for the house, and discounting for—"

"There's nothing but pure gold in that poke," King interrupted coolly, "and you know it. Not even a speck of black sand. No discount, or I'll take my gold and my business down the street."

The bartender shrugged as though he had heard it all before, but he didn't argue. He rang a brass bell that announced another free round for the house and did a quick head count. When he had finished, he shook a handful of smooth yellow nuggets out of King's poke and weighed them.

"You're a half-ounce over," the bartender said.

"Keep it and buy yourself a woman. Sure as hell, that's the only way a man with your disposition will ever get one."

"At least I don't have to consort with wolverines to get company," the bartender retorted as he tipped the extra gold into his own poke.

King laughed, gave Poke a bottle of scotch, and pushed past the crowd of drinkers to the back of the bar. Throughout the winter, the Elite had been a dark log cabin with a heavy iron stove for heat and only one window. But now, in the heady warmth of summer, the owners had knocked out the back wall and thrown canvas over a rough lumber framework to keep out the mosquitoes. The summer sun shone nearly all the time, allowing poker games to be played without lamps at midnight.

The first table was full. The game had started out in conventional fashion, with poker chips and glasses of beer, but now the contestants were down to poke bags and bottles of bourbon. King's practiced eye estimated the pile of nuggets in the center of the table as worth about five thousand dollars. One of the miners checked his hole card and then shoved a fat, sausage-shaped poke into the pot, raising the stakes by at least a thousand dollars.

A murmur went through the kibitzers; five years of Outside wages were riding on the turn of a card.

"I was going to join you," King said, "but it'd take a wheelbarrow for me to carry enough of my gold in here to match the pot."

"Wouldn't need a wheelbarrow if your claim had more gold and less brass shavings," one of the players said, smiling slyly.

"Brass shavings, huh?" King said easily. "No wonder you lost the drift on your claim, Ned. You can't tell shit from shoe polish."

Chuckles went around the table, and Ned laughed the loudest.

"Don't go away, Wolverine," Ned said. "You can have my chair as soon as I clean out this here pocket."

That boast brought a round of hoots from the other players. The men were a mix of prospectors who had staked their own claims last year and shrewd traders who had picked up abandoned claims and turned them into paying ones or bought paying claims and turned them into wealthy oncs. Despite the men's ragged appearance, every one of them was worth at least a hundred thousand dollars—or had been before he sat down yesterday to play poker at the sourdoughs' special table in the back of the Elite Bar.

King had no better idea of his own net worth at the moment than he did that of the other prospectors sitting around the table. In the first four months after he had staked his claim, he had taken out a little over twenty thousand dollars, mostly in pure nuggets rather than in the harder-to-mine "dust." By the time the freeze had come last fall, drying up the tiny creeks he used to run his Sierra rocker, King had known his claim was a good one, but not how good.

During the winter, he had set out to discover the extent of the riches he had claimed. He had sunk three more shafts down to the pay-dirt level. Each shaft had proven richer, more viable, than the previous one. Prospecting had been reduced to a monotony that was no longer broken by the unexpected gleam of gold; gold was everywhere. There was no thrill to shooting golden fish in such a well-stocked barrel.

At the moment, King's claim was covered with pay dirt waiting to be washed out. The little creek that gave him sluice water had begun to flow again, but after he had found the third five-hundred dollar pan of nuggets in a row, he knew all that he needed to know: He was richer than he ever had been or ever had hoped to be. He could drink scotch whiskey at two hundred dollars a bottle and eat fried eggs by the dozen at a dollar apiece, and have thirty-dollar haircuts and two-hundred-dollar whores.

And King would have traded it all to be where he had been last year, ass-deep in a shaft where gold was unexpected.

Restless, irritable as a bear in spring, King abandoned the poker table's rough camaraderie. His path out of the bar took him past the canvas wall where three women sat on stools. Known as the Belgian Draft Horses, the women were the Elite's prostitutes. Ten minutes with one of them in a tent behind the log cabin cost a pinch of gold from a prospector's poke. It was widely rumored that the pimp had selected the three women not for their looks but for the size of their thumbs. The women had thick, strong bodies and few words of English. They had walked overland from Edmonton to Dawson with their pimp the previous fall, and they looked strong and coarse enough to walk right out again, carrying their own considerable weight in gold on their broad backs.

King left the saloon and walked through the town that had once been his and now belonged to history. The midnight sky was the color of evening and filled with the high-pitched frenzy of mosquitoes. The boardwalk along Front Street was filled with the high-pitched expectancy of men who were certain that wealth lay just outside Dawson's gumbo streets and ragtag tent city—and if not there, then certainly over the next hill, around the next bend in the stream, up the mountain.

Somewhere.

When King reached the river, he was suddenly walking among mounds of abandoned goods. The Mounties' requirement that each man bring a year's worth of supplies to Dawson had resulted in a glut. Food, shovels, even complete kits, were suddenly worth ten cents on the dollar.

A crowd of people milled around a rowboat that had just docked. Originally, the men had gathered because the boat's sails consisted of female undergarments. Once it was learned that the underwear belonged to a wife rather than to a prostitute, interest had waned until a crate of leggy kittens was heaved onto the dock, setting off a yowling and spitting fight inside the slats. The crate's owner reached inside and dragged out a gray, tiger-striped kitten by the scruff.

"Who wants it?" the man called out. "They'll keep your tent free of mice and warm your lap to boot. Ten dollars a head or take your pick for twenty dollars."

The crowd was composed largely of chechakos who hadn't had time to become accustomed to Dawson's outrageous prices. Ten dollars was a month's groceries on the Outside. For an alley cat that any farmer would have drowned at birth, it was an absurd price.

The tiger-striped kitten twisted and struggled to free itself from its handler, and finally managed to hook a paw into the man's thumb. He yelped and let go. The cat landed on a gunwale of the rowboat, then leaped twelve feet and landed in front of King. Reflexively, he reached down and scooped up the fleeing animal.

The kitten twisted again, lashing out with its claws, but King's hand was so callused from digging out half-frozen gravel that the tiny, sharp claws and teeth were all but useless. King shifted his grip and rested the cat on the palm of his other hand. When the creature tried to attack again, King rapped its nose once with the callused end of his index finger. The kitten stopped struggling, sat up in King's large palm and regarded him with clear, unblinking golden eyes.

"This is my pick," King said.

He dug out a nugget that felt like an ounce of gold and flipped it to the man in the rowboat. Without waiting for the man's response, King walked away down the waterfront, stroking the kitten's soft gray fur and talking to it in a soothing voice.

"Where'd you get that cat, Wolverine?" called a ragged man who had been dickering over a new shovel from a pile of abandoned goods.

"Rowboat, back up the way a bit."

Word of the kittens passed quickly. Prospectors who had wintered over in Dawson started for the rowboat at a trot, starved for something new, living, a furry bit of company that wouldn't complain about hearing a joke for the hundredth time.

King ignored the minor stampede he had begun. Cat in hand, he wandered the riverfront. The midnight sun's twilight gave magic to the crowded waterfront. Boats and rafts were tied six deep and gunwale to gunwale. Out on the river, dozens more boats were turning from the fast currents of the center channel and heading toward shore. Others were just reaching the shore, and still others had been tied up long enough to begin unloading.

Rumbling to the kitten in a low, gentle voice, stroking it, smiling when the kitten rubbed its head against his finger, King continued walking until he drew abreast of a large raft that had been tied up at the stub end of a makeshift dock.

The craft was sturdy, well-built, and sported a sizable shack amidships.

A cabin door opened, a woman emerged, and King stopped as though nailed to the dock.

"God in heaven," he breathed reverently, staring—and wondering how he could have forgotten just how beautiful Tea Rose was.

81

The raft of Chinese prostitutes quickly attracted a crowd, which had been Tan's purpose in tying up along the muddy trail known as Front Street. Dressed in bright, colorful silks cut in Western style, their hair carefully curled and styled in Western fashion, wide-brimmed hats fluttering in the breeze, the Chinese girls looked like exotic flowers. Jasmine was not among them, for no footbound female could have made the crossing over the Chilkoot, a fact that had made Wing even surlier than normal. Under his watchful eyes, the girls who spoke a few gutter phrases of English were teasing the men on the docks.

Tea Rose stood alone by the cabin, dressed in Chinese clothes, as though to warn the gawking white men that she wasn't a sing-song girl available for a pinch of gold. She had remained separate from the saltwater whores from the beginning. She was Tan Feng's virgin paramour, a precious oddity. Even if Tan had permitted Tea Rose to mix with the other prostitutes, there would have been little time for her to make friends. The trail to the lakes had been cold and rigorous, but nothing short of death stopped the stampeders' sexual urges completely. The prostitutes had been very busy. Already, Tan had recouped the cost of his supplies; in Dawson, he would begin reaping enormous profits.

"Tea Rose! My God, is it really you?"

Tea Rose turned at the call and instantly saw King. Taller than most men, stronger, he stood out above the crowd. Even if he had been short or stooped, Tea Rose would have spotted him; in the odd light of the midnight sun, King's mahogany beard smoldered like a banked fire. He was leaner than she remembered, and his face was burned dark by the long hours of summer sun. His clothes were ragged, but his eyes had the clarity and brilliance of fine emeralds.

As Tea Rose looked across the ten-foot gap separating her from King, she fought a fierce struggle to maintain her self-control. The past year had not been wasted; when Tan Feng emerged from the cabin behind her, there was nothing in her face or body to suggest that King was anything to her but a diversion.

"Yes, King Duran, it's really your little sister," she said, bowing politely over her hands.

"What the hell are you doing here?" demanded King. "Didn't you get my message?"

Before Tea Rose could say anything more, Tan Feng stepped from behind the cabin door, grabbed her arm, and spun her around to face him.

"You are not a saltwater whore dressed in white devil clothes and staked out like a goat to lure tigers. Why do you flaunt yourself in front of these miserable wretches? Go back into the cabin, and stay there until you are given permission to leave."

"What the hell's going on?" King demanded.

Tan's head snapped around. The two men had met only a few times, and in far more civilized dress and surroundings, but each recognized his adversary immediately.

"Tan Feng! You back-stabbing son of a bitch!"

The epithet didn't disturb Tan, even though he understood enough gutter English to know that he had just been insulted. An almost sexual thrill of pleasure went through him when he realized that the game he had longed for had begun so quickly upon his arrival. He had hoped King would still be in Dawson, but there had been no way to be certain.

"Speak to him, black butterfly. Invite him aboard," Tan said, his eyes heavy-lidded. He turned Tea Rose around to face King. "Tell him how very carefully I have clipped your silky wings."

King didn't wait to be invited aboard. He was up the ramp and standing in front of Tea Rose before anyone could object. Not that Tan would have; he was delighted to have the opportunity to show King just how futile all the maneuvering had been back in Seattle.

The Durans had lost. Tan Feng had won. Tea Rose was his.

Tea Rose knew Tan far too well to miss the feline pleasure beneath his outward impassivity as he watched King. She wished that King were less transparent, more like Jared, a rapier of ice rather than unpredictable lightning. But King was what he was; she had used his recklessness before. Now, she must use it again, but very, very carefully.

"King," Tea Rose said quickly, hoping that she was speaking too rapidly for Tan to follow, "don't lose your temper. That will only help Tan and hurt me. Do you understand?"

King's eyes narrowed. He nodded curtly.

"Officially, I'm Wing's wife. Unofficially, I'm Tan Feng's concubine. Wait! There's nothing you can do right now, so just listen, please." Tea Rose stood with breath held until she saw the savage light diminish in King's eyes.

"All right," he said evenly. "We'll try it your way. This time. Just so long as you understand that I've never turned my back on a debt or a partner and sure as hell don't plan to start now."

Tea Rose let out a soft trickle of air and forced a calm, polite smile onto her face. She was both relieved and appalled to discover that King was going to uphold his end of the bargain they had made more than a year ago and a thousand miles distant. Relieved, because marriage to him was her only rational chance of escape. Appalled, because if Tan Feng found out that she was King's partner in the claim, and his fiancée as well, Tan would put such a high price on her that even King's gold mine wouldn't be able to buy her freedom.

For it wasn't money alone that Tan Feng wanted. Money, he could get from any man who had a stiff penis. Revenge was a different matter entirely. Revenge could be had only from humiliating the Duran brothers.

Speaking quickly, softly, running her words together until even a native speaker would have had trouble understanding them, Tea Rose said, "Tan knows nothing of our agreement, and he must not find out."

After a moment of sorting out the rushed words, King nodded his understanding.

Tea Rose hid her relief, knowing that Tan Feng would be watching her as intently as he was listening. And he would be enjoying every instant, as well—a puppet-master twitching strings and smiling, sucking the sweat of revenge from his victims' writhing bodies.

Mother, help me to be as strong as you were. Fox Woman, listen to your daughter. Help me be as cold as Tan Feng is cruel.

"Tan plans to sell my maidenhead to the highest bidder," Tea Rose continued, her face and voice calm.

"Then he's a dead man walking."

"It's a piece of skin for which I have no use. No, listen to me, King."

"You listen to me, sugar. No Chink pimp sells my partner and gets away with it."

"My price will drop when I'm no longer a virgin. Then you can buy me."

King looked from Tea Rose to Tan. "Does he want you himself?"

Tea Rose wondered which answer would suit her purposes more, but there was no way to find out. She settled for the truth, which she had learned could be far more deadly than any careful lie.

"Yes."

King grunted. "Then it won't work. Once you're just

another whore, he can have you as often as he wants and not cut your value by a penny. He won't sell you outright to me any more than he would sell Lilac to Cassie's father."

Tea Rose didn't argue. What King had said was the very thing that she feared herself.

"You mustn't appear eager to buy me," Tea Rose said. "It will only raise my price. If you want me too much, Tan will simply keep you dangling, promising me and never selling me. He has done it before whenever he knew that a man wanted one of his prostitutes very badly."

Frowning, King stroked the kitten with his thumb, thinking quickly, wishing that Jared were here, Jared the planner and general.

"Be a hell of a lot easier just to shoot the bastard and be done with it," King said matter-of-factly.

"There are nine other men with Tan. They are tong warriors."

"Christ," hissed King. "How long has he had you?"

"Since the day the *Portland* docked in Seattle."

"That's more than a year ago! Where the hell is Jared? Why hasn't he done something?"

"He has. He ran Tan out of Seattle, nearly ruining him. After that, no matter where Tan hid or whom he bribed, Jared and Cass eventually found him. They came very close to finding me in Vancouver." Memories of that day swept through Tea Rose without warning—clouds and rain and the savage gall of defeat and ecstasy. "Tan decided he could wait no longer. We left for the Klondike that day."

The kitten batted softly at King's finger with sheathed claws, then settled down to gnawing on his thumb. Seeing how little impact the kitten was having, Tea Rose smiled with a mixture of amusement and despair, feeling a shaft of empathy for the small scrap of life buffeted by incomprehensible forces.

King saw Tea Rose's look and held the kitten out to her.

"Here," King said. "I'm not much good with soft things."

Tea Rose took the kitten, held it in her cupped hands, and

smiled as it stropped itself under her chin, liking her scent. Her smile reminded King of how young Tea Rose was, and how extraordinarily beautiful.

"I'll get you out of this," King promised softly.

Tea Rose looked up from the cat's face, both surprised and warmed by the quiet vow.

Tan saw both Tea Rose's beautiful, spontaneous smile and its effect on King Duran. Anticipation expanded through Tan. King was coming to Tea Rose like a fish rising to a lantern held above dark water.

And like a fish, King had no idea of the spear waiting in the fisherman's hand.

"Want buy miserable female, you?" Tan asked in English, watching King with unblinking black eyes.

It took King a moment to sort out the meaning of the heavily accented words.

"I might," King said casually.

There was a burst of Mandarin from Tan. Tea Rose translated as though the object of the discussion were not her own sale.

"Women are very expensive in Dawson," Tea Rose murmured. "Even the most miserable saltwater whore can cost two hundred dollars a night. As I am a virgin and beautiful, I'm worth ten times that—two thousand dollars for a single night."

The sharp crack of King's laughter made a few heads turn their way. Neither King nor Tan noticed.

"Sugar, not even Dawson can support that kind of greed from your pimp." King's hands flashed out without warning, lifting Tea Rose and then setting her back on her feet before Tan could move to intervene. "But you're a pretty little thing. Tell Tan I'll buy you outright for your weight in gold."

"King, don't let him know how much—"

"Tell him," King interrupted. The flat demand was echoed by the line of King's mouth.

Tea Rose translated, listened to Tan, and then turned to King once more.

"For my weight in gold, you may have me for a month of nights. It's a bargain he would offer only to an old friend such as you—one thousand dollars a night."

King looked at Tan. "We can do this one of two ways. I can buy her outright for twice her weight in gold, or I can kill you and take her for nothing."

When Tea Rose finished translating, Tan looked at King. "Ten time," he said, holding up both hands with fingers widespread.

"Three," King said, showing three fingers. "Three hundred pounds."

"You no have," Tan said flatly.

King stared at him with cold green eyes.

"Think get brother, yes?" Tan said. "Have debt you."

"What the hell are you talking about?"

Frustrated by his inability to communicate, Tan turned to Tea Rose and said in Mandarin, "Miserable female, tell that pile of pig shit what his brother did to ruin him. Tell him so that I can understand your words. Do you hear me, wretched one?"

"Yes, lord." Tea Rose turned to King. "Tan wants me to tell you how your stock became worthless back in Seattle."

"What the hell for?"

"Tan thinks that you plan to get money from Jared in order to buy me," Tea Rose said, speaking slowly, distinctly. "So?"

"Tan wants you to know that your brother is the one who ruined you."

King went very still. "What?"

"Jared bought the traction company and then closed it down, making the stock worthless."

"Why the hell would he do that? He lost more than I did!"

"In that venture, yes. He had many other ventures."

"It still doesn't make sense."

Tea Rose felt like laughing at King, but knew he wouldn't understand that, either. "Your brother wanted your woman. Can you understand that?"

For a long minute, King said nothing, but the furious

glitter of his eyes told Tea Rose that now he understood quite well. She nodded. Tan spoke quickly to her.

"Tan asks if you still want to go to Jared for money," Tea Rose said.

"I wouldn't ask Jared for the time of day," King responded bitterly. "I don't need him. This is my town, not his."

"Five time," Tan said, holding up five fingers. "Two week. Yes yes?"

"Four times," King said flatly.

"Yes," Tan said. "Two week?"

"What?"

Tan spoke rapidly to Tea Rose.

"Two weeks," she said to King, her voice soft, bleak. "You must have the whole price in gold, not paper. If you can't meet the price in two weeks, he'll sell me to someone else for whatever he can get."

"Two weeks? Hell, that's not enough time to wash out hundreds of pounds of gold!"

Tan's smile was like a knife sliding free of its sheath, revealing the naked intent of the blade. "Too bad. Sell her someone other. You watch."

"Sell her to someone else and I'll kill you."

Without another word, King turned and headed for his mine. He had a lot of work to do. And while he did it, he would think very hard about Jared's treachery and the golden woman who had once been King's.

82

The slats of the shallow-draught paddle wheel beat the muddy Yukon water to a froth, going full speed astern. The boat remained stuck fast to the bar.

"She'll not take any more, Mr. Duran," the captain reported. "Those boilers are brand-new. They'll crack if we aren't careful."

"Shut them down and heave more whiskey barrels overboard. Just get us out of this damned slough before we're bled dry by the mosquitoes."

The captain went off, muttering about almost a thousand gallons of good whiskey being fed to the Yukon fish.

Jared left the *Denali*'s bridge and walked back along the main deck of the steamer to the pistons that ran the stern wheel. He checked the steam fittings and the bearings on the drivers. He had put intense pressure on the captain for maximum speed all the way from St. Michael to Dawson. As a result, the *Denali* had been fighting through the shallow, braided river courses and pothole lakes of the Yukon Flats, halfway to Dawson, under more steam than was advisable for the shifting channel. The captain assumed that Jared was merely racing the other boats from St. Michael in order to be the first steamboat in Dawson after the breakup, thus getting top prices for the cargo that was stacked everywhere on *Denali* and on her sister ship, *McKinley*.

That was part of Jared's motive. The other part was the woman who lay below, sleeping beneath swaths of mosquito netting. He had promised himself he wouldn't touch Cass until she had seen King again and had confronted her feelings for him. Yet, it was becoming impossible for Jared to keep his hands off Cass, who had made it clear that she loved him, wanted him, needed him.

Yes—but how much? Enough that you won't take one look at King and be drawn helplessly again, moth to flame?

Jared wanted to believe that Cass wouldn't go to King. He wanted to believe it so much that he didn't trust his own judgment anymore. That had never happened to Jared before; but then, he had never loved a woman before—not like this, body and mind and soul.

He crossed to the port side and checked the towline that connected the *Denali* to the *McKinley*, which was still in the deep-water channel, lending its power to the job of refloating the grounded lead steamer. The heavy towline was stretched and humming with strain. The deckhand on

497

watch was huddled behind a ventilator. He looked at Jared and shook his head.

"She's holding, but I'd hate to sit too close to the cleat," the man said. "There's a wire core in that line that'll take your head off if it breaks."

From amid ships came the grumbling sound of full barrels of whiskey being rolled across the deck. Jared watched while two crewmen pushed first one barrel, then another, through a gap in the rail. He turned away and took a sighting on a snag on the opposite bank. More barrels went into the river while the deck trembled with the beating of the engines. Long minutes later, the snag seemed to shiver and then move an inch, two inches, a hand-span. By slow increments, the *Denali* was breaking free of the mud.

"More power!" Jared yelled through the open door to the engine room. "She's moving!"

The vibrations coming through the deck increased. The paddle wheel slapped viciously at the water, churning up the muddy bottom of the river. Gradually, then more quickly, the *Denali* slipped backward until it floated free. A ragged cheer came down from the wheelhouse, and an answering one drifted over from the *McKinley*. The *Denali* turned and began steaming upriver once more.

Wearily, Jared stretched. It had been twenty hours since he had last slept. He hoped that nothing more would go wrong for the next five or six hours. But as tired as he was, he couldn't resist pausing at the door to Cass's cabin. He listened, but heard nothing beyond the throbbing of the ship's powerful engines.

The brass door handle moved soundlessly beneath his hand. He pushed the door open with gentle care. In the odd light of a dawn that hadn't followed darkness, he saw Cass asleep beneath white veils of mosquito netting. Quietly, he closed the door behind him, crossed the small room and stood looking down at her.

Even now, weeks after Jared had found Cass cold and motionless in the Chilkoot, there were times when he had to see her in order to convince himself that she was truly alive.

He had worked a lifetime to cultivate the cool, dispassionate side of his nature, yet he had only to see Cass to know the same kind of elemental need that drove King to run forever after tomorrow's sun. King would die unfulfilled, his dreams receding in front of him, untouchable.

And Jared was afraid he would die the same way, reaching for the woman who would never truly be his. He had been seduced and teased, and merely serviced, by some of the most experienced and skillful prostitutes in the world. He had been lover to women he cared about and who cared about him. None of them had prepared him for the depth of passion and tenderness Cass called out of him.

Would Cass die reaching for King, the unattainable, her untouchable dream?

Knowing he should turn and leave, unable to force himself to do it, Jared picked up a round-backed captain's chair and placed it soundlessly beside Cass's berth. Telling himself that he would stay only for a few minutes, just long enough to assure himself that she was truly alive, Jared sank wearily into the chair.

A few moments later, Cass began to move restlessly, whimpering softly, then more clearly. As Jared leaned toward her, he realized that there were tears on her face, and that the word she was repeating over and over was his name. Suddenly, she sat upright, calling him with chilling urgency.

Jared ripped aside the netting and pulled Cass into his arms. "Cass, sweetheart, wake up. It's all right. I'm here, love. I'm here. You're safe."

He repeated the words over and over until he felt her shudder violently. She put her arms around him and clung as though he were a lifeline and she were drowning.

"J-Jay?" she asked uncertainly after a moment. "Am I still dreaming?"

Smiling sadly, he stroked her hair. "I hope not, Cass. The dream you were having wasn't very happy."

She shuddered again. "I dreamed I was back on the mountain, and I was running and running, but I was standing still, and snow buried me—and then I screamed for you, and I screamed and I screamed, and there was no answer—"

Jared closed his eyes on the wave of anguish that went through him when he thought of Cass trapped, screaming for him, screaming, and finally dying, alone. He whispered her name over and over, holding her, being held in turn; and he kept thinking of her dream, of her calling for him.

Not for King. For Jared. Cass had believed she was dying, and it was to Jared she had turned. He hadn't known that. He hadn't even dared dream of it.

"Cass?" he asked softly, pulling back, trying to see her eyes.

Her arms tightened around him. "Not yet, Jay," she said in a husky voice. "Please, don't let go of me yet. When I sleep, I'm back on the mountain, and it happens all over again. I can't bear it anymore. Just hold me a little while longer. Please, Jay. Just a little more."

Jared pulled Cass even closer, buried his face against her neck, and breathed in her scent as though it were life itself. When his lips brushed against her warm skin, they also felt the metal links of the heavy gold chain around her neck, King's nuggets and life encircling her always, even when she was in Jared's arms. A shudder of protest went through him, a cry that never passed his lips.

Are you sure, Cass? Are you really sure? I don't care about your first love, as long as I'm your last.

"I love you," Jared said, kissing warm skin and golden chain alike.

Cass went utterly still, then clung even more tightly to Jared—laughing, crying, whispering her love of him again and again, until he quieted her with a deep kiss. He had meant to ask no more of her, just her taste spreading through him like a benediction; but when her body moved against his, he groaned. Then her hands slid over his clothes, searching for him, finding him, caressing him with open joy, and he was lost. Within moments, he was naked, sliding beneath the mosquito netting, sheathing himself in her, pulling the netting like a silk veil over their joined bodies, rocking, feeling her satin heat bathe him even as he poured himself into her.

Sleep came to them as ecstasy had, simultaneously, deeply, completely. The next time the mountain swept down around Cass in her dreams, Jared was with her, holding her, and she didn't die.

83

King wiped his face on his sleeve, smearing dirt and blood and mosquitoes across his skin. He tipped the last of the cleanup onto the balance scales, sending a shimmering cascade of gold into the round pan. Carefully, he piled brass-plated weights into the other pan until the two sides balanced. He read the weight, wrote it down, and poured the small mound of gold into a partly filled poke. Frowning, he added up eight days' worth of yield from his claim. After wages were taken out, he had netted seventy-one pounds, four and three-quarters ounces of pure gold.

It was an enormous amount, the result of crews of men working around the clock on all four shafts of King's China Girl mine. Added to the gold he had saved from last summer, when only he and Poke had worked, King had two hundred and eighty-eight pounds, thirteen and one-eighth ounces.

To buy Tea Rose, he would need one hundred and eleven pounds, two and seven-eighths ounces more, and he had only six days in which to mine that much gold.

King thought of hiring more men, but he knew that would be futile. There simply wasn't room for any more miners in the cramped, frozen tunnels, nor was there enough time left to justify sinking more shafts, which might or might not intersect the white gravel bed of the ancient river course, but which would cost gold in wages no matter what the new shafts yielded.

King went over the figures again, as though hoping to find

an error. There was none. The China Girl simply wasn't yielding enough to buy its namesake in the time remaining.

Goddamn it, the gold is there. I know it.

The men had been having trouble getting the feeder creek to run through the flume to the sluice box. At least, that's what they had told King when he'd commented about the low yield. He was beginning to believe that he was being robbed. Yet, he couldn't be everywhere at once. He couldn't determine the lie of the drift at the bottom of the shafts and be at the sluice box, too. He could only check on the men at random, and hope that they weren't holding any unscheduled cleanups of the sluice's riffles.

"Sure is pretty, ain't it?" Poke asked, grinning as he watched lantern light run over the mound of gold in flickering tongues of light.

"It's not enough," King said grimly, his voice hoarse from lack of sleep and from crawling through smoky tunnels in search of the richest places to mine. "I've got to bring it up to eighteen pounds of gold a day."

Poke looked at King as though he had lost his mind. "Not enough?" Poke started to say more, but found no words to express his disbelief. "You gone plumb crazy?" he asked finally. "There's not a man jack out there what wouldn't kiss Satan's red cheeks for that kind of take!"

Not answering, King strode out of the lean-to he had built on the claim and back to the third shaft of the China Girl. The yield from that shaft had dropped in the past four days. It was time to decide in which direction the tunnel should be dug in the hope of more closely matching the drift of the pay dirt—right, left, center, up, or down. Somewhere amid the smoke and frozen earth, more golden tears were trapped. Somewhere, the bitch goddess lay waiting for him. He had only to find her.

"Hey, Wolverine! Ain't you gonna sleep?" Poke yelled.

There was no answer.

Shaking his head, Poke watched as King grabbed the windlass rope on the third shaft, vaulted over the side, and lowered himself into the frozen darkness.

Two hours later, he climbed out again. Without a word to anyone, he headed into Dawson. Once there, he quickly found the big white tent that had become one of the trading centers of the city. There, Jonathan McFarland sat in solitary splendor, his clothes impeccable and his cheeks closely shaven. An advance man for a syndicate of Toronto investors, McFarland was buying claims and shares in claims at a brisk rate. He was the leading edge of what would become a breaking wave of businessmen, the kind of men King hated, the men who would change the Stampede into an orderly march toward Progress. McFarland had marched cross-country from Edmonton with nothing more than a pack on his back and letters of credit from the Royal Dominion Bank.

It had been enough.

"I'm Kingston Duran. I own the China Girl."

McFarland stood, shook hands, and settled into an office chair that had come over the Chilkoot on some anonymous packer's back.

"Sit down," McFarland offered.

King shook his head. "What I have to say won't take long. I want you to loan me one hundred pounds of gold. By September, I'll pay you back two hundred pounds."

Slowly, McFarland shook his head. "I don't lend gold. I buy it."

"Fine. You can have 5 percent of the China Girl in exchange for one hundred pounds of gold."

"Are you serious?"

King just looked at him.

"Ten percent," McFarland said.

"Done."

Smiling, McFarland stood up, his hand held out. "I haven't heard the latest rate for an ounce of gold. As soon as I do, I'll have a check made out for—"

"No," King said curtly. "No paper. One hundred pounds of gold, or there's no deal."

"Why would a man who owns one of the Klondike's best claims want gold?"

King looked at McFarland with eyes like splintered green crystal and said nothing.

"Yes, well," McFarland said, shooting the right sleeve of his suit over his immaculate starched cuff, "whatever you say. It will take time for me to collect that much gold from my various mining interests."

"How long?"

"Oh, no more than three weeks."

"It has to be within six days."

"That's unreasonable."

"Six days or no deal."

McFarland's eyes narrowed. "Why?" Then, at the visible hardening of King's expression, the financier added, "Sorry, I should know better than to ask a miner anything but the weight of his poke." McFarland sighed. "It's a bad time to sell claims for gold, Mr. Duran. Men with that much ore are heading Outside to spend it, and chechakos who want claims are trying to buy in by trading their labor. As for me," he shrugged, "I'm tapped out of cash, and so is every other man who buys and sells claims in Dawson. Two weeks from now, the story will be quite different. There were at least six syndicates forming on the East Coast when I left last summer. You can be sure that I won't be the only source of capital in the Yukon Territory for very much longer."

"I know all about the empire builders," King said bitterly. "They've been stepping on my shadow all my life. I'll rot in hell before I take their money."

King stalked out of the tent and into the bright sunshine of 6:00 A.M. For a moment, he stared off across the slowly churning Yukon, letting his tired eyes adjust to the long view of humpbacked mountains and cloudless sky. The closest mountain slopes had been scoured clean, as Dawson's exploding population leveled acre after acre of forest for firewood and building material. But the farthest slopes were still dark with evergreens and white with snow. In the brilliant morning light, the distant country looked pristine, alluring, shimmering with undiscovered secrets.

King longed to be among them.

With an abrupt movement, he turned away from the horizon and strode toward the Celestial Palace, home of Tan Feng's hotel, restaurant, casino, bath- and whorehouse. On the way, he passed a line of sleepy men and half-drunk chechakos who were waiting outside a big fly tent. Inside, two ugly sisters from Saskatchewan served waffles, side meat, and coffee at two dollars a plate—ten times what it would cost Outside.

A snarling, cursing tangle of dogs and men erupted from the tent and boiled toward King. Silence was restored when a gray-bearded miner kicked apart the fighting malamutes and grabbed the prize, a sawdust-coated piece of side meat.

The Celestial Palace was much more peaceful than Dawson's streets. Burning joss sticks both perfumed the air and thinned out the mosquito and black fly population. The casino was down to only a handful of grim gamblers intent on getting gold the easy way. Wing watched over them with black eyes that missed nothing. The two dealers were white, recruited from the ranks of disappointed chechakos.

Wing recognized the new arrival instantly. He went to Tan's office, which also served as his bedroom, and knocked on the door. A few moments later, Wing returned to the casino, signaled to a sing-song girl, and gave rapid orders. She walked to King, bowed, and began speaking in soft, accented English.

"Tea Rose see you," she said.

"I came to see Tan Feng."

"Tea Rose, please?"

King started to object, shrugged, and followed the girl, who led him to the slat-floored lean-to where baths could be purchased. In the center of the area, two large hip tubs steamed invitingly. Between them stood Tea Rose, wearing peach silk pajamas.

"Good morning," she said, bowing. "Your bath is ready."

"I don't remember ordering one."

"It is Tan Feng's gift to the man who will bring him a mountain of gold," Tea Rose said.

She went to King and began unfastening his clothing.

"What the hell—"

Tea Rose looked up at King. "In the Celestial Palace, no man bathes alone. I will wash you as I have so many times before."

"Not quite, sugar," he said flatly, staring at her exquisite face. "I'm real healthy now."

Tea Rose's smile was as sultry as the air. "I hope so."

King said nothing more, simply watched as her fragile, graceful hands made short work of his clothes. He was aroused long before he was naked. When his muddy boots and clothes lay on the floor, Tea Rose stroked him admiringly from navel to knees and smiled at the visible leap of his response.

"What a pity you may not take me as a man takes a woman," Tea Rose said, glancing up at King through a fringe of midnight eyelashes.

King's smile was as much a warning as a malamute's snarl. "Don't bet on it. I don't tease worth a damn."

"There are a hundred roads to the Ultimate," Tea Rose said, caressing and testing his erection with skilled fingertips. "Only one of them is closed to us. Come. Let's find how many roads we can travel before you tire of the journey."

King grabbed Tea Rose's hand and held it away from his body. "Why is Tan making you do this?"

"He wants you to know what you have lost when you fail to meet my price," she said in a calm voice. "Your memory of this morning will be his vengeance for the trouble you have caused him. As for Tan 'making' me touch you—" Tea Rose laughed and shook her head as she began undoing her own clothes. "Ah, King, I've always wanted to undress you, to caress you, to drink your essence. You should have turned to me long ago, before you ever saw my sister with her hair and eyes of gold. All of our lives might have been much easier."

Before King could answer, Tea Rose stepped out of her pajamas. His breath came in with a sharp, hissing sound. He had expected her to be as slender as her fingers. She wasn't. Her breasts were full and perfectly formed, as were her hips.

Her nipples were dusky rose, her skin had the warm sheen of ivory, and the black hair at the apex of her thighs was as soft as mink.

"My God," King breathed, caressing Tea Rose, curling his fingers against her warmth and softness.

"I'm glad you find me beautiful."

Tea Rose led King to the bath, where she washed his hair and beard and then his body, while he nuzzled and nibbled on her breasts and her mouth and her arms.

"Come," Tea Rose said, urging King from the soapy water to stand beside the second tub. "The ice has been very cruel to your body. This will soothe you."

"I know something that will soothe me a hell of a lot more," he muttered, standing.

Tea Rose rinsed King with small buckets dipped from the oiled, scented water of the second tub. Then she massaged more oil into King's body, working down his muscular length until she was kneeling in front of him. With sensual deliberation, she caressed his erection, playing over his exquisitely sensitive surfaces with changing pressures of her mouth. Using all her skill, she brought him to a peak of arousal that was greater than any she had ever seen in a man. She released him very slowly and admired the results of her training, feeling tremors of delight that were both sensual and vindictive, for she suspected that Tan Feng was watching through one of the spyholes that riddled the Celestial Palace. When he saw King's proportions, she doubted that Tan would be pleased.

Suddenly, King's hands fastened on Tea Rose, pulling her to her feet. Deliberately, he probed between her legs, felt her liquid response and the taut maidenhead shielding her sultry depths, and withdrew his fingers. His hands fastened beneath her rib cage, and he lifted her until she was at his eye level.

"You're a virgin, sugar, but you're a long way from innocent. Tell me one reason why I shouldn't take you right now, standing up, and to hell with the other ninety-nine ways to the Ultimate."

Jared wouldn't have had to ask that question, but the man holding Tea Rose was very different from his brother. She kissed King's cheek just above the soft edge of his beard.

"It's very simple," she said. "Tan Feng doesn't believe that you will have my price in gold, but he can't be certain. If you buy me, I will be lost to him; he will never know what it is to take me as a man takes a woman. He wants that, King. He wants that more than you can imagine. If you break my maidenhead, Tan will have the full use of me for six more days and perhaps have my full price in gold from you as well. Even if you don't meet the full price, he will get two thousand dollars from you for my maidenhead alone."

"Right now, it sounds like a bargain," King said. "Put your legs around my waist, sugar."

Tea Rose obeyed, but her voice went on relentlessly while King probed between her thighs with his fingers, testing her sultry depths.

"Tan is counting on your inability to see beyond the instant to tomorrow. Were you Jared, Tan would never have tried such a maneuver. But you are King, who lives only in the moment, with no regard for the moment after, when Tan's smile will overflow with vengeance, and he will fuck me until we both bleed; and you will be made to watch, so that you will see him in me every time you come to lie between my legs."

With a brutal curse and a sharp twisting motion of his body, King yanked Tea Rose away and set her on her feet. Instantly, she spun and stood behind him, wrapping her arms around his hips and her hands around the blunt, hard flesh that had come so close to tearing through her maidenhead.

"God damn it," King said savagely, reaching for Tea Rose's hands. "Stop teasing me!"

The sudden, erotic pressure of her teeth on the small of his back riveted King, as did the hot, oiled glide of her hands and the dark, savage huskiness of her voice urging him to come and end his torment. Inevitably, he responded, giving himself to her helplessly; and still she continued, shifting her position until her skilled hands and mouth could draw him into hardness once again, even before the last after-shocks of his first climax had stilled. Groaning, trying to say her name, he sank to his knees beneath the onslaught of his own release.

Tea Rose moved with him, tugging on him, turning him, lying on the cool wooden floor with him, kneading his hot flesh, caressing him with tongue and teeth until he was thick and hard once more. She held him, teased him, pleasured him, admired him, and laughed to taste his essence yet again. He would have spoken if he could, but he couldn't form the words, couldn't move, couldn't think. Wrapped in endless, hammering pleasure, he lay supine while Tea Rose's mouth loved him, and her oiled hands kneaded his thighs, his testicles, his buttocks, probing the deep cleft until she found the key, and shock waves of adrenaline slammed through him, bringing him to repeated shattering climax, his hoarse cries of agony and ecstasy echoing in the steamy room.

And then she held him, soothing him, stroking his face, calming him, murmuring to him gently, until he gave a final, bone-deep shudder and fell asleep against her perfect breasts.

84

The shrill whistle of the *Denali* was answered by a ragged cheer from the miners thronging the muddy bank.

"Brace yourself," Jared said.

Even as he warned Cass, he braced her against the railing with his body, as the flat-bottomed steamer ran gently aground. For an instant, he closed his eyes, memorizing the feel and scent of Cass pressed against his full length, for the part of him that had always stood in King's shadow was certain that such intimacy would never come with her again.

When Jared's eyes opened, he scanned the miners intently, looking for a man who was stronger than most, taller, a man with distant horizons in his eyes and sunlight in his smile. King wasn't in the crowd waiting for the first steamer to reach Dawson since the melt. Jared turned to Cass. He wanted to leave her aboard ship, where it was safe, while he went to look for King; but Jared knew Cass would refuse to stay behind. She was taut, vibrating with her urgency to get to Tea Rose.

Or King.

No matter how often Cass said that she loved Jared, part of him still expected Cass to take one look at King and long for the hot currents of life that ran so violently through him, the same wild force that once had compelled her so deeply that she had given her untried body to him. It wasn't that Jared didn't believe Cass's words of love; it was simply that all his life he had been eclipsed by his older brother's presence. Next to King, other people simply faded into insignificance. Jared understood the force of King's charisma. Given that, how could Jared reasonably expect Cass to love him more than she loved King?

I can't expect it. But God, how I want it.

The steamer's short, wide gangplank rolled out like an impudent tongue. Cass walked down quickly, skirt held to midcalf, revealing the incongruous boots she had last worn in the Chilkoot. When the miners saw her blond hair coming unraveled in the wind, they leaned forward to get a better look. Their catcalls and coarse comments died when Jared came down the gangplank, close behind her.

Cass barely noticed the roughly dressed men. Like Jared, she had scanned the crowd for a tall, familiar figure and had found only strangers.

"Are you sure you won't at least wait at the hotel?" Jared asked.

Cass gave him a sideways, exasperated kind of look that made him smile, despite the fear gnawing at him.

"All right," Jared said. He brushed a kiss over her lips and tied the mosquito netting that was part of her hat into place. "Let's get it over with."

510

Cass said nothing while she walked at Jared's side through the town and out the other side. Only when there were no more buildings in sight did she speak.

"Are the Chinese forced to build beyond Dawson's city limits?" she asked.

"No. Why?"

"It's unlike Tan to make his customers walk a step farther than they have to," Cass said dryly.

"But not unlike King."

Jared felt the tightening of Cass's fingers on his arm and wondered for the first time if he were doing the right thing, if moths feared the very flames that drew them.

"I'm sorry," Jared said. "If you don't want—"

"No," Cass said quickly, cutting across his words. "You're right. It has to be done. I'm just afraid Tan might have told King about that traction company."

"Thanks to that traction company, King has one of the best claims in the Klondike," Jared said dryly. "I don't think he's going to hold twenty thousand dollars against me when he's worth at least twenty times that now."

"That won't take care of the fact that King will feel betrayed by you."

"Then there should be no problem," Jared said in a clipped voice. "When it comes to betrayal, the honors between King and me are about even. He knew I wanted you as a wife, not a mistress. He took you anyway, as a mistress, not a wife."

Cass's eyelids flinched at the pain coursing through her as she realized anew how much her misjudgment of King and herself had cost. "King didn't mean it that way, not as a slap at you," she said in a low voice.

"Didn't he?" Jared's smile was thin and cool. "In some ways, King has always resented my building a life beyond the reach of his shadow. Things were so much easier for him when I was around to order supplies and run mining crews; when I took the weight of gold off his hands so that he could chase the sun, while I hunkered down and built toward my own dream. Then he would come back from the chase, and he'd go through my friends like lightning, especially the women."

Cass started to speak, hesitated, and said nothing.

"Go ahead," Jared said. "Say it. I'm damn sick and tired of King being the Great Unspoken in our life."

For a moment, tears constricted her throat, making speech impossible. Then she said, "The candle doesn't burn to destroy moths. It burns because it must."

"And moths go to the flame for the same reason," Jared said bleakly. He brought Cass's gloved hand to his lips, brushed against the soft skin at her wrist and said, "Whatever happens, I'll always remember your gift for loving generously, if not wisely."

"Jay," she whispered. "I love you more than—"

"No," he said gently, refusing to let her finish. "No promises, nothing to haunt you in the future. You don't owe me anything. Think of that when you look at King, and remember what it was like to touch the hot currents of life you saw pouring through him—because you will look at him, Cass, and you will remember."

Jared curled his hand around Cass's neck, feeling the heavy, bittersweet familiarity of the necklace beneath, his older brother's life told in chain links and nuggets of solid gold. Instead of freeing the mosquito netting so that he could kiss Cass again, Jared stroked the nape of her neck gently and released her.

Wanting to say something, anything, Cass tried not to show her pain. She knew that her words would carry no weight until she had seen King. Nor did she blame Jared for not trusting in her love; her first choice had been King, and nothing she could ever say or do would change that unhappy truth. There was no way for her to convince Jared of the depth of her love for him, except to love him and keep on loving him.

And pray that, in time, he would believe in her love.

So Cass said nothing, concentrating instead on keeping her footing along the muddy, rocky trail leading to King's claim. Up on the bench, men were scattered across the ruined landscape in twos and fives, according to the wealth or persistence of the man who held each individual claim. Stones grated over other stones as buckets of pay dirt were dumped into sluices. There the gravel was washed over the riffles, so that gold was trapped and concentrated, in small imitation of the vastly larger force of a flowing river.

The China Girl was easy to find. Every man on the bench knew which claim belonged to Wolverine Duran. Just as Cass and Jared reached the number three shaft, a man clambered out, took one look at Cass, and let out a long howl of delight.

"Hey, Wolverine!" he said turning and yelling down the shaft. "C'mon up! The first steamship done come in!"

"You gone crazy, Poke?" King shouted back. "It's days too early!"

At the sound of King's voice, Jared turned and walked away, so quietly that Cass didn't even know he had gone.

"Then God took pity on us and sent a sweet angel," Poke yelled back, flushing when Cass smiled at him.

"What the hell are you yowling about!" bellowed King.

"Come on up and see! I got another shaft to check on!" Poke smiled shyly, lifted his muddy hat, and muttered, "Been a pleasure, ma'am," as he retreated toward the second shaft.

Cass wasn't alone long. King was up the ladder and over the side of the shaft with the muscular ease of a man who had repeated the same motions hundreds of times. The bright sun was like a blow after the smoky, ill-lit darkness of the tunnels in the frozen earth. Blinking, King looked around.

"Poke? Where the—"

King's vision cleared, and his question was forgotten. He could barely believe what his eyes were telling him. A woman stood between him and the sun, a woman whose silhouette was outlined by a shimmering nimbus of gold. For an instant, there was no earth beneath King's feet, no air in his lungs, just the golden light and the dream-memories enveloping him; he breathed in her fragrance once more, felt her generous love all around him, tasted her on his tongue, knew her even in the marrow of his bones. He had forgotten what it was like to be in the presence of her gentle, radiant femininity. Now, he remembered, and he wondered how it had ever slipped his mind.

"Cassie."

With the motions of a sleepwalker, King approached her. He reached out to touch her cheek and felt the gauzy interference of mosquito netting. With a single quick motion, he tore the veil away.

"My God," he breathed. "It really is you."

"Yes, it really is," Cass said, searching King's eyes, not understanding his reaction, knowing only that his hand had trembled when he reached toward her. "King? Are you all right?"

Being the focus of the emerald fire of King's eyes was like touching a bare electrical wire. Cass felt once more the savage vitality of him, the primal restlessness that would never be quenched short of death.

"My own sweet sugar girl," King said in disbelief, reaching for Cass once more.

Smiling despite the tears burning in her eyes, Cass caught King's hand in her own, and rested her chin on his fingers. "That was a long time ago, Kingston."

King felt the heat of her body, the softness beneath her skin, and something else, something smooth and hard and heavy. Before she could stop him, his index finger flicked between the buttons and found gold nuggets as warm as her skin.

"Some things are like gold," King said simply. "They last forever."

Cass shook her head, making no effort to conceal the slow trail of tears down her cheeks. "Sugar girls don't last. They dissolve."

King searched the golden eyes that had haunted his memories and dreams, whispering to him of things that were just beyond his reach—unattainable.

"Do you hate me, Cassie?" King asked, his voice strained.

"I deserve it, but I can't bear knowing that you do. I loved you the only way I could." His smile was brief, crooked. "I'm just not worth a damn at loving, am I?"

"I don't hate you."

King's smile changed, becoming dark. "Sugar girl, you came a long way for a woman who doesn't hate me."

Cass smiled sadly. "I care for you, King. Very much." She took a deep breath and continued softly. "But not in the same way I once did. I'm not intoxicated with you any more. The sun doesn't rise and set in your smile. I still love you, though. I always will. Just the way Jay will always love you, no matter what, because you have the gift and curse of touching people far more deeply than they can ever touch you."

King's eyes narrowed when he heard his brother's name. "Jay, huh?"

"Yes," Cass said simply. "Jay."

The certainty that had always eluded King lay in the serenity of Cass's golden eyes, in her smile, in her voice as she spoke Jared's name. Abruptly, King looked away from Cass for the first time since he had seen her, surrounded by golden light.

Jared was forty feet down the slope, standing by the sluice, where the sound of rushing water would drown out their conversation. His back was turned, as it had been since Cass had first clasped King's hand in her own. Jared didn't hear King striding toward him across the China Girl's stony earth. The first warning Jared had of his brother's presence was the hard hand on his shoulder, spinning him around, and the even harder fist rushing toward him.

Instinctively, Jared kept spinning, taking the impact on his upper arm. The force of the blow sent him sprawling in the mud and gravel below the sluice. He rolled aside and came to his feet in a crouched position in the muck. An instant later, he exploded forward in a tackle that sent both brothers skidding across the muddy ground.

"You treacherous son of a bitch," King snarled, grunting and panting as he tried to get Jared in a hammerlock. "All my life you've been dogging my shadow, working my played-out claims, getting more out of them than I ever did!" King shifted his grip and bore Jared down into the muck. "You ever think how goddamned tired a man gets of being shown up by his little brother?"

Jared arched his back, scissored his legs, and bucked King face down into the mud. Panting, swearing viciously, Jared planted one knee in the middle of King's back, grabbed his right wrist, and dragged it upward, barring his arm behind his back.

"About as goddamned tired—" Jared panted, "as a man might get—of standing in his big brother's shadow." He twisted the fingers of his left hand into King's hair and yanked backward until King's neck was all but bent double. Jared leaned over until his muddy cheek was alongside King's. "They dug Cass out—of an avalanche—in the Chilkoot," Jared said, his breath sawing harshly. "She was stone cold. Trying to get to you. I wanted to kill you. Still do. But I won't. For Cass—not for you."

Jared snapped King's head forward, came to his feet, and leaped aside in a single rushing movement. King lunged to his feet with catlike swiftness and began circling Jared warily.

"Stop it, both of you!" Cass said furiously. "I was trying to reach Tea Rose, but Jared won't believe that. So go ahead. Beat the hell out of each other. It's what I'd do if I were strong enough."

"What?" King asked.

"Beat the hell out of both of you!" Cass said, her voice shaking. She was frightened, angry, and frustrated all at once—there was blood on both men, they were too well matched, she couldn't make them stop, and she couldn't bear watching them hurt one another over a past that couldn't be changed. "Is Tea Rose here?"

King shook his head sharply, as though to clear his ears of mud. "She's back in Dawson," he said, turning to Cass. "A place called the Celestial Palace. Jay can take you there."

"Jay can go to hell, and you can go with him."

Crying silently, furiously, Cass turned and stalked off the bench.

Jared looked at King. "Go with her. She's yours."

"Like hell she is," King said, turning aside to spit out blood. "Turned me down flatter than yesterday's beer."

"It didn't look like that from where I was standing."

"Then you're a fool."

"I'd be a bigger fool to ignore your chain around her neck."

King started to say something, gave Jared a wary look, and shrugged. "Even if Cassie were mine—which she isn't—I wouldn't go with her to the Celestial Palace."

"Why?"

Shaking his head, smiling a slow, remembering kind of smile, King said, "Last time I saw Tea Rose, she worked me over better than you just did. Thought I'd died and gone to heaven—and maybe a hot little slice of hell, too, just to keep things interesting."

For an instant, Jared looked blank. Then understanding came: Tea Rose had finally gotten her elegant, clever hands on King. Jared threw back his head and laughed as though he were his brother—wildly, irresistibly. King snickered, then joined in the laughter. The rich, masculine sounds echoed across the bench and down the ravine, stopping Cass in midstride. She turned and stared back up the trail in disbelief.

The two brothers were standing at the edge of the bench, bleeding, holding on to one another, and laughing fit to die.

85

Tea Rose sat beside the embroidery frame, working quickly, neatly, putting the final peaks on the phoenix's consuming fire. As she stitched, gold threat glittered and gleamed against scarlet silk, setting off the ivory grace of her hands. Tan Feng watched from the vantage point of Tea Rose's low, rumpled couch. His body was wholly sated at the moment, but his mind was restive.

What will I do if King Duran somehow finds Tea Rose's price?

The obvious answer—go back to the Celestial Empire with four hundred pounds of gold—didn't appease Tan's restlessness as it should have. He had been thirty years a sojourner. His wife was dead, his children were grown, and they were doing as well as could be expected under his elder brother's tutelage. With Tan's new wealth, his children's status would improve greatly. Tan could even marry again and have more children. There were several suitable alliances awaiting him in China.

Unfortunately, nothing that awaited him had the obsessive appeal of Tea Rose. Nor was there any realistic remedy to his problem, as Tan well knew. He could not have both Tea Rose and the Celestial Empire. In fact, he was becoming increasingly certain that he could not have both Tea Rose and his own soul.

But he could not bear to release her a moment before he must.

"The abscess upon my crotch is back," Tan said, breaking a long silence.

Tea Rose's hand hesitated minutely before it continued plying the steel needle. She had wondered if Cass would somehow find her again, and if so, when.

"Is Jared Duran with my sister?" Tea Rose asked.

Nothing in Tea Rose's voice or body gave any indication of her feelings. She could just as well have been talking about the temperature of her bath water.

Tan grunted. "The two steamships that arrived this morning are his. He and his brother fought at the China Girl."

Tea Rose no more showed her discouragement at the news than she had shown her hope a moment before. She stitched quickly, bringing one flame to an elegant peak, and wondered why Tan was telling her that Cass and Jared had come to Dawson only to fight with King.

"I sent word to the China Girl," Tan continued. "If any attempt is made to cheat me, I will cut your throat and feed your wretched corpse to the Yukon in pieces so small that even fish will spurn them. Then, I shall finally be free of the Fox Woman's daughter sucking on my jade stem."

Tea Rose knotted the thread on the reverse side of the fabric, nipped off the gold, and picked up a freshly threaded needle. She neither spoke nor looked at Tan.

"In that way," he said, "your miserable soul will also be lost, for it must have a whole body to take into the next world. If you die in pieces, your soul will not be able to slide into warm flesh again, arousing men to madness."

"You go to unnecessary trouble, great lord. A sing-song girl has no soul against which a man must protect himself."

"Is that what your mother tells you when she whispers to you in the night?"

"There is little night here, generous lord, and in any case, my mother is dead."

Tan didn't argue, even though he knew quite well that Lilac Rain wasn't dead. She lived just beyond his reach, beckoning to him from the edge of his vision, laughing when he turned suddenly yet never fast enough to surprise her into visibility. But she was nearby. He knew it. Because of her, he awakened sweating and fully aroused, smelling her, tasting her, his essence spurting into emptiness where her sleek, pulsing warmth should have been.

In the daytime, he could spend himself within Tea Rose. But a man must sleep, and with sleep came Lilac Rain. Fox Woman pursued him, closed hotly around him, consumed him repeatedly until he wept blood—and she licked it from his skin and grew ever stronger.

With a quick, jerky movement, Tan sat up. "Your half sister wants to see you."

Tea Rose said nothing, concentrating only on the flame licking in delicate shades of gold up the phoenix's straining body.

"Do you wish to see that miserable abscess?" Tan asked sharply.

"If you wish me to see my sister, I will. If you wish me not to see her, I will not."

"When you see her, be certain she understands that your continued life depends on my not being cheated."

"As always, great lord, you are generous. I will be pleased to see the only other person who shares blood in common with my wretched self."

Never had Tea Rose's outer surface been so smooth, so polished. And never had Tan been more certain of the black flames burning beneath her satin exterior. As always, the knowledge of her defiance sent a sexual thrill through him. The familiar rush of blood that followed invigorated him, making him feel completely alive, omnipotent. Smiling, savoring the hardening of his penis, he drew aside his clothes just as the sound of footsteps rang in the hall beyond Tea Rose's door.

"Tea Rose?" called Cass urgently. "Are you there? Are you all right?" Then, "One more step, Wing, and I'll shoot you."

Tan called instructions to Wing even as Tea Rose said quickly, "A moment please, sister, and then I'll be permitted to see you."

Cass barely concealed the relief that went through her. The gun she held on Wing didn't waver. After sucking through his teeth in loud insult, Wing turned his back on her small pistol and walked off, leaving her outside Tea Rose's door.

Carefully, Cass tried the door, but found it locked. From inside the room she heard a rapid exchange of Chinese, then Tan's voice alone, then a brief silence, ended by a harsh, gutteral sound. Moments later, Tea Rose unlocked and opened the door. As Cass stepped in, the door to the adjoining room closed behind Tan. Cass barely noticed it. She had eyes only for the exquisite, deceptively fragile face of her half sister.

"Are you all right?" Cass asked, searching Tea Rose's clear black eyes. "Has Tan Feng—that is, are you—? Oh, Tea Rose, I've tried so hard to find you!"

Tea Rose looked at her sister's pale, tear-streaked face and felt an unaccustomed emotion. Impulsively, Tea Rose held out her arms and knew again the warm, rose-scented embrace of her father's other daughter.

"I'm so sorry," Cass said, holding Tea Rose tightly. "I never should have left you alone in the wagon. I never should have been King's lover. I never should—"

"No," interrupted Tea Rose. "If you had been a different woman, you never would have taken me into your home and heart in the first place. If my mother had been a different woman, I would have ended as a pool of blood between her knees. If I had been a different woman, Jared would have purchased and married me, and none of this would have happened. But we are what we are, and," she smiled sadly, "is that such a bad thing after all?"

"Jared? I don't understand."

"Tan wanted a spy within a powerful white household. Jared wanted a woman with whom he could share his name, his soul, his children. But I could not love in that way. He understood that and loved me differently, as a father or brother." Tea Rose sighed and stepped away from Cass. "We are what we are."

Tea Rose's words brought back another time, Jared explaining what Cass had come to understand too late; and with that memory came more tears.

"What you are is intelligent and beautiful and resilient," Cass said in a low voice. "Those aren't bad things at all."

For long moments, Tea Rose searched Cass's haunted eyes. Then Tea Rose held out her hand and said softly, "Thank you, sister. Come, let me show you my wedding dress."

"A true wedding?" Cass said, startled.

"Perhaps."

"Tan Feng?" Cass persisted, remembering what Tea Rose

had once told her; if Tan had asked Tea Rose to be his wife, she would have gone back to him.

"No. King." Tea Rose saw shock on Cass's face, but no other emotion. No anger, jealousy, resentment—nothing but transparent confusion and surprise. Tea Rose's smile was also transparent, revealing the irony of bitter and sweet, beginnings and endings, dreams and the reality of defeat. "When I gave King the locket that financed his claim, he had to agree to two things. The first was to give up half of what he found to me. The second was to marry me, for only that way would I ever be free. The night you added a nugget to your necklace was the night I knew King would keep the bargain."

Unconsciously, Cass's fingers went to her throat, where the golden necklace lay heavy and smooth, warm with the heat of her body; it was so little to have of the two men she had loved and had somehow failed. So little, and yet so heavy a burden.

"Has Tan Feng agreed?" Cass asked.

"After a fashion. If King gives Tan four times my weight in gold by midnight Saturday, I am free."

"Four times—but that's an impossible amount."

"Yes. King won't admit that. He believes that his bitch goddess gold loves him as much as he loves her. Tan is very shrewd, sister. He has watched King carefully. He knows King's weaknesses and strengths better than anyone except Jared." Tea Rose looked up from the embroidery. "I doubt that it will do any good, but please warn King. Tan expects King to fail and then to be so furious over failing that he will lose his head, pull a gun, and try to kill Tan. At that instant, Wing or one of the other tong men will kill King."

"Tan told you this?" Cass asked, appalled.

"It is what I would do if I were confronted by an enemy whom I couldn't openly murder," Tea Rose said. After a moment, she added quietly, "Warn Jared as well. Tan has hated him for many, many years."

"Why?"

"Lilac Rain."

Cass closed her eyes and told herself it was futile to be jealous of a dead woman; but she was jealous, and she couldn't conceal it.

"So," Tea Rose said, smiling sadly as she ran her fingertips over the cool golden thread of the flames, "you've finally discovered which of the two brothers is able to love in your way, body and soul, for better or for worse. I'm happy for you, sister, but I'm even more happy for Jared. It has taken him a lifetime to find a woman he could trust with his soul."

"He doesn't trust me that way," Cass said, her voice husky. "He believes I still love King."

"Do you?"

"I can't hate him."

Tea Rose looked at Cass for a long, silent minute. "You don't have to hate King. All you have to do is to let go of the past."

"I don't know what you mean."

"Jared once told me that King and my father were a lot alike in one way. Both of them acted without thought because they were very intensely alive, as lightning is intensely alive. They lived in the *now,* without plans for the future or regrets for the past. Men like that bring beauty to the lives around them, and, ultimately, madness. To have such a man for a father—" Tea Rose shrugged. "It must have been like living with the phoenix, forever burning, forever trying to break free. The phoenix sees nothing but the flames that consume him, not even the other souls there who are also burning. I think you must have been very lonely."

"So was my father. He was searching for your mother. If he had found her, life would have been very different for all of us. He would have settled down, and I wouldn't have had a childhood ruled by loneliness and the sound of wagon wheels turning. All my father needed was someone to build a life around. I wasn't enough."

"Is that why King was so irresistible to you? Did you think you could heal the past by giving him what your father had never had?"

"I thought King needed me, wanted me, loved me," Cass said.

"He did for a time, and then he needed, wanted, and loved his bitch goddess more." Tea Rose saw the flinch that Cass couldn't completely hide. "Why does that still distress you?"

"Nobody likes to be reminded of failure," Cass said, her voice raw.

"Failure? Then you really do believe that there was some lack in you that made it impossible for your father or King to build a life around you?" Tea Rose asked curiously.

"Of course there was—and is—such a lack," Cass said, closing her eyes.

Tea Rose smiled, then laughed softly, unhappily. "Open your eyes, sister. Every lock isn't identical. All locks don't open to the same key. Is that the fault of the key or of the lock? Or is it no one's fault? We are what we are—and we are different." Tea Rose's fingers stroked the embroidery absently, as though testing the height and smoothness of the flames. "In any case, the past is beyond healing, so we might as well let go of it. The future will have its own ill-fitting keys and locks to trouble us."

Cass looked at the crimson wedding dress. "Do you love King?"

"I would care for him better than a woman who loved him, because I would demand less of him. But don't worry, sister. You won't have to decide whether to laugh or cry at my wedding. Even King Duran can't coax four hundred pounds of gold from the frozen earth."

"What will happen?"

"After King fails, Tan will sell my maidenhead to the highest bidder. He will skim the cream of my value, then keep me for himself for a time, as he did my mother." Tea Rose's brief, shadowed smile came again. "Don't look so shocked, Cass. It's the life I was trained to lead, just as I was trained to embroider." She stroked the flames and the tormented phoenix trapped within. "I began embroidering my wedding dress before my mother died. See the richness I built, one frail stitch at a time!"

Thoughtfully, Cass looked up at Tea Rose, whose attention was focused solely on the crimson dress. There was no single difference Cass could point to, simply a pervasive feeling that the Tea Rose who stood before her was in some fundamental way different from the girl who had been kidnapped by Tan Feng.

"I'm told that Western women wear white on their wedding day, to symbolize their purity of body and spirit," Tea Rose said. "Celestial women wear red for their wedding, to symbolize their rebirth into a new family, for any birth is accomplished only in blood. Against all custom, I used only one color of thread, because of all colors, gold is the only one that matters for a sing-song girl."

As Tea Rose spoke, her delicate fingertips stroked the embroidery in mute remembrance of a time that would never come again—her mother's laughter and precise advice, her gentle hugs, and a knife blade held against a throat in a dark alley.

"I chose the phoenix design even before my mother died."

And then Cass knew how Tea Rose had changed. In voice and gesture, movement and stillness, smile and silence; in all those things, she was her mother reborn.

"You have become very much like Lilac Rain," Cass said quietly.

Tea Rose glanced up, surprised. "Thank you. Many times lately I've wished she were still alive. I understand her much better now. There are many things we could share. But the past is what it is, beyond reach."

Cass looked at the phoenix, writhing within the embrace of golden flames, and wondered why the elegantly stylized symbol made her want to weep rather than to celebrate the implication of immortality.

86

"What's this?" Jared said, looking at the poke King had just tossed to him.

"Same wages and percentage I'd give to any sluice boss," King said, turning away abruptly.

Jared waited until his brother was across the lean-to, then said harshly, "King!"

With a hard sideways motion of his arm, Jared fired the poke at King. Turning, his brother reflexively caught the heavy leather sack, then looked at it in his hand.

"Keep it," Jared said.

"Like hell I will." King threw the poke back, hard. It struck the ground in front of Jared and opened, spilling a trail of gold. "I'm not taking anything from you, little brother. Not your steamships, your money, or your sweat. You work for me, you get paid. You don't get paid, you don't work."

Jared looked at King's narrowed green eyes and knew that arguing would be worse than futile—it would waste time and energy, and they didn't have enough of either. The tacit truce they had reached after their fight on the bench was as fragile as hoarfrost. Both of them knew it. Both of them also knew if they didn't work together, Tea Rose was doomed. King couldn't chase elusive pay dirt in the tunnels and oversee the sluice at the same time.

"Get some sleep," Jared said in a clipped voice, as he tied the poke to his belt with swift, vicious motions. "You haven't had any for three days."

"I can sleep after midnight tomorrow."

"That's stupid."

"According to you, being stupid is what I'm best at."

"Then let me dig while you run the sluice," Jared said, barely hanging onto his temper. "If the drift changes direction, we can trade places."

Both brothers glared at each other. They were cold, hungry, exhausted, and generally in a murderous frame of mind. Despite the fabulous riches King had found concentrated within the third shaft's rediscovered drift, he was still short more than thirty-eight pounds of gold. He was also unwilling to cede the least bit of control to his younger brother. It wasn't a matter of trust—it was sheer, stubborn pride. Finally, reluctantly, King nodded. Jared could shovel out more pay dirt than any three men, and King knew it.

"Did you try swapping the China Girl straight across for Tea Rose?" Jared asked.

"Yes."

"What happened?"

"Just what you predicted," King said savagely. "Tan Feng laughed at me. I'd have killed him, but being a law-abiding man, I didn't carry my pistol into town. I won't make that mistake again."

"That's just what Tan wants," Jared said tiredly. "He's goading you, King. He hopes if he leans hard enough, you'll make a try for him. He'd rather have an excuse to kill you—and then me, when I come after him—than all the gold in the China Girl."

"Then the next time I see him, it just might be Christmas come early for that Manchu son of a bitch."

"For the love of God," Jared exploded. "For once in your life, look beyond the moment! The best revenge you could have on Tan would be to walk away with Tea Rose in one hand and the China Girl in the other! Why can't you see that?"

There was a taut, electric silence before King said deliberately, "You seen Cassie lately?"

After another silence, Jared accepted the change of subject. "Not for a while. Why?"

"This is a rough town for a woman alone."

"She's not alone. Two Pinkertons are with her. I thought they'd be more use guarding her than watching the Celestial Palace."

King grunted, turned to his bunk, and stretched out.

"Three hours," he said. "Then it's your turn. And you'll sleep, if I have to hold a gun on you the whole time."

King was snoring before Jared trusted himself to answer.

Muttering under his breath about wolverine bait, Jared left the lean-to, walked the short distance to the third shaft, and lowered himself into the smoky, lantern-lit gloom.

"Yo, Poke!"

"Over here."

Jared turned toward Poke's voice, stooped, and began crawling through one of the ragged tunnels that radiated out from the shaft. Working in the frozen ground had many disadvantages, but it had one great advantage—none of the tunnels had to be reinforced with timber, for once the fire was removed, the ground returned to its rocklike state.

Poke crawled forward to meet Jared. "Time to start the fire again, Wolverine," Poke said. "She's froze tight." Then he realized that it was Jared, not King crawling toward him. "Who's running the sluice?"

"You are for the next three hours." Jared paused. "There might be a man coming up from town. Call me if he does come. And wake King in three hours."

Poke scrambled past Jared. "Number five tunnel looked right promising last time," Poke offered. "Might want to work it whilst the other thaws. Sure do hope the man from town comes on my shift. I hear the cleanup gets real rich when he's around."

"Just so King doesn't hear it," Jared said flatly.

"Won't come from me."

"Good."

Jared watched Poke vanish up the shaft and sighed. Sooner or later, King would find out that Cass was in Dawson, selling off cargo—and shares in the steamers themselves—to anyone who could pay in gold. Once a day, one of the Pinkertons would come up to where Jared was working the sluice. Once a day, the proceeds of the cargo sale were calmly poured into the sluice, there to blend untraceably with the China Girl's own gold. The men working the sluice knew what was happening, but Jared had made it plain that there would be bloody trouble for any man who told King.

Jared crawled to a recently thawed tunnel where pale streaks of pay dirt gleamed in the dim light. He began shovelling, working hard and steadily, despite the cramped conditions and the smoke, sweat, and dirt that kept trickling into his eyes. He kept four men busy just hauling away the pay dirt he dug, but he never paused, for in the back of his mind was the knowledge of how few hours were left in which to dig Tea Rose's freedom from the frozen mountain of gold.

Jared didn't know how long he had been digging when Poke's voice hollered him out of the tunnel with the news that something had gone wrong with the sluice. Swearing tiredly, Jared pulled himself up the ladder, wondering if the flume from the feeder creek had come apart, or if the sluice itself had broken under the constant washing.

No sooner had Jared's shoulders cleared the shaft than King reached down, yanked him out, and knocked him flat with a single blow. Several fat pokes rained down and thumped onto Jared's prostrate body.

"Some damn fool was pouring your gold into my sluice," King said coldly.

Slowly, Jared sat up. "I'm getting real tired of being sucker-punched by you. If it happens again, I'm going to take a shovel and bend it over your thick skull."

"It won't happen. You're going to take your gold and your sneaking Pinkertons, and get the hell off my claim."

Jared came to his feet, ignoring the pokes that fell off his body into the dirt. "Half the claim belongs to Tea Rose. Maybe you should ask her before you kick her representative off the China Girl."

"Are you saying this is her idea?"

"I'm saying that you own only half of the China Girl. Do you think Tea Rose would refuse me?"

"I said I didn't want any of your damned money!"

"I'm not giving it to you. I'm giving it to Tea Rose. If you don't like it, don't chew on me—chew on her." Jared smiled coldly and added, "If you think you have the teeth—"

Frustrated, King ran a muddy hand through his hair, making it stick out in wild disarray. Then he spoke in a low, savage voice, putting into words what was really angering him; his golden bitch goddess had let him down.

"It doesn't matter. Nothing matters. *There just isn't enough gold.*"

87

By eleven-thirty on Saturday night, the casino and bar of the Celestial Palace were packed with roughly dressed men. Most of them were recent arrivals in Dawson, high on hopes and low on cash. A few were veteran miners who could afford to buy one of Tan's women for several hours at a time. All of the men were gambling hard and drinking harder, for they had only thirty minutes left in which to rid their pockets and pokes of gold before the Mounties closed down the town for the Sabbath.

Tea Rose heard the raucous laughter and drunken curses as though they were coming from a great distance. She was lightheaded from lack of food and liquid, a self-imposed, three-day fast that was all she could do to help King meet Tan's price. The emetic she had taken, plus her own mounting anxiety, had combined to make it impossible for her to keep anything down.

When Tan came toward Tea Rose with yet another cup of tea, she drank it without protest, then promptly vomited into the metal basin that had been her constant companion for the past thirty hours. The liquid that came from her mouth was as clear as when it had been poured from the teapot.

After she had finished, she sat back and watched Tan with unblinking black eyes, quietly defying him with every breath she took. He returned her stare with equal impassivity, despite the rage and desire knotting his gut at her intransigence.

"I am sorry, great lord," Tea Rose murmured, her voice softly pleading and utterly deceptive. "I have tried, but neither food nor drink stays within me."

Tan made no answer as he stared at Fox Woman reborn, haunting him, thwarting him, drawing him in agony on a rack of lust.

From beyond the room came a sudden silence, then a turmoil of sound that told Tan the Duran brothers had arrived.

"Finish covering your wretched body," Tan said in a harsh voice.

Tea Rose reached for the many layers of her clothing. The heavy crimson silk weighed more than she had remembered. For the first time, she regretted the thick gold embroidery and dense, lush folds of cloth. Slowly, she wrapped the red fabric around her body. The silk was of such high quality that it made almost no sound as it rubbed over itself, draping her in riches. Her fingers trembled over each fastening, until Tan pushed her hands aside impatiently and finished the task himself.

When he was satisfied, he secured her shimmering, softly chiming, pearl-encrusted headdress in place. For a moment, he became very still as he looked down at her. Then he cupped his hands around her cheeks, tilted her face up to his, and studied her as though he had never seen her before.

She had never been more beautiful.

"My exquisite warrior," Tan whispered.

Very gently, he kissed her eyelids, savoring the quivering warmth of her skin.

The piercing tenderness of Tan's kiss was unlike anything Tea Rose had ever experienced. It transfixed her. Long before he lifted his head, she was trembling with conflicting emotions, terrified by the very man she had believed she knew so well.

"Sweetest of poisons," Tan murmured against her lips, "black butterfly of death and desire—fly fast and fly far, for someday I will kill you."

Tan kissed Tea Rose again, a soft ravishment that left her

shaking. Then he turned and walked away without looking at her again. It was several moments before she gathered herself enough to follow him to the door. Tan opened it and stood impassively as she walked past him into the scarlet-draped casino.

The first person Tea Rose saw was King. Big, gaunt, haunted, his face still streaked with the sweat and soil of his labors within the frozen earth, King loomed over the gamblers. When he saw Tea Rose, he became very still. Framed by a fringe of pearls above and crimson silk below, her features drawn by fasting, and her eyes burning with a hope she refused to acknowledge even to herself, Tea Rose was a shuttered goddess.

In absolute silence, she walked to the bar that ran down the back of the room. At a harsh command from Tan, two tong men went into his office. They emerged, carrying between them a brass-plated commercial scale whose twin pans were big enough to balance sacks of flour weighing one hundred pounds each. With quick efficiency, the two men set up the scale on top of the bar, where every man could see without crowding forward.

The balance pans seesawed for a few moments before settling into exact horizontal alignment. King checked the scale by forcing one arm all the way to the polished wood of the bar and then releasing it suddenly. The pans bobbed wildly but settled once more into precise alignment. King signaled his satisfaction by shrugging his shoulders in a motion that shed the small pack he had been carrying on his back. It was the fourth such pack that had been carried into the Celestial Palace.

The meaty thump of the pack as it landed next to the three others on the polished wood brought a rising murmur of sound from the crowd. Only one thing in Dawson was that heavy for its size.

Gold.

Tea Rose walked up to King and watched him with black eyes that refused to ask anything of life. He smiled slowly at her, a smile as reckless as the glittering green of his eyes.

"It's a good thing beauty doesn't weigh extra," King

drawled. "There wouldn't be enough gold in the whole damn world to buy you." As he bent and lifted Tea Rose to the bar, he whispered very softly, "I don't have enough gold, sugar. When I give the signal, you dive toward Jay. See him? He's at that side door. He'll get you out."

"No." Tea Rose's slender arms went around King's neck. She held on with astonishing strength. "If I'm not a wife, I'll never be free, and it has all been for nothing."

King shuddered with the force of the emotions he was keeping in check. "Goddamn you," he said through clenched teeth. "And goddamn Jay, too. He knew you'd refuse to leave without me. Look around, sing-song girl. I don't have a chance in hell of getting you out of here. Jay does."

"Tan has five tong men hidden," Tea Rose said, speaking softly, urgently. "If either of you draws a gun, you'll both be killed where you stand. And so will I."

Tea Rose watched the knowledge of defeat change King. As she looked into the shattering violence of his eyes, she felt compassion stir for the kindred, savage spirit that animated him, a spirit forever trapped within the limitations of human flesh. She laid her cheek along the softness of King's beard, breathed in the richness of sweat and earth and life emanating from him, and felt an immense calm come to her.

"It's all right," Tea Rose whispered, brushing her mouth over King's. "I'll show you the way out of the trap."

Refusing to say any more, Tea Rose stepped from King's arms onto one of the scale's broad pans. With a graceful movement, she knelt and sat on her heels, hands folded, head partially bowed, the image of Celestial submission. But her eyes remained unquenched, feral—Fox Woman watching the human world from bottomless, dark pools.

King turned to his backpack, opened it, and began pulling out fat leather pokes. One after another, he turned them inside out, spilling their contents into the broad, empty pan that was at his eye level. A small mound of gold grew moment by moment as King poured precious nuggets and soft metallic dust from the pokes. Slowly, almost imperceptibly, the golden mound began to sink lower and Tea Rose's pan began to rise. When space showed beneath Tea Rose, men began talking to each other, speculating on the probable worth of the gold and the amount of time King was buying with the beautiful Chinese prostitute.

When the two pans were in balance, King turned and looked at Tan Feng, who was standing twenty feet away, his back to the closed office door and Wing at his side. Tan gestured abruptly. Wing bowed and went to the bar. When he was satisfied that the scale was indeed balanced, he began scooping gold into one of the discarded pokes.

"It will be midnight before you're done," King snarled.

He reached up and tipped the pan so that it spilled its contents onto the bar in a heavy rush of gold. As the gold poured out, he exerted counterpressure, easing Tea Rose's descent to the surface of the bar.

At a sharp word from Tan, Wing retreated. Without pausing, King went to work on the second pack, emptying pokes, measuring out Tea Rose's weight in gold once more.

From the corner of his eye, Jared watched the tiny golden streams issuing from the pokes. The rest of his attention was fixed on the men in the room. The miners and chechakos didn't worry Jared; despite the presence of so much gold, the men were more bemused by the spectacle than intent upon interfering in any way. What bothered Jared was the five missing tong men. He had no doubt that they were waiting in ambush nearby. Nor did he have any doubt that Tea Rose had refused King's wild plan for her escape; a single look at the bleak set of King's face had told Jared that his brother was tasting defeat.

Suddenly, there was a stir at the front door of the Celestial Palace. Cass rushed in, followed by two Mounties. They stationed themselves on either side of the door. The taller officer pulled a watch from his bright jacket pocket, checked the time, and returned the watch to its place. Cass spotted Jared and walked to him between the casino tables, her face pale except for the red stain of anger that rode high on her cheekbones.

"They won't do one damn thing except make sure that the

Celestial Palace closes at midnight as required by law," Cass said bitterly.

"Yes, they will. They'll keep Tan from killing King. As for stopping Tea Rose's sale and giving her to you—" Jared smiled grimly. "They let white women raffle themselves off to the highest bidder for a winter's 'housekeeping.' Why should they care how a China girl spends her time?"

There was another flurry of movement at the front door as Poke and ten more of King's mining crew marched into the casino. The Mounties gave them a hard look, saw no weapons, and ignored the men from the China Girl.

King never so much as looked up from his task. He poured out gold with complete concentration, letting it spill onto the top of the building mound, letting nuggets dance and bounce musically against the metal pan.

Tea Rose remained motionless, her eyes fixed on a distant, darkly beckoning horizon only she could see. Her head was cocked in the attitude of one who was listening intently. It wasn't the music of pouring gold that whispered within her mind, however; it was Lilac Rain.

I will hug you and tickle you and comb your hair into a beautiful maiden's coil. Then I will take your hand and lead you into the Good Lady's Night, where women are free.

The second pan of gold cascaded heavily over the first, creating a large, smooth-topped mound on the bar. Without a pause, King opened the third pack and began refilling the pan, working steadily. His eyes were as savage as the half-snarl that had been fixed on his lips since he had known the first bitter foretaste of defeat.

A third pan of gold grew beneath King's callused hands as he ripped open pokes and dumped out their gleaming contents with reckless disregard for the gold's worth. When the third pan was being dumped onto the small mountain that had grown on the bar, voices rose in the room as gamblers kicked back in their chairs, assuming that three times her weight in gold had been the beautiful prostitute's price.

When Tea Rose made no move to leave the scale, a rumble of disbelief rose from the watching men. When King turned to the fourth and final backpack and pulled out a fat poke, the rumble turned into a roar.

Calmly, the taller Mountie pulled out his watch, called "Ten minutes to Sabbath," and pocketed the watch once more.

King worked like a machine, opening a poke, pouring the nuggets in flashing golden arcs into the pan, opening and pouring, opening and pouring, until there were no pokes left in the fourth backpack.

Tea Rose's side of the scale rested solidly on the bar. With a choked sound, King grabbed the backpack and ripped it apart in savage fury, as though he couldn't believe there was no more gold inside.

"Hold on, Wolverine," Poke yelled, hurrying forward. "It ain't over yet. Help me with these here pokes."

"What—?" King shook his head.

"It come from the China Girl. We all figured it should go the same way."

"I'll double whatever you give me," King said hoarsely. "I swear it."

"Weren't for you, we'd be like those fellows sleeping in the street—poor as piss and twice as useless," Poke said matter-of-factly, as he handed over fat pokes.

"Five minutes to Sabbath!" called the Mountie.

One by one, the miners came up to King and returned to him the wages they had earned working the China Girl's frozen tunnels. With each poke emptied onto the pile, the righthand pan dipped a fraction lower.

It still wasn't enough. Tea Rose's side of the scale remained motionless on the bar, as though the gold were being poured into her hands rather than onto the opposite side of the scale.

When the last poke had been emptied onto the yellow mound, the pan holding Tea Rose quivered and shifted. Tan's hand twitched, as though he would prevent the scale's rise, then he subsided into complete stillness. The scale wavered, dipped—and lowered Tea Rose gently onto the bar once more.

Cass closed her eyes and prayed as she had as a child,

fervently, helplessly—wanting something that seemed forever beyond her reach—prayers like dust in her mouth, and her ears filled with the sound of steel wagon wheels grinding up the past and scattering it to the wind.

"Hell, Wolverine, throw my winnings into the pot," called one of the gamblers. "Can't drink it all 'tween now an' Sunday closing anyhow."

Hands passed the small poke forward. Like a magnet, it drew others from nearby tables. Frantically, King opened pokes and poured them out. The scale shifted and shivered and shifted again, and the watching men spoke with a single rising and falling groan that echoed Tea Rose's rise and fall.

"One minute to closing!"

The pans dipped and bobbed and passed each other in an agonizing motion, Tea Rose on one side and gold on the other. Cass watched without breathing as Tea Rose ascended and then dropped in diminishing arcs.

A chill moved over Cass. She was certain that when the scale was motionless once more, there wouldn't be enough gold to redeem the mistakes of the past. Breath wedged in her throat, choking her, and she saw in her mind the next instant or the next, when King's emotions would overrule his control, and he would reach in helpless fury for a gun, triggering his own death, dragging Tea Rose and Jared after him into darkness.

"No," Cass said, her voice raw.

Her cry galvanized Tea Rose. For the first time since she had climbed onto the scale, her eyes focused on something within the room. It wasn't her sister who drew Tea Rose's attention, nor was it King. It was Tan Feng. Slowly, Tea Rose turned her head toward him, opening her mouth and arching her tongue outward in a glistening invitation to annihilation.

"No!" Cass screamed, pulling on her necklace. "Oh God, get it off me! It belongs to them, not to me!"

Jared looked down and saw Cass yanking savagely at the thick gold chain around her neck, but the heavy links remained intact, resisting her effort. He grabbed the chain in both hands and twisted, tearing links apart.

"King!" Jared yelled.

King spun around at the sound of his brother's voice and saw something flashing and twisting over the crowd toward him. He leaped up and combed the chain out of the air with fingers that were still gritty from the China Girl's frozen womb. The chain dropped instantly from his hand onto the top of the seesawing mound of gold.

The scale hesitated, shuddered, and then the gold-filled pan settled onto the bar with a thump.

The gamblers roared victoriously, but Tea Rose didn't hear, didn't see. She had eyes only for Tan Feng and the past.

"Tea Rose!" King yelled over the noise. "Look at the gold, Tea Rose! You're free!"

Slowly, Tea Rose's head turned. She couldn't understand his words above the cheering of the miners, but she recognized the victory blazing in King's eyes. She looked back to Tan Feng, whose smile was as enigmatic as Lilac Rain's had once been. Then Tea Rose looked to Jared, who was touching Cass's bare neck and smiling as victoriously as King.

Abruptly, Tea Rose's whole body shuddered violently, as though she had just climbed out of cold water and were shaking off the clinging drops. Her lips closed around her tongue as she turned to King, trying to smile, crying instead. With a powerful motion, King lifted Tea Rose from the scale. She turned her face against his chest, letting him carry her from the Celestial Palace, free—as her mother had never been.

As they passed Jared, he turned and looked at Cass. She was looking only at him, and tears of joy flowed down her cheeks. He bent and kissed the faint marks on her skin where golden chains had rested. When he straightened again, his eyes were brilliant with emotion. Smiling, holding tightly to one another, Jared and Cass walked through the dispersing crowd and into the luminous night.

No one looked back to where Tan Feng stood alone, chained to the past by his mountain of gold.